THE HIDDEN
LOUISA MAY ALCOTT

Louisa May Alcott

THE HIDDEN
LOUISA MAY ALCOTT

A COLLECTION OF HER UNKNOWN THRILLERS

Two Volumes in One

Edited and with Introductions by
Madeleine Stern

AVENEL BOOKS
New York

Originally published in two separate volumes entitled:
Behind a Mask: The Unknown Thrillers of Louisa May Alcott Introduction Copyright ©
1975 by Madeleine B. Stern
Plots and Counterplots: More Unknown Thrillers of Louisa May Alcott Copyright © 1976
by Madeleine B. Stern

This 1984 edition is published by Avenel Books, distributed by Crown Publishers, Inc.,
by arrangement with William Morrow & Company, Inc.

Manufactured in the United States of America

Library of Congress Cataloging in Publication Data

Alcott, Louisa May, 1832–1888.
  The hidden Louisa May Alcott.

   I. Stern, Madeleine Bettina, 1912–   . II. Alcott, Louisa May, 1832–1888.
Behind a mask. 1975.   III. Alcott, Louisa May, 1832–1888. Plots and counterplots.
1977. IV. Title.
PS1016.S73   1984   813'.4   84-21707
ISBN: 0-517-464667

h g f e d c b a

❧ Contents ❧

VOLUME ONE

Behind a Mask

❧ *Introduction* ❧

BY MADELEINE STERN

I intend to illuminate the Ledger with a blood & thunder tale as they are easy to "compoze" & are better paid than moral & elaborate works of Shakespeare so dont be shocked if I send you a paper containing a picture of Indians, pirates, wolves, bears & distressed damsels in a grand tableau over a title like this "The Maniac Bride" or The Bath of Blood A Thrilling Tale of Passion.

The quotation is not by a writer associated with the gore of Gothic romance but by the future author of a domestic novel known to all the world as *Little Women*. On June 22, 1862, Louisa May Alcott wrote those lines to a young man named Alf Whitman, whose charms she would one day incorporate into the fictional character of Laurie.[1]

The statement itself evinces her powers, for within the briefest compass it touches upon her facility in composition, her ostensible motive, and the type of periodical or audience at which she aimed. The fact that Louisa May Alcott—"The Children's Friend"—let down her literary hair and wrote blood-and-thunder thrillers in secret is in itself a disconcerting if titillating shock to readers in search of consistency. Like Dr. Johnson's dog that stood upon its hind legs, it is *per se* remarkable. Equally remarkable is the story of their discovery, an intriguing byway in literary detection. Most remarkable of all perhaps is the fact that those gory, gruesome novelettes—written anonymously or pseudonymously, for the most part—were and still are extremely good: well

(ix)

paced, suspenseful, skillfully executed, and peopled with characters of flesh and blood.

Now, for the first time, after more than a century, they are reprinted—a belated though well-deserved tribute to a multifaceted genius who hailed from Concord, Massachusetts. They merit not only the avid attention of the general reader, whose appetite will grow with what it feeds on, but closer study by the astonished yet delighted critic, who may wonder precisely why and when, how and for whom these colorful forays into an exotic world were written. The analysis will disclose not only the nature of the creation but the nature of the creator, for Louisa May Alcott brought to this genre of escapist literature both an economic and a psychological need.

There is no doubt the economic need was there. The four "little women" whose name was not March but Alcott—Anna, Louisa, Abby, and Elizabeth—grew up not only in the climate of love but in the colder climate of poverty. Their father, Amos Bronson Alcott, the Concord seer, who was sometimes regarded as a seer-sucker, had many gifts but none for making money. As Louisa put it in a letter to a publisher: "I too am sure that 'he who giveth to the poor lendeth to the Lord' & on that principle devote time & earnings to the care of my father & mother, for one possesses no gift for money making & the other is now too old to work any longer for those who are happy & able to work for her." [2]

The cost of coal, the price of shoes, discussions of ways and means, all the essentials of living formed an obbligato to Louisa's early years, a background as basic to her life as romps with the neighboring Emerson children, berrying excursions with Henry David Thoreau, glimpses of a mysterious Hawthorne hovering in the Old Manse, and echoes of her father's lofty discourses on universal love and Pythagorean diet. Returned from a lecture tour in the West, Bronson Alcott was asked, "Well, did people pay you?" He opened his pocketbook, flourished a single dollar bill, and replied, "Only that! My overcoat was stolen, and I had to buy a shawl. Many promises were not kept, and travelling is costly; but I have opened the way, and another year shall do better." [3] He was the recipient of gifts from his wife's distinguished relatives, the Mays or Sewalls, or from his friend and neighbor the illustrious Ralph Waldo Emerson, who would place a bill under a book or behind a candlestick "when he thinks Father wants a little money, and no one will help him earn." [4]

To solve the mundane question of ways and means, to pay the family debts and end the necessity for a charitable Alcott Sinking Fund, Louisa May Alcott was prepared to do any kind of work that offered, menial or mental. "Though an *Alcott*"—and Louisa underlined not the condition but the name—she would prove she could support herself. "I will make a battering-ram of my head," she wrote in her journal, "and make a way through this rough-and-tumble world." [5]

She tried what was available, and what was not she tried to make available: teaching, working as a seamstress or as second girl, doing the wash at two dollars a week. At midcentury the family poverty had never been more extreme. At this juncture Louisa went out to service and garnered from her experience no money but a villain for her tales and a consuming inner fury to explode.

The full story of what might be entitled "The Humiliation at Dedham" has never been told, although Louisa herself years later wrote a bowdlerized account of it in "How I Went Out to Service." Since it was grist for the mill of a writer of thrillers, it merits recounting. [6] At the difficult midcentury the Alcotts lived for a time in Boston, for it was better to be earning a living in a city than to be starving in a country paradise. Mrs. Alcott, the Marmee of the as yet unwritten *Little Women*, worked as a city missionary and opened an intelligence office. When an ancient gentleman from Dedham applied for a companion for his sister, Louisa decided to take the position herself. The gentleman—now for the first time identified as the Honorable James Richardson, Dedham lawyer, president of a local fire-insurance company, author of several orations, and devotee of the Muses—seemed to her tall, ministerial, refined. Waving black-gloved hands about, he assured her that his home was graced by books and pictures, flowers, a piano, the best of society. She would be one of the family, required to help only in the lighter work.

Fortified by those assurances, Louisa in 1851, age nineteen, went out to service. The Richardson home was not precisely as it had been represented. The light housework included not only bed making but the kindling of fires and the destruction of cobwebs. What was more, Louisa was expected to play audience to Hon. James Richardson, who invited her into his study for oral readings or metaphysical discussions. The aged Richardson's attentions soon became maudlin. He plied her with poems while she washed the dishes and he left reproachful little notes under her door. Stranded on an island of water in a sea of soapsuds, Louisa finally delivered an ultimatum: she had come to serve as companion to Hon. James Richardson's sister, not to him. As a result of her display of independence, all the household work was assigned to her: digging paths through the snow, fetching water from the well, splitting the kindling, and sifting the ashes. The final degradation was the command to polish the master's muddy boots with the blacking hose, at which the young domestic balked. After seven weeks of drudgery she announced her intention of leaving. Richardson shut himself up in sulky retirement while his sister tucked a sixpenny pocketbook into Louisa's chilblained hands. The pocketbook contained four dollars, which the outraged Alcotts returned to Dedham. Although Louisa subsequently made light of this experience in "How I Went Out to Service," there can be no doubt that from her humiliation an anger was born that would express itself both obliquely and directly when she sat down to write her blood-and-thunder tales.

Another devastating experience a few years later could also be caught in a net of words, provided the author remained anonymous. Frustrated in her attempts to find work—teaching Alice Lovering, sewing for Mrs. Reed or Mrs. Sargent—Louisa found that her courage had all but failed. As she looked at the waters of the Mill Dam she was tempted to find the solution of her problems in their oblivion. Though her immediate problem was resolved, surely that "Temptation at the Mill Dam," however fleeting, became, along with the "Humiliation at Dedham," part of the psychological equipment of a young woman who would shortly take her pen as her bridegroom.[7]

There was much else in Louisa's life in Concord or Boston that formed part of that equipment. There were characters not merely in books but in life—like Hawthorne, whose dark figure had glided through the entry of a somber Manse, a fitting shadow to inhabit a house of shadows. There were fugitive slaves who passed through the village, a stop on the Underground Railway. There were the ghost stories with which Louisa thrilled the boys of Frank Sanborn's school as apples and ginger cakes rounded out an Alcott Monday Evening. Surely the report of Professor Webster's hanging for the murder of George Parkman at Harvard provided her with a store of bloodcurdling detail. Louisa's short but indelible service as a nurse in the Civil War brought her a harvest of characters along with a shattering illness in which delirium alternated with unconsciousness, aspects of disease most adaptable to the blood-and-thunder variety of fiction. As companion to a sickly young woman, Louisa went abroad in 1865. Europe yielded her dramatis personae ranging from a Russian baron to an English colonel, from a mysterious lady resembling Marie Antoinette to a charming Polish boy. There too she saw Mazzini, pallid, diaphanous, wearing deep mourning for his country, the perfect hero for a dramatic destiny in a sensational story. For a Louisa Alcott who never stopped taking notes, Europe provided also a panorama of backgrounds—exotic, colorful, romantic. As her father wrote to her: "Your visit to Chillon and description of . . . the Prison, is as good for the romancer as for the poet, and this with the legend the best matereal [*sic*] for a story by the former." [8]

Bronson Alcott called his scribbling daughter "an arsenal of powers." [9] In that arsenal was stored still another personal source for stories. All her life the redoubtable Louisa May Alcott had gone barnstorming and all her life she had dreamed of the ten dramatic passions.[10] The "Louy Alcott troupe," of which Louisa May, age ten, was author-director, gave way to family tableaux and dramatic performances in the Hillside barn. At fifteen Louisa dipped her pen into gaudy ink as, with her sister Anna, she wrote the scripts of a succession of melodramas whose titles and subtitles foreshadow those of the thrillers that were to come: "Norna; or, The Witch's Curse"; "The Captive of Castile; or, The Moorish Maiden's Vow." The props and appurtenances, the backgrounds and characters of these early plays staged for the Concord neighbors are familiar to readers of blood-and-thunder tales: ghosts and stolen scrolls, duels and magic potions, dungeon cells and gloomy woods, murder and suicide.

Throughout her life Louisa carried the theater with her wherever she went. She took the roles of director, author, and actress in drawing-room charades or plays in the Boston kitchen. With lightning changes of costume she ranged from a prince in silver armor to a murderer in chains, until she confided to her journal that she would be a Siddons if she could. From her later work in the Amateur Dramatic Company of Walpole and the Concord Dramatic Union, Louisa gained a certain professionalism in her attitude toward the theater. In 1860 her farce, *Nat Bachelor's Pleasure Trip,* was actually staged at the Howard Athenaeum, Boston, and the playwright received a bouquet as she viewed the performance from a private parlor box. Louisa received more than a bouquet from her experience in theatricals and her romance with greasepaint. She developed a skill in lively dialogue, in suspenseful plotting, and in broad-stroke character delineation, skills she would one day apply to her blood-and-thunder tales. "I fancy 'lurid' things," she wrote in her 1850 journal, "if true and strong also"[11]—a fancy she would gratify a decade later. Like many of the episodes of her life, Louisa's addiction to the theater provided both a source and a training ground for what would follow.

So too did her reading. Dickens she devoured, reading aloud with her sister Anna the dialogue of Sairey Gamp and Betsey Prig, thrilling to the tale of Reuben Haredale's murder, reinaugurating the Pickwick Club in Concord. Books from Emerson's study could be borrowed: Dante and Shakespeare, Carlyle and Goethe. "R.W.E. gave me 'Wilhelm Meister,'" she noted, "and from that day Goethe has been my chief idol."[12] (Her chief idol, it needs no reminding, had delved into matters alchemical and antiquarian, and his Faust had made a world-famous pact with the devil.) *The Heir of Redclyffe* was a favorite of Louisa's and so too was Hawthorne's *Scarlet Letter*. Indeed, she was so enthralled by novels that in one lofty moment she "made a resolution to read fewer novels, and those only of the best."[13]

There can be no doubt at all that the fiction addict Louisa Alcott dipped from time to time into the gore of the Gothic novel. In America that type of romance was so enthusiastically received that as early as 1797 both "dairymaid and hired hand" amused themselves "into an agreeable terror with the haunted houses and hobgoblins of Mrs. Radcliffe."[14] By the time she had become an omnivorous reader a host of Gothic novels was available to her in English or in English translation. In their pages Louisa could envision settings, mouth language, and cogitate themes. She could wander from ruined abbey to frowning castle, from haunted gallery and feudal hall to pathless forest and chilly catacomb. She could savor romantic words—*repasts, casements, chambers*. She could revel in unholy themes—deals with the devil and the raising of the dead, secret sects and supernatural agencies. Horace Walpole's marvelous machinery, Mrs. Ann Radcliffe's ghosts, Monk Lewis's horrors, William Beckford's Oriental terror, Ludwig Tieck's vampires were all available to her. So too, of course, were the strange stories of Washington Irving, the haunting stories of Nathaniel Hawthorne, the subtle tales of Poe the master, whose horrors were the unknown horrors of the mind.[15]

Probably Louisa Alcott had been moved to write as soon as she had learned to read. The compulsion was hers early to combine threads of her own experience with the threads of the books she had read and interweave them into a fabric of her own creating.[16] Her first published work was a poem, entitled "Sunlight," that appeared in the September, 1851, issue of *Peterson's Magazine*. Interestingly, it was pseudonymous, for it was signed "Flora Fairfield." The poem was followed in May, 1852, by Louisa's first published prose narrative, "The Rival Painters: A Tale of Rome," for which the author received five dollars along with the delight of seeing her initials in print.

Despite a devastating rebuke from the publisher James T. Fields, who advised her, "Stick to your teaching, Miss Alcott. You can't write," Louisa persisted. In 1854 "Flora Fairfield" adorned the *Saturday Evening Gazette* with "The Rival Prima Donnas," a tale of vengeance in which one singer crushed her competitor to death by means of an iron ring placed upon her head. In the garret with her papers around her and a pile of apples nearby, the twenty-two-year-old spinner of tales evolved plots about strong-minded women and poor lost creatures until she became the mainstay of the *Gazette*.

At the same time, in 1855, her full name appeared as the author of her first published book, *Flower Fables*, "legends of faery land" she had devised for Emerson's daughter Ellen. The book netted her thirty-two dollars. In the sky parlor of a Boston boardinghouse Louisa continued to write when she was not teaching or sewing. "Love and Self-Love," the story of an attempted suicide woven from her own temptation at the Mill Dam, was accepted by James Russell Lowell, editor of *The Atlantic Monthly*. "M. L.," a story of slavery and abolition, was rejected. The author went on consuming piles of paper. She had caught the writing fever and boasted to Alf Whitman, "My 'works of art' are in such demand that I shall be one great blot soon."[17] She worked on two novels: *Moods*, a medley of death, sleepwalking, and shipwreck; and *Success* (later changed to *Work*), an autobiographical romance in which she would one day insert a chapter on insanity, suicide, and thwarted love. After her brief service as a Civil War nurse, Louisa converted her experience into a realistic narrative, *Hospital Sketches*, first serialized in *The Commonwealth* and subsequently published in book form.

Seated at her desk, an old green-and-red party wrap draped around her as a "glory cloak," Louisa pondered in groves of manuscripts. In 1855 her earnings included fifty dollars from teaching, fifty dollars from sewing, and twenty dollars from stories.[18] Yet she not only preferred pen and ink to birch and book—or needle—she was committed. Her pen was never and would never be idle. She lived in her inkstand. Some years later, when she supplied *The New York Ledger* with an article on "Happy Women," [19] she would include a sketch of herself as the scribbling spinster.

The scribbling spinster had already had a variety of writing experience. From flower fables to realistic hospital sketches, from tales of virtue rewarded to tales of violence, she had tried her ink-stained hand. Now, in her early thirties, she would attempt still another experiment. The letter to Alf Whitman revealed the plan: "I intend to illuminate the Ledger with a blood & thunder tale as they are easy to 'compoze' & are better paid than moral . . . works." For Louisa May Alcott they were indeed easy to compose. She could stir in her witch's caldron a brew concocted from her own experience, her observations and needs, as well as from the books she had read, for, like Washington Irving, she had "read somewhat, heard and seen more, and dreamt more than all." Louisa's blood-and-thunder tales would be not only "necessity stories" produced for money—from fifty to seventy-five dollars each— but a psychological catharsis. What is more, although their author never publicly acknowledged them, these experiments would stand the test of time. The future author of *Little Women* added much of her own to the genre. Indeed, had she persisted in the writing of thrillers, the name of Louisa May Alcott may well have conjured up the rites of a Walpurgis Night instead of the wholesome domesticities of a loving family.

In 1862, in the midst of the Civil War, *Frank Leslie's Illustrated Newspaper,* a popular New York weekly devoted to alluring pictures, gossip, and murder trials, offered a one-hundred-dollar prize for a story. To pay the family debts and at the same time to give vent to the pent-up emotions of her thirty years, Louisa Alcott wrote the first of her blood-and-thunder tales. Though it would be published anonymously, "Pauline's Passion and Punishment" [20] bore the stamp of its author, who immediately developed her own technique and outlined a theme to which she would often return. While her plots were violent enough and her backdrops remote enough to merit classification in the Gothic genre, Louisa was principally concerned with character. Of all the characters she adumbrated in these narratives the one who came most completely to life and who obviously was as intriguing to her author as to readers was the passionate, richly sexual *femme fatale* who had a mysterious past, an electrifying present, and a revengeful future. In such a heroine—so different from the submissive heroine of the Gothic formula—Louisa May Alcott could distill her passion for dramatics and her feminist anger at a world of James Richardsons. At the same time she could win a sorely needed hundred dollars.

In "Pauline's Passion and Punishment," as in all the Alcott thrillers, the reader is immediately introduced to problems of character rather than of plot. The suspense lies less in what the heroine will *do* than in what the heroine *is,* although both considerations become entwined as the character develops and the plot advances. In a fascinating opening, the anonymous author places onstage her Pauline, a proud and passionate woman who has lost all—fortune and, as a result of one man's perfidy, love. She is left with her fury and her desire for revenge, emotions which become the motivating forces in an ironic plot.

Against the background of an exotic paradise, a green wilderness where the tamarind vies with the almond tree, the spotlight falls upon Pauline Valary, pacing "to and fro, like a wild creature in its cage," a "handsome woman, with bent head, locked hands, and restless steps." She is a woman scorned by her lover, Gilbert Redmond, who has abandoned her for a moneyed bride. In swift course she arouses the devotion of the sensitive, young, southern romantic Manuel, who, attracted by her implicit sexuality, becomes not only her husband but her accomplice in the intended destruction of Gilbert Redmond. She does not plan Gilbert's murder but some more subtle revenge. "There are fates more terrible than death, weapons more keen than poniards, more noiseless than pistols. . . . Leave Gilbert to remorse—and me." And so, on page 1 of her thriller, the already skillful author has sketched in her characters, spotlighted her heroine, set her scene, and suggested a suspenseful plot.

The suspense mounts in the search for Gilbert and the dramatic encounter with him and his bride. The character is embroidered as Pauline's "woman's tongue" avenges her and "with feminine skill" she "mutely conveys the rebuke she would not trust herself to utter, by stripping the glove from the hand he had touched, and dropping it disdainfully." The meeting of Gilbert and Pauline is the meeting of man and woman, a meeting in which Pauline silently accepts Gilbert's challenge to the "tournament so often held between man and woman —a tournament where the keen tongue is the lance, pride the shield, passion the fiery steed, and the hardest heart the winner of the prize, which seldom fails to prove a barren honor, ending in remorse." And so faint alarms and excursions subtly suggest without overtly revealing the denouement.

Pauline's inexorable anger intensifies until she is possessed by a devil—not one with a cloven hoof but a subtle psychological force for evil. Her little stage performance and "drama of deceit"—all Louisa's heroines are actresses on the stage or off—her machinations to bankrupt Gilbert "in love, honor, liberty, and hope" fail utterly in the end.

The winner of Frank Leslie's one-hundred-dollar prize adopted the pseudonym of A. M. Barnard for a tale she submitted to another flamboyant weekly, *The Flag of Our Union*. Despite her preoccupation with passionate and angry heroines, Louisa was already too skillful a writer to repeat herself without variation. "The Abbot's Ghost: or, Maurice Treherne's Temptation" [21] is set in no exotic Cuban paradise but a haunted English abbey replete with screaming peacocks, thick-walled gallery and arched stone roof, armored figures and an abbot's ghost. A Dickensian flavor attaches to these Gothic appurtenances as, sitting round the hall fire, the dramatis personae tell tales of ghosts and coffins, skeletons and haunted houses. The star of that dramatis personae is less the hero of the title than the magnificent Edith Snowden, a strong-willed woman burdened by a heavy cross, a mysterious past, and jealousies that conflict with "contending emotions of . . . remorse and despair." "The Abbot's Ghost" is filled with psychological insights that illuminate the subtle relationships of the characters. The plot, revolving principally about the sudden cure of the crippled Maurice Treherne and ending with a triple wedding in the abbey, is basically a love story narrated against a strongly Gothic background. It comes to life through the brilliant depiction of a woman of passion and power whose furies are banked by her innate nobility.

Unlike the anonymous "Pauline's Passion" and the pseudonymous "Abbot's Ghost," *The Mysterious Key* [22] has a male hero, a charming young Italianate Englishman, and unlike either of those narratives, *The Mysterious Key* was published over the name of Louisa May Alcott. The possibility suggests itself that Louisa insisted upon secrecy less for her blood-and-thunder stories in general than for her passionate and angry heroines in particular.

The hero of *The Mysterious Key* combines a touch of that Polish boy who, with Alf Whitman, was to become the Laurie of *Little*

Women, and a strong hint of the pale and ardent Italian patriot Mazzini. Paul's appearance at the Trevlyn home in Warwickshire—an estate adequately equipped with haunted room and state chamber—touches off an elaborate plot. Well paced, it depends for its unfoldment upon a prophetic rhyme and a mysterious black-bearded visitor, a sealed letter and an ancient family volume, pretended sleepwalking, a touch of bigamy and a blind ward, Helen. The silver key that opens the Trevlyn tomb and discloses a mildewed paper proving Helen's identity is less mysterious and less intriguing than the hero Paul who, as Paolo, had been—like Mazzini—a hero in the Italian Revolution. All loose ends—and there are many—are neatly tied as the silver key slips into the door of a grisly tomb unlocking "a tragedy of life and death."

Between "Pauline's Passion," written in 1862, and *The Mysterious Key,* which appeared in 1867, Louisa wrote other gaudy, gruesome, and psychologically perceptive thrillers. Sitting incognito behind her pen, she produced "V. V.: or, Plots and Counterplots," an involved tale about a danseuse, Virginie Varens, whose flesh bore the tattooed letters *V. V.* above a lover's knot. A mysterious iron ring, drugged coffee, four violent deaths, and a viscount parading as a deaf-and-dumb Indian servant were the ingredients of this heady witch's broth. Poison vied with pistols or daggers for "the short road to . . . revenge," garments were dyed with blood, the heroine concluded her dark bargain, and the author doubtless recalled with nostalgia the comic tragedies of her childhood. This flight into the all-but-impossible not only emblazoned the pages of a sensational newspaper but was reprinted as a ten-cent novelette.[23]

Like "V. V.," "A Marble Woman: or, The Mysterious Model"[24] was filled with a variety of plots and counterplots as well as a colorful cast of characters that included a sculptor, Bazil Yorke, and an opium-eating heroine. The plight of Mme. Mathilde Arnheim was pursued by the indefatigable writer in *The Skeleton in the Closet,*[25] the narrative of a woman married to an idiot husband and bound to him by a tie which death alone could sever.

Of all the blood-and-thunder tales conceived by Louisa May Alcott when her hair was down and her dander up, the most extraordinary—in this critic's opinion at least—is the one that gives this book its title. "Behind a Mask: or, A Woman's Power"[26] is not only *per se* a suspenseful story recounted in a masterly manner; it fuses in its crucible many of the elements that had gone into the life of its author.

It engrosses the reader while it makes use of and reflects the experiences and emotions of its creator. "Behind a Mask" is therefore a Gothic *roman à clef,* a fast-moving narrative whose episodes unlock the past not only of the heroine Jean Muir but of the writer Louisa Alcott. Behind this mask, perhaps, the future author of *Little Women* sits for a dark but revealing portrait.

Jean Muir is many things: a woman bent, like Pauline Valary, upon revenge; a woman who, to achieve her ends, resorts to all sorts of coquetries and subterfuges including the feigning of an attempted suicide; a woman filled with anger directed principally against the male lords of creation. But she is primarily an actress.

The arrival of a new governess at the ancestral Coventry estate in England—a role played by Jean Muir—sets the plot in motion. She appears, pale-faced, small, and thin, not more than nineteen years old, and the first scene she enacts is an effective, sympathy-arousing faint. "Scene first, very well done," murmurs the astute Gerald, to which she replies, "The last scene shall be still better."

The mystery is suggested, the suspense begun, the plot laid down when, in the privacy of her room, Miss Muir proceeds to open a flask and drink "some ardent cordial," remove the braids from her head, wipe the pink from her face, take out "several pearly teeth" and emerge "a haggard, worn, and moody woman of thirty. . . . The metamorphosis was wonderful. . . . her mobile features settled into their natural expression, weary, hard, bitter. . . . brooding over some wrong, or loss, or disappointment which had darkened all her life."

Very gradually Miss Muir's transformation is made intelligible until she develops into one of Miss Alcott's most fascinating heroines. Like Pauline Valary she is, of course, a *femme fatale* with whom every male member of the Coventry household, including the fifty-five-year-old Sir John Coventry, falls madly in love. Her background is mysterious. She has lived in Paris, traveled in Russia, can sing brilliant Italian airs and read character. Her powers are fatal. She confesses to one of her lovers, "I *am* a witch, and one day my disguise will drop away and you will see me as I am, old, ugly, bad and lost."

Jean Muir is indeed a psychological if not a Gothic witch. Proud and passionate, mysterious and mocking, she wields a subtle spell. Motivated like Pauline by thwarted love, she carries out her intention of ruining the Coventry family with deliberation, using all the dramatic skills known to the theater. She lies or cries at will, feigns timidity or imperiousness to suit her needs. In a remarkable episode, when impromptu tableaux are performed in the great saloon of Coventry Hall, Miss Muir darkens her skin, paints her brows, and writes hatred on her face. Success crowns all her efforts for she captures her prize —the middle-aged head of the House of Coventry and with him a title and an estate. Meanwhile her secret is out. And what a feminist secret it is!

The temptation at the Mill Dam, the humiliation at Dedham, the theatrical barnstorming, the readings in Gothic romances were all stirred in the caldron of "Behind a Mask." So too were Louisa's conflicting emotions, her hates and her loves, her challenge to fortune. Weaving from these varied threads a tale of evil and passion, of fury and revenge, A. M. Barnard had used her sources well.

Just why Louisa May Alcott selected that pseudonym remains conjectural. "A.M." were her mother's initials—Abigail May; "Barnard" might have been suggested by the distinguished Connecticut educator Henry Barnard, who was a family friend. For the most part, the thrillers, whether pseudonymous, anonymous, or upon one or two occasions in her own name, were issued by two publishing firms. One of them boasted an editor who was as much of a *femme fatale* as L. M. Alcott could conjure up. The other included a partner whose life strongly suggested the episodes of a sensational novel. In her editorial and publishing negotiations therefore, A. M. Barnard—whether she was aware of it or not—was among kindred spirits.

"Wrote two tales for L.," Louisa noted in her 1862 journal. "I enjoy romancing to suit myself; and though my tales are silly, they are not bad; and my sinners always have a good spot somewhere. I hope it is good drill for fancy and language, for I can do it fast; and Mr. L. says my tales are so 'dramatic, vivid, and full of plot,' they are just what he wants." And a few months later: "Rewrote the last story, and sent it to L., who wants more than I can send him." [27]

1862 was the year of Antietam and Fredericksburg. It was not for the home circle alone that so-called family newspapers and cheap paperbacks were printed, but for soldiers in camp who could while away tedious hours between battles by escaping to an ancestral estate in Britain or a tropical paradise in Cuba. As the war gathered momentum, the market for such literature widened and with it the need for new authors and new stories.

The "L." of Louisa's journal, to whom she offered "Pauline's Passion" in competition for the announced hundred-dollar prize, was well aware of this need. Frank Leslie,[28] publisher of *Frank Leslie's Illustrated Newspaper,* had his hand on the public pulse. He had begun life as Henry Carter, wood engraver in England, adopted the pseudonym of Frank Leslie, and migrated to America. Ruddy, black-bearded, aggressive, dynamic, he had in 1855 launched his *Illustrated Newspaper,* a project that was to make him a power on New York's Publishers' Row. With its graphic cuts of murders and assassinations, prizefights and fires, the weekly was to dominate the field of illustrated journalism for nearly three-quarters of a century. It sported just enough text to float the pictures instead of just enough pictures to float the text. Thanks to a clever and ingenious device, Leslie was able to produce his pictures—sometimes mammoth double-page engravings—with unprecedented speed. Thanks to his editorial staff, he was able to select text that titillated an ever-expanding readership whether it gathered at hearth or campfire.

It was E. G. Squier who wrote to Louisa May Alcott in December, 1862, when she herself was nursing at the Union Hotel Hospital: "Your tale 'Pauline' this morning was awarded the $100 prize for the best short tale for Mr. Leslie's newspaper, and you will hear from him in due course in reference to what you may regard as an essential part of the matter. I presume that it will be on hand for those little Christmas purchases. Allow me to congratulate you on your success and to recommend you to submit whatever you may hereafter have of the same sort for Mr. Leslie's acceptance." [29]

E. G. Squier, scholar-archaeologist serving temporarily as a Leslie editor, was married to another Leslie protégée who could have served as prototype for every one of Louisa's *femmes fatales*. Miriam Florence Squier [30] had been born in New Orleans in 1836, and throughout a stormy, flamboyant, and successful life in the North she remained a southern belle. Much of that life would have fascinated A. M. Barnard. Between Miriam's first two marriages she had gone barnstorming with Lola Montez under the stage name of Minnie Montez. As knowledgeable editor of the House of Leslie she sported a blue stocking on one leg, but her other leg was encased in a stocking as scarlet as any worn by Pauline Valary or Jean Muir. Eventually Mrs. Squier would marry not only Frank Leslie but his publishing domain, becoming a *grande dame* and a forcible power as head of the House of Leslie before going on to other conquests marital and extramarital.

In A. M. Barnard's heyday, during the early 1860's, this was the colorful trio who managed the Leslie publications. With the new year of 1863 *Frank Leslie's Illustrated Newspaper* announced that, after deliberating over the moral tendency and artistic merit of over two hundred manuscripts, the editor had decided to award the first prize to "a lady of Massachusetts" for "Pauline's Passion and Punishment." [31] In the next number, the first half of a story of "exceeding power, brilliant description, thrilling incident and unexceptionable moral" was anonymously published, with appropriate illustrations of "Manuel reading Gilbert's Letter" and "Gilbert's Despair at Pauline's Final Rejection." "Received $100 from F.L.," Louisa commented in her journal, "for a tale which won the prize last January; paid debts, and was glad that my winter bore visible fruit." [32]

Other seasons also bore visible fruit that ripened in the Leslie periodicals. "A Whisper in the Dark," [33] a tale too mild for A. M. Barnard but too lurid for L. M. Alcott, and "Enigmas," [34] a mystery about Italian refugees, a spy and a woman disguised as a man, made their bows in the *Illustrated Newspaper*. In 1866 Miriam Squier reminded Louisa May Alcott that Frank Leslie would be glad to receive a sensational story from her every month at fifty dollars each. [35]

By that time the tireless author was receiving between two and three dollars a column for thrillers produced for a Boston publishing firm headed by yet another remarkable trio. In the ears of those three gentlemen the call of the wild still echoed, for one had edited tales that embodied it, a second had yielded to it by sailing to New Granada aboard the *Crescent City*, and a third had been the hero of a sensational novel which, if written, would have included chapters on the conquest of California, gold digging, a jaunt to the Sandwich and Fiji islands, China, and Australia. If A. M. Barnard was ever at a loss for a plot she needed merely to hearken to the lives of Messrs. Elliott, Thomes, and Talbot of Boston. [36] William Henry Thomes, who had succumbed to gold fever, had also encountered Indians, coyotes, and grizzlies, had sailed aboard an opium smuggler that plied between China and California, and was himself a mine of suggestions for authors whose thrilling romances he would publish. As publisher of the *True Flag*, James R. Elliott had edited the type of story William

Thomes had lived. The two formed a publishing partnership in 1861, a year after the New York firm of Beadle had introduced their dime-novel series to an avid American reading public. Joined by Newton Talbot, who had listed to the call of the wild by sailing to New Granada, the trio set out their shingle on Boston's Washington Street and, like the House of Leslie in New York, proceeded to issue a chain of periodicals and novelettes that would bring adventure and romance to a nation at war.

The mainstay of their business was *The Flag of Our Union*,[37] a miscellaneous weekly designed for the home circle. Though, according to its publishers, it contained "not one vulgar word or line," it did seem to specialize in violent narratives peopled with convicts and opium addicts. It was for that periodical that Louisa May Alcott under the pseudonym of A. M. Barnard produced her bloodiest and most thunderous thrillers.

A series of five letters from James R. Elliott to Louisa M. Alcott written between 1865 and 1866 reveals her relations with the Boston trio, their terms, and their reactions to her effusions:

> *Jan. 5. 1865.*
>
> *I forward you this evening the 3 first copies of the "Flag" in its new form.*
>
> *I think it is now a literary paper that none need to blush for, and a credit to contribute to its columns, rather than otherwise.*
>
> *Now I have a proposition to make you. I want to publish your story "V.V." in it, in place of publishing it as a Novelette in cheap style, as I had intended, and will give you $25. more for the story provided I can publish it under your own name.*
>
> *Please look the "Flag" over & let me know as early as Saturday. . . .*[38]

Louisa resisted the additional twenty-five dollars and "V.V.: or, Plots and Counterplots," its authorship unacknowledged, appeared as a four-part serial in *The Flag of Our Union* in February, 1865. It was later reprinted as No. 80 in the firm's series of *Ten Cent Novelettes of Standard American Authors*—this standard author bearing the name of A. M. Barnard. Elliott's subsequent letters reflect his own growing addiction for the productions of that standard author and his repeated desire to use the name of Louisa May Alcott, known now for her *Hospital Sketches,* in place of A. M. Barnard:

Jan. 7. 1865.

I should be pleased to have you write me some stories for the Flag, of about 25 to 40 pages of such Ms. as "V.V." I want them over your own name of course, & will give you $2.00 a column (short columns you will notice) for them. That rate will be fully equal to $16.00 for a first page story in the "American Union" . . . I have entered your name on our gratis list, & you will receive the "Flag" regularly. . . .

P.S. I will purchase another Novelette of you at any time you may wish to dispose of one. . . .

On January 21, 1865, Elliott followed this with the brief but revealing note that was to provide the clue to the Alcott pseudonym:

You may send me anything in either the sketch or Novelette line that you do not wish to "father", or that you wish A. M. Barnard, or "any other man" to be responsible for, & if they suit me I will purchase them.

. . . I will give you $3,00 per column (run in inside length) for sketches under your own name.

Let me hear from you.

Between January and June of 1865, when the next extant letter is dated, Elliott did indeed hear from Miss Alcott, for her "Marble Woman" was run in May and June. The insatiable publisher demanded more, writing on June 15:

Have you written anything in the novel line you would like to have me publish "by A M. Barnard, author of "V.V." "The Marble Woman" &c. &c.? If not can you furnish me with a sensation story of about 145 to 150 pages such Mss. as your last "The Marble Woman" so that I can have it by the middle of July? I don't care about even any particular name, if you prefer any other nome [sic] de plume for this one story, use it, as it is for one of my cheap Novelettes.

I will give you $50. for such a story, & don't want it to exceed 150 pages of Mss. the size of "The Marble Woman," 140 pages will answer, or 145 will be better.

By the way my friends think the "Marble Woman" is just splendid; & I think no author of novels need be ashamed to own it for a bantling. I am sorry you should have had any feeling in regard to the nome [sic] de plume. I am sure that I have not given currency to the idea that "A. M. Barnard" & yourself were identical.

Please let me hear from you by return mail, if possible; in regard to the short novel.

In August, 1866, the last extant letter in this extraordinary correspondence was written:

The story entitled "Behind A Mask" is accepted. I think it a story of peculiar power, and have no doubt but my readers will be quite as much fascinated with it as I was myself while reading the Ms. I will give you $65. for it. . . .
I should like another by the 20th of September.
Can I have one? . . .

The source of supply seemed as limitless as the demand. "The Abbot's Ghost" followed "Behind a Mask," and in 1867 both *The Skeleton in the Closet* and *The Mysterious Key* appeared in paperback—the former in the *Ten Cent Novelettes* series as No. 49 along with Perley Parker's *The Foundling* and the latter as No. 50.

There is little doubt that Louisa enjoyed not only the monetary rewards for her surreptitious labors but the use of a pseudonym, the secret correspondence with her publishers—the whole clandestine procedure involved in producing thrillers from "behind a mask." There is little doubt too that she would have enjoyed the story of the discovery of her pseudonym and of her anonymous and pseudonymous narratives. If the ghost of A. M. Barnard still haunts an earthly realm it will surely hover close at hand as that mystery is unraveled.

The unmasking of Louisa May Alcott took place while the country was engaged in another conflict, the Second World War. I was at work on a biography of Louisa May Alcott. With my lifelong friend and future business partner—Dr. Leona Rostenberg, printing historian and founder of our firm, Leona Rostenberg—Rare Books—I visited a distinguished Alcott collector. Carroll Atwood Wilson was a handsome and urbane gentleman, an attorney and a bibliophile who showed his bookish treasures with an enthusiasm equaled only by our intense interest.[39] He knew his Alcott well, and his Alcott characters, especially Jo March of *Little Women*, who, it will be recalled, offered sensational stories to the publishers of the *Weekly Volcano* and *Blarneystone Banner*. Mr. Wilson showed us many volumes by Louisa May Alcott, among them the copy of *The Mysterious Key* that was used in the preparation of the present collection. And as he dusted off the books, handing them to us one by one, he remarked, "Miss Stern, you must get yourself a Guggenheim Fellowship and complete your biography of Louisa May Alcott." Then, mindful of Leona Rostenberg's preoccupation with bibliographical problems and printing history, he turned to her. "Miss Rostenberg, we know that Louisa Alcott wrote blood-and-thunder stories just as Jo March did. And we know she had some sort of pseudonym. We don't know what the pseudonym was and we don't know anything about the stories. You identify the pseudonym and locate the stories."

Both Miss Stern and Miss Rostenberg proceeded to carry out Mr. Wilson's injunctions. At Houghton Library, Harvard University, where we delved through piles of manuscript and mountains of family letters, Leona came upon the five letters from James R. Elliott of Elliott, Thomes & Talbot to Louisa May Alcott that revealed the pseudonym, the titles of three of the thrillers and the name of the periodical that issued them. For the Sherlock Holmes of Houghton Library the rest was elementary—or would have been elementary had the exigencies of war not intervened.

The Flag of Our Union, it appeared, was and is, in the language of booksellers, an uncommon periodical. The Library of Congress boasts one of the more complete runs. To wartime Washington, therefore, Sherlock Rostenberg repaired, having paved the way with the necessary correspondence. Armed with her deerstalker and her magnifying glass, not to mention the all but intolerable anticipatory palpitations of the scholar bent on discovery, she awaited the arrival of the Civil War run of *The Flag of Our Union,* only to be informed that the periodical had been placed in safekeeping "for the duration." Despite this frustration, Leona Rostenberg was able to announce her extraordinary discovery in an article entitled "Some Anonymous and Pseudonymous Thrillers of Louisa M. Alcott," published in the *Papers* of the Bibliographical Society of America in 1943.[40] In the thirty years that have followed that announcement the discovery has been referred to in bibliographies, biographies, and publishing histories. But it is not until now that the stories themselves have been unearthed and reprinted.

The author herself, whose secret was so well hidden, viewed her clandestine productions with some ambivalence. Like her illustrious mentor Ralph Waldo Emerson, many critics objected strongly to the "yellow-covered literature of the Sylvanus Cobb, Jr. stamp," and Louisa was sometimes inclined to agree with this denunciation. When she converted *The Flag of Our Union* into the *Blarneystone Banner* and *Frank Leslie's Illustrated Newspaper* into the *Weekly Volcano* as media for Jo March's "necessity stories," she might have had her tongue in cheek but she was also looking down her nose. Later, reprinting "The Baron's Gloves" in a collection of *Proverb Stories*, she explained her motive: "As many girls have asked to see what sort of tales Jo March wrote at the beginning of her career, I have added 'The Baron's Gloves,' as a sample of the romantic rubbish which paid so well once upon a time. If it shows them what *not* to write it will not have been rescued from oblivion in vain."[41]

Yet there was another side to the complex Louisa May Alcott. Her thrillers were "necessity stories" of course, but the necessity was not merely monetary. In a revealing conversation she once doffed her mask and confessed her addiction to blood-and-thunder:

> I think my natural ambition is for the lurid style. I indulge in gorgeous fancies and wish that I dared inscribe them upon my pages and set them before the public. . . . How should I dare to interfere with the proper grayness of old Concord? The dear old town has never known a startling hue since the redcoats were there. Far be it from me to inject an inharmonious color into the neutral tint. And my favorite characters! Suppose they went to cavorting at their own sweet will, to the infinite horror of dear Mr. Emerson, who never imagined a Concord person as walking off a plumb line stretched between two pearly clouds in the empyrean. To have had Mr. Emerson for an intellectual god all one's life is to be invested with a chain armor of propriety. . . . And what would my own good father think of me . . . if I set folks to doing the things that I have a longing to see my people do? No, my dear, I shall always be a wretched victim to the respectable traditions of Concord.[42]

Actually, Louisa May Alcott was a victim less to "the respectable traditions of Concord" than to her own success. In September of 1867 she noted in her journal, "Niles, partner of Roberts, asked me to write a girls' book. Said I'd try."[43] The result was *Little Women*, the first part of which appeared in 1868, the second in 1869. The families of New England, the merchants of Boston, in time the American public itself laughed and cried over a story destined to become a perennial best seller. The girl who had gone out to service and hemmed pillow-cases to fill the gaps in the Alcott Sinking Fund had made her fortune. At the same time, the author who had dispatched thrillers to Frank Leslie and James R. Elliott had presumably found her style. The niche she had walked into with *Little Women* was too comfortable to abandon. Henceforth Louisa May Alcott would have neither the necessity nor the time to play A. M. Barnard.

Only when her publishers, Roberts Brothers of Boston, projected a "No Name Series" would the author of *Little Women* revert to the literary subterfuge of the author of "Behind a Mask." In *A Modern Mephistopheles*, published anonymously in that series in 1877, Louisa Alcott fused the influences of Hawthorne and Goethe and added to her cast of "lurid" characters the pagan figure of Felix Canaris, who sold liberty and love for fame; the sybarite Jasper Helwyze, her "modern Mephistopheles," who sought out the evil in mankind; and Olivia the mellow beauty. "It has been simmering," the author wrote in her journal, "ever since I read Faust last year. Enjoyed doing it, being tired of providing moral pap for the young." [44] Surely The Children's Friend must have found nostalgic pleasure in returning to the ingredients of earlier caldrons: hashish enclosed in a tortoiseshell bonbonnière; mesmerism; "skins mooned and barred with black upon the tawny velvet"; a heroine who walked, as Pauline Valary had done, with the "restless grace of a leopardess pacing its cage."

Yet No. 6 in the "No Name Series" could not restore the past to the author of No. 50 in the *Ten Cent Novelettes* series. The past was buried between the fading blue wrappers of those *Ten Cent Novelettes* or in the dusty pages of the once gaudy weeklies *The Flag of Our Union, Frank Leslie's Illustrated Newspaper*. It is time to brush the dust away, for the stories are better than their author realized and their reprinting is long overdue.

Although they are rare and all but impossible to find today, rarity alone would not entitle them to the wide readership which should be accorded this collection. Like all the authors of sensational literature, Louisa Alcott was equipped with a riotous imagination, a dramatic instinct, and an indefatigable right hand. If she borrowed from other Gothic romancers the trappings of a rich aristocracy in which she could forget her own penury, if her language upon occasion was high-style pompous and her themes ghostly-gruesome, she nonetheless added much of her own to the genre she had adopted. Her plotting was tight and well paced and she used the serial form to heighten the mounting suspense of her narratives. Her characterizations were natural and subtle and her gallery of *femmes fatales* forms a suite of flesh-and-blood portraits. Her own anger at an unjust world she transformed into the anger of her heroines, who made of it a powerful weapon with which to challenge fate. The psychological insights of A. M. Barnard disclose the darker side of the character of Louisa May Alcott, and so her stories must appeal enormously to all who have been enthralled by the life and work of the author of *Little Women*. Since those same psychological insights reveal her as intensely modern, intensely if obliquely feminist, her stories must command an immediate response today. They are rich with interest for those in search of current themes and preoccupations as well as for those in search of Louisa May Alcott. And for those who seek merely the thrills of the cliff-hanger, they bring the delights of the suspenseful tale well told.

The four narratives selected for *Behind a Mask* are, it is hoped, an earnest, a foretaste of others that will follow. For Louisa Alcott was indeed a natural—an almost limitless—"source of stories." Here her "gorgeous fancies" and her flamboyant characters do "cavort at their own sweet will." And here, in an extraordinary union, the excitements of escape are coupled with the excitements of self-discovery. She writes in a vortex behind her mask and she proves, if proof is needed, that "the writers of sensation novels are wiser in their generation than the children of sweetness and light."[45]

NOTES

[1] Louisa May Alcott to Alf Whitman, Concord, June 22 [1862] (Houghton Library, Harvard University).

[2] Louisa May Alcott to James Redpath, n.p., n.d. (New York Historical Society).

[3] Ednah D. Cheney, ed., *Louisa May Alcott: Her Life, Letters, and Journals* (Boston, 1889) p. 70 [hereinafter Cheney]. For biographical details about Louisa May Alcott, see also Madeleine B. Stern, *Louisa May Alcott* (Norman, Okla., 1971).

[4] Cheney, pp. 124–125.

[5] *Ibid.*, p. 89.

[6] Louisa May Alcott, "How I Went Out to Service," *The Independent*, XXVI:1331 (June 4, 1874); Stern, *Louisa May Alcott*, pp. 64–66. The Dedham family was identified with the help of the late Mr. Frank W. Kimball and Dr. Arthur M. Worthington, both of Dedham, Mass. In *An Address . . . before . . . the Massachusetts Charitable Fire Society* (Boston, 1810), James Richardson announced, "Benevolence is both a sentiment and a duty." See also Alvan Lamson, *A Discourse on The Life and Character of Hon. James Richardson* (Boston, 1858).

According to "Gossip," *Frank Leslie's Lady's Journal*, XIX:476 (December 25, 1880), p. 115, Louisa May Alcott had worked as a servant in a former Senator's household. A young theological student who boarded with the family asked her to black his boots shortly after her term as a servant had expired. Her reply was that while studying divinity he should have learned humanity. Despite inaccuracies, this is an interesting record, especially since it appeared in a Leslie periodical.

[7] Stern, *Louisa May Alcott*, pp. 89–91.

[8] A. Bronson Alcott to Louisa, Concord, December 17, 1865, in Richard L. Herrnstadt, ed., *The Letters of A. Bronson Alcott* (Ames, Iowa [1969]), p. 379.

[9] A. Bronson Alcott to Mrs. A. Bronson Alcott, St. Louis, November 30, 1866, *ibid.*, p. 397.

[10] *Comic Tragedies Written by "Jo" and "Meg" and Acted by the "Little Women"* (Boston, 1893); Stern, *Louisa May Alcott, passim;* Madeleine B. Stern, "Louisa Alcott, Trouper," *The New England Quarterly*, XVI:2 (June, 1943); Madeleine B. Stern, "The Witch's Cauldron to the Family Hearth: Louisa M. Alcott's Literary Development, 1848–1868," *More Books, The Bulletin of the Boston Public Library* (October, 1943), p. 363.

[11] Cheney, p. 63.

[12] *Ibid.*, p. 45.

[13] *Ibid.*, p. 68.

[14] Edith Birkhead, *The Tale of Terror: A Study of the Gothic Romance* (New York [1920]), p. 197.

[15] For a fine anthology of Gothic novels with extremely informative introductions, see Peter Haining, ed., *Gothic Tales of Terror*, I and II (Baltimore, 1973).

[16] For Louisa May Alcott's writings, see the Bibliography appended to Stern, *Louisa May Alcott*, pp. 342–360; Madeleine B. Stern, *Louisa's Wonder Book: A Newly Discovered Alcott Juvenile* (Mount Pleasant, Mich., 1975); Jacob Blanck, *Bibliography of American Literature* (New Haven, 1955), I, 27–45.

[17] Louisa May Alcott to Alf Whitman, April 5 [1860] (Houghton Library), quoted in Stern, *Louisa May Alcott*, p. 97.

[18] Cheney, p. 80.

[19] Louisa May Alcott, "Happy Women," *The New York Ledger*, XXIV:7 (April 11, 1868).

[20] "Pauline's Passion and Punishment," *Frank Leslie's Illustrated Newspaper*, XV:379 and 380 (January 3 and 10, 1863). Published anonymously. Now reprinted from issues at the New York Public Library and the New York Historical Society Library.

21 "The Abbot's Ghost: or, Maurice Treherne's Temptation," *The Flag of Our Union*, XXII:1, 2, 3, and 4 (January 5, 12, 19, 26, 1867). Published under the pseudonym of A. M. Barnard. Now reprinted through the courtesy of Mr. William Matheson, Chief, Rare Book Division, Library of Congress.

22 L. M. Alcott, *The Mysterious Key, and What It Opened* (Boston: Elliott, Thomes & Talbot, [1867]). Issued as No. 50 in the *Ten Cent Novelettes* of *Standard American Authors* series. Reprinted as No. 382 in *The Leisure Hour Library* by F. M. Lupton of New York, ca. 1900. For bibliographical details, see Blanck, *op. cit.*, No. 152 and No. 231. Now reprinted through the courtesy of Dr. Julius P. Barclay, Curator of Rare Books, and Miss Joan Crane, Alderman Library, University of Virginia. The copy at the University of Virginia had belonged to Carroll Atwood Wilson.

23 "V. V.: or, Plots and Counterplots," *The Flag of Our Union*, XX:5, 6, 7, 8 (February 4, 11, 18, 25, 1865). Reprinted as No. 80 in the *Ten Cent Novelettes* of *Standard American Authors* series under the pseudonym of A. M. Barnard. For bibliographical details, see Blanck, *op. cit.*, No. 165.

24 "A Marble Woman: or, The Mysterious Model," *The Flag of Our Union*, XX: 20, 21, 22, 23 (May 20, 27, June 3, 10, 1865). Published under the pseudonym of A. M. Barnard.

25 L. M. Alcott, *The Skeleton in the Closet*. Published with Perley Parker, *The Foundling* (Boston: Elliott, Thomes & Talbot [1867]), as No. 49 in the *Ten Cent Novelettes* of *Standard American Authors* series. For bibliographical details, see Blanck, *op cit.*, No. 151.

26 "Behind a Mask: or, A Woman's Power," *The Flag of Our Union*, XXI:41, 42, 43, 44 (October 13, 20, 27, November 3, 1866). Published under the pseudonym of A. M. Barnard. Now reprinted through the courtesy of Dr. Marc A. McCorison, American Antiquarian Society, Worcester, Mass.

27 Cheney, p. 131.

28 For details of Frank Leslie and his *Illustrated Newspaper*, see Frank Luther Mott, *A History of American Magazines 1850–1865* (Cambridge, Mass., 1957) II, 452–465; Madeleine B. Stern, *Imprints on History: Book Publishers and American Frontiers* (Bloomington, Ind., 1956), pp. 221–232; Madeleine B. Stern, *Purple Passage: The Life of Mrs. Frank Leslie* (Norman, Okla., 1970), *passim*; John

Tebbel, *A History of Book Publishing in the United States* (New York and London, 1972) I, 357–358.

[29] E. G. Squier to Louisa May Alcott, ca. December 18, 1862 (Orchard House, Concord, Mass.). Quoted in Leona Rostenberg, "Some Anonymous and Pseudonymous Thrillers of Louisa M. Alcott," *Papers* of the Bibliographical Society of America, XXXVII:2 (1943). See also Stern, *Louisa May Alcott*, p. 123.

[30] For Miriam Squier's tumultuous life and career, see Stern, *Purple Passage, passim.*

[31] Stern, *Louisa May Alcott*, p. 128.

[32] Cheney, p. 151.

[33] "A Whisper in the Dark," *Frank Leslie's Illustrated Newspaper*, XVI:401 and 402 (June 6 and 13, 1863). Reprinted in *A Modern Mephistopheles and A Whisper in the Dark* (Boston, 1889).

[34] "Enigmas," *Frank Leslie's Illustrated Newspaper*, XVIII:450 and 451 (May 14 and 21, 1864).

[35] Miriam F. Squier to Louisa May Alcott, New Rochelle, September 17, 1866 (Houghton Library, Harvard University). See also Stern, *Purple Passage*, p. 220.

[36] For Elliott, Thomes & Talbot, see Rostenberg, "Some Anonymous and Pseudonymous Thrillers of Louisa M. Alcott," *passim;* Stern, *Imprints on History*, pp. 206–220; Tebbel, *A History of Book Publishing in the United States* I, 438–440.

[37] The periodical ran from 1846 to 1870. See Mott, *A History of American Magazines* II, 35.

[38] The letters, which were found in the Louisa M. Alcott MSS., Box II (Houghton Library, Harvard University), were first printed in Rostenberg, *op. cit.* Quotations have been made from their text, and two of the letters have been reproduced by permission of the Harvard College Library.

[39] See Carroll A. Wilson, *Thirteen Author Collections of the Nineteenth Century and Five Centuries of Familiar Quotations.* Edited by Jean C. S. Wilson and David A. Randall (New York, 1950).

[40] Rostenberg, *op. cit.*

[41] Louisa May Alcott, Preface, *Proverb Stories* (Boston, 1882). See Madeleine B. Stern, "Louisa M. Alcott's Self-Criticism," *More Books, The Bulletin of the Boston Public Library*, XX:8 (October, 1945), p. 341.

[42] From a conversation with Louisa May Alcott. See L. C. Pickett, *Across My Path: Memories of People I Have Known* (New York, 1916), pp. 107–108. See also Stern, "Louisa M. Alcott's Self-Criticism," *loc. cit.*, p. 341.

[43] Cheney, p. 186.

[44] *Ibid.*, p. 296. See also Stern, *Louisa May Alcott*, pp. 264–265; Madeleine B. Stern, "Louisa M. Alcott: An Appraisal," *The New England Quarterly*, XXII:4 (December, 1949), pp. 494–496.

[45] Dorothy L. Sayers and Robert Eustace, *The Documents in the Case* (New York, [1972]), p. 81.

AMERICAN UNION,
    Three Dollars a year.
FLAG OF OUR UNION,
    Four Dollars a year.
MONTHLY NOVELETTE,
    Two Dollars a year.
DOLLAR MONTHLY,
    $1.50 a year.
OFFICE OF **Elliott, Thomes & Talbot's Publications,**
63 CONGRESS STREET,

Boston, Aug. 11 1866,

Dear Miss Alcott,

The story entitled "Behind A Mask" is accepted. I think it a story of peculiar power, and have no doubt but my readers will be quite as much fascinated with it as I was myself while reading the Ms. I will give you $65. for it. That amt awaits your order.

I should like another by the 20th of September. Can I have one? I shd be happy to pay you $5. each for two or three poems by Miss Alcott.

Very Truly Yours
J. R. Elliott.

Boston Jan. 21. 1865.

Dear Miss Alcott,

You may send me anything in either the sketch or Novelette line that you do not wish to "father", or that you wish A. M. Barnard, or "any other man" to be responsible for, & if they suit me I will purchase them.

I will pay for poems under your own name. Also I will give you $3.00 per Column (Union inside length) for sketches under your own name.

Let me hear from you.

Very Truly Yours

J. R. Elliott

Behind a Mask

or

A WOMAN'S POWER

BY A. M. BARNARD

≈ *chapter I* ≈

JEAN MUIR

"HAS she come?"

"No, Mamma, not yet."

"I wish it were well over. The thought of it worries and excites me. A cushion for my back, Bella."

And poor, peevish Mrs. Coventry sank into an easy chair with a nervous sigh and the air of a martyr, while her pretty daughter hovered about her with affectionate solicitude.

"Who are they talking of, Lucia?" asked the languid young man lounging on a couch near his cousin, who bent over her tapestry work with a happy smile on her usually haughty face.

"The new governess, Miss Muir. Shall I tell you about her?"

"No, thank you. I have an inveterate aversion to the whole tribe. I've often thanked heaven that I had but one sister, and she a spoiled child, so that I have escaped the infliction of a governess so long."

"How will you bear it now?" asked Lucia.

"Leave the house while she is in it."

"No, you won't. You're too lazy, Gerald," called out a younger and more energetic man, from the recess where he stood teasing his dogs.

"I'll give her a three days' trial; if she proves endurable I shall not disturb myself; if, as I am sure, she is a bore, I'm off anywhere, anywhere out of her way."

"I beg you won't talk in that depressing manner, boys. I dread the coming of a stranger more than you possibly can, but Bella *must* not be neglected; so I have nerved myself to endure this woman, and Lucia is good enough to say she will attend to her after tonight."

"Don't be troubled, Mamma. She is a nice person, I dare say, and when once we are used to her, I've no doubt we shall be glad to have her, it's so dull here just now. Lady Sydney said she was a quiet, accomplished, amiable girl, who needed a home, and would be a help to poor stupid me, so try to like her for my sake."

"I will, dear, but isn't it getting late? I do hope nothing has happened. Did you tell them to send a carriage to the station for her, Gerald?"

"I forgot it. But it's not far, it won't hurt her to walk" was the languid reply.

"It was indolence, not forgetfulness, I know. I'm very sorry; she will think it so rude to leave her to find her way so late. Do go and see to it, Ned."

"Too late, Bella, the train was in some time ago. Give your orders to me next time. Mother and I'll see that they are obeyed," said Edward.

"Ned is just at an age to make a fool of himself for any girl who comes in his way. Have a care of the governess, Lucia, or she will bewitch him."

Gerald spoke in a satirical whisper, but his brother heard him and answered with a good-humored laugh.

"I wish there was any hope of your making a fool of yourself in that way, old fellow. Set me a good example, and I promise to follow it. As for the governess, she is a woman, and should be treated with common civility. I should say a little extra kindness wouldn't be amiss, either, because she is poor, and a stranger."

"That is my dear, good-hearted Ned! We'll stand by poor little Muir, won't we?" And running to her brother, Bella stood on tiptoe to offer him a kiss which he could not refuse, for the rosy lips were pursed up invitingly, and the bright eyes full of sisterly affection.

"I do hope she has come, for, when I make an effort to see anyone, I hate to make it in vain. Punctuality is *such* a virtue, and I know this woman hasn't got it, for she promised to be here at seven, and now it is long after," began Mrs. Coventry, in an injured tone.

Before she could get breath for another complaint, the clock struck seven and the doorbell rang.

"There she is!" cried Bella, and turned toward the door as if to go and meet the newcomer.

But Lucia arrested her, saying authoritatively, "Stay here, child. It is her place to come to you, not yours to go to her."

"Miss Muir," announced a servant, and a little black-robed figure stood in the doorway. For an instant no one stirred, and the governess had time to see and be seen before a word was uttered. All looked at her, and she cast on the household group a keen glance that impressed them curiously; then her eyes fell, and bowing slightly she walked in. Edward came forward and received her with the frank cordiality which nothing could daunt or chill.

"Mother, this is the lady whom you expected. Miss Muir, allow me to apologize for our apparent neglect in not sending for you. There was a mistake about the carriage, or, rather, the lazy fellow to whom the order was given forgot it. Bella, come here."

"Thank you, no apology is needed. I did not expect to be sent for." And the governess meekly sat down without lifting her eyes.

"I am glad to see you. Let me take your things," said Bella, rather shyly, for Gerald, still lounging, watched the fireside group with languid interest, and Lucia never stirred. Mrs. Coventry took a second survey and began:

"You were punctual, Miss Muir, which pleases me. I'm a sad invalid, as Lady Sydney told you, I hope; so that Miss Coventry's lessons will be directed by my niece, and you will go to her for directions, as she knows what I wish. You will excuse me if I ask you a few questions, for Lady Sydney's note was very brief, and I left everything to her judgment."

"Ask anything you like, madam," answered the soft, sad voice.

"You are Scotch, I believe."

"Yes, madam."

"Are your parents living?"

"I have not a relation in the world."

"Dear me, how sad! Do you mind telling me your age?"

"Nineteen." And a smile passed over Miss Muir's lips, as she folded her hands with an air of resignation, for the catechism was evidently to be a long one.

"So young! Lady Sydney mentioned five-and-twenty, I think, didn't she, Bella?"

"No, Mamma, she only said she thought so. Don't ask such questions. It's not pleasant before us all," whispered Bella.

A quick, grateful glance shone on her from the suddenly lifted eyes of Miss Muir, as she said quietly, "I wish I was thirty, but, as I am not, I do my best to look and seem old."

Of course, every one looked at her then, and all felt a touch of pity at the sight of the pale-faced girl in her plain black dress, with no ornament but a little silver cross at her throat. Small, thin, and colorless she was, with yellow hair, gray eyes, and sharply cut, irregular, but very expressive features. Poverty seemed to have set its bond stamp upon her, and life to have had for her more frost than sunshine. But something in the lines of the mouth betrayed strength, and the clear, low voice had a curious mixture of command and entreaty in its varying tones. Not an attractive woman, yet not an ordinary one; and, as she sat there with her delicate hands lying in her lap, her head bent, and a bitter look on her thin face, she was more interesting than many a blithe and blooming girl. Bella's heart warmed to her at once, and she drew her seat nearer, while Edward went back to his dogs that his presence might not embarrass her.

"You have been ill, I think," continued Mrs. Coventry, who considered this fact the most interesting of all she had heard concerning the governess.

"Yes, madam, I left the hospital only a week ago."

"Are you quite sure it is safe to begin teaching so soon?"

"I have no time to lose, and shall soon gain strength here in the country, if you care to keep me."

"And you are fitted to teach music, French, and drawing?"

"I shall endeavor to prove that I am."

"Be kind enough to go and play an air or two. I can judge by your touch; I used to play finely when a girl."

Miss Muir rose, looked about her for the instrument, and seeing it at the other end of the room went toward it, passing Gerald and Lucia as if she did not see them. Bella followed, and in a moment forgot everything in admiration. Miss Muir played like one who loved music and was perfect mistress of her art. She charmed them all by the magic of this spell; even indolent Gerald sat up to listen, and Lucia put down her needle, while Ned watched the slender white fingers as they flew, and wondered at the strength and skill which they possessed.

"Please sing," pleaded Bella, as a brilliant overture ended.

With the same meek obedience Miss Muir complied, and began a little Scotch melody, so sweet, so sad, that the girl's eyes filled, and Mrs. Coventry looked for one of her many pocket-handkerchiefs. But suddenly the music ceased, for, with a vain attempt to support herself, the singer slid from her seat and lay before the startled listeners, as white and rigid as if struck with death. Edward caught her up, and, ordering his brother off the couch, laid her there, while Bella chafed her hands, and her mother rang for her maid. Lucia bathed the poor girl's temples, and Gerald, with unwonted energy, brought a glass of wine. Soon Miss Muir's lips trembled, she sighed, then murmured, tenderly, with a pretty Scotch accent, as if wandering in the past, "Bide wi' me, Mither, I'm sae sick an sad here all alone."

"Take a sip of this, and it will do you good, my dear," said Mrs. Coventry, quite touched by the plaintive words.

The strange voice seemed to recall her. She sat up, looked about her, a little wildly, for a moment, then collected herself and said, with a pathetic look and tone, "Pardon me. I have been on my feet all day, and, in my eagerness to keep my appointment, I forgot to eat since morning. I'm better now; shall I finish the song?"

"By no means. Come and have some tea," said Bella, full of pity and remorse.

"Scene first, very well done," whispered Gerald to his cousin.

Miss Muir was just before them, apparently listening to Mrs. Coventry's remarks upon fainting fits; but she heard, and looked over her shoulders with a gesture like Rachel. Her eyes were gray, but at that instant they seemed black with some strong emotion of anger, pride, or defiance. A curious smile passed over her face as she bowed, and said in her penetrating voice, "Thanks. The last scene shall be still better."

Young Coventry was a cool, indolent man, seldom conscious of any emotion, any passion, pleasurable or otherwise; but at the look, the tone of the governess, he experienced a new sensation, indefinable, yet strong. He colored and, for the first time in his life, looked abashed. Lucia saw it, and hated Miss Muir with a sudden hatred; for, in all the years she had passed with her cousin, no look or word of hers had possessed such power. Coventry was himself again in an instant, with no trace of that passing change, but a look of interest in his usually dreamy eyes, and a touch of anger in his sarcastic voice.

"What a melodramatic young lady! I shall go tomorrow."

Lucia laughed, and was well pleased when he sauntered away to bring her a cup of tea from the table where a little scene was just taking place. Mrs. Coventry had sunk into her chair again, exhausted by the flurry of the fainting fit. Bella was busied about her; and Edward, eager to feed the pale governess, was awkwardly trying to make the tea, after a beseeching glance at his cousin which she did not choose to answer. As he upset the caddy and uttered a despairing exclamation, Miss Muir quietly took her place behind the urn, saying with a smile, and a shy glance at the young man, "Allow me to assume my duty at once, and serve you all. I understand the art of making people comfortable in this way. The scoop, please. I can gather this up quite well alone, if you will tell me how your mother likes her tea."

Edward pulled a chair to the table and made merry over his mishaps, while Miss Muir performed her little task with a skill and grace that made it pleasant to watch her. Coventry lingered a moment after she had given him a steaming cup, to observe her more nearly, while he asked a question or two of his brother. She took no more notice of him than if he had been a statue, and in the middle of the one remark he addressed to her, she rose to take the sugar basin to Mrs. Coventry, who was quite won by the modest, domestic graces of the new governess.

"Really, my dear, you are a treasure; I haven't tasted such tea since my poor maid Ellis died. Bella never makes it good, and Miss Lucia always forgets the cream. Whatever you do you seem to do well, and that is *such* a comfort."

"Let me always do this for you, then. It will be a pleasure, madam." And Miss Muir came back to her seat with a faint color in her cheek which improved her much.

"My brother asked if young Sydney was at home when you left," said Edward, for Gerald would not take the trouble to repeat the question.

Miss Muir fixed her eyes on Coventry, and answered with a slight tremor of the lips, "No, he left home some weeks ago."

The young man went back to his cousin, saying, as he threw himself down beside her, "I shall not go tomorrow, but wait till the three days are out."

"Why?" demanded Lucia.

Lowering his voice he said, with a significant nod toward the governess, "Because I have a fancy that she is at the bottom of Sydney's mystery. He's not been himself lately, and now he is gone without a word. I rather like romances in real life, if they are not too long, or difficult to read."

"Do you think her pretty?"

"Far from it, a most uncanny little specimen."

"Then why fancy Sydney loves her?"

"He is an oddity, and likes sensations and things of that sort."

"What do you mean, Gerald?"

"Get the Muir to look at you, as she did at me, and you will understand. Will you have another cup, Juno?"

"Yes, please." She liked to have him wait upon her, for he did it to no other woman except his mother.

Before he could slowly rise, Miss Muir glided to them with another cup on the salver; and, as Lucia took it with a cold nod, the girl said under her breath, "I think it honest to tell you that I possess a quick ear, and cannot help hearing what is said anywhere in the room. What you say of me is of no consequence, but you may speak of things which you prefer I should not hear; therefore, allow me to warn you." And she was gone again as noiselessly as she came.

"How do you like that?" whispered Coventry, as his cousin sat looking after the girl, with a disturbed expression.

"What an uncomfortable creature to have in the house! I am very sorry I urged her coming, for your mother has taken a fancy to her, and it will be hard to get rid of her," said Lucia, half angry, half amused.

"Hush, she hears every word you say. I know it by the expression of her face, for Ned is talking about horses, and she looks as haughty as ever you did, and that is saying much. Faith, this is getting interesting."

"Hark, she is speaking; I want to hear," and Lucia laid her hand on her cousin's lips. He kissed it, and then idly amused himself with turning the rings to and fro on the slender fingers.

"I have been in France several years, madam, but my friend died and I came back to be with Lady Sydney, till—" Muir paused an instant, then added, slowly, "till I fell ill. It was a contagious fever, so I went of my own accord to the hospital, not wishing to endanger her."

"Very right, but are you sure there is no danger of infection now?" asked Mrs. Coventry anxiously.

"None, I assure you. I have been well for some time, but did not leave because I preferred to stay there, than to return to Lady Sydney."

"No quarrel, I hope? No trouble of any kind?"

"No quarrel, but—well, why not? You have a right to know, and I will not make a foolish mystery out of a very simple thing. As your family, only, is present, I may tell the truth. I did not go back on the young gentleman's account. Please ask no more."

"Ah, I see. Quite prudent and proper, Miss Muir. I shall never allude to it again. Thank you for your frankness. Bella, you will be careful not to mention this to your young friends; girls gossip sadly, and it would annoy Lady Sydney beyond everything to have this talked of."

"Very neighborly of Lady S. to send the dangerous young lady here, where there are *two* young gentlemen to be captivated. I wonder why she didn't keep Sydney after she had caught him," murmured Coventry to his cousin.

"Because she had the utmost contempt for a titled fool." Miss Muir dropped the words almost into his ear, as she bent to take her shawl from the sofa corner.

"How the deuce did she get there?" ejaculated Coventry, looking as if he had received another sensation. "She has spirit, though, and upon my word I pity Sydney, if he did try to dazzle her, for he must have got a splendid dismissal."

"Come and play billiards. You promised, and I hold you to your word," said Lucia, rising with decision, for Gerald was showing too much interest in another to suit Miss Beaufort.

"I am, as ever, your most devoted. My mother is a charming woman, but I find our evening parties slightly dull, when only my own family are present. Good night, Mamma." He shook hands with his mother, whose pride and idol he was, and, with a comprehensive nod to the others, strolled after his cousin.

"Now they are gone we can be quite cozy, and talk over things, for I don't mind Ned any more than I do his dogs," said Bella, settling herself on her mother's footstool.

"I merely wish to say, Miss Muir, that my daughter has never had a governess and is sadly backward for a girl of sixteen. I want you to pass the mornings with her, and get her on as rapidly as possible. In the afternoon you will walk or drive with her, and in the evening sit with us here, if you like, or amuse yourself as you please. While in the country we are very quiet, for I cannot bear much company, and when my sons want gaiety, they go away for it. Miss Beaufort oversees the servants, and takes my place as far as possible. I am very delicate and keep my room till evening, except for an airing at noon. We will try each other for a month, and I hope we shall get on quite comfortably together."

"I shall do my best, madam."

One would not have believed that the meek, spiritless voice which uttered these words was the same that had startled Coventry a few minutes before, nor that the pale, patient face could ever have kindled with such sudden fire as that which looked over Miss Muir's shoulder when she answered her young host's speech.

Edward thought within himself, Poor little woman! She has had a hard life. We will try and make it easier while she is here; and began his charitable work by suggesting that she might be tired. She acknowledged she was, and Bella led her away to a bright, cozy room, where with a pretty little speech and a good-night kiss she left her.

When alone Miss Muir's conduct was decidedly peculiar. Her first act was to clench her hands and mutter between her teeth, with passionate force, "I'll not fail again if there is power in a woman's wit and will!" She stood a moment motionless, with an expression of almost fierce disdain on her face, then shook her clenched hand as if menacing some unseen enemy. Next she laughed, and shrugged her shoulders with a true French shrug, saying low to herself, "Yes, the last scene *shall* be better than the first. *Mon dieu,* how tired and hungry I am!"

Kneeling before the one small trunk which held her worldly possessions, she opened it, drew out a flask, and mixed a glass of some ardent cordial, which she seemed to enjoy extremely as she sat on the carpet, musing, while her quick eyes examined every corner of the room.

"Not bad! It will be a good field for me to work in, and the harder the task the better I shall like it. *Merci,* old friend. You put heart and courage into me when nothing else will. Come, the curtain is down, so I may be myself for a few hours, if actresses ever are themselves."

Still sitting on the floor she unbound and removed the long

abundant braids from her head, wiped the pink from her face, took out several pearly teeth, and slipping off her dress appeared herself indeed, a haggard, worn, and moody woman of thirty at least. The metamorphosis was wonderful, but the disguise was more in the expression she assumed than in any art of costume or false adornment. Now she was alone, and her mobile features settled into their natural expression, weary, hard, bitter. She had been lovely once, happy, innocent, and tender; but nothing of all this remained to the gloomy woman who leaned there brooding over some wrong, or loss, or disappointment which had darkened all her life. For an hour she sat so, sometimes playing absently with the scanty locks that hung about her face, sometimes lifting the glass to her lips as if the fiery draught warmed her cold blood; and once she half uncovered her breast to eye with a terrible glance the scar of a newly healed wound. At last she rose and crept to bed, like one worn out with weariness and mental pain.

✦ *chapter II* ✦

A GOOD BEGINNING

O NLY the housemaids were astir when Miss Muir left her room next morning and quietly found her way into the garden. As she walked, apparently intent upon the flowers, her quick eye scrutinized the fine old house and its picturesque surroundings.

"Not bad," she said to herself, adding, as she passed into the adjoining park, "but the other may be better, and I will have the best."

Walking rapidly, she came out at length upon the wide green lawn which lay before the ancient hall where Sir John Coventry lived in solitary splendor. A stately old place, rich in oaks, well-kept shrubberies, gay gardens, sunny terraces, carved gables, spacious rooms, liveried servants, and every luxury befitting the ancestral home of a rich and honorable race. Miss Muir's eyes brightened as she looked, her step grew firmer, her carriage prouder, and a smile broke over her face; the smile of one well pleased at the prospect of the success of some cherished hope. Suddenly her whole air changed, she pushed back her hat, clasped her hands loosely before her, and seemed absorbed in girlish admiration of the fair scene that could not fail to charm any beauty-loving eye. The cause of this rapid change soon appeared. A hale, handsome man, between fifty and sixty, came through the little gate leading to the park, and, seeing the young stranger, paused to examine her. He had only time for a glance, however; she seemed conscious of his presence in a moment, turned with a startled look, uttered an exclamation of surprise, and looked as if hesitating whether to speak or run away. Gallant Sir John took off his hat and said, with the old-fashioned courtesy which became him well, "I beg your pardon for disturbing you, young lady. Allow me to atone for it by inviting you to walk where you will, and gather what flowers you like. I see you love them, so pray make free with those about you."

With a charming air of maidenly timidity and artlessness, Miss Muir replied, "Oh, thank you, sir! But it is I who should ask pardon for trespassing. I never should have dared if I had not known that Sir John was absent. I always wanted to see this fine old place, and ran over the first thing, to satisfy myself."

"And *are* you satisfied?" he asked, with a smile.

"More than satisfied—I'm charmed; for it is the most beautiful spot I ever saw, and I've seen many famous seats, both at home and abroad," she answered enthusiastically.

"The Hall is much flattered, and so would its master be if he heard you," began the gentleman, with an odd expression.

"I should not praise it to him—at least, not as freely as I have to you, sir," said the girl, with eyes still turned away.

"Why not?" asked her companion, looking much amused.

"I should be afraid. Not that I dread Sir John; but I've heard so many beautiful and noble things about him, and respect him so highly, that I should not dare to say much, lest he should see how I admire and—"

"And what, young lady? Finish, if you please."

"I was going to say, love him. I will say it, for he is an old man, and one cannot help loving virtue and bravery."

Miss Muir looked very earnest and pretty as she spoke, standing there with the sunshine glinting on her yellow hair, delicate face, and downcast eyes. Sir John was not a vain man, but he found it pleasant to hear himself commended by this unknown girl, and felt redoubled curiosity to learn who she was. Too well-bred to ask, or to abash her by avowing what she seemed unconscious of, he left both discoveries to chance; and when she turned, as if to retrace her steps, he offered her the handful of hothouse flowers which he held, saying, with a gallant bow, "In Sir John's name let me give you my little nosegay, with thanks for your good opinion, which, I assure you, is not entirely deserved, for I know him well."

Miss Muir looked up quickly, eyed him an instant, then dropped her eyes, and, coloring deeply, stammered out, "I did not know—I beg your pardon—you are too kind, Sir John."

He laughed like a boy, asking, mischievously, "Why call me Sir John? How do you know that I am not the gardener or the butler?"

"I did not see your face before, and no one but yourself would say that any praise was undeserved," murmured Miss Muir, still overcome with girlish confusion.

"Well, well, we will let that pass, and the next time you come we will be properly introduced. Bella always brings her friends to the Hall, for I am fond of young people."

"I am not a friend. I am only Miss Coventry's governess." And Miss Muir dropped a meek curtsy. A slight change passed over Sir John's manner. Few would have perceived it, but Miss Muir felt it at once, and bit her lips with an angry feeling at her heart. With a curious air of pride, mingled with respect, she accepted the still offered bouquet, returned Sir John's parting bow, and tripped away, leaving the old gentleman to wonder where Mrs. Coventry found such a piquant little governess.

"That is done, and very well for a beginning," she said to herself as she approached the house.

In a green paddock close by fed a fine horse, who lifted up his head and eyed her inquiringly, like one who expected a greeting. Following a sudden impulse, she entered the paddock and, pulling a handful of clover, invited the creature to come and eat. This was evidently a new proceeding on the part of a lady, and the horse careered about as if bent on frightening the newcomer away.

"I see," she said aloud, laughing to herself. "I am not your master, and you rebel. Nevertheless, I'll conquer you, my fine brute."

Seating herself in the grass, she began to pull daisies, singing idly the while, as if unconscious of the spirited prancings of the horse. Presently he drew nearer, sniffing curiously and eyeing her with surprise. She took no notice, but plaited the daisies and sang on as if he was not there. This seemed to pique the petted creature, for, slowly approaching, he came at length so close that he could smell her little foot and nibble at her dress. Then she offered the clover, uttering caressing words and making soothing sounds, till by degrees and with much coquetting, the horse permitted her to stroke his glossy neck and smooth his mane.

It was a pretty sight—the slender figure in the grass, the high-spirited horse bending his proud head to her hand. Edward Coventry, who had watched the scene, found it impossible to restrain himself any longer and, leaping the wall, came to join the group, saying, with mingled admiration and wonder in countenance and voice, "Good morning, Miss Muir. If I had not seen your skill and courage proved before my eyes, I should be alarmed for your safety. Hector is a wild, wayward beast, and has damaged more than one groom who tried to conquer him."

"Good morning, Mr. Coventry. Don't tell tales of this noble creature, who has not deceived my faith in him. Your grooms did not know how to win his heart, and so subdue his spirit without breaking it."

Miss Muir rose as she spoke, and stood with her hand on Hector's neck while he ate the grass which she had gathered in the skirt of her dress.

"You have the secret, and Hector is your subject now, though heretofore he has rejected all friends but his master. Will you give him his morning feast? I always bring him bread and play with him before breakfast."

"Then you are not jealous?" And she looked up at him with eyes so bright and beautiful in expression that the young man wondered he had not observed them before.

"Not I. Pet him as much as you will; it will do him good. He is a solitary fellow, for he scorns his own kind and lives alone, like his master," he added, half to himself.

"Alone, with such a happy home, Mr. Coventry?" And a softly compassionate glance stole from the bright eyes.

"That was an ungrateful speech, and I retract it for Bella's sake. Younger sons have no position but such as they can make for themselves, you know, and I've had no chance yet."

"Younger sons! I thought—I beg pardon." And Miss Muir paused, as if remembering that she had no right to question.

Edward smiled and answered frankly, "Nay, don't mind me. You thought I was the heir, perhaps. Whom did you take my brother for last night?"

"For some guest who admired Miss Beaufort. I did not hear his name, nor observe him enough to discover who he was. I saw only your kind mother, your charming little sister, and—"

She stopped there, with a half-shy, half-grateful look at the young man which finished the sentence better than any words. He was still a boy, in spite of his one-and-twenty years, and a little color came into his brown cheek as the eloquent eyes met his and fell before them.

"Yes, Bella is a capital girl, and one can't help loving her. I know you'll get her on, for, really, she is the most delightful little dunce. My mother's ill health and Bella's devotion to her have prevented our attending to her education before. Next winter, when we go to town, she is to come out, and must be prepared for that great event, you know," he said, choosing a safe subject.

"I shall do my best. And that reminds me that I should report myself to her, instead of enjoying myself here. When one has been ill and shut up a long time, the country is so lovely one is apt to forget duty for pleasure. Please remind me if I am negligent, Mr. Coventry."

"That name belongs to Gerald. I'm only Mr. Ned here," he said as they walked toward the house, while Hector followed to the wall and sent a sonorous farewell after them.

Bella came running to meet them, and greeted Miss Muir as if she had made up her mind to like her heartily. "What a lovely bouquet you have got! I never can arrange flowers prettily, which vexes me, for Mamma is so fond of them and cannot go out herself. You have charming taste," she said, examining the graceful posy which Miss Muir had much improved by adding feathery grasses, delicate ferns, and fragrant wild flowers to Sir John's exotics.

Putting them into Bella's hand, she said, in a winning way, "Take them to your mother, then, and ask her if I may have the pleasure of making her a daily nosegay; for I should find real delight in doing it, if it would please her."

"How kind you are! Of course it would please her. I'll take them to her while the dew is still on them." And away flew Bella, eager to give both the flowers and the pretty message to the poor invalid.

Edward stopped to speak to the gardener, and Miss Muir went up the steps alone. The long hall was lined with portraits, and pacing slowly down it she examined them with interest. One caught her eye, and, pausing before it, she scrutinized it carefully. A young, beautiful, but very haughty female face. Miss Muir suspected at once who it was, and gave a decided nod, as if she saw and caught at some unexpected chance. A soft rustle behind her made her look around, and, seeing Lucia, she bowed, half turned, as if for another glance at the picture, and said, as if involuntarily, "How beautiful it is! May I ask if it is an ancestor, Miss Beaufort?"

"It is the likeness of my mother" was the reply, given with a softened voice and eyes that looked up tenderly.

"Ah, I might have known, from the resemblance, but I scarcely saw you last night. Excuse my freedom, but Lady Sydney treated me as a friend, and I forget my position. Allow me."

As she spoke, Miss Muir stooped to return the handkerchief which had fallen from Lucia's hand, and did so with a humble mien which touched the other's heart; for, though a proud, it was also a very generous one.

"Thank you. Are you better, this morning?" she said, graciously. And having received an affirmative reply, she added, as she walked on, "I will show you to the breakfast room, as Bella is not here. It is a very informal meal with us, for my aunt is never down and my cousins are very irregular in their hours. You can always have yours when you like, without waiting for us if you are an early riser."

Bella and Edward appeared before the others were seated, and Miss Muir quietly ate her breakfast, feeling well satisfied with her hour's work. Ned recounted her exploit with Hector, Bella delivered her mother's thanks for the flowers, and Lucia more than once recalled, with pardonable vanity, that the governess had compared her to her lovely mother, expressing by a look as much admiration for the living likeness as for the painted one. All kindly did their best to make the pale girl feel at home, and their cordial manner seemed to warm and draw her out; for soon she put off her sad, meek air and entertained them with gay anecdotes of her life in Paris, her travels in Russia when governess in Prince Jermadoff's family, and all manner of witty stories that kept them interested and merry long after the meal was over. In the middle of an absorbing adventure, Coventry came in, nodded lazily, lifted his brows, as if surprised at seeing the governess there, and began his breakfast as if the ennui of another day had already taken possession of him. Miss Muir stopped short, and no entreaties could induce her to go on.

"Another time I will finish it, if you like. Now Miss Bella and I should be at our books." And she left the room, followed by her pupil, taking no notice of the young master of the house, beyond a graceful bow in answer to his careless nod.

"Merciful creature! she goes when I come, and does not make life unendurable by moping about before my eyes. Does she belong to the moral, the melancholy, the romantic, or the dashing class, Ned?" said Gerald, lounging over his coffee as he did over everything he attempted.

"To none of them; she is a capital little woman. I wish you had seen her tame Hector this morning." And Edward repeated his story.

"Not a bad move on her part," said Coventry in reply. "She must be an observing as well as an energetic young person, to discover your chief weakness and attack it so soon. First tame the horse, and then the master. It will be amusing to watch the game, only I shall be under the painful necessity of checkmating you both, if it gets serious."

"You needn't exert yourself, old fellow, on my account. If I was not above thinking ill of an inoffensive girl, I should say you were the prize best worth winning, and advise you to take care of your own heart, if you've got one, which I rather doubt."

"I often doubt it, myself; but I fancy the little Scotchwoman will not be able to satisfy either of us upon that point. How does your highness like her?" asked Coventry of his cousin, who sat near him.

"Better than I thought I should. She is well-bred, unassuming, and very entertaining when she likes. She has told us some of the wittiest stories I've heard for a long time. Didn't our laughter wake you?" replied Lucia.

"Yes. Now atone for it by amusing me with a repetition of these witty tales."

"That is impossible; her accent and manner are half the charm," said Ned. "I wish you had kept away ten minutes longer, for your appearance spoilt the best story of all."

"Why didn't she go on?" asked Coventry, with a ray of curiosity.

"You forget that she overheard us last night, and must feel that you consider her a bore. She has pride, and no woman forgets speeches like those you made," answered Lucia.

"Or forgives them, either, I believe. Well, I must be resigned to languish under her displeasure then. On Sydney's account I take a slight interest in her; not that I expect to learn anything from her, for a woman with a mouth like that never confides or confesses anything. But I have a fancy to see what captivated him; for captivated he was, beyond a doubt, and by no lady whom he met in society. Did you ever hear anything of it, Ned?" asked Gerald.

"I'm not fond of scandal or gossip, and never listen to either." With which remark Edward left the room.

Lucia was called out by the housekeeper a moment after, and

Coventry left to the society most wearisome to him, namely his own. As he entered, he had caught a part of the story which Miss Muir had been telling, and it had excited his curiosity so much that he found himself wondering what the end could be and wishing that he might hear it.

What the deuce did she run away for, when I came in? he thought. If she *is* amusing, she must make herself useful; for it's intensely dull, I own, here, in spite of Lucia. Hey, what's that?

It was a rich, sweet voice, singing a brilliant Italian air, and singing it with an expression that made the music doubly delicious. Stepping out of the French window, Coventry strolled along the sunny terrace, enjoying the song with the relish of a connoisseur. Others followed, and still he walked and listened, forgetful of weariness or time. As one exquisite air ended, he involuntarily applauded. Miss Muir's face appeared for an instant, then vanished, and no more music followed, though Coventry lingered, hoping to hear the voice again. For music was the one thing of which he never wearied, and neither Lucia nor Bella possessed skill enough to charm him. For an hour he loitered on the terrace or the lawn, basking in the sunshine, too indolent to seek occupation or society. At length Bella came out, hat in hand, and nearly stumbled over her brother, who lay on the grass.

"You lazy man, have you been dawdling here all this time?" she said, looking down at him.

"No, I've been very busy. Come and tell me how you've got on with the little dragon."

"Can't stop. She bade me take a run after my French, so that I might be ready for my drawing, and so I must."

"It's too warm to run. Sit down and amuse your deserted brother, who has had no society but bees and lizards for an hour."

He drew her down as he spoke, and Bella obeyed; for, in spite of his indolence, he was one to whom all submitted without dreaming of refusal.

"What have you been doing? Muddling your poor little brains with all manner of elegant rubbish?"

"No, I've been enjoying myself immensely. Jean is *so* interesting, so kind and clever. She didn't bore me with stupid grammar, but just talked to me in such pretty French that I got on capitally, and like it as I never expected to, after Lucia's dull way of teaching it."

"What did you talk about?"

"Oh, all manner of things. She asked questions, and I answered, and she corrected me."

"Questions about our affairs, I suppose?"

"Not one. She don't care two sous for us or our affairs. I thought she might like to know what sort of people we were, so I told her about Papa's sudden death, Uncle John, and you, and Ned; but in the midst of it she said, in her quiet way, 'You are getting too confidential, my dear. It is not best to talk too freely of one's affairs to strangers. Let us speak of something else.'"

"What were you talking of when she said that, Bell?"

"You."

"Ah, then no wonder she was bored."

"She was tired of my chatter, and didn't hear half I said; for she was busy sketching something for me to copy, and thinking of something more interesting than the Coventrys."

"How do you know?"

"By the expression of her face. Did you like her music, Gerald?"

"Yes. Was she angry when I clapped?"

"She looked surprised, then rather proud, and shut the piano at once, though I begged her to go on. Isn't Jean a pretty name?"

"Not bad; but why don't you call her Miss Muir?"

"She begged me not. She hates it, and loves to be called Jean, alone. I've imagined such a nice little romance about her, and someday I shall tell her, for I'm sure she has had a love trouble."

"Don't get such nonsense into your head, but follow Miss Muir's well-bred example and don't be curious about other people's affairs. Ask her to sing tonight; it amuses me."

"She won't come down, I think. We've planned to read and work in my boudoir, which is to be our study now. Mamma will stay in her room, so you and Lucia can have the drawing room all to yourselves."

"Thank you. What will Ned do?"

"He will amuse Mamma, he says. Dear old Ned! I wish you'd stir about and get him his commission. He is so impatient to be doing something and yet so proud he won't ask again, after you have neglected it so many times and refused Uncle's help."

"I'll attend to it very soon; don't worry me, child. He will do very well for a time, quietly here with us."

"You always say that, yet you know he chafes and is unhappy at being dependent on you. Mamma and I don't mind; but he is a man, and it frets him. He said he'd take matters into his own hands soon, and then you may be sorry you were so slow in helping him."

"Miss Muir is looking out of the window. You'd better go and take your run, else she will scold."

"Not she. I'm not a bit afraid of her, she's so gentle and sweet. I'm fond of her already. You'll get as brown as Ned, lying here in the sun. By the way, Miss Muir agrees with me in thinking him handsomer than you."

"I admire her taste and quite agree with her."

"She said he was manly, and that was more attractive than beauty in a man. She does express things so nicely. Now I'm off." And away danced Bella, humming the burden of Miss Muir's sweetest song.

" 'Energy is more attractive than beauty in a man.' She is right, but how the deuce *can* a man be energetic, with nothing to expend his energies upon?" mused Coventry, with his hat over his eyes.

A few moments later, the sweep of a dress caught his ear. Without stirring, a sidelong glance showed him Miss Muir coming across the terrace, as if to join Bella. Two stone steps led down to the lawn. He lay near them, and Miss Muir did not see him till close upon him. She started and slipped on the last step, recovered herself, and glided on, with a glance of unmistakable contempt as she passed the recumbent figure of the apparent sleeper. Several things in Bella's report had nettled him, but this look made him angry, though he would not own it, even to himself.

"Gerald, come here, quick!" presently called Bella, from the rustic seat where she stood beside her governess, who sat with her hand over her face as if in pain.

Gathering himself up, Coventry slowly obeyed, but involuntarily quickened his pace as he heard Miss Muir say, "Don't call him; *he* can do nothing"; for the emphasis on the word "he" was very significant.

"What is it, Bella?" he asked, looking rather wider awake than usual.

"You startled Miss Muir and made her turn her ankle. Now help her to the house, for she is in great pain; and don't lie there anymore to frighten people like a snake in the grass," said his sister petulantly.

"I beg your pardon. Will you allow me?" And Coventry offered his arm.

Miss Muir looked up with the expression which annoyed him and answered coldly, "Thank you, Miss Bella will do as well."

"Permit me to doubt that." And with a gesture too decided to be resisted, Coventry drew her arm through his and led her into the house. She submitted quietly, said the pain would soon be over, and when settled on the couch in Bella's room dismissed him with the briefest thanks. Considering the unwonted exertion he had made, he thought she might have been a little more grateful, and went away to Lucia, who always brightened when he came.

No more was seen of Miss Muir till teatime; for now, while the family were in retirement, they dined early and saw no company. The governess had excused herself at dinner, but came down in the evening a little paler than usual and with a slight limp in her gait. Sir John was there, talking with his nephew, and they merely acknowledged her presence by the sort of bow which gentlemen bestow on governesses. As she slowly made her way to her place behind the urn, Coventry said to his brother, "Take her a footstool, and ask her how she is, Ned." Then, as if necessary to account for his politeness to his uncle, he explained how he was the cause of the accident.

"Yes, yes. I understand. Rather a nice little person, I fancy. Not exactly a beauty, but accomplished and well-bred, which is better for one of her class."

"Some tea, Sir John?" said a soft voice at his elbow, and there was Miss Muir, offering cups to the gentlemen.

"Thank you, thank you," said Sir John, sincerely hoping she had overheard him.

As Coventry took his, he said graciously, "You are very forgiving, Miss Muir, to wait upon me, after I have caused you so much pain."

"It is my duty, sir" was her reply, in a tone which plainly said, "but not my pleasure." And she returned to her place, to smile, and chat, and be charming, with Bella and her brother.

Lucia, hovering near her uncle and Gerald, kept them to herself, but was disturbed to find that their eyes often wandered to the cheerful group about the table, and that their attention seemed distracted by the frequent bursts of laughter and fragments of animated conversation which reached them. In the midst of an account of a tragic affair which she endeavored to make as interesting and pathetic as possible, Sir John burst into a hearty laugh, which betrayed that he had been listening to a livelier story than her own. Much annoyed, she said hastily, "I knew it would be so! Bella has no idea of the proper manner in which to treat a governess. She and Ned will forget the difference of rank and spoil that person for her work. She is inclined to be presumptuous already, and if my aunt won't trouble herself to give Miss Muir a hint in time, I shall."

"Wait till she has finished that story, I beg of you," said Coventry, for Sir John was already off.

"If you find that nonsense so entertaining, why don't you follow Uncle's example? I don't need you."

"Thank you. I will." And Lucia was deserted.

But Miss Muir had ended and, beckoning to Bella, left the room, as if quite unconscious of the honor conferred upon her or the dullness she left behind her. Ned went up to his mother, Gerald returned to make his peace with Lucia, and, bidding them good-night, Sir John turned homeward. Strolling along the terrace, he came to the lighted window of Bella's study, and wishing to say a word to her, he half pushed aside the curtain and looked in. A pleasant little scene. Bella working busily, and near her in a low chair, with the light falling on her fair hair and delicate profile, sat Miss Muir, reading aloud. "Novels!" thought Sir John, and smiled at them for a pair of romantic girls. But pausing to listen a moment before he spoke, he found it was no novel, but history, read with a fluency which made every fact interesting, every sketch of character memorable, by the dramatic effect given to it. Sir John was fond of history, and failing eyesight often curtailed his favorite amusement. He had tried readers, but none suited him, and he had given up the plan. Now as he listened, he thought how pleasantly the smoothly flowing voice would wile away his evenings, and he envied Bella her new acquisition.

A bell rang, and Bella sprang up, saying, "Wait for me a minute. I must run to Mamma, and then we will go on with this charming prince."

Away she went, and Sir John was about to retire as quietly as he came, when Miss Muir's peculiar behavior arrested him for an instant. Dropping the book, she threw her arms across the table, laid her head down upon them, and broke into a passion of tears, like one who could bear restraint no longer. Shocked and amazed, Sir John stole away; but all that night the kindhearted gentleman puzzled his brains with conjectures about his niece's interesting young governess, quite unconscious that she intended he should do so.

❧ chapter III ❦

PASSION AND PIQUE

FOR several weeks the most monotonous tranquillity seemed to reign at Coventry House, and yet, unseen, unsuspected, a storm was gathering. The arrival of Miss Muir seemed to produce a change in everyone, though no one could have explained how or why. Nothing could be more unobtrusive and retiring than her manners. She was devoted to Bella, who soon adored her, and was only happy when in her society. She ministered in many ways to Mrs. Coventry's comfort, and that lady declared there never was such a nurse. She amused, interested and won Edward with her wit and womanly sympathy. She made Lucia respect and envy her for her accomplishments, and piqued indolent Gerald by her persistent avoidance of him, while Sir John was charmed with her respectful deference and the graceful little attentions she paid him in a frank and artless way, very winning to the lonely old man. The very servants liked her; and instead of being, what most governesses are, a forlorn creature hovering between superiors and inferiors, Jean Muir was the life of the house, and the friend of all but two.

Lucia disliked her, and Coventry distrusted her; neither could exactly say why, and neither owned the feeling, even to themselves. Both watched her covertly yet found no shortcoming anywhere. Meek, modest, faithful, and invariably sweet-tempered—they could complain of nothing and wondered at their own doubts, though they could not banish them.

It soon came to pass that the family was divided, or rather that two members were left very much to themselves. Pleading timidity, Jean Muir kept much in Bella's study and soon made it such a pleasant little nook that Ned and his mother, and often Sir John, came in to enjoy the music, reading, or cheerful chat which made the evenings so gay. Lucia at first was only too glad to have her cousin to herself, and he too lazy to care what went on about him. But presently he wearied of her society, for she was not a brilliant girl, and possessed few of those winning arts which charm a man and steal into his heart. Rumors of the merrymakings that went on reached him and made him curious to share them; echoes of fine music went sounding through the house, as he lounged about the empty drawing room; and peals of laughter reached him while listening to Lucia's grave discourse.

She soon discovered that her society had lost its charm, and the more eagerly she tried to please him, the more signally she failed. Before long Coventry fell into a habit of strolling out upon the terrace of an evening, and amusing himself by passing and repassing the window of Bella's room, catching glimpses of what was going on and reporting the result of his observations to Lucia, who was too proud to ask admission to the happy circle or to seem to desire it.

"I shall go to London tomorrow, Lucia," Gerald said one evening, as he came back from what he called "a survey," looking very much annoyed.

"To London?" exclaimed his cousin, surprised.

"Yes, I must bestir myself and get Ned his commission, or it will be all over with him."

"How do you mean?"

"He is falling in love as fast as it is possible for a boy to do it. That girl has bewitched him, and he will make a fool of himself very soon, unless I put a stop to it."

"I was afraid she would attempt a flirtation. These persons always do, they are such a mischief-making race."

"Ah, but there you are wrong, as far as little Muir is concerned. She does not flirt, and Ned has too much sense and spirit to be caught by a silly coquette. She treats him like an elder sister, and mingles the most attractive friendliness with a quiet dignity that captivates the boy. I've been watching them, and there he is, devouring her with his eyes, while she reads a fascinating novel in the most fascinating style.

Bella and Mamma are absorbed in the tale, and see nothing; but Ned makes himself the hero, Miss Muir the heroine, and lives the love scene with all the ardor of a man whose heart has just waked up. Poor lad! Poor lad!"

Lucia looked at her cousin, amazed by the energy with which he spoke, the anxiety in his usually listless face. The change became him, for it showed what he might be, making one regret still more what he was. Before she could speak, he was gone again, to return presently, laughing, yet looking a little angry.

"What now?" she asked.

" 'Listeners never hear any good of themselves' is the truest of proverbs. I stopped a moment to look at Ned, and heard the following flattering remarks. Mamma is gone, and Ned was asking little Muir to sing that delicious barcarole she gave us the other evening.

" 'Not now, not here,' she said.

" 'Why not? You sang it in the drawing room readily enough,' said Ned, imploringly.

" 'That is a very different thing,' and she looked at him with a little shake of the head, for he was folding his hands and doing the passionate pathetic.

" 'Come and sing it there then,' said innocent Bella. 'Gerald likes your voice so much, and complains that you will never sing to him.'

" 'He never asks me,' said Muir, with an odd smile.

" 'He is too lazy, but he wants to hear you.'

" 'When he asks me, I will sing—if I feel like it.' And she shrugged her shoulders with a provoking gesture of indifference.

" 'But it amuses him, and he gets so bored down here,' began stupid little Bella. 'Don't be shy or proud, Jean, but come and enter- tain the poor old fellow.'

" 'No, thank you. I engaged to teach Miss Coventry, not to amuse Mr. Coventry' was all the answer she got.

" 'You amuse Ned, why not Gerald? Are you afraid of him?' asked Bella.

"Miss Muir laughed, such a scornful laugh, and said, in that peculiar tone of hers, 'I cannot fancy anyone being *afraid* of your elder brother.'

" 'I am, very often, and so would you be, if you ever saw him angry.' And Bella looked as if I'd beaten her.

" 'Does he ever wake up enough to be angry?' asked that girl, with an air of surprise. Here Ned broke into a fit of laughter, and they are at it now, I fancy, by the sound."

"Their foolish gossip is not worth getting excited about, but I certainly would send Ned away. It's no use trying to get rid of 'that girl,' as you say, for my aunt is as deluded about her as Ned and Bella, and she really does get the child along splendidly. Dispatch Ned, and then she can do no harm," said Lucia, watching Coventry's altered face as he stood in the moonlight, just outside the window where she sat.

"Have you no fears for me?" he asked smiling, as if ashamed of his momentary petulance.

"No, have you for yourself?" And a shade of anxiety passed over her face.

"I defy the Scotch witch to enchant me, except with her music," he added, moving down the terrace again, for Jean was singing like a nightingale.

As the song ended, he put aside the curtain, and said, abruptly, "Has anyone any commands for London? I am going there tomorrow."

"A pleasant trip to you," said Ned carelessly, though usually his brother's movements interested him extremely.

"I want quantities of things, but I must ask Mamma first." And Bella began to make a list.

"May I trouble you with a letter, Mr. Coventry?"

Jean Muir turned around on the music stool and looked at him with the cold keen glance which always puzzled him.

He bowed, saying, as if to them all, "I shall be off by the early train, so you must give me your orders tonight."

"Then come away, Ned, and leave Jean to write her letter."

And Bella took her reluctant brother from the room.

"I will give you the letter in the morning," said Miss Muir, with a curious quiver in her voice, and the look of one who forcibly suppressed some strong emotion.

"As you please." And Coventry went back to Lucia, wondering who Miss Muir was going to write to. He said nothing to his brother of the purpose which took him to town, lest a word should produce the catastrophe which he hoped to prevent; and Ned, who now lived in a sort of dream, seemed to forget Gerald's existence altogether.

With unwonted energy Coventry was astir seven next morning. Lucia gave him his breakfast, and as he left the room to order the carriage, Miss Muir came gliding downstairs, very pale and heavy-eyed (with a sleepless, tearful night, he thought) and, putting a delicate little letter into his hand, said hurriedly, "Please leave this at Lady Sydney's, and if you see her, say 'I have remembered.'"

Her peculiar manner and peculiar message struck him. His eye involuntarily glanced at the address of the letter and read young Sydney's name. Then, conscious of his mistake, he thrust it into his pocket with a hasty "Good morning," and left Miss Muir standing with one hand pressed on her heart, the other half extended as if to recall the letter.

All the way to London, Coventry found it impossible to forget the almost tragical expression of the girl's face, and it haunted him through the bustle of two busy days. Ned's affair was put in the way of being speedily accomplished, Bella's commissions were executed, his mother's pet delicacies provided for her, and a gift for Lucia, whom the family had given him for his future mate, as he was too lazy to choose for himself.

Jean Muir's letter he had not delivered, for Lady Sydney was in the country and her townhouse closed. Curious to see how she would receive his tidings, he went quietly in on his arrival at home. Everyone had dispersed to dress for dinner except Miss Muir, who was in the garden, the servant said.

"Very well, I have a message for her"; and, turning, the "young master," as they called him, went to seek her. In a remote corner he saw her sitting alone, buried in thought. As his step roused her, a look of surprise, followed by one of satisfaction, passed over her face, and, rising, she beckoned to him with an almost eager gesture. Much amazed, he went to her and offered the letter, saying kindly, "I regret that I could not deliver it. Lady Sydney is in the country, and I did not like to post it without your leave. Did I do right?"

"Quite right, thank you very much—it is better so." And with an air of relief, she tore the letter to atoms, and scattered them to the wind.

More amazed than ever, the young man was about to leave her when she said, with a mixture of entreaty and command, "Please stay a moment. I want to speak to you."

He paused, eyeing her with visible surprise, for a sudden color dyed her cheeks, and her lips trembled. Only for a moment, then she was quite self-possessed again. Motioning him to the seat she had left, she remained standing while she said, in a low, rapid tone full of pain and of decision:

"Mr. Coventry, as the head of the house I want to speak to you, rather than to your mother, of a most unhappy affair which has occurred during your absence. My month of probation ends today; your mother wishes me to remain; I, too, wish it sincerely, for I am happy here, but I ought not. Read this, and you will see why."

She put a hastily written note into his hand and watched him intently while he read it. She saw him flush with anger, bite his lips, and knit his brows, then assume his haughtiest look, as he lifted his eyes and said in his most sarcastic tone, "Very well for a beginning. The boy has eloquence. Pity that it should be wasted. May I ask if you have replied to this rhapsody?"

"I have."

"And what follows? He begs you 'to fly with him, to share his fortunes, and be the good angel of his life.' Of course you consent?"

There was no answer, for, standing erect before him, Miss Muir regarded him with an expression of proud patience, like one who expected reproaches, yet was too generous to resent them. Her manner had its effect. Dropping his bitter tone, Coventry asked briefly, "Why do you show me this? What can I do?"

"I show it that you may see how much in earnest 'the boy' is, and how open I desire to be. You can control, advise, and comfort your brother, and help me to see what is my duty."

"You love him?" demanded Coventry bluntly.

"No!" was the quick, decided answer.

"Then why make him love you?"

"I never tried to do it. Your sister will testify that I have endeavored to avoid him as I—" And he finished the sentence with an unconscious tone of pique, "As you have avoided me."

She bowed silently, and he went on:

"I will do you the justice to say that nothing can be more blameless than your conduct toward myself; but why allow Ned to haunt you evening after evening? What could you expect of a romantic boy who had nothing to do but lose his heart to the first attractive woman he met?"

A momentary glisten shone in Jean Muir's steel-blue eyes as the last words left the young man's lips; but it was gone instantly, and her voice was full of reproach, as she said, steadily, impulsively, "If the 'romantic boy' had been allowed to lead the life of a man, as he longed to do, he would have had no time to lose his heart to the first sorrowful girl whom he pitied. Mr. Coventry, the fault is yours. Do not blame your brother, but generously own your mistake and retrieve it in the speediest, kindest manner."

For an instant Gerald sat dumb. Never since his father died had anyone reproved him; seldom in his life had he been blamed. It was a new experience, and the very novelty added to the effect. He saw his fault, regretted it, and admired the brave sincerity of the girl in telling him of it. But he did not know how to deal with the case, and was forced to confess not only past negligence but present incapacity. He was as honorable as he was proud, and with an effort he said frankly, "You are right, Miss Muir. I *am* to blame, yet as soon as I saw the danger, I tried to avert it. My visit to town was on Ned's account; he will have his commission very soon, and then he will be sent out of harm's way. Can I do more?"

"No, it is too late to send him away with a free and happy heart. He must bear his pain as he can, and it may help to make a man of him," she said sadly.

"He'll soon forget," began Coventry, who found the thought of gay Ned suffering an uncomfortable one.

"Yes, thank heaven, that is possible, for men."

Miss Muir pressed her hands together, with a dark expression on her half-averted face. Something in her tone, her manner, touched Coventry; he fancied that some old wound bled, some bitter memory awoke at the approach of a new lover. He was young, heart-whole, and romantic, under all his cool nonchalance of manner. This girl, who he fancied loved his friend and who was beloved by his brother, became an object of interest to him. He pitied her, desired to help her, and regretted his past distrust, as a chivalrous man always regrets injustice to a woman. She was happy here, poor, homeless soul, and she should stay. Bella loved her, his mother took comfort in her, and when Ned was gone, no one's peace would be endangered by her winning ways, her rich accomplishments. These thoughts swept through his mind during a brief pause, and when he spoke, it was to say gently:

"Miss Muir, I thank you for the frankness which must have been painful to you, and I will do my best to be worthy of the confidence which you repose in me. You were both discreet and kind to speak only to me. This thing would have troubled my mother extremely, and have done no good. I shall see Ned, and try and repair my long neglect as promptly as possible. I know you will help me, and in return let me beg of you to remain, for he will soon be gone."

She looked at him with eyes full of tears, and there was no coolness in the voice that answered softly, "You are too kind, but I had better go; it is not wise to stay."

"Why not?"

She colored beautifully, hesitated, then spoke out in the clear, steady voice which was her greatest charm, "If I had known there were sons in this family, I never should have come. Lady Sydney spoke only of your sister, and when I found two gentlemen, I was troubled, because—I am so unfortunate—or rather, people are so kind as to like me more than I deserve. I thought I could stay a month, at least, as your brother spoke of going away, and you were already affianced, but—"

"I am not affianced."

Why he said that, Coventry could not tell, but the words passed his lips hastily and could not be recalled. Jean Muir took the announcement oddly enough. She shrugged her shoulders with an air of extreme annoyance, and said almost rudely, "Then you should be; you will be soon. But that is nothing to me. Miss Beaufort wishes me gone, and I am too proud to remain and become the cause of disunion in a happy family. No, I will go, and go at once."

She turned away impetuously, but Edward's arm detained her, and Edward's voice demanded, tenderly, "Where will you go, my Jean?"

The tender touch and name seemed to rob her of her courage and calmness, for, leaning on her lover, she hid her face and sobbed audibly.

"Now don't make a scene, for heaven's sake," began Coventry impatiently, as his brother eyed him fiercely, divining at once what had passed, for his letter was still in Gerald's hand and Jean's last words had reached her lover's ear.

"Who gave you the right to read that, and to interfere in my affairs?" demanded Edward hotly.

"Miss Muir" was the reply, as Coventry threw away the paper.

"And you add to the insult by ordering her out of the house," cried Ned with increasing wrath.

"On the contrary, I beg her to remain."

"The deuce you do! And why?"

"Because she is useful and happy here, and I am unwilling that your folly should rob her of a home which she likes."

"You are very thoughtful and devoted all at once, but I beg you will not trouble yourself. Jean's happiness and home will be my care now."

"My dear boy, do be reasonable. The thing is impossible. Miss Muir sees it herself; she came to tell me, to ask how best to arrange matters without troubling my mother. I've been to town to attend to your affairs, and you may be off now very soon."

"I have no desire to go. Last month it was the wish of my heart. Now I'll accept nothing from you." And Edward turned moodily away from his brother.

"What folly! Ned, you *must* leave home. It is all arranged and cannot be given up now. A change is what you need, and it will make a man of you. We shall miss you, of course, but you will be where you'll see something of life, and that is better for you than getting into mischief here."

"Are you going away, Jean?" asked Edward, ignoring his brother entirely and bending over the girl, who still hid her face and wept. She did not speak, and Gerald answered for her.

"No, why should she if you are gone?"

"Do you mean to stay?" asked the lover eagerly of Jean.

"I wish to remain, but—" She paused and looked up. Her eyes went from one face to the other, and she added, decidedly, "Yes, I must go, it is not wise to stay even when you are gone."

Neither of the young men could have explained why that hurried glance affected them as it did, but each felt conscious of a willful desire to oppose the other. Edward suddenly felt that his brother loved Miss Muir, and was bent on removing her from his way. Gerald had a vague idea that Miss Muir feared to remain on his account, and he longed to show her that he was quite safe. Each felt angry, and each showed it in a different way, one being violent, the other satirical.

"You are right, Jean, this is not the place for you; and you must let me see you in a safer home before I go," said Ned, significantly.

"It strikes me that this will be a particularly safe home when your dangerous self is removed," began Coventry, with an aggravating smile of calm superiority.

"And *I* think that I leave a more dangerous person than myself behind me, as poor Lucia can testify."

"Be careful what you say, Ned, or I shall be forced to remind you that I am master here. Leave Lucia's name out of this disagreeable affair, if you please."

"You *are* master here, but not of me, or my actions, and you have no right to expect obedience or respect, for you inspire neither. Jean, I asked you to go with me secretly; now I ask you openly to share my fortune. In my brother's presence I ask, and *will* have an answer."

He caught her hand impetuously, with a defiant look at Coventry, who still smiled, as if at boy's play, though his eyes were kindling and his face changing with the still, white wrath which is more terrible than any sudden outburst. Miss Muir looked frightened; she shrank away from her passionate young lover, cast an appealing glance at Gerald, and seemed as if she longed to claim his protection yet dared not.

"Speak!" cried Edward, desperately. "Don't look to him, tell me truly, with your own lips, do you, can you love me, Jean?"

"I have told you once. Why pain me by forcing another hard reply," she said pitifully, still shrinking from his grasp and seeming to appeal to his brother.

"You wrote a few lines, but I'll not be satisfied with that. You shall answer; I've seen love in your eyes, heard it in your voice, and I know it is hidden in your heart. You fear to own it; do not hesitate, no one can part us—speak, Jean, and satisfy me."

Drawing her hand decidedly away, she went a step nearer Coventry, and answered, slowly, distinctly, though her lips trembled, and she evidently dreaded the effect of her words, "I will speak, and speak truly. You have seen love in my face; it is in my heart, and I do not hesitate to own it, cruel as it is to force the truth from me, but this love is not for you. Are you satisfied?"

He looked at her with a despairing glance and stretched his hand toward her beseechingly. She seemed to fear a blow, for suddenly she clung to Gerald with a faint cry. The act, the look of fear, the protecting gesture Coventry involuntarily made were too much for Edward, already excited by conflicting passions. In a paroxysm of blind wrath, he caught up a large pruning knife left there by the gardener, and would have dealt his brother a fatal blow had he not warded it off with his arm. The stroke fell, and another might have followed had not Miss Muir with unexpected courage and strength wrested the knife from Edward and flung it into the little pond near by. Coventry dropped down upon the seat, for the blood poured from a deep wound in his arm, showing by its rapid flow that an artery had been severed. Edward stood aghast, for with the blow his fury passed, leaving him overwhelmed with remorse and shame.

Gerald looked up at him, smiled faintly, and said, with no sign of reproach or anger, "Never mind, Ned. Forgive and forget. Lend me a hand to the house, and don't disturb anyone. It's not much, I dare say." But his lips whitened as he spoke, and his strength failed him. Edward sprang to support him, and Miss Muir, forgetting her terrors, proved herself a girl of uncommon skill and courage.

"Quick! Lay him down. Give me your handkerchief, and bring some water," she said, in a tone of quiet command. Poor Ned obeyed and watched her with breathless suspense while she tied the handkerchief tightly around the arm, thrust the handle of his riding whip underneath, and pressed it firmly above the severed artery to stop the dangerous flow of blood.

"Dr. Scott is with your mother, I think. Go and bring him here" was the next order; and Edward darted away, thankful to do anything to ease the terror which possessed him. He was gone some minutes, and while they waited Coventry watched the girl as she knelt beside him, bathing his face with one hand while with the other she held the bandage firmly in its place. She was pale, but quite steady and self-possessed, and her eyes shone with a strange brilliancy as she looked down at him. Once, meeting his look of grateful wonder, she smiled a reassuring smile that made her lovely, and said, in a soft, sweet tone never used to him before, "Be quiet. There is no danger. I will stay by you till help comes."

Help did come speedily, and the doctor's first words were "Who improvised that tourniquet?"

"She did," murmured Coventry.

"Then you may thank her for saving your life. By Jove! It was capitally done"; and the old doctor looked at the girl with as much admiration as curiosity in his face.

"Never mind that. See to the wound, please, while I run for bandages, and salts, and wine."

Miss Muir was gone as she spoke, so fleetly that it was in vain to call her back or catch her. During her brief absence, the story was told by repentant Ned and the wound examined.

"Fortunately I have my case of instruments with me," said the doctor, spreading on the bench a long array of tiny, glittering implements of torture. "Now, Mr. Ned, come here, and hold the arm in that way, while I tie the artery. Hey! That will never do. Don't tremble so, man, look away and hold it steadily."

"I can't!" And poor Ned turned faint and white, not at the sight but with the bitter thought that he had longed to kill his brother.

"I will hold it," and a slender white hand lifted the bare and bloody arm so firmly, steadily, that Coventry sighed a sigh of relief, and Dr. Scott fell to work with an emphatic nod of approval.

It was soon over, and while Edward ran in to bid the servants beware of alarming their mistress, Dr. Scott put up his instruments and Miss Muir used salts, water, and wine so skillfully that Gerald was able to walk to his room, leaning on the old man, while the girl supported the wounded arm, as no sling could be made on the spot. As he entered the chamber, Coventry turned, put out his left hand, and with much feeling in his fine eyes said simply, "Miss Muir, I thank you."

The color came up beautifully in her pale cheeks as she pressed the hand and without a word vanished from the room. Lucia and the housekeeper came bustling in, and there was no lack of attendance on the invalid. He soon wearied of it, and sent them all away but Ned, who remorsefully haunted the chamber, looking like a comely young Cain and feeling like an outcast.

"Come here, lad, and tell me all about it. I was wrong to be domineering. Forgive me, and believe that I care for your happiness more sincerely than for my own."

These frank and friendly words healed the breach between the two brothers and completely conquered Ned. Gladly did he relate his love passages, for no young lover ever tires of that amusement if he has a sympathizing auditor, and Gerald *was* sympathetic now. For an hour did he lie listening patiently to the history of the growth of his brother's passion. Emotion gave the narrator eloquence, and Jean Muir's character was painted in glowing colors. All her unsuspected kindness to those about her was dwelt upon; all her faithful care, her sisterly interest in Bella, her gentle attentions to their mother, her sweet forbearance with Lucia, who plainly showed her dislike, and most of all, her friendly counsel, sympathy, and regard for Ned himself.

"She would make a man of me. She puts strength and courage into me as no one else can. She is unlike any girl I ever saw; there's no sentimentality about her; she is wise, and kind, and sweet. She says what she means, looks you straight in the eye, and is as true as steel. I've tried her, I know her, and—ah, Gerald, I love her so!"

Here the poor lad leaned his face into his hands and sighed a sigh that made his brother's heart ache.

"Upon my soul, Ned, I feel for you; and if there was no obstacle on her part, I'd do my best for you. She loves Sydney, and so there is nothing for it but to bear your fate like a man."

"Are you sure about Sydney? May it not be some one else?" and Ned eyed his brother with a suspicious look.

Coventry told him all he knew and surmised concerning his friend, not forgetting the letter. Edward mused a moment, then seemed relieved, and said frankly, "I'm glad it's Sydney and not you. I can bear it better."

"Me!" ejaculated Gerald, with a laugh.

"Yes, you; I've been tormented lately with a fear that you cared for her, or rather, she for you."

"You jealous young fool! We never see or speak to one another scarcely, so how could we get up a tender interest?"

"What do you lounge about on that terrace for every evening? And why does she get fluttered when your shadow begins to come and go?" demanded Edward.

"I like the music and don't care for the society of the singer, that's why I walk there. The fluttering is all your imagination; Miss Muir isn't a woman to be fluttered by a man's shadow." And Coventry glanced at his useless arm.

"Thank you for that, and for not saying 'little Muir,' as you generally do. Perhaps it was my imagination. But she never makes fun of you now, and so I fancied she might have lost her heart to the 'young master.' Women often do, you know."

"She used to ridicule me, did she?" asked Coventry, taking no notice of the latter part of his brother's speech, which was quite true nevertheless.

"Not exactly, she was too well-bred for that. But sometimes when

Bella and I joked about you, she'd say something so odd or witty that it was irresistible. You're used to being laughed at, so you don't mind, I know, just among ourselves."

"Not I. Laugh away as much as you like," said Gerald. But he did mind, and wanted exceedingly to know what Miss Muir had said, yet was too proud to ask. He turned restlessly and uttered a sigh of pain.

"I'm talking too much; it's bad for you. Dr. Scott said you must be quiet. Now go to sleep, if you can."

Edward left the bedside but not the room, for he would let no one take his place. Coventry tried to sleep, found it impossible, and after a restless hour called his brother back.

"If the bandage was loosened a bit, it would ease my arm and then I could sleep. Can you do it, Ned?"

"I dare not touch it. The doctor gave orders to leave it till he came in the morning, and I shall only do harm if I try."

"But I tell you it's too tight. My arm is swelling and the pain is intense. It can't be right to leave it so. Dr. Scott dressed it in a hurry and did it too tight. Common sense will tell you that," said Coventry impatiently.

"I'll call Mrs. Morris; she will understand what's best to be done." And Edward moved toward the door, looking anxious.

"Not she, she'll only make a stir and torment me with her chatter. I'll bear it as long as I can, and perhaps Dr. Scott will come tonight. He said he would if possible. Go to your dinner, Ned. I can ring for Neal if I need anything. I shall sleep if I'm alone, perhaps."

Edward reluctantly obeyed, and his brother was left to himself. Little rest did he find, however, for the pain of the wounded arm grew unbearable, and, taking a sudden resolution, he rang for his servant.

"Neal, go to Miss Coventry's study, and if Miss Muir is there, ask her to be kind enough to come to me. I'm in great pain, and she understands wounds better than anyone else in the house."

With much surprise in his face, the man departed and a few moments after the door noiselessly opened and Miss Muir came in. It had been a very warm day, and for the first time she had left off her plain black dress. All in white, with no ornament but her fair hair, and a fragrant posy of violets in her belt, she looked a different woman from the meek, nunlike creature one usually saw about the house. Her face was as altered as her dress, for now a soft color glowed in her cheeks, her eyes smiled shyly, and her lips no longer wore the firm look of one who forcibly repressed every emotion. A fresh, gentle, and charming woman she seemed, and Coventry found the dull room suddenly brightened by her presence. Going straight to him, she said simply, and with a happy, helpful look very comforting to see, "I'm glad you sent for me. What can I do for you?"

He told her, and before the complaint was ended, she began loosening the bandages with the decision of one who understood what was to be done and had faith in herself.

"Ah, that's relief, that's comfort!" ejaculated Coventry, as the last tight fold fell away. "Ned was afraid I should bleed to death if he touched me. What will the doctor say to us?"

"I neither know nor care. I shall say to him that he is a bad surgeon to bind it so closely, and not leave orders to have it untied if necessary. Now I shall make it easy and put you to sleep, for that is what you need. Shall I? May I?"

"I wish you would, if you can."

And while she deftly rearranged the bandages, the young man watched her curiously. Presently he asked, "How came you to know so much about these things?"

"In the hospital where I was ill, I saw much that interested me, and when I got better, I used to sing to the patients sometimes."

"Do you mean to sing to me?" he asked, in the submissive tone men unconsciously adopt when ill and in a woman's care.

"If you like it better than reading aloud in a dreamy tone," she answered, as she tied the last knot.

"I do, much better," he said decidedly.

"You are feverish. I shall wet your forehead, and then you will be quite comfortable." She moved about the room in the quiet way which made it a pleasure to watch her, and, having mingled a little cologne with water, bathed his face as unconcernedly as if he had been a child. Her proceedings not only comforted but amused Coventry, who mentally contrasted her with the stout, beer-drinking matron who had ruled over him in his last illness.

"A clever, kindly little woman," he thought, and felt quite at his ease, she was so perfectly easy herself.

"There, now you look more like yourself," she said with an approving nod as she finished, and smoothed the dark locks off his forehead with a cool, soft hand. Then seating herself in a large chair near by, she began to sing, while tidily rolling up the fresh bandages which had been left for the morning. Coventry lay watching her by the dim light that burned in the room, and she sang on as easily as a bird, a dreamy, low-toned lullaby, which soothed the listener like a spell. Presently, looking up to see the effect of her song, she found the young man wide awake, and regarding her with a curious mixture of pleasure, interest, and admiration.

"Shut your eyes, Mr. Coventry," she said, with a reproving shake of the head, and an odd little smile.

He laughed and obeyed, but could not resist an occasional covert glance from under his lashes at the slender white figure in the great velvet chair. She saw him and frowned.

"You are very disobedient; why won't you sleep?"

"I can't, I want to listen. I'm fond of nightingales."

"Then I shall sing no more, but try something that has never failed yet. Give me your hand, please."

Much amazed, he gave it, and, taking it in both her small ones, she sat down behind the curtain and remained as mute and motionless as a statue. Coventry smiled to himself at first, and wondered which would tire first. But soon a subtle warmth seemed to steal from the soft palms that enclosed his own, his heart beat quicker, his breath grew unequal, and a thousand fancies danced through his brain. He sighed, and said dreamily, as he turned his face toward her, "I like this." And in the act of speaking, seemed to sink into a soft cloud which encompassed him about with an atmosphere of perfect repose. More than this he could not remember, for sleep, deep and dreamless, fell upon him, and when he woke, daylight was shining in between the curtains, his hand lay alone on the coverlet, and his fair-haired enchantress was gone.

≥ *chapter IV* ≤

A DISCOVERY

FOR several days Coventry was confined to his room, much against his will, though everyone did their best to lighten his irksome captivity. His mother petted him, Bella sang, Lucia read, Edward was devoted, and all the household, with one exception, were eager to serve the young master. Jean Muir never came near him, and Jean Muir alone seemed to possess the power of amusing him. He soon tired of the others, wanted something new; recalled the piquant character of the girl and took a fancy into his head that she would lighten his ennui. After some hesitation, he carelessly spoke of her to Bella, but nothing came of it, for Bella only said Jean was well, and very busy doing something lovely to surprise Mamma with. Edward complained that he never saw her, and Lucia ignored her existence altogether. The only intelligence the invalid received was from the gossip of two housemaids over their work in the next room. From them he learned that the governess had been "scolded" by Miss Beaufort for going to Mr. Coventry's room; that she had taken it very sweetly and kept herself carefully out of the way of both young gentlemen, though it was plain to see that Mr. Ned was dying for her.

Mr. Gerald amused himself by thinking over this gossip, and quite annoyed his sister by his absence of mind.

"Gerald, do you know Ned's commission has come?"

"Very interesting. Read on, Bella."

"You stupid boy! You don't know a word I say," and she put down the book to repeat her news.

"I'm glad of it; now we must get him off as soon as possible—that is, I suppose he will want to be off as soon as possible." And Coventry woke up from his reverie.

"You needn't check yourself, I know all about it. I think Ned was very foolish, and that Miss Muir has behaved beautifully. It's quite impossible, of course, but I wish it wasn't, I do so like to watch lovers. You and Lucia are so cold you are not a bit interesting."

"You'll do me a favor if you'll stop all that nonsense about Lucia and me. We are not lovers, and never shall be, I fancy. At all events, I'm tired of the thing, and wish you and Mamma would let it drop, for the present at least."

"Oh Gerald, you know Mamma has set her heart upon it, that Papa desired it, and poor Lucia loves you so much. How can you speak of dropping what will make us all so happy?"

"It won't make me happy, and I take the liberty of thinking that this is of some importance. I'm not bound in any way, and don't intend to be till I am ready. Now we'll talk about Ned."

Much grieved and surprised, Bella obeyed, and devoted herself to Edward, who very wisely submitted to his fate and prepared to leave home for some months. For a week the house was in a state of excitement about his departure, and everyone but Jean was busied for him. She was scarcely seen; every morning she gave Bella her lessons, every afternoon drove out with Mrs. Coventry, and nearly every evening went up to the Hall to read to Sir John, who found his wish granted without exactly knowing how it had been done.

The day Edward left, he came down from bidding his mother good-bye, looking very pale, for he had lingered in his sister's little room with Miss Muir as long as he dared.

"Good-bye, dear. Be kind to Jean," he whispered as he kissed his sister.

"I will, I will," returned Bella, with tearful eyes.

"Take care of Mamma, and remember Lucia," he said again, as he touched his cousin's beautiful cheek.

"Fear nothing. I will keep them apart," she whispered back, and Coventry heard it.

Edward offered his hand to his brother, saying, significantly, as he looked him in the eye, "I trust you, Gerald."

"You may, Ned."

Then he went, and Coventry tired himself with wondering what Lucia meant. A few days later he understood.

Now Ned is gone, little Muir will appear, I fancy, he said to himself; but "little Muir" did not appear, and seemed to shun him more carefully than she had done her lover. If he went to the drawing room in the evening hoping for music, Lucia alone was there. If he tapped at Bella's door, there was always a pause before she opened it, and no sign of Jean appeared though her voice had been audible when he knocked. If he went to the library, a hasty rustle and the sound of flying feet betrayed that the room was deserted at his approach. In the garden Miss Muir never failed to avoid him, and if by chance they met in hall or breakfast room, she passed him with downcast eyes and the briefest, coldest greeting. All this annoyed him intensely, and the more she eluded him, the more he desired to see her—from a spirit of opposition, he said, nothing more. It fretted and yet it entertained him, and he found a lazy sort of pleasure in thwarting the girl's little maneuvers. His patience gave out at last, and he resolved to know what was the meaning of this peculiar conduct. Having locked and taken away the key of one door in the library, he waited till Miss Muir went in to get a book for his uncle. He had heard her speak to Bella of it, knew that she believed him with his mother, and smiled to himself as he stole after her. She was standing in a chair, reaching up, and he had time to see a slender waist, a pretty foot, before he spoke.

"Can I help you, Miss Muir?"

She started, dropped several books, and turned scarlet, as she said hurriedly, "Thank you, no; I can get the steps."

"My long arm will be less trouble. I've got but one, and that is tired of being idle, so it is very much at your service. What will you have?"

"I—I—you startled me so I've forgotten." And Jean laughed, nervously, as she looked about her as if planning to escape.

"I beg your pardon, wait till you remember, and let me thank you for the enchanted sleep you gave me ten days ago. I've had no chance yet, you've shunned me so pertinaciously."

"Indeed I try not to be rude, but—" She checked herself, and turned her face away, adding, with an accent of pain in her voice, "It is not my fault, Mr. Coventry. I only obey orders."

"Whose orders?" he demanded, still standing so that she could not escape.

"Don't ask; it is one who has a right to command where you are concerned. Be sure that it is kindly meant, though it may seem folly to us. Nay, don't be angry, laugh at it, as I do, and let me run away, please."

She turned, and looked down at him with tears in her eyes, a smile on her lips, and an expression half sad, half arch, which was altogether charming. The frown passed from his face, but he still looked grave and said decidedly, "No one has a right to command in this house but my mother or myself. Was it she who bade you avoid me as if I was a madman or a pest?"

"Ah, don't ask. I promised not to tell, and you would not have me break my word, I know." And still smiling, she regarded him with a look of merry malice which made any other reply unnecessary. It was Lucia, he thought, and disliked his cousin intensely just then. Miss Muir moved as if to step down; he detained her, saying earnestly, yet with a smile, "Do you consider me the master here?"

"Yes," and to the word she gave a sweet, submissive intonation which made it expressive of the respect, regard, and confidence which men find pleasantest when women feel and show it. Unconsciously his face softened, and he looked up at her with a different glance from any he had ever given her before.

"Well, then, will you consent to obey me if I am not tyrannical or unreasonable in my demands?"

"I'll try."

"Good! Now frankly, I want to say that all this sort of thing is very disagreeable to me. It annoys me to be a restraint upon anyone's liberty or comfort, and I beg you will go and come as freely as you like, and not mind Lucia's absurdities. She means well, but hasn't a particle of penetration or tact. Will you promise this?"

"No."

"Why not?"

"It is better as it is, perhaps."

"But you called it folly just now."

"Yes, it seems so, and yet—" She paused, looking both confused and distressed.

Coventry lost patience, and said hastily, "You women are such enigmas I never expect to understand you! Well, I've done my best to make you comfortable, but if you prefer to lead this sort of life, I beg you will do so."

"I *don't* prefer it; it is hateful to me. I like to be myself, to have my liberty, and the confidence of those about me. But I cannot think it kind to disturb the peace of anyone, and so I try to obey. I've promised Bella to remain, but I will go rather than have another scene with Miss Beaufort or with you."

Miss Muir had burst out impetuously, and stood there with a sudden fire in her eyes, sudden warmth and spirit in her face and voice that amazed Coventry. She was angry, hurt, and haughty, and the change only made her more attractive, for not a trace of her former meek self remained. Coventry was electrified, and still more surprised when she added, imperiously, with a gesture as if to put him aside, "Hand me that book and move away. I wish to go."

He obeyed, even offered his hand, but she refused it, stepped lightly down, and went to the door. There she turned, and with the same indignant voice, the same kindling eyes and glowing cheeks, she said rapidly, "I know I have no right to speak in this way. I restrain myself as long as I can, but when I can bear no more, my true self breaks loose, and I defy everything. I am tired of being a cold, calm machine; it is impossible with an ardent nature like mine, and I shall try no longer. I cannot help it if people love me. I don't want their love. I only ask to be left in peace, and why I am tormented so I cannot see. I've neither beauty, money, nor rank, yet every foolish boy mistakes my frank interest for something warmer, and makes me miserable. It is my misfortune. Think of me what you will, but beware of me in time, for against my will I may do you harm."

Almost fiercely she had spoken, and with a warning gesture she hurried from the room, leaving the young man feeling as if a sudden thunder-gust had swept through the house. For several minutes he sat in the chair she left, thinking deeply. Suddenly he rose, went to his sister, and said, in his usual tone of indolent good nature, "Bella, didn't I hear Ned ask you to be kind to Miss Muir?"

"Yes, and I try to be, but she is so odd lately."

"Odd! How do you mean?"

"Why, she is either as calm and cold as a statue, or restless and queer; she cries at night, I know, and sighs sadly when she thinks I don't hear. Something is the matter."

"She frets for Ned perhaps," began Coventry.

"Oh dear, no; it's a great relief to her that he is gone. I'm afraid that she likes someone very much, and someone don't like her. Can it be Mr. Sydney?"

"She called him a 'titled fool' once, but perhaps that didn't mean anything. Did you ever ask her about him?" said Coventry, feeling rather ashamed of his curiosity, yet unable to resist the temptation of questioning unsuspecting Bella.

"Yes, but she only looked at me in her tragical way, and said, so pitifully, 'My little friend, I hope you will never have to pass through the scenes I've passed through, but keep your peace unbroken all your life.' After that I dared say no more. I'm very fond of her, I want to make her happy, but I don't know how. Can you propose anything?"

"I was going to propose that you make her come among us more, now Ned is gone. It must be dull for her, moping about alone. I'm sure it is for me. She is an entertaining little person, and I enjoy her music very much. It's good for Mamma to have gay evenings; so you bestir yourself, and see what you can do for the general good of the family."

"That's all very charming, and I've proposed it more than once, but Lucia spoils all my plans. She is afraid you'll follow Ned's example, and that is so silly."

"Lucia is a—no, I won't say fool, because she has sense enough when she chooses; but I wish you'd just settle things with Mamma, and then Lucia can do nothing but submit," said Gerald angrily.

"I'll try, but she goes up to read to Uncle, you know, and since he has had the gout, she stays later, so I see little of her in the evening. There she goes now. I think she will captivate the old one as well as the young one, she is so devoted."

Coventry looked after her slender black figure, just vanishing through the great gate, and an uncomfortable fancy took possession of him, born of Bella's careless words. He sauntered away, and after eluding his cousin, who seemed looking for him, he turned toward the Hall, saying to himself, I will see what is going on up here. Such things have happened. Uncle is the simplest soul alive, and if the girl is ambitious, she can do what she will with him.

Here a servant came running after him and gave him a letter, which he thrust into his pocket without examining it. When he reached the Hall, he went quietly to his uncle's study. The door was ajar, and looking in, he saw a scene of tranquil comfort, very pleasant to watch. Sir John leaned in his easy chair with one foot on a cushion. He was dressed with his usual care and, in spite of the gout, looked like a handsome, well-preserved old gentleman. He was smiling as he listened, and his eyes rested complacently on Jean Muir, who sat near him reading in her musical voice, while the sunshine glittered on her hair and the soft rose of her cheek. She read well, yet Coventry thought her heart was not in her task, for once when she paused, while Sir John spoke, her eyes had an absent expression, and she leaned her head upon her hand, with an air of patient weariness.

Poor girl! I did her great injustice; she has no thought of captivating the old man, but amuses him from simple kindness. She is tired. I'll put an end to her task; and Coventry entered without knocking.

Sir John received him with an air of polite resignation, Miss Muir with a perfectly expressionless face.

"Mother's love, and how are you today, sir?"

"Comfortable, but dull, so I want you to bring the girls over this evening, to amuse the old gentleman. Mrs. King has got out the antique costumes and trumpery, as I promised Bella she should have them, and tonight we are to have a merrymaking, as we used to do when Ned was here."

"Very well, sir, I'll bring them. We've all been out of sorts since the lad left, and a little jollity will do us good. Are you going back, Miss Muir?" asked Coventry.

"No, I shall keep her to give me my tea and get things ready. Don't read anymore, my dear, but go and amuse yourself with the pictures, or whatever you like," said Sir John; and like a dutiful daughter she obeyed, as if glad to get away.

"That's a very charming girl, Gerald," began Sir John as she left the room. "I'm much interested in her, both on her own account and on her mother's."

"Her mother's! What do you know of her mother?" asked Coventry, much surprised.

"Her mother was Lady Grace Howard, who ran away with a poor Scotch minister twenty years ago. The family cast her off, and she lived and died so obscurely that very little is known of her except that she left an orphan girl at some small French pension. This is the girl, and a fine girl, too. I'm surprised that you did not know this."

"So am I, but it is like her not to tell. She is a strange, proud creature. Lady Howard's daughter! Upon my word, that is a discovery," and Coventry felt his interest in his sister's governess much increased by this fact; for, like all wellborn Englishmen, he valued rank and gentle blood even more than he cared to own.

"She has had a hard life of it, this poor little girl, but she has a brave spirit, and will make her way anywhere," said Sir John admiringly.

"Did Ned know this?" asked Gerald suddenly.

"No, she only told me yesterday. I was looking in the *Peerage* and chanced to speak of the Howards. She forgot herself and called Lady Grace her mother. Then I got the whole story, for the lonely little thing was glad to make a confidant of someone."

"That accounts for her rejection of Sydney and Ned: she knows she is their equal and will not snatch at the rank which is hers by right. No, she's not mercenary or ambitious."

"What do you say?" asked Sir John, for Coventry had spoken more to himself than to his uncle.

"I wonder if Lady Sydney was aware of this?" was all Gerald's answer.

"No, Jean said she did not wish to be pitied, and so told nothing to the mother. I think the son knew, but that was a delicate point, and I asked no questions."

"I shall write to him as soon as I discover his address. We have been so intimate I can venture to make a few inquiries about Miss Muir, and prove the truth of her story."

"Do you mean to say that you doubt it?" demanded Sir John angrily.

"I beg your pardon, Uncle, but I must confess I have an instinctive distrust of that young person. It is unjust, I dare say, yet I cannot banish it."

"Don't annoy me by expressing it, if you please. I have some penetration and experience, and I respect and pity Miss Muir heartily. This dislike of yours may be the cause of her late melancholy, hey, Gerald?" And Sir John looked suspiciously at his nephew.

Anxious to avert the rising storm, Coventry said hastily as he turned away, "I've neither time nor inclination to discuss the matter now, sir, but will be careful not to offend again. I'll take your message to Bella, so good-bye for an hour, Uncle."

And Coventry went his way through the park, thinking within himself, The dear old gentleman is getting fascinated, like poor Ned. How the deuce does the girl do it? Lady Howard's daughter, yet never told us; I don't understand that.

⋟ *chapter V* ⋞

HOW THE GIRL DID IT

A T home he found a party of young friends, who hailed with
delight the prospect of a revel at the Hall. An hour later, the
blithe company trooped into the great saloon, where preparations had already been made for a dramatic evening.

Good Sir John was in his element, for he was never so happy as
when his house was full of young people. Several persons were chosen,
and in a few moments the curtains were withdrawn from the first
of these impromptu tableaux. A swarthy, darkly bearded man lay
asleep on a tiger skin, in the shadow of a tent. Oriental arms and
drapery surrounded him; an antique silver lamp burned dimly on a
table where fruit lay heaped in costly dishes, and wine shone redly in
half-emptied goblets. Bending over the sleeper was a woman robed
with barbaric splendor. One hand turned back the embroidered sleeve
from the arm which held a scimitar; one slender foot in a scarlet
sandal was visible under the white tunic; her purple mantle swept
down from snowy shoulders; fillets of gold bound her hair, and jewels
shone on neck and arms. She was looking over her shoulder toward
the entrance of the tent, with a steady yet stealthy look, so effective
that for a moment the spectators held their breath, as if they also
heard a passing footstep.

"Who is it?" whispered Lucia, for the face was new to her.

"Jean Muir," answered Coventry, with an absorbed look.

"Impossible! She is small and fair," began Lucia, but a hasty "Hush, let me look!" from her cousin silenced her.

Impossible as it seemed, he was right nevertheless; for Jean Muir it was. She had darkened her skin, painted her eyebrows, disposed some wild black locks over her fair hair, and thrown such an intensity of expression into her eyes that they darkened and dilated till they were as fierce as any southern eyes that ever flashed. Hatred, the deepest and bitterest, was written on her sternly beautiful face, courage glowed in her glance, power spoke in the nervous grip of the slender hand that held the weapon, and the indomitable will of the woman was expressed—even the firm pressure of the little foot half hidden in the tiger skin.

"Oh, isn't she splendid?" cried Bella under her breath.

"She looks as if she'd use her sword well when the time comes," said someone admiringly.

"Good night to Holofernes; his fate is certain," added another.

"He is the image of Sydney, with that beard on."

"Doesn't she look as if she really hated him?"

"Perhaps she does."

Coventry uttered the last exclamation, for the two which preceded it suggested an explanation of the marvelous change in Jean. It was not all art: the intense detestation mingled with a savage joy that the object of her hatred was in her power was too perfect to be feigned; and having the key to a part of her story, Coventry felt as if he caught a glimpse of the truth. It was but a glimpse, however, for the curtain dropped before he had half analyzed the significance of that strange face.

"Horrible! I'm glad it's over," said Lucia coldly.

"Magnificent! Encore! Encore!" cried Gerald enthusiastically.

But the scene was over, and no applause could recall the actress. Two or three graceful or gay pictures followed, but Jean was in none, and each lacked the charm which real talent lends to the simplest part.

"Coventry, you are wanted," called a voice. And to everyone's surprise, Coventry went, though heretofore he had always refused to exert himself when handsome actors were in demand.

"What part am I to spoil?" he asked, as he entered the green room, where several excited young gentlemen were costuming and attitudinizing.

"A fugitive cavalier. Put yourself into this suit, and lose no time asking questions. Miss Muir will tell you what to do. She is in the tableau, so no one will mind you," said the manager pro tem, throwing a rich old suit toward Coventry and resuming the painting of a moustache on his own boyish face.

A gallant cavalier was the result of Gerald's hasty toilet, and when he appeared before the ladies a general glance of admiration was bestowed upon him.

"Come along and be placed; Jean is ready on the stage." And Bella ran before him, exclaiming to her governess, "Here he is, quite splendid. Wasn't he good to do it?"

Miss Muir, in the charmingly prim and puritanical dress of a Roundhead damsel, was arranging some shrubs, but turned suddenly and dropped the green branch she held, as her eye met the glittering figure advancing toward her.

"You!" she said with a troubled look, adding low to Bella, "Why did you ask *him?* I begged you not."

"He is the only handsome man here, and the best actor if he likes. He won't play usually, so make the most of him." And Bella was off to finish powdering her hair for "The Marriage à la Mode."

"I was sent for and I came. Do you prefer some other person?" asked Coventry, at a loss to understand the half-anxious, half-eager expression of the face under the little cap.

It changed to one of mingled annoyance and resignation as she said, "It is too late. Please kneel here, half behind the shrubs; put down your hat, and—allow me—you are too elegant for a fugitive."

As he knelt before her, she disheveled his hair, pulled his lace collar awry, threw away his gloves and sword, and half untied the cloak that hung about his shoulders.

"That is better; your paleness is excellent—nay, don't spoil it. We are to represent the picture which hangs in the Hall. I need tell you no more. Now, Roundheads, place yourselves, and then ring up the curtain."

With a smile, Coventry obeyed her; for the picture was of two lovers, the young cavalier kneeling, with his arm around the waist of the girl, who tries to hide him with her little mantle, and presses his head to her bosom in an ecstasy of fear, as she glances back at the approaching pursuers. Jean hesitated an instant and shrank a little as his hand touched her; she blushed deeply, and her eyes fell before his. Then, as the bell rang, she threw herself into her part with sudden spirit. One arm half covered him with her cloak, the other pillowed his head on the muslin kerchief folded over her bosom, and she looked backward with such terror in her eyes that more than one chivalrous young spectator longed to hurry to the rescue. It lasted but a moment; yet in that moment Coventry experienced another new sensation. Many women had smiled on him, but he had remained heart-whole, cool, and careless, quite unconscious of the power which a woman possesses and knows how to use, for the weal or woe of man. Now, as he knelt there with a soft arm about him, a slender waist yielding to his touch, and a maiden heart throbbing against his cheek, for the first time in his life he felt the indescribable spell of womanhood, and looked the ardent lover to perfection. Just as his face assumed this new and most becoming aspect, the curtain dropped, and clamorous encores recalled him to the fact that Miss Muir was trying to escape from his hold, which had grown painful in its unconscious pressure. He sprang up, half bewildered, and looking as he had never looked before.

"Again! Again!" called Sir John. And the young men who played the Roundheads, eager to share in the applause begged for a repetition in new attitudes.

"A rustle has betrayed you, we have fired and shot the brave girl, and she lies dying, you know. That will be effective; try it, Miss Muir," said one. And with a long breath, Jean complied.

The curtain went up, showing the lover still on his knees, unmindful of the captors who clutched him by the shoulder, for at his feet the girl lay dying. Her head was on his breast, now, her eyes looked full into his, no longer wild with fear, but eloquent with the love which even death could not conquer. The power of those tender eyes thrilled Coventry with a strange delight, and set his heart beating as rapidly as hers had done. She felt his hands tremble, saw the color flash into his cheek, knew that she had touched him at last, and when she rose it was with a sense of triumph which she found it hard to conceal. Others thought it fine acting; Coventry tried to believe so; but Lucia set her teeth, and, as the curtain fell on that second picture, she left her place to hurry behind the scenes, bent on putting an end to such dangerous play. Several actors were complimenting the mimic lovers. Jean took it merrily, but Coventry, in spite of himself, betrayed that he was excited by something deeper than mere gratified vanity.

As Lucia appeared, his manner changed to its usual indifference; but he could not quench the unwonted fire of his eyes, or keep all trace of emotion out of his face, and she saw this with a sharp pang.

"I have come to offer my help. You must be tired, Miss Muir. Can I relieve you?" said Lucia hastily.

"Yes, thank you. I shall be very glad to leave the rest to you, and enjoy them from the front."

So with a sweet smile Jean tripped away, and to Lucia's dismay Coventry fellowed.

"I want you, Gerald; please stay," she cried.

"I've done my part—no more tragedy for me tonight." And he was gone before she could entreat or command.

There was no help for it; she must stay and do her duty, or expose her jealousy to the quick eyes about her. For a time she bore it; but the sight of her cousin leaning over the chair she had left and chatting with the governess, who now filled it, grew unbearable, and she dispatched a little girl with a message to Miss Muir.

"Please, Miss Beaufort wants you for Queen Bess, as you are the only lady with red hair. Will you come?" whispered the child, quite unconscious of any hidden sting in her words.

"Yes, dear, willingly though I'm not stately enough for Her Majesty, nor handsome enough," said Jean, rising with an untroubled face, though she resented the feminine insult.

"Do you want an Essex? I'm all dressed for it," said Coventry, following to the door with a wistful look.

"No, Miss Beaufort said *you* were not to come. She doesn't want you both together," said the child decidedly.

Jean gave him a significant look, shrugged her shoulders, and went away smiling her odd smile, while Coventry paced up and down the hall in a curious state of unrest, which made him forgetful of everything till the young people came gaily out to supper.

"Come, bonny Prince Charlie, take me down, and play the lover as charmingly as you did an hour ago. I never thought you had so much warmth in you," said Bella, taking his arm and drawing him on against his will.

"Don't be foolish, child. Where is—Lucia?"

Why he checked Jean's name on his lips and substituted an-other's, he could not tell; but a sudden shyness in speaking of her possessed him, and though he saw her nowhere, he would not ask for her. His cousin came down looking lovely in a classical costume; but Gerald scarcely saw her, and, when the merriment was at its height, he slipped away to discover what had become of Miss Muir.

Alone in the deserted drawing room he found her, and paused to watch her a moment before he spoke; for something in her attitude and face struck him. She was leaning wearily back in the great chair which had served for a throne. Her royal robes were still unchanged, though the crown was off and all her fair hair hung about her shoulders. Excitement and exertion made her brilliant, the rich dress became her wonderfully, and an air of luxurious indolence changed the meek governess into a charming woman. She leaned on the velvet cushions as if she were used to such support; she played with the jewels which had crowned her as carelessly as if she were born to wear them; her attitude was full of negligent grace, and the expression of her face half proud, half pensive, as if her thoughts were bitter-sweet.

One would know she was wellborn to see her now. Poor girl, what a burden a life of dependence must be to a spirit like hers! I wonder what she is thinking of so intently. And Coventry indulged in another look before he spoke.

"Shall I bring you some supper, Miss Muir?"

"Supper!" she ejaculated, with a start. "Who thinks of one's body when one's soul is—" She stopped there, knit her brows, and laughed faintly as she added, "No, thank you. I want nothing but advice, and that I dare not ask of anyone."

"Why not?"

"Because I have no right."

"Everyone has a right to ask help, especially the weak of the strong. Can I help you? Believe me, I most heartily offer my poor services."

"Ah, you forget! This dress, the borrowed splendor of these jewels, the freedom of this gay evening, the romance of the part you played, all blind you to the reality. For a moment I cease to be a servant, and for a moment you treat me as an equal."

It was true; he *had* forgotten. That soft, reproachful glance touched him, his distrust melted under the new charm, and he answered with real feeling in voice and face, "I treat you as an equal because you *are* one; and when I offer help, it is not to my sister's governess alone, but to Lady Howard's daughter."

"Who told you that?" she demanded, sitting erect.

"My uncle. Do not reproach him. It shall go no further, if you forbid it. Are you sorry that I know it?"

"Yes."

"Why?"

"Because I will not be pitied!" And her eyes flashed as she made a half-defiant gesture.

"Then, if I may not pity the hard fate which has befallen an innocent life, may I admire the courage which meets adverse fortune so bravely, and conquers the world by winning the respect and regard of all who see and honor it?"

Miss Muir averted her face, put up her hand, and answered hastily, "No, no, not that! Do not be kind; it destroys the only barrier now left between us. Be cold to me as before, forget what I am, and let me go on my way, unknown, unpitied, and unloved!"

Her voice faltered and failed as the last word was uttered, and she bent her face upon her hand. Something jarred upon Coventry in this speech, and moved him to say, almost rudely, "You need have no fears for me. Lucia will tell you what an iceberg I am."

"Then Lucia would tell me wrong. I have the fatal power of reading character; I know you better than she does, and I see—" There she stopped abruptly.

"What? Tell me and prove your skill," he said eagerly.

Turning, she fixed her eyes on him with a penetrating power that made him shrink as she said slowly, "Under the ice I see fire, and warn you to beware lest it prove a volcano."

For a moment he sat dumb, wondering at the insight of the girl; for she was the first to discover the hidden warmth of a nature too proud to confess its tender impulses, or the ambitions that slept till some potent voice awoke them. The blunt, almost stern manner in which she warned him away from her only made her more attractive; for there was no conceit or arrogance in it, only a foreboding fear emboldened by past suffering to be frank. Suddenly he spoke impetuously:

"You are right! I am not what I seem, and my indolent indifference is but the mask under which I conceal my real self. I could be as passionate, as energetic and aspiring as Ned, if I had any aim in life. I have none, and so I am what you once called me, a thing to pity and despise."

"I never said that!" cried Jean indignantly.

"Not in those words, perhaps; but you looked it and thought it, though you phrased it more mildly. I deserved it, but I shall deserve it no longer. I am beginning to wake from my disgraceful idleness, and long for some work that shall make a man of me. Why do you go? I annoy you with my confessions. Pardon me. They are the first I ever made; they shall be the last."

"No, oh no! I am too much honored by your confidence; but is it wise, is it loyal to tell *me* your hopes and aims? Has not Miss Beaufort the first right to be your confidante?"

Coventry drew back, looking intensely annoyed, for the name recalled much that he would gladly have forgotten in the novel excitement of the hour. Lucia's love, Edward's parting words, his own reserve so strangely thrown aside, so difficult to resume. What he would have said was checked by the sight of a half-open letter which fell from Jean's dress as she moved away. Mechanically he took it up to return it, and, as he did so, he recognized Sydney's handwriting. Jean snatched it from him, turning pale to the lips as she cried, "Did you read it? What did you see? Tell me, tell me, on your honor!"

"On my honor, I saw nothing but this single sentence, 'By the love I bear you, believe what I say.' No more, as I am a gentleman. I know the hand, I guess the purport of the letter, and as a friend of Sydney, I earnestly desire to help you, if I can. Is this the matter upon which you want advice?"

"Yes."

"Then let me give it?"

"You cannot, without knowing all, and it is so hard to tell!"

"Let me guess it, and spare you the pain of telling. May I?" And Coventry waited eagerly for her reply, for the spell was still upon him.

Holding the letter fast, she beckoned him to follow, and glided before him to a secluded little nook, half boudoir, half conservatory. There she paused, stood an instant as if in doubt, then looked up at him with confiding eyes and said decidedly, "I will do it; for, strange as it may seem, you are the only person to whom I *can* speak. You know Sydney, you have discovered that I am an equal, you have offered your help. I accept it; but oh, do not think me unwomanly!

Remember how alone I am, how young, and how much I rely upon your sincerity, your sympathy!"

"Speak freely. I am indeed your friend." And Coventry sat down beside her, forgetful of everything but the soft-eyed girl who confided in him so entirely.

Speaking rapidly, Jean went on, "You know that Sydney loved me, that I refused him and went away. But you do not know that his importunities nearly drove me wild, that he threatened to rob me of my only treasure, my good name, and that, in desperation, I tried to kill myself. Yes, mad, wicked as it was, I did long to end the life which was, at best, a burden, and under his persecution had become a torment. You are shocked, yet what I say is the living truth. Lady Sydney will confirm it, the nurses at the hospital will confess that it was not a fever which brought me there; and here, though the external wound is healed, my heart still aches and burns with the shame and indignation which only a proud woman can feel."

She paused and sat with kindling eyes, glowing cheeks, and both hands pressed to her heaving bosom, as if the old insult roused her spirit anew. Coventry said not a word, for surprise, anger, incredulity, and admiration mingled so confusedly in his mind that he forgot to speak, and Jean went on, "That wild act of mine convinced him of my indomitable dislike. He went away, and I believed that this stormy love of his would be cured by absence. It is not, and I live in daily fear of fresh entreaties, renewed persecution. His mother promised not to betray where I had gone, but he found me out and wrote to me. The letter I asked you to take to Lady Sydney was a reply to his, imploring him to leave me in peace. You failed to deliver it, and I was glad, for I thought silence might quench hope. All in vain; this is a more passionate appeal than ever, and he vows he will never desist from his endeavors till I give another man the right to protect me. I *can* do this—I am sorely tempted to do it, but I rebel against the cruelty. I love my freedom, I have no wish to marry at this man's bidding. What can I do? How can I free myself? Be my friend, and help me!"

Tears streamed down her cheeks, sobs choked her words, and she clasped her hands imploringly as she turned toward the young man in all the abandonment of sorrow, fear, and supplication. Coventry found it hard to meet those eloquent eyes and answer calmly, for he had no experience in such scenes and knew not how to play his part. It is this absurd dress and that romantic nonsense which makes me feel so unlike myself, he thought, quite unconscious of the dangerous power which the dusky room, the midsummer warmth and fragrance, the memory of the "romantic nonsense," and, most of all, the presence of a beautiful, afflicted woman had over him. His usual self-possession deserted him, and he could only echo the words which had made the strongest impression upon him:

"You *can* do this, you are tempted to do it. Is Ned the man who can protect you?"

"No" was the soft reply.

"Who then?"

"Do not ask me. A good and honorable man; one who loves me well, and would devote his life to me; one whom once it would have been happiness to marry, but now—"

There her voice ended in a sigh, and all her fair hair fell down about her face, hiding it in a shining veil.

"Why not now? This is a sure and speedy way of ending your distress. Is it impossible?"

In spite of himself, Gerald leaned nearer, took one of the little hands in his, and pressed it as he spoke, urgently, compassionately, nay, almost tenderly. From behind the veil came a heavy sigh, and the brief answer, "It is impossible."

"Why, Jean?"

She flung her hair back with a sudden gesture, drew away her hand, and answered, almost fiercely, "Because I do not love him! Why do you torment me with such questions? I tell you I am in a sore strait and cannot see my way. Shall I deceive the good man, and secure peace at the price of liberty and truth? Or shall I defy Sydney and lead a life of dread? If he menaced my life, I should not fear; but he menaces that which is dearer than life—my good name. A look, a word can tarnish it; a scornful smile, a significant shrug can do me more harm than any blow; for I am a woman—friendless, poor, and at the mercy of his tongue. Ah, better to have died, and so have been saved the bitter pain that has come now!"

She sprang up, clasped her hands over her head, and paced despairingly through the little room, not weeping, but wearing an expression more tragical than tears. Still feeling as if he had suddenly stepped into a romance, yet finding a keen pleasure in the part assigned him, Coventry threw himself into it with spirit, and heartily did his best to console the poor girl who needed help so much. Going to her, he said as impetuously as Ned ever did, "Miss Muir—nay, I will say Jean, if that will comfort you—listen, and rest assured that no harm shall touch you if I can ward it off. You are needlessly alarmed. Indignant you may well be, but, upon my life, I think you wrong Sydney. He is violent, I know, but he is too honorable a man to injure you by a light word, an unjust act. He did but threaten, hoping to soften you. Let me see him, or write to him. He is my friend; he will listen to me. Of that I am sure."

"Be sure of nothing. When a man like Sydney loves and is thwarted in his love, nothing can control his headstrong will. Promise me you will not see or write to him. Much as I fear and despise him, I will submit, rather than any harm should befall you—or your brother. You promise me, Mr. Coventry?"

He hesitated. She clung to his arm with unfeigned solicitude in her eager, pleading face, and he could not resist it.

"I promise; but in return you must promise to let me give what help I can; and, Jean, never say again that you are friendless."

"You are so kind! God bless you for it. But I dare not accept your friendship; *she* will not permit it, and I have no right to mar her peace."

"Who will not permit it?" he demanded hotly.

"Miss Beaufort."

"Hang Miss Beaufort!" exclaimed Coventry, with such energy that Jean broke into a musical laugh, despite her trouble. He joined in it, and, for an instant they stood looking at one another as if the last barrier were down, and they were friends indeed. Jean paused suddenly, with the smile on her lips, the tears still on her cheek, and made a warning gesture. He listened: the sound of feet mingled with calls and laughter proved that they were missed and sought.

"That laugh betrayed us. Stay and meet them. I cannot." And Jean darted out upon the lawn. Coventry followed; for the thought of confronting so many eyes, so many questions, daunted him, and he fled like a coward. The sound of Jean's flying footsteps guided him, and he overtook her just as she paused behind a rose thicket to take breath.

"Fainthearted knight! You should have stayed and covered my retreat. Hark! they are coming! Hide! Hide!" she panted, half in fear, half in merriment, as the gay pursuers rapidly drew nearer.

"Kneel down; the moon is coming out and the glitter of your embroidery will betray you," whispered Jean, as they cowered behind the roses.

"Your arms and hair will betray you. 'Come under my plaiddie,' as the song says." And Coventry tried to make his velvet cloak cover the white shoulders and fair locks.

"We are acting our parts in reality now. How Bella will enjoy the thing when I tell her!" said Jean as the noises died away.

"Do not tell her," whispered Coventry.

"And why not?" she asked, looking up into the face so near her own, with an artless glance.

"Can you not guess why?"

"Ah, you are so proud you cannot bear to be laughed at."

"It is not that. It is because I do not want you to be annoyed by silly tongues; you have enough to pain you without that. I am your friend, now, and I do my best to prove it."

"So kind, so kind! How can I thank you?" murmured Jean. And she involuntarily nestled closer under the cloak that sheltered both.

Neither spoke for a moment, and in the silence the rapid beating of two hearts was heard. To drown the sound, Coventry said softly, "Are you frightened?"

"No, I like it," she answered, as softly, then added abruptly, "But why do we hide? There is nothing to fear. It is late. I must go. You are kneeling on my train. Please rise."

"Why in such haste? This flight and search only adds to the charm of the evening. I'll not get up yet. Will you have a rose, Jean?"

"No, I will not. Let me go, Mr. Coventry, I insist. There has been enough of this folly. You forget yourself."

She spoke imperiously, flung off the cloak, and put him from her. He rose at once, saying, like one waking suddenly from a pleasant dream, "I do indeed forget myself."

Here the sound of voices broke on them, nearer than before. Pointing to a covered walk that led to the house, he said, in his usually cool, calm tone, "Go in that way; I will cover your retreat." And turning, he went to meet the merry hunters.

Half an hour later, when the party broke up, Miss Muir joined them in her usual quiet dress, looking paler, meeker, and sadder than usual. Coventry saw this, though he neither looked at her nor addressed her. Lucia saw it also, and was glad that the dangerous girl had fallen back into her proper place again, for she had suffered much that night. She appropriated her cousin's arm as they went through the park, but he was in one of his taciturn moods, and all her attempts at conversation were in vain. Miss Muir walked alone, singing softly to herself as she followed in the dusk. Was Gerald so silent because he listened to that fitful song? Lucia thought so, and felt her dislike rapidly deepening to hatred.

When the young friends were gone, and the family were exchanging good-nights among themselves, Jean was surprised by Coventry's offering his hand, for he had never done it before, and whispering, as he held it, though Lucia watched him all the while, "I have not given my advice, yet."

"Thanks, I no longer need it. I have decided for myself."

"May I ask how?"

"To brave my enemy."

"Good! But what decided you so suddenly?"

"The finding of a friend." And with a grateful glance she was gone.

‰ *chapter VI* ‰

ON THE WATCH

"IF you please, Mr. Coventry, did you get the letter last night?" were the first words that greeted the "young master" as he left his room next morning.

"What letter, Dean? I don't remember any," he answered, pausing, for something in the maid's manner struck him as peculiar.

"It came just as you left for the Hall, sir. Benson ran after you with it, as it was marked 'Haste.' Didn't you get it, sir?" asked the woman, anxiously.

"Yes, but upon my life, I forgot all about it till this minute. It's in my other coat, I suppose, if I've not lost it. That absurd masquerading put everything else out of my head." And speaking more to himself than to the maid, Coventry turned back to look for the missing letter.

Dean remained where she was, apparently busy about the arrangement of the curtains at the hall window, but furtively watching meanwhile with a most unwonted air of curiosity.

"Not there, I thought so!" she muttered, as Coventry impatiently thrust his hand into one pocket after another. But as she spoke, an expression of amazement appeared in her face, for suddenly the letter was discovered.

"I'd have sworn it wasn't there! I don't understand it, but she's a deep one, or I'm much deceived." And Dean shook her head like one perplexed, but not convinced.

Coventry uttered an exclamation of satisfaction on glancing at the address and, standing where he was, tore open the letter.

Dear C:
    I'm off to Baden. Come and join me, then you'll be out of harm's way; for if you fall in love with J. M. (and you can't escape if you stay where she is), you will incur the trifling inconvenience of having your brains blown out by
                               Yours truly, F. R. Sydney

"The man is mad!" ejaculated Coventry, staring at the letter while an angry flush rose to his face. "What the deuce does he mean by writing to me in that style? Join him—not I! And as for the threat, I laugh at it. Poor Jean! This headstrong fool seems bent on tormenting her. Well, Dean, what are you waiting for?" he demanded, as if suddenly conscious of her presence.

"Nothing, sir; I only stopped to see if you found the letter. Beg pardon, sir."

And she was moving on when Coventry asked, with a suspicious look, "What made you think it was lost? You seem to take an uncommon interest in my affairs today."

"Oh dear, no, sir. I felt a bit anxious, Benson is so forgetful, and it was me who sent him after you, for I happened to see you go out, so I felt responsible. Being marked that way, I thought it might be important so I asked about it."

"Very well, you can go, Dean. It's all right, you see."

"I'm not so sure of that," muttered the woman, as she curtsied respectfully and went away, looking as if the letter had *not* been found.

Dean was Miss Beaufort's maid, a grave, middle-aged woman with keen eyes and a somewhat grim air. Having been long in the family, she enjoyed all the privileges of a faithful and favorite servant. She loved her young mistress with an almost jealous affection. She watched over her with the vigilant care of a mother and resented any attempt at interference on the part of others. At first she had pitied and liked Jean Muir, then distrusted her, and now heartily hated her, as the cause of the increased indifference of Coventry toward his cousin. Dean knew the depth of Lucia's love, and though no man, in her eyes, was worthy of her mistress, still, having honored him with her regard, Dean felt bound to like him, and the late change in his manner disturbed the maid almost as much as it did the mistress. She watched Jean narrowly, causing that amiable creature much amusement but little annoyance, as yet, for Dean's slow English wit was no match for the subtle mind of the governess. On the preceding night, Dean had been sent up to the Hall with costumes and had there seen something which much disturbed her. She began to speak of it while undressing her mistress, but Lucia, being in an unhappy mood, had so sternly ordered her not to gossip that the tale remained untold, and she was forced to bide her time.

Now I'll see how *she* looks after it; though there's not much to be got out of *her* face, the deceitful hussy, thought Dean, marching down the corridor and knitting her black brows as she went.

"Good morning, Mrs. Dean. I hope you are none the worse for last night's frolic. You had the work and we the play," said a blithe voice behind her; and turning sharply, she confronted Miss Muir. Fresh and smiling, the governess nodded with an air of cordiality which would have been irresistible with anyone but Dean.

"I'm quite well, thank you, miss," she returned coldly, as her keen eye fastened on the girl as if to watch the effect of her words. "I had a good rest when the young ladies and gentlemen were at supper, for while the maids cleared up, I sat in the 'little anteroom.'"

"Yes, I saw you, and feared you'd take cold. Very glad you didn't. How is Miss Beaufort? She seemed rather poorly last night" was the tranquil reply, as Jean settled the little frills about her delicate wrists. The cool question was a return shot for Dean's hint that she had been where she could oversee the interview between Coventry and Miss Muir.

"She is a bit tired, as any *lady* would be after such an evening. People who are *used* to *play-acting* wouldn't mind it, perhaps, but Miss Beaufort don't enjoy *romps* as much as *some* do."

The emphasis upon certain words made Dean's speech as impertinent as she desired. But Jean only laughed, and as Coventry's step was heard behind them, she ran downstairs, saying blandly, but with a wicked look, "I won't stop to thank you now, lest Mr. Coventry should bid me good-morning, and so increase Miss Beaufort's indisposition."

Dean's eyes flashed as she looked after the girl with a wrathful face, and went her way, saying grimly, "I'll bide my time, but I'll get the better of her yet."

Fancying himself quite removed from "last night's absurdity," yet curious to see how Jean would meet him, Coventry lounged into the breakfast room with his usual air of listless indifference. A languid nod and murmur was all the reply he vouchsafed to the greetings of cousin, sister, and governess as he sat down and took up his paper.

"Have you had a letter from Ned?" asked Bella, looking at the note which her brother still held.

"No" was the brief answer.

"Who then? You look as if you had received bad news."

There was no reply, and, peeping over his arm, Bella caught sight of the seal and exclaimed, in a disappointed tone, "It is the Sydney crest. I don't care about the note now. Men's letters to each other are not interesting."

Miss Muir had been quietly feeding one of Edward's dogs, but at the name she looked up and met Coventry's eyes, coloring so distressfully that he pitied her. Why he should take the trouble to cover her confusion, he did not stop to ask himself, but seeing the curl of Lucia's lip, he suddenly addressed her with an air of displeasure, "Do you know that Dean is getting impertinent? She presumes too much on her age and your indulgence, and forgets her place."

"What has she done?" asked Lucia coldly.

"She troubles herself about my affairs and takes it upon herself to keep Benson in order."

Here Coventry told about the letter and the woman's evident curiosity.

"Poor Dean, she gets no thanks for reminding you of what you had forgotten. Next time she will leave your letters to their fate, and perhaps it will be as well, if they have such a bad effect upon your temper, Gerald."

Lucia spoke calmly, but there was an angry color in her cheek as she rose and left the room. Coventry looked much annoyed, for on Jean's face he detected a faint smile, half pitiful, half satirical, which disturbed him more than his cousin's insinuation. Bella broke the awkward silence by saying, with a sigh, "Poor Ned! I do so long to hear again from him. I thought a letter had come for some of us. Dean said she saw one bearing his writing on the hall table yesterday."

"She seems to have a mania for inspecting letters. I won't allow it. Who was the letter for, Bella?" said Coventry, putting down his paper.

"She wouldn't or couldn't tell, but looked very cross and told me to ask you."

"Very odd! I've had none," began Coventry.

"But I had one several days ago. Will you please read it, and my reply?" And as she spoke, Jean laid two letters before him.

"Certainly not. It would be dishonorable to read what Ned intended for no eyes but your own. You are too scrupulous in one way, and not enough so in another, Miss Muir." And Coventry offered both the letters with an air of grave decision, which could not conceal the interest and surprise he felt.

"You are right. Mr. Edward's note *should* be kept sacred, for in it the poor boy has laid bare his heart to me. But mine I beg you will read, that you may see how well I try to keep my word to you. Oblige me in this, Mr. Coventry; I have a right to ask it of you."

So urgently she spoke, so wistfully she looked, that he could not refuse and, going to the window, read the letter. It was evidently an answer to a passionate appeal from the young lover, and was written with consummate skill. As he read, Gerald could not help thinking, If this girl writes in this way to a man whom she does *not* love, with what a world of power and passion would she write to one whom she *did* love. And this thought kept returning to him as his eye went over line after line of wise argument, gentle reproof, good counsel, and friendly regard. Here and there a word, a phrase, betrayed what she had already confessed, and Coventry forgot to return the letter, as he stood wondering who was the man whom Jean loved.

The sound of Bella's voice recalled him, for she was saying, half kindly, half petulantly, "Don't look so sad, Jean. Ned will outlive it, I dare say. You remember you said once men never died of love, though women might. In his one note to me, he spoke so beautifully of you, and begged me to be kind to you for his sake, that I try to be with all my heart, though if it was anyone but you, I really think I should hate them for making my dear boy so unhappy."

"You are too kind, Bella, and I often think I'll go away to relieve you of my presence; but unwise and dangerous as it is to stay, I haven't the courage to go. I've been so happy here." And as she spoke, Jean's head dropped lower over the dog as it nestled to her affectionately.

Before Bella could utter half the loving words that sprang to her lips, Coventry came to them with all languor gone from face and mien, and laying Jean's letter before her, he said, with an undertone of deep feeling in his usually emotionless voice, "A right womanly and eloquent letter, but I fear it will only increase the fire it was meant to quench. I pity my brother more than ever now."

"Shall I send it?" asked Jean, looking straight up at him, like one who had entire reliance on his judgment.

"Yes, I have not the heart to rob him of such a sweet sermon upon self-sacrifice. Shall I post it for you?"

"Thank you; in a moment." And with a grateful look, Jean dropped her eyes. Producing her little purse, she selected a penny, folded it in a bit of paper, and then offered both letter and coin to Coventry, with such a pretty air of business, that he could not control a laugh.

"So you won't be indebted to me for a penny? What a proud woman you are, Miss Muir."

"I am; it's a family failing." And she gave him a significant glance, which recalled to him the memory of who she was. He understood her feeling, and liked her the better for it, knowing that he would have done the same had he been in her place. It was a little thing, but if done for effect, it answered admirably, for it showed a quick insight into his character on her part, and betrayed to him the existence of a pride in which he sympathized heartily. He stood by Jean a moment, watching her as she burnt Edward's letter in the blaze of the spirit lamp under the urn.

"Why do you do that?" he asked involuntarily.

"Because it is my duty to forget" was all her answer.

"Can you always forget when it becomes a duty?"

"I wish I could! I wish I could!"

She spoke passionately, as if the words broke from her against her will, and, rising hastily, she went into the garden, as if afraid to stay.

"Poor, dear Jean is very unhappy about something, but I can't discover what it is. Last night I found her crying over a rose, and now she runs away, looking as if her heart was broken. I'm glad I've got no lessons."

"What kind of a rose?" asked Coventry from behind his paper as Bella paused.

"A lovely white one. It must have come from the Hall; we have none like it. I wonder if Jean was ever going to be married, and lost her lover, and felt sad because the flower reminded her of bridal roses."

Coventry made no reply, but felt himself change countenance as he recalled the little scene behind the rose hedge, where he gave Jean the flower which she had refused yet taken. Presently, to Bella's surprise, he flung down the paper, tore Sydney's note to atoms, and rang for his horse with an energy which amazed her.

"Why, Gerald, what has come over you? One would think Ned's restless spirit had suddenly taken possession of you. What are you going to do?"

"I'm going to work" was the unexpected answer, as Coventry turned toward her with an expression so rarely seen on his fine face.

"What has waked you up all at once?" asked Bella, looking more and more amazed.

"You did," he said, drawing her toward him.

"I! When? How?"

"Do you remember saying once that energy was better than beauty in a man, and that no one could respect an idler?"

"I never said anything half so sensible as that. Jean said something like it once, I believe, but I forgot. Are you tired of doing nothing, at last, Gerald?"

"Yes, I neglected my duty to Ned, till he got into trouble, and now I reproach myself for it. It's not too late to do other neglected tasks, so I'm going at them with a will. Don't say anything about it to anyone, and don't laugh at me, for I'm in earnest, Bell."

"I know you are, and I admire and love you for it, my dear old boy," cried Bella enthusiastically, as she threw her arms about his neck and kissed him heartily. "What will you do first?" she asked, as he stood thoughtfully smoothing the bright head that leaned upon his shoulder, with that new expression still clear and steady in his face.

"I'm going to ride over the whole estate, and attend to things as a master should; not leave it all to Bent, of whom I've heard many complaints, but have been too idle to inquire about them. I shall consult Uncle, and endeavor to be all that my father was in his time. Is that a worthy ambition, dear?"

"Oh, Gerald, let me tell Mamma. It will make her so happy. You are her idol, and to hear you say these things, to see you look so like dear Papa, would do more for her spirits than all the doctors in England."

"Wait till I prove what my resolution is worth. When I have

really done something, then I'll surprise Mamma with a sample of my work."

"Of course you'll tell Lucia?"

"Not on any account. It is a little secret between us, so keep it till I give you leave to tell it."

"But Jean will see it at once; she knows everything that happens, she is so quick and wise. Do you mind her knowing?"

"I don't see that I can help it if she is so wonderfully gifted. Let her see what she can, I don't mind her. Now I'm off." And with a kiss to his sister, a sudden smile on his face, Coventry sprang upon his horse and rode away at a pace which caused the groom to stare after him in blank amazement.

Nothing more was seen of him till dinnertime, when he came in so exhilarated by his brisk ride and busy morning that he found some difficulty in assuming his customary manner, and more than once astonished the family by talking animatedly on various subjects which till now had always seemed utterly uninteresting to him. Lucia was amazed, his mother delighted, and Bella could hardly control her desire to explain the mystery; but Jean took it very calmly and regarded him with the air of one who said, "I understand, but you will soon tire of it." This nettled him more than he would confess, and he exerted himself to silently contradict that prophecy.

"Have you answered Mr. Sydney's letter?" asked Bella, when they were all scattered about the drawing room after dinner.

"No," answered her brother, who was pacing up and down with restless steps, instead of lounging near his beautiful cousin.

"I ask because I remembered that Ned sent a message for him in my last note, as he thought you would know Sydney's address. Here it is, something about a horse. Please put it in when you write," and Bella laid the note on the writing table nearby.

"I'll send it at once and have done with it," muttered Coventry and, seating himself, he dashed off a few lines, sealed and sent the letter, and then resumed his march, eyeing the three young ladies with three different expressions, as he passed and repassed. Lucia sat apart, feigning to be intent upon a book, and her handsome face looked almost stern in its haughty composure, for though her heart ached, she was too proud to own it. Bella now lay on the sofa, half asleep, a rosy little creature, as unconsciously pretty as a child. Miss Muir sat in the recess of a deep window, in a low lounging chair, working at an embroidery frame with a graceful industry pleasant to see. Of late she had worn colors, for Bella had been generous in gifts, and the pale blue muslin which flowed in soft waves about her was very becoming to her fair skin and golden hair. The close braids were gone, and loose curls dropped here and there from the heavy coil wound around her well-shaped head. The tip of one dainty foot was visible, and a petulant litle gesture which now and then shook back the falling sleeve gave glimpses of a round white arm. Ned's great hound lay nearby, the sunshine flickered on her through the leaves, and as she sat smiling to herself, while the dexterous hands shaped leaf and flower, she made a charming picture of all that is most womanly and winning; a picture which few men's eyes would not have liked to rest upon.

Another chair stood near her, and as Coventry went up and down, a strong desire to take it possessed him. He was tired of his thoughts and wished to be amused by watching the changes of the girl's expressive face, listening to the varying tones of her voice, and trying to discover the spell which so strongly attracted him in spite of himself. More than once he swerved from his course to gratify his whim, but Lucia's presence always restrained him, and with a word to the dog, or a glance from the window, as pretext for a pause, he resumed his walk again. Something in his cousin's face reproached him, but her manner of late was so repellent that he felt no desire to resume their former familiarity, and, wishing to show that he did not consider himself bound, he kept aloof. It was a quiet test of the power of each woman over this man; they instinctively felt it, and both tried to conquer. Lucia spoke several times, and tried to speak frankly and affably; but her manner was constrained, and Coventry, having answered politely, relapsed into silence. Jean said nothing, but silently appealed to eye and ear by the pretty picture she made of herself, the snatches of song she softly sang, as if forgetting that she was not alone, and a shy glance now and then, half wistful, half merry, which was more alluring than graceful figure or sweet voice. When she had tormented Lucia and tempted Coventry long enough, she quietly asserted her supremacy in a way which astonished her rival, who knew nothing of the secret of her birth, which knowledge did much to attract and charm the young man. Letting a ball of silk escape from her lap, she watched it roll toward the promenader, who caught and returned it with an alacrity which added grace to the trifling service.

As she took it, she said, in the frank way that never failed to win him, "I think you must be tired; but if exercise is necessary, employ your energies to some purpose and put your mother's basket of silks in order. They are in a tangle, and it will please her to know that you did it, as your brother used to do."

"Hercules at the distaff," said Coventry gaily, and down he sat in the long-desired seat. Jean put the basket on his knee, and as he surveyed it, as if daunted at his task, she leaned back, and indulged in a musical little peal of laughter charming to hear. Lucia sat dumb with surprise, to see her proud, indolent cousin obeying the commands of a governess, and looking as if he heartily enjoyed it. In ten minutes she was as entirely forgotten as if she had been miles away; for Jean seemed in her wittiest, gayest mood, and as she now treated the "young master" like an equal, there was none of the former meek timidity. Yet often her eyes fell, her color changed, and the piquant sallies faltered on her tongue, as Coventry involuntarily looked deep into the fine eyes which had once shone on him so tenderly in that mimic tragedy. He could not forget it, and though neither alluded to it, the memory of the previous evening seemed to haunt both and lend a secret charm to the present moment. Lucia bore this as long as she could, and then left the room with the air of an insulted princess; but Coventry did not, and Jean feigned not to see her go. Bella was fast asleep, and before he knew how it came to pass, the young man was listening to the story of his companion's life. A sad tale, told with wonderful skill, for soon he was absorbed in it. The basket slid unobserved from his knee, the dog was pushed away, and, leaning forward, he listened eagerly as the girl's low voice recounted all the hardships, loneliness, and grief of her short life. In the midst of a touching episode she started, stopped, and looked straight before her, with an intent expression which changed to one of intense contempt, and her eye turned to Coventry's, as she said, pointing to the window behind him, "We are watched."

"By whom?" he demanded, starting up angrily.

"Hush, say nothing, let it pass. I am used to it."

"But *I* am not, and I'll not submit to it. Who was it, Jean?" he answered hotly.

She smiled significantly at a knot of rose-colored ribbon, which a little gust was blowing toward them along the terrace. A black frown darkened the young man's face as he sprang out of the long window and went rapidly out of sight, scrutinizing each green nook as he passed. Jean laughed quietly as she watched him, and said softly to herself, with her eyes on the fluttering ribbon, "That was a fortunate accident, and a happy inspiration. Yes, my dear Mrs. Dean, you will find that playing the spy will only get your mistress as well as yourself into trouble. You would not be warned, and you must take the consequences, reluctant as I am to injure a worthy creature like yourself."

Soon Coventry was heard returning. Jean listened with suspended breath to catch his first words, for he was not alone.

"Since you insist that it was you and not your mistress, I let it pass, although I still have my suspicions. Tell Miss Beaufort I desire to see her for a few moments in the library. Now go, Dean, and be careful for the future, if you wish to stay in my house."

The maid retired, and the young man came in looking both ireful and stern.

"I wish I had said nothing, but I was startled, and spoke involuntarily. Now you are angry, and I have made fresh trouble for poor Miss Lucia. Forgive me as I forgive her, and let it pass. I have learned to bear this surveillance, and pity her causeless jealousy," said Jean, with a self-reproachful air.

"I will forgive the dishonorable act, but I cannot forget it, and I intend to put a stop to it. I am not betrothed to my cousin, as I told you once, but you, like all the rest, seem bent on believing that I am. Hitherto I have cared too little about the matter to settle it, but now I shall prove beyond all doubt that I am free."

As he uttered the last word, Coventry cast on Jean a look that affected her strangely. She grew pale, her work dropped on her lap, and her eyes rose to his, with an eager, questioning expression, which slowly changed to one of mingled pain and pity, as she turned her face away, murmuring in a tone of tender sorrow, "Poor Lucia, who will comfort her?"

For a moment Coventry stood silent, as if weighing some fateful purpose in his mind. As Jean's rapt sigh of compassion reached his ear, he had echoed it within himself, and half repented of his resolution; then his eye rested on the girl before him looking so lonely in her sweet sympathy for another that his heart yearned toward her. Sudden fire shot into his eye, sudden warmth replaced the cold sternness of his face, and his steady voice faltered suddenly, as he said, very low, yet very earnestly, "Jean, I have tried to love her, but I cannot. Ought I to deceive her, and make myself miserable to please my family?"

"She is beautiful and good, and loves you tenderly; is there no hope for her?" asked Jean, still pale, but very quiet, though she held one hand against her heart, as if to still or hide its rapid beating.

"None," answered Coventry.

"But can you not learn to love her? Your will is strong, and most men would not find it a hard task."

"I cannot, for something stronger than my own will controls me."

"What is that?" And Jean's dark eyes were fixed upon him, full of innocent wonder.

His fell, and he said hastily, "I dare not tell you yet."

"Pardon! I should not have asked. Do not consult me in this matter; I am not the person to advise you. I can only say that it seems to me as if any man with an empty heart would be glad to have so beautiful a woman as your cousin."

"My heart is not empty," began Coventry, drawing a step nearer, and speaking in a passionate voice. "Jean, I *must* speak; hear me. I cannot love my cousin, because I love you."

"Stop!" And Jean sprang up with a commanding gesture. "I will not hear you while any promise binds you to another. Remember your mother's wishes, Lucia's hopes, Edward's last words, your own pride, my humble lot. You forget yourself, Mr. Coventry. Think well before you speak, weigh the cost of this act, and recollect who I am before you insult me by any transient passion, any false vows."

"I have thought, I do weigh the cost, and I swear that I desire to woo you as humbly, honestly as I would any lady in the land. You speak of my pride. Do I stoop in loving my equal in rank? You speak of your lowly lot, but poverty is no disgrace, and the courage with which you bear it makes it beautiful. I should have broken with Lucia before I spoke, but I could not control myself. My mother loves you, and will be happy in my happiness. Edward must forgive me, for I have tried to do my best, but love is irresistible. Tell me, Jean, is there any hope for me?"

He had seized her hand and was speaking impetuously, with ardent face and tender tone, but no answer came, for as Jean turned her eloquent countenance toward him, full of maiden shame and timid love, Dean's prim figure appeared at the door, and her harsh voice broke the momentary silence, saying, sternly, "Miss Beaufort is waiting for you, sir."

"Go, go at once, and be kind, for my sake, Gerald," whispered

Jean, for he stood as if deaf and blind to everything but her voice, her face.

As she drew his head down to whisper, her cheek touched his, and regardless of Dean, he kissed it, passionately, whispering back, "My little Jean! For your sake I can be anything."

"Miss Beaufort is waiting. Shall I say you will come, sir?" demanded Dean, pale and grim with indignation.

"Yes, yes, I'll come. Wait for me in the garden, Jean." And Coventry hurried away, in no mood for the interview but anxious to have it over.

As the door closed behind him, Dean walked up to Miss Muir, trembling with anger, and laying a heavy hand on her arm, she said below her breath, "I've been expecting this, you artful creature. I saw your game and did my best to spoil it, but you are too quick for me. You think you've got him. There you are mistaken; for as sure as my name is Hester Dean, I'll prevent it, or Sir John shall."

"Take your hand away and treat me with proper respect, or you will be dismissed from this house. Do you know who I am?" And Jean drew herself up with a haughty air, which impressed the woman more deeply than her words. "I am the daughter of Lady Howard and, if I choose it, can be the wife of Mr. Coventry."

Dean drew back amazed, yet not convinced. Being a well-trained servant, as well as a prudent woman, she feared to overstep the bounds of respect, to go too far, and get her mistress as well as herself into trouble. So, though she still doubted Jean, and hated her more than ever, she controlled herself. Dropping a curtsy, she assumed her usual air of deference, and said, meekly, "I beg pardon, miss. If I'd known, I should have conducted myself differently, of course, but ordinary governesses make so much mischief in a house, one can't help mistrusting them. I don't wish to meddle or be overbold, but being fond of my dear young lady, I naturally take her part, and must say that Mr. Coventry has not acted like a gentleman."

"Think what you please, Dean, but I advise you to say as little as possible if you wish to remain. I have not accepted Mr. Coventry yet, and if he chooses to set aside the engagement his family made for him, I think he has a right to do so. Miss Beaufort would hardly care to marry him against his will, because he pities her for her unhappy love," and with a tranquil smile, Miss Muir walked away.

❧ chapter VII ❧

THE LAST CHANCE

"SHE will tell Sir John, will she? Then I must be before her, and hasten events. It will be as well to have all sure before there can be any danger. My poor Dean, you are no match for me, but you may prove annoying, nevertheless."

These thoughts passed through Miss Muir's mind as she went down the hall, pausing an instant at the library door, for the murmur of voices was heard. She caught no word, and had only time for an instant's pause as Dean's heavy step followed her. Turning, Jean drew a chair before the door, and, beckoning to the woman, she said, smiling still, "Sit here and play watchdog. I am going to Miss Bella, so you can nod if you will."

"Thank you, miss. I will wait for my young lady. She may need me when this hard time is over." And Dean seated herself with a resolute face.

Jean laughed and went on; but her eyes gleamed with sudden malice, and she glanced over her shoulder with an expression which boded ill for the faithful old servant.

"I've got a letter from Ned, and here is a tiny note for you," cried Bella as Jean entered the boudoir. "Mine is a very odd, hasty letter, with no news in it, but his meeting with Sydney. I hope yours is better, or it won't be very satisfactory."

As Sydney's name passed Bella's lips, all the color died out of Miss Muir's face, and the note shook with the tremor of her hand.

Her very lips were white, but she said calmly, "Thank you. As you are busy, I'll go and read my letter on the lawn." And before Bella could speak, she was gone.

Hurrying to a quiet nook, Jean tore open the note and read the few blotted lines it contained.

> *I have seen Sydney; he has told me all; and, hard as I found it to believe, it was impossible to doubt, for he has discovered proofs which cannot be denied. I make no reproaches, shall demand no confession or atonement, for I cannot forget that I once loved you. I give you three days to find another home, before I return to tell the family who you are. Go at once, I beseech you, and spare me the pain of seeing your disgrace.*

Slowly, steadily she read it twice over, then sat motionless, knitting her brows in deep thought. Presently she drew a long breath, tore up the note, and rising, went slowly toward the Hall, saying to herself, "Three days, only three days! Can it be accomplished in so short a time? It shall be, if wit and will can do it, for it is my last chance. If this fails, I'll not go back to my old life, but end all at once."

Setting her teeth and clenching her hands, as if some memory stung her, she went on through the twilight, to find Sir John waiting to give her a hearty welcome.

"You look tired, my dear. Never mind the reading tonight; rest yourself, and let the book go," he said kindly, observing her worn look.

"Thank you, sir. I am tired, but I'd rather read, else the book will not be finished before I go."

"Go, child! Where are you going?" demanded Sir John, looking anxiously at her as she sat down.

"I will tell you by-and-by, sir." And opening the book, Jean read for a little while.

But the usual charm was gone; there was no spirit in the voice of the reader, no interest in the face of the listener, and soon he said, abruptly, "My dear, pray stop! I cannot listen with a divided mind. What troubles you? Tell your friend, and let him comfort you."

As if the kind words overcame her, Jean dropped the book, covered up her face, and wept so bitterly that Sir John was much alarmed; for such a demonstration was doubly touching in one who usually was all gaiety and smiles. As he tried to soothe her, his words grew tender, his solicitude full of a more than paternal anxiety, and his kind heart overflowed with pity and affection for the weeping girl. As she grew calmer, he urged her to be frank, promising to help and counsel her, whatever the affliction or fault might be.

"Ah, you are too kind, too generous! How can I go away and leave my one friend?" sighed Jean, wiping the tears away and looking up at him with grateful eyes.

"Then you do care a little for the old man?" said Sir John with an eager look, an involuntary pressure of the hand he held.

Jean turned her face away, and answered, very low, "No one ever was so kind to me as you have been. Can I help caring for you more than I can express?"

Sir John was a little deaf at times, but he heard that, and looked well pleased. He had been rather thoughtful of late, had dressed with unusual care, been particularly gallant and gay when the young ladies visited him, and more than once, when Jean paused in the reading to ask a question, he had been forced to confess that he had not been listening; though, as she well knew, his eyes had been fixed upon her. Since the discovery of her birth, his manner had been peculiarly benignant, and many little acts had proved his interest and goodwill. Now, when Jean spoke of going, a panic seized him, and desolation seemed about to fall upon the old Hall. Something in her unusual agitation struck him as peculiar and excited his curiosity. Never had she seemed so interesting as now, when she sat beside him with tearful eyes, and some soft trouble in her heart which she dared not confess.

"Tell me everything, child, and let your friend help you if he can." Formerly he said "father" or "the old man," but lately he always spoke of himself as her "friend."

"I will tell you, for I have no one else to turn to. I must go away because Mr. Coventry has been weak enough to love me."

"What, Gerald?" cried Sir John, amazed.

"Yes; today he told me this, and left me to break with Lucia; so I ran to you to help me prevent him from disappointing his mother's hopes and plans."

Sir John had started up and paced down the room, but as Jean paused he turned toward her, saying, with an altered face, "Then you do not love him? Is it possible?"

"No, I do not love him," she answered promptly.

"Yet he is all that women usually find attractive. How is it that you have escaped, Jean?"

"I love someone else" was the scarcely audible reply.

Sir John resumed his seat with the air of a man bent on getting at a mystery, if possible.

"It will be unjust to let you suffer for the folly of these boys, my little girl. Ned is gone, and I was sure that Gerald was safe; but now that his turn has come, I am perplexed, for he cannot be sent away."

"No, it is I who must go; but it seems so hard to leave this safe and happy home, and wander away into the wide, cold world again. You have all been too kind to me, and now separation breaks my heart."

A sob ended the speech, and Jean's head went down upon her hands again. Sir John looked at her a moment, and his fine old face was full of genuine emotion, as he said slowly, "Jean, will you stay and be a daughter to the solitary old man?"

"No, sir" was the unexpected answer.

"And why not?" asked Sir John, looking surprised, but rather pleased than angry.

"Because I could not be a daughter to you; and even if I could, it would not be wise, for the gossips would say you were not old enough to be the adopted father of a girl like me. Sir John, young as I am, I know much of the world, and am sure that this kind plan is impractical; but I thank you from the bottom of my heart."

"Where will you go, Jean?" asked Sir John, after a pause.

"To London, and try to find another situation where I can do no harm."

"Will it be difficult to find another home?"

"Yes. I cannot ask Mrs. Coventry to recommend me, when I have innocently brought so much trouble into her family; and Lady Sydney is gone, so I have no friend."

"Except John Coventry. I will arrange all that. When will you go, Jean?"

"Tomorrow."

"So soon!" And the old man's voice betrayed the trouble he was trying to conceal.

Jean had grown very calm, but it was the calmness of desperation. She had hoped that the first tears would produce the avowal for which she waited. It had not, and she began to fear that her last chance was slipping from her. Did the old man love her? If so, why did he not speak? Eager to profit by each moment, she was on the alert for any hopeful hint, any propitious word, look, or act, and every nerve was strung to the utmost.

"Jean, may I ask one question?" said Sir John.

"Anything of me, sir."

"This man whom you love—can he not help you?"

"He could if he knew, but he must not."

"If he knew what? Your present trouble?"

"No. My love."

"He does know this, then?"

"No, thank heaven! And he never will."

"Why not?"

"Because I am too proud to own it."

"He loves you, my child?"

"I do not know—I dare not hope it," murmured Jean.

"Can I not help you here? Believe me, I desire to see you safe and happy. Is there nothing I can do?"

"Nothing, nothing."

"May I know the name?"

"No! No! Let me go; I cannot bear this questioning!" And Jean's distressful face warned him to ask no more.

"Forgive me, and let me do what I may. Rest here quietly. I'll write a letter to a good friend of mine, who will find you a home, if you leave us."

As Sir John passed into his inner study, Jean watched him with despairing eyes and wrung her hands, saying to herself, Has all my skill deserted me when I need it most? How can I make him understand, yet not overstep the bounds of maiden modesty? He is so blind, so timid, or so dull he will not see, and time is going fast. What shall I do to open his eyes?

Her own eyes roved about the room, seeking for some aid from inanimate things, and soon she found it. Close behind the couch where she sat hung a fine miniature of Sir John. At first her eye rested on it as she contrasted its placid comeliness with the unusual pallor and disquiet of the living face seen through the open door, as the old man sat at his desk trying to write and casting covert glances at the girlish figure he had left behind him. Affecting unconsciousness of this, Jean gazed on as if forgetful of everything but the picture, and suddenly, as if obeying an irresistible impulse, she took it down, looked long and fondly at it, then, shaking her curls about her face, as if to hide the act, pressed it to her lips and seemed to weep over it in an uncontrollable paroxysm of tender grief. A sound startled her, and like a guilty thing, she turned to replace the picture; but it dropped from her hand as she uttered a faint cry and hid her face, for Sir John stood before her, with an expression which she could not mistake.

"Jean, why did you do that?" he asked, in an eager, agitated voice.

No answer, as the girl sank lower, like one overwhelmed with shame. Laying his hand on the bent head, and bending his own, he whispered, "Tell me, is the name John Coventry?"

Still no answer, but a stifled sound betrayed that his words had gone home.

"Jean, shall I go back and write the letter, or may I stay and tell you that the old man loves you better than a daughter?"

She did not speak, but a little hand stole out from under the falling hair, as if to keep him. With a broken exclamation he seized it, drew her up into his arms, and laid his gray head on her fair one, too happy for words. For a moment Jean Muir enjoyed her success; then, fearing lest some sudden mishap should destroy it, she hastened to make all secure. Looking up with well-feigned timidity and half-confessed affection, she said softly, "Forgive me that I could not hide this better. I meant to go away and never tell it, but you were so kind it made the parting doubly hard. Why did you ask such dangerous questions? Why did you look, when you should have been writing my dismissal?"

"How could I dream that you loved me, Jean, when you refused the only offer I dared make? Could I be presumptuous enough to fancy you would reject young lovers for an old man like me?" asked Sir John, caressing her.

"You are not old, to me, but everything I love and honor!" interrupted Jean, with a touch of genuine remorse, as this generous, honorable gentleman gave her both heart and home, unconscious of deceit. "It is I who am presumptuous, to dare to love one so far above me. But I did not know how dear you were to me till I felt that I must go. I ought not to accept this happiness. I am not worthy of it; and you will regret your kindness when the world blames you for giving a home to one so poor, and plain, and humble as I."

"Hush, my darling. I care nothing for the idle gossip of the world. If you are happy here, let tongues wag as they will. I shall be too busy enjoying the sunshine of your presence to heed anything that goes on about me. But, Jean, you are sure you love me? It seems incredible that I should win the heart that has been so cold to younger, better men than I."

"Dear Sir John, be sure of this, I love you truly. I will do my best to be a good wife to you, and prove that, in spite of my many faults, I possess the virtue of gratitude."

If he had known the strait she was in, he would have understood the cause of the sudden fervor of her words, the intense thankfulness that shone in her face, the real humility that made her stoop and kiss the generous hand that gave so much. For a few moments she enjoyed and let him enjoy the happy present, undisturbed. But the anxiety which devoured her, the danger which menaced her, soon recalled her, and forced her to wring yet more from the unsuspicious heart she had conquered.

"No need of letters now," said Sir John, as they sat side by side, with the summer moonlight glorifying all the room. "You have found a home for life; may it prove a happy one."

"It is not mine yet, and I have a strange foreboding that it never will be," she answered sadly.

"Why, my child?"

"Because I have an enemy who will try to destroy my peace, to poison your mind against me, and to drive me out from my paradise, to suffer again all I have suffered this last year."

"You mean that mad Sydney of whom you told me?"

"Yes. As soon as he hears of this good fortune to poor little Jean, he will hasten to mar it. He is my fate; I cannot escape him, and wherever he goes my friends desert me; for he has the power and uses it for my destruction. Let me go away and hide before he comes, for, having shared your confidence, it will break my heart to see you distrust and turn from me, instead of loving and protecting."

"My poor child, you are superstitious. Be easy. No one can harm you now, no one would dare attempt it. And as for my deserting you, that will soon be out of my power, if I have my way."

"How, dear Sir John?" asked Jean, with a flutter of intense relief at her heart, for the way seemed smoothing before her.

"I will make you my wife at once, if I may. This will free you from Gerald's love, protect you from Sydney's persecution, give you a safe home, and me the right to cherish and defend with heart and hand. Shall it be so, my child?"

"Yes; but oh, remember that I have no friend but you! Promise me to be faithful to the last—to believe in me, to trust me, protect and love me, in spite of all misfortunes, faults, and follies. I will be true as steel to you, and make your life as happy as it deserves to be. Let us promise these things now, and keep the promises unbroken to the end."

Her solemn air touched Sir John. Too honorable and upright himself to suspect falsehood in others, he saw only the natural impulse of a lovely girl in Jean's words, and, taking the hand she gave him in both of his, he promised all she asked, and kept that promise to the end. She paused an instant, with a pale, absent expression, as if she searched herself, then looked up clearly in the confiding face above her, and promised what she faithfully performed in afteryears.

"When shall it be, little sweetheart? I leave all to you, only let it be soon, else some gay young lover will appear, and take you from me," said Sir John, playfully, anxious to chase away the dark expression which had stolen over Jean's face.

"Can you keep a secret?" asked the girl, smiling up at him, all her charming self again.

"Try me."

"I will. Edward is coming home in three days. I must be gone before he comes. Tell no one of this; he wishes to surprise them. And if you love me, tell nobody of your approaching marriage. Do not betray that you care for me until I am really yours. There will be such a stir, such remonstrances, explanations, and reproaches that I shall be worn out, and run away from you all to escape the trial. If I could have my wish, I would go to some quiet place tomorrow and wait till you come for me. I know so little of such things, I cannot tell how soon we may be married; not for some weeks, I think."

"Tomorrow, if we like. A special license permits people to marry when and where they please. My plan is better than yours. Listen, and tell me if it can be carried out. I will go to town tomorrow, get the license, invite my friend, the Reverend Paul Fairfax, to return with me, and tomorrow evening you come at your usual time, and, in the presence of my discreet old servants, make me the happiest man in England. How does this suit you, my little Lady Coventry?"

The plan which seemed made to meet her ends, the name which was the height of her ambition, and the blessed sense of safety which came to her filled Jean Muir with such intense satisfaction that tears of real feeling stood in her eyes, and the glad assent she gave was the truest word that had passed her lips for months.

"We will go abroad or to Scotland for our honeymoon, till the storm blows over," said Sir John, well knowing that this hasty marriage would surprise or offend all his relations, and feeling as glad as Jean to escape the first excitement.

"To Scotland, please. I long to see my father's home," said Jean, who dreaded to meet Sydney on the continent.

They talked a little longer, arranging all things, Sir John so intent on hurrying the event that Jean had nothing to do but give a ready assent to all his suggestions. One fear alone disturbed her. If Sir John went to town, he might meet Edward, might hear and believe his statements. Then all would be lost. Yet this risk must be incurred, if the marriage was to be speedily and safely accomplished; and to guard against the meeting was Jean's sole care. As they went through the park—for Sir John insisted upon taking her home—she said, clinging to his arm:

"Dear friend, bear one thing in mind, else we shall be much annoyed, and all our plans disarranged. Avoid your nephews; you are so frank your face will betray you. They both love me, are both hot-tempered, and in the first excitement of the discovery might be violent. You must incur no danger, no disrespect for my sake; so shun them both till we are safe—particularly Edward. He will feel that his brother has wronged him, and that you have succeeded where he failed. This will irritate him, and I fear a stormy scene. Promise to avoid both for a day or two; do not listen to them, do not see them, do not write to or receive letters from them. It is foolish, I know; but you are all I have, and I am haunted by a strange foreboding that I am to lose you."

Touched and flattered by her tender solicitude, Sir John promised everything, even while he laughed at her fears. Love blinded the good gentleman to the peculiarity of the request; the novelty, romance, and secrecy of the affair rather bewildered though it charmed him; and the knowledge that he had outrivaled three young and ardent lovers gratified his vanity more than he would confess. Parting from the girl at the garden gate, he turned homeward, feeling like a boy again, and loitered back, humming a love lay, quite forgetful of evening damps, gout, and the five-and-fifty years which lay so lightly on his shoulders since Jean's arms had rested there. She hurried toward the house, anxious to escape Coventry; but he was waiting for her, and she was forced to meet him.

"How could you linger so long, and keep me in suspense?" he said reproachfully, as he took her hand and tried to catch a glimpse of her face in the shadow of her hat brim. "Come and rest in the grotto. I have so much to say, to hear and enjoy."

"Not now; I am too tired. Let me go in and sleep. Tomorrow we will talk. It is damp and chilly, and my head aches with all this worry." Jean spoke wearily, yet with a touch of petulance, and Coventry, fancying that she was piqued at his not coming for her, hastened to explain with eager tenderness.

"My poor little Jean, you do need rest. We wear you out, among us, and you never complain. I should have come to bring you home, but Lucia detained me, and when I got away I saw my uncle had forestalled me. I shall be jealous of the old gentleman, if he is so devoted. Jean, tell me one thing before we part; I am free as air, now, and have a right to speak. Do you love me? Am I the happy man who has won your heart? I dare to think so, to believe that this telltale face of yours has betrayed you, and to hope that I have gained what poor Néd and wild Sydney have lost."

"Before I answer, tell me of your interview with Lucia. I have a right to know," said Jean.

Coventry hesitated, for pity and remorse were busy at his heart when he recalled poor Lucia's grief. Jean was bent on hearing the humiliation of her rival. As the young man paused, she frowned, then lifted up her face wreathed in softest smiles, and laying her hand on his arm, she said, with most effective emphasis, half shy, half fond, upon his name, "Please tell me, Gerald!"

He could not resist the look, the touch, the tone, and taking the little hand in his, he said rapidly, as if the task was distasteful to him, "I told her that I did not, could not love her; that I had submitted to my mother's wish, and, for a time, had felt tacitly bound to her, though no words had passed between us. But now I demanded my liberty, regretting that the separation was not mutually desired."

"And she—what did she say? How did she bear it?" asked Jean, feeling in her own woman's heart how deeply Lucia's must have been wounded by that avowal.

"Poor girl! It was hard to bear, but her pride sustained her to the end. She owned that no pledge tied me, fully relinquished any claim my past behavior had seemed to have given her, and prayed that I might find another woman to love me as truly, tenderly as she had done. Jean, I felt like a villain; and yet I never plighted my word to her, never really loved her, and had a perfect right to leave her, if I would."

"Did she speak of me?"

"Yes."

"What did she say?"

"Must I tell you?"

"Yes, tell me everything. I know she hates me and I forgive her, knowing that I should hate any woman whom *you* loved."

"Are you jealous, dear?"

"Of you, Gerald?" And the fine eyes glanced up at him, full of a brilliancy that looked like the light of love.

"You make a slave of me already. How do you do it? I never obeyed a woman before. Jean, I think you are a witch. Scotland is the home of weird, uncanny creatures, who take lovely shapes for the bedevilment of poor weak souls. Are you one of those fair deceivers?"

"You are complimentary," laughed the girl. "I *am* a witch, and one day my disguise will drop away and you will see me as I am, old, ugly, bad and lost. Beware of me in time. I've warned you. Now love me at your peril."

Coventry had paused as he spoke, and eyed her with an unquiet look, conscious of some fascination which conquered yet brought no happiness. A feverish yet pleasurable excitement possessed him; a reckless mood, making him eager to obliterate the past by any rash act, any new experience which his passion brought. Jean regarded him with a wistful, almost woeful face, for one short moment; then a strange smile broke over it, as she spoke in a tone of malicious mockery, under which lurked the bitterness of a sad truth. Coventry looked half bewildered, and his eye went from the girl's mysterious face to a dimly lighted window, behind whose curtains poor Lucia hid her aching heart, praying for him the tender prayers that loving women give to those whose sins are all forgiven for love's sake. His heart smote him, and a momentary feeling of repulsion came over him, as he looked at Jean. She saw it, felt angry, yet conscious of a sense of relief; for now that her own safety was so nearly secured, she felt no wish to do mischief, but rather a desire to undo what was already done, and be at peace with all the world. To recall him to his allegiance, she sighed and walked on, saying gently yet coldly, "Will you tell me what I ask before I answer your question, Mr. Coventry?"

"What Lucia said of you? Well, it was this. 'Beware of Miss Muir. We instinctively distrusted her when we had no cause. I believe in instincts, and mine have never changed, for she has not tried to delude me. Her art is wonderful; I feel yet cannot explain or detect it, except in the working of events which her hand seems to guide. She has brought sorrow and dissension into this hitherto happy family. We are all changed, and this girl has done it. Me she can harm no further; you she will ruin, if she can. Beware of her in time, or you will bitterly repent your blind infatuation!'"

"And what answer did you make?" asked Jean, as the last words came reluctantly from Coventry's lips.

"I told her that I loved you in spite of myself, and would make you my wife in the face of all opposition. Now, Jean, your answer."

"Give me three days to think of it. Good night." And gliding from him, she vanished into the house, leaving him to roam about half the night, tormented with remorse, suspense, and the old distrust which would return when Jean was not there to banish it by her art.

≽ *chapter VIII* ≼

SUSPENSE

ALL the next day, Jean was in a state of the most intense anxiety, as every hour brought the crisis nearer, and every hour might bring defeat, for the subtlest human skill is often thwarted by some unforeseen accident. She longed to assure herself that Sir John was gone, but no servants came or went that day, and she could devise no pretext for sending to glean intelligence. She dared not go herself, lest the unusual act should excite suspicion, for she never went till evening. Even had she determined to venture, there was no time, for Mrs. Coventry was in one of her nervous states, and no one but Miss Muir could amuse her; Lucia was ill, and Miss Muir must give orders; Bella had a studious fit, and Jean must help her. Coventry lingered about the house for several hours, but Jean dared not send him, lest some hint of the truth might reach him. He had ridden away to his new duties when Jean did not appear, and the day dragged on wearisomely. Night came at last, and as Jean dressed for the late dinner, she hardly knew herself when she stood before her mirror, excitement lent such color and brilliancy to her countenance. Remembering the wedding which was to take place that evening, she put on a simple white dress and added a cluster of white roses in bosom and hair. She often wore flowers, but in spite of her desire to look and seem as usual, Bella's first words as she entered the drawing room were

"Why, Jean, how like a bride you look; a veil and gloves would make you quite complete!"

"You forget one other trifle, Bell," said Gerald, with eyes that brightened as they rested on Miss Muir.

"What is that?"asked his sister.

"A bridegroom."

Bella looked to see how Jean received this, but she seemed quite composed as she smiled one of her sudden smiles, and merely said, "That trifle will doubtless be found when the time comes. Is Miss Beaufort too ill for dinner?"

"She begs to be excused, and said you would be willing to take her place, she thought."

As innocent Bella delivered this message, Jean glanced at Coventry, who evaded her eye and looked ill at ease.

A little remorse will do him good, and prepare him for repentance after the grand *coup,* she said to herself, and was particularly gay at dinnertime, though Coventry looked often at Lucia's empty seat, as if he missed her. As soon as they left the table, Miss Muir sent Bella to her mother; and, knowing that Coventry would not linger long at his wine, she hurried away to the Hall. A servant was lounging at the door, and of him she asked, in a tone which was eager in spite of all efforts to be calm, "Is Sir John at home?"

"No, miss, he's just gone to town."

"Just gone! When do you mean?" cried Jean, forgetting the relief she felt in hearing of his absence in surprise at his late departure.

"He went half an hour ago, in the last train, miss."

"I thought he was going early this morning; he told me he should be back this evening."

"I believe he did mean to go, but was delayed by company. The steward came up on business, and a load of gentlemen called, so Sir John could not get off till night, when he wasn't fit to go, being worn out, and far from well."

"Do you think he will be ill? Did he look so?" And as Jean spoke, a thrill of fear passed over her, lest death should rob her of her prize.

"Well, you know, miss, hurry of any kind is bad for elderly gentlemen inclined to apoplexy. Sir John was in a worry all day, and not like himself. I wanted him to take his man, but he wouldn't; and drove off looking flushed and excited like. I'm anxious about him, for I know something is amiss to hurry him off in this way."

"When will he be back, Ralph?"

"Tomorrow noon, if possible; at night, certainly, he bid me tell anyone that called."

"Did he leave no note or message for Miss Coventry, or someone of the family?"

"No, miss, nothing."

"Thank you." And Jean walked back to spend a restless night and rise to meet renewed suspense.

The morning seemed endless, but noon came at last, and under the pretense of seeking coolness in the grotto, Jean stole away to a slope whence the gate to the Hall park was visible. For two long hours she watched, and no one came. She was just turning away when a horseman dashed through the gate and came galloping toward the Hall. Heedless of everything but the uncontrollable longing to gain some tidings, she ran to meet him, feeling assured that he brought ill news. It was a young man from the station, and as he caught sight of her, he drew bridle, looking agitated and undecided.

"Has anything happened?" she cried breathlessly.

"A dreadful accident on the railroad, just the other side of Croydon. News telegraphed half an hour ago," answered the man, wiping his hot face.

"The noon train? Was Sir John in it? Quick, tell me all!"

"It was that train, miss, but whether Sir John was in it or not, we don't know; for the guard is killed, and everything is in such confusion that nothing can be certain. They are at work getting out the dead and wounded. We heard that Sir John was expected, and I came up to tell Mr. Coventry, thinking he would wish to go down. A train leaves in fifteen minutes; where shall I find him? I was told he was at the Hall."

"Ride on, ride on! And find him if he is there. I'll run home and look for him. Lose no time. Ride! Ride!" And turning, Jean sped back like a deer, while the man tore up the avenue to rouse the Hall.

Coventry was there, and went off at once, leaving both Hall and house in dismay. Fearing to betray the horrible anxiety that possessed her, Jean shut herself up in her room and suffered untold agonies as the day wore on and no news came. At dark a sudden cry rang through the house, and Jean rushed down to learn the cause. Bella was standing in the hall, holding a letter, while a group of excited servants hovered near her.

"What is it?" demanded Miss Muir, pale and steady, though her heart died within her as she recognized Gerald's handwriting. Bella gave her the note, and hushed her sobbing to hear again the heavy tidings that had come.

> *Dear Bella:*
>
> *Uncle is safe; he did not go in the noon train. But several persons are sure that Ned was there. No trace of him as yet, but many bodies are in the river, under the ruins of the bridge, and I am doing my best to find the poor lad, if he is there. I have sent to all his haunts in town, and as he has not been seen, I hope it is a false report and he is safe with his regiment. Keep this from my mother till we are sure. I write you, because Lucia is ill. Miss Muir will comfort and sustain you. Hope for the best, dear.*
>
> *Yours, G. C.*

Those who watched Miss Muir as she read these words wondered at the strange expressions which passed over her face, for the joy which appeared there as Sir John's safety was made known did not change to grief or horror at poor Edward's possible fate. The smile died on her lips, but her voice did not falter, and in her downcast eyes shone an inexplicable look of something like triumph. No wonder, for if this was true, the danger which menaced her was averted for a time, and the marriage might be consummated without such desperate haste. This sad and sudden event seemed to her the mysterious fulfilment of a secret wish; and though startled she was not daunted but inspirited, for fate seemed to favor her designs. She did comfort Bella, control the excited household, and keep the rumors from Mrs. Coventry all that dreadful night.

At dawn Gerald came home exhausted, and bringing no tiding of the missing man. He had telegraphed to the headquarters of the regiment and received a reply, stating that Edward had left for London the previous day, meaning to go home before returning. The fact of his having been at the London station was also established, but whether he left by the train or not was still uncertain. The ruins were still being searched, and the body might yet appear.

"Is Sir John coming at noon?" asked Jean, as the three sat together in the rosy hush of dawn, trying to hope against hope.

"No, he had been ill, I learned from young Gower, who is just from town, and so had not completed his business. I sent him word to wait till night, for the bridge won't be passable till then. Now I must try and rest an hour; I've worked all night and have no strength left. Call me the instant any messenger arrives."

With that Coventry went to his room, Bella followed to wait on him, and Jean roamed through house and grounds, unable to rest. The morning was far spent when the messenger arrived. Jean went to receive his tidings, with the wicked hope still lurking at her heart.

"Is he found?" she asked calmly, as the man hesitated to speak.

"Yes, ma'am."

"You are sure?"

"I am certain, ma'am, though some won't say till Mr. Coventry comes to look."

"Is he alive?" And Jean's white lips trembled as she put the question.

"Oh no, ma'am, that warn't possible, under all them stones and water. The poor young gentleman is so wet, and crushed, and torn, no one would know him, except for the uniform, and the white hand with the ring on it."

Jean sat down, very pale, and the man described the finding of the poor shattered body. As he finished, Coventry appeared, and with one look of mingled remorse, shame, and sorrow, the elder brother went away, to find and bring the younger home. Jean crept into the garden like a guilty thing, trying to hide the satisfaction which struggled with a woman's natural pity, for so sad an end for this brave young life.

"Why waste tears or feign sorrow when I must be glad?" she muttered, as she paced to and fro along the terrace. "The poor boy is out of pain, and I am out of danger."

She got no further, for, turning as she spoke, she stood face to face with Edward! Bearing no mark of peril on dress or person, but stalwart and strong as ever, he stood there looking at her, with contempt and compassion struggling in his face. As if turned to stone, she remained motionless, with dilated eyes, arrested breath, and paling cheek. He did not speak but watched her silently till she put out a trembling hand, as if to assure herself by touch that it was really he. Then he drew back, and as if the act convinced as fully as words, she said slowly, "They told me you were dead."

"And you were glad to believe it. No, it was my comrade, young Courtney, who unconsciously deceived you all, and lost his life, as I should have done, if I had not gone to Ascot after seeing him off yesterday."

"To Ascot?" echoed Jean, shrinking back, for Edward's eye was on her, and his voice was stern and cold.

"Yes; you know the place. I went there to make inquiries concerning you and was well satisfied. Why are you still here?"

"The three days are not over yet. I hold you to your promise. Before night I shall be gone; till then you will be silent, if you have honor enough to keep your word."

"I have." Edward took out his watch and, as he put it back, said with cool precision, "It is now two, the train leaves for London at half-past six; a carriage will wait for you at the side door. Allow me to advise you to go then, for the instant dinner is over I shall speak." And with a bow he went into the house, leaving Jean nearly suffocated with a throng of contending emotions.

For a few minutes she seemed paralyzed; but the native energy of the woman forbade utter despair, till the last hope was gone. Frail as that now was, she still clung to it tenaciously, resolving to win the game in defiance of everything. Springing up, she went to her room, packed her few valuables, dressed herself with care, and then sat down to wait. She heard a joyful stir below, saw Coventry come hurrying back, and from a garrulous maid learned that the body was that of young Courtney. The uniform being the same as Edward's and the ring, a gift from him, had caused the men to believe the disfigured corpse to be that of the younger Coventry. No one but the maid came near her; once Bella's voice called her, but some one checked the girl, and the call was not repeated. At five an envelope was brought her, directed in Edward's hand, and containing a check which more than paid a year's salary. No word accompanied the gift, yet the generosity of it touched her, for Jean Muir had the relics of a once honest nature, and despite her falsehood could still admire nobleness and respect virtue. A tear of genuine shame dropped on the paper, and real gratitude filled her heart, as she thought that even if all else failed, she was not thrust out penniless into the world, which had no pity for poverty.

As the clock struck six, she heard a carriage drive around and went down to meet it. A servant put on her trunk, gave the order, "To the station, James," and she drove away without meeting anyone, speaking to anyone, or apparently being seen by anyone. A sense of utter weariness came over her, and she longed to lie down and forget. But the last chance still remained, and till that failed, she would not give up. Dismissing the carriage, she seated herself to watch for the quarter-past-six train from London, for in that Sir John would come if he came at all that night. She was haunted by the fear that Edward had met and told him. The first glimpse of Sir John's frank face would betray the truth. If he knew all, there was no hope, and she would go her way alone. If he knew nothing, there was yet time for the marriage; and once his wife, she knew she was safe, because for the honor of his name he would screen and protect her.

Up rushed the train, out stepped Sir John, and Jean's heart died within her. Grave, and pale, and worn he looked, and leaned heavily on the arm of a portly gentleman in black. The Reverend Mr. Fairfax, why has he come, if the secret is out? thought Jean, slowly advancing to meet them and fearing to read her fate in Sir John's face. He saw her, dropped his friend's arm, and hurried forward with the ardor of a young man, exclaiming, as he seized her hand with a beaming face, a glad voice, "My little girl! Did you think I would never come?"

She could not answer, the reaction was too strong, but she clung to him, regardless of time or place, and felt that her last hope had not failed. Mr. Fairfax proved himself equal to the occasion. Asking no questions, he hurried Sir John and Jean into a carriage and stepped in after them with a bland apology. Jean was soon herself again, and, having told her fears at his delay, listened eagerly while he related the various mishaps which had detained him.

"Have you seen Edward?" was her first question.

"Not yet, but I know he has come, and have heard of his narrow escape. I should have been in that train, if I had not been delayed by the indisposition which I then cursed, but now bless. Are you ready, Jean? Do you repent your choice, my child?"

"No, no! I am ready, I am only too happy to become your wife, dear, generous Sir John," cried Jean, with a glad alacrity, which touched the old man to the heart, and charmed the Reverend Mr. Fairfax, who concealed the romance of a boy under his clerical suit.

They reached the Hall. Sir John gave orders to admit no one and after a hasty dinner sent for his old housekeeper and his steward, told them of his purpose, and desired them to witness his marriage. Obedience had been the law of their lives, and Master could do nothing wrong in their eyes, so they played their parts willingly, for Jean was a favorite at the Hall. Pale as her gown, but calm and steady, she stood beside Sir John, uttering her vows in a clear tone and taking upon herself the vows of a wife with more than a bride's usual docility. When the ring was fairly on, a smile broke over her face. When Sir John kissed and called her his "little wife," she shed a tear or two of sincere happiness; and when Mr. Fairfax addressed her as "my lady," she laughed her musical laugh, and glanced up at a picture of Gerald with eyes full of exultation. As the servants left the room, a message was brought from Mrs. Coventry, begging Sir John to come to her at once.

"You will not go and leave me so soon?" pleaded Jean, well knowing why he was sent for.

"My darling, I must." And in spite of its tenderness, Sir John's manner was too decided to be withstood.

"Then I shall go with you," cried Jean, resolving that no earthly power should part them.

≳ *chapter IX* ≴

LADY COVENTRY

WHEN the first excitement of Edward's return had subsided, and before they could question him as to the cause of this unexpected visit, he told them that after dinner their curiosity should be gratified, and meantime he begged them to leave Miss Muir alone, for she had received bad news and must not be disturbed. The family with difficulty restrained their tongues and waited impatiently. Gerald confessed his love for Jean and asked his brother's pardon for betraying his trust. He had expected an outbreak, but Edward only looked at him with pitying eyes, and said sadly, "You too! I have no reproaches to make, for I know what you will suffer when the truth is known."

"What do you mean?" demanded Coventry.

"You will soon know, my poor Gerald, and we will comfort one another."

Nothing more could be drawn from Edward till dinner was over, the servants gone, and all the family alone together. Then pale and grave, but very self-possessed, for trouble had made a man of him, he produced a packet of letters, and said, addressing himself to his brother, "Jean Muir has deceived us all. I know her story; let me tell it before I read her letters."

"Stop! I'll not listen to any false tales against her. The poor girl has enemies who belie her!" cried Gerald, starting up.

"For the honor of the family, you must listen, and learn what fools she has made of us. I can prove what I say, and convince you that she has the art of a devil. Sit still ten minutes, then go, if you will."

Edward spoke with authority, and his brother obeyed him with a foreboding heart.

"I met Sydney, and he begged me to beware of her. Nay, listen, Gerald! I know she has told her story, and that you believe it; but her own letters convict her. She tried to charm Sydney as she did us, and nearly succeeded in inducing him to marry her. Rash and wild as he is, he is still a gentleman, and when an incautious word of hers roused his suspicions, he refused to make her his wife. A stormy scene ensued, and, hoping to intimidate him, she feigned to stab herself as if in despair. She did wound herself, but failed to gain her point and insisted upon going to a hospital to die. Lady Sydney, good, simple soul, believed the girl's version of the story, thought her son was in the wrong, and when he was gone, tried to atone for his fault by finding Jean Muir another home. She thought Gerald was soon to marry Lucia, and that I was away, so sent her here as a safe and comfortable retreat."

"But, Ned, are you sure of all this? Is Sydney to be believed?" began Coventry, still incredulous.

"To convince you, I'll read Jean's letters before I say more. They were written to an accomplice and were purchased by Sydney. There was a compact between the two women, that each should keep the other informed of all adventures, plots and plans, and share whatever good fortune fell to the lot of either. Thus Jean wrote freely, as you shall judge. The letters concern us alone. The first was written a few days after she came.

"*Dear Hortense:*

"*Another failure. Sydney was more wily than I thought. All was going well, when one day my old fault beset me, I took too much wine, and I carelessly owned that I had been an actress. He was shocked, and retreated. I got up a scene, and gave myself a safe little wound, to frighten him. The brute was not frightened, but coolly left me to my fate. I'd have died to spite him, if I dared, but as I didn't, I lived to torment him. As yet, I have had no chance, but I will not forget him. His mother is a poor, weak creature, whom I could use as I would, and through her I found an excellent place. A sick mother, silly daughter, and two eligible sons. One is engaged to a handsome iceberg, but that only renders him more interesting in my eyes, rivalry adds so much to the charm of one's conquests. Well, my dear, I went, got up in the meek style, intending to do the pathetic; but before I saw the family, I was so angry I could hardly control myself. Through the indolence of Monsieur the young master, no carriage was sent for me, and I intend he shall atone for that rudeness by-and-by. The younger son, the mother, and the girl received me patronizingly, and I understood the simple souls at once. Monsieur (as I shall call him, as names are unsafe) was unapproachable, and took no pains to conceal his dislike of governesses. The cousin was lovely, but detestable with her pride, her coldness, and her very visible adoration of Monsieur, who let her worship him, like an inanimate idol as he is. I hated them both, of course, and in return for their insolence shall torment her with jealousy, and teach him how to woo a woman by making his heart ache. They are an intensely proud family, but I can humble them all, I think, by captivating the sons, and when they have committed themselves, cast them off, and marry the old uncle, whose title takes my fancy."*

"She never wrote that! It is impossible. A woman could not do it," cried Lucia indignantly, while Bella sat bewildered and Mrs. Coventry supported herself with salts and fan. Coventry went to his brother, examined the writing, and returned to his seat, saying, in a tone of suppressed wrath, "She did write it. I posted some of those letters myself. Go on, Ned."

"I made myself useful and agreeable to the amiable ones, and overheard the chat of the lovers. It did not suit me, so I fainted away to stop it, and excite interest in the provoking pair. I thought I had succeeded, but Monsieur suspected me and showed me that he did. I forgot my meek role and gave him a stage look. It had a good effect, and I shall try it again. The man is well worth winning, but I prefer the title, and as the uncle is a hale, handsome gentleman, I can't wait for him to die, though Monsieur is very charming, with his elegant languor, and his heart so fast asleep no woman has had power to wake it yet. I told my story, and they believed it, though I had the audacity to say I was but nineteen, to talk Scotch, and bashfully confess that Sydney wished to marry me. Monsieur knows S. and evidently suspects something. I must watch him and keep the truth from him, if possible.

"I was very miserable that night when I got alone. Something in the atmosphere of this happy home made me wish I was anything but what I am. As I sat there trying to pluck up my spirits, I thought of the days when I was lovely and young, good and gay. My glass showed me an old woman of thirty, for my false locks were off, my paint gone, and my face was without its mask. Bah! how I hate sentiment! I drank your health from your own little flask, and went to bed to dream that I was playing Lady Tartuffe—as I am. Adieu, more soon."

No one spoke as Edward paused, and taking up another letter, he read on:

"My Dear Creature:

"All goes well. Next day I began my task, and having caught a hint of the character of each, tried my power over them. Early in the morning I ran over to see the Hall. Approved of it highly, and took the first step toward becoming its mistress, by piquing the curiosity and flattering the pride of its master. His estate is his idol; I praised it with a few artless compliments to himself, and he was charmed. The cadet of the family adores horses. I risked my neck to pet his beast, and he was charmed. The little girl is romantic about flowers; I made a posy and was sentimental, and she was charmed. The fair icicle loves her departed mamma, I had raptures over an old picture, and she thawed. Monsieur is used to being worshipped. I took no notice of him, and by the natural perversity of human nature, he began to take notice of me. He likes music; I sang, and stopped when he'd listened long enough to want more. He is lazily fond of being amused; I showed him my skill, but refused to exert it in his behalf. In short, I gave him no peace till he began to wake up. In order to get rid of the boy, I fascinated him, and he was sent away. Poor lad, I rather liked him, and if the title had been nearer would have married him.

"Many thanks for the honor." And Edward's lip curled with intense scorn. But Gerald sat like a statue, his teeth set, his eyes fiery, his brows bent, waiting for the end.

"The passionate boy nearly killed his brother, but I turned the affair to good account, and bewitched Monsieur by playing nurse, till Vashti (the icicle) interfered. Then I enacted injured virtue, and kept out of his way, knowing that he would miss me. I mystified him about S. by sending a letter where S. would not get it, and got up all manner of soft scenes to win this proud

*creature. I get on well and meanwhile privately fascinate Sir J.
by being daughterly and devoted. He is a worthy old man, simple
as a child, honest as the day, and generous as a prince. I shall be
a happy woman if I win him, and you shall share my good fortune; so wish me success.*

"This is the third, and contains something which will surprise
you," Edward said, as he lifted another paper.

"Hortense:

*"I've done what I once planned to do on another occasion.
You know my handsome, dissipated father married a lady of rank
for his second wife. I never saw Lady H_____d but once, for
I was kept out of the way. Finding that this good Sir J. knew
something of her when a girl, and being sure that he did not
know of the death of her little daughter, I boldly said I was the
child, and told a pitiful tale of my early life. It worked like a
charm; he told Monsieur, and both felt the most chivalrous compassion for Lady Howard's daughter, though before they had
secretly looked down on me, and my real poverty and my lowliness. That boy pitied me with an honest warmth and never waited
to learn my birth. I don't forget that and shall repay it if I can.
Wishing to bring Monsieur's affair to a successful crisis, I got up
a theatrical evening and was in my element. One little event I
must tell you, because I committed an actionable offense and was
nearly discovered. I did not go down to supper, knowing that the
moth would return to flutter about the candle, and preferring that
the fluttering should be done in private, as Vashti's jealousy is
getting uncontrollable. Passing through the gentlemen's dressing
room, my quick eye caught sight of a letter lying among the costumes. It was no stage affair, and an odd sensation of fear ran
through me as I recognized the hand of S. I had feared this, but
I believe in chance; and having found the letter, I examined it.
You know I can imitate almost any hand. When I read in this
paper the whole story of my affair with S., truly told, and also
that he had made inquiries into my past life and discovered the
truth, I was in a fury. To be so near success and fail was terrible,
and I resolved to risk everything. I opened the letter by means of
a heated knife blade under the seal, therefore the envelope was
perfect; imitating S.'s hand, I penned a few lines in his hasty
style, saying he was at Baden, so that if Monsieur answered, the
reply would not reach him, for he is in London, it seems. This
letter I put into the pocket whence the other must have fallen,*

*and was just congratulating myself on this narrow escape, when
Dean, the maid of Vashti, appeared as if watching me. She had
evidently seen the letter in my hand, and suspected something.
I took no notice of her, but must be careful, for she is on the
watch. After this the evening closed with strictly private theatricals, in which Monsieur and myself were the only actors. To make
sure that he received my version of the story first, I told him a
romantic story of S.'s persecution, and he believed it. This I followed up by a moonlight episode behind a rose hedge, and sent
the young gentleman home in a half-dazed condition. What fools
men are!"*

"She is right!" muttered Coventry, who had flushed scarlet with
shame and anger, as his folly became known and Lucia listened in
astonished silence.

"Only one more, and my distasteful task will be nearly over," said
Edward, unfolding the last of the papers. "This is not a letter, but a
copy of one written three nights ago. Dean boldly ransacked Jean
Muir's desk while she was at the Hall, and, fearing to betray the deed
by keeping the letter, she made a hasty copy which she gave me today,
begging me to save the family from disgrace. This makes the chain
complete. Go now, if you will, Gerald. I would gladly spare you the
pain of hearing this."

"I will not spare myself; I deserve it. Read on," replied Coventry,
guessing what was to follow and nerving himself to hear it. Reluctantly
his brother read these lines:

*"The enemy has surrendered! Give me joy, Hortense; I can
be the wife of this proud monsieur, if I will. Think what an
honor for the divorced wife of a disreputable actor. I laugh at the
farce and enjoy it, for I only wait till the prize I desire is fairly
mine, to turn and reject this lover who has proved himself false
to brother, mistress, and his own conscience. I resolved to be revenged on both, and I have kept my word. For my sake he cast
off the beautiful woman who truly loved him; he forgot his promise to his brother, and put by his pride to beg of me the worn-out
heart that is not worth a good man's love. Ah well, I am satisfied,
for Vashti has suffered the sharpest pain a proud woman can endure, and will feel another pang when I tell her that I scorn her
recreant lover, and give him back to her, to deal with as she will."*

Coventry started from his seat with a fierce exclamation, but

Lucia bowed her face upon her hands, weeping, as if the pang had been sharper than even Jean foresaw.

"Send for Sir John! I am mortally afraid of this creature. Take her away; do something to her. My poor Bella, what a companion for you! Send for Sir John at once!" cried Mrs. Coventry incoherently, and clasped her daughter in her arms, as if Jean Muir would burst in to annihilate the whole family. Edward alone was calm.

"I have already sent, and while we wait, let me finish this story. It is true that Jean is the daughter of Lady Howard's husband, the pretended clergyman, but really a worthless man who married her for her money. Her own child died, but this girl, having beauty, wit and a bold spirit, took her fate into her own hands, and became an actress. She married an actor, led a reckless life for some years; quarreled with her husband, was divorced, and went to Paris; left the stage, and tried to support herself as governess and companion. You know how she fared with the Sydneys, how she has duped us, and but for this discovery would have duped Sir John. I was in time to prevent this, thank heaven. She is gone; no one knows the truth but Sydney and ourselves; he will be silent, for his own sake; we will be for ours, and leave this dangerous woman to the fate which will surely overtake her."

"Thank you, it has overtaken her, and a very happy one she finds it."

A soft voice uttered the words, and an apparition appeared at the door, which made all start and recoil with amazement—Jean Muir leaning on the arm of Sir John.

"How dare you return?" began Edward, losing the self-control so long preserved. "How dare you insult us by coming back to enjoy the mischief you have done? Uncle, you do not know that woman!"

"Hush, boy, I will not listen to a word, unless you remember where you are," said Sir John, with a commanding gesture.

"Remember your promise: love me, forgive me, protect me, and do not listen to their accusations," whispered Jean, whose quick eye had discovered the letters.

"I will; have no fears, my child," he answered, drawing her nearer as he took his accustomed place before the fire, always lighted when Mrs. Coventry was down.

Gerald, who had been pacing the room excitedly, paused behind Lucia's chair as if to shield her from insult; Bella clung to her mother;

and Edward, calming himself by a strong effort, handed his uncle the letters, saying briefly, "Look at those, sir, and let them speak."

"I will look at nothing, hear nothing, believe nothing which can in any way lessen my respect and affection for this young lady. She has prepared me for this. I know the enemy who is unmanly enough to belie and threaten her. I know that you both are unsuccessful lovers, and this explains your unjust, uncourteous treatment now. We all have committed faults and follies. I freely forgive Jean hers, and desire to know nothing of them from your lips. If she has innocently offended, pardon it for my sake, and forget the past."

"But, Uncle, we have proofs that this woman is not what she seems. Her own letters convict her. Read them, and do not blindly deceive yourself," cried Edward, indignant at his uncle's words.

A low laugh startled them all, and in an instant they saw the cause of it. While Sir John spoke, Jean had taken the letters from the hand which he had put behind him, a favorite gesture of his, and, unobserved, had dropped them on the fire. The mocking laugh, the sudden blaze, showed what had been done. Both young men sprang forward, but it was too late; the proofs were ashes, and Jean Muir's bold, bright eyes defied them, as she said, with a disdainful little gesture, "Hands off, gentlemen! You may degrade yourselves to the work of detectives, but I am not a prisoner yet. Poor Jean Muir you might harm, but Lady Coventry is beyond your reach."

"Lady Coventry!" echoed the dismayed family, in varying tones of incredulity, indignation, and amazement.

"Aye, my dear and honored wife," said Sir John, with a protecting arm about the slender figure at his side; and in the act, the words, there was a tender dignity that touched the listeners with pity and respect for the deceived man. "Receive her as such, and for my sake, forbear all further accusation," he continued steadily. "I know what I have done. I have no fear that I shall repent it. If I am blind, let me remain so till time opens my eyes. We are going away for a little while, and when we return, let the old life return again, unchanged, except that Jean makes sunshine for me as well as for you."

No one spoke, for no one knew what to say. Jean broke the silence, saying coolly, "May I ask how those letters came into your possession?"

"In tracing out your past life, Sydney found your friend Hortense.

She was poor, money bribed her, and your letters were given up to him as soon as received. Traitors are always betrayed in the end," replied Edward sternly.

Jean shrugged her shoulders, and shot a glance at Gerald, saying with her significant smile, "Remember that, monsieur, and allow me to hope that in wedding you will be happier than in wooing. Receive my congratulations, Miss Beaufort, and let me beg of you to follow my example, if you would keep your lovers."

Here all the sarcasm passed from her voice, the defiance from her eye, and the one unspoiled attribute which still lingered in this woman's artful nature shone in her face, as she turned toward Edward and Bella at their mother's side.

"You have been kind to me," she said, with grateful warmth. "I thank you for it, and will repay it if I can. To you I will acknowledge that I am not worthy to be this good man's wife, and to you I will solemnly promise to devote my life to his happiness. For his sake forgive me, and let there be peace between us."

There was no reply, but Edward's indignant eyes fell before hers. Bella half put out her hand, and Mrs. Coventry sobbed as if some regret mingled with her resentment. Jean seemed to expect no friendly demonstration, and to understand that they forbore for Sir John's sake, not for hers, and to accept their contempt as her just punishment.

"Come home, love, and forget all this," said her husband, ringing the bell, and eager to be gone. "Lady Coventry's carriage."

And as he gave the order, a smile broke over her face, for the sound assured her that the game was won. Pausing an instant on the threshold before she vanished from their sight, she looked backward, and fixing on Gerald the strange glance he remembered well, she said in her penetrating voice, "Is not the last scene better than the first?"

Pauline's Passion
~ *and* ~
PUNISHMENT

≫ *chapter I* ≪

TO and fro, like a wild creature in its cage, paced that handsome woman, with bent head, locked hands, and restless steps. Some mental storm, swift and sudden as a tempest of the tropics, had swept over her and left its marks behind. As if in anger at the beauty now proved powerless, all ornaments had been flung away, yet still it shone undimmed, and filled her with a passionate regret. A jewel glittered at her feet, leaving the lace rent to shreds on the indignant bosom that had worn it; the wreaths of hair that had crowned her with a woman's most womanly adornment fell disordered upon shoulders that gleamed the fairer for the scarlet of the pomegranate flowers clinging to the bright meshes that had imprisoned them an hour ago; and over the face, once so affluent in youthful bloom, a stern pallor had fallen like a blight, for pride was slowly conquering passion, and despair had murdered hope.

Pausing in her troubled march, she swept away the curtain swaying in the wind and looked out, as if imploring help from Nature, the great mother of us all. A summer moon rode high in a cloudless heaven, and far as eye could reach stretched the green wilderness of a Cuban *cafetal*. No forest, but a tropical orchard, rich in lime, banana, plantain, palm, and orange trees, under whose protective shade grew the evergreen coffee plant, whose dark-red berries are the fortune of their possessor, and the luxury of one-half the world. Wide avenues diverging from the mansion, with its belt of brilliant shrubs and

flowers, formed shadowy vistas, along which, on the wings of the wind, came a breath of far-off music, like a wooing voice; for the magic of night and distance lulled the cadence of a Spanish *contra-danza* to a trance of sound, soft, subdued, and infinitely sweet. It was a southern scene, but not a southern face that looked out upon it with such unerring glance; there was no southern languor in the figure, stately and erect; no southern swarthiness on fairest cheek and arm; no southern darkness in the shadowy gold of the neglected hair; the light frost of northern snows lurked in the features, delicately cut, yet vividly alive, betraying a temperament ardent, dominant, and subtle. For passion burned in the deep eyes, changing their violet to black. Pride sat on the forehead, with its dark brows; all a woman's sweetest spells touched the lips, whose shape was a smile; and in the spirited carriage of the head appeared the freedom of an intellect ripened under colder skies, the energy of a nature that could wring strength from suffering, and dare to act where feebler souls would only dare desire.

Standing thus, conscious only of the wound that bled in that high heart of hers, and the longing that gradually took shape and deepened to a purpose, an alien presence changed the tragic atmosphere of that still room and woke her from her dangerous mood. A wonderfully winning guise this apparition wore, for youth, hope, and love endowed it with the charm that gives beauty to the plainest, while their reign endures. A boy in any other climate, in this his nineteen years had given him the stature of a man; and Spain, the land of romance, seemed embodied in this figure, full of the lithe slenderness of the whispering palms overhead, the warm coloring of the deep-toned flowers sleeping in the room, the native grace of the tame antelope lifting its human eyes to his as he lingered on the threshold in an attitude eager yet timid, watching that other figure as it looked into the night and found no solace there.

"Pauline!"

She turned as if her thought had taken voice and answered her, regarded him a moment, as if hesitating to receive the granted wish, then beckoned with the one word.

"Come!"

Instantly the fear vanished, the ardor deepened, and with an imperious "Lie down!" to his docile attendant, the young man obeyed with equal docility, looking as wistfully toward his mistress as the brute toward her master, while he waited proudly humble for her commands.

"Manuel, why are you here?"

"Forgive me! I saw Dolores bring a letter; you vanished, an hour passed, I could wait no longer, and I came."

"I am glad, I needed my one friend. Read that."

She offered a letter, and with her steady eyes upon him, her purpose strengthening as she looked, stood watching the changes of that expressive countenance. This was the letter:

> Pauline—
>
> Six months ago I left you, promising to return and take you home my wife; I loved you, but I deceived you; for though my heart was wholly yours, my hand was not mine to give. This it was that haunted me through all that blissful summer, this that marred my happiness when you owned you loved me, and this drove me from you, hoping I could break the tie with which I had rashly bound myself. I could not, I am married, and there all ends. Hate me, forget me, solace your pride with the memory that none knew your wrong, assure your peace with the knowledge that mine is destroyed forever, and leave my punishment to remorse and time.
>
> Gilbert

With a gesture of wrathful contempt, Manuel flung the paper from him as he flashed a look at his companion, muttering through his teeth, "Traitor! Shall I kill him?"

Pauline laughed low to herself, a dreary sound, but answered with a slow darkening of the face that gave her words an ominous significance. "Why should you? Such revenge is brief and paltry, fit only for mock tragedies or poor souls who have neither the will to devise nor the will to execute a better. There are fates more terrible than death; weapons more keen than poniards, more noiseless than pistols. Women use such, and work out a subtler vengeance than men can conceive. Leave Gilbert to remorse—and me."

She paused an instant, and by some strong effort banished the black frown from her brow, quenched the baleful fire of her eyes, and left nothing visible but the pale determination that made her beautiful face more eloquent than her words.

"Manuel, in a week I leave the island."

"Alone, Pauline?"

"No, not alone."

A moment they looked into each other's eyes, each endeavoring to read the other. Manuel saw some indomitable purpose, bent on conquering all obstacles. Pauline saw doubt, desire, and hope; knew that a word would bring the ally she needed; and, with a courage as native to her as her pride, resolved to utter it.

Seating herself, she beckoned her companion to assume the place beside her, but for the first time he hesitated. Something in the unnatural calmness of her manner troubled him, for his southern temperament was alive to influences whose presence would have been unfelt by one less sensitive. He took the cushion at her feet, saying, half tenderly, half reproachfully, "Let me keep my old place till I know in what character I am to fill the new. The man you trusted has deserted you; the boy you pitied will prove loyal. Try him, Pauline."

"I will."

And with the bitter smile unchanged upon her lips, the low voice unshaken in its tones, the deep eyes unwavering in their gaze, Pauline went on:

"You know my past, happy as a dream till eighteen. Then all was swept away, home, fortune, friends, and I was left, like an unfledged bird, without even the shelter of a cage. For five years I have made my life what I could, humble, honest, but never happy, till I came here, for here I saw Gilbert. In the poor companion of your guardian's daughter he seemed to see the heiress I had been, and treated me as such. This flattered my pride and touched my heart. He was kind, I grateful; then he loved me, and God knows how utterly I loved him! A few months of happiness the purest, then he went to make home ready for me, and I believed him; for where I wholly love I wholly trust. While my own peace was undisturbed, I learned to read the language of your eyes, Manuel, to find the boy grown into the man, the friend warmed into a lover. Your youth had kept me blind too long. Your society had grown dear to me, and I loved you like a sister for your unvarying kindness to the solitary woman who earned her bread and found it bitter. I told you my secret to prevent the utterance of your own. You remember the promise you made me then, keep it still, and bury the knowledge of my lost happiness deep in your pitying heart, as I shall in my proud one. Now the storm is over, and I am ready for my work again, but it must be a new task in a new scene. I hate this house, this room, the faces I must meet, the duties

I must perform, for the memory of that traitor haunts them all. I see a future full of interest, a stage whereon I could play a stirring part. I long for it intensely, yet cannot make it mine alone. Manuel, do you love me still?"

Bending suddenly, she brushed back the dark hair that streaked his forehead and searched the face that in an instant answered her. Like a swift rising light, the eloquent blood rushed over swarthy cheek and brow, the slumberous softness of the eyes kindled with a flash, and the lips, sensitive as any woman's, trembled yet broke into a rapturous smile as he cried, with fervent brevity, "I would die for you!"

A look of triumph swept across her face, for with this boy, as chivalrous as ardent, she knew that words were not mere breath. Still, with her stern purpose uppermost, she changed the bitter smile into one half-timid, half-tender, as she bent still nearer, "Manuel, in a week I leave the island. Shall I go alone?"

"No, Pauline."

He understood her now. She saw it in the sudden paleness that fell on him, heard it in the rapid beating of his heart, felt it in the strong grasp that fastened on her hand, and knew that the first step was won. A regretful pang smote her, but the dark mood which had taken possession of her stifled the generous warnings of her better self and drove her on.

"Listen, Manuel. A strange spirit rules me tonight, but I will have no reserves from you, all shall be told; then, if you will come, be it so; if not, I shall go my way as solitary as I came. If you think that this loss has broken my heart, undeceive yourself, for such as I live years in an hour and show no sign. I have shed no tears, uttered no cry, asked no comfort; yet, since I read that letter, I have suffered more than many suffer in a lifetime. I am not one to lament long over any hopeless sorrow. A single paroxysm, sharp and short, and it is over. Contempt has killed my love, I have buried it, and no power can make it live again, except as a pale ghost that will not rest till Gilbert shall pass through an hour as bitter as the last."

"Is that the task you give yourself, Pauline?"

The savage element that lurks in southern blood leaped up in the boy's heart as he listened, glittered in his eye, and involuntarily found expression in the nervous grip of the hands that folded a fairer one between them. Alas for Pauline that she had roused the sleeping devil, and was glad to see it!

"Yes, it is weak, wicked, and unwomanly; yet I persist as relentlessly as any Indian on a war trail. See me as I am, not the gay girl you have known, but a revengeful woman with but one tender spot now left in her heart, the place you fill. I have been wronged, and I long to right myself at once. Time is too slow; I cannot wait, for that man must be taught that two can play at the game of hearts, taught soon and sharply. I can do this, can wound as I have been wounded, can sting him with contempt, and prove that I too can forget."

"Go on, Pauline. Show me how I am to help you."

"Manuel, I want fortune, rank, splendor, and power; you can give me all these, and a faithful friend beside. I desire to show Gilbert the creature he deserted no longer poor, unknown, unloved, but lifted higher than himself, cherished, honored, applauded, her life one of royal pleasure, herself a happy queen. Beauty, grace, and talent you tell me I possess; wealth gives them luster, rank exalts them, power makes them irresistible. Place these worldly gifts in my hand and that hand is yours. See, I offer it."

She did so, but it was not taken. Manuel had left his seat and now stood before her, awed by the undertone of strong emotion in her calmly spoken words, bewildered by the proposal so abruptly made, longing to ask the natural question hovering on his lips, yet too generous to utter it. Pauline read his thought, and answered it with no touch of pain or pride in the magical voice that seldom spoke in vain.

"I know your wish; it is as just as your silence is generous, and I reply to it in all sincerity. You would ask, 'When I have given all that I possess, what do I receive in return?' This—a wife whose friendship is as warm as many a woman's love; a wife who will give you all the heart still left her, and cherish the hope that time may bring a harvest of real affection to repay you for the faithfulness of years; who, though she takes the retribution of a wrong into her hands and executes it in the face of heaven, never will forget the honorable name you give into her keeping or blemish it by any act of hers. I can promise no more. Will this content you, Manuel?"

Before she ended his face was hidden in his hands, and tears streamed through them as he listened, for like a true child of the south each emotion found free vent and spent itself as swiftly as it rose. The reaction was more than he could bear, for in a moment his life was changed, months of hopeless longing were banished with a word, a blissful yes canceled the hard no that had been accepted as inexorable, and Happiness, lifting her full cup to his lips, bade him drink. A moment he yielded to the natural relief, then dashed his tears away and threw himself at Pauline's feet in that attitude fit only for a race as graceful as impassioned.

"Forgive me! Take all I have—fortune, name, and my poor self; use us as you will, we are proud and happy to be spent for you! No service will be too hard, no trial too long if in the end you learn to love me with one tithe of the affection I have made my life. Do you mean it? Am I to go with you? To be near you always, to call you wife, and know we are each other's until death? What have I ever done to earn a fate like this?"

Fast and fervently he spoke, and very winsome was the glad abandonment of this young lover, half boy, half man, possessing the simplicity of the one, the fervor of the other. Pauline looked and listened with a soothing sense of consolation in the knowledge that this loyal heart was all her own, a sweet foretaste of the devotion which henceforth was to shelter her from poverty, neglect, and wrong, and turn life's sunniest side to one who had so long seen only its most bleak and barren. Still at her feet, his arms about her waist, his face flushed and proud, lifted to hers, Manuel saw the cold mask soften, the stern eyes melt with a sudden dew as Pauline watched him, saying, "Dear Manuel, love me less; I am not worth such ardent and entire faith. Pause and reflect before you take this step. I will not bind you to my fate too soon lest you repent too late. We both stand alone in the world, free to make or mar our future as we will. I have chosen my lot. Recall all it may cost you to share it and be sure the price is not too high a one. Remember I am poor, you the possessor of one princely fortune, the sole heir to another."

"The knowledge of this burdened me before; now I glory in it because I have the more for you."

"Remember, I am older than yourself, and may early lose the beauty you love so well, leaving an old wife to burden your youth."

"What are a few years to me? Women like you grow lovelier with age, and you shall have a strong young husband to lean on all your life."

"Remember, I am not of your faith, and the priests will shut me out from your heaven."

"Let them prate as they will. Where you go I will go; Santa Paula shall be my madonna!"

"Remember, I am a deserted woman, and in the world we are

going to my name may become the sport of that man's cruel tongue. Could you bear that patiently, and curb your fiery pride if I desired it?"

"Anything for you, Pauline!"

"One thing more. I give you my liberty; for a time give me forbearance in return, and though wed in haste woo me slowly, lest this sore heart of mine find even your light yoke heavy. Can you promise this, and wait till time has healed my wound, and taught me to be meek?"

"I swear to obey you in all things; make me what you will, for soul and body I am wholly yours henceforth."

"Faithful and true! I knew you would not fail me. Now go, Manuel. Tomorrow do your part resolutely as I shall do mine, and in a week we will begin the new life together. Ours is a strange betrothal, but it shall not lack some touch of tenderness from me. Love, good night."

Pauline bent till her bright hair mingled with the dark, kissed the boy on lips and forehead as a fond sister might have done, then put him gently from her; and like one in a blessed dream he went away to pace all night beneath her window, longing for the day.

As the echo of his steps died along the corridor, Pauline's eye fell on the paper lying where her lover flung it. At this sight all the softness vanished, the stern woman reappeared, and, crushing it in her hand with slow significance, she said low to herself, "This is an old, old story, but it shall have a new ending."

❧ *chapter II* ❦

"WHAT jewels will the señora wear tonight?"

"None, Dolores. Manuel has gone for flowers—he likes them best. You may go."

"But the señora's toilette is not finished; the sandals, the gloves, the garland yet remain."

"Leave them all; I shall not go down. I am tired of this endless folly. Give me that book and go."

The pretty Creole obeyed; and careless of Dolores' work, Pauline sank into the deep chair with a listless mien, turned the pages for a little, then lost herself in thoughts that seemed to bring no rest.

Silently the young husband entered and, pausing, regarded his wife with mingled pain and pleasure—pain to see her so spiritless, pleasure to see her so fair. She seemed unconscious of his presence till the fragrance of his floral burden betrayed him, and looking up to smile a welcome she met a glance that changed the sad dreamer into an excited actor, for it told her that the object of her search was found. Springing erect, she asked eagerly, "Manuel, is he here?"

"Yes."

"Alone?"

"His wife is with him."

"Is she beautiful?"

"Pretty, petite, and petulant."

"And he?"

"Unchanged: the same imposing figure and treacherous face, the same restless eye and satanic mouth. Pauline, let me insult him!"

"Not yet. Were they together?"

"Yes. He seemed anxious to leave her, but she called him back imperiously, and he came like one who dared not disobey."

"Did he see you?"

"The crowd was too dense, and I kept in the shadow."

"The wife's name? Did you learn it?"

"Barbara St. Just."

"Ah! I knew her once and will again. Manuel, am I beautiful tonight?"

"How can you be otherwise to me?"

"That is not enough. I must look my fairest to others, brilliant and blithe, a happy-hearted bride whose honeymoon is not yet over."

"For his sake, Pauline?"

"For yours. I want him to envy you your youth, your comeliness, your content; to see the man he once sneered at the husband of the woman he once loved; to recall impotent regret. I know his nature, and can stir him to his heart's core with a look, revenge myself with a word, and read the secrets of his life with a skill he cannot fathom."

"And when you have done all this, shall you be happier, Pauline?"

"Infinitely; our three weeks' search is ended, and the real interest of the plot begins. I have played the lover for your sake, now play the man of the world for mine. This is the moment we have waited for. Help me to make it successful. Come! Crown me with your garland, give me the bracelets that were your wedding gift—none can be too brilliant for tonight. Now the gloves and fan. Stay, my sandals—you shall play Dolores and tie them on."

With an air of smiling coquetry he had never seen before, Pauline stretched out a truly Spanish foot and offered him its dainty covering. Won by the animation of her manner, Manuel forgot his misgivings and played his part with boyish spirit, hovering about his stately wife as no assiduous maid had ever done; for every flower was fastened with a word sweeter than itself, the white arms kissed as the ornaments went on, and when the silken knots were deftly accomplished, the lighthearted bridegroom performed a little dance of triumph about his idol, till she arrested him, beckoning as she spoke.

"Manuel, I am waiting to assume the last best ornament you have given me, my handsome husband." Then, as he came to her laughing with frank pleasure at her praise, she added, "You, too, must look your best and bravest now, and remember you must enact the man tonight. Before Gilbert wear your stateliest aspect, your tenderest to me, your courtliest to his wife. You possess dramatic skill. Use it for my sake, and come for your reward when this night's work is done."

The great hotel was swarming with life, ablaze with light, resonant with the tread of feet, the hum of voices, the musical din of the band, and full of the sights and sounds which fill such human hives at a fashionable watering place in the height of the season. As Manuel led his wife along the grand hall thronged with promenaders, his quick ear caught the whispered comments of the passers-by, and the fragmentary rumors concerning themselves amused him infinitely.

"*Mon ami!* There are five bridal couples here tonight, and there is the handsomest, richest, and most enchanting of them all. The groom is not yet twenty, they tell me, and the bride still younger. Behold them!"

Manuel looked down at Pauline with a mirthful glance, but she had not heard.

"See, Belle! Cubans; own half the island between them. Splendid, aren't they? Look at the diamonds on her lovely arms, and his ravishing moustache. Isn't he your ideal of Prince Djalma, in *The Wandering Jew?*"

A pretty girl, forgetting propriety in interest, pointed as they passed. Manuel half-bowed to the audible compliment, and the blushing damsel vanished, but Pauline had not seen.

"Jack, there's the owner of the black span you fell into raptures over. My lord and lady look as highbred as their stud. We'll patronize them!"

Manuel muttered a disdainful *"Impertinente!"* between his teeth as he surveyed a brace of dandies with an air that augured ill for the patronage of Young America, but Pauline was unconscious of both criticism and reproof. A countercurrent held them stationary for a moment, and close behind them sounded a voice saying, confidentially, to some silent listener, "The Redmonds are here tonight, and I am curious to see how he bears his disappointment. You know he married for money, and was outwitted in the bargain; for his wife's fortune not only proves to be much less than he was led to believe, but is so tied up that he is entirely dependent upon her, and the bachelor debts he sold himself to liquidate still harass him, with a wife's reproaches to augment the affliction. To be ruled by a spoiled child's whims is a fit punishment for a man whom neither pride nor principle could curb before. Let us go and look at the unfortunate."

Pauline heard now. Manuel felt her start, saw her flush and pale, then her eye lit, and the dark expression he dreaded to see settled on her face as she whispered, like a satanic echo, "Let us also go and look at this unfortunate."

A jealous pang smote the young man's heart as he recalled the past.

"You pity him, Pauline, and pity is akin to love."

"I only pity what I respect. Rest content, my husband."

Steadily her eyes met his, and the hand whose only ornament was a wedding ring went to meet the one folded on his arm with a confiding gesture that made the action a caress.

"I will try to be, yet mine is a hard part," Manuel answered with a sigh, then silently they both paced on.

Gilbert Redmond lounged behind his wife's chair, looking intensely bored.

"Have you had enough of this folly, Babie?"

"No, we have but just come. Let us dance."

"Too late; they have begun."

"Then go about with me. It's very tiresome sitting here."

"It is too warm to walk in all that crowd, child."

"You are so indolent! Tell me who people are as they pass. I know no one here."

"Nor I."

But his act belied the words, for as they passed his lips he rose erect, with a smothered exclamation and startled face, as if a ghost had suddenly confronted him. The throng had thinned, and as his wife followed the direction of his glance, she saw no uncanny apparition to cause such evident dismay, but a woman fair-haired, violet-eyed, blooming and serene, sweeping down the long hall with noiseless grace. An air of sumptuous life pervaded her, the shimmer of bridal snow surrounded her, bridal gifts shone on neck and arms, and bridal happiness seemed to touch her with its tender charm as she looked up at her companion, as if there were but one human being in the world to her. This companion, a man slender and tall, with a face delicately dark as a fine bronze, looked back at her with eyes as eloquent as her own, while both spoke rapidly and low in the melodious language which seems made for lover's lips.

"Gilbert, who are they?"

There was no answer, and before she could repeat the question the approaching pair paused before her, and the beautiful woman offered her hand, saying, with inquiring smiles, "Barbara, have you forgotten your early friend, Pauline?"

Recognition came with the familiar name, and Mrs. Redmond welcomed the newcomer with a delight as unrestrained as if she were still the schoolgirl, Babie. Then, recovering herself, she said, with a pretty attempt at dignity, "Let me present my husband. Gilbert, come and welcome my friend Pauline Valary."

Scarlet with shame, dumb with conflicting emotions, and utterly deserted by self-possession, Redmond stood with downcast eyes and agitated mien, suffering a year's remorse condensed into a moment. A mute gesture was all the greeting he could offer. Pauline slightly bent her haughty head as she answered, in a voice frostily sweet, "Your wife mistakes. Pauline Valary died three weeks ago, and Pauline Laroche rose from her ashes. Manuel, my schoolmate, Mrs. Redmond; Gilbert you already know."

With the manly presence he could easily assume and which was henceforth to be his role in public, Manuel bowed courteously to the lady, coldly to the gentleman, and looked only at his wife. Mrs. Redmond, though childish, was observant; she glanced from face to face, divined a mystery, and spoke out at once.

"Then you have met before? Gilbert, you have never told me this."

"It was long ago—in Cuba. I believed they had forgotten me."

"I never forget." And Pauline's eye turned on him with a look he dared not meet.

Unsilenced by her husband's frown, Mrs. Redmond, intent on pleasing herself, drew her friend to the seat beside her as she said petulantly, "Gilbert tells me nothing, and I am constantly discovering things which might have given me pleasure had he only chosen to be frank. I've spoken of you often, yet he never betrayed the least knowledge of you, and I take it very ill of him, because I am sure he has not forgotten you. Sit here, Pauline, and let me tease you with questions, as I used to do so long ago. You were always patient with me, and though far more beautiful, your face is still the same kind one that comforted the little child at school. Gilbert, enjoy your friend, and leave us to ourselves until the dance is over."

Pauline obeyed; but as she chatted, skillfully leading the young wife's conversation to her own affairs, she listened to the two voices behind her, watched the two figures reflected in the mirror before her, and felt a secret pride in Manuel's address, for it was evident that the former positions were renewed.

The timid boy who had feared the sarcastic tongue of his guardian's guest, and shrunk from his presence to conceal the jealousy that was his jest, now stood beside his formal rival, serene and self-possessed, by far the manliest man of the two, for no shame daunted him, no fear oppressed him, no dishonorable deed left him at the mercy of another's tongue.

Gilbert Redmond felt this keenly, and cursed the falsehood which had placed him in such an unenviable position. It was vain to assume the old superiority that was forfeited; but too much a man of the world to be long discomforted by any contretemps like this, he rapidly regained his habitual ease of manner, and avoiding the perilous past clung to the safer present, hoping, by some unguarded look or word, to fathom the purpose of his adversary, for such he knew the husband of Pauline must be at heart. But Manuel schooled his features, curbed his tongue, and when his hot blood tempted him to point his smooth speech with a taunt, or offer a silent insult with the eye, he remembered Pauline, looked down on the graceful head below, and forgot all other passions in that of love.

"Gilbert, my shawl. The sea air chills me."

"I forgot it, Babie."

"Allow me to supply the want."

Mindful of his wife's commands, Manuel seized this opportunity to win a glance of commendation from her. And taking the downy mantle that hung upon his arm, he wrapped the frail girl in it with a care that made the act as cordial as courteous. Mrs. Redmond felt the charm of his manner with the quickness of a woman, and sent a reproachful glance at Gilbert as she said plantively, "Ah! It is evident that my honeymoon is over, and the assiduous lover replaced by the negligent husband. Enjoy your midsummer night's dream while you may, Pauline, and be ready for the awakening that must come."

"Not to her, madame, for our honeymoon shall last till the golden wedding day comes round. Shall it not, *cariña?*"

"There is no sign of waning yet, Manuel," and Pauline looked up into her husband's face with a genuine affection which made her own more beautiful and filled his with a visible content. Gilbert read the glance, and in that instant suffered the first pang of regret that Pauline had foretold. He spoke abruptly, longing to be away.

"Babie, we may dance now, if you will."

"I am going, but not with you—so give me my fan, and entertain Pauline till my return."

He unclosed his hand, but the delicately carved fan fell at his feet in a shower of ivory shreds—he had crushed it as he watched his first love with the bitter thought "It might have been!"

"Forgive me, Babie, it was too frail for use; you should choose a stronger."

"I will next time, and a gentler hand to hold it. Now, Monsieur Laroche, I am ready."

Mrs. Redmond rose in a small bustle of satisfaction, shook out her flounces, glanced at the mirror, then Manuel led her away; and the other pair were left alone. Both felt a secret agitation quicken their breath and thrill along their nerves, but the woman concealed it best. Gilbert's eye wandered restlessly to and fro, while Pauline fixed her own on his as quietly as if he were the statue in the niche behind him. For a moment he tried to seem unconscious of it, then essayed to meet and conquer it, but failed signally and, driven to his last resources by that steady gaze, resolved to speak out and have all over before his wife's return. Assuming the seat beside her, he said, impetuously, "Pauline, take off your mask as I do mine—we are alone now, and may see each other as we are."

Leaning deep into the crimson curve of the couch, with the indolent grace habitual to her, yet in strong contrast to the vigilant gleam of her eye, she swept her hand across her face as if obeying him, yet no change followed, as she said with a cold smile, "It is off; what next?"

"Let me understand you. Did my letter reach your hands?"

"A week before my marriage."

He drew a long breath of relief, yet a frown gathered as he asked, like one loath and eager to be satisfied, "Your love died a natural death, then, and its murder does not lie at my door?"

Pointing to the shattered toy upon the ground, she only echoed his own words. "It was too frail for use—I chose a stronger."

It wounded, as she meant it should; and the evil spirit to whose guidance she had yielded herself exulted to see his self-love bleed, and pride vainly struggle to conceal the stab. He caught the expression in her averted glance, bent suddenly a fixed and scrutinizing gaze upon her, asking, below his breath, "Then why are you here to tempt me with the face that tempted me a year ago?"

"I came to see the woman to whom you sold yourself. I have seen her, and am satisfied."

Such quiet contempt iced her tones, such pitiless satisfaction shone through the long lashes that swept slowly down, after her eye had met and caused his own to fall again, that Gilbert's cheek burned as if the words had been a blow, and mingled shame and anger trembled in his voice.

"Ah, you are quick to read our secret, for you possess the key. Have you no fear that I may read your own, and tell the world you sold your beauty for a name and fortune? Your bargain is a better one than mine, but I know you too well, though your fetters are diamonds and your master a fond boy."

She had been prepared for this, and knew she had a shield in the real regard she bore her husband, for though sisterly, it was sincere. She felt its value now, for it gave her courage to confront the spirit of retaliation she had roused, and calmness to answer the whispered taunt with an unruffled mien, as lifting her white arm she let its single decoration drop glittering to her lap.

"You see my 'fetters' are as loose as they are light, and nothing binds me but my will. Read my heart, if you can. You will find there contempt for a love so poor that it feared poverty; pity for a man who dared not face the world and conquer it, as a girl had done before him, and gratitude that I have found my 'master' in a truehearted boy, not a falsehearted man. If I am a slave, I never know it. Can you say as much?"

Her woman's tongue avenged her, and Gilbert owned his defeat. Pain quenched the ire of his glance, remorse subdued his pride, self-condemnation compelled him to ask, imploringly, "Pauline, when may I hope for pardon?"

"Never."

The stern utterance of the word dismayed him, and, like one shut

out from hope, he rose, as if to leave her, but paused irresolutely, looked back, then sank down again, as if constrained against his will by a longing past control. If she had doubted her power this action set the doubt at rest, as the haughtiest nature she had known confessed it by a bittersweet complaint. Eyeing her wistfully, tenderly, Gilbert murmured, in the voice of long ago, "Why do I stay to wound and to be wounded by the hand that once caressed me? Why do I find more pleasure in your contempt than in another woman's praise, and feel myself transported into the delights of that irrecoverable past, now grown the sweetest, saddest memory of my life? Send me away, Pauline, before the old charm asserts its power, and I forget that I am not the happy lover of a year ago."

"Leave me then, Gilbert. Good night."

Half unconsciously, the former softness stole into her voice as it lingered on his name. The familiar gesture accompanied the words, the old charm did assert itself, and for an instant changed the cold woman into the ardent girl again. Gilbert did not go but, with a hasty glance down the deserted hall behind him, captured and kissed the hand he had lost, passionately whispering, "Pauline, I love you still, and that look assures me that you have forgiven, forgotten, and kept a place for me in that deep heart of yours. It is too late to deny it. I have seen the tender eyes again, and the sight has made me the proudest, happiest man that walks the world tonight, slave though I am."

Over cheek and forehead rushed the treacherous blood as the violet eyes filled and fell before his own, and in the glow of mingled pain and fear that stirred her blood, Pauline, for the first time, owned the peril of the task she had set herself, saw the dangerous power she possessed, and felt the buried passion faintly moving in its grave. Indignant at her own weakness, she took refuge in the memory of her wrong, controlled the rebel color, steeled the front she showed him, and with feminine skill mutely conveyed the rebuke she would not trust herself to utter, by stripping the glove from the hand he had touched and dropping it disdainfully as if unworthy of its place. Gilbert had not looked for such an answer, and while it baffled him it excited his man's spirit to rebel against her silent denial. With a bitter laugh he snatched up the glove.

"I read a defiance in your eye as you flung this down. I accept the challenge, and will keep gage until I prove myself the victor. I have asked for pardon. You refuse it. I have confessed my love. You scorn it. I have possessed myself of your secret, yet you deny it. Now we will try our strength together, and leave those children to their play."

"We are the children, and we play with edge tools. There has been enough of this, there must be no more." Pauline rose with her haughtiest mien, and the brief command, "Take me to Manuel."

Silently Gilbert offered his arm, and silently she rejected it.

"Will you accept nothing from me?"

"Nothing."

Side by side they passed through the returning throng till Mrs. Redmond joined them, looking blithe and bland with the exhilaration of gallantry and motion. Manuel's first glance was at Pauline, his second at her companion; there was a shadow upon the face of each, which seemed instantly to fall upon his own as he claimed his wife with a masterful satisfaction as novel as becoming, and which prompted her to whisper, "You enact your role to the life, and shall enjoy a fore-taste of your reward at once. I want excitement; let us show these graceless, frozen people the true art of dancing, and electrify them with the life and fire of a Cuban valse."

Manuel kindled at once, and Pauline smiled stealthily as she glanced over her shoulder from the threshold of the dancing hall, for her slightest act, look, and word had their part to play in that night's drama.

"Gilbert, if you are tired I will go now."

"Thank you, I begin to find it interesting. Let us watch the dancers."

Mrs. Redmond accepted the tardy favor, wondering at his un-wonted animation, for never had she seen such eagerness in his coun-tenance, such energy in his manner as he pressed through the crowd and won a place where they could freely witness one of those exhibi-tions of fashionable figurante which are nightly to be seen at such resorts. Many couples were whirling around the white hall, but among them one pair circled with slowly increasing speed, in perfect time to the inspiring melody of trumpet, flute, and horn, that seemed to sound for them alone. Many paused to watch them, for they gave to the graceful pastime the enchantment which few have skill enough to lend it, and made it a spectacle of life-enjoying youth, to be remem-bered long after the music ceased and the agile feet were still.

Gilbert's arm was about his little wife to shield her from the pressure of the crowd, and as they stood his hold unconsciously tightened, till, marveling at this unwonted care, she looked up to thank him with a happy glance and discovered that his eye rested on a single pair, kindling as they approached, keenly scanning every gesture as they floated by, following them with untiring vigilance through the many-colored mazes they threaded with such winged steps, while his breath quickened, his hand kept time, and every sense seemed to own the intoxication of the scene. Sorrowfully she too watched this pair, saw their grace, admired their beauty, envied their happiness; for, short as her wedded life had been, the thorns already pierced her through the roses, and with each airy revolution of those figures, dark and bright, her discontent increased, her wonder deepened, her scrutiny grew keener, for she knew no common interest held her husband there, fascinated, flushed, and excited as if his heart beat responsive to the rhythmic rise and fall of that booted foot and satin slipper. The music ended with a crash, the crowd surged across the floor, and the spell was broken. Like one but half disenchanted, Gilbert stood a moment, then remembered his wife, and looking down met brown eyes, full of tears, fastened on his face.

"Tired so soon, Babie? Or in a pet because I cannot change myself into a thistledown and float about with you, like Manuel and Pauline?"

"Neither; I was only wishing that you loved me as he loves her, and hoping he would never tire of her, they are so fond and charming now. How long have you known them—and where?"

"I shall have no peace until I tell you. I passed a single summer with them in a tropical paradise, where we swung half the day in hammocks, under tamarind and almond trees; danced half the night to music, of which this seems but a faint echo; and led a life of luxurious delight in an enchanted climate, where all is so beautiful and brilliant that its memory haunts a life as pressed flowers sweeten the leaves of a dull book."

"Why did you leave it then?"

"To marry you, child."

"That was a regretful sigh, as if I were not worth the sacrifice. Let us go back and enjoy it together."

"If you were dying for it, I would not take you to Cuba. It would be purgatory, not paradise, now."

"How stern you look, how strangely you speak. Would you not go to save your own life, Gilbert?"

"I would not cross the room to do that much, less the sea."

"Why do you both love and dread it? Don't frown, but tell me. I have a right to know."

"Because the bitterest blunder of my life was committed there—a blunder that I never can repair in this world, and may be damned for in the next. Rest satisfied with this, Babie, lest you prove like Bluebeard's wife, and make another skeleton in my closet, which has enough already."

Strange regret was in his voice, strange gloom fell upon his face; but though rendered doubly curious by the change, Mrs. Redmond dared not question further and, standing silent, furtively scanned the troubled countenance beside her. Gilbert spoke first, waking out of his sorrowful reverie with a start.

"Pauline is coming. Say adieu, not au revoir, for tomorrow we must leave this place."

His words were a command, his aspect one of stern resolve, though the intensest longing mingled with the dark look he cast on the approaching pair. The tone, the glance displeased his willful wife, who loved to use her power and exact obedience where she had failed to win affection, often ruling imperiously when a tender word would have made her happy to submit.

"Gilbert, you take no thought for my pleasures though you pursue your own at my expense. Your neglect forces me to find solace and satisfaction where I can, and you have forfeited your right to command or complain. I love Pauline, I am happy with her, therefore I shall stay until we tire of one another. I am a burden to you; go if you will."

"You know I cannot without you, Babie. I ask it as a favor. For my sake, for your own, I implore you to come away."

"Gilbert, do you love her?"

She seized his arm and forced an answer by the energy of her sharply whispered question. He saw that it was vain to dissemble, yet replied with averted head, "I did and still remember it."

"And she? Did she return your love?"

"I believed so; but she forgot me when I went. She married Manuel and is happy. Babie, let me go!"

"No! you shall stay and feel a little of the pain I feel when I look into your heart and find I have no place there. It is this which has stood between us and made all my efforts vain. I see it now and despise you for the falsehood you have shown me, vowing you loved no one but me until I married you, then letting me so soon discover that I was only an encumbrance to your enjoyment of the fortune I possessed. You treat me like a child, but I suffer like a woman, and you shall share my suffering, because you might have spared me, and you did not. Gilbert, you shall stay."

"Be it so, but remember I have warned you."

An exultant expression broke through the gloom of her husband's face as he answered with the grim satisfaction of one who gave restraint to the mind, and stood ready to follow whatever impulse should sway him next. His wife trembled inwardly at what she had done, but was too proud to recall her words and felt a certain bitter pleasure in the excitement of the new position she had taken, the new interest given to her listless life.

Pauline and Manuel found them standing silently together, for a moment had done the work of years and raised a barrier between them never to be swept away.

Mrs. Redmond spoke first, and with an air half resentful, half triumphant:

"Pauline, this morose husband of mine says we must leave tomorrow. But in some things I rule; this is one of them. Therefore we remain and go with you to the mountains when we are tired of the gay life here. So smile and submit, Gilbert, else these friends will count your society no favor. Would you not fancy, from the aspect he thinks proper to assume, that I had sentenced him to a punishment, not a pleasure?"

"Perhaps you have unwittingly, Babie. Marriage is said to cancel the follies of the past, but not those of the future, I believe; and, as there are many temptations to an idle man in a place like this, doubtless your husband is wise enough to own that he dares not stay but finds discretion the better part of valor."

Nothing could be softer than the tone in which these words were uttered, nothing sharper than the hidden taunt conveyed, but Gilbert only laughed a scornful laugh as he fixed his keen eyes full upon her and took her bouquet with the air of one assuming former rights.

"My dear Pauline, discretion is the last virtue I should expect to be accused of by you; but if valor consists in daring all things, I may lay claim to it without its 'better part,' for temptation is my delight—the stronger the better. Have no fears for me, my friend. I gladly accept Babie's decree and, ignoring the last ten years, intend to begin life anew, having discovered a *sauce piquante* which will give the stalest pleasures a redoubled zest. I am unfortunate tonight, and here is a second wreck; this I can rebuild happily. Allow me to do so, for I remember you once praised my skill in floral architecture."

With an air of eager gallantry in strange contrast to the malign expression of his countenance, Gilbert knelt to regather the flowers which a careless gesture of his own had scattered from their jeweled holder. His wife turned to speak to Manuel, and, yielding to the unconquerable anxiety his reckless manner awoke, Pauline whispered below her breath as she bent as if to watch the work, "Gilbert, follow your first impulse, and go tomorrow."

"Nothing shall induce me to."

"I warn you harm will come of it."

"Let it come; I am past fear now."

"Shun me for Babie's sake, if not for your own."

"Too late for that; she is headstrong—let her suffer."

"Have you no power, Gilbert?"

"None over her, much over you."

"We will prove that!"

"We will!"

Rapidly as words could shape them, these questions and answers fell, and with their utterance the last generous feeling died in Pauline's breast; for as she received the flowers, now changed from a love token to a battle gage, she saw the torn glove still crushed in Gilbert's hand, and silently accepted his challenge to the tournament so often held between man and woman—a tournament where the keen tongue is the lance, pride the shield, passion the fiery steed, and the hardest heart the winner of the prize, which seldom fails to prove a barren honor, ending in remorse.

❧ *chapter III* ❧

FOR several days the Cubans were almost invisible, appearing only for a daily drive, a twilight saunter on the beach, or a brief visit to the ballroom, there to enjoy the excitement of the pastime in which they both excelled. Their apartments were in the quietest wing of the hotel, and from the moment of their occupancy seemed to acquire all the charms of home. The few guests admitted felt the atmosphere of poetry and peace that pervaded the nest which Love, the worker of miracles, had built himself even under that tumultuous roof. Strollers in the halls or along the breezy verandas often paused to listen to the music of instrument or voice which came floating out from these sequestered rooms. Frequent laughter and the murmur of conversation proved that ennui was unknown, and a touch of romance inevitably enhanced the interest wakened by the beautiful young pair, always together, always happy, never weary of the *dolce far niente* of this summer life.

In a balcony like a hanging garden, sheltered from the sun by blossoming shrubs and vines that curtained the green nook with odorous shade, Pauline lay indolently swinging in a gaily fringed hammock as she had been wont to do in Cuba, then finding only pleasure in the luxury of motion which now failed to quiet her unrest. Manuel had put down the book to which she no longer listened and, leaning his head upon his hand, sat watching her as she swayed to and fro with thoughtful eyes intent upon the sea, whose murmurous

voice possessed a charm more powerful than his own. Suddenly he spoke:

"Pauline, I cannot understand you! For three weeks we hurried east and west to find this man, yet when found you shun him and seem content to make my life a heaven upon earth. I sometimes fancy that you have resolved to let the past sleep, but the hope dies as soon as born, for in moments like this I see that, though you devote yourself to me, the old purpose is unchanged, and I marvel why you pause."

Her eyes came back from their long gaze and settled on him full of an intelligence which deepened his perplexity. "You have not learned to know me yet; death is not more inexorable or time more tireless than I. This week has seemed one of indolent delight to you. To me it has been one of constant vigilance and labor, for scarcely a look, act, or word of mine has been without effect. At first I secluded myself that Gilbert might contrast our life with his and, believing us all and all to one another, find impotent regret his daily portion. Three days ago accident placed an unexpected weapon in my hand which I have used in silence, lest in spite of promises you should rebel and end his trial too soon. Have you no suspicion of my meaning?"

"None. You are more mysterious than ever, and I shall, in truth, believe you are the enchantress I have so often called you if your spells work invisibly."

"They do not, and I use no supernatural arts, as I will prove to you. Take my lorgnette that lies behind you, part the leaves where the green grapes hang thickest, look up at the little window in the shadowy angle of the low roof opposite, and tell me what you see."

"Nothing but a half-drawn curtain."

"Ah! I must try the ruse that first convinced me. Do not show yourself, but watch, and if you speak, let it be in Spanish."

Leaving her airy cradle, Pauline bent over the balcony as if to gather the climbing roses that waved their ruddy clusters in the wind. Before the third stem was broken Manuel whispered, "I see the curtain move; now comes the outline of a head, and now a hand, with some bright object in it. Santo Pablo! It is a man staring at you as coolly as if you were a lady in a balcony. What prying rascal is it?"

"Gilbert."

"Impossible! He is a gentleman."

"If gentlemen play the traitor and the spy, then he is one. I am not mistaken; for since the glitter of his glass first arrested me I have watched covertly, and several trials as successful as the present have confirmed the suspicion which Babie's innocent complaints of his long absences aroused. Now do you comprehend why I remained in these rooms with the curtains seldom drawn? Why I swung the hammock here and let you sing and read to me while I played with your hair or leaned upon your shoulder? Why I have been all devotion and made this balcony a little stage for the performance of our version of the honeymoon for one spectator?"

Still mindful of the eager eyes upon her, Pauline had been fastening the roses in her bosom as she spoke, and ended with a silvery laugh that made the silence musical with its heartsome sound. As she paused, Manuel flung down the lorgnette and was striding past her with ireful impetuosity, but the white arms took him captive, adding another figure to the picture framed by the green arch as she whispered decisively, "No farther! There must be no violence. You promised obedience and I exact it. Do you think detection to a man so lost to honor would wound as deeply as the sights which make his daily watch a torment? Or that a blow would be as hard to bear as the knowledge that his own act has placed you where you are and made him what he is? Silent contempt is the law now, so let this insult pass, unclench your hand and turn that defiant face to me, while I console you for submission with a kiss."

He yielded to the command enforced by the caress but drew her jealously from sight, and still glanced rebelliously through the leaves, asking with a frown, "Why show me this if I may not resent it? How long must I bear with this man? Tell me your design, else I shall mar it in some moment when hatred of him conquers love of you."

"I will, for it is time, because though I have taken the first step you must take the second. I showed you this that you might find action pleasanter than rest, and you must bear with this man a little longer for my sake, but I will give you an amusement to beguile the time. Long ago you told me that Gilbert was a gambler. I would not believe it then, now I can believe anything, and you can convince the world of this vice of his as speedily as you will."

"Do you wish me to become a gambler that I may prove him one? I also told you that he was suspected of dishonorable play—shall I load the dice and mark the cards to catch him in his own snares?"

Manuel spoke bitterly, for his high spirit chafed at the task assigned him; womanly wiles seemed more degrading than the masculine method of retaliation, in which strength replaces subtlety and speedier vengeance brings speedier satisfaction. But Pauline, fast learning to play upon that mysterious instrument, the human heart, knew when to stimulate and when to soothe.

"Do not reproach me that I point out a safer mode of operation than your own. You would go to Gilbert and by a hot word, a rash act, put your life and my happiness into his hands, for though dueling is forbidden here, he would not hesitate to break all laws, human or divine, if by so doing he could separate us. What would you gain by it? If you kill him he is beyond our reach forever, and a crime remains to be atoned for. If he kill you your blood will be upon my head, and where should I find consolation for the loss of the one heart always true and tender?"

With the inexplicable prescience which sometimes foreshadows coming ills, she clung to him as if a vision of the future dimly swept before her, but he only saw the solicitude it was a sweet surprise to find he had awakened, and in present pleasure forgot past pain.

"You shall not suffer from this man any grief that I can shield you from, rest assured of that, my heart. I will be patient, though your ways are not mine, for the wrong was yours, and the retribution shall be such as you decree."

"Then hear your task and see the shape into which circumstances have molded my design. I would have you exercise a self-restraint that shall leave Gilbert no hold upon you, accept all invitations like that which you refused when we passed him on the threshold of the billiard room an hour ago, and seem to find in such amusements the same fascination as himself. Your skill in games of chance excels his, as you proved at home where these pastimes lose their disreputable aspect by being openly enjoyed. Therefore I would have you whet this appetite of his by losing freely at first—he will take a grim delight in lessening the fortune he covets—then exert all your skill till he is deeply in your debt. He has nothing but what is doled out to him by Babie's father, I find; he dare not ask help there for such a purpose; other resources have failed else he would not have married; and if the sum be large enough, it lays him under an obligation which will be a thorn in his flesh, the sharper for your knowledge of his impotence to draw it out. When this is done, or even while it is in progress, I would have you add the pain of a new jealousy to the old. He neglects this young wife of his, and she is eager to recover the affections she believes she once possessed. Help her, and teach Gilbert the value of what he now despises. You are young, comely, accomplished, and possessed of many graces more attractive than you are conscious of; your southern birth and breeding gift you with a winning warmth of manners in strong contrast to the colder natures around you; and your love for me lends an almost tender deference to your intercourse with all womankind. Amuse, console this poor girl, and show her husband what he should be; I have no fear of losing your heart nor need you fear for hers; she is one of those spaniel-like creatures who love the hand that strikes them and fawn upon the foot that spurns them."

"Am I to be the sole actor in the drama of deceit? While I woo Babie, what will you do, Pauline?"

"Let Gilbert woo me—have patience till you understand my meaning; he still loves me and believes I still return that love. I shall not undeceive him yet, but let silence seem to confess what I do not own in words. He fed me with false promises, let me build my life's happiness on baseless hopes, and rudely woke me when he could delude no longer, leaving me to find I had pursued a shadow. I will do the same. He shall follow me undaunted, undeterred by all obstacles, all ties; shall stake his last throw and lose it, for when the crowning moment comes I shall show him that through me he is made bankrupt in love, honor, liberty, and hope, tell him I am yours entirely and forever, then vanish like an *ignis-fatuus*, leaving him to the darkness of despair and defeat. Is not this a better retribution than the bullet that would give him peace at once?"

Boy, lover, husband though he was, Manuel saw and stood aghast at the baleful spirit which had enslaved this woman, crushing all generous impulses, withering all gentle charities, and making her the saddest spectacle this world can show—one human soul rebelling against Providence, to become the nemesis of another. Involuntarily he recoiled from her, exclaiming, "Pauline! Are you possessed of a devil?"

"Yes! One that will not be cast out till every sin, shame, and sorrow mental ingenuity can conceive and inflict has been heaped on that man's head. I thought I should be satisfied with one accusing look, one bitter word; I am not, for the evil genii once let loose cannot be recaptured. Once I ruled it, now it rules me, and there is no turning back. I have come under the law of fate, and henceforth the powers I possess will ban, not bless, for I am driven to whet and wield them as weapons which may win me success at the price of my salvation. It is not yet too late for you to shun the spiritual contagion I bear about me. Choose now, and abide by that choice without a shadow of turning, as I abide by mine. Take me as I am; help me willingly and unwillingly; and in the end receive the promised gift—years like the days you have called heaven upon earth. Or retract the vows you plighted, receive again the heart and name you gave me, and live unvexed by the stormy nature time alone can tame. Here is the ring. Shall I restore or keep it, Manuel?"

Never had she looked more beautiful as she stood there, an image of will, daring, defiant, and indomitable, with eyes darkened by intensity of emotion, voice half sad, half stern, and outstretched hand on which the wedding ring no longer shone. She felt her power, yet was wary enough to assure it by one bold appeal to the strongest element of her husband's character: passions, not principles, were the allies she desired, and before the answer came she knew that she had gained them at the cost of innocence and self-respect.

As Manuel listened, an expression like a dark reflection of her own settled on his face; a year of youth seemed to drop away; and with the air of one who puts fear behind him, he took the hand, replaced the ring, resolutely accepted the hard conditions, and gave all to love, only saying as he had said before, "Soul and body, I belong to you; do with me as you will."

A fortnight later Pauline sat alone, waiting for her husband. Under the pretext of visiting a friend, she had absented herself a week, that Manuel might give himself entirely to the distasteful task she set him. He submitted to the separation, wrote daily, but sent no tidings of his progress, told her nothing when they met that night, and had left her an hour before asking her to have patience till he could show his finished work. Now, with her eye upon the door, her ear alert to catch the coming step, her mind disturbed by contending hopes and fears, she sat waiting with the vigilant immobility of an Indian on the watch. She had not long to look and listen. Manuel entered hastily, locked the door, closed the windows, dropped the curtains, then paused in the middle of the room and broke into a low, triumphant laugh as he eyed his wife with an expression she had never seen in those dear eyes before. It startled her, and, scarcely knowing what to desire or dread, she asked eagerly, "You are come to tell me you have prospered."

"Beyond your hopes, for the powers of darkness seem to help us, and lead the man to his destruction faster than any wiles of ours can do. I am tired, let me lie here and rest. I have earned it, so when I have told all say, 'Love, you have done well,' and I am satisfied."

He threw himself along the couch where she still sat and laid his head in her silken lap, her cool hand on his hot forehead, and continued in a muffled voice.

"You know how eagerly Gilbert took advantage of my willingness to play, and soon how recklessly he pursued it, seeming to find the satisfaction you foretold, till, obeying your commands, I ceased losing and won sums which surprised me. Then you went, but I was not idle, and in the effort to extricate himself, Gilbert plunged deeper into debt; for my desire to please you seemed to gift me with redoubled skill. Two days ago I refused to continue the unequal conflict, telling him to give himself no uneasiness, for I could wait. You were right in thinking it would oppress him to be under any obligation to me, but wrong in believing he would endure, and will hardly be prepared for the desperate step he took to free himself. That night he played falsely, was detected, and though his opponent generously promised silence for Babie's sake, the affair stole out—he is shunned and this resource has failed. I thought he had no other, but yesterday he came to me with a strange expression of relief, discharged the debt to the last farthing, then hinted that my friendship with his wife was not approved by him and must cease. This proves that I have obeyed you in all things, though the comforting of Babie was an easy task, for, both loving you, our bond of sympathy and constant theme has been Pauline and her perfections."

"Hush! No praise—it is a mockery. I am what one man's perfidy has made; I may yet learn to be worthy of another man's devotion. What more, Manuel?"

"I thought I should have only a defeat to show you, but today has given me a strange success. At noon a gentleman arrived and asked for Gilbert. He was absent, but upon offering information relative to the time of his return, which proved my intimacy with him, this Seguin entered into conversation with me. His evident desire to avoid Mrs. Redmond and waylay her husband interested me, and when he

questioned me somewhat closely concerning Gilbert's habits and movements of late, my suspicions were roused; and on mentioning the debt
so promptly discharged, I received a confidence that startled me. In
a moment of despair Gilbert had forged the name of his former friend,
whom he believed abroad, had drawn the money and freed himself
from my power, but not for long. The good fortune which has led him
safely through many crooked ways seems to have deserted him in this
strait. For the forgery was badly executed, inspection raised doubts,
and Seguin, just returned, was at his banker's an hour after Gilbert,
to prove the fraud; he came hither at once to accuse him of it and
made me his confidant. What would you have had me do, Pauline?
Time was short, and I could not wait for you."

"How can I tell at once? Why pause to ask? What did you do?"

"Took a leaf from your book and kept accusation, punishment,
and power in my own hands, to be used in your behalf. I returned
the money, secured the forged check, and prevailed on Seguin to leave
the matter in my hands, while he departed as quietly as he had come.
Babie's presence when we met tonight prevented my taking you into
my counsels. I had prepared this surprise for you and felt a secret pride
in working it out alone. An hour ago I went to watch for Gilbert. He
came, I took him to his rooms, told him what I had done, added that
compassion for his wife had actuated me. I left him saying the possession of the check was a full equivalent for the money, which I now
declined to receive from such dishonorable hands. Are you satisfied,
Pauline?"

With countenance and gestures full of exultation she sprang up
to pace the room, exclaiming, as she seized the forged paper, "Yes, that
stroke was superb! How strangely the plot thickens. Surely the powers
of darkness are working with us and have put this weapon in our hands
when that I forged proved useless. By means of this we have a hold
upon him which nothing can destroy unless he escape by death. Will
he, Manuel?"

"No; there was more wrath than shame in his demeanor when I
accused him. He hates me too much to die yet, and had I been the only
possessor of this fatal fact, I fancy it might have gone hard with me;
for if ever there was murder in a man's heart it was in his when I
showed him that paper and then replaced it next the little poniard
you smile at me for wearing. This is over. What next, my queen?"

There was energy in the speaker's tone but none in attitude or aspect, as, still lying where she had left him, he pillowed his head upon his arm and turned toward her a face already worn and haggard with the feverish weariness that had usurped the blithe serenity which had been his chiefest charm a month ago. Pausing in her rapid walk, as if arrested by the change that seemed to strike her suddenly, she recalled her thoughts from the dominant idea of her life and, remembering the youth she was robbing of its innocent delights, answered the wistful look which betrayed the hunger of a heart she had never truly fed, as she knelt beside her husband and, laying her soft cheek to his, whispered in her tenderest accents, "I am not wholly selfish or ungrateful, Manuel. You shall rest now while I sing to you, and tomorrow we will go away among the hills and leave behind us for a time the dark temptation which harms you through me."

"No! Finish what you have begun. I will have all or nothing, for if we pause now you will bring me a divided mind, and I shall possess only the shadow of a wife. Take Gilbert and Babie with us, and end this devil's work without delay. Hark! What is that?"

Steps came flying down the long hall, a hand tried the lock, then beat impetuously upon the door, and a low voice whispered with shrill importunity, "Let me in! Oh, let me in!"

Manuel obeyed the urgent summons, and Mrs. Redmond, half dressed, with streaming hair and terror-stricken face, fled into Pauline's arms, crying incoherently, "Save me! Keep me! I never can go back to him; he said I was a burden and a curse, and wished I never had been born!"

"What has happened, Babie? We are your friends. Tell us, and let us comfort and protect you if we can."

But for a time speech was impossible, and the poor girl wept with a despairing vehemence sad to see, till their gentle efforts soothed her; and, sitting by Pauline, she told her trouble, looking oftenest at Manuel, who stood before them, as if sure of redress from him.

"When I left here an hour or more ago I found my rooms still empty, and, though I had not seen my husband since morning, I knew he would be displeased to find me waiting, so I cried myself to sleep and dreamed of the happy time when he was kind, till the sound of voices woke me. I heard Gilbert say, 'Babie is with your wife, her maid tells me; therefore we are alone here. What is this mysterious affair, Laroche?' That tempted me to listen, and then, Manuel, I learned all the shame and misery you so generously tried to spare me. How can I ever repay you, ever love and honor you enough for such care of one so helpless and forlorn as I?"

"I am repaid already. Let that pass, and tell what brings you here with such an air of fright and fear?"

"When you were gone he came straight to the inner room in search of something, saw me, and knew I must have heard all he had concealed from me so carefully. If you have ever seen him when that fierce temper of his grows ungovernable, you can guess what I endured. He said such cruel things I could not bear it, and cried out that I would come to you, for I was quite wild with terror, grief, and shame, that seemed like oil to fire. He swore I should not, and oh, Pauline, he struck me! See, if I do not tell the living truth!"

Trembling with excitement, Mrs. Redmond pushed back the wide sleeve of her wrapper and showed the red outline of a heavy hand. Manuel set his teeth and stamped his foot into the carpet with an indignant exclamation and the brief question, "Then you left him, Babie?"

"Yes, although he locked me in my room, saying the law gave him the right to teach obedience. I flung on these clothes, crept noiselessly along the balcony till the hall window let me in, and then I ran to you. He will come for me. Can he take me away? Must I go back to suffer any more?"

In the very act of uttering the words, Mrs. Redmond clung to Manuel with a cry of fear, for on the threshold stood her husband. A comprehensive glance seemed to stimulate his wrath and lend the hardihood wherewith to confront the three, saying sternly as he beckoned, "Babie, I am waiting for you."

She did not speak, but still clung to Manuel as if he were her only hope. A glance from Pauline checked the fiery words trembling on his lips, and he too stood silent while she answered with a calmness that amazed him:

"Your wife has chosen us her guardians, and I think you will scarcely venture to use force again with two such witnesses as these to prove that you have forfeited your right to her obedience and justify the step she has taken."

With one hand she uncovered the discolored arm, with the other held the forgery before him. For a moment Gilbert stood daunted by these mute accusations, but just then his ire burned hottest against Manuel; and believing that he could deal a double blow by wounding

Pauline through her husband, he ignored her presence and, turning to the young man, asked significantly, "Am I to understand that you refuse me my wife, and prefer to abide by the consequences of such an act?"

Calmed by Pauline's calmness, Manuel only drew the trembling creature closer, and answered with his haughtiest mien, "I do; spare yourself the labor of insulting me, for having placed yourself beyond the reach of a gentleman's weapon, I shall accept no challenge from a——"

A soft hand at his lips checked the opprobrious word, as Babie, true woman through it all, whispered with a broken sob, "Spare him, for I loved him once."

Gilbert Redmond had a heart, and, sinful though it was, this generous forbearance wrung it with a momentary pang of genuine remorse, too swiftly followed by a selfish hope that all was not lost if through his wife he could retain a hold upon the pair which now possessed for him the strong attraction of both love and hate. In that brief pause this thought came, was accepted and obeyed, for, as if yielding to an uncontrollable impulse of penitent despair, he stretched his arms to his wife, saying humbly, imploringly, "Babie, come back to me, and teach me how I may retrieve the past. I freely confess I bitterly repent my manifold transgressions, and submit to your decree alone; but in executing justice, oh, remember mercy! Remember that I was too early left fatherless, motherless, and went astray for want of some kind heart to guide and cherish me. There is still time. Be compassionate and save me from myself. Am I not punished enough? Must death be my only comforter? Babie, when all others cast me off, will you too forsake me?"

"No, I will not! Only love me, and I can forgive, forget, and still be happy!"

Pauline was right. The spaniel-like nature still loved the hand that struck it, and Mrs. Redmond joyfully returned to the arms from which she had so lately fled. The tenderest welcome she had ever received from him welcomed the loving soul whose faith was not yet dead, for Gilbert felt the value this once neglected possession had suddenly acquired, and he held it close; yet as he soothed with gentle touch and tone, could not forbear a glance of triumph at the spectators of the scene.

Pauline met it with that inscrutable smile of hers, and a look of intelligence toward her husband, as she said, "Did I not prophesy truly, Manuel? Be kind to her, Gilbert, and when next we meet show us a happier wife than the one now sobbing on your shoulder. Babie, good night and farewell, for we are off to the mountains in the morning."

"Oh, let us go with you as you promised! You know our secret, you pity me and will help Gilbert to be what he should. I cannot live at home, and places like this will seem so desolate when you and Manuel are gone. May we, can we be with you a little longer?"

"If Gilbert wishes it and Manuel consents, we will bear and forbear much for your sake, my poor child."

Pauline's eye said, "Dare you go?" and Gilbert's answered, "Yes," as the two met with a somber fire in each; but his lips replied, "Anywhere with you, Babie," and Manuel took Mrs. Redmond's hand with a graceful warmth that touched her deeper than his words.

"Your example teaches me the beauty of compassion, and Pauline's friends are mine."

"Always so kind to me! Dear Manuel, I never can forget it, though I have nothing to return but this," and, like a grateful child, she lifted up her innocent face so wistfully he could only bend his tall head to receive the kiss she offered.

Gilbert's black brows lowered ominously at the sight, but he never spoke; and, when her good-nights were over, bowed silently and carried his little wife away, nestling to him as if all griefs and pains were banished by returning love.

"Poor little heart! She should have a smoother path to tread. Heaven grant she may hereafter; and this sudden penitence prove no sham." Manuel paused suddenly, for as if obeying an unconquerable impulse, Pauline laid a hand on either shoulder and searched his face with an expression which baffled his comprehension, though he bore it steadily till her eyes fell before his own, when he asked smilingly:

"Is the doubt destroyed, *cariña?*"

"No; it is laid asleep."

Then as he drew her nearer, as if to make his peace for his unknown offense, she turned her cheek away and left him silently. Did she fear to find Babie's kiss upon his lips?

≽ *chapter IV* ≼

THE work of weeks is soon recorded, and when another month
was gone these were the changes it had wrought. The four so
strangely bound together by ties of suffering and sin went on
their way, to the world's eye, blessed with every gracious gift, but
below the tranquil surface rolled that undercurrent whose mysterious
tides ebb and flow in human hearts unfettered by race or rank or time.
Gilbert was a good actor, but, though he curbed his fitful temper,
smoothed his mien, and sweetened his manner, his wife soon felt the
vanity of hoping to recover that which never had been hers. Silently
she accepted the fact and, uttering no complaint, turned to others for
the fostering warmth without which she could not live. Conscious of
a hunger like her own, Manuel could offer her sincerest sympathy, and
soon learned to find a troubled pleasure in the knowledge that she loved
him and her husband knew it, for his life of the emotions was rapidly
maturing the boy into the man, as the fierce ardors of his native skies
quicken the growth of wondrous plants that blossom in a night. Mrs.
Redmond, as young in character as in years, felt the attraction of a
nature generous and sweet, and yielded to it as involuntarily as an
unsupported vine yields to the wind that blows it to the strong arms
of a tree, still unconscious that a warmer sentiment than gratitude
made his companionship the sunshine of her life. Pauline saw this,
and sometimes owned within herself that she had evoked spirits which
she could not rule, but her purpose drove her on, and in it she found

a charm more perilously potent than before. Gilbert watched the three
with a smile darker than a frown, yet no reproach warned his wife
of the danger which she did not see; no jealous demonstration roused
Manuel to rebel against the oppression of a presence so distasteful to
him; no rash act or word gave Pauline power to banish him, though
the one desire of his soul became the discovery of the key to the inscrutable expression of her eyes as they followed the young pair, whose
growing friendship left their mates alone. Slowly her manner softened
toward him, pity seemed to bridge across the gulf that lay between
them, and in rare moments time appeared to have retraced its steps,
leaving the tender woman of a year ago. Nourished by such unexpected hope, the early passion throve and strengthened until it became
the mastering ambition of his life, and, only pausing to make assurance
doubly sure, he waited the advent of the hour when he could "put his
fortune to the touch and win or lose it all."

"Manuel, are you coming?"
He was lying on the sward at Mrs. Redmond's feet, and, waking
from the reverie that held him, while his companion sang the love lay
he was teaching her, he looked up to see his wife standing on the green
slope before him. A black lace scarf lay over her blonde hair as Spanish
women wear their veils, below it the violet eyes shone clear, the cheek
glowed with the color fresh winds had blown upon their paleness, the
lips parted with a wistful smile, and a knot of bright-hued leaves upon
her bosom made a mingling of snow and fire in the dress, whose white
folds swept the grass. Against a background of hoary cliffs and somber
pines, this figure stood out like a picture of blooming womanhood, but
Manuel saw three blemishes upon it—Gilbert had sketched her with
that shadowy veil upon her head, Gilbert had swung himself across
a precipice to reach the scarlet nosegay for her breast, Gilbert stood
beside her with her hand upon his arm; and troubled by the fear that
often haunted him since Pauline's manner to himself had grown so
shy and sad, Manuel leaned and looked forgetful of reply, but Mrs.
Redmond answered blithely:
"He is coming, but with me. You are too grave for us, so go your
ways, talking wisely of heaven and earth, while we come after, enjoying both as we gather lichens, chase the goats, and meet you at the
waterfall. Now señor, put away guitar and book, for I have learned

my lesson; so help me with this unruly hair of mine and leave the Spanish for today."

They looked a pair of lovers as Manuel held back the long locks blowing in the wind, while Babie tied her hat, still chanting the burthen of the tender song she had caught so soon. A voiceless sigh stirred the ruddy leaves on Pauline's bosom as she turned away, but Gilbert embodied it in words, "They are happier without us. Let us go."

Neither spoke till they reached the appointed tryst. The others were not there, and, waiting for them, Pauline sat on a mossy stone, Gilbert leaned against the granite boulder beside her, and both silently surveyed a scene that made the heart glow, the eye kindle with delight as it swept down from that airy height, across valleys dappled with shadow and dark with untrodden forests, up ranges of majestic mountains, through gap after gap, each hazier than the last, far out into that sea of blue which rolls around all the world. Behind them roared the waterfall swollen with autumn rains and hurrying to pour itself into the rocky basin that lay boiling below, there to leave its legacy of shattered trees, then to dash itself into a deeper chasm, soon to be haunted by a tragic legend and go glittering away through forest, field, and intervale to join the river rolling slowly to the sea. Won by the beauty and the grandeur of the scene, Pauline forgot she was not alone, till turning, she suddenly became aware that while she scanned the face of nature her companion had been scanning hers. What he saw there she could not tell, but all restraint had vanished from his manner, all reticence from his speech, for with the old ardor in his eye, the old impetuosity in his voice, he said, leaning down as if to read her heart, "This is the moment I have waited for so long. For now you see what I see, that both have made a bitter blunder, and may yet repair it. Those children love each other; let them love, youth mates them, fortune makes them equals, fate brings them together that we may be free. Accept this freedom as I do, and come out into the world with me to lead the life you were born to enjoy."

With the first words he uttered Pauline felt that the time had come, and in the drawing of a breath was ready for it, with every sense alert, every power under full control, every feature obedient to the art which had become a second nature. Gilbert had seized her hand, and she did not draw it back; the sudden advent of the instant which must end her work sent an unwonted color to her cheek, and she did avert it;

the exultation which flashed into her eyes made it unsafe to meet his own, and they drooped before him as if in shame or fear, her whole face woke and brightened with the excitement that stirred her blood. She did not seek to conceal it, but let him cheat himself with the belief that love touched it with such light and warmth, as she softly answered in a voice whose accents seemed to assure his hope.

"You ask me to relinquish much. What do you offer in return, Gilbert, that I may not for a second time find love's labor lost?"

It was a wily speech, though sweetly spoken, for it reminded him how much he had thrown away, how little now remained to give, but her mien inspired him, and nothing daunted, he replied more ardently than ever:

"I can offer you a heart always faithful in truth though not in seeming, for I never loved that child. I would give years of happy life to undo that act and be again the man you trusted. I can offer you a name which shall yet be an honorable one, despite the stain an hour's madness cast upon it. You once taunted me with cowardice because I dared not face the world and conquer it. I dare do that now; I long to escape from this disgraceful servitude, to throw myself into the press, to struggle and achieve for your dear sake. I can offer you strength, energy, devotion—three gifts worthy any woman's acceptance who possesses power to direct, reward, and enjoy them as you do, Pauline. Because with your presence for my inspiration, I feel that I can retrieve my faultful past, and with time become God's noblest work—an honest man. Babie never could exert this influence over me. You can, you will, for now my earthly hope is in your hands, my soul's salvation in your love."

If that love had not died a sudden death, it would have risen up to answer him as the one sincere desire of an erring life cried out to her for help, and this man, as proud as sinful, knelt down before her with a passionate humility never paid at any other shrine, human or divine. It seemed to melt and win her, for he saw the color ebb and flow, heard the rapid beating of her heart, felt the hand tremble in his own, and received no denial but a lingering doubt, whose removal was a keen satisfaction to himself.

"Tell me, before I answer, are you sure that Manuel loves Babie?"

"I am; for every day convinces me that he has outlived the brief delusion, and longs for liberty, but dares not ask it. Ah! that pricks pride! But it is so. I have watched with jealous vigilance and let no sign escape me; because in his infidelity to you lay my chief hope. Has he not grown melancholy, cold, and silent? Does he not seek Babie and, of late, shun you? Will he not always yield his place to me without a token of displeasure or regret? Has he ever uttered reproach, warning, or command to you, although he knows I was and am your lover? Can you deny these proofs, or pause to ask if he will refuse to break the tie that binds him to a woman, whose superiority in all things keeps him a subject where he would be a king? You do not know the heart of man if you believe he will not bless you for his freedom."

Like the cloud which just then swept across the valley, blotting out its sunshine with a gloomy shadow, a troubled look flitted over Pauline's face. But if the words woke any sleeping fear she cherished, it was peremptorily banished, for scarcely had the watcher seen it than it was gone. Her eyes still shone upon the ground, and still she prolonged the bittersweet delight at seeing this humiliation of both soul and body by asking the one question whose reply would complete her sad success.

"Gilbert, do you believe I love you still?"

"I know it! Can I not read the signs that proved it to me once? Can I forget that, though you followed me to pity and despise, you have remained to pardon and befriend? Am I not sure that no other power could work the change you have wrought in me? I was learning to be content with slavery, and slowly sinking into that indolence of will which makes submission easy. I was learning to forget you, and be resigned to hold the shadow when the substance was gone, but you came, and with a look undid my work, with a word destroyed my hard-won peace, with a touch roused the passion which was not dead but sleeping, and have made this month of growing certainty to be the sweetest in my life—for I believed all lost, and you showed me that all was won. Surely that smile is propitious! and I may hope to hear the happy confirmation of my faith from lips that were formed to say 'I love!' "

She looked up then, and her eyes burned on him, with an expression which made his heart leap with expectant joy, as over cheek and forehead spread a glow of womanly emotion too genuine to be feigned, and her voice thrilled with the fervor of that sentiment which blesses life and outlives death.

"Yes, I love; not as of old, with a girl's blind infatuation, but with the warmth and wisdom of heart, mind, and soul—love made up of honor, penitence and trust, nourished in secret by the better self which lingers in the most tried and tempted of us, and now ready to blossom and bear fruit, if God so wills. I have been once deceived, but faith still endures, and I believe that I may yet earn this crowning gift of a woman's life for the man who shall make my happiness as I make his —who shall find me the prouder for past coldness, the humbler for past pride—whose life shall pass serenely loving. And that beloved is—my husband."

If she had lifted her white hand and stabbed him, with that smile upon her face, it would not have shocked him with a more pale dismay than did those two words as Pauline shook him off and rose up, beautiful and stern as an avenging angel. Dumb with an amazement too fathomless for words, he knelt there motionless and aghast. She did not speak. And, passing his hand across his eyes as if he felt himself the prey to some delusion, he rose slowly, asking, half incredulously, half imploringly, "Pauline, this is a jest?"

"To me it is; to you—a bitter earnest."

A dim foreboding of the truth fell on him then, and with it a strange sense of fear; for in this apparition of human judgment he seemed to receive a premonition of the divine. With a sudden gesture of something like entreaty, he cried out, as if his fate lay in her hands, "How will it end? how will it end?"

"As it began—in sorrow, shame and loss."

Then, in words that fell hot and heavy on the sore heart made desolate, she poured out the dark history of the wrong and the atonement wrung from him with such pitiless patience and inexorable will. No hard fact remained unrecorded, no subtle act unveiled, no hint of her bright future unspared to deepen the gloom of his. And when the final word of doom died upon the lips that should have awarded pardon, not punishment, Pauline tore away the last gift he had given, and dropping it to the rocky path, set her foot upon it, as if it were the scarlet badge of her subjection to the evil spirit which had haunted her so long, now cast out and crushed forever.

Gilbert had listened with a slowly gathering despair, which deepened to the blind recklessness that comes to those whose passions are their masters, when some blow smites but cannot subdue. Pale to his very lips, with the still white wrath, so much more terrible to witness than the fiercest ebullition of the ire that flames and feeds like a sudden fire, he waited till she ended, then used the one retaliation she had left

him. His hand went to his breast, a tattered glove flashed white against the cliff as he held it up before her, saying, in a voice that rose gradually till the last words sounded clear above the waterfall's wild song:

"It was well and womanly done, Pauline, and I could wish Manuel a happy life with such a tender, frank, and noble wife; but the future which you paint so well never shall be his. For, by the Lord that hears me! I swear I will end this jest of yours in a more bitter earnest than you prophesied. Look; I have worn this since the night you began the conflict, which has ended in defeat to me, as it shall to you. I do not war with women, but you shall have one man's blood upon your soul, for I will goad that tame boy to rebellion by flinging this in his face and taunting him with a perfidy blacker than my own. Will that rouse him to forget your commands and answer like a man?"

"Yes!"

The word rang through the air sharp and short as a pistol shot, a slender brown hand wrenched the glove away, and Manuel came between them. Wild with fear, Mrs. Redmond clung to him. Pauline sprang before him, and for a moment the two faced each other, with a year's smoldering jealousy and hate blazing in fiery eyes, trembling in clenched hands, and surging through set teeth in defiant speech.

"This is the gentleman who gambles his friend to desperation, and skulks behind a woman, like the coward he is," sneered Gilbert.

"Traitor and swindler, you lie!" shouted Manuel, and, flinging his wife behind him, he sent the glove, with a stinging blow, full in his opponent's face.

Then the wild beast that lurks in every strong man's blood leaped up in Gilbert Redmond's, as, with a single gesture of his sinewy right arm he swept Manuel to the verge of the narrow ledge, saw him hang poised there one awful instant, struggling to save the living weight that weighed him down, heard a heavy plunge into the black pool below, and felt that thrill of horrible delight which comes to murderers alone.

So swift and sure had been the act it left no time for help. A rush, a plunge, a pause, and then two figures stood where four had been—a man and woman staring dumbly at each other, appalled at the dread silence that made high noon more ghostly than the deepest night. And with that moment of impotent horror, remorse, and woe, Pauline's long punishment began.

The Mysterious Key

~ and ~

WHAT IT OPENED

BY L. M. ALCOTT

❧ *chapter I* ❧

THE PROPHECY

Trevlyn lands and Trevlyn gold,
Heir nor heiress e'er shall hold,
Undisturbed, till, spite of rust,
Truth is found in Trevlyn dust.

"THIS is the third time I've found you poring over that old rhyme. What is the charm, Richard? Not its poetry I fancy." And the young wife laid a slender hand on the yellow, time-worn page where, in Old English text, appeared the lines she laughed at.

Richard Trevlyn looked up with a smile and threw by the book, as if annoyed at being discovered reading it. Drawing his wife's hand through his own, he led her back to her couch, folded the soft shawls about her, and, sitting in a low chair beside her, said in a cheerful tone, though his eyes betrayed some hidden care, "My love, that book is a history of our family for centuries, and that old prophecy has never yet been fulfilled, except the 'heir and heiress' line. I am the last Trevlyn, and as the time draws near when my child shall be born, I naturally think of his future, and hope he will enjoy his heritage in peace."

"God grant it!" softly echoed Lady Trevlyn, adding, with a look askance at the old book, "I read that history once, and fancied it must be a romance, such dreadful things are recorded in it. Is it all true, Richard?"

"Yes, dear. I wish it was not. Ours has been a wild, unhappy race till the last generation or two. The stormy nature came in with old Sir Ralph, the fierce Norman knight, who killed his only son in a fit of wrath, by a blow with his steel gauntlet, because the boy's strong will would not yield to his."

"Yes, I remember, and his daughter Clotilde held the castle during a siege, and married her cousin, Count Hugo. 'Tis a warlike race, and I like it in spite of the mad deeds."

"Married her cousin! That has been the bane of our family in times past. Being too proud to mate elsewhere, we have kept to ourselves till idiots and lunatics began to appear. My father was the first who broke the law among us, and I followed his example: choosing the freshest, sturdiest flower I could find to transplant into our exhausted soil."

"I hope it will do you honor by blossoming bravely. I never forget that you took me from a very humble home, and have made me the happiest wife in England."

"And I never forget that you, a girl of eighteen, consented to leave your hills and come to cheer the long-deserted house of an old man like me," returned her husband fondly.

"Nay, don't call yourself old, Richard; you are only forty-five, the boldest, handsomest man in Warwickshire. But lately you look worried; what is it? Tell me, and let me advise or comfort you."

"It is nothing, Alice, except my natural anxiety for you— Well, Kingston, what do you want?"

Trevlyn's tender tones grew sharp as he addressed the entering servant, and the smile on his lips vanished, leaving them dry and white as he glanced at the card he handed him. An instant he stood staring at it, then asked, "Is the man here?"

"In the library, sir."

"I'll come."

Flinging the card into the fire, he watched it turn to ashes before he spoke, with averted eyes: "Only some annoying business, love; I shall soon be with you again. Lie and rest till I come."

With a hasty caress he left her, but as he passed a mirror, his wife saw an expression of intense excitement in his face. She said nothing, and lay motionless for several minutes evidently struggling with some strong impulse.

"He is ill and anxious, but hides it from me; I have a right to know, and he'll forgive me when I prove that it does no harm."

As she spoke to herself she rose, glided noiselessly through the hall, entered a small closet built in the thickness of the wall, and, bending to the keyhole of a narrow door, listened with a half-smile on her lips at the trespass she was committing. A murmur of voices met her ear. Her husband spoke oftenest, and suddenly some word of his dashed the smile from her face as if with a blow. She started, shrank, and shivered, bending lower with set teeth, white cheeks, and panic-stricken heart. Paler and paler grew his lips, wilder and wilder her eyes, fainter and fainter her breath, till, with a long sigh, a vain effort to save herself, she sank prone upon the threshold of the door, as if struck down by death.

"Mercy on us, my lady, are you ill?" cried Hester, the maid, as her mistress glided into the room looking like a ghost, half an hour later.

"I am faint and cold. Help me to my bed, but do not disturb Sir Richard."

A shiver crept over her as she spoke, and, casting a wild, woeful look about her, she laid her head upon the pillow like one who never cared to lift it up again. Hester, a sharp-eyed, middle-aged woman, watched the pale creature for a moment, then left the room muttering, "Something is wrong, and Sir Richard must know it. That black-bearded man came for no good, I'll warrant."

At the door of the library she paused. No sound of voices came from within; a stifled groan was all she heard; and without waiting to knock she went in, fearing she knew not what. Sir Richard sat at his writing table pen in hand, but his face was hidden on his arm, and his whole attitude betrayed the presence of some overwhelming despair.

"Please, sir, my lady is ill. Shall I send for anyone?"

No answer. Hester repeated her words, but Sir Richard never stirred. Much alarmed, the woman raised his head, saw that he was unconscious, and rang for help. But Richard Trevlyn was past help, though he lingered for some hours. He spoke but once, murmuring faintly, "Will Alice come to say good-bye?"

"Bring her if she can come," said the physician.

Hester went, found her mistress lying as she left her, like a figure carved in stone. When she gave the message, Lady Trevlyn answered sternly, "Tell him I will not come," and turned her face to the wall, with an expression which daunted the woman too much for another word.

Hester whispered the hard answer to the physician, fearing to utter it aloud, but Sir Richard heard it, and died with a despairing prayer for pardon on his lips.

When day dawned Sir Richard lay in his shroud and his little daughter in her cradle, the one unwept, the other unwelcomed by the wife and mother, who, twelve hours before, had called herself the happiest woman in England. They thought her dying, and at her own command gave her the sealed letter bearing her address which her husband left behind him. She read it, laid it in her bosom, and, waking from the trance which seemed to have so strongly chilled and changed her, besought those about her with passionate earnestness to save her life.

For two days she hovered on the brink of the grave, and nothing but the indomitable will to live saved her, the doctors said. On the third day she rallied wonderfully, and some purpose seemed to gift her with unnatural strength. Evening came, and the house was very still, for all the sad bustle of preparation for Sir Richard's funeral was over, and he lay for the last night under his own roof. Hester sat in the darkened chamber of her mistress, and no sound broke the hush but the low lullaby the nurse was singing to the fatherless baby in the adjoining room. Lady Trevlyn seemed to sleep, but suddenly put back the curtain, saying abruptly, "Where does he lie?"

"In the state chamber, my lady," replied Hester, anxiously watching the feverish glitter of her mistress's eye, the flush on her cheek, and the unnatural calmness of her manner.

"Help me to go there; I must see him."

"It would be your death, my lady. I beseech you, don't think of it," began the woman; but Lady Trevlyn seemed not to hear her, and something in the stern pallor of her face awed the woman into submission.

Wrapping the slight form of her mistress in a warm cloak, Hester half-led, half-carried her to the state room, and left her on the threshold.

"I must go in alone; fear nothing, but wait for me here," she said, and closed the door behind her.

Five minutes had not elapsed when she reappeared with no sign of grief on her rigid face.

"Take me to my bed and bring my jewel box," she said, with a shuddering sigh, as the faithful servant received her with an exclamation of thankfulness.

When her orders had been obeyed, she drew from her bosom the portrait of Sir Richard which she always wore, and, removing the ivory oval from the gold case, she locked the former in a tiny drawer of the casket, replaced the empty locket in her breast, and bade Hester give the jewels to Watson, her lawyer, who would see them put in a safe place till the child was grown.

"Dear heart, my lady, you'll wear them yet, for you're too young to grieve all your days, even for so good a man as my blessed master. Take comfort, and cheer up, for the dear child's sake if no more."

"I shall never wear them again" was all the answer as Lady Trevlyn drew the curtains, as if to shut out hope.

Sir Richard was buried and, the nine days' gossip over, the mystery of his death died for want of food, for the only person who could have explained it was in a state which forbade all allusion to that tragic day.

For a year Lady Trevlyn's reason was in danger. A long fever left her so weak in mind and body that there was little hope of recovery, and her days were passed in a state of apathy sad to witness. She seemed to have forgotten everything, even the shock which had so sorely stricken her. The sight of her child failed to rouse her, and month after month slipped by, leaving no trace of their passage on her mind, and but slightly renovating her feeble body.

Who the stranger was, what his aim in coming, or why he never reappeared, no one discovered. The contents of the letter left by Sir Richard were unknown, for the paper had been destroyed by Lady Trevlyn and no clue could be got from her. Sir Richard had died of heart disease, the physicians said, though he might have lived years had no sudden shock assailed him. There were few relatives to make investigations, and friends soon forgot the sad young widow; so the years rolled on, and Lillian the heiress grew from infancy to childhood in the shadow of this mystery.

≥ *chapter II* ≤

PAUL

"COME, child, the dew is falling, and it is time we went in."
"No, no, Mamma is not rested yet, so I may run down
to the spring if I like." And Lillian, as willful as winsome,
vanished among the tall ferns where deer couched and rabbits hid.

Hester leisurely followed, looking as unchanged as if a day instead
of twelve years had passed since her arms received the little mistress,
who now ruled her like a tyrant. She had taken but a few steps when
the child came flying back, exclaiming in an excited tone, "Oh, come
quick! There's a man there, a dead man. I saw him and I'm frightened!"

"Nonsense, child, it's one of the keepers asleep, or some stroller
who has no business here. Take my hand and we'll see who it is."

Somewhat reassured, Lillian led her nurse to one of the old oaks
beside the path, and pointed to a figure lying half hidden in the fern.
A slender, swarthy boy of sixteen, with curly black hair, dark brows,
and thick lashes, a singularly stern mouth, and a general expression of
strength and pride, which added character to his boyish face and dignified his poverty. His dress betrayed that, being dusty and threadbare,
his shoes much worn, and his possessions contained in the little bundle
on which he pillowed his head. He was sleeping like one quite spent

with weariness, and never stirred, though Hester bent away the ferns and examined him closely.

"He's not dead, my deary; he's asleep, poor lad, worn out with his day's tramp, I dare say."

"I'm glad he's alive, and I wish he'd wake up. He's a pretty boy, isn't he? See what nice hands he's got, and his hair is more curly than mine. Make him open his eyes, Hester," commanded the little lady, whose fear had given place to interest.

"Hush, he's stirring. I wonder how he got in, and what he wants," whispered Hester.

"I'll ask him," and before her nurse could arrest her, Lillian drew a tall fern softly over the sleeper's face, laughing aloud as she did so.

The boy woke at the sound, and without stirring lay looking up at the lovely little face bent over him, as if still in a dream.

"Bella cara," he said, in a musical voice. Then, as the child drew back abashed at the glance of his large, bright eyes, he seemed to wake entirely and, springing to his feet, looked at Hester with a quick, searching glance. Something in his face and air caused the woman to soften her tone a little, as she said gravely, "Did you wish to see any one at the Hall?"

"Yes. Is Lady Trevlyn here?" was the boy's answer, as he stood cap in hand, with the smile fading already from his face.

"She is, but unless your business is very urgent you had better see Parks, the keeper; we don't trouble my lady with trifles."

"I've a note for her from Colonel Daventry; and as it is *not* a trifle, I'll deliver it myself, if you please."

Hester hesitated an instant, but Lillian cried out, "Mamma is close by, come and see her," and led the way, beckoning as she ran.

The lad followed with a composed air, and Hester brought up the rear, taking notes as she went with a woman's keen eye.

Lady Trevlyn, a beautiful, pale woman, delicate in health and melancholy in spirit, sat on a rustic seat with a book in her hand; not reading, but musing with an absent mind. As the child approached, she held out her hand to welcome her, but neither smiled nor spoke.

"Mamma, here is a—a person to see you," cried Lillian, rather at a loss how to designate the stranger, whose height and gravity now awed her.

"A note from Colonel Daventry, my lady," and with a bow the boy delivered the missive.

Scarcely glancing at him, she opened it and read:

My Dear Friend,

The bearer of this, Paul Jex, has been with me some months and has served me well. I brought him from Paris, but he is English born, and, though friendless, prefers to remain here, even after we leave, as we do in a week. When I last saw you you mentioned wanting a lad to help in the garden; Paul is accustomed to that employment, though my wife used him as a sort of page in the house. Hoping you may be able to give him shelter, I venture to send him. He is honest, capable, and trustworthy in all respects. Pray try him, and oblige,

Yours sincerely,

J. R. Daventry

"The place is still vacant, and I shall be very glad to give it to you, if you incline to take it," said Lady Trevlyn, lifting her eyes from the note and scanning the boy's face.

"I do, madam," he answered respectfully.

"The colonel says you are English," added the lady, in a tone of surprise.

The boy smiled, showing a faultless set of teeth, as he replied, "I am, my lady, though just now I may not look it, being much tanned and very dusty. My father was an Englishman, but I've lived abroad a good deal since he died, and got foreign ways, perhaps."

As he spoke without any accent, and looked full in her face with a pair of honest blue eyes under the dark lashes, Lady Trevlyn's momentary doubt vanished.

"Your age, Paul?"

"Sixteen, my lady."

"You understand gardening?"

"Yes, my lady."

"And what else?"

"I can break horses, serve at table, do errands, read aloud, ride after a young lady as groom, illuminate on parchment, train flowers, and make myself useful in any way."

The tone, half modest, half eager, in which the boy spoke, as well as the odd list of his accomplishments, brought a smile to Lady Trevlyn's lips, and the general air of the lad prepossessed her.

"I want Lillian to ride soon, and Roger is rather old for an escort to such a little horsewoman. Don't you think we might try Paul?" she said, turning to Hester.

The woman gravely eyed the lad from head to foot, and shook her head, but an imploring little gesture and a glance of the handsome eyes softened her heart in spite of herself.

"Yes, my lady, if he does well about the place, and Parks thinks he's steady enough, we might try it by-and-by."

Lillian clapped her hands and, drawing nearer, exclaimed confidingly, as she looked up at her new groom, "I know he'll do, Mamma. I like him very much, and I hope you'll let him train my pony for me. Will you, Paul?"

"Yes."

As he spoke very low and hastily, the boy looked away from the eager little face before him, and a sudden flush of color crossed his dark cheek.

Hester saw it and said within herself, "That boy has good blood in his veins. He's no clodhopper's son, I can tell by his hands and feet, his air and walk. Poor lad, it's hard for him, I'll warrant, but he's not too proud for honest work, and I like that."

"You may stay, Paul, and we will try you for a month. Hester, take him to Parks and see that he is made comfortable. Tomorrow we will see what he can do. Come, darling, I am rested now."

As she spoke, Lady Trevlyn dismissed the boy with a gracious gesture and led her little daughter away. Paul stood watching her, as if forgetful of his companion, till she said, rather tartly, "Young man, you'd better have thanked my lady while she was here than stare after her now it's too late. If you want to see Parks, you'd best come, for I'm going."

"Is that the family tomb yonder, where you found me asleep?" was the unexpected reply to her speech, as the boy quietly followed her, not at all daunted by her manner.

"Yes, and that reminds me to ask how you got in, and why you were napping there, instead of doing your errand properly?"

"I leaped the fence and stopped to rest before presenting myself, Miss Hester" was the cool answer, accompanied by a short laugh as he confessed his trespass.

"You look as if you'd had a long walk; where are you from?"

"London."

"Bless the boy! It's fifty miles away."

"So my shoes show; but it's a pleasant trip in summer time."

"But why did you walk, child! Had you no money?"

"Plenty, but not for wasting on coaches, when my own stout legs could carry me. I took a two days' holiday and saved my money for better things."

"I like that," said Hester, with an approving nod. "You'll get on, my lad, if that's your way, and I'll lend a hand, for laziness is my abomination, and one sees plenty nowadays."

"Thank you. That's friendly, and I'll prove that I am grateful. Please tell me, is my lady ill?"

"Always delicate since Sir Richard died."

"How long ago was that?"

"Ten years or more."

"Are there no young gentlemen in the family?"

"No, Miss Lillian is an only child, and a sweet one, bless her!"

"A proud little lady, I should say."

"And well she may be, for there's no better blood in England than the Trevlyns, and she's heiress to a noble fortune."

"Is that the Trevlyn coat of arms?" asked the boy abruptly, pointing to a stone falcon with the motto ME AND MINE carved over the gate through which they were passing.

"Yes. Why do you ask?"

"Mere curiosity; I know something of heraldry and often paint these things for my own pleasure. One learns odd amusements abroad," he added, seeing an expression of surprise on the woman's face.

"You'll have little time for such matters here. Come in and report yourself to the keeper, and if you'll take my advice ask no questions of him, for you'll get no answers."

"I seldom ask questions of men, as *they* are not fond of gossip." And the boy nodded with a smile of mischievous significance as he entered the keeper's lodge.

A sharp lad and a saucy, if he likes. I'll keep my eye on him, for my lady takes no more thought of such things than a child, and Lillian cares for nothing but her own will. He has a taking way with him, though, and knows how to flatter. It's well he does, poor lad, for life's a hard matter to a friendless soul like him.

As she thought these thoughts Hester went on to the house, leaving Paul to win the good graces of the keeper, which he speedily did by assuming an utterly different manner from that he had worn with the woman.

That night, when the boy was alone in his own room, he wrote a long letter in Italian describing the events of the day, enclosed a sketch of the falcon and motto, directed it to "Father Cosmo Carmela, Genoa," and lay down to sleep, muttering, with a grim look and a heavy sigh, "So far so well; I'll not let my heart be softened by pity, or my purpose change till my promise is kept. Pretty child, I wish I had never seen her!"

৯ *chapter III* ৯

SECRET SERVICE

I N a week Paul was a favorite with the household; even prudent
Hester felt the charm of his presence, and owned that Lillian
was happier for a young companion in her walks. Hitherto the
child had led a solitary life, with no playmates of her own age, such
being the will of my lady; therefore she welcomed Paul as a new
and delightful amusement, considering him her private property and
soon transferring his duties from the garden to the house. Satisfied
of his merits, my lady yielded to Lillian's demands, and Paul was
installed as page to the young lady. Always respectful and obedient,
he never forgot his place, yet seemed unconsciously to influence all
who approached him, and win the goodwill of everyone.

My lady showed unusual interest in the lad, and Lillian openly
displayed her admiration for his accomplishments and her affection
for her devoted young servitor. Hester was much flattered by the
confidence he reposed in her, for to her alone did he tell his story,
and of her alone asked advice and comfort in his various small straits.
It was as she suspected: Paul was a gentleman's son, but misfortune
had robbed him of home, friends, and parents, and thrown him upon
the world to shift for himself. This sad story touched the woman's
heart, and the boy's manly spirit won respect. She had lost a son years
ago, and her empty heart yearned over the motherless lad. Ashamed
to confess the tender feeling, she wore her usual severe manner to

him in public, but in private softened wonderfully and enjoyed the boy's regard heartily.

"Paul, come in. I want to speak with you a moment," said my lady, from the long window of the library to the boy who was training vines outside.

Dropping his tools and pulling off his hat, Paul obeyed, looking a little anxious, for the month of trial expired that day. Lady Trevlyn saw and answered the look with a gracious smile.

"Have no fears. You are to stay if you will, for Lillian is happy and I am satisfied with you."

"Thank you, my lady." And an odd glance of mingled pride and pain shone in the boy's downcast eyes.

"That is settled, then. Now let me say what I called you in for. You spoke of being able to illuminate on parchment. Can you restore this old book for me?"

She put into his hand the ancient volume Sir Richard had been reading the day he died. It had lain neglected in a damp nook for years till my lady discovered it, and, sad as were the associations connected with it, she desired to preserve it for the sake of the weird prophecy if nothing else. Paul examined it, and as he turned it to and fro in his hands it opened at the page oftenest read by its late master. His eye kindled as he looked, and with a quick gesture he turned as if toward the light, in truth to hide the flash of triumph that passed across his face. Carefully controlling his voice, he answered in a moment, as he looked up, quite composed, "Yes, my lady, I can retouch the faded colors on these margins and darken the pale ink of the Old English text. I like the work, and will gladly do it if you like."

"Do it, then, but be very careful of the book while in your hands. Provide what is needful, and name your own price for the work," said his mistress.

"Nay, my lady, I am already paid—"

"How so?" she asked, surprised.

Paul had spoken hastily, and for an instant looked embarrassed, but answered with a sudden flush on his dark cheeks, "You have been kind to me, and I am glad to show my gratitude in any way, my lady."

"Let that pass, my boy. Do this little service for me and we will see about the recompense afterward." And with a smile Lady Trevlyn left him to begin his work.

The moment the door closed behind her a total change passed over Paul. He shook his clenched hand after her with a gesture of menace, then tossed up the old book and caught it with an exclamation of delight, as he reopened it at the worn page and reread the inexplicable verse.

"Another proof, another proof! The work goes bravely on, Father Cosmo; and boy as I am, I'll keep my word in spite of everything," he muttered.

"What is that you'll keep, lad?" said a voice behind him.

"I'll keep my word to my lady, and do my best to restore this book, Mrs. Hester," he answered, quickly recovering himself.

"Ah, that's the last book poor Master read. I hid it away, but my lady found it in spite of me," said Hester, with a doleful sigh.

"Did he die suddenly, then?" asked the boy.

"Dear heart, yes; I found him dying in this room with the ink scarce dry on the letter he left for my lady. A mysterious business and a sad one."

"Tell me about it. I like sad stories, and I already feel as if I belonged to the family, a loyal retainer as in the old times. While you dust the books and I rub the mold off this old cover, tell me the tale, please, Mrs. Hester."

She shook her head, but yielded to the persuasive look and tone of the boy, telling the story more fully than she intended, for she loved talking and had come to regard Paul as her own, almost.

"And the letter? What was in it?" asked the boy, as she paused at the catastrophe.

"No one ever knew but my lady."

"She destroyed it, then?"

"I thought so, till a long time afterward, one of the lawyers came pestering me with questions, and made me ask her. She was ill at the time, but answered with a look I shall never forget, 'No, it's not burnt, but no one shall ever see it.' I dared ask no more, but I fancy she has it safe somewhere and if it's ever needed she'll bring it out. It was only some private matters, I fancy."

"And the stranger?"

"Oh, he vanished as oddly as he came, and has never been found. A strange story, lad. Keep silent, and let it rest."

"No fear of my tattling," and the boy smiled curiously to himself as he bent over the book, polishing the brassbound cover.

"What are you doing with that pretty white wax?" asked Lillian the next day, as she came upon Paul in a quiet corner of the garden and found him absorbed in some mysterious occupation.

With a quick gesture he destroyed his work, and, banishing a momentary expression of annoyance, he answered in his accustomed tone as he began to work anew, "I am molding a little deer for you, Miss Lillian. See, here is a rabbit already done, and I'll soon have a stag also."

"It's very pretty! How many nice things you can do, and how kind you are to think of my liking something new. Was this wax what you went to get this morning when you rode away so early?" asked the child.

"Yes, Miss Lillian. I was ordered to exercise your pony and I made him useful as well. Would you like to try this? It's very easy."

Lillian was charmed, and for several days wax modeling was her favorite play. Then she tired of it, and Paul invented a new amusement, smiling his inexplicable smile as he threw away the broken toys of wax.

"You are getting pale and thin, keeping such late hours, Paul. Go to bed, boy, go to bed, and get your sleep early," said Hester a week afterward, with a motherly air, as Paul passed her one morning.

"And how do you know I don't go to bed?" he asked, wheeling about.

"My lady has been restless lately, and I sit up with her till she sleeps. As I go to my room, I see your lamp burning, and last night I got as far as your door, meaning to speak to you, but didn't, thinking you'd take it amiss. But really you are the worse for late hours, child."

"I shall soon finish restoring the book, and then I'll sleep. I hope I don't disturb you. I have to grind my colors, and often make more noise than I mean to."

Paul fixed his eyes sharply on the woman as he spoke, but she seemed unconscious of it, and turned to go on, saying indifferently, "Oh, that's the odd sound, is it? No, it doesn't trouble me, so grind away, and make an end of it as soon as may be."

An anxious fold in the boy's forehead smoothed itself away as he left her, saying to himself with a sigh of relief, "A narrow escape; it's well I keep the door locked."

The boy's light burned no more after that, and Hester was content till a new worry came to trouble her. On her way to her room late one night, she saw a tall shadow flit down one of the side corridors that branched from the main one. For a moment she was startled, but, being a woman of courage, she followed noiselessly, till the shadow seemed to vanish in the gloom of the great hall.

"If the house ever owned a ghost I'd say that's it, but it never did, so I suspect some deviltry. I'll step to Paul. He's not asleep, I dare say. He's a brave and a sensible lad, and with him I'll quietly search the house."

Away she went, more nervous than she would own, and tapped at the boy's door. No one answered, and, seeing that it was ajar, Hester whisked in so hurriedly that her candle went out. With an impatient exclamation at her carelessness she glided to the bed, drew the curtain, and put forth her hand to touch the sleeper. The bed was empty. A disagreeable thrill shot through her, as she assured herself of the fact by groping along the narrow bed. Standing in the shadow of the curtain, she stared about the dusky room, in which objects were visible by the light of a new moon.

"Lord bless me, what is the boy about! I do believe it was him I saw in the—" She got no further in her mental exclamation for the sound of light approaching footsteps neared her. Slipping around the bed she waited in the shadow, and a moment after Paul appeared, looking pale and ghostly, with dark, disheveled hair, wide-open eyes, and a cloak thrown over his shoulders. Without a pause he flung it off, laid himself in bed, and seemed to sleep at once.

"Paul! Paul!" whispered Hester, shaking him, after a pause of astonishment at the whole proceeding.

"Hey, what is it?" And he sat up, looking drowsily about him.

"Come, come, no tricks, boy. What are you doing, trailing about the house at this hour and in such trim?"

"Why, Hester, is it you?" he exclaimed with a laugh, as he shook off her grip and looked up at her in surprise.

"Yes, and well it is me. If it had been any of those silly girls, the house would have been roused by this time. What mischief is afoot that you leave your bed and play ghost in this wild fashion?"

"Leave my bed! Why, my good soul, I haven't stirred, but have been dreaming with all my might these two hours. What do you mean, Hester?"

She told him as she relit her lamp, and stood eyeing him sharply the while. When she finished he was silent a minute, then said, looking half vexed and half ashamed, "I see how it is, and I'm glad you alone have found me out. I walk in my sleep sometimes, Hester, that's the truth. I thought I'd got over it, but it's come back, you see, and I'm sorry for it. Don't be troubled. I never do any mischief or come to any harm. I just take a quiet promenade and march back to bed again. Did I frighten you?"

"Just a trifle, but it's nothing. Poor lad, you'll have to have a bedfellow or be locked up; it's dangerous to go roaming about in this way," said Hester anxiously.

"It won't last long, for I'll get more tired and then I shall sleep sounder. Don't tell anyone, please, else they'll laugh at me, and that's not pleasant. I don't mind your knowing for you seem almost like a mother, and I thank you for it with all my heart."

He held out his hand with the look that was irresistible to Hester. Remembering only that he was a motherless boy, she stroked the curly hair off his forehead, and kissed him, with the thought of her own son warm at her heart.

"Good night, dear. I'll say nothing, but give you something that will ensure quiet sleep hereafter."

With that she left him, but would have been annoyed could she have seen the convulsion of boyish merriment which took possession of him when alone, for he laughed till the tears ran down his cheeks.

≥ *chapter IV* ≤

VANISHED

"HE'S a handsome lad, and one any woman might be proud
to call her son," said Hester to Bedford, the stately butler,
as they lingered at the hall door one autumn morning to
watch their young lady's departure on her daily ride.

"You are right, Mrs. Hester, he's a fine lad, and yet he seems
above his place, though he does look the very picture of a lady's groom,"
replied Bedford approvingly.

So he did, as he stood holding the white pony of his little mistress,
for the boy gave an air to whatever he wore and looked like a gentleman even in his livery. The dark-blue coat with silver buttons, the
silver band about his hat, his white-topped boots and bright spurs,
spotless gloves, and tightly drawn belt were all in perfect order, all
becoming, and his handsome, dark face caused many a susceptible
maid to blush and simper as they passed him. "Gentleman Paul" as
the servants called him, was rather lofty and reserved among his
mates, but they liked him nonetheless, for Hester had dropped hints
of his story and quite a little romance had sprung up about him. He
stood leaning against the docile creature, sunk in thought, and quite
unconscious of the watchers and whisperers close by. But as Lillian
appeared he woke up, attended to his duties like a well-trained
groom, and lingered over his task as if he liked it. Down the avenue
he rode behind her, but as they turned into a shady lane Lillian

(172)

beckoned, saying, in the imperious tone habitual to her, "Ride near me. I wish to talk."

Paul obeyed, and amused her with the chat she liked till they reached a hazel copse; here he drew rein, and, leaping down, gathered a handful of ripe nuts for her.

"How nice. Let us rest a minute here, and while I eat a few, please pull some of those flowers for Mamma. She likes a wild nosegay better than any I can bring her from the garden."

Lillian ate her nuts till Paul came to her with a hatful of late flowers and, standing by her, held the impromptu basket while she made up a bouquet to suit her taste.

"You shall have a posy, too; I like you to wear one in your buttonhole as the ladies' grooms do in the Park," said the child, settling a scarlet poppy in the blue coat.

"Thanks, Miss Lillian, I'll wear your colors with all my heart, especially today, for it is my birthday." And Paul looked up at the blooming little face with unusual softness in his keen blue eyes.

"Is it? Why, then, you're seventeen; almost a man, aren't you?"

"Yes, thank heaven," muttered the boy, half to himself.

"I wish I was as old. I shan't be in my teens till autumn. I must give you something, Paul, because I like you very much, and you are always doing kind things for me. What shall it be?" And the child held out her hand with a cordial look and gesture that touched the boy.

With one of the foreign fashions which sometimes appeared when he forgot himself, he kissed the small hand, saying impulsively, "My dear little mistress, I want nothing but your goodwill—and your forgiveness," he added, under his breath.

"You have that already, Paul, and I shall find something to add to it. But what is that?" And she laid hold of a little locket which had slipped into sight as Paul bent forward in his salute.

He thrust it back, coloring so deeply that the child observed it, and exclaimed, with a mischievous laugh, "It is your sweetheart, Paul. I heard Bessy, my maid, tell Hester she was sure you had one because you took no notice of them. Let me see it. Is she pretty?"

"Very pretty," answered the boy, without showing the picture.

"Do you like her very much?" questioned Lillian, getting interested in the little romance.

"Very much," and Paul's black eyelashes fell.

"Would you die for her, as they say in the old songs?" asked the girl, melodramatically.

"Yes, Miss Lillian, or live for her, which is harder."

"Dear me, how very nice it must be to have anyone care for one so much," said the child innocently. "I wonder if anybody ever will for me?"

> *"Love comes to all soon or late,*
> *And maketh gay or sad;*
> *For every bird will find its mate,*
> *And every lass a lad,"*

sang Paul, quoting one of Hester's songs, and looking relieved that Lillian's thoughts had strayed from him. But he was mistaken.

"Shall you marry this sweetheart of yours someday?" asked Lillian, turning to him with a curious yet wistful look.

"Perhaps."

"You look as if there was no 'perhaps' about it," said the child, quick to read the kindling of the eye and the change in the voice that accompanied the boy's reply.

"She is very young and I must wait, and while I wait many things may happen to part us."

"Is she a lady?"

"Yes, a wellborn, lovely little lady, and I'll marry her if I live." Paul spoke with a look of decision, and a proud lift of the head that contrasted curiously with the badge of servitude he wore.

Lillian felt this, and asked, with a sudden shyness coming over her, "But you are a gentleman, and so no one will mind even if you are not rich."

"How do you know what I am?" he asked quickly.

"I heard Hester tell the housekeeper that you were not what you seemed, and one day she hoped you'd get your right place again. I asked Mamma about it, and she said she would not let me be with you so much if you were not a fit companion for me. I was not to speak of it, but she means to be your friend and help you by-and-by."

"Does she?"

And the boy laughed an odd, short laugh that jarred on Lillian's ear and made her say reprovingly, "You are proud, I know, but you'll let us help you because we like to do it, and I have no brother to share my money with."

"Would you like one, or a sister?" asked Paul, looking straight into her face with his piercing eyes.

"Yes, indeed! I long for someone to be with me and love me, as Mamma can't."

"Would you be willing to share everything with another person —perhaps have to give them a great many things you like and now have all to yourself?"

"I think I should. I'm selfish, I know, because everyone pets and spoils me, but if I loved a person dearly I'd give up anything to them. Indeed I would, Paul, pray believe me."

She spoke earnestly, and leaned on his shoulder as if to enforce her words. The boy's arm stole around the little figure in the saddle, and a beautiful bright smile broke over his face as he answered warmly, "I do believe it, dear, and it makes me happy to hear you say so. Don't be afraid, I'm your equal, but I'll not forget that you are my little mistress till I can change from groom to gentleman."

He added the last sentence as he withdrew his arm, for Lillian had shrunk a little and blushed with surprise, not anger, at this first breach of respect on the part of her companion. Both were silent for a moment, Paul looking down and Lillian busy with her nosegay. She spoke first, assuming an air of satisfaction as she surveyed her work.

"That will please Mamma, I'm sure, and make her quite forget my naughty prank of yesterday. Do you know I offended her dreadfully by peeping into the gold case she wears on her neck? She was asleep and I was sitting by her. In her sleep she pulled it out and said something about a letter and Papa. I wanted to see Papa's face, for I never did, because the big picture of him is gone from the gallery where the others are, so I peeped into the case when she let it drop and was so disappointed to find nothing but a key."

"A key! What sort of a key?" cried Paul in an eager tone.

"Oh, a little silver one like the key of my piano, or the black cabinet. She woke and was very angry to find me meddling."

"What did it belong to?" asked Paul.

"Her treasure box, she said, but I don't know where or what that is, and I dare not ask any more, for she forbade my speaking to her about it. Poor Mamma! I'm always troubling her in some way or other."

With a penitent sigh, Lillian tied up her flowers and handed them to Paul to carry. As she did so, the change in his face struck her.

"How grim and old you look," she exclaimed. "Have I said anything that troubles you?"

"No, Miss Lillian. I'm only thinking."

"Then I wish you wouldn't think, for you get a great wrinkle in your forehead, your eyes grow almost black, and your mouth looks fierce. You are a very odd person, Paul; one minute as gay as any boy, and the next as grave and stern as a man with a deal of work to do."

"I *have* got a deal of work to do, so no wonder I look old and grim."

"What work, Paul?"

"To make my fortune and win my lady."

When Paul spoke in that tone and wore that look, Lillian felt as if they had changed places, and he was the master and she the servant. She wondered over this in her childish mind, but proud and willful as she was, she liked it, and obeyed him with unusual meekness when he suggested that it was time to return. As he rode silently beside her, she stole covert glances at him from under her wide hat brim, and studied his unconscious face as she had never done before. His lips moved now and then but uttered no audible sound, his black brows were knit, and once his hand went to his breast as if he thought of the little sweetheart whose picture lay there.

He's got a trouble. I wish he'd tell me and let me help him if I can. I'll make him show me that miniature someday, for I'm interested in that girl, thought Lillian with a pensive sigh.

As he held his hand for her little foot in dismounting her at the hall door, Paul seemed to have shaken off his grave mood, for he looked up and smiled at her with his blithest expression. But Lillian appeared to be the thoughtful one now and with an air of dignity, very pretty and becoming, thanked her young squire in a stately manner and swept into the house, looking tall and womanly in her flowing skirts.

Paul laughed as he glanced after her and, flinging himself onto his horse, rode away to the stables at a reckless pace, as if to work off some emotion for which he could find no other vent.

"Here's a letter for you, lad, all the way from some place in Italy. Who do you know there?" said Bedford, as the boy came back.

With a hasty "Thank you," Paul caught the letter and darted away to his own room, there to tear it open and, after reading a single line, to drop into a chair as if he had received a sudden blow. Growing paler and paler he read on, and when the letter fell from his hands he exclaimed, in a tone of despair, "How could he die at such a time!"

For an hour the boy sat thinking intently, with locked door, curtained window, and several papers strewn before him. Letters, memoranda, plans, drawings, and bits of parchment, all of which he took from a small locked portfolio always worn about him. Over these he pored with a face in which hope, despondency, resolve, and regret alternated rapidly. Taking the locket out he examined a ring which lay in one side, and the childish face which smiled on him from the other. His eyes filled as he locked and put it by, saying tenderly, "Dear little heart! I'll not forget or desert her whatever happens. Time must help me, and to time I must leave my work. One more attempt and then I'm off."

"I'll go to bed now, Hester; but while you get my things ready I'll take a turn in the corridor. The air will refresh me."

As she spoke, Lady Trevlyn drew her wrapper about her and paced softly down the long hall lighted only by fitful gleams of moonlight and the ruddy glow of the fire. At the far end was the state chamber, never used now, and never visited except by Hester, who occasionally went in to dust and air it, and my lady, who always passed the anniversary of Sir Richard's death alone there. The gallery was very dark, and she seldom went farther than the last window in her restless walks, but as she now approached she was startled to see a streak of yellow light under the door. She kept the key herself and neither she nor Hester had been there that day. A cold shiver passed over her for, as she looked, the shadow of a foot darkened the light for a moment and vanished as if someone had noiselessly passed. Obeying a sudden impulse, my lady sprang forward and tried to open the door. It was locked, but as her hand turned the silver knob a sound as if a drawer softly closed met her ear. She stooped to the keyhole but it was dark, a key evidently being in the lock. She drew back and flew to her room, snatched the key from her dressing table, and, bidding Hester follow, returned to the hall.

"What is it, my lady?" cried the woman, alarmed at the agitation of her mistress.

"A light, a sound, a shadow in the state chamber. Come quick!" cried Lady Trevlyn, adding, as she pointed to the door, "There, there, the light shines underneath. Do you see it?"

"No, my lady, it's dark," returned Hester.

It was, but never pausing my lady thrust in the key, and to her surprise it turned, the door flew open, and the dim, still room was before them. Hester boldly entered, and while her mistress slowly followed, she searched the room, looking behind the tall screen by the hearth, up the wide chimney, in the great wardrobe, and under the ebony cabinet, where all the relics of Sir Richard were kept. Nothing appeared, not even a mouse, and Hester turned to my lady with an air of relief. But her mistress pointed to the bed shrouded in dark velvet hangings, and whispered breathlessly, "You forgot to look there."

Hester had not forgotten, but in spite of her courage and good sense she shrank a little from looking at the spot where she had last seen her master's dead face. She believed the light and sound to be phantoms of my lady's distempered fancy, and searched merely to satisfy her. The mystery of Sir Richard's death still haunted the minds of all who remembered it, and even Hester felt a superstitious dread of that room. With a nervous laugh she looked under the bed and, drawing back the heavy curtains, said soothingly, "You see, my lady, there's nothing there."

But the words died on her lips, for, as the pale glimmer of the candle pierced the gloom of that funeral couch, both saw a face upon the pillow: a pale face framed in dark hair and beard, with closed eyes and the stony look the dead wear. A loud, long shriek that roused the house broke from Lady Trevlyn as she fell senseless at the bedside, and dropping both curtain and candle Hester caught up her mistress and fled from the haunted room, locking the door behind her.

In a moment a dozen servants were about them, and into their astonished ears Hester poured her story while vainly trying to restore her lady. Great was the dismay and intense the unwillingness of anyone to obey when Hester ordered the men to search the room again, for she was the first to regain her self-possession.

"Where's Paul? He's the heart of a man, boy though he is," she said angrily as the men hung back.

"He's not here. Lord! Maybe it was him a-playing tricks, though it ain't like him," cried Bessy, Lillian's little maid.

"No, it can't be him, for I locked him in myself. He walks in his sleep sometimes, and I was afraid he'd startle my lady. Let him sleep; this would only excite him and set him to marching again. Follow me, Bedford and James, I'm not afraid of ghosts or rogues."

With a face that belied her words Hester led the way to the awful room, and flinging back the curtain resolutely looked in. The bed was empty, but on the pillow was plainly visible the mark of a head and a single scarlet stain, as of blood. At that sight Hester turned pale and caught the butler's arm, whispering with a shudder, "Do you remember the night we put him in his coffin, the drop of blood that fell from his white lips? Sir Richard has been here."

"Good Lord, ma'am, don't say that! We can never rest in our beds if such things are to happen," gasped Bedford, backing to the door.

"It's no use to look, we've found all we shall find so go your ways and tell no one of this," said the woman in a gloomy tone, and, having assured herself that the windows were fast, Hester locked the room and ordered everyone but Bedford and the housekeeper to bed. "Do you sit outside my lady's door till morning," she said to the butler, "and you, Mrs. Price, help me to tend my poor lady, for if I'm not mistaken this night's work will bring on the old trouble."

Morning came, and with it a new alarm; for, though his door was fast locked and no foothold for even a sparrow outside the window, Paul's room was empty, and the boy nowhere to be found.

≽ *chapter V* ≼

A HERO

FOUR years had passed, and Lillian was fast blooming into a lovely woman: proud and willful as ever, but very charming, and already a belle in the little world where she still reigned a queen. Owing to her mother's ill health, she was allowed more freedom than is usually permitted to an English girl of her age; and, during the season, often went into company with a friend of Lady Trevlyn's who was chaperoning two young daughters of her own. To the world Lillian seemed a gay, free-hearted girl; and no one, not even her mother, knew how well she remembered and how much she missed the lost Paul. No tidings of him had ever come, and no trace of him was found after his flight. Nothing was missed, he went without his wages, and no reason could be divined for his departure except the foreign letter. Bedford remembered it, but forgot what postmark it bore, for he had only been able to decipher "Italy." My lady made many inquiries and often spoke of him; but when month after month passed and no news came, she gave him up, and on Lillian's account feigned to forget him. Contrary to Hester's fear, she did not seem the worse for the nocturnal fright, but evidently connected the strange visitor with Paul, or, after a day or two of nervous exhaustion, returned to her usual state of health. Hester had her own misgivings, but, being forbidden to allude to the subject, she held her peace, after emphatically declaring that Paul would yet appear to set her mind at rest.

"Lillian, Lillian, I've such news for you! Come and hear a charming little romance, and prepare to see the hero of it!" cried Maud Churchill, rushing into her friend's pretty boudoir one day in the height of the season.

Lillian lay on a couch, rather languid after a ball, and listlessly begged Maud to tell her story, for she was dying to be amused.

"Well, my dear, just listen and you'll be as enthusiastic as I am," cried Maud. And throwing her bonnet on one chair, her parasol on another, and her gloves anywhere, she settled herself on the couch and began: "You remember reading in the papers, some time ago, that fine account of the young man who took part in the Italian revolution and did that heroic thing with the bombshell?"

"Yes, what of him?" asked Lillian, sitting up.

"He is my hero, and we are to see him tonight."

"Go on, go on! Tell all, and tell it quickly," she cried.

"You know the officers were sitting somewhere, holding a council, while the city (I forget the name) was being bombarded, and how a shell came into the midst of them, how they sat paralyzed, expecting it to burst, and how this young man caught it up and ran out with it, risking his own life to save theirs?"

"Yes, yes, I remember!" And Lillian's listless face kindled at the recollection.

"Well, an Englishman who was there was so charmed by the act that, finding the young man was poor and an orphan, he adopted him. Mr. Talbot was old, and lonely, and rich, and when he died, a year after, he left his name and fortune to this Paolo."

"I'm glad, I'm glad!" cried Lillian, clapping her hands with a joyful face. "How romantic and charming it is!"

"Isn't it? But, my dear creature, the most romantic part is to come. Young Talbot served in the war, and then came to England to take possession of his property. It's somewhere down in Kent, a fine place and good income, all his; and he deserves it. Mamma heard a deal about him from Mrs. Langdon, who knew old Talbot and has seen the young man. Of course all the girls are wild to behold him, for he is very handsome and accomplished, and a gentleman by birth. But the dreadful part is that he is already betrothed to a lovely Greek girl, who came over at the same time, and is living in London with a

companion; quite elegantly, Mrs. Langdon says, for she called and
was charmed. This girl has been seen by some of our gentlemen
friends, and they already rave about the 'fair Helene,' for that's her
name."

Here Maud was forced to stop for breath, and Lillian had a
chance to question her.

"How old is she?"

"About eighteen or nineteen, they say."

"Very pretty?"

"Ravishing, regularly Greek and divine, Fred Raleigh says."

"When is she to be married?"

"Don't know; when Talbot gets settled, I fancy."

"And he? Is he as charming as she?"

"Quite, I'm told. He's just of age, and is, in appearance as in
everything else, a hero of romance."

"How came your mother to secure him for tonight?"

"Mrs. Langdon is dying to make a lion of him, and begged to
bring him. He is very indifferent on such things and seems intent on
his own affairs. Is grave and old for his years, and doesn't seem to
care much for pleasure and admiration, as most men would after a
youth like his, for he has had a hard time, I believe. For a wonder, he
consented to come when Mrs. Langdon asked him, and I flew off at
once to tell you and secure you for tonight."

"A thousand thanks. I meant to rest, for Mamma frets about my
being so gay; but she won't object to a quiet evening with you. What
shall we wear?" And here the conversation branched off on the all-
absorbing topic of dress.

When Lillian joined her friend that evening, the hero had already arrived, and, stepping into a recess, she waited to catch a glimpse
of him. Maud was called away, and she was alone when the crowd
about the inner room thinned and permitted young Talbot to be
seen. Well for Lillian that no one observed her at that moment, for
she grew pale and sank into a chair, exclaiming below her breath,
"It is Paul—*my* Paul!"

She recognized him instantly, in spite of increased height, a dark
moustache, and martial bearing. It was Paul, older, graver, handsomer,
but still "her Paul," as she called him, with a flush of pride and delight as she watched him, and felt that of all there she knew him best

and loved him most. For the childish affection still existed, and this discovery added a tinge of romance that made it doubly dangerous as well as doubly pleasant.

Will he know me? she thought, glancing at a mirror which reflected a slender figure with bright hair, white arms, and brilliant eyes; a graceful little head, proudly carried, and a sweet mouth, just then very charming, as it smiled till pearly teeth shone between the ruddy lips.

I'm glad I'm not ugly, and I hope he'll like me, she thought, as she smoothed the golden ripples on her forehead, settled her sash, and shook out the folds of her airy dress in a flutter of girlish excitement. "I'll pretend not to know him, when we meet, and see what he will do," she said, with a wicked sense of power; for being forewarned she was forearmed, and, fearing no betrayal of surprise on her own part, was eager to enjoy any of which he might be guilty.

Leaving her nook, she joined a group of young friends and held herself prepared for the meeting. Presently she saw Maud and Mrs. Langdon approaching, evidently intent on presenting the hero to the heiress.

"Mr. Talbot, Miss Trevlyn," said the lady. And looking up with a well-assumed air of indifference, Lillian returned the gentleman's bow with her eyes fixed full upon his face.

Not a feature of that face changed, and so severely unconscious of any recognition was it that the girl was bewildered. For a moment she fancied she had been mistaken in his identity, and a pang of disappointment troubled her; but as he moved a chair for Maud, she saw on the one ungloved hand a little scar which she remembered well, for he received it in saving her from a dangerous fall. At the sight all the happy past rose before her, and if her telltale eyes had not been averted they would have betrayed her. A sudden flush of maidenly shame dyed her cheek as she remembered that last ride, and the childish confidences then interchanged. This Helen was the little sweetheart whose picture he wore, and now, in spite of all obstacles, he had won both fortune and ladylove. The sound of his voice recalled her thoughts, and glancing up she met the deep eyes fixed on her with the same steady look they used to wear. He had addressed her, but what he said she knew not, beyond a vague idea that it was some slight allusion to the music going on in the next room. With a smile which would serve for an answer to almost any remark, she hastily plunged into conversation with a composure that did her credit in the eyes of her friends, who stood in awe of the young hero, for all were but just out.

"Mr. Talbot hardly needs an introduction here, for his name is well-known among us, though this is perhaps his first visit to England?" she said, flattering herself that this artful speech would entrap him into the reply she wanted.

With a slight frown, as if the allusion to his adventure rather annoyed him, and a smile that puzzled all but Lillian, he answered very simply, "It is not my first visit to this hospitable island. I was here a few years ago, for a short time, and left with regret."

"Then you have old friends here?" And Lillian watched him as she spoke.

"I had. They have doubtless forgotten me now," he said, with a sudden shadow marring the tranquillity of his face.

"Why doubt them? If they were true friends, they will not forget."

The words were uttered impulsively, almost warmly, but Talbot made no response, except a polite inclination and an abrupt change in the conversation.

"That remains to be proved. Do you sing, Miss Trevlyn?"

"A little." And Lillian's tone was both cold and proud.

"A great deal, and very charmingly," added Maud, who took pride in her friend's gifts both of voice and beauty. "Come, dear, there are so few of us you will sing, I know. Mamma desired me to ask you when Edith had done."

To her surprise Lillian complied, and allowed Talbot to lead her to the instrument. Still hoping to win some sign of recognition from him, the girl chose an air he taught her and sang it with a spirit and skill that surprised the listeners who possessed no key to her mood. At the last verse her voice suddenly faltered, but Talbot took up the song and carried her safely through it with his well-tuned voice.

"You know the air then?" she said in a low tone, as a hum of commendation followed the music.

"All Italians sing it, though few do it like yourself," he answered quietly, restoring the fan he had held while standing beside her.

Provoking boy! why won't he know me? thought Lillian. And her tone was almost petulant as she refused to sing again.

Talbot offered his arm and led her to a seat, behind which stood a little statuette of a child holding a fawn by a daisy chain.

"Pretty, isn't it?" she said, as he paused to look at it instead of taking the chair before her. "I used to enjoy modeling tiny deer and hinds in wax, as well as making daisy chains. Is sculpture among the many accomplishments which rumor tells us you possess?"

"No. Those who, like me, have their own fortunes to mold find time for little else," he answered gravely, still examining the marble group.

Lillian broke her fan with an angry flirt, for she was tired of her trial, and wished she had openly greeted him at the beginning; feeling now how pleasant it would have been to sit chatting of old times, while her friends dared hardly address him at all. She was on the point of calling him by his former name, when the remembrance of what he had been arrested the words on her lips. He was proud; would he not dread to have it known that, in his days of adversity, he had been a servant? For if she betrayed her knowledge of his past, she would be forced to tell where and how that knowledge was gained. No, better wait till they met alone, she thought; he would thank her for her delicacy, and she could easily explain her motive. He evidently wished to seem a stranger, for once she caught a gleam of the old, mirthful mischief in his eye, as she glanced up unexpectedly. He did remember her, she was sure, yet was trying her, perhaps, as she tried him. Well, she would stand the test and enjoy the joke by-and-by. With this fancy in her head she assumed a gracious air and chatted away in her most charming style, feeling both gay and excited, so anxious was she to please, and so glad to recover her early friend. A naughty whim seized her as her eye fell on a portfolio of classical engravings which someone had left in disorder on a table near her. Tossing them over she asked his opinion of several, and then handed him one in which Helen of Troy was represented as giving her hand to the irresistible Paris.

"Do you think her worth so much bloodshed, and deserving so much praise?" she asked, vainly trying to conceal the significant smile that would break loose on her lips and sparkle in her eyes.

Talbot laughed the short, boyish laugh so familiar to her ears, as he glanced from the picture to the arch questioner, and answered in a tone that made her heart beat with a nameless pain and pleasure, so full of suppressed ardor was it:

"Yes! 'All for love or the world well lost' is a saying I heartily agree to. La belle Hélène is my favorite heroine, and I regard Paris as the most enviable of men."

"I should like to see her."

The wish broke from Lillian involuntarily, and she was too much confused to turn it off by any general expression of interest in the classical lady.

"You may sometime," answered Talbot, with an air of amusement; adding, as if to relieve her, "I have a poetical belief that all the lovely women of history or romance will meet, and know, and love each other in some charming hereafter."

"But I'm no heroine and no beauty, so I shall never enter your poetical paradise," said Lillian, with a pretty affectation of regret.

"Some women are beauties without knowing it, and the heroines of romances never given to the world. I think you and Helen will yet meet, Miss Trevlyn."

As he spoke, Mrs. Langdon beckoned, and he left her pondering over his last words, and conscious of a secret satisfaction in his implied promise that she should see his betrothed.

"How do you like him?" whispered Maud, slipping into the empty chair.

"Very well," was the composed reply; for Lillian enjoyed her little mystery too much to spoil it yet.

"What did you say to him? I longed to hear, for you seemed to enjoy yourselves very much, but I didn't like to be a marplot."

Lillian repeated a part of the conversation, and Maud professed to be consumed with jealousy at the impression her friend had evidently made.

"It is folly to try to win the hero, for he is already won, you know," answered Lillian, shutting the cover on the pictured Helen with a sudden motion as if glad to extinguish her.

"Oh dear, no; Mrs. Langdon just told Mamma that she was mistaken about their being engaged; for she asked him and he shook his head, saying Helen was his ward."

"But that is absurd, for he's only a boy himself. It's very odd, isn't it? Never mind, I shall soon know all about it."

"How?" cried Maud, amazed at Lillian's assured manner.

"Wait a day or two, and I'll tell you a romance in return for yours. Your mother beckons to me, so I know Hester has come. Good night. I've had a charming time."

And with this tantalizing adieu, Lillian slipped away. Hester was waiting in the carriage, but as Lillian appeared, Talbot put aside the footman and handed her in, saying very low, in the well-remembered tone:

"Good night, my little mistress."

❧ *chapter VI* ❦

FAIR HELEN

TO no one but her mother and Hester did Lillian confide the discovery she had made. None of the former servants but old Bedford remained with them, and till Paul chose to renew the old friendship it was best to remain silent. Great was the surprise and delight of our lady and Hester at the good fortune of their protégé, and many the conjectures as to how he would explain his hasty flight.

"You will go and see him, won't you, Mamma, or at least inquire about him?" said Lillian, eager to assure the wanderer of a welcome, for those few words of his had satisfied her entirely.

"No, dear, it is for him to seek us, and till he does, I shall make no sign. He knows where we are, and if he chooses he can renew the acquaintance so strangely broken off. Be patient, and above all things remember, Lillian, that you are no longer a child," replied my lady, rather disturbed by her daughter's enthusiastic praises of Paul.

"I wish I was, for then I might act as I feel, and not be afraid of shocking the proprieties." And Lillian went to bed to dream of her hero.

For three days she stayed at home, expecting Paul, but he did not come, and she went out for her usual ride in the Park, hoping to meet him. An elderly groom now rode behind her, and she surveyed him with extreme disgust, as she remembered the handsome lad who had once filled that place. Nowhere did Paul appear, but in the

Ladies' Mile she passed an elegant brougham in which sat a very lovely girl and a mild old lady.

"That is Talbot's fiancée," said Maud Churchill, who had joined her. "Isn't she beautiful?"

"Not at all—yes, very," was Lillian's somewhat peculiar reply, for jealousy and truth had a conflict just then.

"He's so perfectly absorbed and devoted that I am sure that story is true, so adieu to our hopes," laughed Maud.

"Did you have any? Good-bye, I must go." And Lillian rode home at a pace which caused the stout groom great distress.

"Mamma, I've seen Paul's betrothed!" she cried, running into her mother's boudoir.

"And I have seen Paul himself," replied my lady, with a warning look, for there he stood, with half-extended hand, as if waiting to be acknowledged.

Lillian forgot her embarrassment in her pleasure, and made him an elaborate curtsy, saying, with a half-merry, half-reproachful glance, "Mr. Talbot is welcome in whatever guise he appears."

"I choose to appear as Paul, then, and offer you a seat, Miss Lillian," he said, assuming as much of his boyish manner as he could.

Lillian took it and tried to feel at ease, but the difference between the lad she remembered and the man she now saw was too great to be forgotten.

"Now tell us your adventures, and why you vanished away so mysteriously four years ago," she said, with a touch of the childish imperiousness in her voice, though her frank eyes fell before his.

"I was about to do so when you appeared with news concerning my cousin," he began.

"Your cousin!" exclaimed Lillian.

"Yes, Helen's mother and my own were sisters. Both married Englishmen, both died young, leaving us to care for each other. We were like a brother and sister, and always together till I left her to serve Colonel Daventry. The death of the old priest to whom I entrusted her recalled me to Genoa, for I was then her only guardian. I meant to have taken leave of you, my lady, properly, but the consequences of that foolish trick of mine frightened me away in the most unmannerly fashion."

"Ah, it was you, then, in the state chamber; I always thought so," and Lady Trevlyn drew a long breath of relief.

"Yes, I heard it whispered among the servants that the room was haunted, and I felt a wish to prove the truth of the story and my own courage. Hester locked me in, for fear of my sleepwalking; but I lowered myself by a rope and then climbed in at the closet window of the state chamber. When you came, my lady, I thought it was Hester, and slipped into the bed, meaning to give her a fright in return for her turning the key on me. But when your cry showed me what I had done, I was filled with remorse, and escaped as quickly and quietly as possible. I should have asked pardon before; I do now, most humbly, my lady, for it was sacrilege to play pranks *there.*"

During the first part of his story Paul's manner had been frank and composed, but in telling the latter part, his demeanor underwent a curious change. He fixed his eyes on the ground and spoke as if repeating a lesson, while his color varied, and a half-proud, half-submissive expression replaced the former candid one. Lillian observed this, and it disturbed her, but my lady took it for shame at his boyish freak and received his confession kindly, granting a free pardon and expressing sincere pleasure at his amended fortunes. As he listened, Lillian saw him clench his hand hard and knit his brows, assuming the grim look she had often seen, as if trying to steel himself against some importunate emotion or rebellious thought.

"Yes, half my work is done, and I have a home, thanks to my generous benefactor, and I hope to enjoy it well and wisely," he said in a grave tone, as if the fortune had not yet brought him his heart's desire.

"And when is the other half of the work to be accomplished, Paul? That depends on your cousin, perhaps." And Lady Trevlyn regarded him with a gleam of womanly curiosity in her melancholy eyes.

"It does, but not in the way you fancy, my lady. Whatever Helen may be, she is not my fiancée yet, Miss Lillian." And the shadow lifted as he laughed, looking at the young lady, who was decidedly abashed, in spite of a sense of relief caused by his words.

"I merely accepted the world's report," she said, affecting a nonchalant air.

"The world is a liar, as you will find in time" was his abrupt reply.

"I hope to see this beautiful cousin, Paul. Will she receive us as old friends of yours?"

"Thanks, not yet, my lady. She is still too much a stranger here to enjoy new faces, even kind ones. I have promised perfect rest and freedom for a time, but you shall be the first whom she receives."

Again Lillian detected the secret disquiet which possessed him, and her curiosity was roused. It piqued her that this Helen felt no desire to meet her and chose to seclude herself, as if regardless of the interest and admiration she excited. "I *will* see her in spite of her refusal, for I only caught a glimpse in the Park. Something is wrong, and I'll discover it, for it evidently worries Paul, and perhaps I can help him."

As this purpose sprang up in the warm but willful heart of the girl, she regained her spirits and was her most charming self while the young man stayed. They talked of many things in a pleasant, confidential manner, though when Lillian recalled that hour, she was surprised to find how little Paul had really told them of his past life or future plans. It was agreed among them to say nothing of their former relations, except to old Bedford, who was discretion itself, but to appear to the world as new-made friends—thus avoiding unpleasant and unnecessary explanations which would only excite gossip. My lady asked him to dine, but he had business out of town and declined, taking his leave with a lingering look, which made Lillian steal away to study her face in the mirror and wonder if she looked her best, for in Paul's eyes she had read undisguised admiration.

Lady Trevlyn went to her room to rest, leaving the girl free to ride, drive, or amuse herself as she liked. As if fearing her courage would fail if she delayed, Lillian ordered the carriage, and, bidding Hester mount guard over her, she drove away to St. John's Wood.

"Now, Hester, don't lecture or be prim when I tell you that we are going on a frolic," she began, after getting the old woman into an amiable mood by every winning wile she could devise. "I think you'll like it, and if it's found out I'll take the blame. There is some mystery about Paul's cousin, and I'm going to find it out."

"Bless you, child, how?"

"She lives alone here, is seldom seen, and won't go anywhere or receive anyone. That's not natural in a pretty girl. Paul won't talk about her, and, though he's fond of her, he always looks grave and grim when I ask questions. That's provoking, and I won't hear it. Maud is engaged to Raleigh, you know; well, he confided to her that he and a friend had found out where Helen was, had gone to the next villa, which is empty, and under pretense of looking at it got a peep at the girl in her garden. I'm going to do the same."

"And what am *I* to do?" asked Hester, secretly relishing the prank, for she was dying with curiosity to behold Paul's cousin.

"You are to do the talking with the old woman, and give me a chance to look. Now say you will, and I'll behave myself like an angel in return."

Hester yielded, after a few discreet scruples, and when they reached Laburnum Lodge played her part so well that Lillian soon managed to stray away into one of the upper rooms which overlooked the neighboring garden. Helen was there, and with eager eyes the girl scrutinized her. She was very beautiful, in the classical style; as fair and finely molded as a statue, with magnificent dark hair and eyes, and possessed of that perfect grace which is as effective as beauty. She was alone, and when first seen was bending over a flower which she caressed and seemed to examine with great interest as she stood a long time motionless before it. Then she began to pace slowly around and around the little grass plot, her hands hanging loosely clasped before her, and her eyes fixed on vacancy as if absorbed in thought. But as the first effect of her beauty passed away, Lillian found something peculiar about her. It was not the somewhat foreign dress and ornaments she wore; it was in her face, her movements, and the tone of her voice, for as she walked she sang a low, monotonous song, as if unconsciously. Lillian watched her keenly, marking the aimless motions of the little hands, the apathy of the lovely face, and the mirthless accent of the voice; but most of all the vacant fixture of the great dark eyes. Around and around she went, with an elastic step and a mechanical regularity wearisome to witness.

What is the matter with her? thought Lillian anxiously, as this painful impression increased with every scrutiny of the unconscious girl. So abashed was she that Hester's call was unheard, and Hester was unseen as she came and stood beside her. Both looked a moment, and as they looked an old lady came from the house and led Helen in, still murmuring her monotonous song and moving her hands as if to catch and hold the sunshine.

"Poor dear, poor dear. No wonder Paul turns sad and won't talk of her, and that she don't see anyone," sighed Hester pitifully.

"What is it? I see, but don't understand," whispered Lillian.

"She's an innocent, deary, an idiot, though that's a hard word for a pretty creature like her."

"How terrible! Come away, Hester, and never breathe to anyone what we have seen." And with a shudder and sense of pain and pity lying heavy at her heart, she hurried away, feeling doubly guilty in the discovery of this affliction. The thought of it haunted her continually; the memory of the lonely girl gave her no peace; and a consciousness of deceit burdened her unspeakably, especially in Paul's presence. This lasted for a week, then Lillian resolved to confess, hoping that when he found she knew the truth he would let her share his cross and help to lighten it. Waiting her opportunity, she seized a moment when her mother was absent, and with her usual frankness spoke out impetuously.

"Paul, I've done wrong, and I can have no peace till I am pardoned. I have seen Helen."

"Where, when, and how?" he asked, looking disturbed and yet relieved.

She told him rapidly, and as she ended she looked up at him with her sweet face, so full of pity, shame, and grief it would have been impossible to deny her anything.

"Can you forgive me for discovering this affliction?"

"I think I could forgive you a far greater fault, Lillian," he answered, in a tone that said many things.

"But deceit is so mean, so dishonorable and contemptible, how can you so easily pardon it in me?" she asked, quite overcome by this forgiveness, granted without any reproach.

"Then you would find it hard to pardon such a thing in another?" he said, with the expression that always puzzled her.

"Yes, it would be hard; but in those I loved, I could forgive much for love's sake."

With a sudden gesture he took her hand saying, impulsively, "How little changed you are! Do you remember that last ride of ours nearly five years ago?"

"Yes, Paul," she answered, with averted eyes.

"And what we talked of?"

"A part of that childish gossip I remember well."

"Which part?"

"The pretty little romance you told me." And Lillian looked up now, longing to ask if Helen's childhood had been blighted like her youth.

Paul dropped her hand as if he read her thoughts, and his own hand went involuntarily toward his breast, betraying that the locket still hung there.

"What did I say?" he asked, smiling at her sudden shyness.

"You vowed you'd win and wed your fair little ladylove if you lived."

"And so I will," he cried, with sudden fire in his eyes.

"What, marry her?"

"Aye, that I will."

"Oh Paul, will you tie yourself for life to a—" The word died on her lips, but a gesture of repugnance finished the speech.

"A what?" he demanded, excitedly.

"An innocent, one bereft of reason," stammered Lillian, entirely forgetting herself in her interest for him.

"Of whom do you speak?" asked Paul, looking utterly bewildered.

"Of poor Helen."

"Good heavens, who told you that base lie?" And his voice deepened with indignant pain.

"I saw her, you did not deny her affliction; Hester said so, and I believed it. Have I wronged her, Paul?"

"Yes, cruelly. She is blind, but no idiot, thank God."

There was such earnestness in his voice, such reproach in his words, and such ardor in his eye, that Lillian's pride gave way, and with a broken entreaty for pardon, she covered up her face, weeping the bitterest tears she ever shed. For in that moment, and the sharp pang it brought her, she felt how much she loved Paul and how hard it was to lose him. The childish affection had blossomed into a woman's passion, and in a few short weeks had passed through many phases of jealousy, hope, despair, and self-delusion. The joy she felt on seeing him again, the pride she took in him, the disgust Helen caused her, the relief she had not dared to own even to herself, when she fancied fate had put an insurmountable barrier between Paul and his cousin, the despair at finding it only a fancy, and the anguish of hearing him declare his unshaken purpose to marry his first love—all these conflicting emotions had led to this hard moment, and now self-control deserted her in her need. In spite of her efforts the passionate tears would have their way, though Paul soothed her with assurances of entire forgiveness, promises of Helen's friendship, and every gentle device he could imagine. She commanded herself at last by a strong effort, murmuring eagerly as she shrank from the hand that put back her fallen hair, and the face so full of tender sympathy bending over her:

"I am so grieved and ashamed at what I have said and done. I shall never dare to see Helen. Forgive me, and forget this folly. I'm sad and heavyhearted just now; it's the anniversary of Papa's death, and Mamma always suffers so much at such times that I get nervous."

"It is your birthday also. I remembered it, and ventured to bring a little token in return for the one you gave me long ago. This is a talisman, and tomorrow I will tell you the legend concerning it. Wear it for my sake, and God bless you, dear."

The last words were whispered hurriedly; Lillian saw the glitter of an antique ring, felt the touch of bearded lips on her hand, and Paul was gone.

But as he left the house he set his teeth, exclaiming low to himself, "Yes, tomorrow there shall be an end of this! We must risk everything and abide the consequences now. I'll have no more torment for any of us."

⇘ chapter VII ⇙

THE SECRET KEY

"IS Lady Trevlyn at home, Bedford?" asked Paul, as he presented himself at an early hour next day, wearing the keen, stern expression which made him look ten years older than he was.

"No, sir, my lady and Miss Lillian went down to the Hall last night."

"No ill news, I hope?" And the young man's eye kindled as if he felt a crisis at hand.

"Not that I heard, sir. Miss Lillian took one of her sudden whims and would have gone alone, if my lady hadn't given in much against her will, this being a time when she is better away from the place."

"Did they leave no message for me?"

"Yes, sir. Will you step in and read the note at your ease. We are in sad confusion, but this room is in order."

Leading the way to Lillian's boudoir, the man presented the note and retired. A few hasty lines from my lady, regretting the necessity of this abrupt departure, yet giving no reason for it, hoping they might meet next season, but making no allusion to seeing him at the Hall, desiring Lillian's thanks and regards, but closing with no hint of Helen, except compliments. Paul smiled as he threw it into the fire, saying to himself, "Poor lady, she thinks she has escaped the danger by flying, and Lillian tries to hide her trouble from me. Tender little heart! I'll comfort it without delay."

He sat looking about the dainty room still full of tokens of her presence. The piano stood open with a song he liked upon the rack; a bit of embroidery, whose progress he had often watched, lay in her basket with the little thimble near it; there was a strew of papers on the writing table, torn notes, scraps of drawing, and ball cards; a pearl-colored glove lay on the floor; and in the grate the faded flowers he had brought two days before. As his eye roved to and fro, he seemed to enjoy some happy dream, broken too soon by the sound of servants shutting up the house. He arose but lingered near the table, as if longing to search for some forgotten hint of himself.

"No, there has been enough lock picking and stealthy work; I'll do no more for her sake. This theft will harm no one and tell no tales." And snatching up the glove, Paul departed.

"Helen, the time has come. Are you ready?" he asked, entering her room an hour later.

"I am ready." And rising, she stretched her hand to him with a proud expression, contrasting painfully with her helpless gesture.

"They have gone to the Hall, and we must follow. It is useless to wait longer; we gain nothing by it, and the claim must stand on such proof as we have, or fall for want of that one link. I am tired of disguise. I want to be myself and enjoy what I have won, unless I lose it all."

"Paul, whatever happens, remember we cling together and share good or evil fortune as we always have done. I am a burden, but I cannot live without you, for you are my world. Do not desert me."

She groped her way to him and clung to his strong arm as if it was her only stay. Paul drew her close, saying wistfully, as he caressed the beautiful sightless face leaning on his shoulder, "*Mia cara*, would it break your heart, if at the last hour I gave up all and let the word remain unspoken? My courage fails me, and in spite of the hard past I would gladly leave them in peace."

"No, no, you shall not give it up!" cried Helen almost fiercely, while the slumbering fire of her southern nature flashed into her face. "You have waited so long, worked so hard, suffered so much, you must not lose your reward. You promised, and you must keep the promise."

"But it is so beautiful, so noble to forgive, and return a blessing for a curse. Let us bury the old feud, and right the old wrong in a new way. Those two are so blameless, it is cruel to visit the sins of the dead on their innocent heads. My lady has suffered enough already, and Lillian is so young, so happy, so unfit to meet a storm like this. Oh, Helen, mercy is more divine than justice."

Something moved Paul deeply, and Helen seemed about to yield, when the name of Lillian wrought a subtle change in her. The color died out of her face, her black eyes burned with a gloomy fire, and her voice was relentless as she answered, while her frail hands held him fast, "I will not let you give it up. We are as innocent as they; we have suffered more; and we deserve our rights, for we have no sin to expiate. Go on, Paul, and forget the sentimental folly that unmans you."

Something in her words seemed to sting or wound him. His face darkened, and he put her away, saying briefly, "Let it be so then. In an hour we must go."

On the evening of the same day, Lady Trevlyn and her daughter sat together in the octagon room at the Hall. Twilight was falling and candles were not yet brought, but a cheery fire blazed in the wide chimney, filling the apartment with a ruddy glow, turning Lillian's bright hair to gold and lending a tinge of color to my lady's pallid cheeks. The girl sat on a low lounging chair before the fire, her head on her hand, her eyes on the red embers, her thoughts—where? My lady lay on her couch, a little in the shadow, regarding her daughter with an anxious air, for over the young face a somber change had passed which filled her with disquiet.

"You are out of spirits, love," she said at last, breaking the long silence, as Lillian gave an unconscious sigh and leaned wearily into the depths of her chair.

"Yes, Mamma, a little."

"What is it? Are you ill?"

"No, Mamma; I think London gaiety is rather too much for me. I'm too young for it, as you often say, and I've found it out."

"Then it is only weariness that makes you so pale and grave, and so bent on coming back here?"

Lillian was the soul of truth, and with a moment's hesitation answered slowly, "Not that alone, Mamma. I'm worried about other things. Don't ask me what, please."

"But I must ask. Tell me, child, what things? Have you seen any one? Had letters, or been annoyed in any way about—anything?"

My lady spoke with sudden energy and rose on her arm, eyeing the girl with unmistakable suspicion and excitement.

"No, Mamma, it's only a foolish trouble of my own," answered Lillian, with a glance of surprise and a shamefaced look as the words reluctantly left her lips.

"Ah, a love trouble, nothing more? Thank God for that!" And my lady sank back as if a load was off her mind. "Tell me all, my darling; there is no confidante like a mother."

"You are very kind, and perhaps you can cure my folly if I tell it, and yet I am ashamed," murmured the girl. Then yielding to an irresistible impulse to ask help and sympathy, she added, in an almost inaudible tone, "I came away to escape from Paul."

"Because he loves you, Lillian?" asked my lady, with a frown and a half smile.

"Because he does *not* love me, Mamma." And the poor girl hid her burning cheeks in her hands, as if overwhelmed with maidenly shame at the implied confession of her own affection.

"My child, how is this? I cannot but be glad that he does *not* love you; yet it fills me with grief to see that this pains you. He is not a mate for you, Lillian. Remember this, and forget the transient regard that has sprung up from that early intimacy of yours."

"He is wellborn, and now my equal in fortune, and oh, so much my superior in all gifts of mind and heart," sighed the girl, still with hidden face, for tears were dropping through her slender fingers.

"It may be, but there is a mystery about him; and I have a vague dislike to him in spite of all that has passed. But, darling, are you sure he does not care for you? I fancied I read a different story in his face, and when you begged to leave town so suddenly, I believed that you had seen this also, and kindly wished to spare him any pain."

"It was to spare myself. Oh, Mamma, he loves Helen, and will marry her although she is blind. He told me this, with a look I could not doubt, and so I came away to hide my sorrow," sobbed poor Lillian in despair.

Lady Trevlyn went to her and, laying the bright head on her motherly bosom, said soothingly as she caressed it, "My little girl, it is too soon for you to know these troubles, and I am punished for yielding to your entreaties for a peep at the gay world. It is now too late to spare you this; you have had your wish and must pay its price, dear. But, Lillian, call pride to aid you, and conquer this fruitless love. It cannot be very deep as yet, for you have known Paul, the man, too short a time to be hopelessly enamored. Remember, there are others, better, braver, more worthy of you; that life is long, and full of pleasure yet untried."

"Have no fears for me, Mamma. I'll not disgrace you or myself by any sentimental folly. I do love Paul, but I can conquer it, and I will. Give me a little time, and you shall see me quite myself again."

Lillian lifted her head with an air of proud resolve that satisfied her mother, and with a grateful kiss stole away to ease her full heart alone. As she disappeared Lady Trevlyn drew a long breath and, clasping her hands with a gesture of thanksgiving, murmured to herself in an accent of relief, "Only a love sorrow! I feared it was some new terror like the old one. Seventeen years of silence, seventeen years of secret dread and remorse for me," she said, pacing the room with tightly locked hands and eyes full of unspeakable anguish. "Oh, Richard, Richard! I forgave you long ago, and surely I have expiated my innocent offense by these years of suffering! For her sake I did it, and for her sake I still keep dumb. God knows I ask nothing for myself but rest and oblivion by your side."

Half an hour later, Paul stood at the hall door. It was ajar, for the family had returned unexpectedly, as was evident from the open doors and empty halls. Entering unseen, he ascended to the room my lady usually occupied. The fire burned low, Lillian's chair was empty, and my lady lay asleep, as if lulled by the sighing winds without and the deep silence that reigned within. Paul stood regarding her with a great pity softening his face as he marked the sunken eyes, pallid cheeks, locks too early gray, and restless lips muttering in dreams.

"I wish I could spare her this," he sighed, stooping to wake her with a word. But he did not speak, for, suddenly clutching the chain about her neck, she seemed to struggle with some invisible foe and beat it off, muttering audibly as she clenched her thin hands on the golden case. Paul leaned and listened as if the first word had turned him to stone, till the paroxysm had passed, and with a heavy sigh my lady sank into a calmer sleep. Then, with a quick glance over his shoulder, Paul skillfully opened the locket, drew out the silver key, replaced it with one from the piano close by, and stole from the house noiselessly as he had entered it.

That night, in the darkest hour before the dawn, a figure went gliding through the shadowy Park to its most solitary corner. Here stood the tomb of the Trevlyns, and here the figure paused. A dull spark of light woke in its hand, there was a clank of bars, the creak of rusty hinges, then light and figure both seemed swallowed up.

Standing in the tomb where the air was close and heavy, the pale glimmer of the lantern showed piles of moldering coffins in the niches, and everywhere lay tokens of decay and death. The man drew his hat lower over his eyes, pulled the muffler closer about his mouth, and surveyed the spot with an undaunted aspect, though the beating of his heart was heard in the deep silence. Nearest the door stood a long casket covered with black velvet and richly decorated with silver ornaments, tarnished now. The Trevlyns had been a stalwart race, and the last sleeper brought there had evidently been of goodly stature, for the modern coffin was as ponderous as the great oaken beds where lay the bones of generations. Lifting the lantern, the intruder brushed the dust from the shield-shaped plate, read the name RICHARD TREV-LYN and a date, and, as if satisfied, placed a key in the lock, half-raised the lid, and, averting his head that he might not see the ruin seventeen long years had made, he laid his hand on the dead breast and from the folded shroud drew a mildewed paper. One glance sufficed, the casket was relocked, the door rebarred, the light extinguished, and the man vanished like a ghost in the darkness of the wild October night.

❧ *chapter VIII* ❧

WHICH?

"A GENTLEMAN, my lady."

Taking a card from the silver salver on which the servant offered it, Lady Trevlyn read, "Paul Talbot," and below the name these penciled words, "I beseech you to see me." Lillian stood beside her and saw the line. Their eyes met, and in the girl's face was such a sudden glow of hope, and love, and longing, that the mother could not doubt or disappoint her wish.

"I will see him," she said.

"Oh, Mamma, how kind you are!" cried the girl with a passionate embrace, adding breathlessly, "He did not ask for me. I cannot see him yet. I'll hide in the alcove, and can appear or run away as I like when we know why he comes."

They were in the library, for, knowing Lillian's fondness for the room which held no dark memories for her, my lady conquered her dislike and often sat there. As she spoke, the girl glided into the deep recess of a bay window and drew the heavy curtains just as Paul's step sounded at the door.

Hiding her agitation with a woman's skill, my lady rose with outstretched hand to welcome him. He bowed but did not take the hand, saying, in a voice of grave respect in which was audible an undertone of strong emotion, "Pardon me, Lady Trevlyn. Hear what I have to say; and then if you offer me your hand, I shall gratefully receive it."

She glanced at him, and saw that he was very pale, that his eye glittered with suppressed excitement, and his whole manner was that of a man who had nerved himself up to the performance of a difficult but intensely interesting task. Fancying these signs of agitation only natural in a young lover coming to woo, my lady smiled, reseated herself, and calmly answered, "I will listen patiently. Speak freely, Paul, and remember I am an old friend."

"I wish I could forget it. Then my task would be easier," he murmured in a voice of mingled regret and resolution, as he leaned on a tall chair opposite and wiped his damp forehead, with a look of such deep compassion that her heart sank with a nameless fear.

"I must tell you a long story, and ask your forgiveness for the offenses I committed against you when a boy. A mistaken sense of duty guided me, and I obeyed it blindly. Now I see my error and regret it," he said earnestly.

"Go on," replied my lady, while the vague dread grew stronger, and she braced her nerves as for some approaching shock. She forgot Lillian, forgot everything but the strange aspect of the man before her, and the words to which she listened like a statue. Still standing pale and steady, Paul spoke rapidly, while his eyes were full of mingled sternness, pity, and remorse.

"Twenty years ago, an English gentleman met a friend in a little Italian town, where he had married a beautiful wife. The wife had a sister as lovely as herself, and the young man, during that brief stay, loved and married her—in a very private manner, lest his father should disinherit him. A few months passed, and the Englishman was called home to take possession of his title and estates, the father being dead. He went alone, promising to send for the wife when all was ready. He told no one of his marriage, meaning to surprise his English friends by producing the lovely woman unexpectedly. He had been in England but a short time when he received a letter from the old priest of the Italian town, saying the cholera had swept through it, carrying off half its inhabitants, his wife and friend among others. This blow prostrated the young man, and when he recovered he hid his grief, shut himself up in his country house, and tried to forget. Accident threw in his way another lovely woman, and he married again. Before the first year was out, the friend whom he supposed was dead appeared, and told him that his wife still lived, and had borne him a child. In the terror and confusion of the plague, the priest had mistaken one sister for the other, as the elder did die."

"Yes, yes, I know; go on!" gasped my lady, with white lips, and eyes that never left the narrator's face.

"This friend had met with misfortune after flying from the doomed village with the surviving sister. They had waited long for letters, had written, and, when no answer came, had been delayed by illness and poverty from reaching England. At this time the child was born, and the friend, urged by the wife and his own interest, came here, learned that Sir Richard was married, and hurried to him in much distress. We can imagine the grief and horror of the unhappy man. In that interview the friend promised to leave all to Sir Richard, to preserve the secret till some means of relief could be found; and with this promise he returned, to guard and comfort the forsaken wife. Sir Richard wrote the truth to Lady Trevlyn, meaning to kill himself, as the only way of escape from the terrible situation between two women, both so beloved, both so innocently wronged. The pistol lay ready, but death came without its aid, and Sir Richard was spared the sin of suicide."

Paul paused for breath, but Lady Trevlyn motioned him to go on, still sitting rigid and white as the marble image near her.

"The friend only lived to reach home and tell the story. It killed the wife, and she died, imploring the old priest to see her child righted and its father's name secured to it. He promised; but he was poor, the child was a frail baby, and he waited. Years passed, and when the child was old enough to ask for its parents and demand its due, the proofs of the marriage were lost, and nothing remained but a ring, a bit of writing, and the name. The priest was very old, had neither friends, money, nor proofs to help him; but I was strong and hopeful, and though a mere boy I resolved to do the work. I made my way to England, to Trevlyn Hall, and by various stratagems (among which, I am ashamed to say, were false keys and feigned sleepwalking) I collected many proofs, but nothing which would satisfy a court, for no one but you knew where Sir Richard's confession was. I searched every nook and corner of the Hall, but in vain, and began to despair, when news of the death of Father Cosmo recalled me to Italy; for Helen was left to my care then. The old man had faithfully recorded the facts and left witnesses to prove the truth of his story; but for four years I never used it, never made any effort to secure the title or estates."

"Why not?" breathed my lady in a faint whisper, as hope suddenly revived.

"Because I was grateful," and for the first time Paul's voice faltered. "I was a stranger, and you took me in. I never could forget that, nor the many kindnesses bestowed upon the friendless boy. This afflicted me, even while I was acting a false part, and when I was away my heart failed me. But Helen gave me no peace; for my sake, she urged me to keep the vow made to that poor mother, and threatened to tell the story herself. Talbot's benefaction left me no excuse for delaying longer, and I came to finish the hardest task I can ever undertake. I feared that a long dispute would follow any appeal to law, and meant to appeal first to you, but fate befriended me, and the last proof was found."

"Found! Where?" cried Lady Trevlyn, springing up aghast.

"In Sir Richard's coffin, where you hid it, not daring to destroy, yet fearing to keep it."

"Who has betrayed me?" And her eye glanced wildly about the room, as if she feared to see some spectral accuser.

"Your own lips, my lady. Last night I came to speak of this. You lay asleep, and in some troubled dream spoke of the paper, safe in its writer's keeping, and your strange treasure here, the key of which you guarded day and night. I divined the truth. Remembering Hester's stories, I took the key from your helpless hand, found the paper on Sir Richard's dead breast, and now demand that you confess your part in this tragedy."

"I do, I do! I confess, I yield, I relinquish everything, and ask pity only for my child."

Lady Trevlyn fell upon her knees before him, with a submissive gesture, but imploring eyes, for, amid the wreck of womanly pride and worldly fortune, the mother's heart still clung to its idol.

"Who should pity her, if not I? God knows I would have spared her this blow if I could; but Helen would not keep silent, and I was driven to finish what I had begun. Tell Lillian this, and do not let her hate me."

As Paul spoke, tenderly, eagerly, the curtain parted, and Lillian appeared, trembling with the excitement of that interview, but conscious of only one emotion as she threw herself into his arms, crying in a tone of passionate delight, "Brother! Brother! Now I may love you!"

Paul held her close, and for a moment forgot everything but the joy of that moment. Lillian spoke first, looking up through tears of tenderness, her little hand laid caressingly against his cheek, as she whispered with sudden bloom in her own, "Now I know why I loved you so well, and now I can see you marry Helen without breaking my heart. Oh, Paul, you are still mine, and I care for nothing else."

"But, Lillian, I am not your brother."

"Then, in heaven's name, who are you?" she cried, tearing herself from his arms.

"Your lover, dear!"

"Who, then, is the heir?" demanded Lady Trevlyn, springing up, as Lillian turned to seek shelter with her mother.

"I am."

Helen spoke, and Helen stood on the threshold of the door, with a hard, haughty look upon her beautiful face.

"You told your story badly, Paul," she said, in a bitter tone. "You forgot me, forgot my affliction, my loneliness, my wrongs, and the natural desire of a child to clear her mother's honor and claim her father's name. I am Sir Richard's eldest daughter. I can prove my birth, and I demand my right with his own words to sustain me."

She paused, but no one spoke; and with a slight tremor in her proud voice, she added, "Paul has done the work; he shall have the reward. I only want my father's name. Title and fortune are nothing to one like me. I coveted and claimed them that I might give them to you, Paul, my one friend, always, so tender and so true."

"I'll have none of it," he answered, almost fiercely. "I have kept my promise, and am free. You chose to claim your own, although I offered all I had to buy your silence. It is yours by right—take it, and enjoy it if you can. I'll have no reward for work like this."

He turned from her with a look that would have stricken her to the heart could she have seen it. She felt it, and it seemed to augment some secret anguish, for she pressed her hands against her bosom with an expression of deep suffering, exclaiming passionately, "Yes, I *will* keep it, since I am to lose all else. I am tired of pity. Power is sweet, and I will use it. Go, Paul, and be happy if you can, with a nameless wife, and the world's compassion or contempt to sting your pride."

"Oh, Lillian, where shall we go? This is no longer our home, but who will receive us now?" cried Lady Trevlyn, in a tone of despair, for her spirit was utterly broken by the thought of the shame and sorrow in store for this beloved and innocent child.

"I will." And Paul's face shone with a love and loyalty they could not doubt. "My lady, you gave me a home when I was homeless; now let me pay my debt. Lillian, I have loved you from the time when, a romantic boy, I wore your little picture in my breast, and vowed to win you if I lived. I dared not speak before, but now, when other hearts may be shut against you, mine stands wide open to welcome you. Come, both. Let me protect and cherish you, and so atone for the sorrow I have brought you."

It was impossible to resist the sincere urgency of his voice, the tender reverence of his manner, as he took the two forlorn yet innocent creatures into the shelter of his strength and love. They clung to him instinctively, feeling that there still remained to them one staunch friend whom adversity could not estrange.

An eloquent silence fell upon the room, broken only by sobs, grateful whispers, and the voiceless vows that lovers plight with eyes, and hands, and tender lips. Helen was forgotten, till Lillian, whose elastic spirit threw off sorrow as a flower sheds the rain, looked up to thank Paul, with smiles as well as tears, and saw the lonely figure in the shadow. Her attitude was full of pathetic significance; she still stood on the threshold, for no one had welcomed her, and in the strange room she knew not where to go; her hands were clasped before her face, as if those sightless eyes had seen the joy she could not share, and at her feet lay the time-stained paper that gave her a barren title, but no love. Had Lillian known how sharp a conflict between passion and pride, jealousy and generosity, was going on in that young heart, she could not have spoken in a tone of truer pity or sincerer goodwill than that in which she softly said, "Poor girl! We must not forget her, for, with all her wealth, she is poor compared to us. We both had one father, and should love each other in spite of this misfortune. Helen, may I call you sister?"

"Not yet. Wait till I deserve it."

As if that sweet voice had kindled an answering spark of nobleness in her own heart, Helen's face changed beautifully, as she tore the paper to shreds, saying in a glad, impetuous tone, while the white flakes fluttered from her hands, "I, too, can be generous. I, too, can forgive. I bury the sad past. See! I yield my claim, I destroy my proofs, I promise eternal silence, and keep 'Paul's cousin' for my only title. Yes, you are happy, for you love one another!" she cried, with a sudden passion of tears. "Oh, forgive me, pity me, and take me in, for I am all alone and in the dark!"

There could be but one reply to an appeal like that, and they gave it, as they welcomed her with words that sealed a household league of mutual secrecy and sacrifice.

They *were* happy, for the world never knew the hidden tie that bound them so faithfully together, never learned how well the old prophecy had been fulfilled, or guessed what a tragedy of life and death the silver key unlocked.

The Abbot's Ghost

~ or ~

MAURICE TREHERNE'S TEMPTATION

A Christmas Story

BY A. M. BARNARD

⊱ *chapter I* ⊰

DRAMATIS PERSONAE

"HOW goes it, Frank? Down first, as usual."

"The early bird gets the worm, Major."

"Deuced ungallant speech, considering that the lovely Octavia is the worm," and with a significant laugh the major assumed an Englishman's favorite attitude before the fire.

His companion shot a quick glance at him, and an expression of anxiety passed over his face as he replied, with a well-feigned air of indifference, "You are altogether too sharp, Major. I must be on my guard while you are in the house. Any new arrivals? I thought I heard a carriage drive up not long ago."

"It was General Snowdon and his charming wife. Maurice Treherne came while we were out, and I've not seen him yet, poor fellow!"

"Aye, you may well say that; his is a hard case, if what I heard is true. I'm not booked up in the matter, and I should be, lest I make some blunder here, so tell me how things stand, Major. We've a good half hour before dinner. Sir Jasper is never punctual."

"Yes, you've a right to know, if you are going to try your fortune with Octavia."

The major marched through the three drawing rooms to see that no inquisitive servant was eavesdropping, and, finding all deserted, he resumed his place, while young Annon lounged on a couch as he listened with intense interest to the major's story.

"You know it was supposed that old Sir Jasper, being a bachelor, would leave his fortune to his two nephews. But he was an oddity, and as the title *must* go to young Jasper by right, the old man said Maurice should have the money. He was poor, young Jasper rich, and it seemed but just, though Madame Mère was very angry when she learned how the will was made."

"But Maurice didn't get the fortune. How was that?"

"There was some mystery there which I shall discover in time. All went smoothly till that unlucky yachting trip, when the cousins were wrecked. Maurice saved Jasper's life, and almost lost his own in so doing. I fancy he wishes he had, rather than remain the poor cripple he is. Exposure, exertion, and neglect afterward brought on paralysis of the lower limbs, and there he is—a fine, talented, spirited fellow tied to that cursed chair like a decrepit old man."

"How does he bear it?" asked Annon, as the major shook his gray head, with a traitorous huskiness in his last words.

"Like a philosopher or a hero. He is too proud to show his despair at such a sudden end to all his hopes, too generous to complain, for Jasper is desperately cut up about it, and too brave to be daunted by a misfortune which would drive many a man mad."

"Is it true that Sir Jasper, knowing all this, made a new will and left every cent to his namesake?"

"Yes, and there lies the mystery. Not only did he leave it away from poor Maurice, but so tied it up that Jasper cannot transfer it, and at his death it goes to Octavia."

"The old man must have been demented. What in heaven's name did he mean by leaving Maurice helpless and penniless after all his devotion to Jasper? Had he done anything to offend the old party?"

"No one knows; Maurice hasn't the least idea of the cause of this sudden whim, and the old man would give no reason for it. He died soon after, and the instant Jasper came to the title and estate he brought his cousin home, and treats him like a brother. Jasper is a noble fellow, with all his faults, and this act of justice increases my respect for him," said the major heartily.

"What will Maurice do, now that he can't enter the army as he intended?" asked Annon, who now sat erect, so full of interest was he.

"Marry Octavia, and come to his own, I hope."

"An excellent little arrangement, but Miss Treherne may object," said Annon, rising with sudden kindling of the eye.

"I think not, if no one interferes. Pity, with women, is akin to love, and she pities her cousin in the tenderest fashion. No sister could be more devoted, and as Maurice is a handsome, talented fellow, one can easily foresee the end, if, as I said before, no one interferes to disappoint the poor lad again."

"You espouse his cause, I see, and tell me this that I may stand aside. Thanks for the warning, Major; but as Maurice Treherne is a man of unusual power in many ways, I think we are equally matched, in spite of his misfortune. Nay, if anything, he has the advantage of me, for Miss Treherne pities him, and that is a strong ally for my rival. I'll be as generous as I can, but I'll *not* stand aside and relinquish the woman I love without a trial first."

With an air of determination Annon faced the major, whose keen eyes had read the truth which he had but newly confessed to himself. Major Royston smiled as he listened, and said briefly, as steps approached, "Do your best. Maurice will win."

"We shall see," returned Annon between his teeth.

Here their host entered, and the subject of course was dropped. But the major's words rankled in the young man's mind, and would have been doubly bitter had he known that their confidential conversation had been overheard. On either side of the great fireplace was a door leading to a suite of rooms which had been old Sir Jasper's. These apartments had been given to Maurice Treherne, and he had just returned from London, whither he had been to consult a certain famous physician. Entering quietly, he had taken possession of his rooms, and having rested and dressed for dinner, rolled himself into the library, to which led the curtained door on the right. Sitting idly in his light, wheeled chair, ready to enter when his cousin appeared, he had heard the chat of Annon and the major. As he listened, over his usually impassive face passed varying expressions of anger, pain, bitterness, and defiance, and when the young man uttered his almost fierce "We shall see," Treherne smiled a scornful smile and clenched his pale hand with a gesture which proved that a year of suffering had not conquered the man's spirit, though it had crippled his strong body.

A singular face was Maurice Treherne's; well-cut and somewhat haughty features; a fine brow under the dark locks that carelessly streaked it; and remarkably piercing eyes. Slight in figure and wasted by pain, he still retained the grace as native to him as the stern fortitude which enabled him to hide the deep despair of an ambitious

nature from every eye, and bear his affliction with a cheerful philos-
ophy more pathetic than the most entire abandonment to grief. Carefully dressed, and with no hint at invalidism but the chair, he bore
himself as easily and calmly as if the doom of lifelong helplessness
did not hang over him. A single motion of the hand sent him rolling
noiselessly to the curtained door, but as he did so, a voice exclaimed
behind him, "Wait for me, cousin." And as he turned, a young girl
approached, smiling a glad welcome as she took his hand, adding in a
tone of soft reproach, "Home again, and not let me know it, till I heard
the good news by accident."

"Was it good news, Octavia?" and Maurice looked up at the
frank face with a new expression in those penetrating eyes of his. His
cousin's open glance never changed as she stroked the hair off his forehead with the caress one often gives a child, and answered eagerly,
"The best to me; the house is dull when you are away, for Jasper
always becomes absorbed in horses and hounds, and leaves Mamma
and me to mope by ourselves. But tell me, Maurice, what they said
to you, since you would not write."

"A little hope, with time and patience. Help me to wait, dear,
help me to wait."

His tone was infinitely sad, and as he spoke, he leaned his cheek
against the kind hand he held, as if to find support and comfort
there. The girl's face brightened beautifully, though her eyes filled, for
to her alone did he betray his pain, and in her alone did he seek
consolation.

"I will, I will with heart and hand! Thank heaven for the hope,
and trust me it shall be fulfilled. You look very tired, Maurice. Why
go in to dinner with all those people? Let me make you cozy here,"
she added anxiously.

"Thanks, I'd rather go in, it does me good; and if I stay away,
Jasper feels that he must stay with me. I dressed in haste, am I right,
little nurse?"

She gave him a comprehensive glance, daintily settled his cravat,
brushed back a truant lock, and, with a maternal air that was charming, said, "My boy is always elegant, and I'm proud of him. Now we'll
go in." But with her hand on the curtain she paused, saying quickly,
as a voice reached her, "Who is that?"

"Frank Annon. Didn't you know he was coming?" Maurice eyed
her keenly.

"No, Jasper never told me. Why did he ask him?"

"To please you."

"Me! When he knows I detest the man. No matter, I've got on the color he hates, so he won't annoy me, and Mrs. Snowdon can amuse herself with him. The general has come, you know?"

Treherne smiled, well pleased, for no sign of maiden shame or pleasure did the girl's face betray, and as he watched her while she peeped, he thought with satisfaction, Annon is right, I have the advantage, and I'll keep it at all costs.

"Here is Mamma. We must go in," said Octavia, as a stately old lady made her appearance in the drawing room.

The cousins entered together and Annon watched them covertly, while seemingly intent on paying his respects to Madame Mère, as his hostess was called by her family.

"Handsomer than ever," he muttered, as his eye rested on the blooming girl, looking more like a rose than ever in the peach-colored silk which he had once condemned because a rival admired it. She turned to reply to the major, and Annon glanced at Treherne with an irrepressible frown, for sickness had not marred the charm of that peculiar face, so colorless and thin that it seemed cut in marble; but the keen eyes shone with a wonderful brilliancy, and the whole countenance was alive with a power of intellect and will which made the observer involuntarily exclaim, "That man must suffer a daily martyrdom, so crippled and confined; if it last long he will go mad or die."

"General and Mrs. Snowdon," announced the servant, and a sudden pause ensued as everyone looked up to greet the newcomers.

A feeble, white-haired old man entered, leaning on the arm of an indescribably beautiful woman. Not thirty yet, tall and nobly molded, with straight black brows over magnificent eyes; rippling dark hair gathered up in a great knot, and ornamented with a single band of gold. A sweeping dress of wine-colored velvet, set off with a dazzling neck and arms decorated like her stately head with ornaments of Roman gold. At the first glance she seemed a cold, haughty creature, born to dazzle but not to win. A deeper scrutiny detected lines of suffering in that lovely face, and behind the veil of reserve, which pride forced her to wear, appeared the anguish of a strong-willed woman burdened by a heavy cross. No one would dare express pity or offer sympathy, for her whole air repelled it, and in her gloomy eyes sat scorn of herself mingled with defiance of the scorn of others. A strange, almost tragical-looking woman, in spite of beauty, grace, and the cold sweetness of her manner. A faint smile parted her lips as she greeted those about her, and as her husband seated himself beside Lady Treherne, she lifted her head with a long breath, and a singular expression of relief, as if a burden was removed, and for the time being she was free. Sir Jasper was at her side, and as she listened, her eye glanced from face to face.

"Who is with you now?" she asked, in a low, mellow voice that was full of music.

"My sister and my cousin are yonder. You may remember Tavia as a child, she is little more now. Maurice is an invalid, but the finest fellow breathing."

"I understand," and Mrs. Snowdon's eyes softened with a sudden glance of pity for one cousin and admiration for the other, for she knew the facts.

"Major Royston, my father's friend, and Frank Annon, my own. Do you know him?" asked Sir Jasper.

"No."

"Then allow me to make him happy by presenting him, may I?"

"Not now. I'd rather see your cousin."

"Thanks, you are very kind. I'll bring him over."

"Stay, let me go to him," began the lady, with more feeling in face and voice than one would believe her capable of showing.

"Pardon, it will offend him, he will not be pitied, or relinquish any of the duties or privileges of a gentleman which he can possibly perform. He is proud, we can understand the feeling, so let us humor the poor fellow."

Mrs. Snowdon bowed silently, and Sir Jasper called out in his hearty, blunt way, as if nothing was amiss with his cousin, "Maurice, I've an honor for you. Come and receive it."

Divining what it was, Treherne noiselessly crossed the room, and with no sign of self-consciousness or embarrassment, was presented to the handsome woman. Thinking his presence might be a restraint, Sir Jasper went away. The instant his back was turned, a change came over both: an almost grim expression replaced the suavity of Treherne's face, and Mrs. Snowdon's smile faded suddenly, while a deep flush rose to her brow, as her eyes questioned his beseechingly.

"How dared you come?" he asked below his breath.

"The general insisted."

"And you could not change his purpose; poor woman!"

"You will not be pitied, neither will I," and her eyes flashed; then the fire was quenched in tears, and her voice lost all its pride in a pleading tone.

"Forgive me, I longed to see you since your illness, and so I 'dared' to come."

"You shall be gratified; look, quite helpless, crippled for life, perhaps."

The chair was turned from the groups about the fire, and as he spoke, with a bitter laugh Treherne threw back the skin which covered his knees, and showed her the useless limbs once so strong and fleet. She shrank and paled, put out her hand to arrest him, and cried in an indignant whisper, "No, no, not that! You know I never meant such cruel curiosity, such useless pain to both—"

"Be still, someone is coming," he returned inaudibly; adding aloud, as he adjusted the skin and smoothed the rich fur as if speaking of it, "Yes, it is a very fine one, Jasper gave it to me. He spoils me, like a dear, generous-hearted fellow as he is. Ah, Octavia, what can I do for you?"

"Nothing, thank you. I want to recall myself to Mrs. Snowdon's memory, if she will let me."

"No need of that; I never forget happy faces and pretty pictures. Two years ago I saw you at your first ball, and longed to be a girl again."

As she spoke, Mrs. Snowdon pressed the hand shyly offered, and smiled at the spirited face before her, though the shadow in her own eyes deepened as she met the bright glance of the girl.

"How kind you were that night! I remember you let me chatter away about my family, my cousin, and my foolish little affairs with the sweetest patience, and made me very happy by your interest. I was homesick, and Aunt could never bear to hear of those things. It was before your marriage, and all the kinder, for you were the queen of the night, yet had a word for poor little me."

Mrs. Snowdon was pale to the lips, and Maurice impatiently tapped the arm of his chair, while the girl innocently chatted on.

"I am sorry the general is such an invalid; yet I dare say you find great happiness in taking care of him. It is so pleasant to be of use to those we love." And as she spoke, Octavia leaned over her cousin to hand him the glove he had dropped.

The affectionate smile that accompanied the act made the color deepen again in Mrs. Snowdon's cheek, and lit a spark in her softened eyes. Her lips curled and her voice was sweetly sarcastic as she answered, "Yes, it is charming to devote one's life to these dear invalids, and find one's reward in their gratitude. Youth, beauty, health, and happiness are small sacrifices if one wins a little comfort for the poor sufferers."

The girl felt the sarcasm under the soft words and drew back with a troubled face.

Maurice smiled, and glanced from one to the other, saying significantly, "Well for me that my little nurse loves her labor, and finds no sacrifice in it. I am fortunate in my choice."

"I trust it may prove so—" Mrs. Snowdon got no further, for at that moment dinner was announced, and Sir Jasper took her away. Annon approached with him and offered his arm to Miss Treherne, but with an air of surprise, and a little gesture of refusal, she said coldly:

"My cousin always takes me in to dinner. Be good enough to escort the major." And with her hand on the arm of the chair, she walked away with a mischievous glitter in her eyes.

Annon frowned and fell back, saying sharply, "Come, Major, what are you doing there?"

"Making discoveries."

≈ chapter II ≈

BYPLAY

A RIGHT splendid old dowager was Lady Treherne, in her black velvet and point lace, as she sat erect and stately on a couch by the drawing-room fire, a couch which no one dare occupy in her absence, or share uninvited. The gentlemen were still over their wine, and the three ladies were alone. My lady never dozed in public, Mrs. Snowdon never gossiped, and Octavia never troubled herself to entertain any guests but those of her own age, so long pauses fell, and conversation languished, till Mrs. Snowdon roamed away into the library. As she disappeared, Lady Treherne beckoned to her daughter, who was idly making chords at the grand piano. Seating herself on the ottoman at her mother's feet, the girl took the still handsome hand in her own and amused herself with examining the old-fashioned jewels that covered it, a pretext for occupying her telltale eyes, as she suspected what was coming.

"My dear, I'm not pleased with you, and I tell you so at once, that you may amend your fault," began Madame Mère in a tender tone, for though a haughty, imperious woman, she idolized her children.

"What have I done, Mamma?" asked the girl.

"Say rather, what have you left undone. You have been very rude to Mr. Annon. It must not occur again; not only because he is a guest, but because he is your—brother's friend."

My lady hesitated over the word "lover," and changed it, for to

(219)

her Octavia still seemed a child, and though anxious for the alliance, she forbore to speak openly, lest the girl should turn willful, as she inherited her mother's high spirit.

"I'm sorry, Mamma. But how can I help it, when he teases me so that I detest him?" said Octavia, petulantly.

"How tease, my love?"

"Why, he follows me about like a dog, puts on a sentimental look when I appear; blushes, and beams, and bows at everything I say, if I am polite; frowns and sighs if I'm not; and glowers tragically at every man I speak to, even poor Maurice. Oh, Mamma, what foolish creatures men are!" And the girl laughed blithely, as she looked up for the first time into her mother's face.

My mother smiled, as she stroked the bright head at her knee, but asked quickly, "Why say 'even poor Maurice,' as if it were impossible for anyone to be jealous of him?"

"But isn't it, Mamma? I thought strong, well men regarded him as one set apart and done with, since his sad misfortune."

"Not entirely; while women pity and pet the poor fellow, his comrades will be jealous, absurd as it is."

"No one pets him but me, and I have a right to do it, for he is my cousin," said the girl, feeling a touch of jealousy herself.

"Rose and Blanche Talbot outdo you, my dear, and there is no cousinship to excuse them."

"Then let Frank Annon be jealous of them, and leave me in peace. They promised to come today; I'm afraid something has happened to prevent them." And Octavia gladly seized upon the new subject. But my lady was not to be eluded.

"They said they could not come till after dinner. They will soon arrive. Before they do so, I must say a few words, Tavia, and I beg you to give heed to them. I desire you to be courteous and amiable to Mr. Annon, and before strangers to be less attentive and affectionate to Maurice. You mean it kindly, but it looks ill, and causes disagreeable remarks."

"Who blames me for being devoted to my cousin? Can I ever do enough to repay him for his devotion? Mamma, you forget he saved your son's life."

Indignant tears filled the girl's eyes, and she spoke passionately, forgetting that Mrs. Snowdon was within earshot of her raised voice. With a frown my lady laid her hand on her daughter's lips, saying

coldly, "I do not forget, and I religiously discharge my every obligation
by every care and comfort it is in my power to bestow. You are young,
romantic, and tender-hearted. You think you must give your time and
health, must sacrifice your future happiness to this duty. You are
wrong, and unless you learn wisdom in season, you will find that you
have done harm, not good."

"God forbid! How can I do that? Tell me, and I will be wise
in time."

Turning the earnest face up to her own, Lady Treherne whispered anxiously, "Has Maurice ever looked or hinted anything of love
during this year he has been with us, and you his constant companion?"

"Never, Mamma; he is too honorable and too unhappy to speak
or think of that. I am his little nurse, sister, and friend, no more, nor
ever shall be. Do not suspect us, or put such fears into my mind, else
all our comfort will be spoiled."

Flushed and eager was the girl, but her clear eyes betrayed no
tender confusion as she spoke, and all her thought seemed to be to
clear her cousin from the charge of loving her too well. Lady Treherne
looked relieved, paused a moment, then said, seriously but gently,
"This is well, but, child, I charge you tell me at once, if ever he forgets
himself, for this thing cannot be. Once I hoped it might, now it is
impossible; remember that he continue a friend and cousin, nothing
more. I warn you in time, but if you neglect the warning, Maurice
must go. No more of this; recollect my wish regarding Mr. Annon,
and let your cousin amuse himself without you in public."

"Mamma, do you wish me to like Frank Annon?"

The abrupt question rather disturbed my lady, but knowing her
daughter's frank, impetuous nature, she felt somewhat relieved by this
candor, and answered decidedly, "I do. He is your equal in all respects; he loves you, Jasper desires it, I approve, and you, being heart-
whole, can have no just objection to the alliance."

"Has he spoken to you?"

"No, to your brother."

"You wish this much, Mamma?"

"Very much, my child."

"I will try to please you, then." And stifling a sigh, the girl
kissed her mother with unwonted meekness in tone and manner.

"Now I am well pleased. Be happy, my love. No one will urge

or distress you. Let matters take their course, and if this hope of ours can be fulfilled, I shall be relieved of the chief care of my life."

A sound of girlish voices here broke on their ears, and springing up, Octavia hurried to meet her friends, exclaiming joyfully, "They have come! they have come!"

Two smiling, blooming girls met her at the door, and, being at an enthusiastic age, they gushed in girlish fashion for several minutes, making a pretty group as they stood in each other's arms, all talking at once, with frequent kisses and little bursts of laughter, as vents for their emotion. Madame Mère welcomed them and then went to join Mrs. Snowdon, leaving the trio to gossip unrestrained.

"My dearest creature, I thought we never should get here, for Papa had a tiresome dinner party, and we were obliged to stay, you know," cried Rose, the lively sister, shaking out the pretty dress and glancing at herself in the mirror as she fluttered about the room like a butterfly.

"We were dying to come, and so charmed when you asked us, for we haven't seen you this age, darling," added Blanche, the pensive one, smoothing her blond curls after a fresh embrace.

"I'm sorry the Ulsters couldn't come to keep Christmas with us, for we have no gentlemen but Jasper, Frank Annon, and the major. Sad, isn't it?" said Octavia, with a look of despair, which caused a fresh peal of laughter.

"One apiece, my dear, it might be worse." And Rose privately decided to appropriate Sir Jasper.

"Where is your cousin?" asked Blanche, with a sigh of sentimental interest.

"He is here, of course. I forget him, but he is not on the flirting list, you know. We must amuse him, and not expect him to amuse us, though really, all the capital suggestions and plans for merrymaking always come from him."

"He is better, I hope?" asked both sisters with real sympathy, making their young faces womanly and sweet.

"Yes, and has hopes of entire recovery. At least, they tell him so, though Dr. Ashley said there was no chance of it."

"Dear, dear, how sad! Shall we see him, Tavia?"

"Certainly; he is able to be with us now in the evening, and enjoys society as much as ever. But please take no notice of his infirmity, and make no inquiries beyond the usual 'How do you do.'

He is sensitive, and hates to be considered an invalid more than ever."

"How charming it must be to take care of him, he is so accomplished and delightful. I quite envy you," said Blanche pensively.

"Sir Jasper told us that the General and Mrs. Snowdon were coming. I hope they will, for I've a most intense curiosity to see her—" began Rose.

"Hush, she is here with Mamma! Why curious? What is the mystery? For you look as if there was one," questioned Octavia under her breath.

The three charming heads bent toward one another as Rose replied in a whisper, "If I knew, I shouldn't be inquisitive. There was a rumor that she married the old general in a fit of pique, and now repents. I asked Mamma once, but she said such matters were not for young girls to hear, and not a word more would she say. *N'importe,* I have wits of my own, and I can satisfy myself. The gentlemen are coming! Am I all right, dear?" And the three glanced at one another with a swift scrutiny that nothing could escape, then grouped themselves prettily, and waited, with a little flutter of expectation in each young heart.

In came the gentlemen, and instantly a new atmosphere seemed to pervade the drawing room, for with the first words uttered, several romances began. Sir Jasper was taken possession of by Rose, Blanche intended to devote herself to Maurice Treherne, but Annon intercepted her, and Octavia was spared any effort at politeness by this unexpected move on the part of her lover.

"He is angry, and wishes to pique me by devoting himself to Blanche. I wish he would, with all my heart, and leave me in peace. Poor Maurice, he expects me, and I long to go to him, but must obey Mamma." And Octavia went to join the group formed by my lady, Mrs. Snowdon, the general, and the major.

The two young couples flirted in different parts of the room, and Treherne sat alone, watching them all with eyes that pierced below the surface, reading the hidden wishes, hopes, and fears that ruled them. A singular expression sat on his face as he turned from Octavia's clear countenance to Mrs. Snowdon's gloomy one. He leaned his head upon his hand and fell into deep thought, for he was passing through one of those fateful moments which come to us all, and which may make or mar a life. Such moments come when least looked for: an unexpected meeting, a peculiar mood, some trivial circumstance, or careless word produces it, and often it is gone before we realize its presence, leaving aftereffects to show us what we have gained or lost. Treherne was conscious that the present hour, and the acts that filled it, possessed unusual interest, and would exert an unusual influence on his life. Before him was the good and evil genius of his nature in the guise of those two women. Edith Snowdon had already tried her power, and accident only had saved him. Octavia, all unconscious as she was, never failed to rouse and stimulate the noblest attributes of mind and heart. A year spent in her society had done much for him, and he loved her with a strange mingling of passion, reverence, and gratitude. He knew why Edith Snowdon came, he felt that the old fascination had not lost its charm, and though fear was unknown to him, he was ill pleased at the sight of the beautiful, dangerous woman. On the other hand, he saw that Lady Treherne desired her daughter to shun him and smile on Annon; he acknowledged that he had no right to win the young creature, crippled and poor as he was, and a pang of jealous pain wrung his heart as he watched her.

Then a sense of power came to him, for helpless, poor, and seemingly an object of pity, he yet felt that he held the honor, peace, and happiness of nearly every person present in his hands. It was a strong temptation to this man, so full of repressed passion and power, so set apart and shut out from the more stirring duties and pleasures of life. A few words from his lips, and the pity all felt for him would be turned to fear, respect, and admiration. Why not utter them, and enjoy all that was possible? He owed the Trehernes nothing; why suffer injustice, dependence, and the compassion that wounds a proud man deepest? Wealth, love, pleasure might be his with a breath. Why not secure them now?

His pale face flushed, his eye kindled, and his thin hand lay clenched like a vise as these thoughts passed rapidly through his mind. A look, a word at that moment would sway him; he felt it, and leaned forward, waiting in secret suspense for the glance, the speech which should decide him for good or ill. Who shall say what subtle instinct caused Octavia to turn and smile at him with a wistful, friendly look that warmed his heart? He met it with an answering glance, which thrilled her strangely, for love, gratitude, and some mysterious intelligence met and mingled in the brilliant yet soft expression which swiftly shone and faded in her face. What it was she could not tell;

she only felt that it filled her with an indescribable emotion never experienced before. In an instant it all passed, Lady Treherne spoke to her, and Blanche Talbot addressed Maurice, wondering, as she did so, if the enchanting smile he wore was meant for her.

"Mr. Annon having mercifully set me free, I came to try to cheer your solitude; but you look as if solitude made you happier than society does the rest of us," she said without her usual affectation, for his manner impressed her.

"You are very kind and very welcome. I do find pleasures to beguile my loneliness, which gayer people would not enjoy, and it is well that I can, else I should turn morose and tyrannical, and doom some unfortunate to entertain me all day long." He answered with a gentle courtesy which was his chief attraction to womankind.

"Pray tell me some of your devices. I'm often alone in spirit, if not so in the flesh, for Rose, though a dear girl, is not congenial, and I find no kindred soul."

A humorous glimmer came to Treherne's eyes, as the sentimental damsel heaved a soft sigh and drooped her long lashes effectively. Ignoring the topic of "kindred souls," he answered coldly, "My favorite amusement is studying the people around me. It may be rude, but tied to my corner, I cannot help watching the figures around me, and discovering their little plots and plans. I'm getting very expert, and really surprise myself sometimes by the depth of my researches."

"I can believe it; your eyes look as if they possessed that gift. Pray don't study *me*." And the girl shrank away with an air of genuine alarm.

Treherne smiled involuntarily, for he had read the secret of that shallow heart long ago, and was too generous to use the knowledge, however flattering it might be to him. In a reassuring tone he said, turning away the keen eyes she feared, "I give you my word I never will, charming as it might be to study the white pages of a maidenly heart. I find plenty of others to read, so rest tranquil, Miss Blanche."

"Who interests you most just now?" asked the girl, coloring with pleasure at his words. "Mrs. Snowdon looks like one who has a romance to be read, if you have the skill."

"I have read it. My lady is my study just now. I thought I knew her well, but of late she puzzles me. Human minds are more full of mysteries than any written book and more changeable than the cloud shapes in the air."

"A fine old lady, but I fear her so intensely I should never dare to try to read her, as you say." Blanche looked toward the object of discussion as she spoke, and added, "Poor Tavia, how forlorn she seems. Let me ask her to join us, may I?"

"With all my heart" was the quick reply.

Blanche glided away but did not return, for my lady kept her as well as her daughter.

"That test satisfies me; well, I submit for a time, but I think I can conquer my aunt yet." And with a patient sigh Treherne turned to observe Mrs. Snowdon.

She now stood by the fire, talking with Sir Jasper, a handsome, reckless, generous-hearted young gentleman, who very plainly showed his great admiration for the lady. When he came, she suddenly woke up from her listless mood and became as brilliantly gay as she had been unmistakably melancholy before. As she chatted, she absently pushed to and fro a small antique urn of bronze on the chimneypiece, and in doing so she more than once gave Treherne a quick, significant glance, which he answered at last by a somewhat haughty nod. Then, as if satisfied, she ceased toying with the ornament and became absorbed in Sir Jasper's gallant badinage.

The instant her son approached Mrs. Snowdon, Madame Mère grew anxious, and leaving Octavia to her friends and lover, she watched Jasper. But her surveillance availed little, for she could neither see nor hear anything amiss, yet could not rid herself of the feeling that some mutual understanding existed between them. When the party broke up for the night, she lingered till all were gone but her son and nephew.

"Well, Madame Ma Mère, what troubles you?" asked Sir Jasper, as she looked anxiously into his face before bestowing her good-night kiss.

"I cannot tell, yet I feel ill at ease. Remember, my son, that you are the pride of my heart, and any sin or shame of yours would kill me. Good night, Maurice." And with a stately bow she swept away.

Lounging with both elbows on the low chimneypiece, Sir Jasper smiled at his mother's fears, and said to his cousin, the instant they were alone, "She is worried about E. S. Odd, isn't it, what instinctive antipathies women take to one another?"

"Why did you ask E. S. here?" demanded Treherne.

"My dear fellow, how could I help it? My mother wanted the

general, my father's friend, and of course his wife must be asked also. I couldn't tell my mother that the lady had been a most arrant coquette, to put it mildly, and had married the old man in a pet, because my cousin and I declined to be ruined by her."

"You *could* have told her what mischief she makes wherever she goes, and for Octavia's sake have deferred the general's visit for a time. I warn you, Jasper, harm will come of it."

"To whom, you or me?"

"To both, perhaps, certainly to you. She was disappointed once when she lost us both by wavering between your title and my supposed fortune. She is miserable with the old man, and her only hope is in his death, for he is very feeble. You are free, and doubly attractive now, so beware, or she will entangle you before you know it."

"Thanks, Mentor. I've no fear, and shall merely amuse myself for a week—they stay no longer." And with a careless laugh, Sir Jasper strolled away.

"Much mischief may be done in a week, and this is the beginning of it," muttered Treherne, as he raised himself to look under the bronze vase for the note. It was gone!

❧ *chapter III* ❧

WHO WAS IT?

WHO had taken it? This question tormented Treherne all that
sleepless night. He suspected three persons, for only these
had approached the fire after the note was hidden. He had
kept his eye on it, he thought, till the stir of breaking up. In that
moment it must have been removed by the major, Frank Annon, or
my lady; Sir Jasper was out of the question, for he never touched an
ornament in the drawing room since he had awkwardly demolished a
whole *étagère* of costly trifles, to his mother's and sister's great grief.
The major evidently suspected something, Annon was jealous, and
my lady would be glad of a pretext to remove her daughter from his
reach. Trusting to his skill in reading faces, he waited impatiently
for morning, resolving to say nothing to anyone but Mrs. Snowdon,
and from her merely to inquire what the note contained.

Treherne usually was invisible till lunch, often till dinner; therefore, fearing to excite suspicion by unwonted activity, he did not appear till noon. The mailbag had just been opened, and everyone was
busy over their letters, but all looked up to exchange a word with the
newcomer, and Octavia impulsively turned to meet him, then checked
herself and hid her suddenly crimsoned face behind a newspaper.
Treherne's eye took in everything, and saw at once in the unusually

late arrival of the mail a pretext for discovering the pilferer of the note.

"All have letters but me, yet I expected one last night. Major, have you got it among yours?" And as he spoke, Treherne fixed his penetrating eyes full on the person he addressed.

With no sign of consciousness, no trace of confusion, the major carefully turned over his pile, and replied in the most natural manner, "Not a trace of it; I wish there was, for nothing annoys me more than any delay or mistake about my letters."

He knows nothing of it, thought Treherne, and turned to Annon, who was deep in a long epistle from some intimate friend, with a talent for imparting news, to judge from the reader's interest.

"Annon, I appeal to you, for I *must* discover who has robbed me of my letter."

"I have but one, read it, if you will, and satisfy yourself" was the brief reply.

"No, thank you. I merely asked in joke; it is doubtless among my lady's. Jasper's letters and mine often get mixed, and my lady takes care of his for him. I think you must have it, Aunt."

Lady Treherne looked up impatiently. "My dear Maurice, what a coil about a letter! We none of us have it, so do not punish us for the sins of your correspondent or the carelessness of the post."

She was not the thief, for she is always intensely polite when she intends to thwart me, thought Treherne, and, apologizing for his rudeness in disturbing them, he rolled himself to his nook in a sunny window and became apparently absorbed in a new magazine.

Mrs. Snowdon was opening the general's letters for him, and, having finished her little task, she roamed away into the library, as if in search of a book. Presently returning with one, she approached Treherne, and, putting it into his hand, said, in her musically distinct voice, "Be so kind as to find for me the passage you spoke of last night. I am curious to see it."

Instantly comprehending her stratagem, he opened it with apparent carelessness, secured the tiny note laid among the leaves, and, selecting a passage at hazard, returned her book and resumed his own. Behind the cover of it he unfolded and read these words:

> *I understand, but do not be anxious; the line I left was merely this—"I must see you alone, tell me when and where." No one can make much of it, and I will discover the thief before*

dinner. Do nothing, but watch to whom I speak first on entering, when we meet in the evening, and beware of that person.

Quietly transferring the note to the fire with the wrapper of the magazine, he dismissed the matter from his mind and left Mrs. Snowdon to play detective as she pleased, while he busied himself about his own affairs.

It was a clear, bright December day, and when the young people separated to prepare for a ride, while the general and the major sunned themselves on the terrace, Lady Treherne said to her nephew, "I am going for an airing in the pony carriage. Will you be my escort, Maurice?"

"With pleasure," replied the young man, well knowing what was in store for him.

My lady was unusually taciturn and grave, yet seemed anxious to say something which she found difficult to utter. Treherne saw this, and ended an awkward pause by dashing boldly into the subject which occupied both.

"I think you want to say something to me about Tavie, Aunt. Am I right?"

"Yes."

"Then let me spare you the pain of beginning, and prove my sincerity by openly stating the truth, as far as I am concerned. I love her very dearly, but I am not mad enough to dream of telling her so. I know that it is impossible, and I relinquish my hopes. Trust me. I will keep silent and see her marry Annon without a word of complaint, if you will it. I see by her altered manner that you have spoken to her, and that my little friend and nurse is to be mine no longer. Perhaps you are wise, but if you do this on my account, it is in vain—the mischief is done, and while I live I shall love my cousin. If you do it to spare her, I am dumb, and will go away rather than cause her a care or pain."

"Do you really mean this, Maurice?" And Lady Treherne looked at him with a changed and softened face.

Turning upon her, Treherne showed her a countenance full of suffering and sincerity, of resignation and resolve, as he said earnestly, "I do mean it; prove me in any way you please. I am not a bad fellow, Aunt, and I desire to be better. Since my misfortune I've had time to test many things, myself among others, and in spite of many faults, I do cherish the wish to keep my soul honest and true, even though my body be a wreck. It is easy to say these things, but in spite of temptation, I think I can stand firm, if you trust me."

"My dear boy, I do trust you, and thank you gratefully for this frankness. I never forget that I owe Jasper's life to you, and never expect to repay that debt. Remember this when I seem cold or unkind, and remember also that I say now, had you been spared this affliction, I would gladly have given you my girl. But—"

"But, Aunt, hear one thing," broke in Treherne. "They tell me that any sudden and violent shock of surprise, joy, or sorrow may do for me what they hope time will achieve. I said nothing of this, for it is but a chance; yet, while there is any hope, need I utterly renounce Octavia?"

"It is hard to refuse, and yet I cannot think it wise to build upon a chance so slight. Once let her have you, and both are made unhappy, if the hope fail. No, Maurice, it is better to be generous, and leave her free to make her own happiness elsewhere. Annon loves her, she is heart-whole, and will soon learn to love him, if you are silent. My poor boy, it seems cruel, but I must say it."

"Shall I go away, Aunt?" was all his answer, very firmly uttered, though his lips were white.

"Not yet, only leave them to themselves, and hide your trouble if you can. Yet, if you prefer, you shall go to town, and Benson shall see that you are comfortable. Your health will be a reason, and I will come, or write often, if you are homesick. It shall depend on you, for I want to be just and kind in this hard case. You shall decide."

"Then I will stay. I can hide my love; and to see them together will soon cease to wound me, if Octavia is happy."

"So let it rest then, for a time. You shall miss your companion as little as possible, for I will try to fill her place. Forgive me, Maurice, and pity a mother's solicitude, for these two are the last of many children, and I am a widow now."

Lady Treherne's voice faltered, and if any selfish hope or plan lingered in her nephew's mind, that appeal banished it and touched his better nature. Pressing her hand he said gently, "Dear Aunt, do not lament over me. I am one set apart for afflictions, yet I will not be conquered by them. Let us forget my youth and be friendly counselors together for the good of the two whom we both love. I must say a word about Jasper, and you will not press me to explain more than I can without breaking my promise."

"Thank you, thank you! It is regarding that woman, I know. Tell me all you can; I will not be importunate, but I disliked her the instant I saw her, beautiful and charming as she seems."

"When my cousin and I were in Paris, just before my illness, we met her. She was with her father then, a gay old man who led a life of pleasure, and was no fit guardian for a lovely daughter. She knew our story and, having fascinated both, paused to decide which she would accept: Jasper, for his title, or me, for my fortune. This was before my uncle changed his will, and I believed myself his heir; but, before she made her choice, something (don't ask me what, if you please) occurred to send us from Paris. On our return voyage we were wrecked, and then came my illness, disinheritance, and helplessness. Edith Dubarry heard the story, but rumor reported it falsely, and she believed both of us had lost the fortune. Her father died penniless, and in a moment of despair she married the general, whose wealth surrounds her with the luxury she loves, and whose failing health will soon restore her liberty—"

"And then, Maurice?" interrupted my lady.

"She hopes to win Jasper, I think."

"Never! We must prevent that at all costs. I had rather see him dead before me, than the husband of such a woman. Why is she permitted to visit homes like mine? I should have been told this sooner," exclaimed my lady angrily.

"I should have told you had I known it, and I reproved Jasper for his neglect. Do not be needlessly troubled, Aunt. There is no blemish on Mrs. Snowdon's name, and, as the wife of a brave and honorable man, she is received without question; for beauty, grace, or tact like hers can make their way anywhere. She stays but a week, and I will devote myself to her; this will save Jasper, and, if necessary, convince Tavie of my indifference—" Then he paused to stifle a sigh.

"But yourself, have you no fears for your own peace, Maurice? You must not sacrifice happiness or honor, for me or mine."

"I am safe; I love my cousin, and that is my shield. Whatever happens remember that I tried to serve you, and sincerely endeavored to forget myself."

"God bless you, my son! Let me call you so, and feel that, though

I deny you my daughter, I give you heartily a mother's care and affection."

Lady Treherne was as generous as she was proud, and her nephew had conquered her by confidence and submission. He acted no part, yet, even in relinquishing all, he cherished a hope that he might yet win the heart he coveted. Silently they parted, but from that hour a new and closer bond existed between the two, and exerted an unsuspected influence over the whole household.

Maurice waited with some impatience for Mrs. Snowdon's entrance, not only because of his curiosity to see if she had discovered the thief, but because of the part he had taken upon himself to play. He was equal to it, and felt a certain pleasure in it for a threefold reason. It would serve his aunt and cousin, would divert his mind from its own cares, and, perhaps by making Octavia jealous, waken love; for, though he had chosen the right, he was but a man, and moreover a lover.

Mrs. Snowdon was late. She always was, for her toilet was elaborate, and she liked to enjoy its effects upon others. The moment she entered Treherne's eye was on her, and to his intense surprise and annoyance she addressed Octavia, saying blandly, "My dear Miss Treherne, I've been admiring your peacocks. Pray let me see you feed them tomorrow. Miss Talbot says it is a charming sight."

"If you are on the terrace just after lunch, you will find them there, and may feed them yourself, if you like" was the cool, civil reply.

"She looks like a peacock herself in that splendid green and gold dress, doesn't she?" whispered Rose to Sir Jasper, with a wicked laugh.

"Faith, so she does. I wish Tavie's birds had voices like Mrs. Snowdon's; their squalling annoys me intensely."

"I rather like it, for it is honest, and no malice or mischief is hidden behind it. I always distrust those smooth, sweet voices; they are insincere. I like a full, clear tone; sharp, if you please, but decided and true."

"Well said, Octavia. I agree with you, and your own is a perfect sample of the kind you describe." And Treherne smiled as he rolled by to join Mrs. Snowdon, who evidently waited for him, while Octavia turned to her brother to defend her pets.

"Are you sure? How did you discover?" said Maurice, affecting to admire the lady's bouquet, as he paused beside her.

"I suspected it the moment I saw her this morning. She is no actress; and dislike, distrust, and contempt were visible in her face when we met. Till you so cleverly told me my note was lost, I fancied she was disturbed about her brother—or you."

A sudden pause and a keen glance followed the last softly uttered word, but Treherne met it with an inscrutable smile and a quiet "Well, what next?"

"The moment I learned that you did not get the note I was sure she had it, and, knowing that she must have seen me put it there, in spite of her apparent innocence, I quietly asked her for it. This surprised her, this robbed the affair of any mystery, and I finished her perplexity by sending it to the major the moment she returned it to me, as if it had been intended for him. She begged pardon, said her brother was thoughtless, and she watched over him lest he should get into mischief; professed to think I meant the line for him, and behaved like a charming simpleton, as she is."

"Quite a tumult about nothing. Poor little Tavie! You doubtlessly frightened her so that we may safely correspond hereafter."

"You may give me an answer, now and here."

"Very well, meet me on the terrace tomorrow morning; the peacocks will make the meeting natural enough. I usually loiter away an hour or two there, in the sunny part of the day."

"But the girl?"

"I'll send her away."

"You speak as if it would be an easy thing to do."

"It will, both easy and pleasant."

"Now you are mysterious or uncomplimentary. You either care nothing for a tête-à-tête with her, or you will gladly send her out of my way. Which is it?"

"You shall decide. Can I have this?"

She looked at him as he touched a rose with a warning glance, for the flower was both an emblem of love and of silence. Did he mean to hint that he recalled the past, or to warn her that someone was near? She leaned from the shadow of the curtain where she sat, and caught a glimpse of a shadow gliding away.

"Who was it?" she asked, below her breath.

"A Rose," he answered, laughing. Then, as if the danger was over, he said, "How will you account to the major for the message you sent him?"

"Easily, by fabricating some interesting perplexity in which I want sage counsel. He will be flattered, and by seeming to take him into my confidence, I can hoodwink the excellent man to my heart's content, for he annoys me by his odd way of mounting guard over me at all times. Now take me in to dinner, and be your former delightful self."

"That is impossible," he said, yet proved that it was not.

≈ *chapter IV* ≈

FEEDING THE
PEACOCKS

IT was indeed a charming sight, the twelve stately birds perched
on the broad stone balustrade, or prancing slowly along the terrace, with the sun gleaming on their green and golden necks
and the glories of their gorgeous plumes, widespread, or sweeping like
rich trains behind them. In pretty contrast to the splendid creatures
was their young mistress, in her simple morning dress and fur-trimmed
hood and mantle, as she stood feeding the tame pets from her hand,
calling their fanciful names, laughing at their pranks, and heartily
enjoying the winter sunshine, the fresh wind, and the girlish pastime.
As Treherne slowly approached, he watched her with lover's eyes, and
found her very sweet and blithe, and dearer in his sight than ever.
She had shunned him carefully all the day before, had parted at night
with a hasty handshake, and had not come as usual to bid him good-
morning in the library. He had taken no notice of the change as yet,
but now, remembering his promise to his aunt, he resolved to let the
girl know that he fully understood the relation which henceforth was
to exist between them.

"Good morning, cousin. Shall I drive you away, if I take a turn
or two here?" he said, in a cheerful tone, but with a half-reproachful
glance.

She looked at him an instant, then went to him with extended
hand and cheeks rosier than before, while her frank eyes filled, and

her voice had a traitorous tremor in it, as she said, impetuously: "I *will* be myself for a moment, in spite of everything. Maurice, don't think me unkind, don't reproach me, or ask my leave to come where I am. There is a reason for the change you see in me; it's not caprice, it is obedience."

"My dear girl, I know it. I meant to speak of it, and show you that I understand. Annon is a good fellow, as worthy of you as any man can be, and I wish you all the happiness you deserve."

"Do you?" And her eyes searched his face keenly.

"Yes; do you doubt it?" And so well did he conceal his love, that neither face, voice, nor manner betrayed a hint of it.

Her eyes fell, a cloud passed over her clear countenance, and she withdrew her hand, as if to caress the hungry bird that gently pecked at the basket she held. As if to change the conversation, she said playfully, "Poor Argus, you have lost your fine feathers, and so all desert you, except kind little Juno, who never forgets her friends. There, take it all, and share between you."

Treherne smiled, and said quickly, "I am a human Argus, and you have been a kind little Juno to me since I lost my plumes. Continue to be so, and you will find me a very faithful friend."

"I will." And as she answered, her old smile came back and her eyes met his again.

"Thanks! Now we shall get on happily. I don't ask or expect the old life—that is impossible. I knew that when lovers came, the friend would fall into the background; and I am content to be second, where I have so long been first. Do not think you neglect me; be happy with your lover, dear, and when you have no pleasanter amusement, come and see old Maurice."

She turned her head away, that he might not see the angry color in her cheeks, the trouble in her eyes, and when she spoke, it was to say petulantly, "I wish Jasper and Mamma would leave me in peace. I hate lovers and want none. If Frank teases, I'll go into a convent and so be rid of him."

Maurice laughed, and turned her face toward himself, saying, in his persuasive voice, "Give him a trial first, to please your mother. It can do no harm and may amuse you. Frank is already lost, and, as you are heart-whole, why not see what you can do for him? I shall have a new study, then, and not miss you so much."

"You are very kind; I'll do my best. I wish Mrs. Snowdon would come, if she is coming; I've an engagement at two, and Frank will look tragical if I'm not ready. He is teaching me billiards, and I really like the game, though I never thought I should."

"That looks well. I hope you'll learn a double lesson, and Annon find a docile pupil in both."

"You are very pale this morning; are you in pain, Maurice?" suddenly asked Octavia, dropping the tone of assumed ease and gaiety under which she had tried to hide her trouble.

"Yes, but it will soon pass. Mrs. Snowdon is coming. I saw her at the hall door a moment ago. I will show her the peacocks, if you want to go. She won't mind the change, I dare say, as you don't like her, and I do."

"No, I am sure of that. It was an arrangement, perhaps? I understand. I will not play Mademoiselle De Trop."

Sudden fire shone in the girl's eyes, sudden contempt curled her lip, and a glance full of meaning went from her cousin to the door, where Mrs. Snowdon appeared, waiting for her maid to bring her some additional wrappings.

"You allude to the note you stole. How came you to play that prank, Tavie?" asked Treherne tranquilly.

"I saw her put it under the urn. I thought it was for Jasper, and I took it," she said boldly.

"Why for Jasper?"

"I remembered his speaking of meeting her long ago, and describing her beauty enthusiastically—and so did you."

"You have a good memory."

"I have for everything concerning those I love. I observed her manner of meeting my brother, his devotion to her, and, when they stood laughing together before the fire, I felt sure that she wished to charm him again."

"Again? Then she did charm him once?" asked Treherne, anxious to know how much Jasper had told his sister.

"He always denied it, and declared that you were the favorite."

"Then why not think the note for me?" he asked.

"I do now" was the sharp answer.

"But she told you it was for the major, and sent it."

"She deceived me; I am not surprised. I am glad Jasper is safe, and I wish you a pleasant tête-à-tête."

Bowing with unwonted dignity, Octavia set down her basket,

and walked away in one direction as Mrs. Snowdon approached in another.

"I have done it now," sighed Treherne, turning from the girlish figure to watch the stately creature who came sweeping toward him with noiseless grace.

Brilliancy and splendor became Mrs. Snowdon; she enjoyed luxury, and her beauty made many things becoming which in a plainer woman would have been out of taste, and absurd. She had wrapped herself in a genuine Eastern burnous of scarlet, blue, and gold; the hood drawn over her head framed her fine face in rich hues, and the great gilt tassels shone against her rippling black hair. She wore it with grace, and the barbaric splendor of the garment became her well. The fresh air touched her cheeks with a delicate color; her usually gloomy eyes were brilliant now, and the smile that parted her lips was full of happiness.

"Welcome, Cleopatra!" cried Treherne, with difficulty repressing a laugh, as the peacocks screamed and fled before the rustling amplitude of her drapery.

"I might reply by calling you Thaddeus of Warsaw, for you look very romantic and Polish with your pale, pensive face, and your splendid furs," she answered, as she paused beside him with admiration very visibly expressed in her eyes.

Treherne disliked the look, and rather abruptly said, as he offered her the basket of bread, "I have disposed of my cousin, and offered to do the honors of the peacocks. Here they are—will you feed them?"

"No, thank you—I care nothing for the fowls, as you know; I came to speak to you," she said impatiently.

"I am at your service."

"I wish to ask you a question or two—is it permitted?"

"What man ever refused Mrs. Snowdon a request?"

"Nay, no compliments; from you they are only satirical evasions. I was deceived when abroad, and rashly married that old man. Tell me truly how things stand."

"Jasper has all. I have nothing."

"I am glad of it."

"Many thanks for the hearty speech. You at least speak sincerely," he said bitterly.

"I do, Maurice—I do; let me prove it."

Treherne's chair was close beside the balustrade. Mrs. Snowdon leaned on the carved railing, with her back to the house and her face screened by a tall urn. Looking steadily at him, she said rapidly and low, "You thought I wavered between you and Jasper, when we parted two years ago. I did; but it was not between title and fortune that I hesitated. It was between duty and love. My father, a fond, foolish old man, had set his heart on seeing me a lady. I was his all; my beauty was his delight, and no untitled man was deemed worthy of me. I loved him tenderly. You may doubt this, knowing how selfish, reckless, and vain I am, but I have a heart, and with better training had been a better woman. No matter, it is too late now. Next my father, I loved you. Nay, hear me—I *will* clear myself in your eyes. I mean no wrong to the general. He is kind, indulgent, generous; I respect him—I am grateful, and while he lives, I shall be true to him."

"Then be silent now. Do not recall the past, Edith; let it sleep, for both our sakes," began Treherne; but she checked him imperiously.

"It shall, when I am done. I loved you, Maurice; for, of all the gay, idle, pleasure-seeking men I saw about me, you were the only one who seemed to have a thought beyond the folly of the hour. Under the seeming frivolity of your life lay something noble, heroic, and true. I felt that you had a purpose, that your present mood was but transitory—a young man's holiday, before the real work of his life began. This attracted, this won me; for even in the brief regard you then gave me, there was an earnestness no other man had shown. I wanted your respect; I longed to earn your love, to share your life, and prove that even in my neglected nature slept the power of canceling a frivolous past by a noble future. Oh, Maurice, had you lingered one week more, I never should have been the miserable thing I am!"

There her voice faltered and failed, for all the bitterness of lost love, peace, and happiness sounded in the pathetic passion of that exclamation. She did not weep, for tears seldom dimmed those tragical eyes of hers; but she wrung her hands in mute despair, and looked down into the frost-blighted gardens below, as if she saw there a true symbol of her own ruined life. Treherne uttered not a word, but set his teeth with an almost fierce glance toward the distant figure of Sir Jasper, who was riding gaily away, like one unburdened by a memory or a care.

Hurriedly Mrs. Snowdon went on, "My father begged and commanded me to choose your cousin. I could not break his heart, and asked for time, hoping to soften him. While I waited, that mysterious affair hurried you from Paris, and then came the wreck, the illness, and the rumor that old Sir Jasper had disinherited both nephews. They told me you were dying, and I became a passive instrument in my father's hands. I promised to recall and accept your cousin, but the old man died before it was done, and then I cared not what became of me.

"General Snowdon was my father's friend; he pitied me; he saw my desolate, destitute state, my despair and helplessness. He comforted, sustained, and saved me. I was grateful; and when he offered me his heart and home, I accepted them. He knew I had no love to give; but as a friend, a daughter, I would gladly serve him, and make his declining years as happy as I could. It was all over, when I heard that you were alive, afflicted, and poor. I longed to come and live for you. My new bonds became heavy fetters then, my wealth oppressed me, and I was doubly wretched—for I dared not tell my trouble, and it nearly drove me mad. I have seen you now; I know that you are happy; I read your cousin's love and see a peaceful life in store for you. This must content me, and I must learn to bear it as I can."

She paused, breathless and pale, and walked rapidly along the terrace, as if to hide or control the agitation that possessed her.

Treherne still sat silent, but his heart leaped within him, as he thought, "She sees that Octavia loves me! A woman's eye is quick to detect love in another, and she asserts what I begin to hope. My cousin's manner just now, her dislike of Annon, her new shyness with me; it may be true, and if it is— Heaven help me—what am I saying! I must not hope, nor wish, nor dream; I must renounce and forget."

He leaned his head upon his hand, and sat so till Mrs. Snowdon rejoined him, pale, but calm and self-possessed. As she drew near, she marked his attitude, the bitter sadness of his face, and hope sprang up within her. Perhaps she was mistaken; perhaps he did not love his cousin; perhaps he still remembered the past, and still regretted the loss of the heart she had just laid bare before him. Her husband was failing, and might die any day. And then, free, rich, beautiful, and young, what might she not become to Treherne, helpless, poor, and ambitious? With all her faults, she was generous, and this picture charmed her fancy, warmed her heart, and comforted her pain.

"Maurice," she said softly, pausing again beside him, "If I mistake you and your hopes, it is because I dare ask nothing for myself;

but if ever a time shall come when I have liberty to give or help, ask of me *anything,* and it is gladly yours."

He understood her, pitied her, and, seeing that she found consolation in a distant hope, he let her enjoy it while she might. Gravely, yet gratefully, he spoke, and pressed the hand extended to him with an impulsive gesture.

"Generous as ever, Edith, and impetuously frank. Thank you for your sincerity, your kindness, and the affection you once gave me. I say 'once,' for now duty, truth, and honor bar us from each other. My life must be solitary, yet I shall find work to do, and learn to be content. You owe all devotion to the good old man who loves you, and will not fail him, I am sure. Leave the future and the past, but let us make the present what it may be—a time to forgive and forget, to take heart and begin anew. Christmas is a fitting time for such resolves, and the birth of friendship such as ours may be."

Something in his tone and manner struck her, and, eyeing him with soft wonder, she exclaimed, "How changed you are!"

"Need you tell me that?" And he glanced at his helpless limbs with a bitter yet pathetic look of patience.

"No, no—not so! I mean in mind, not body. Once you were gay and careless, eager and fiery, like Jasper; now you are grave and quiet, or cheerful, and so very kind. Yet, in spite of illness and loss, you seem twice the man you were, and something wins respect, as well as admiration—and love."

Her dark eyes filled as the last word left her lips, and the beauty of a touched heart shone in her face. Maurice looked up quickly, asking with sudden earnestness, "Do you see it? Then it is true. Yes, I *am* changed, thank God! And she has done it."

"Who?" demanded his companion jealously.

"Octavia. Unconsciously, yet surely, she has done much for me, and this year of seeming loss and misery has been the happiest, most profitable of my life. I have often heard that afflictions were the best teachers, and I believe it now."

Mrs. Snowdon shook her head sadly.

"Not always; they are tormentors to some. But don't preach, Maurice. I am still a sinner, though you incline to sainthood, and I have one question more to ask. What was it that took you and Jasper so suddenly away from Paris?"

"That I can never tell you."

"I shall discover it for myself, then."

"It is impossible."

"Nothing is impossible to a determined woman."

"You can neither wring, surprise, nor bribe this secret from the two persons who hold it. I beg of you to let it rest," said Treherne earnestly.

"I have a clue, and I shall follow it; for I am convinced that something is wrong, and you are—"

"Dear Mrs. Snowdon, are you so charmed with the birds that you forget your fellow-beings, or so charmed with one fellow-being that you forget the birds?"

As the sudden question startled both, Rose Talbot came along the terrace, with hands full of holly and a face full of merry mischief, adding as she vanished, "I shall tell Tavie that feeding the peacocks is such congenial amusement for lovers, she and Mr. Annon had better try it."

"Saucy gypsy!" muttered Treherne.

But Mrs. Snowdon said, with a smile of double meaning, "Many a true word is spoken in jest."

≥ *chapter V* ≤

UNDER THE
MISTLETOE

UNUSUALLY gay and charming the three young friends looked, dressed alike in fleecy white with holly wreaths in their hair, as they slowly descended the wide oaken stairway arm in arm. A footman was lighting the hall lamps, for the winter dusk gathered early, and the girls were merrily chatting about the evening's festivity when suddenly a loud, long shriek echoed through the hall. A heavy glass shade fell from the man's hand with a crash, and the young ladies clung to one another aghast, for mortal terror was in the cry, and a dead silence followed it.

"What was it, John?" demanded Octavia, very pale, but steady in a moment.

"I'll go and see, miss." And the man hurried away.

"Where did the dreadful scream come from?" asked Rose, collecting her wits as rapidly as possible.

"Above us somewhere. Oh, let us go down among people; I am frightened to death," whispered Blanche, trembling and faint.

Hurrying into the parlor, they found only Annon and the major, both looking startled, and both staring out of the windows.

"Did you hear it? What could it be? Don't go and leave us!" cried the girls in a breath, as they rushed in.

The gentlemen had heard, couldn't explain the cry, and were

quite ready to protect the pretty creatures who clustered about them like frightened fawns. John speedily appeared, looking rather wild, and as eager to tell his tale as they to listen.

"It's Patty, one of the maids, miss, in a fit. She went up to the north gallery to see that the fires was right, for it takes a power of wood to warm the gallery even enough for dancing, as you know, miss. Well, it was dark, for the fires was low and her candle went out as she whisked open the door, being flurried, as the maids always is when they go in there. Halfway down the gallery she says she heard a rustling, and stopped. She's the pluckiest of 'em all, and she called out, 'I see you!' thinking it was some of us trying to fright her. Nothing answered, and she went on a bit, when suddenly the fire flared up one flash, and there right before her was the ghost."

"Don't be foolish, John. Tell us what it was," said Octavia sharply, though her face whitened and her heart sank as the last word passed the man's lips.

"It was a tall, black figger, miss, with a dead-white face and a black hood. She see it plain, and turned to go away, but she hadn't gone a dozen steps when there it was again before her, the same tall, dark thing with the dead-white face looking out from the black hood. It lifted its arm as if to hold her, but she gave a spring and dreadful screech, and ran to Mrs. Benson's room, where she dropped in a fit."

"How absurd to be frightened by the shadows of the figures in armor that stand along the gallery!" said Rose, boldly enough, though she would have declined entering the gallery without a light.

"Nay, I don't wonder, it's a ghostly place at night. How is the poor thing?" asked Blanche, still hanging on the major's arm in her best attitude.

"If Mamma knows nothing of it, tell Mrs. Benson to keep it from her, please. She is not well, and such things annoy her very much," said Octavia, adding as the man turned away, "Did anyone look in the gallery after Patty told her tale?"

"No, miss. I'll go and do it myself; I'm not afraid of man, ghost, or devil, saving your presence, ladies," replied John.

"Where is Sir Jasper?" suddenly asked the major.

"Here I am. What a deuce of a noise someone has been making. It disturbed a capital dream. Why, Tavie, what is it?" And Sir Jasper came out of the library with a sleepy face and tumbled hair.

They told him the story, whereat he laughed heartily, and said the maids were a foolish set to be scared by a shadow. While he still laughed and joked, Mrs. Snowdon entered, looking alarmed, and anxious to know the cause of the confusion.

"How interesting! I never knew you kept a ghost. Tell me all about it, Sir Jasper, and soothe our nerves by satisfying our curiosity," she said in her half-persuasive, half-commanding way, as she seated herself on Lady Treherne's sacred sofa.

"There's not much to tell, except that this place used to be an abbey, in fact as well as in name. An ancestor founded it, and for years the monks led a jolly life here, as one may see, for the cellar is twice as large as the chapel, and much better preserved. But another ancestor, a gay and gallant baron, took a fancy to the site for his castle, and, in spite of prayers, anathemas, and excommunication, he turned the poor fellows out, pulled down the abbey, and built this fine old place. Abbot Boniface, as he left his abbey, uttered a heavy curse on all who should live here, and vowed to haunt us till the last Treherne vanished from the face of the earth. With this amiable threat the old party left Baron Roland to his doom, and died as soon as he could in order to begin his cheerful mission."

"Did he haunt the place?" asked Blanche eagerly.

"Yes, most faithfully from that time to this. Some say many of the monks still glide about the older parts of the abbey, for Roland spared the chapel and the north gallery which joined it to the modern building. Poor fellows, they are welcome, and once a year they shall have a chance to warm their ghostly selves by the great fires always kindled at Christmas in the gallery."

"Mrs. Benson once told me that when the ghost walked, it was a sure sign of a coming death in the family. Is that true?" asked Rose, whose curiosity was excited by the expression of Octavia's face, and a certain uneasiness in Sir Jasper's manner in spite of his merry mood.

"There is a stupid superstition of that sort in the family, but no one except the servants believes it, of course. In times of illness some silly maid or croaking old woman can easily fancy they see a phantom, and, if death comes, they are sure of the ghostly warning. Benson saw it before my father died, and old Roger, the night my uncle was seized with apoplexy. Patty will never be made to believe that this warning does not forebode the death of Maurice or myself, for the gallant spirit leaves the ladies of our house to depart in peace. How does it strike you, Cousin?"

Turning as he spoke, Sir Jasper glanced at Treherne, who had entered while he spoke.

"I am quite skeptical and indifferent to the whole affair, but I agree with Octavia that it is best to say nothing to my aunt if she is ignorant of the matter. Her rooms are a long way off, and perhaps she did not hear the confusion."

"You seem to hear everything; you were not with us when I said that." And Octavia looked up with an air of surprise.

Smiling significantly, Treherne answered, "I hear, see, and understand many things that escape others. Jasper, allow me to advise you to smooth the hair which your sleep has disarranged. Mrs. Snowdon, permit me. This rich velvet catches the least speck." And with his handkerchief he delicately brushed away several streaks of white dust which clung to the lady's skirt.

Sir Jasper turned hastily on his heel and went to remake his toilet; Mrs. Snowdon bit her lip, but thanked Treherne sweetly and begged him to fasten her glove. As he did so, she said softly, "Be more careful next time. Octavia has keen eyes, and the major may prove inconvenient."

"I have no fear that *you* will," he whispered back, with a malicious glance.

Here the entrance of my lady put an end to the ghostly episode, for it was evident that she knew nothing of it. Octavia slipped away to question John, and learn that no sign of a phantom was to be seen. Treherne devoted himself to Mrs. Snowdon, and the major entertained my lady, while Sir Jasper and the girls chatted apart.

It was Christmas Eve, and a dance in the great gallery was the yearly festival at the abbey. All had been eager for it, but the maid's story seemed to have lessened their enthusiasm, though no one would own it. This annoyed Sir Jasper, and he exerted himself to clear the atmosphere by affecting gaiety he did not feel. The moment the gentlemen came in after dinner he whispered to his mother, who rose, asked the general for his arm, and led the way to the north gallery, whence the sound of music now proceeded. The rest followed in a merry procession, even Treherne, for two footmen carried him up the great stairway, chair and all.

Nothing could look less ghostly now than the haunted gallery. Fires roared up a wide chimney at either end, long rows of figures clad in armor stood on each side, one mailed hand grasping a lance, the other bearing a lighted candle, a device of Sir Jasper's. Narrow windows pierced in the thick walls let in gleams of wintry moonlight; ivy, holly, and evergreen glistened in the ruddy glow of mingled fire-light and candle shine. From the arched stone roof hung tattered banners, and in the midst depended a great bunch of mistletoe. Red-cushioned seats stood in recessed window nooks, and from behind a high-covered screen of oak sounded the blithe air of Sir Roger de Coverley.

With the utmost gravity and stateliness my lady and the general led off the dance, for, according to the good old fashion, the men and maids in their best array joined the gentlefolk and danced with their betters in a high state of pride and bashfulness. Sir Jasper twirled the old housekeeper till her head spun around and around and her deco-rous skirts rustled stormily; Mrs. Snowdon captivated the gray-haired butler by her condescension; and John was made a proud man by the hand of his young mistress. The major came out strong among the pretty maids, and Rose danced the footmen out of breath long before the music paused.

The merriment increased from that moment, and when the general surprised my lady by gallantly saluting her as she uncon-sciously stood under the mistletoe, the applause was immense. Every-one followed the old gentleman's example as fast as opportunities occurred, and the young ladies soon had as fine a color as the house-maids. More dancing, games, songs, and all manner of festival devices filled the evening, yet under cover of the gaiety more than one little scene was enacted that night, and in an hour of seeming frivolity the current of several lives was changed.

By a skillful maneuver Annon led Octavia to an isolated recess, as if to rest after a brisk game, and, taking advantage of the auspicious hour, pleaded his suit. She heard him patiently and, when he paused, said slowly, yet decidedly, and with no sign of maiden hesitation, "Thanks for the honor you do me, but I cannot accept it, for I do not love you. I think I never can."

"Have you tried?" he asked eagerly.

"Yes, indeed I have. I like you as a friend, but no more. I know Mamma desires it, that Jasper hopes for it, and I try to please them, but love will not be forced, so what can I do?" And she smiled in spite of herself at her own blunt simplicity.

"No, but it can be cherished, strengthened, and in time won, with patience and devotion. Let me try, Octavia; it is but fair, unless you have already learned from another the lesson I hope to teach. Is it so?"

"No, I think not. I do not understand myself as yet, I am so young, and this so sudden. Give me time, Frank."

She blushed and fluttered now, looked half angry, half beseeching, and altogether lovely.

"How much time shall I give? It cannot take long to read a heart like yours, dear." And fancying her emotion a propitious omen, he assumed the lover in good earnest.

"Give me time till the New Year. I will answer then, and, meantime, leave me free to study both myself and you. We have known each other long, I own, but, still, this changes everything, and makes you seem another person. Be patient, Frank, and I will try to make my duty a pleasure."

"I will. God bless you for the kind hope, Octavia. It has been mine for years, and if I lose it, it will go hardly with me."

Later in the evening General Snowdon stood examining the antique screen. In many places carved oak was pierced quite through, so that voices were audible from behind it. The musicians had gone down to supper, the young folk were quietly busy at the other end of the hall, and as the old gentleman admired the quaint carving, the sound of his own name caught his ear. The housekeeper and butler still remained, though the other servants had gone, and sitting cosily behind the screen chatted in low tones believing themselves secure.

"It *was* Mrs. Snowdon, Adam, as I'm a living woman, though I wouldn't say it to anyone but you. She and Sir Jasper were here wrapped in cloaks, and up to mischief, I'll be bound. She is a beauty, but I don't envy her, and there'll be trouble in the house if she stays long."

"But how do you know, Mrs. Benson, she was here? Where's your proof, mum?" asked the pompous butler.

"Look at this, and then look at the outlandish trimming of the lady's dress. You men are so dull about such matters you'd never observe these little points. Well, I was here first after Patty, and my light shone on this jet ornament lying near where she saw the spirit. No one has any such tasty trifles but Mrs. Snowdon, and these are all over her gown. If that ain't proof, what is?"

"Well, admitting it, I then say what on earth should she and master be up here for, at such a time?" asked the slow-witted butler.

"Adam, we are old servants of the family, and to you I'll say what tortures shouldn't draw from to another. Master has been wild, as you know, and it's my belief that he loved this lady abroad. There was a talk of some mystery, or misdeed, or misfortune, more than a year ago, and she was in it. I'm loath to say it, but I think Master loves her still, and she him. The general is an old man, she is but young, and so spirited and winsome she can't in reason care for him as for a fine, gallant gentleman like Sir Jasper. There's trouble brewing, Adam, mark my words. There's trouble brewing for the Trehernes."

So low had the voices fallen that the listener could not have caught the words had not his ear been strained to the utmost. He did hear all, and his wasted face flashed with the wrath of a young man, then grew pale and stern as he turned to watch his wife. She stood apart from the others talking to Sir Jasper, who looked unusually handsome and debonair as he fanned her with a devoted air.

Perhaps it is true, thought the old man bitterly. They are well matched, were lovers once, no doubt, and long to be so again. Poor Edith, I was very blind. And with his gray head bowed upon his breast the general stole away, carrying an arrow in his brave old heart.

"Blanche, come here and rest, you will be ill tomorrow; and I promised Mamma to take care of you." With which elder-sisterly command Rose led the girl to an immense old chair, which held them both. "Now listen to me and follow my advice, for I am wise in my generation, though not yet gray. They are all busy, so leave them alone and let me show you what is to be done."

Rose spoke softly, but with great resolution, and nodded her pretty head so energetically that the holly berries came rolling over her white shoulders.

"We are not as rich as we might be, and must establish ourselves as soon and as well as possible. I intend to be Lady Treherne. You can be the Honorable Mrs. Annon, if you give your mind to it."

"My dear child, are you mad?" whispered Blanche.

"Far from it, but you will be if you waste your time on Maurice. He is poor, and a cripple, though very charming, I admit. He loves Tavie, and she will marry him, I am sure. She can't endure Frank, but tries to because my lady commands it. Nothing will come of it, so try your fascinations and comfort the poor man; sympathy now will foster love hereafter."

"Don't talk so here, Rose, someone will hear us," began her sister, but the other broke in briskly.

"No fear, a crowd is the best place for secrets. Now remember what I say, and make your game while the ball is rolling. Other people are careful not to put their plans into words, but I'm no hypocrite, and say plainly what I mean. Bear my sage counsel in mind and act wisely. Now come and begin."

Treherne was sitting alone by one of the great fires, regarding the gay scene with serious air. For him there was neither dancing nor games; he could only roam about catching glimpses of forbidden pleasures, impossible delights, and youthful hopes forever lost to him. Sad but not morose was his face, and to Octavia it was a mute reproach which she could not long resist. Coming up as if to warm herself, she spoke to him in her usually frank and friendly way, and felt her heart beat fast when she saw how swift a change her cordial manner wrought in him.

"How pretty your holly is! Do you remember how we used to go and gather it for festivals like this, when we were happy children?" he asked, looking up at her with eyes full of tender admiration.

"Yes, I remember. Everyone wears it tonight as a badge, but you have none. Let me get you a bit, I like to have you one of us in all things."

She leaned forward to break a green sprig from the branch over the chimneypiece; the strong draft drew in her fleecy skirt, and in an instant she was enveloped in flames.

"Maurice, save me, help me!" cried a voice of fear and agony, and before anyone could reach her, before he himself knew how the deed was done, Treherne had thrown himself from his chair, wrapped the tiger skin tightly about her, and knelt there clasping her in his arms heedless of fire, pain, or the incoherent expressions of love that broke from his lips.

≈ *chapter VI* ≈

MIRACLES

G REAT was the confusion and alarm which reigned for many
minutes, but when the panic subsided two miracles appeared
Octavia was entirely uninjured, and Treherne was standing
on his feet, a thing which for months he had not done without
crutches. In the excitement of the moment, no one observed the wonder; all were crowding about the girl, who, pale and breathless but now
self-possessed, was the first to exclaim, pointing to her cousin, who
had drawn himself up, with the help of his chair, and leaned there
smiling, with a face full of intense delight.

"Look at Maurice! Oh, Jasper, help him or he'll fall!"

Sir Jasper sprung to his side and put a strong arm about him,
while a chorus of wonder, sympathy, and congratulations rose about
them.

"Why, lad, what does it mean? Have you been deceiving us all
this time?" cried Jasper, as Treherne leaned on him, looking exhausted but truly happy.

"It means that I am not to be a cripple all my life; that they did
not deceive me when they said a sudden shock might electrify me
with a more potent magnetism than any they could apply. It *has*, and
if I am cured I owe it all to you, Octavia."

He stretched his hands to her with a gesture of such passionate
gratitude that the girl covered her face to hide its traitorous tenderness, and my lady went to him, saying brokenly, as she embraced him

with maternal warmth, "God bless you for this act, Maurice, and reward you with a perfect cure. To you I owe the lives of both my children; how can I thank you as I ought?"

"I dare not tell you yet," he whispered eagerly, then added, "I am growing faint, Aunt. Get me away before I make a scene."

This hint recalled my lady to her usual state of dignified self-possession. Bidding Jasper and the major help Treherne to his room without delay, she begged Rose to comfort her sister, who was sobbing hysterically, and as they all obeyed her, she led her daughter away to her own apartment, for the festivities of the evening were at an end.

At the same time Mrs. Snowdon and Annon bade my lady good-night, as if they also were about to retire, but as they reached the door of the gallery Mrs. Snowdon paused and beckoned Annon back. They were alone now, and, standing before the fire which had so nearly made that Christmas Eve a tragical one, she turned to him with a face full of interest and sympathy as she said, nodding toward the blackened shreds of Octavia's dress, and the scorched tiger skin which still lay at their feet, "That was both a fortunate and an unfortunate little affair, but I fear Maurice's gain will be your loss. Pardon my frankness for Octavia's sake; she is a fine creature, and I long to see her given to one worthy of her. I am a woman to read faces quickly; I know that your suit does not prosper as you would have it, and I desire to help you. May I?"

"Indeed you may, and command any service of me in return. But to what do I owe this unexpected friendliness?" cried Annon, both grateful and surprised.

"To my regard for the young lady, my wish to save her from an unworthy man."

"Do you mean Treherne?" asked Annon, more and more amazed.

"I do. Octavia must not marry a gambler!"

"My dear lady, you labor under some mistake; Treherne is by no means a gambler. I owe him no goodwill, but I cannot hear him slandered."

"You are generous, but I am not mistaken. Can you, on your honor, assure me that Maurice never played?"

Mrs. Snowdon's keen eyes were on him, and he looked embarrassed for a moment, but answered with some hesitation, "Why, no, I cannot say that, but I can assure you that he is not an habitual gambler. All young men of his rank play more or less, especially abroad. It is merely an amusement with most, and among men is not considered dishonorable or dangerous. Ladies think differently, I believe, at least in England."

At the word "abroad," Mrs. Snowdon's face brightened, and she suddenly dropped her eyes, as if afraid of betraying some secret purpose.

"Indeed we do, and well we may, many of us having suffered from this pernicious habit. I have had special cause to dread and condemn it, and the fear that Octavia should in time suffer what I have suffered as a girl urges me to interfere where otherwise I should be dumb. Mr. Annon, there was a rumor that Maurice was forced to quit Paris, owing to some dishonorable practices at the gaming table. Is this true?"

"Nay, don't ask me; upon my soul I cannot tell you. I only know that something was amiss, but what I never learned. Various tales were whispered at the clubs, and Sir Jasper indignantly denied them all. The bravery with which Maurice saved his cousin, and the sad affliction which fell upon him, silenced the gossip, and it was soon forgotten."

Mrs. Snowdon remained silent for a moment, with brows knit in deep thought, while Annon uneasily watched her. Suddenly she glanced over her shoulder, drew nearer, and whispered cautiously, "Did the rumors of which you speak charge him with—" and the last word was breathed into Annon's ear almost inaudibly.

He started, as if some new light broke on him, and stared at the speaker with a troubled face for an instant, saying hastily, "No, but now you remind me that when an affair of that sort was discussed the other day Treherne looked very odd, and rolled himself away, as if it didn't interest him. I can't believe it, and yet it may be something of the kind. That would account for old Sir Jasper's whim, and Treherne's steady denial of any knowledge of the cause. How in heaven's name did you learn this?"

"My woman's wit suggested it, and my woman's will shall confirm or destroy the suspicion. My lady and Octavia evidently know nothing, but they shall if there is any danger of the girl's being won by him."

"You would not tell her!" exclaimed Annon.

"I will, unless you do it" was the firm answer.

"Never! To betray a friend, even to gain the woman I love, is a thing I cannot do; my honor forbids it."

Mrs. Snowdon smiled scornfully.

"Men's code of honor is a strong one, and we poor women suffer from it. Leave this to me; do your best, and if all other means fail, you may be glad to try my device to prevent Maurice from marrying his cousin. Gratitude and pity are strong allies, and if he recovers, his strong will will move heaven and earth to gain her. Good night." And leaving her last words to rankle in Annon's mind, Mrs. Snowdon departed to endure sleepless hours full of tormenting memories, newborn hopes, and alternations of determination and despair.

Treherne's prospect of recovery filled the whole house with delight, for his patient courage and unfailing cheerfulness had endeared him to all. It was no transient amendment, for day by day he steadily gained strength and power, passing rapidly from chair to crutches, from crutches to a cane and a friend's arm, which was always ready for him. Pain returned with returning vitality, but he bore it with a fortitude that touched all who witnessed it. At times motion was torture, yet motion was necessary lest the torpidity should return, and Treherne took his daily exercise with unfailing perseverance, saying with a smile, though great drops stood upon his forehead, "I have something dearer even than health to win. Hold me up, Jasper, and let me stagger on, in spite of everything, till my twelve turns are made."

He remembered Lady Treherne's words, "If you were well, I'd gladly give my girl to you." This inspired him with strength, endurance, and a happiness which could not be concealed. It overflowed in looks, words, and acts; it infected everyone, and made these holidays the blithest the old abbey had seen for many a day.

Annon devoted himself to Octavia, and in spite of her command to be left in peace till the New Year, she was very kind—so kind that hope flamed up in his heart, though he saw that something like compassion often shone on him from her frank eyes, and her compliance had no touch of the tender docility which lovers long to see. She still avoided Treherne, but so skillfully that few observed the change but Annon and himself. In public Sir Jasper appeared to worship at the sprightly Rose's shrine, and she fancied her game was prospering well.

But had any one peeped behind the scenes it would have been

discovered that during the half hour before dinner, when everyone was in their dressing rooms and the general taking his nap, a pair of ghostly black figures flitted about the haunted gallery, where no servant ventured without orders. The major fancied himself the only one who had made this discovery, for Mrs. Snowdon affected Treherne's society in public, and was assiduous in serving and amusing the "dear convalescent," as she called him. But the general did not sleep; he too watched and waited, longing yet dreading to speak, and hoping that this was but a harmless freak of Edith's, for her caprices were many, and till now he had indulged them freely. This hesitation disgusted the major, who, being a bachelor, knew little of women's ways, and less of their powers of persuasion. The day before New Year he took a sudden resolution, and demanded a private interview with the general.

"I have come on an unpleasant errand, sir," he abruptly began, as the old man received him with an expression which rather daunted the major. "My friendship for Lady Treherne, and my guardianship of her children, makes me jealous of the honor of the family. I fear it is in danger, sir; pardon me for saying it, but your wife is the cause."

"May I trouble you to explain, Major Royston" was all the general's reply, as his old face grew stern and haughty.

"I will, sir, briefly. I happen to know from Jasper that there were love passages between Miss Dubarry and himself a year or more ago in Paris. A whim parted them, and she married. So far no reproach rests upon either, but since she came here it has been evident to others as well as myself that Jasper's affection has revived, and that Mrs. Snowdon does not reject and reprove it as she should. They often meet, and from Jasper's manner I am convinced that mischief is afloat. He is ardent, headstrong, and utterly regardless of the world's opinion in some cases. I have watched them, and what I tell you is true."

"Prove it."

"I will. They meet in the north gallery, wrapped in dark cloaks, and play ghost if anyone comes. I concealed myself behind the screen last evening at dusk, and satisfied myself that my suspicions were correct. I heard little of their conversation, but that little was enough."

"Repeat it, if you please."

"Sir Jasper seemed pleading for some promise which she reluctantly gave, saying, 'While you live I will be true to my word with everyone but him. He will suspect, and it will be useless to keep it from him.'

" 'He will shoot me for this if he knows I am the traitor,' expostulated Jasper.

" 'He shall not know that; I can hoodwink him easily, and serve my purpose also.'

" 'You are mysterious, but I leave all to you and wait for my reward. When shall I have it, Edith?' She laughed, and answered so low I could not hear, for they left the gallery as they spoke. Forgive me, General, for the pain I inflict. You are the only person to whom I have spoken, and you are the only person who can properly and promptly prevent this affair from bringing open shame and scandal on an honorable house. To you I leave it, and will do my part with this infatuated young man if you will withdraw the temptation which will ruin him."

"I will. Thank you, Major. Trust to me, and by tomorrow I will prove that I can act as becomes me."

The grief and misery in the general's face touched the major; he silently wrung his hand and went away, thanking heaven more fervently than ever that no cursed coquette of a woman had it in her power to break his heart.

While this scene was going on above, another was taking place in the library. Treherne sat there alone, thinking happy thoughts evidently, for his eyes shone and his lips smiled as he mused, while watching the splendors of a winter sunset. A soft rustle and the faint scent of violets warned him of Mrs. Snowdon's approach, and a sudden foreboding told him that danger was near. The instant he saw her face his fear was confirmed, for exultation, resolve, and love met and mingled in the expression it wore. Leaning in the window recess, where the red light shone full on her lovely face and queenly figure, she said, softly yet with a ruthless accent below the softness, "Dreaming dreams, Maurice, which will never come to pass, unless I will it. I know your secret, and I shall use it to prevent the fulfillment of the foolish hope you cherish."

"Who told you?" he demanded, with an almost fierce flash of the eye and an angry flush.

"I discovered it, as I warned you I should. My memory is good, I recall the gossip of long ago, I observe the faces, words, and acts of those whom I suspect, and unconscious hints from them give me the truth."

"I doubt it," and Treherne smiled securely.

She stooped and whispered one short sentence into his ear. Whatever it was it caused him to start up with a pale, panic-stricken face, and eye her as if she had pronounced his doom.

"Do you doubt it now?" she asked coldly.

"He told you! Even your skill and craft could not discover it alone," he muttered.

"Nay, I told you nothing was impossible to a determined woman. I needed no help, for I knew more than you think."

He sank down again in a despairing attitude and hid his face, saying mournfully, "I might have known you would hunt me down and dash my hopes when they were surest. How will you use this unhappy secret?"

"I will tell Octavia, and make her duty less hard. It will be kind to both of you, for even with her this memory would mar your happiness; and it saves her from the shame and grief of discovering, when too late, that she has given herself to a———"

"Stop!" he cried, in a tone that made her start and pale, as he rose out of his chair white with a stern indignation which awed her for a moment. "You shall not utter that word—you know but half the truth, and if you wrong me or trouble the girl I will turn traitor also, and tell the general the game you are playing with my cousin. You feign to love me as you feigned before, but his title is the bait now as then, and you fancy that by threatening to mar my hopes you will secure my silence, and gain your end."

"Wrong, quite wrong. Jasper is nothing to me; I use *him* as a tool, not you. If I threaten, it is to keep you from Octavia, who cannot forgive the past and love you for yourself, as I have done all these miserable months. You say I know but half the truth. Tell me the whole and I will spare you."

If ever a man was tempted to betray a trust it was Treherne then. A word, and Octavia might be his; silence, and she might be lost; for this woman was in earnest, and possessed the power to ruin his good name forever. The truth leaped to his lips and would have passed them, had not his eye fallen on the portrait of Jasper's father. This man had loved and sheltered the orphan all his life, had made of him a son, and, dying, urged him to guard and serve and save the rebellious youth he left, when most needing a father's care.

"I promised, and I will keep my promise at all costs," sighed Treherne, and with a gesture full of pathetic patience he waved the fair tempter from him, saying steadily, "I will never tell you, though you rob me of that which is dearer than my life. Go and work your will, but remember that when you might have won the deepest gratitude of the man you profess to love, you chose instead to earn his hatred and contempt."

Waiting for no word of hers, he took refuge in his room, and Edith Snowdon sank down upon the couch, struggling with contending emotions of love and jealousy, remorse and despair. How long she sat there she could not tell; an approaching step recalled her to herself, and looking up she saw Octavia. As the girl approached down the long vista of the drawing rooms, her youth and beauty, innocence and candor touched that fairer and more gifted woman with an envy she had never known before. Something in the girl's face struck her instantly: a look of peace and purity, a sweet serenity more winning than loveliness, more impressive than dignity or grace. With a smile on her lips, yet a half-sad, half-tender light in her eyes, and a cluster of pale winter roses in her hand, she came on till she stood before her rival and, offering the flowers, said, in words as simple as sincere, "Dear Mrs. Snowdon, I cannot let the last sun of the old year set on any misdeeds of mine for which I may atone. I have disliked, distrusted, and misjudged you, and now I come to you in all humility to say forgive me."

With the girlish abandon of her impulsive nature Octavia knelt down before the woman who was plotting to destroy her happiness, laid the roses like a little peace offering on her lap, and with eloquently pleading eyes waited for pardon. For a moment Mrs. Snowdon watched her, fancying it a well-acted ruse to disarm a dangerous rival; but in that sweet face there was no art; one glance showed her that. The words smote her to the heart and won her in spite of pride or passion, as she suddenly took the girl into her arms, weeping repentant tears. Neither spoke, but in the silence each felt the barrier which had stood between them vanishing, and each learned to know the other better in that moment than in a year of common life. Octavia rejoiced that the instinct which had prompted her to make this appeal had not misled her, but assured her that behind the veil of coldness, pride, and levity which this woman wore there was a heart aching for sympathy and help and love. Mrs. Snowdon felt her worser self slip from her, leaving all that was true and noble to make her worthy of the test applied. Art she could meet with equal art, but nature conquered her. For spite of her misspent life and faulty character, the germ of virtue, which lives in the worst, was there, only waiting for the fostering sun and dew of love to strengthen it, even though the harvest be a late one.

"Forgive you!" she cried, brokenly. "It is I who should ask forgiveness of you—I who should atone, confess, and repent. Pardon *me,* pity me, love me, for I am more wretched than you know."

"Dear, I do with heart and soul. Believe it, and let me be your friend" was the soft answer.

"God knows I need one!" sighed the poor woman, still holding fast the only creature who had wholly won her. "Child, I am not good, but not so bad that I dare not look in your innocent face and call you friend. I never had one of my own sex. I never knew my mother; and no one ever saw in me the possibility of goodness, truth, and justice but you. Trust and love and help me, Octavia, and I will reward you with a better life, if I can do no more."

"I will, and the new year shall be happier than the old."

"God bless you for that prophecy; may I be worthy of it."

Then as a bell warned them away, the rivals kissed each other tenderly, and parted friends. As Mrs. Snowdon entered her room, she saw her husband sitting with his gray head in his hands, and heard him murmur despairingly to himself, "My life makes her miserable. But for the sin of it I'd die to free her."

"No, live for me, and teach me to be happy in your love." The clear voice startled him, but not so much as the beautiful changed face of the wife who laid the gray head on her bosom, saying tenderly, "My kind and patient husband, you have been deceived. From me you shall know all the truth, and when you have forgiven my faulty past, you shall see how happy I will try to make your future."

➢ *chapter VII* ➢

A GHOSTLY REVEL

"BLESS me, how dull we all are tonight!" exclaimed Rose, as the younger portion of the party wandered listlessly about the drawing rooms that evening, while my lady and the major played an absorbing game of piquet, and the general dozed peacefully at last.

"It is because Maurice is not here; he always keeps us going, for he is a fellow of infinite resources," replied Sir Jasper, suppressing a yawn.

"Have him out then," said Annon.

"He won't come. The poor lad is blue tonight, in spite of his improvement. Something is amiss, and there is no getting a word from him."

"Sad memories afflict him, perhaps," sighed Blanche.

"Don't be absurd, dear, sad memories are all nonsense; melancholy is always indigestion, and nothing is so sure a cure as fun," said Rose briskly. "I'm going to send in a polite invitation begging him to come and amuse us. He'll accept, I haven't a doubt."

The message was sent, but to Rose's chagrin a polite refusal was returned.

"He *shall* come. Sir Jasper, do you and Mr. Annon go as a deputation from us, and return without him at your peril" was her command.

They went, and while waiting their reappearance the sisters spoke of what all had observed.

"How lovely Mrs. Snowdon looks tonight. I always thought she owed half her charms to her skill in dress, but she never looked so beautiful as in that plain black silk, with those roses in her hair," said Rose.

"What has she done to herself?" replied Blanche. "I see a change, but can't account for it. She and Tavie have made some beautifying discovery, for both look altogether uplifted and angelic all of a sudden."

"Here come the gentlemen, and, as I'm a Talbot, they haven't got him!" cried Rose as the deputation appeared, looking very crestfallen. "Don't come near me," she added, irefully, "you are disloyal cowards, and I doom you to exile till I want you. *I* am infinite in resources as well as this recreant man, and come he shall. Mrs. Snowdon, would you mind asking Mr. Treherne to suggest something to wile away the rest of this evening? We are in despair, and can think of nothing, and you are all-powerful with him."

"I must decline, since he refuses you" was the decided answer, as Mrs. Snowdon moved away.

"Tavie, dear, do go; we *must* have him; he always obeys you, and you would be such a public benefactor, you know."

Without a word Octavia wrote a line and sent it by a servant. Several minutes passed, and the gentlemen began to lay wagers on the success of her trial. "He will not come for me, you may be sure," said Octavia. As the words passed her lips he appeared.

A general laugh greeted him, but, taking no notice of the jests at his expense, he turned to Octavia, saying quietly, "What can I do for you, Cousin?"

His colorless face and weary eyes reproached her for disturbing him, but it was too late for regret, and she answered hastily, "We are in want of some new and amusing occupation to wile away the evening. Can you suggest something appropriate?"

"Why not sit round the hall fire and tell stories, while we wait to see the old year out, as we used to do long ago?" he asked, after a moment's thought.

"I told you so! There it is, just what we want." And Sir Jasper looked triumphant.

"It's capital—let us begin at once. It is after ten now, so we shall not have long to wait," cried Rose, and, taking Sir Jasper's arm, she led the way to the hall.

A great fire always burned there, and in wintertime thick carpets and curtains covered the stone floor and draped the tall windows. Plants blossomed in the warm atmosphere, and chairs and lounges stood about invitingly. The party was soon seated, and Treherne was desired to begin.

"We must have ghost stories, and in order to be properly thrilling and effective, the lights must be put out," said Rose, who sat next him, and spoke first, as usual.

This was soon done, and only a ruddy circle of firelight was left to oppose the rapt gloom that filled the hall, where shadows now seemed to lurk in every corner.

"Don't be very dreadful, or I shall faint away," pleaded Blanche, drawing nearer to Annon, for she had taken her sister's advice, and laid close siege to that gentleman's heart.

"I think your nerves will bear my little tale," replied Treherne. "When I was in India, four years ago, I had a very dear friend in my regiment—a Scotchman; I'm half Scotch myself, you know, and clannish, of course. Gordon was sent up the country on a scouting expedition, and never returned. His men reported that he left them one evening to take a survey, and his horse came home bloody and riderless. We searched, but could not find a trace of him, and I was desperate to discover and avenge his murder. About a month after his disappearance, as I sat in my tent one fearfully hot day, suddenly the canvas door flap was raised and there stood Gordon. I saw him as plainly as I see you, Jasper, and should have sprung to meet him, but something held me back. He was deathly pale, dripping with water, and in his bonny blue eyes was a wild, woeful look that made my blood run cold. I stared dumbly, for it was awful to see my friend so changed and so unearthly. Stretching his arm to me he took my hand, saying solemnly, 'Come!' The touch was like ice; an ominous thrill ran through me; I started up to obey, and he was gone."

"A horrid dream, of course. Is that all?" asked Rose.

With his eyes on the fire and his left hand half extended, Treherne went on as if he had not heard her.

"I thought it was a fancy, and soon recovered myself, for no one had seen or heard anything of Gordon, and my native servant lay just outside my tent. A strange sensation remained in the hand the phantom touched. It was cold, damp, and white. I found it vain to try to forget this apparition; it took strong hold of me; I told Yermid, my man, and he bade me consider it a sign that I was to seek my friend. That night I dreamed I was riding up the country in hot haste; what led me I know not, but I pressed on and on, longing to reach the end. A half-dried river crossed my path, and, riding down the steep bank to ford it, I saw Gordon's body lying in the shallow water looking exactly as the vision looked. I woke in a strange mood, told the story to my commanding officer, and, as nothing was doing just then, easily got leave of absence for a week. Taking Yermid, I set out on my sad quest. I thought it folly, but I could not resist the impulse that drew me on. For seven days I searched, and the strangest part of the story is that all that time I went on exactly as in the dream, seeing what I saw then, and led by the touch of a cold hand on mine. On the seventh day I reached the river, and found my friend's body."

"How horrible! Is it really true?" cried Mrs. Snowdon.

"As true as I am a living man. Nor is that all: this left hand of mine never has been warm since that time. See and feel for yourselves."

He opened both hands, and all satisfied themselves that the left was smaller, paler, and colder than the right.

"Pray someone tell another story to put this out of my mind; it makes me nervous," said Blanche.

"I'll tell one, and you may laugh to quiet your nerves. I want to have mine done with, so that I can enjoy the rest with a free mind." With these words Rose began her tale in the good old fashion.

"Once upon a time, when we were paying a visit to my blessed grandmamma, I saw a ghost in this wise: The dear old lady was ill with a cold and kept her room, leaving us to mope, for it was very dull in the great lonely house. Blanche and I were both homesick, but didn't like to leave till she was better, so we ransacked the library and solaced ourselves with all manner of queer books. One day I found Grandmamma very low and nervous, and evidently with something on her mind. She would say nothing, but the next day was worse, and I insisted on knowing the cause, for the trouble was evidently mental. Charging me to keep it from Blanche, who was, and is, a sad coward, she told me that a spirit had appeared to her two successive nights. 'If it comes a third time, I shall prepare to die,' said the foolish old lady.

" 'No, you won't, for I'll come and stay with you and lay your ghost,' I said. With some difficulty I made her yield, and after Blanche was asleep I slipped away to Grandmamma, with a book and candle for a long watch, as the spirit didn't appear till after midnight. She usually slept with her door unlocked, in case of fire or fright, and her maid was close by. That night I locked the door, telling her that spirits could come through the oak if they chose, and I preferred to have a fair trial. Well, I read and chatted and dozed till dawn and nothing appeared, so I laughed at the whole affair, and the old lady pretended to be convinced that it was all a fancy.

"Next night I slept in my own room, and in the morning was told that not only Grandmamma but Janet had seen the spirit. All in white, with streaming hair, a pale face, and a red streak at the throat. It came and parted the bed-curtains, looking in a moment, and then vanished. Janet had slept with Grandmamma and kept a lamp burning on the chimney, so both saw it.

"I was puzzled, but not frightened; I never am, and I insisted on trying again. The door was left unlocked, as on the previous night, and I lay with Grandmamma, a light burning as before. About two she clutched me as I was dropping off. I looked, and there, peeping in between the dark curtains, was a pale face with long hair all about it, and a red streak at the throat. It was very dim, the light being low, but I saw it, and after one breathless minute sprang up, caught my foot, fell down with a crash, and by the time I was around the bed, not a vestige of the thing appeared. I was angry, and vowed I'd succeed at all hazards, though I'll confess I was just a bit daunted.

"Next time Janet and I sat up in easy chairs, with bright lights burning, and both wide awake with the strongest coffee we could make. As the hour drew near we got nervous, and when the white shape came gliding in Janet hid her face. I didn't, and after one look was on the point of laughing, for the spirit was Blanche walking in her sleep. She wore a coral necklace in those days, and never took it off, and her long hair half hid her face, which had the unnatural, uncanny look somnambulists always wear. I had the sense to keep still and tell Janet what to do, so the poor child went back unwaked, and Grandmamma's spirit never walked again for I took care of that."

"Why did you haunt the old lady?" asked Annon, as the laughter ceased.

"I don't know, unless it was that I wanted to ask leave to go home, and was afraid to do it awake, so tried when asleep. I shall not tell any story, as I was the heroine of this, but will give my turn to you, Mr. Annon," said Blanche, with a soft glance, which was quite thrown away, for the gentleman's eyes were fixed on Octavia, who sat on a low ottoman at Mrs. Snowdon's feet in the full glow of the firelight.

"I've had very small experience in ghosts, and can only recall a little fright I once had when a boy at college. I'd been out to a party, got home tired, couldn't find my matches, and retired in the dark. Toward morning I woke, and glancing up to see if the dim light was dawn or moonshine I was horrified to see a coffin standing at the bed's foot. I rubbed my eyes to be sure I was awake, and looked with all my might. There it was, a long black coffin, and I saw the white plate in the dusk, for the moon was setting and my curtain was not drawn. 'It's some trick of the fellows,' I thought; 'I'll not betray myself, but keep cool.' Easy to say but hard to do, for it suddenly flashed into my mind that I might be in the wrong room. I glanced about, but there were the familiar objects as usual, as far as the indistinct light allowed me to see, and I made sure by feeling on the wall at the bed's head for my watchcase. It was there, and mine beyond a doubt, being peculiar in shape and fabric. Had I been to a college wine party I could have accounted for the vision, but a quiet evening in a grave professor's well-conducted family could produce no ill effects. 'It's an optical illusion, or a prank of my mates; I'll sleep and forget it,' I said, and for a time endeavored to do so, but curiosity overcame my resolve, and soon I peeped again. Judge of my horror when I saw the sharp white outline of a dead face, which seemed to be peeping up from the coffin. It gave me a terrible shock for I was but a lad and had been ill. I hid my face and quaked like a nervous girl, still thinking it some joke and too proud to betray fear lest I should be laughed at. How long I lay there I don't know, but when I looked again the face was farther out and the whole figure seemed rising slowly. The moon was nearly down, I had no lamp, and to be left in the dark with that awesome thing was more than I could bear. Joke or earnest, I must end the panic, and bolting out of my room I roused my neighbor. He told me I was mad or drunk, but lit a lamp and returned with me, to find my horror only a heap of clothes thrown on the table in such a way that, as the moon's pale light shot it, it struck upon my black student's gown, with a white card lying on it, and produced the effect of a coffin and plate. The face was a crumpled handkerchief, and what seemed hair a brown muffler. As the moon sank, these outlines changed and, incredible as it may seem, grew like a face. My friend not having had the fright enjoyed the joke, and 'Coffins' was my sobriquet for a long while."

"You get worse and worse. Sir Jasper, do vary the horrors by a touch of fun, or I shall run away," said Blanche, glancing over her shoulder nervously.

"I'll do my best, and tell a story my uncle used to relate of his young days. I forget the name of the place, but it was some little country town famous among anglers. My uncle often went to fish, and always regretted that a deserted house near the trout stream was not occupied, for the inn was inconveniently distant. Speaking of this one evening as he lounged in the landlady's parlor, he asked why no one took it and let the rooms to strangers in the fishing season. 'For fear of the ghostissess, your honor,' replied the woman, and proceeded to tell him that three distinct spirits haunted the house. In the garret was heard the hum of a wheel and the tap of high-heeled shoes, as the ghostly spinner went to and fro. In a chamber sounded the sharpening of a knife, followed by groans and the drip of blood. The cellar was made awful by a skeleton sitting on a half-buried box and chuckling fiendishly. It seems a miser lived there once, and was believed to have starved his daughter in the garret, keeping her at work till she died. The second spirit was that of the girl's rejected lover, who cut his throat in the chamber, and the third of the miser who was found dead on the money chest he was too feeble to conceal. My uncle laughed at all this, and offered to lay the ghosts if anyone would take the house.

"This offer got abroad, and a crusty old fellow accepted it, hoping to turn a penny. He had a pretty girl, whose love had been thwarted by the old man, and whose lover was going to sea in despair. My uncle knew this and pitied the young people. He had made acquaintance with a wandering artist, and the two agreed to conquer the prejudices against the house by taking rooms there. They did so, and after satisfying themselves regarding the noises, consulted a wise old woman as to the best means of laying the ghosts. She told them if any young girl would pass a night in each haunted room, praying piously the while, that all would be well. Peggy was asked if she would do it, and being a stouthearted lass she consented, for a round sum, to try it.

The first night was in the garret, and Peggy, in spite of the prophecies of the village gossips, came out alive, though listeners at the door heard the weird humming and tapping all night long. The next night all went well, and from that time no more sharpening, groaning, or dripping was heard. The third time she bade her friends good-bye and, wrapped in her red cloak, with a lamp and prayer book, went down into the cellar. Alas for pretty Peggy! When day came she was gone, and with her the miser's empty box, though his bones remained to prove how well she had done her work.

"The town was in an uproar, and the old man furious. Some said the devil had flown away with her, others that the bones were hers, and all agreed that henceforth another ghost would haunt the house. My uncle and the artist did their best to comfort the father, who sorely reproached himself for thwarting the girl's love, and declared that if Jack would find her he should have her. But Jack had sailed, and the old man 'was left lamenting.' The house was freed from its unearthly visitors, however, for no ghost appeared; and when my uncle left, old Martin found money and letter informing him that Peggy had spent her first two nights preparing for flight, and on the third had gone away to marry and sail with Jack. The noises had been produced by the artist, who was a ventriloquist, the skeleton had been smuggled from the surgeons, and the whole thing was a conspiracy to help Peggy and accommodate the fishermen."

"It is evident that roguery is hereditary," laughed Rose as the narrator paused.

"I strongly suspect that Sir Jasper the second was the true hero of that story," added Mrs. Snowdon.

"Think what you like, I've done my part, and leave the stage for you, madam."

"I will come last. It is your turn, dear."

As Mrs. Snowdon softly uttered the last word, and Octavia leaned upon her knee with an affectionate glance, Treherne leaned forward to catch a glimpse of the two changed faces, and looked as if bewildered when both smiled at him, as they sat hand in hand while the girl told her story.

"Long ago a famous actress suddenly dropped dead at the close of a splendidly played tragedy. She was carried home, and preparations were made to bury her. The play had been gotten up with great care and expense, and a fine actor was the hero. The public demanded a repetition, and an inferior person was engaged to take the dead lady's part. A day's delay had been necessary, but when the night came the house was crowded. They waited both before and behind the curtain for the debut of the new actress, with much curiosity. She stood waiting for her cue, but as it was given, to the amazement of all, the great tragedienne glided upon the stage. Pale as marble, and with a strange fire in her eyes, strange pathos in her voice, strange power in her acting, she went through her part, and at the close vanished as mysteriously as she came. Great was the excitement that night, and intense the astonishment and horror next day when it was whispered abroad that the dead woman never had revived, but had lain in her coffin before the eyes of watchers all the evening, when hundreds fancied they were applauding her at the theater. The mystery never was cleared up, and Paris was divided by two opinions: one that some person marvelously like Madame Z. had personated her for the sake of a sensation; the other that the ghost of the dead actress, unable to free itself from the old duties so full of fascination to an ambitious and successful woman, had played for the last time the part which had made her famous."

"Where did you find that, Tavie? It's very French, and not bad if you invented it," said Sir Jasper.

"I read it in an old book, where it was much better told. Now, Edith, there is just time for your tale."

As the word "Edith" passed her lips, again Treherne started and eyed them both, and again they smiled, as Mrs. Snowdon caressed the smooth cheek leaning on her knee, and looking full at him began the last recital.

"You have been recounting the pranks of imaginary ghosts; let me show you the workings of some real spirits, evil and good, that haunt every heart and home, making its misery or joy. At Christmas-time, in a country house, a party of friends met to keep the holidays, and very happily they might have done so had not one person marred the peace of several. Love, jealousy, deceit, and nobleness were the spirits that played their freaks with these people. The person of whom I speak was more haunted than the rest, and much tormented, being willful, proud, and jealous. Heaven help her, she had had no one to exorcise these ghosts for her, and they goaded her to do much harm. Among these friends there were more than one pair of lovers, and much tangling of plots and plans, for hearts are wayward and mysterious things, and cannot love as duty bids or prudence counsels. This woman held the key to all the secrets of the house, and, having a purpose to gain, she used her power selfishly, for a time. To satisfy a doubt, she feigned a fancy for a gentleman who once did her the honor of admiring her, and, to the great scandal of certain sage persons, permitted him to show his regard for her, knowing that it was but a transient amusement on his part as well as upon hers. In the hands of this woman lay a secret which could make or mar the happiness of the best and dearest of the party. The evil spirits which haunted her urged her to mar their peace and gratify a sinful hope. On the other side, honor, justice, and generosity prompted her to make them happy, and while she wavered there came to her a sweet enchantress who, with a word, banished the tormenting ghosts forever, and gave the haunted woman a talisman to keep her free henceforth."

There the earnest voice faltered, and with a sudden impulse Mrs. Snowdon bent her head and kissed the fair forehead which had bent lower and lower as she went on. Each listener understood the truth, lightly veiled in that hasty fable, and each found in it a different meaning. Sir Jasper frowned and bit his lips, Annon glanced anxiously from face to face, Octavia hid hers, and Treherne's flashed with sudden intelligence, while Rose laughed low to herself, enjoying the scene. Blanche, who was getting sleepy, said, with a stifled gape, "That is a very nice, moral little story, but I wish there had been some real ghosts in it."

"There was. Will you come and see them?"

As she put the question, Mrs. Snowdon rose abruptly, wishing to end the séance, and beckoning them to follow glided up the great stairway. All obeyed, wondering what whim possessed her, and quite ready for any jest in store for them.

≽ *chapter VIII* ≼

JASPER

S HE led them to the north gallery and, pausing at the door, said merrily, "The ghost—or ghosts rather, for there were two—which frightened Patty were Sir Jasper and myself, meeting to discuss certain important matters which concerned Mr. Treherne. If you want to see spirits we will play phantom for you, and convince you of our power."

"Good, let us go and have a ghostly dance, as a proper finale of our revel," answered Rose as they flocked into the long hall.

At that moment the great clock struck twelve, and all paused to bid the old year adieu. Sir Jasper was the first to speak, for, angry with Mrs. Snowdon, yet thankful to her for making a jest to others of what had been earnest to him, he desired to hide his chagrin under a gay manner; and taking Rose around the waist was about to waltz away as she proposed, saying cheerily, "'Come one and all, and dance the new year in,'" when a cry from Octavia arrested him, and turning he saw her stand, pale and trembling, pointing to the far end of the hall.

Eight narrow Gothic windows pierced either wall of the north gallery. A full moon sent her silvery light strongly in upon the eastern side, making broad bars of brightness across the floor. No fires burned there now, and wherever the moonlight did not fall deep shadows lay. As Octavia cried out, all looked, and all distinctly saw a tall, dark figure moving noiselessly across the second bar of light far down the hall.

"Is it some jest of yours?" asked Sir Jasper of Mrs. Snowdon, as the form vanished in the shadow.

"No, upon my honor, I know nothing of it! I only meant to relieve Octavia's superstitious fears by showing her our pranks" was the whispered reply as Mrs. Snowdon's cheek paled, and she drew nearer to Jasper.

"Who is there?" called Treherne in a commanding tone.

No answer, but a faint, cold breath of air seemed to sigh along the arched roof and die away as the dark figure crossed the third streak of moonlight. A strange awe fell upon them all, and no one spoke, but stood watching for the appearance of the shape. Nearer and nearer it came, with soundless steps, and as it reached the sixth window its outlines were distinctly visible. A tall, wasted figure, all in black, with a rosary hanging from the girdle, and a dark beard half concealing the face.

"The Abbot's ghost, and very well got up," said Annon, trying to laugh but failing decidedly, for again the cold breath swept over them, causing a general shudder.

"Hush!" whispered Treherne, drawing Octavia to his side with a protecting gesture.

Once more the phantom appeared and disappeared, and as they waited for it to cross the last bar of light that lay between it and them, Mrs. Snowdon stepped forward to the edge of the shadow in which they stood, as if to confront the apparition alone. Out of the darkness it came, and in the full radiance of the light it paused. Mrs. Snowdon, being nearest, saw the face first, and uttering a faint cry dropped down upon the stone floor, covering up her eyes. Nothing human ever wore a look like that of the ghastly, hollow-eyed, pale-lipped countenance below the hood. All saw it and held their breath as it slowly raised a shadowy arm and pointed a shriveled finger at Sir Jasper.

"Speak, whatever you are, or I'll quickly prove whether you are man or spirit!" cried Jasper fiercely, stepping forward as if to grasp the extended arm that seemed to menace him alone.

An icy gust swept through the hall, and the phantom slowly receded into the shadow. Jasper sprang after it, but nothing crossed the second stream of light, and nothing remained in the shade. Like one possessed by a sudden fancy he rushed down the gallery to find all fast and empty, and to return looking very strangely. Blanche had fainted away and Annon was bearing her out of the hall. Rose was clinging to Mrs. Snowdon, and Octavia leaned against her cousin, saying in a fervent whisper, "Thank God it did not point at you!"

"Am I then dearer than your brother?" he whispered back.

There was no audible reply, but one little hand involuntarily pressed his, though the other was outstretched toward Jasper, who came up white and startled but firm and quiet. Affecting to make light of it, he said, forcing a smile as he raised Mrs. Snowdon, "It is some stupid joke of the servants. Let us think no more of it. Come, Edith, this is not like your usual self."

"It was nothing human, Jasper; you know it as well as I. Oh, why did I bring you here to meet the warning phantom that haunts your house!"

"Nay, if my time is near the spirit would have found me out wherever I might be. I have no faith in that absurd superstition—I laugh at and defy it. Come down and drink my health in wine from the Abbot's own cellar."

But no one had heart for further gaiety, and, finding Lady Treherne already alarmed by Annon, they were forced to tell her all, and find their own bewilderment deepened by her unalterable belief in the evil omen.

At her command the house was searched, the servants cross-questioned, and every effort made to discover the identity of the apparition. All in vain; the house was as usual, and not a man or maid but turned pale at the idea of entering the gallery at midnight. At my lady's request, all promised to say no more upon the mystery, and separated at last to such sleep as they could enjoy.

Very grave were the faces gathered about the breakfast table next morning, and very anxious the glances cast on Sir Jasper as he came in, late as usual, looking uncommonly blithe and well. Nothing serious ever made a deep impression on his mercurial nature. Treherne had more the air of a doomed man, being very pale and worn, in spite of an occasional gleam of happiness as he looked at Octavia. He haunted Jasper like a shadow all the morning, much to that young gentleman's annoyance, for both his mother and sister hung about him with faces of ill-dissembled anxiety. By afternoon his patience gave out, and he openly rebelled against the tender guard kept over him. Ringing for his horse he said decidedly, "I'm bored to death with the solemnity which pervades the house today, so I'm off for a brisk gallop, before I lose my temper and spirits altogether."

"Come with me in the pony carriage, Jasper. I've not had a drive with you for a long while, and should enjoy it so much," said my lady, detaining him.

"Mrs. Snowdon looks as if she needed air to revive her roses, and the pony carriage is just the thing for her, so I will cheerfully resign my seat to her," he answered laughing, as he forced himself from his mother's hand.

"Take the girls in the clarence. We all want a breath of air, and you are the best whip we know. Be gallant and say yes, dear."

"No, thank you, Tavie, that won't do. Rose and Blanche are both asleep, and you are dying to go and do likewise, after your vigils last night. As a man and a brother I beg you'll do so, and let me ride as I like."

"Suppose you ask Annon to join you—" began Treherne with well-assumed indifference; but Sir Jasper frowned and turned sharply on him, saying, half-petulantly, half-jocosely:

"Upon my life I should think I was a boy or a baby, by the manner in which you mount guard over me today. If you think I'm going to live in daily fear of some mishap, you are all much mistaken. Ghost or no ghost, I shall make merry while I can; a short life and a jolly one has always been my motto, you know, so fare you well till dinnertime."

They watched him gallop down the avenue, and then went their different ways, still burdened with a nameless foreboding. Octavia strolled into the conservatory, thinking to refresh herself with the balmy silence which pervaded the place, but Annon soon joined her, full of a lover's hopes and fears.

"Miss Treherne, I have ventured to come for my answer. Is my New Year to be a blissful or a sad one?" he asked eagerly.

"Forgive me if I give you an unwelcome reply, but I must be true, and so regretfully refuse the honor you do me," she said sorrowfully.

"May I ask why?"

"Because I do not love you."

"And you do love your cousin," he cried angrily, pausing to watch her half-averted face.

She turned it fully toward him and answered, with her native sincerity, "Yes, I do, with all my heart, and now my mother will not thwart me, for Maurice has saved my life, and I am free to devote it all to him."

"Happy man, I wish I had been a cripple!" sighed Annon. Then with a manful effort to be just and generous, he added heartily, "Say no more, he deserves you; I want no sacrifice to duty; I yield, and go away, praying heaven to bless you now and always."

He kissed her hand and left her to seek my lady and make his adieus, for no persuasion could keep him. Leaving a note for Sir Jasper, he hurried away, to the great relief of Treherne and the deep regret of Blanche, who, however, lived in hopes of another trial later in the season.

"Here comes Jasper, Mamma, safe and well," cried Octavia an hour or two later, as she joined her mother on the terrace, where my lady had been pacing restlessly to and fro nearly ever since her son rode away.

With a smile of intense relief she waved her handkerchief as he came clattering up the drive, and seeing her he answered with hat and hand. He usually dismounted at the great hall door, but a sudden whim made him ride along the wall that lay below the terrace, for he was a fine horseman, and Mrs. Snowdon was looking from her window. As he approached, the peacocks fled screaming, and one flew up just before the horse's eyes as his master was in the act of dismounting. The spirited creature was startled, sprang partway up the low, broad steps of the terrace, and, being sharply checked, slipped, fell, and man and horse rolled down together.

Never did those who heard it forget the cry that left Lady Treherne's lips as she saw the fall. It brought out both guests and servants, to find Octavia recklessly struggling with the frightened horse, and my lady down upon the stones with her son's bleeding head in her arms.

They bore in the senseless, shattered body, and for hours tried everything that skill and science could devise to save the young man's life. But every effort was in vain, and as the sun set Sir Jasper lay dying. Conscious at last, and able to speak, he looked about him with a troubled glance, and seemed struggling with some desire that overmastered pain and held death at bay.

"I want Maurice," he feebly said, at length.

"Dear lad, I'm here," answered his cousin's voice from a seat in the shadow of the half-drawn curtains.

"Always near when I need you. Many a scrape have you helped me out of, but this is beyond your power," and a faint smile passed over Jasper's lips as the past flitted before his mind. But the smile died, and a groan of pain escaped him as he cried suddenly, "Quick! Let me tell it before it is too late! Maurice never will, but bear the shame all his life that my dead name may be untarnished. Bring Edith; she must hear the truth."

She was soon there, and, lying in his mother's arms, one hand in his cousin's, and one on his sister's bent head, Jasper rapidly told the secret which had burdened him for a year.

"I did it; I forged my uncle's name when I had lost so heavily at play that I dared not tell my mother, or squander more of my own fortune. I deceived Maurice, and let him think the check a genuine one; I made him present it and get the money, and when all went well I fancied I was safe. But my uncle discovered it secretly, said nothing, and, believing Maurice the forger, disinherited him. I never knew this till the old man died, and then it was too late. I confessed to Maurice, and he forgave me. He said, 'I am helpless now, shut out from the world, with nothing to lose or gain, and soon to be forgotten by those who once knew me, so let the suspicion of shame, if any such there be, still cling to me, and do you go your way, rich, happy, honorable, and untouched by any shadow on your fame.' Mother, I let him do it, unconscious as he was that many knew the secret sin and fancied him the doer of it."

"Hush, Jasper, let it pass. I can bear it; I promised your dear father to be your staunch friend through life, and I have only kept my word."

"God knows you have, but now my life ends, and I cannot die till you are cleared. Edith, I told you half the truth, and you would have used it against him had not some angel sent this girl to touch your heart. You have done your part to atone for the past, now let me do mine. Mother, Tavie loves him, he has risked life and honor for me. Repay him generously and give him this."

With feeble touch Sir Jasper tried to lay his sister's hand in Treherne's as he spoke; Mrs. Snowdon helped him, and as my lady bowed her head in silent acquiescence, a joyful smile shone on the dying man's face.

"One more confession, and then I am ready," he said, looking up into the face of the woman whom he had loved with all the power of a shallow nature. "It was a jest to you, Edith, but it was bitter earnest to me, for I loved you, sinful as it was. Ask your husband to forgive me, and tell him it was better I should die than live to mar a good man's peace. Kiss me once, and make him happy for my sake."

She touched his cold lips with remorseful tenderness, and in the same breath registered a vow to obey that dying prayer.

"Tavie dear, Maurice, my brother, God bless you both. Good-bye, Mother. He will be a better son than I have been to you." Then, the reckless spirit of the man surviving to the last, Sir Jasper laughed faintly, as he seemed to beckon some invisible shape, and died saying gaily, "Now, Father Abbot, lead on, I'll follow you."

A year later three weddings were celebrated on the same day and in the same church. Maurice Treherne, a well man, led up his cousin. Frank Annon rewarded Blanche's patient siege by an unconditional surrender, and, to the infinite amusement of Mrs. Grundy, Major Royston publicly confessed himself outgeneraled by merry Rose. The triple wedding feast was celebrated at Treherne Abbey, and no uncanny visitor marred its festivities, for never again was the north gallery haunted by the ghostly Abbot.

VOLUME TWO

Plots and Counterplots

⇘ Introduction ⇙

BY MADELEINE STERN

[Jo March] took to writing sensation stories, for in those dark ages, even all-perfect America read rubbish. She told no one, but concocted a "thrilling tale," and boldly carried it herself to . . . [the] editor of the Weekly Volcano. *. . .*

. . . Jo rashly took a plunge into the frothy sea of sensational literature.[1]

When Louisa Alcott adopted the name of Jo March for her own role in *Little Women,* she was not writing "behind a mask." The creation is as vital as the creator and many of the episodes in the life of this flesh-and-blood character are autobiographical. The author herself once listed the "facts in the stories that are true, though often changed as to time and place," and that list included "Jo's literary . . . experiences."[2]

The exact nature of Louisa's clandestine "literary experiences"—the discovery of her pseudonym, the identification of her Gothic effusions— was all revealed in *Behind a Mask.*[3] There four of her thrillers were reprinted, suspenseful stories that for over a century had lain unrecognized and unread in the yellowing pages of once gaudy journals. Now the remaining sensational narratives written by Jo March's prototype have been assembled in a companion volume. Again readers may revel in more stories by an L. M. Alcott masked in anonymity or in pseudonymity. From the garret where the author wrote in a vortex flowed the tales emblazoned in flashy weeklies circulated to campfire and hearthstone in the 1860's. Now they can be devoured again—these suspenseful cliff-hangers which are also extraordinary revelations of a writer who turns out to be not simply "The Children's Friend" but a delver in darkness familiar with the passions of the mind.

As a professional who could suit the demands of diverse tastes, Louisa Alcott disdained a precise duplication of her themes and characters. Her repetitions are repetitions with variations. Her heroines—those *femmes fatales* who could manipulate whole families—are in this second volume *femmes fatales* with a difference. Motivated still by jealousy or thwarted love, ambition or innate cruelty, they now take on the texture of marble beneath whose cold white surface the fires of passion flame or are banked. Louisa Alcott's marble women have their variants too: sometimes they have encased themselves in marble the better to execute their purposes; sometimes an attempt is made by a demonic character to transform them into marble. Whatever the nature of their seeming frigidity, they are all extraordinary actresses, mistresses of the arts of disguise who use their props—their bracelets or ebony caskets, their miniatures and keys or bloodstained slippers—with histrionic skill. In one of the narratives of *Plots and Counterplots*, Alcott's most evil heroine has been painted, the dancer Virginie Varens of "V. V.," a creature seductive, viperish, manipulating, who with a lovely bit of irony wins even as she loses in the end.

Here too will be found themes that go beyond the tamer shockers of *Behind a Mask:* the child-bride theme, which had a strange lure for the creator of *Little Women,* stemming perhaps from her early disastrous experience as a domestic in the service of the elderly James Richardson of Dedham; the theme of murder, which appears here in gory splendor; the theme of insanity, which is traced through many variations from a hereditary curse to an attempt at manipulated insanity, a black plot to madden a benighted heroine. The whole psychology of manipulation is presented with singular power in these tales, the drive of one dark mind to shape another, the Pygmalion theme in a somber setting. Finally, in addition to the lure of evil and violence, mental aberrations and mind control, *Plots and Counterplots* will offer to devotees of "The Children's Friend" another sinister theme—drug addiction and experimentation. The creator of Jo March was skilled not only in the wholesome delights of apples and ginger cookies but in the more macabre delights of opium and hashish.

Like the stories presented in *Behind a Mask,* these narratives with their purple passages and their scarlet motifs had their sources not only in the gaudy Gothics which their author devoured but also in the life she had led, the observations she had made, the fantasies she had dreamed. Louisa Alcott was to some extent the Jo March who "like most young scribblers . . . went abroad for her characters and scenery; and banditti, counts, gypsies, nuns, and duchesses appeared upon her stage. . . .

"As thrills could not be produced except by harrowing up the souls of the readers, history and romance, land and sea, science and art, police records and lunatic asylums, had to be ransacked for the purpose. . . . Eager to find material for stories, and bent on making them original in plot, if not masterly in execution, she searched newspapers for accidents, incidents, and crimes; she excited the suspicions of public librarians by asking for works on poisons; she studied faces in the street, and characters, good, bad, and indifferent, all about her; she delved in the dust of ancient times for facts or fictions . . . and introduced herself to folly, sin, and misery." [4]

She delved also into her own "ancient times," dredging up especially the ingredients of those "Comic Tragedies" she had penned as a girl with her sister Anna and produced on the stage of the Hillside barn in Concord.[5] Love scenes and direful lines, dramatic confrontations and disguises, desertions and suicides, magic herbs, love potions and death phials that had been the staples of "The Unloved Wife" or "The Captive of Castile" could be introduced again with alterations. If they had once chilled the blood of an audience of illustrious neighbors, now, having undergone a subtle sea change, they could chill the blood of subscribers to flamboyant weeklies.

Other episodes in Louisa Alcott's past could be served up to readers of sensational stories. In 1858, after her sister Lizzie's death, she had seen a light mist rise from the body. Seven years later a misty apparition would arise from a fictional Alcott grave. Before the Civil War, Louisa had heard tales of Jonathan Walker, whose hand had been branded with the letters S.S. for "Slave Stealer." For the prototype of Jo March's *Blarneystone Banner* or *Weekly Volcano* the initials *V. V.* would be tattooed upon an imaginary wrist. A short period during the summer of 1860, when Louisa had cared for "a young friend during a temporary fit of insanity," would be put to use for lurid excursions into nightmarish derangements.[6]

Louisa Alcott's service as a Civil War nurse in the Union Hotel Hospital, Georgetown, was followed by an illness that provided her with one of the most interesting sources for her tales of violence and revenge. After some six weeks of nursing she succumbed to typhoid pneumonia, a severe attack of which she wrote, "I was never ill before this time, and never well afterward." The bout was accompanied by sinister dreams from which the patient would awaken unrefreshed. Since those dreams, that fevered delirium, would be interwoven into the fabric of her blood-and-thunders, they merit an attention less medical than literary.

> *The most vivid and enduring was the conviction that I had married a stout, handsome Spaniard, dressed in black velvet, with very soft hands, and a voice that was continually saying, "Lie still, my dear!" This was Mother, I suspect; but with all the comfort I often found in her presence, there was blended an awful fear of the Spanish spouse who was always coming after me, appearing out of closets, in at windows, or threatening me dreadfully all night long. . . .*
> *A mob at Baltimore breaking down the door to get me, being hung for a witch, burned, stoned, and otherwise maltreated, were some of my fancies. Also being tempted to join Dr. W. and two of the nurses in worshipping the Devil. Also tending millions of rich men who never died or got well.*

After three weeks of delirium "the old fancies still lingered, seeming so real I believed in them, and deluded Mother and May with the most absurd stories, so soberly told that they thought them true." As her father reported in a letter to Anna in January, 1863, Louisa "asked me to sit near her bedside, and tell her the adventures of our fearful journey home [from Georgetown] . . . and enjoyed the story, laughing over the plot and catastrophe, as if it were a tale of her imagining." [7]

The tales of her imagining would still pay the family bills. The economic necessity that had prompted the stories in *Behind a Mask* prompted those in *Plots and Counterplots*. At times the only breadwinner of the family, Louisa Alcott set about liberating that family from debt with her thrillers, and in so doing she achieved a psychological catharsis that liberated her own mind from its phantasmagorias. Her father had observed in "the elements of your temperament" both the "Spaniard" and the "Saxon." [8] The "Spanish" elements were surely in the ascendancy when she reeled off her " 'thrilling' tales, and mess up my work in a queer but interesting way." She was at this time a compulsive writer, dashing off her narratives "like a thinking machine in full operation." Stories simmered in her brain demanding to be written. "My pen," she despaired, "will not keep in order, and ink has a tendency to splash when used copiously and with rapidity." Once she wrote, "Liberty is a better husband than love to many of us," and often she "longed for a crust in a garret with freedom and a pen." [9]

It was to the office of the *Weekly Volcano* that Jo March boldly ventured with a thrilling tale and "bravely climbed two pairs of dark and dirty stairs to find herself in a disorderly room, a cloud of cigar smoke, and the presence of three gentlemen, sitting with their heels rather higher than their hats."[10] If "Louisa Alcott" is read for "Jo March," then *The Flag of Our Union* may be read for the *Weekly Volcano,* and for the three gentlemen in a cloud of cigar smoke, the three colorful Boston publishers, Messrs. Elliott, Thomes and Talbot, whose "disorderly room" was part of the Journal Building at 118 Washington Street.

Louisa Alcott's first contribution to *The Flag of Our Union* was also the story that flaunted her most unregenerate heroine. "V. V.: or, Plots and Counterplots" "By a Well Known Author"[11] appeared in February, 1865, to titillate readers and divert them from news of the war that would end two months later. A shocker it was, with its heady ingredients—poison in an opal, footprints left by a murderess, drugged coffee, a feigned pistol duel, theatrical props against sketchy theatrical backgrounds of a fancied Spain or India, Paris or Scottish estate. But it is less for its plots and counterplots moving relentlessly on to the "éclat" of a "grand *dénouement*" that "V. V." becomes a fascinating narrative. It is, as in most of the Alcott thrillers, the nature of the heroine that captures the intense interest of the reader.

Virginie Varens is no Jo March. All Spanish, she bears no traces of her author's "Saxon" elements. "A sylph she seemed" in the greenroom of a Paris theater, a seventeen-year-old dancer "costumed in fleecy white and gold . . . flushed and panting, but radiant with the triumphs of the hour." Her cousin and dancing partner, that sinewy, animated flame of fire, Victor, has set his mark upon her—two dark letters "tattooed on the white flesh" of her wrist, the monogram *V. V.*, which she conceals by means of a bracelet fastened with a golden padlock. Virginie is already a *fille* if not a *femme fatale* with many suitors, including a viscount who offers her an establishment and infamy, and the Scot Allan Douglas who offers her an honorable name and a home. "Mercenary, vain, and hollow-hearted" as well as conniving and ambitious, Virginie accepts the latter. Thereupon the "fiery and fierce" Victor, enraged with jealousy, "reckless of life or limb," takes "the short road to his revenge," and "with the bound of a wounded tiger" stabs the bridegroom. As for the heroine, one "night of love, and sin, and death" has transformed her into wife, widow, and, as it turns out, mother too.

So the curtain rises upon a melodrama of deceit and death. Because she is motivated primarily by social ambition, Virginie Varens appears more innately evil than her competitors—those powerful and passionate

Alcott heroines urged on by the more primitive force of jealousy. The remainder of the narrative is set in the Scottish estate of Lady Lennox, where V. V. determines to win Allan Douglas's cousin, a noble Scot also named Douglas who looks like Allan's twin. For this mercenary purpose Virginie assumes several theatrical disguises and perpetrates sins both venial and venal, ranging from peccadillo to crime. Posing as Mrs. Vane—she has been Colonel Vane's mistress in India, not his wife—she captivates every Scot but her target, Cousin Douglas, who astutely detects in her "gliding gait" and "brilliant eyes" the hint of "a little green viper."

The "viper" is accompanied by a deaf-and-dumb servant named Jitomar, supposedly one of Colonel Vane's Indian retainers, actually, of course, the treacherous Victor in Eastern disguise. With his help Virginie lays her plot and spins her counterplots. Her pawn is the lovely Diana Stuart, betrothed to Douglas, who must be eliminated. This V. V. proceeds to accomplish, feigning, lying, conniving, manipulating. To Douglas this female Iago confides that Diana may be the victim of a hereditary curse; to Diana she "proves" that Douglas is already married.

These viperish machinations and the plots they generate are implemented by a succession of fascinating props that recall performances in the Hillside barn: an ancient iron seal ring; a satin slipper with a dull red stain; a bit of black lace. But the most potent dea ex machina is, of course, the heroine herself. She is an exciting *femme fatale*. She has some feminist inclinations although they stem primarily from a basic misanthropy. To Diana she observes, "A man's honor is not tarnished in his eyes by treachery to a woman, and be believes that a woman's peace will not be marred by the knowledge that in God's sight she is not his wife, although she may be in the eyes of the world." Virginie has "the nerves of a man, the quick wit of a woman, and presence of mind enough for . . . all." She has also the malignancy of a Satan and the conniving skills of a Machiavelli. She has both the power and the will to inveigle her rival, Diana, to a loathsome death.

Since crime must in some way, however subtle, be followed by punishment, the counterplots spin on. A surprisingly modern, pre-Sherlockian detective, M. Duprès, is introduced for the purpose—a man who "adore[s] mystery; to fathom a secret, trace a lie, discover a disguise, is my delight . . . this brain of mine is fertile in inventions, and by morning will have been inspired with a design which will enchant you by its daring, its acuteness, its romance."

Against such an agent Virginie, adopting a variety of disguises, continues to weave her deceitful web until, in the "éclat" of the "grand dé-

nouement," that web is broken and the spinner brought to judgment. "A hunted creature driven to bay," she is arrogant, audacious, and conniving to the end. In a final confrontation Douglas condemns her: "Your treachery, your craft, your sin deserve nothing but the heavy retribution you have brought upon yourself." Her disguises—her "artifices of costume, cosmetics, and consummate acting"—have all been penetrated. Her plots and counterplots have been unraveled. "Virginie, this night your long punishment begins"—a punishment intolerable to contemplate, a punishment from which "escape is impossible," but from which, in her ultimate triumph, Virginie Varens, the most Mephistophelian of Louisa Alcott's heroines, does in her way escape.

This was doubtless one of the tales the author had in mind when, in January, 1865, she recorded in her journal: "Fell back on rubbishy tales, for they pay best, and I can't afford to starve on praise, when sensation stories are written in half the time and keep the family cosey." [12] As for Jo March, "She . . . began to feel herself a power in the house, for by the magic of a pen, her 'rubbish' turned into comforts for them all. *The Duke's Daughter* paid the butcher's bill, *A Phantom Hand* put down a new carpet, and the *Curse of the Coventrys* proved the blessing of the Marches in the way of groceries and gowns." [13]

If "V. V.: or, Plots and Counterplots" is "rubbish," then it is superb rubbish. Though the heart of the heroine may be molded of marble, she is a creature of flesh and blood who, in the very act of appalling, enchants. The plots and counterplots, though derivative, are inventive enough to lure the reader on. As star of this page-turner, Virginie Varens merits a lead position in the Alcott gallery of *femmes fatales*.

The first of the Alcott contributions to *The Flag of Our Union* was by no means the last. The delighted editor James R. Elliott assured his new author that he "should be pleased to have you write me some stories for the Flag, of about 25 to 40 pages of such Ms. as 'V. V.'" [14] Using the pseudonym of A. M. Barnard, she obliged; and three months after "V. V.'s" bow, "A Marble Woman: or, The Mysterious Model" appeared in the pages of Elliott's weekly.

Richmond had been taken in April, and Louisa had gone to Boston "and enjoyed the grand jollification. Saw Booth again in Hamlet." [15] Less than a week after Appomattox came news of Lincoln's assassination. Despite, or perhaps because of, the crisis and grief of the Union, the story papers churned out their narratives for avid readers in search of escape. On May 20, *The Flag of Our Union* carried the first installment of "A Marble Woman: or, The Mysterious Model. A Novel of Absorbing Interest. By A. M. Barnard, Author of 'V. V.: or, Plots and Counterplots.'"[16]

Into this remarkable tale the author injected a delectable combination of themes, including the Pygmalion-Galatea motif, the concept of the child-bride, a hint at incest, and a brief but intriguing bout with opium addiction. Add to these the enigma of the "mysterious model," a masquerade, a chase at sea, and a satisfactory dénouement, and the result is a story as varied in its episodes as it is absorbing in its totality.

Of all the themes used by A. M. Barnard one of the most interesting is her variation on the Pygmalion and Galatea motif—her depiction of the woman who is molded into marble by a sculptor whose clay is flesh and blood. The "marble woman" first appears on stage as a twelve-year-old orphan, Cecilia Bazil Stein, whose dying mother has selected as her guardian a former lover, the genius sculptor Bazil Yorke. Against a Gothic background replete with ancient furniture, dark window hangings, gloomy pictures, a great dog on a "tawny tiger skin," and a spiral staircase leading to Bazil's tower studio, the child and her artist guardian interact. Bazil Yorke bears "traces of deep suffering, latent passion, and a strange wistfulness, as if the lonely eyes were forever seeking something they had lost." To crush his rising affection for the child of the woman he once loved and lost, the sculptor attempts to stifle her warmth and remold her into marble. "If I had power to kill the savage beast, skill to subdue the fierce dog, surely I can mold the child as I will, and make the daughter pay the mother's debt." Bazil's ruthless purpose is complicated by the third actor in this melodrama, who appears at first as a face at a window—"a strange, uncanny face, half concealed by a black beard that made the pallor of the upper part more striking'—the face of the hidden watcher or mysterious model, whose identity is suspensefully withheld until an appropriate time.

In the tower studio Yorke models from a handful of clay. The long large room is "filled with busts, statues, uncut blocks, tools, dust, and disorder." Young Cecil—for so Yorke calls her—learns the art of modeling, and there is no doubt that A. M. Barnard borrowed for the sequences in the tower studio the knowledge of art that Louisa Alcott had acquired from observing her artist sister May. Indeed, Dr. William Rimmer, May's anatomical drawing teacher, was one day to be incorporated into the character of Professor Bhaer in *Little Women*.[17]

Meanwhile, five years pass and a different kind of modeling is attempted by the sculptor in flesh and blood. Cecil, dressed in white from neck to ankle, has no companions but marble men and women. She is cautioned to live without love. "Be what I would have you," Yorke commands, to which she replies, "A marble woman like your Psyche, with no heart to love you, only grace and beauty to please your eye and bring you honor. . . ."

"Yes," says Yorke, "I would have you beautiful and passionless as Psyche. . . . I am done with love."

The experiment all but succeeds. As Yorke's wife in name only, Cecil becomes "Yorke's statue," "his best work." Yorke has married "one of his marble goddesses. . . . He fell in love with her beauty, and is as proud of it as if he had carved the fine curves of her figure and cut the clear outline of her face." But the snow image is not marble yet. Out of her unsatisfied human desires arises one of the most interesting episodes in the Alcott blood-and-thunders, an episode concerned with drug addiction. The theme engrossed A. M. Barnard, who would return to it, with fascinating variations, later on.

As narrated in "A Marble Woman," Yorke gives the sleepless Cecil a bitter, dark liquid that will bring her "deep and dreamless sleep." She recalls that her mother had taken laudanum for pain and that she herself has "often tasted it." After the unconsummated marriage with her sculptor Cecil develops a growing taciturnity, takes short unexplained flights, and ventures upon mysterious errands. She appears "dreamy, yet intense, blissfully calm, yet full of a mysterious brightness that made her face strangely beautiful." An unnatural inner excitement is followed by "an unconquerable drowsiness" that overpowers her. A "restless sleep" deepens into a "deathlike immobility; the feverish flush was gone, and violet shadows gave her closed eyes a sunken look; through her pale lips slow breaths came and went." A physician recognizes immediately that Cecil has taken an overdose of laudanum and that she has survived the overdose because she is addicted.

"Your wife eats opium, I suspect."

The suspicion is verified. For a year Cecil has had the habit, which "grew upon me unconsciously, and became so fascinating I could not resist it." She eats her opium in the form of little comfits that leave traces of "grayish crumbs" and an "acrid odor." Her need for this "dangerous comforter" is clearly traced to the secluded life forced upon her as the teen-age virgin bride of a thirty-eight-year-old recluse. She has found it too "hard to tame myself to the quiet, lonely life you wish me to lead."

The opium episode is pivotal to the plot of "A Marble Woman" and its dénouement. But its interest is not literary alone. As the concoction of the future author of *Little Women* it raises the eyebrows. The fact that Louisa May Alcott concerned herself with drug addiction is a shocker which, today especially, requires some analysis and investigation.

Bazil Yorke's library—and doubtless Louisa Alcott's—contained a copy of De Quincey's *Confessions of an Opium-Eater*. But the opium poppy, *Papaver somniferum*, played a less bookish part in many nineteenth-century American lives.[18] Indeed, some of the great New England fortunes accrued from the shipping industry in which opium trade with China was often involved. A. M. Barnard's publisher, William Henry Thomes of Elliott, Thomes & Talbot, had sailed aboard an opium smuggler that plied between China and California.[19] Little more than a month after "A Marble Woman" completed its run in his paper, Louisa Alcott would go abroad as companion to a young woman whose father, William Fletcher Weld, owned a fleet of ships that flew the Black Horse flag to Hong Kong and Manila.[20] Obviously the opium trade was familiar to her.

Laudanum—tincture of opium—was part of the pharmacopoeia of every nineteenth-century physician except those who eschewed medicine of every kind. It was freely prescribed for coughs and digestive disorders, arthritis and rheumatism, and despite the Alcott preference for homeopathic medicine, there is a strong possibility that at some stage of Louisa's typhoid pneumonia some derivative of the opium poppy had been administered to her. During her brief but disastrous period as a nurse in the Civil War, she had certainly observed the use of morphine as a narcotic for wounded soldiers and was perforce aware of the morphine addiction that sometimes followed and was known as "soldier's disease." With the influx of Chinese laborers on expanding American railways, tales of Oriental opium dens in the West provided grist for the mill of sensation writers in the East.

And so for A. M. Barnard laudanum or opium was not merely surcease from pain but a useful narrative device. She applied it skillfully in "A Marble Woman," in which Cecil's addiction softens and transforms Yorke into a human being who can react to love. The inevitable Alcott masquerade party; a mad chase in a storm at sea against a backdrop of buffeting gusts, torrential rain, and thick mists; the identification of the mysterious model and the hint of incestuous love this entails—all lead to a satisfactory conclusion. By curtainfall the marble has been reconverted into very human clay and, as her publisher assured her, "my friends think the 'Marble Woman' is just splendid; & I think no author of novels need be ashamed to own it for a bantling."[21]

The conclusion of "A Marble Woman" by A. M. Barnard appeared in *The Flag of Our Union* on June 10, 1865. On July 19, Louisa M.

Alcott, traveling companion, sailed aboard the *China* bound for Liverpool and her first journey abroad. Her travels were productive for they yielded a partial prototype for Laurie in *Little Women* as well as romantic backgrounds for Gothic tales—castles and towers, gardens and lighthouses on moon-shaped bays. They produced also an urgent compulsion to write, for her mother had borrowed money to keep the traveler in London after she had left her charge. According to her father, Mr. Weld had complacently remarked, "Miss Alcott can easily pay all her travelling expenses by contributing to some newspapers." [22] Shortly after her return she "fell to work on some stories, for things were, as I expected, behindhand when the money-maker was away. Found plenty to do, as orders from E. . . . and several other offers waited for me." [23]

One of the stories she produced at this time for "E." (James R. Elliott) was a short but dramatic narrative in which the heroine is a self-made marble woman. She is also, it develops, a woman of noble character, and so Louisa M. Alcott allowed her name to appear as the author of *The Skeleton in the Closet* [24] when Elliott, Thomes & Talbot issued it in November, 1867. It is, like most of the Alcott thrillers, a page-turner. It is also of more than ordinary interest for its variation on the marble-woman theme and for its description of a mind unhinged.

Mme. Mathilde Arnheim, "the loveliest widow in all France," graces a château which, although she "desires no Adam," she has converted into an Eden. With its "airy balconies" and "inviting apartments," its "rare pictures" and "graceful statues," its "light draperies" swaying before "open casements" and "leafy shadows" flickering on a marble floor, Madame's château was surely based upon some villa the scribbling traveling companion had seen on her recent journey. As for Madame herself, she is slender and white-robed, wearing a black lace scarf in the Spanish style, an Italian greyhound tripping daintily beside her. She seems "a marble image, beautiful and cold, though there are rare flashes of warmth that win, a softness that enchants, which make her doubly dangerous." Her eyes are lustrous, dark, "filled with the soft gloom of a patient grief." She calls herself a widow. Like V. V. she wears a steel bracelet clasped by a golden lock, the key of which hangs by a golden chain. But unlike V. V., Mme. Arnheim is an *involuntary femme fatale* who lives in seclusion guarding her secret—the skeleton in her closet.

Despite the isolation of this "loveliest spot in France," Madame attracts a lover. Gustave Novaire's jealousy is aroused when he glimpses an apparent rival whose arm encircles "her graceful neck," whose hand plays "idly with a tress of sunny hair." Gustave spies his beloved "pacing to and fro with clasped hands and streaming eyes, as if full of some pas-

sionate despair." He sees her "strike her fettered arm" upon the balcony
and knows that the bracelet binds her to a dire fate. The mystery is at
length revealed—"the secret anguish of my life, the haunting specter of
my home, the stern fate which makes all love a bitter mockery, and
leaves me desolate." At sixteen—again the child-bride theme—Mathilde
was married to the victim of a "fearful malady," "a hereditary curse"—a
"wreck of manhood" afflicted with a weakened brain. Having learned
of her plan to commit suicide to escape this "marriage mockery," Reinhold Arnheim suffers further mental derangement until he becomes an
imbecile mouthing senseless words, smiling a vacant smile.

Now Mathilde is "bound by a tie which death alone can sever; till
then I wear this fetter, placed here by a husband's hand nine years ago;
it is a symbol of my life, a mute monitor of duty. . . . I have thrown
away the key, and its place is here till this arm lies powerless, or is
stretched free and fetterless."

After the passage of three years and the machinations of two artful
villains, Mathilde's loathsome tie is broken and the steel bracelet is replaced by a slender chain of gold. The heroine has been faithful unto
death, and so the author's sally into the nightmare of mental aberration
could be acknowledged.

Several years before, Louisa Alcott had ventured more boldly into
a similar region of the mind. Six months after her prize story, "Pauline's
Passion and Punishment," [25] had appeared in *Frank Leslie's Illustrated
Newspaper,* Prize Story No. 17—the anonymous "A Whisper in the
Dark" [26]—was emblazoned in the columns of that gaudy weekly. The
narrative goes far beyond the effort at mind control that provides the
basis for the plot of "A Marble Woman." Here the reader is regaled with
the lowest form of psychological manipulation—an attempt, for mercenary purposes, to drive the heiress heroine insane so that her inheritance will be denied her. Interwoven in this black fabric are several
scarlet threads: suicidal thoughts and chemical experiments, sleepwalking and the hint of sexual attraction between a forty-five-year-old adopted
uncle-guardian and the heroine, Sybil, who is not quite eighteen. With
an unusual last will and testament, a large measure of maternal love,
and a house of horrors for background, "A Whisper in the Dark" becomes not only an engrossing gruesome Gothic but an interesting foray
into the disorders of the mind.

The teen-age orphan Sybil is thrust almost immediately into the
clutches of her so-called uncle, who "regarded me mutely for an instant, then, holding me fast, deliberately returned my salute on lips,

cheeks, and forehead, with such warmth that I turned scarlet and struggled to free myself, while he laughed that mirthless laugh of his till my
shame turned to anger, and I imperiously commanded him to let me go.

"'Not yet, young lady. You came here for your own pleasure, but
shall stay for mine, till I tame you as I see you must be tamed. . . . Chut!
What a little fury it is!'

"I was just then; for exasperated at his coolness . . . I had suddenly stooped and bitten the . . . hand that held both my own. I had
better have submitted; for . . . it had an influence on my afterlife. . . ."

Although Sybil is betrothed to her adopted uncle's son, Guy, she is
at first not averse to trying her "power over them both." Before the plot
advances she sits on "Uncle's" knee and smokes "a cigarette of his own
offering . . . then I slept on his arm an hour, and he was fatherly
kind."

"Uncle's" fatherly kindness is soon exposed for the dastardly mercenary sham it is. When Sybil refuses the role of child-bride and rejects
her "uncle"—"I had rather die than marry you!"—her fate is sealed.

Now, with the aid of the "stealthy, sallow-faced Spaniard," Dr.
Karnac, "Uncle" resorts to mind control. If he can unhinge Sybil's mind,
he—not she—will receive the inheritance. And so the horrors accumulate.
Spirited away in a drugged sleep to a nightmarish domain "twenty miles
from the Moors," she is placed in a dreary room, its door locked, its
window grated. "An ominous foreboding thrilled cold through nerves
and blood, as, for the first time, I felt the paralyzing touch of fear." A
great hound guards the room above where a mysterious occupant paces,
a ghostly hand emerges, a whisper sounds through a keyhole. Sybil walks
in her sleep through the haunted house. Since "madness seemed [her]
inevitable fate," she resolves to commit suicide. Instead, she elucidates
the mystery of the room above, learning that if she is "not already mad,
[she] will be . . . [she was] sent here to be made so; for the air is poison,
the solitude is fatal, and Karnac remorseless in his mania for prying into
the mysteries of human minds."

Despite the terrors of this dark plot, "A Whisper in the Dark" has
moral overtones, thanks to which Louisa Alcott eventually found it possible to acknowledge its authorship. Twenty-five years after its initial
appearance she agreed to reprint "A Whisper in the Dark" with a new
edition of her *Modern Mephistopheles*.

Only by means of initials did Louisa acknowledge authorship of
the final story in *Plots and Counterplots*. "Perilous Play" [27] by "L. M. A."

appeared not in *Frank Leslie's Illustrated Newspaper* but in another of Leslie's expanding chain of periodicals. Issued in February, 1869, shortly after she had completed the second part of her perennial best seller *Little Women,* it was the last of Jo March's necessity stories.

In January, 1865, Louisa had written in her journal: "L. asked me to be a regular contributor to his new paper, and I agreed if he'd pay beforehand; he said he would, and bespoke two tales at once, $50 each . . . Alcott brains seem in demand, whereat I sing 'Hallyluyer' and fill up my inkstand." [28]

Frank Leslie's "new paper" was actually his present mistress's and future wife's new paper. *Frank Leslie's Chimney Corner* [29] had been started, planned, and edited by that *femme fatale* of real life Miriam Squier, who assembled its corps of writers and defined its purpose. It was conceived as a family paper that would appeal to every member of the American home, an illustrated fireside friend in which the mother would find a domestic story, the daughter a romance of love, the son a dramatic escapade, the youngsters adventures and fairy tales. Miriam Squier's flowery prospectus rivaled some of Louisa Alcott's purple passages: "We present herewith, just as the aurora of peace irradiates the horizon, the first number of The Chimney Corner . . . which shall be a welcome messenger of instruction and amusement to the young and old, in the family and by the fireside—that altar around which cluster our holiest and most cherished recollections." The astute editor selected for her "welcome messenger" articles less holy than titillating—sketches of Chinese gamblers or insane monarchs, the original Bluebeard or the werewolf of Dole—along with such stories of engaging violence as "The Queen of the Stranglers" and "The Phantom Hand." "We give," she boasted, "a story a day . . . some to touch by their tragic power, some to thrill with love's vicissitudes, some to hold in suspense with dramatic interest."

"Perilous Play" by L. M. A. could be assigned to this last category when it was run in 1869 in that "Great Family Paper of America." The last, the shortest of the Alcott thrillers, it is also in a way the most dramatic shocker of all, for it is devoted in its entirety to an experiment with hashish.

As usual the now extremely skillful author sketches her dramatis personae with broad brushstrokes, presenting the familiar Alcott heroine, daughter of a Spanish mother and an English father (the "Spanish" and "Saxon" elements are here combined). Rose St. Just is "pale, and yet brilliant" with magnificent "Southern eyes," "clear olive cheeks," "lips like a pomegranate flower." She is attired in an "airy burnoose" and she wears a bracelet of Arabian coins. She reads the legend of "The Lotus Eaters."

To while away a long afternoon for Rose St. Just and others of the party, Dr. Meredith produces his "little box of tortoiseshell and gold" containing "that Indian stuff which brings one fantastic visions" and is called hashish. The clever and ingenious twist that L. M. A. gives to this experiment results in a story of delicate charm that is also a page-turner. But it is the experiment itself that transcends the interest of the plot, for in "Perilous Play" the twentieth-century reader familiar with marijuana can be introduced to the nineteenth-century attitude toward hashish.

Although *Cannabis sativa,* the source of hashish and marijuana, is one of the oldest drugs known to man, it has been stated that "the only account of the use of this drug in the United States prior to the twentieth century" is an autobiographical work by Fitz Hugh Ludlow entitled *The Hasheesh Eater: Being Passages from the Life of a Pythagorean,* published anonymously in New York in 1857.[30]

Now another nineteenth-century account of the drug has been unearthed—authored by "The Children's Friend"! Had Louisa Alcott ever used hashish? It was freely available at six cents a stick. Had Louisa Alcott ever heard of the Hashish Club of writers and artists modeled in the 1850's upon the French Club des Hashishins? Had she pondered upon the "joy-giver" of the Hindu sages, Rabelais's "Herb Pantagruelion" that induced "cerebral excitation"?

Her description of the effects of hashish in "Perilous Play" certainly suggests either an incomparable imagination or a familiarity with the drug. According to Dr. Meredith, "Six ["comfits"] can do no harm. . . . I take twenty before I can enjoy myself. . . . I've tried many experiments, both on the sick and the well, and nothing ever happened amiss, though the demonstrations were immensely interesting. . . . A heavenly drowsiness comes over one, in which they move as if on air. Everything is calm and lovely to them: no pain, no care, no fear of anything, and while it lasts one feels like an angel half asleep." The trance comes on "about three hours after you take your dose. . . . Your pulse will rise, heart beat quickly, eyes darken and dilate, and an uplifted sensation will pervade you generally. Then these symptoms change, and the bliss begins. I've seen people sit or lie in one position for hours, rapt in a delicious dream, and wake from it as tranquil as if they had not a nerve in their bodies." As for an overdose, that is "not so pleasant, unless one likes phantoms, frenzies, and a touch of nightmare, which seems to last a thousand years."

And so the experiment is made. Rose St. Just is offered "a taste of Elysium," which she secretly accepts. Her lover, Mark Done, is maddened by both love and hashish, and the two are caught not only in a gathering storm at sea but in the unnatural and wild excitement induced by *Cannabis sativa*. "Every nerve was overstrained, every pulse beating like a trip-hammer, and everything . . . was intensified and exaggerated with awful power. The thundershower seemed a wild hurricane, the quaint room a wilderness peopled with tormenting phantoms." All night Mark "lay motionless, with staring eyes, feverish lips, and a mind on the rack, for the delicate machinery which had been tampered with revenged the wrong by torturing the foolish experimenter." Nevertheless, thanks to the author's ingenuity, the hashish folly ends happily and the Perilous Players can exclaim at curtainfall, "Heaven bless hashish, if its dreams end like this!"

With "Perilous Play" most of Louisa May Alcott's nightmarish dreams—or at least their literary applications—ended. The publication of Part II of *Little Women* in April, 1869, brought her the fame and fortune she coveted and set her on the path of sweetness and light from which she seldom strayed.

Astute and sometimes piratical publishers, however, did not hesitate to reprint the Alcott forays into the realms of darkness and from time to time, without her knowledge, her thrillers reappeared. "Perilous Play," for example, was lifted out of *Frank Leslie's Chimney Corner* and run in November, 1876, in *Frank Leslie's Popular Monthly*. "V. V.: or, Plots and Counterplots" reemerged around 1870 in an altogether new dress, as a *Ten Cent Novelette* by A. M. Barnard. Both *The Mysterious Key, and What It Opened*[31] and *The Skeleton in the Closet* had been issued by Elliott, Thomes & Talbot of Boston in their series of *Ten Cent Novelettes by Standard American Authors*—the latter as the trailer of *The Foundling* by Perley Parker. Now, as the new decade of the 1870's began, the firm—restyled Thomes & Talbot—reprinted *V. V.* under the authorship of A. M. Barnard as No. 80 in that series. The pseudonymous thriller, bound in blue wrappers, took its place in the literature of the dime novel and is today one of the rarest and most desirable of those ephemeral pamphlets thumbed to death in the nineteenth century, treasured in the twentieth.

The dime novel, introduced by the New York firm of Beadle in 1860, caught on. A. M. Barnard's publishers, Elliott, Thomes & Talbot, entered into competition, issuing their first *Ten Cent Novelette* in 1863— *The Golden Eagle* by Sylvanus Cobb, Jr., an author scorned by Louisa Alcott's illustrious neighbor Ralph Waldo Emerson. The *Ten Cent*

Novelettes [32] issued by Elliott, Thomes & Talbot were described as the handsomest and largest ten-cent books ever published. A new one appeared on the last Monday of every month, bound in pink, later in blue paper, and for one dollar subscribers could receive twelve complete choice novels a year. For a country from whose borders romantic adventure was fast disappearing, these stories offered the lure of the distant in time and space, the excitement of conquest and exploration, the color of the gun-toting West, not to mention the lurid delights of *The Black Adder* or *The Dwarf Fiend*.

From their new address at 63 Congress Street, Boston, Thomes & Talbot reissued A. M. Barnard's effusion *V. V.*, and unbeknownst to Louisa May Alcott the violent and elaborate plots and counterplots she had abandoned were again made available to the public. Between the blue wrappers of a dime novel, the Spanish temptress Virginie Varens still danced, still wove her malignant web, still escaped her punishment. That paperback is remarkable indeed, for it tells a tale not only of a Spanish dancer but of a writer from New England whose variety was all but infinite.

Unlike V. V., who embodied corruption, the heroine of "A Whisper in the Dark" was the victim, not the perpetrator, of evil. Partly for this reason Louisa Alcott, toward the end of her life, permitted her publishers to reprint that story under her own name as a trailer to *A Modern Mephistopheles*. On May 7, 1887, she wrote to Thomas Niles, of Roberts Brothers, who had made the suggestion: "'A Whisper' is rather a lurid tale, but might do if I add a few lines to the preface of 'Modern Mephistopheles,' saying that this is put in to fill the volume, or to give a sample of Jo March's necessity stories, which many girls have asked for." [33]

It was eminently fitting to reprint "A Whisper in the Dark" with *A Modern Mephistopheles*. When in 1877 her publishers had proposed that the author of *Little Women* provide an anonymous book for their "No Name Series," Louisa Alcott had dipped her pen into A. M. Barnard's lurid ink and written a novel dreamed by A. M. Barnard's ghost. In *A Modern Mephistopheles* [34] she had reverted to the Gothic technique, incorporating in her novel the Mephistophelian sybarite Jasper Helwyze, who manipulates his victim, Felix Canaris; Gladys, beguiled out of "her tranquil girlhood"; and the familiar lush heroine, Olivia, "a woman in the midsummer of her life, brilliant, strong, and stately . . . passion slept in the Southern eyes . . . and will curved the closely folded lips of vivid red."

In her room at the Bellevue Hotel in Boston the erstwhile con-

tributor to *The Flag of Our Union* rose from the past, dredging up
themes once woven through "A Marble Woman," "A Whisper in the
Dark," and "Perilous Play": mind control and the lure of drugs. Again
she analyzed the "psychological curiosity" that penetrates and violates
"the mysterious mechanism of human nature." And again she described
an elaborate experiment with hashish.

Jasper Helwyze's "little bonbonnière of tortoiseshell and silver"
contained "white comfits"—the "Indian drug," which "made the face of
Coleridge shine." Hashish is given to Gladys who, like Rose St. Just,
experiences "inward excitement . . . a strange chill . . . through her
blood. Everything seemed vast and awful; every sense grew painfully
acute; and she walked as in a dream. . . . Her identity was doubled"
until she floated into "the unconscious stage of the hasheesh dream."

Interspersed though it is with metaphysical borrowings from Goethe
and Hawthorne, *A Modern Mephistopheles* is an A. M. Barnard thriller
in which the now celebrated Louisa May Alcott indulged her "natural
ambition . . . for the lurid" [35] and enjoyed a psychological and literary
catharsis. When it was first published as an anonymous full-length novel
in 1877, the author wrote in her journal: " 'M.M.' appears and causes
much guessing. It is praised and criticised, and I enjoy the fun, especially
when friends say, 'I know *you* didn't write it, for you can't hide your
peculiar style.' " [36]

For some time she hid it successfully, reviewers asking, "Who wrote
this story? Whose hand painted these marvellous pictures of the angel
and the demon striving for the mastery in every human soul?" [37] A decade after its appearance in the "No Name Series," when the author was
paying the penalty of years of overwork and suffering with the cancer
that would soon prove fatal, she agreed to the reprinting of *A Modern
Mephistopheles and A Whisper in the Dark*. The combined volume that
embodied the techniques and preoccupations of her salad days was published posthumously in 1889.

Now "A Whisper in the Dark" has been reprinted once again for
the twentieth-century audience that still clamors for more stories by
Louisa May Alcott. With "V. V.: or, Plots and Counterplots," "A Marble Woman: or, The Mysterious Model," "The Skeleton in the Closet"
and "Perilous Play," it forms a collection that rounds out the stories
introduced in *Behind a Mask*. Always there may be a lingering suspicion
that Louisa Alcott had other masks, that in the brittle pages of sensational nineteenth-century weeklies lurk more of her anonymous and
pseudonymous shockers awaiting excited discovery. The lingering suspicion is really but a persistent hope, for the appetite grows with what it

feeds on. The flamboyant thrillers of *Plots and Counterplots*—narratives delving into violence, mind control, drug experimentation—present in still another, wilder guise the many-sided author of *Little Women*.

The corpus of Louisa Alcott's excursions into the gruesome horrors of the mind has now been completed. The Concord Scheherazade emerges full-face from behind her mask.

NOTES

[1] Louisa May Alcott, *Little Women* (New York and London, [1975]), pp. 382, 385.

[2] Ednah D. Cheney, ed., *Louisa May Alcott: Her Life, Letters, and Journals* (Boston, 1889), p. 193 [hereinafter Cheney].

[3] *Behind a Mask: The Unknown Thrillers of Louisa May Alcott. Edited and with an Introduction by Madeleine Stern* (New York: William Morrow & Company, 1975).

[4] Alcott, *Little Women*, pp. 385–386.

[5] *Comic Tragedies Written by "Jo" and "Meg" and Acted by the "Little Women"* (Boston, 1893); Madeleine B. Stern, *Louisa May Alcott* (Norman, Oklahoma, 1971), p. 54.

[6] Cheney, pp. 97–98, 111; Stern, *Louisa May Alcott*, p. 95.

[7] Bronson Alcott to Anna, Concord, January 29, 1863, in Richard L. Herrnstadt, ed., *The Letters of A. Bronson Alcott* (Ames, Iowa, [1969]), p. 334; Cheney, pp. 137, 145–147; Stern, *Louisa May Alcott*, pp. 129–132; Madeleine B. Stern, "Louisa M. Alcott, Civil War Nurse," *Americana*, XXXVII: 2 (April, 1943), pp. 296–325.

[8] Bronson Alcott to Louisa, Concord, December 17, 1865, in Herrnstadt, *op. cit.*, p. 379.

[9] Cheney, pp. 109, 130, 132, 161, 197.

[10] Alcott, *Little Women*, p. 383.

[11] "V. V.: or, Plots and Counterplots," *The Flag of Our Union*, XX: 5, 6, 7, 8 (February 4, 11, 18, 25, 1865). Reprinted as No. 80 in the *Ten Cent Novelettes* of *Standard American Authors* series *ca.* 1870, under the pseudonym of A. M. Barnard. Now reprinted from the *Novel-*

ette in the New York Public Library, Rare Book Division, through the courtesy of Mrs. Maud Cole, Chief.

[12] Cheney, p. 165.

[13] Alcott, *Little Women,* p. 302.

[14] James R. Elliott to Louisa M. Alcott, Boston, January 7, 1865 (Houghton Library, Harvard University).

[15] Cheney, p. 165.

[16] "A Marble Woman: or, The Mysterious Model," *The Flag of Our Union,* XX: 20, 21, 22, 23 (May 20, 27, June 3, 10, 1865). Published under the pseudonym of A. M. Barnard. Now reprinted from the issues at Houghton Library, Harvard University, through the courtesy of Miss Carolyn Jakeman.

[17] Stern, *Lousia May Alcott,* pp. 138–139, 184.

[18] John Rublowsky, *The Stoned Age: A History of Drugs in America* (New York, [1974]), pp. 35, 117–130.

[19] Madeleine B. Stern, *Imprints on History: Book Publishers and American Frontiers* (Bloomington, Indiana, 1956), p. 208.

[20] Stern, *Louisa May Alcott,* p. 147.

[21] James R. Elliott to Louisa M. Alcott, Boston, June 15, 1865 (Houghton Library, Harvard University).

[22] Bronson Alcott to Louisa, Concord, March 25, 1866, in Herrnstadt, *op. cit.,* p. 391.

[23] Cheney, p. 184; Stern, *Louisa May Alcott,* p. 167.

[24] L. M. Alcott, *The Skeleton in the Closet.* Published with Perley Parker, *The Foundling* (Boston: Elliott, Thomes & Talbot [1867]) as No. 49 in the *Ten Cent Novelettes* of *Standard American Authors* series. Now reprinted through the courtesy of Dr. Julius P. Barclay and Miss Joan Crane, Alderman Library, University of Virginia. For date of deposit, see Jacob Blanck, *Bibliography of American Literature* (New Haven, 1955), I, No. 151.

[25] "Pauline's Passion and Punishment," *Frank Leslie's Illustrated Newspaper,* XV: 379 and 380 (January 3 and 10, 1863). Reprinted in *Behind a Mask.*

[26] "A Whisper in the Dark," *Frank Leslie's Illustrated Newspaper,* XVI: 401 and 402 (June 6 and 13, 1863). Reprinted in *A Modern Mephistopheles and A Whisper in the Dark* (Boston, 1889). Now reprinted from the copy of the latter owned by Madeleine B. Stern. In the periodical version the horse is named Satan, not Sultan. The illustrations are from *Frank Leslie's Illustrated Newspaper* (June 6 and 13, 1863), courtesy New York Historical Society.

[27] "Perilous Play," *Frank Leslie's Chimney Corner,* VIII: 194 (Feb-

ruary 3, 1869). Reprinted in *Frank Leslie's Popular Monthly*, II: 5 (November, 1876). Now reprinted from the periodical *Frank Leslie's Chimney Corner* in the New York Public Library.

[28] Cheney, p. 165.

[29] Madeleine B. Stern, *Purple Passage: The Life of Mrs. Frank Leslie* (Norman, Oklahoma, 1970), pp. 44–46.

[30] Rublowsky, *The Stoned Age*, pp. 35, 94–99.

[31] L. M. Alcott, *The Mysterious Key, and What It Opened* (Boston: Elliott, Thomes & Talbot [1867]). Issued as No. 50 in the *Ten Cent Novelettes* of *Standard American Authors* series. Reprinted as No. 382 in The Leisure Hour Library by F. M. Lupton of New York, *ca.* 1900. Reprinted in *Behind a Mask*.

[32] Stern, *Imprints on History*, pp. 211–214.

[33] Cheney, pp. 379–382.

[34] *A Modern Mephistopheles* (Boston, 1877). Published anonymously. Reprinted as Louisa M. Alcott, *A Modern Mephistopheles and A Whisper in the Dark* (Boston, 1889).

[35] See *Behind a Mask*, p. *xxvi*.

[36] Cheney, p. 297.

[37] Louisa M. Alcott, *A Modern Mephistopheles and A Whisper in the Dark* (Boston, 1889), advertisement at end, quoting from review in *The New Age*.

Old Terms

THE AMERICAN UNION.
Two Dollars a Year.

THE FLAG OF OUR UNION.
Two Dollars a Year.

THE NOVELETTE.
$2 a Year—Four Copies, $6.

THE DOLLAR MONTHLY.
$1 a Year—Six Copies, $5.

OFFICE OF
ELLIOTT, THOMES & TALBOT'S
PUBLICATIONS,
JOURNAL BUILDING, 118 WASHINGTON STREET,
BOSTON, MASS.

J. R. ELLIOTT.   WM. H. THOMES.   NEWTON TALBOT.

☞ We will combine our publications on the following terms:
The Dollar Monthly Magazine and The Novelette, together, for.... $2 50
The Novelette and The Flag of our Union, together, for 3 25
The American Union and Dollar Monthly, together, for........... 2 50
The Flag of our Union and Dollar Monthly, together, for 2 50
The American Union and Flag of our Union, together, for 3 50

Jan. 5. 1865.

Louisa M. Alcott,

   Dear Madam,

        I forward you
this evening the 3 first copies of the
"Flag" in its new form.

    I think it is now a
literary paper that none
need to blush for, and
a credit to contribute
to its columns, rather
than otherwise.

Now I have a proposition
to make you. I want

to publish your story "Y. Y." in it, in place of publishing it as a Novelette in cheap style. as I had intended, and will give you $25. more for the story provided I can publish it under your own name. Please look the "Flag" over & let me know as early as Saturday & oblige

Very Truly Yours

~~Elliott Thompson~~

J. R. Elliott

Edr.

M. ... Elliott

OFFICE OF

ELLIOTT, THOMES & TALBOT'S
PUBLICATIONS,

JOURNAL BUILDING, 118 WASHINGTON STREET.

BOSTON, MASS.

J. R. ELLIOTT.   WM. H. THOMES.   NEWTON TALBOT.

☞ We will combine our publications on the following terms:
The Dollar Monthly Magazine and The Novelette, together, for.... $2 50
The Novelette and The Flag of our Union, together, for.......... 3 25
The American Union and Dollar Monthly, together, for.......... 2 50
The Flag of our Union and Dollar Monthly, together, for 2 50
The American Union and Flag of our Union, together, for........ 3 50

THE AMERICAN UNION.
Two Dollars a Year.

THE FLAG OF OUR UNION.
Two Dollars a Year.

THE NOVELETTE.
$2 a Year—Four Copies, $6.

THE DOLLAR MONTHLY.
$1 a Year—Six Copies, $5.

Jan. 7 1865

Dear Miss Alcott,

I should be pleased
to have you write me some
stories for the Flag, of about
25 to 40 pages of such Ms.
as "V. V." I want them
over your own name of
course, & will give you
$2.00 a column (short columns
you will notice) for them.
That rate will be fully equal
to $16.00 for a first page story
in the "American Union"

which paper I think you
contributed to while it was
under the management
of Messrs. Graves & Weston.
Will you not contribute
a poem or two for the
"Flag" also? I do not know
as that is in your line,
if it is I shall be glad
to receive poems from —
your pen. I have entered
your name on our gratis
list, & you will receive
the "Flag" regularly.
                Very truly Yours
                    J. R. Elliott

P.S. I will purchase another
Novelette of you at any time
you may wish to dispose
of one. "K. V." will be com-
menced in No. 5 about two
week. What title would

you suggest in place of
"V. V?" Or what for a second
title? Please answer at
your earliest convenience
R. W. E.

AMERICAN UNION.
Three Dollars a year.
FLAG OF OUR UNION,
Four Dollars a year.
MONTHLY NOVELETTE.
Two Dollars a year.
DOLLAR MONTHLY,
$1.50 a year.

OFFICE OF **Elliott, Thomes & Talbot's Publications,**

63 CONGRESS STREET,

Boston June 15 1865

Dear Miss Alcott,

Have you written anything in the novel line you would like to have me publish by A M Barnard, author of "V.V." "The Marble Woman" &c, &c.? If not Can you furnish me with a sensation story of about 145 to 150 pages such M.S. as your last "The Marble Woman" so that I can have it by the middle of July? I don't care about even any particular name, if you prefer any other nom de plume for this one story, use it, as it is for one of my cheap novelettes.

I will give you $50. for such a story, & don't want it to exceed 150 pages of Mss. the size of "The Marble Woman," 140 pages will answer, oo 145 will be better.

By the way my friends think the "Marble Woman" is just splendid; & I think no author of Novels need be ashamed to own it for a last thing. I am sorry you should have had any feeling in regard to the nom de plume. I am sure that I have not given currancy to the idea that "A.M. Barnard" & yourself were identical.

Please let me hear from you by return mail, if possible, in regard to the short novel.

Very truly yours
J. R. Elliott

TEN CENT NOVELETTES.

V. V.

By A. M. BARNARD

COMPLETE

STANDARD AMERICAN AUTHORS

THOMES & TALBOT,
63 Congress St., Boston.

V. V.

or

PLOTS
AND COUNTERPLOTS

≫ *Chapter I* ≪

WON AND LOST

IN the greenroom of a Parisian theater a young man was pacing to and fro, evidently waiting with impatience for some expected arrival.

The room was empty, for the last performance of a Grand Spectacle was going on, and the entire strength of the company in demand. Frequent bursts of barbaric music had filled the air; but now a brief lull had fallen, broken only by the soft melody of flutes and horns. Standing motionless, the young man listened with a sudden smile, an involuntary motion of the head, as if in fancy he saw and followed some object of delight. A storm of applause broke in on the last notes of the air. Again and again was it repeated, and when at length it died away, trumpet, clarion, and drum resumed their martial din, and the enchanting episode seemed over.

Suddenly, framed in the dark doorway, upon which the young man's eyes were fixed, appeared an apparition well worth waiting for. A sylph she seemed, costumed in fleecy white and gold; the star that glittered on her forehead was less brilliant than her eyes; the flowers that filled her graceful arms were outrivaled by the blooming face that smiled above them; the ornaments she wore were forgotten in admiration of the long blond tresses that crowned her spirited little head; and when the young man welcomed her she crossed the room as if borne by the shining wings upon her shoulders.

"My Virginie, how long they kept you," began the lover, as this beautiful girl leaned against him, flushed and panting, but radiant with the triumphs of the hour.

"Yes, for they recalled me many times; and see—not one bouquet without a *billet-doux* or gift attached!"

"I have much to say, Virginie, and you give me no time but this. Where is Victor?"

"Safe for many minutes; he is in the 'Pas des Enfers,' and then we are together in the 'Pas des Déesses.' Behold! Another offer from the viscount. Shall I accept?"

While speaking she had been rifling the flowers of their attractive burdens, and now held up a delicately scented note with an air half serious, half gay. Her lover crushed the paper in his hand and answered hotly, "You will refuse, or I shall make the viscount a different sort of offer. His devotion is an insult, for you are mine!"

"Not yet, monsieur. Victor has the first claim. And see, he has set his mark upon me."

Pushing up a bracelet, she showed two dark letters stamped or tattooed on the white flesh.

"And you permitted him to disfigure you? When, Virginie, and why?"

"Ah, that was years ago when I cared nothing for beauty, and clung to Victor as my only friend, letting him do what he would, quite content to please him, for he was very kind, and I, poor child, was nothing but a burden. A year ago we were betrothed, and next year he hopes to marry—for we do well now, and I shall then be eighteen."

"You will not marry him. Then why deceive him, Virginie?"

"Yes, but I may if no one else will offer me a name as he does. I do not love him, but he is useful; he guards me like a dragon, works for me, cherishes me, and keeps me right when from mere youth and gaiety of heart I might go astray. What then? I care nothing for lovers; they are false and vain, they annoy me, waste my time, keep Victor savage, and but for the éclat it gives me, I would banish all but—" She finished the sentence with a caress more eloquent than any words and, before he could speak, added half tenderly, half reproachfully, while the flowers strayed down upon the ground, "Not one of all these came from you. I thought you would remember me on this last night."

Passionately kissing the red lips so near his own, the lover answered, "I did remember you, but kept my gift to offer when we were alone."

"That is so like you! A thousand thanks. Now give it to me."

With a pretty gesture of entreaty she held out her little hand, and the young man put his own into it, saying earnestly, "I offer this in all sincerity, and ask you to be my wife."

A brilliant smile flashed over her face, and something like triumph shone in her eyes as she clasped the hand in both her own, exclaiming with mingled delight and incredulity, "You ask that of me, the *danseuse,* friendless, poor and humble? Do you mean it, Allan? Shall I go with you to Scotland, be 'my lady' by-and-by? *Ciel!* It is incredible."

"Yes, I mean it. Passion has conquered pride, and for love's sake I can forgive, forget anything but degradation. That you shall never know; and I thank Victor that his jealous vigilance has kept you innocent through all the temptation of a life like yours. The viscount offers you an establishment and infamy; I offer you an honorable name and a home with my whole heart. Which shall it be, Virginie?"

She looked at him keenly—saw a young and comely face, now flushed and kindled with the ardor of a first love. She had seen many such waiting for her smile; but beyond this she saw truth in the honest eyes, read a pride on the forehead that no dishonor could stain, and knew that she might trust one whose promises were never broken. With a little cry of joy and gratitude she laid her face down on the generous hand that gave so much, and thanked heaven that the desire of her life was won. Gathering her close, Allan whispered, with a soft cheek against his own, "My darling, we must be married at once, or Victor will discover and betray us. All is arranged, and this very night we may quit Paris for a happy honeymoon in Italy. Say yes, and leave the rest to me."

"It is impossible! I cannot leave my possessions behind me; I must prepare a little. Wait till tomorrow, and give me time to think."

She spoke resolutely; the young man saw that his project would fail unless he yielded the point, and controlling his impatience, he modified his plan and won her by the ease of that concession.

"I will not hurry you, but, Virginie, we must be married tonight, because all is prepared, and delay may ruin us. Once mine, Victor has no control over you, and my friends will have no power to part us. Grant me this boon, and you shall leave Paris when you will."

She smiled and agreed to it, but did not confess that the chief reason of her reluctance to depart so suddenly was a desire to secure the salary which on the morrow would be paid her for a most successful but laborious season. Mercenary, vain, and hollow-hearted as she was, there was something so genuine in the perfect confidence, the ardent affection of her lover, that it won her respect and seemed to gift the rank which she aspired to attain with a redoubled charm.

"Now tell me your plan, and tell me rapidly, lest Victor should divine that we are plotting and disturb us," she said, with the look of exultation still gleaming in her eyes.

"It is this. Your engagement ends tonight, and you have made no new one. You have spoken of going into the country to rest, and when you vanish people will believe that you have gone suddenly to rusticate. Victor is too proud to complain, and we will leave a penitent confession behind us to appease him."

"He will be terrible, Allan."

"You have a right to choose, I to protect you. Have no fear; we shall be far beyond his reach when he discovers his mistake. I asked you of him honorably once, and he refused with anger."

"He never told me that. We are requited, so let him rave. What next?"

"When your last dance is over, change your dress quickly, and instead of waiting here for your cousin, as usual, slip out by the private door. I shall be there with a carriage, and while Victor is detained searching for you, we will be married, and I shall take you home to gather up those precious possessions of yours. You will do this, Virginie?"

"Yes."

"Your courage will not fail when I am gone, and some fear of Victor keep you?"

"Bah! I fear nothing now."

"Then I am sure of you, and I swear you never shall regret your confidence; for as soon as my peace is made at home, you shall be received there as my honored wife."

"Are you very sure that you *will* be forgiven?" she asked anxiously, as if weighing possibilities even then.

"I *am* sure of pardon after the first anger is over, for they love me too much to disinherit or banish me, and they need only see you to be won at once."

"This marriage, Allan—it will be a true one? You will not deceive me; for if I leave Victor I shall have no friend in the wide world but you."

The most disloyal lover could not have withstood the pleading look, the gesture of appeal which accompanied her words, and this one, who harbored no treachery, assured her with solemn protestations and the most binding vows.

A few moments were spent in maturing their plan, and Virginie was just leaving him with the word "Tomorrow" on her lips when an animated flame of fire seemed to dart into the room. It was a youth whose scarlet-and-silver costume glowed and glittered in the light, as with one marvelous bound he crossed the room and stood before them. Supple, sinewy, and slight was the threatening figure which they saw; dark and defiant the face, with fierce black eyes, frowning brows, and the gleam of set teeth between lips parted by a muttered malediction. Lovely as the other apparition had been, this was far more striking, for it seemed full of the strong grace and beauty of the fallen angel whom it represented. The pose was magnificent; a flaming crown shone in the dark hair, and filmy pinions of scarlet flecked with silver drooped from shoulder to heel. So fiery and fierce he looked, it was little wonder that one lover drew back and the other uttered an exclamation of surprise. Instantly recovering herself, however, Virginie broke into a blithe laugh, and airily twirled away beyond the reach of Victor's outstretched hand.

"It is late; you are not dressed—you will be disgraced by a failure. Go!" he said, with an air of command.

"*Au revoir, monsieur;* I leave Paris with you." And as she uttered the words with a glance that pointed their double meaning, Virginie vanished.

Turning to the long mirror behind him, the young gentleman replaced his hat, resettled in his buttonhole the flower just given him, tranquilly drew on his gloves, saying, as he strolled toward the door, "I shall return to my box to witness this famous 'Pas des Déesses.' Virginie, Lucille, and Clotilde, upon my word, Paris, you will find it difficult to decide upon which of the three goddesses to bestow the golden apple."

Not a word spoke Victor, till the sounds of steps died away. Then he departed to his dressing room, moodily muttering as he went, "Tomorrow, she said. They intend to meet somewhere. Good! I will prevent *that*. There has been enough of this—it must end, and Virginie shall keep her promise. I will stand guard tonight and watch them well tomorrow."

Three hours later, breathless and pale with fatigue and rage, Victor sprang up the steps leading to his cousin's chamber in the old house by the Seine. A lamp burned in a niche beside her door; a glass of wine and a plate of fruit stood there also, waiting as usual for him. As his eye fell upon these objects a long sigh of relief escaped him.

"Thank heaven, she has come home then. Yet hold! It may be but a ruse to prevent my discovering her absence. Virginie! Cousin! Are you there?"

He struck upon the door, lightly at first, then vehemently, and to his great joy a soft, sleepy voice replied, "Who calls?"

"It is Victor. I missed you, searched for you, and grew anxious when I found you gone. Why did you not wait, as usual?"

"Mlle. Clotilde offered me a seat in her carriage, and I gladly accepted it. She was set down first, and it is a long distance there and back, you know. Now let me rest; I am very tired."

"Good night, my heart," answered Victor, adding, in a tone of pain and tenderness, as he turned away, *"mon Dieu!* How I love that girl, and how she tortures me! Rest well, my cousin; I shall guard your sleep."

Hour after hour passed, and still a solitary figure paced to and fro with noiseless feet along the narrow terrace that lay between the ancient house and the neglected garden sloping to the river. Dawn was slowly breaking in the east when the window of Virginie's chamber opened cautiously, and her charming head appeared. The light was very dim, and shadows still lay dark upon the house; but Victor, coming from the water gate whither he had been drawn by the sound of a passing boat, heard the soft movement, glided behind a group of shrubs, and eyed the window keenly, remembering that now it was "tomorrow." For a moment the lovely face leaned out, looking anxiously across terrace, street, and garden. The morning air seemed to strike cold on her un-covered shoulders, and with a shiver she was drawing back when a man's hand laid a light cloak about her, and a man's head appeared beside her own.

"Imprudent! Go quickly, or Victor will be stirring. At noon I shall be ready," she said half aloud, and as she withdrew the curtain fell.

With the bound of a wounded tiger, Victor reached the terrace, and reckless of life or limb, took the short road to his revenge. The barred shutters of a lower window, the carved ornaments upon the wall, and the balcony that hung above, all offered foot- and handhold for an agile climber like himself, as, creeping upward like a stealthy shadow, he peered in with a face that would have appalled the lovers had they seen it. They did not, for standing near the half-opened door, they were parting as Romeo and Juliet parted, heart to heart, cheek to cheek, and neither saw nor heard the impending doom until the swift stroke fell. So sure, so sudden was it that Virginie knew nothing, till, with a stifled cry, her lover started, swayed backward from her arms, and dyeing her garments with his blood, fell at her feet stabbed through the heart.

An awful silence followed, for Virginie uttered no cry of alarm, made no gesture of flight, showed no sign of guilt; but stood white and motionless as if turned to stone.

Soon Victor grasped her arm and hissed into her ear, "Traitress! I could find it in my heart to lay you there beside him. But no; you shall live to atone for your falsehood to me and mourn your lover."

Something in the words or tone seemed to recall her scattered senses and rouse her to a passionate abhorrence of him and of his deed. She wrenched herself from his hold, saying vehemently, though instinctively below her breath, "No; it is you who shall atone! He was my husband, not my lover. Look if I lie!"

He did look as a trembling hand was stretched toward him over that dead form. On it he saw a wedding ring, and in it the record of the marriage which in a single night had made her wife and widow. With an ejaculation of despair he snatched the paper as if to tear and scatter it; but some sudden thought flashed into his mind, and putting the record in his bosom, he turned to Virginie with an expression that chilled her by its ominous resolve.

"Listen," he said, "and save yourself while you may; for I swear, if you raise your voice, lift your hand against me, or refuse to obey me now, that I will denounce you as the murderer of that man. You were last seen with him, were missed by others besides me last night. There lies his purse; here is the only proof of your accursed marriage; and if I call in witnesses, which of us looks most like an assassin, you or I?"

She listened with a terror-stricken face, glanced at her bloody garments, knew that she was in the power of a relentless man, and clasped her hands with a gesture of mute supplication and submission.

"You are wise," he said. "Apart, we are both in danger; together we may be strong and safe. I have a plan—hear it and help me to execute it, for time is life now. You have spoken to many of going into the country; it shall be so, but we will give our departure the appearance of a sudden thought, a lover's flight. Leave everything behind you but money and jewels. That purse will more than pay you the sum you cannot claim. While I go to fling this body into the river, to tell no tales till we are safe, destroy all traces of the deed, prepare yourself for traveling, and guard the room in silence until I come. Remember! One sign of treachery, one cry for help, and I denounce you where my word will have much weight and yours none."

She gave him her hand upon the dark bargain, and covering up her face to hide the tragic spectacle, she heard Victor leave the room with his awful burden.

When he returned, she was nearly ready, for though moving like one in a ghastly dream, bewildered by the sudden loss of the long coveted, just won prize, and daunted by the crime whose retribution a word might bring upon herself, she still clung to life and its delights with the tenacity of a selfish nature, a shallow heart. While she finished her hasty preparations, Victor set the room in order, saw that the red witnesses of the crime were burnt, and dashed off a gay note to a friend, enclosing money for all obligations, explaining their sudden flight as an innocent ruse to escape congratulations on their hasty marriage, and promising to send soon for such possessions as were left behind. Then, leaving the quiet room to be forever haunted by the memory of a night of love, and sin, and death, like two pale ghosts they vanished in the dimness of the dawn.

❧ *Chapter II* ❧

EARL'S MYSTERY

FOUR ladies sat in the luxurious privacy of Lady Lennox's boudoir, whiling away the listless hour before dinner with social chat. Dusk was deepening, but firelight filled the room with its warm glow, flickering on mirrors, marbles, rich hues, and graceful forms, and bathing the four faces with unwonted bloom.

Stately Diana Stuart leaned on the high back of the chair in which sat her aunt and chaperon, the Honorable Mrs. Berkeley. On the opposite side of the wide hearth a slender figure lounged in the deep corner of a couch, with a graceful abandon which no Englishwoman could hope to imitate. The face was hidden by a hand-screen, but a pair of ravishing feet were visible, and a shower of golden hair shone against the velvet pillow. Directly before the fire sat Lady Lennox, a comely, hospitable matron who was never so content as when she could gather her female guests about her and refresh herself with a little good-natured gossip. She had evidently been discussing some subject which interested her hearers, for all were intently listening, and all looked eager for more, when she said, with a significant nod:

"Yes, I assure you there is a mystery in that family. Lady Carrick has known them all her life, and from what she has dropped from time to time, I quite agree with her in believing that something has gone wrong."

"Dear Lady Lennox, pray go on! There is nothing so charming as a family mystery when the narrator can give a clue to her audience, as I am sure you can," exclaimed the lady on the couch, in a persuasive voice which had a curious ring to it despite its melody.

"That is just what I cannot do, Mrs. Vane. However, I will gladly tell you all I know. This is in strict confidence, you understand."

"Certainly!" "Upon my honor!" "Not a word shall pass my lips!" murmured the three listeners, drawing nearer, as Lady Lennox fixed her eyes upon the fire and lowered her voice.

"It is the custom in ancient Scottish families for the piper of the house, when dying, to put the pipes into the hand of the heir to name or title. Well, when old Dougal lay on his deathbed, he called for Earl, the fourth son—"

"What a peculiar name!" interrupted Mrs. Berkeley.

"It was not his proper name, but they called him so because of his strong resemblance to the pictures of the great earl, Black Douglass. They continued to call him so to this day, and I really don't know whether his name is Allan, Archie, or Alex, for they are all family names, and one cannot remember which belongs to whom. Now the eldest son was Robert, and Dougal should have called for him, because the title and the fortune always go to the eldest son of the eldest son. But no, Earl must come; and into his hands the pipes were put, with a strange prophecy that no heir would enjoy the title but a year until it came to him."

"Was the prediction fulfilled?" asked Diana.

"To the letter. This was five or six years ago, and not one year has passed without a death, till now a single feeble life is all that stands between Earl and the title. Nor was this all. When his father died, though he had lain insensible for days, he rose up in his bed at the last and put upon Earl's hand the iron ring which is their most precious heirloom, because it belonged to the ancient earl. This, too, should have gone to Robert; but the same gift of second sight seemed given to the father as to the servant, and these strange things made a deep impression upon the family, as you may suppose."

"That is the mystery, then?" said Mrs. Vane, with an accent of disappointment in her voice.

"Only a part of it. I am not superstitious, so the prediction and all the rest of it don't trouble me much, but what occurred afterward does. When Earl was one-and-twenty he went abroad, was gone a year, and came home so utterly and strangely changed that everyone was amazed at the alteration. The death of a cousin just then drew people's attention from him, and when that stir was over the family seemed to be reconciled to the sad change in him. Nothing was said, nothing ever transpired to clear up the matter; and to this day he has remained a cold, grave, peculiar man, instead of the frank, gay fellow he once was."

"He met with some loss in an affair of the heart, doubtless. Such little tragedies often mar a young man's peace for years—perhaps for life."

As Mrs. Vane spoke she lowered her screen, showing a pair of wonderfully keen and brilliant eyes fixed full upon Diana. The young lady was unconscious of this searching glance as she intently regarded Lady Lennox, who said:

"That is my opinion, though Lady Carrick never would confirm it, being hampered by some promise to the family, I suspect, for they are almost as high and haughty now as in the olden time. There was a vague rumor of some serious entanglement at Paris, but it was hushed up at once, and few gave it credence. Still, as year after year passed, and Earl remains unmarried, I really begin to fear there was some truth in what I fancied an idle report."

Something in this speech seemed to ruffle Mrs. Berkeley; a look of intelligence passed between her and her niece as she drew herself up, and before Diana could speak, the elder lady exclaimed, with an air of mystery, "Your ladyship does Mr. Douglas great injustice, and a few months, weeks, perhaps, will quite change your opinion. We saw a good deal of him last season before my poor brother's death took us from town, and I assure you that he is free to address any lady in England. More I am not at liberty to say at present."

Lady Lennox looked politely incredulous, but Diana's eyes fell and a sudden color bathed her face in a still deeper bloom than that which the firelight shed over it. A slight frown contracted Mrs. Vane's beautiful brows as she watched the proud girl's efforts to conceal the secret of her heart. But the frown faded to a smile of intelligent compassion as she said, with a significant glance that stung Diana like an insult, "Dear Miss Stuart, pray take my screen. This glowing fire is ruining your complexion."

"Thank you, I need no screens of any sort."

There was a slight emphasis upon the "I," and a smile of equal significance curled her lips. If any taunt was intended it missed its mark, for Mrs. Vane only assumed a more graceful pose, saying with a provoking little air of superior wisdom, "There you are wrong, for our faces are such traitors, that unless we have learned the art of self-control, it is not best for us to scorn such harmless aids as fans, screens, and veils. Emotions are not well-bred, and their demonstrations are often as embarrassing to others as to ourselves."

"That, doubtless, is the reason why you half conceal your face behind a cloud of curls. It certainly is a most effectual mask at times," replied Diana, pushing back her own smooth bands of hair.

"Thanks for the suggestion. I wonder it never occurred to me before," sweetly answered Mrs. Vane, adding, as she gathered up the disheveled locks, "my poor hair is called a great ornament, but indeed it is a trial both to Gabrielle and to myself."

Lady Lennox touched a long tress that rolled down the pillow, saying with motherly admiration, "My dear, I promised Mrs. Berkeley she should see this wonderful hair of yours, for she could not believe my account of it. The dressing bell will ring directly, so you may gratify us without making more work for Gabrielle."

"Willingly, dear Lady Lennox; anything for you!"

As she spoke with affectionate goodwill, Mrs. Vane rose, drew out a comb or two, and a stream of golden hair rippled far below her knee. Mrs. Berkeley exclaimed, and Diana praised, while watching with a very natural touch of envy the charming picture the firelight showed her. In its full glow stood Mrs. Vane; against the deep purple of her dress glittered the golden mass, and a pair of lovely hands parted the shining veil from a face whose beauty was as peculiar and alluring as the mingled spirit and sweetness of her smile.

"A thousand pardons! I thought your ladyship was alone." A deep voice broke the momentary silence, and a tall figure paused upon the threshold of the softly opened door. All started, and with a little cry of pleasure and surprise, Lady Lennox hurried forward to greet her guest.

"My dear Earl, this is a most inhospitable welcome. George should have apprised me of your arrival."

"He is a lazy fellow, as he bade me find you here. I tapped, but receiving no reply, fancied the room empty and peeped to make sure. Pray accept my apologies, and put me out if I intrude."

The voice of Mr. Douglas was remarkably calm, his manner stately yet cordial, and his dark eyes went rapidly from face to face with a glance that seemed to comprehend the scene at once.

"Not in the least," said Lady Lennox heartily. "Let me present you to Mrs. Berkeley, Miss Stuart, and—why, where is she? The poor little woman has run away in confusion, and must receive your apologies by-and-by."

"We must run away also, for it is quite time to dress." And with a most gracious smile Mrs. Berkeley led her niece away before the gentleman should have time to note her flushed face and telltale eyes.

"You did not mention the presence of those ladies in your ladyship's letter," began Douglas, as his hostess sat down and motioned him to do likewise.

"They came unexpectedly, and you have met before, it seems. You never mentioned that fact, Earl," said Lady Lennox, with a sharp glance.

"Why should I? We only met a few times last winter, and I quite forgot that you knew them. But pray tell me who was the fair one with golden locks, whom I frightened away?"

"The widow of Colonel Vane."

"My dear lady, do you mean to tell me that child is a widow?"

"Yes; and a very lovely one, I assure you. I invited you here expressly to fall in love with her, for George and Harry are too young."

"Thank you. Now be so kind as to tell me all about her, for I knew Vane before he went to India."

"I can only tell you that he married this lady when she was very young, took her to India, and in a year she returned a widow."

"I remember hearing something of an engagement, but fancied it was broken off. Who was the wife?"

"A Montmorenci; noble but poor, you know. The family lost everything in the revolution, and never regained their former grandeur. But one can see at a glance that she is of high birth—high enough to suit even a Douglas."

"Ah, you know our weakness, and I must acknowledge that the best blood in France is not to be despised by the best blood in Scotland. How long have you known her?"

"Only a few months; that charming Countess Camareena brought her from Paris, and left her when she returned. Mrs. Vane seemed lonely for so young a thing; her family are all gone, and she made herself so agreeable, seemed so grateful for any friendship, that I asked her here. She went into very little society in London, and was really suffering for change and care."

"Poor young lady! I will do my best to aid your friendly purpose— for Vane's sake, if not for her own," said Douglas, evidently continuing the subject, lest her ladyship should revert to the former one.

"That reminds me to give you one warning: Never speak to her or before her of the colonel. He died three or four years ago; but when I mentioned him, she implored me to spare her all allusion to that unhappy past, and I have done so. It is my belief that he was not all she believed him to be, and she may have suffered what she is too generous to complain of or confess."

"I doubt that; for when I knew him, though weak on some points, Vane was an excellent fellow. She wears no weeds, I observe."

"You have a quick eye, to discover that in such an instant," replied Lady Lennox, smiling.

"I could scarcely help looking longest at the most striking figure of the group."

"I forgive you for it. She left off her weeds by my advice, for the somber colors seemed to oppress and sadden her. Three or four years are long enough to mourn one whom she did not wholly love, and she is too young to shroud herself in sables for a lifetime."

"Has she fortune?"

"The colonel left her something handsome, I suspect, for she keeps both man and maid, and lives as becomes her rank. I ask no questions, but I feel deeply for the poor child, and do my best for her. Now tell me about home, and your dear mother."

Earl obeyed, and entertained his hostess till the dressing bell rang.

❧ *Chapter III* ❧

THE IRON RING

WHEN Douglas entered the drawing rooms, he was instantly seized upon by Major Mansfield, and while he stood listening with apparent interest to that gentleman's communications, he took a survey of the party before him. The elder ladies were not yet down; Harry Lennox was worshiping Diana with all the frank admiration of a lad of eighteen, and Mrs. Vane was pacing up and down the rooms on the arm of George Lennox, the young master of the house. Few little women would have appeared to advantage beside the tall guardsman; but Mrs. Vane moved with a dignity that seemed to add many inches to her almost fairylike stature, and make her a fit companion for her martial escort. Everything about her was peculiar and piquant. Her dress was of that vivid silvery green which is so ruinous to any but the purest complexion, so ravishing when worn by one whose bloom defies all hues. The skirt swept long behind her, and the Pompadour waist, with its flowing sleeves, displayed a neck and arms of dazzling fairness, half concealed by a film of costly lace. No jewels but an antique opal ring, attached by a slender chain to a singular bracelet, or wide band of enchased gold. A single deep-hued flower glowed on her bosom, and in that wonderful hair of hers a chaplet of delicate ferns seemed to gather back the cloud of curls, and encircle coil upon coil of glossy hair, that looked as if it burdened her small head.

The young man watched her so intently that the major soon observed his preoccupation, and paused in the middle of his account of a review to ask good-naturedly, "Well, what do you think of the bewitching widow?"

"She reminds me of a little green viper," replied Douglas coolly.

"The deuce she does! What put such an odd fancy into your head?" asked the major.

"The color of her gown, her gliding gait, her brilliant eyes, and poor George's evident fascination."

"Faith! I see the resemblance, and you've expressed my feeling exactly. Do you know I've tried to fall in love with that woman, and, upon my soul, I can't do it!"

"She does not care to fascinate you, perhaps."

"Neither does she care to charm George, as I happen to know; yet you see what a deuce of a state he's getting into."

"His youth prevents his seeing the danger before it is too late; and there you have the advantage, Major."

"We shall see how you will prosper, Douglas; for you are not a lad of twenty, like George, or an old fellow of forty, like me, and, if rumor does not lie, you have had 'experiences,' and understand womankind."

Though he spoke in a tone of raillery, the major fixed a curious eye upon his companion's countenance. But the dark handsome face remained inscrutably calm, and the only answer he received was a low—

"Hush! they are coming. Present me, and I'll see what I can make of her."

Now Douglas was undoubtedly the best *parti* of the season, and he knew it. He was not a vain man, but an intensely proud one—proud of his ancient name, his honorable race, his ancestral home, his princely fortune; and he received the homage of both men and women as his due. Great, therefore, was his surprise at the little scene which presently occurred, and very visible was his haughty displeasure.

Lennox and his fair companion approached, the one bending his tall head to listen ardently, the other looking up with a most tempting face, as she talked rapidly, after softening a hard English phrase by an entrancing accent. The major presented his friend with much *empressement*, and Douglas was prepared to receive the gracious greeting which women seldom failed to give him. But scarcely pausing in her progress, Mrs. Vane merely glanced at him, as his name was mentioned, returned his bow with a slight inclination, and rustled on as if quite oblivious that a direct descendant of the great Scotch earl had been presented to her.

The major stifled an irrepressible laugh at this unexpected rebuff, and took a malicious pleasure in watching his friend's eye kindle, his attitude become more stately as he talked on, and deigned to take no notice of an act which evidently much annoyed and amazed him. Just then Lady Lennox entered, and dinner was announced. George beckoned, and Douglas reluctantly joined him.

"As host, I am obliged to take Mrs. Berkeley down; Harry has monopolized Miss Stuart, and the major belongs to my mother—so I must reluctantly relinquish Mrs. Vane to you."

Being a well-bred man, Douglas could only bow, and offer his arm. Mrs. Vane made George happy by a smile, as he left her, then turned to Douglas with a "May I trouble you?" as she gave him her fan and handkerchief to hold, while she gathered up her train and took his arm, as unconcernedly as if he had been a footman. Though rather piqued by her nonchalance, Douglas found something half amusing, half captivating in her demeanor; for, much as he had been courted and admired, few women were quite at ease with the highborn gentleman, whose manners were so coldly charming, whose heart seemed so invulnerable. It was a new sensation to be treated like other men, and set to serve an imperious lady, who leaned upon his arm as if she needed its support, and tranquilly expected the small courtesies which hitherto had been left to his own goodwill and pleasure to offer.

Whatever the secret of his past might be, and however well he might conceal his real self behind a grave demeanor, Douglas had not yet lost his passion for beautiful women, and though no word was spoken during the short transit from drawing room to dinner table, the power of loveliness and womanhood made itself felt beyond a doubt. The touch of a fair hand upon his arm, the dazzle of white shoulders at his side, the soft scent of violets shaken from the folds of lace and cambric which he held, the glimpse of a dainty foot, and the glance of a vivacious eye, all made the little journey memorable. When they took their places, the hauteur had melted from his manner, the coldness from his face, and with his courtliest air he began a conversation which soon became absorbing—for Mrs. Vane talked with the grace of a French woman, and the intelligence of an English woman.

When the gentlemen rejoined the ladies, they were found examining some antique jewels, which Lady Lennox had been prevailed upon to show.

"How well those diamonds look in Diana's dark hair. Ah, my dear, a coronet becomes you vastly. Does it not?" said Mrs. Berkeley, appealing to Douglas, who was approaching.

"So well that I hope you will soon see one rightfully there, madam," he answered, with a glance that made Diana's eyes fall, and Mrs. Berkeley look radiant.

Mrs. Vane saw the look, divined its meaning, and smiled a strange smile, as she looked down upon the jewels that strewed her lap.

Mrs. Berkeley mistook her attitude for one of admiration and envy, and said, "You wear no ornaments but flowers, I observe; from choice, doubtless, for, as you are the last of your race, you must possess many of the family relics."

Mrs. Vane looked up, and answered with an indescribable mixture of simplicity and dignity, "I wear flowers because I have no other ornaments. My family paid the price of loyalty with both life and fortune; but I possess one jewel which I value above all these—a noble name."

A banished princess might have so looked, so spoken, as, gathering up the glittering mass in her white hands, she let it fall again, with an air of gentle pride. Douglas gave her a glance of genuine admiration, and Diana took the diamonds from her hair, as if they burdened her. Mrs. Berkeley saw that her shot had failed, but tried again, only to be more decidedly defeated.

"Very prettily done, my dear; but I really thought you were going to say that your most valuable jewel was the peculiar bracelet you wear. Is there any charming legend or mystery concerning it? I fancied so, because you never take it off, however out of taste it may be; and otherwise your dress is always perfect."

"I wear it in fulfillment of a vow, and the beauty of the ring atones for the ugliness of the bracelet. Does it not?"

As she spoke, Mrs. Vane extended an exquisitely molded arm and hand to Douglas, who answered with most unusual gallantry, "The beauty of the arm would render any fetter an ornament."

He bent to examine the jewel as he spoke, and Mrs. Vane whispered, below her breath, "You have offended Diana; pray make your peace. I should be desolated to think my poor arm had estranged you, even for an hour."

So entirely was he thrown off his guard by this abrupt address, that he whispered eagerly, "Do my actions interest her? Have I any cause for hope? Does she—"

There he paused, recovered his self-possession, but not his countenance—for an angry flush stained his dark cheek, and he fixed a look upon Mrs. Vane that would have daunted any other woman. She did not seem to see it, for her head drooped till her face was hidden, and she sat absently playing with the little chain that shone against her hand. George Lennox looked fiercely jealous; Diana turned pale; Mrs. Berkeley frowned; and good, unconscious Lady Lennox said blandly, "Apropos to heirlooms and relics, I was telling these ladies about your famous iron ring, Earl. I wish you had it here to show them."

"I am happy to be able to gratify your ladyship's wish. I never leave without it, for I use it as my seal. I will ring for it."

Mrs. Vane lifted her head with an air of interest as Douglas gave an order, and his servant presently put a small steel-bound case into his hand. Opening this with a key that hung upon his watch guard, he displayed the famous relic. Antique, rusty, and massive it was, and on its shield the boar's head and the motto of the house.

"You say you use this as a signet ring; why do you not have your arms cut on some jewel, and set in a more graceful setting? This device is almost effaced, and the great ring anything but ornamental to one's hand or chatelaine," said Mrs. Vane, curiously examining the ring as it was passed to her.

"Because I am superstitious and believe that an especial virtue lies in this ancient bit of iron. The legend goes that no harm can befall its possessor, and as I have gone scatheless so far, I hold fast to the old faith."

As Douglas turned to hear and answer Mrs. Vane's question, Harry Lennox, with the freedom of a boy, had thrown back the lid of the case, which had been opened with peculiar care, and, lifting several worn papers, disclosed two objects that drew exclamations of surprise from several of the party. A satin slipper, of fairylike proportions, with a dull red stain upon its sole, and what looked like a ring of massive gold, till the lad lifted it, when coil after coil unwound, till a long curl of human hair touched the ground.

"My faith! That is the souvenir of the beautiful *danseuse* Virginie Varens, about whom you bored me with questions when you showed me that several years ago," said the major, staring with all his eyes.

Mrs. Vane had exclaimed with the rest, but her color faded perceptibly, her eye grew troubled, and when Harry leaned toward her to compare the long tress with her own, she shrank back with a shudder. Diana caught a muttered ejaculation from Douglas, saw Mrs. Vane's discomposure, and fixed a scrutinizing gaze upon her. But in a moment those obedient features resumed their former calm, and, with a little gesture of contrition, Mrs. Vane laid the long curl beside one of her own, saying tranquilly:

"Pardon, that I betrayed an instinctive shrinking from anything plebeian. The hair of the dancer is lighter than mine, you see; for this is pure gold, and mine is fast deepening to brown. Let me atone for my rudeness thus; and believe me, I can sympathize, for I, too, have loved and lost."

While speaking, she had refolded the lock, and, tying it together with a little knot of ribbon from her dress, she laid it back into its owner's hand, with a soft glance and a delicate dropping of the voice at the last words.

If it was a bit of acting, it was marvelously well done, and all believed it to be a genuine touch of nature. Diana looked consumed with curiosity, and Douglas answered hastily, "Thanks for the pity, but I need none. I never saw this girl, and as for love—"

He paused there, as if words unfit for time and place were about to pass his lips. His eye grew fierce, and his black brows lowered heavily, leaving no doubt on the mind of any observer that hate, not love, was the sentiment with which he now regarded the mysterious *danseuse*. An uncomfortable pause followed as Douglas relocked the case and put it in his pocket, forgetting, in his haste, the ring he had slipped upon his finger.

Feeling that some unpleasant theme had been touched upon, Lady Lennox asked for music. Diana coldly declined, but Mrs. Vane readily turned to the piano. The two elder ladies and the major went to chat by the fire; Lennox took his brother aside to administer a reproof; and Douglas, after a moment of moody thoughtfulness, placed himself beside Diana on the couch which stood just behind Mrs. Vane. She had begun with a brilliant overture, but suddenly passed to a softer movement, and filled the room with the whispering melody of a Venetian barcarole. This seeming caprice was caused by an intense desire to overhear the words of the pair behind her. But though she strained her keen ear to the utmost, she caught only broken fragments of their low-toned conversation, and these fragments filled her with disquiet.

"Why so cold, Miss Stuart? One would think you had forgotten me."

"I fancied the forgetfulness was yours."

"I never shall forget the happiest hours of my life. May I hope that you recall those days with pleasure?"

There was no answer, and a backward glance showed Mrs. Vane Diana's head bent low, and Douglas watching the deepening color on her half-averted cheek with an eager, ardent glance. More softly murmured the boat song, and scarcely audible was the whispered entreaty:

"I have much to say; you will hear me tomorrow, early, in the park?"

A mute assent was given, and, with the air of a happy lover, Douglas left her, as if fearing to say more, lest their faces should betray them. Then the barcarole ended as suddenly as it had begun, and Mrs. Vane resumed the stormy overture, playing as if inspired by a musical frenzy. So pale was she when she left the instrument that no one doubted the fact of her needing rest, as, pleading weariness, she sank into a deep chair, and leaning her head upon her hand, sat silent for an hour.

As they separated for the night, and Douglas stood listening to his young host's arrangements for the morrow, a singular-looking man appeared at the door of an anteroom and, seeing them, paused where he stood, as if waiting for them to precede him.

"Who is that, George? What does he want?" said Douglas, drawing his friend's attention to the dark figure, whose gleaming eyes belied his almost servile posture of humility and respect.

"Oh, that is Mrs. Vane's man, Jitomar. He was one of the colonel's Indian servants, I believe. Deaf and dumb, but harmless, devoted, and invaluable—*she* says. A treacherous-looking devil, to my mind," replied Lennox.

"He looks more like an Italian than an Indian, in spite of his Eastern costume and long hair. What is he after now?" asked Earl.

"Going to receive the orders of his mistress. I would gladly change places with him, heathen as he is, for the privilege of serving her. Good night."

As George spoke, they parted, and while the dark servant watched Douglas going up the wide oaken stairs, he shook his clenched hand after the retreating figure, and his lips moved as if he muttered something low between his teeth.

A few moments afterward, as Earl sat musing over his fire, there came a tap at his door. Having vainly bidden the knocker to enter, he answered the summons, and saw Jitomar obsequiously offering a handkerchief. Douglas examined it, found the major's name, and, pointing out that gentleman's room, farther down the corridor, he returned the lost article with a nod of thanks and dismissal. While he had been turning the square of cambric in his hands, the man's keen eyes had explored every corner of the room. Nothing seemed to escape them, from the ashes on the hearth, to a flower which Diana had worn, now carefully preserved in water; and once a gleam of satisfaction glittered in them, as if some desired object had met their gaze. Making a low obeisance, he retired, and Douglas went to bed, to dream waking dreams till far into the night.

The great hall clock had just struck one, and sleep was beginning to conquer love, when something startled him wide awake. What it was he could not tell, but every sense warned him of impending danger. Sitting up in his bed, he pushed back the curtains and looked out. The night lamp burned low, the fire had faded, and the room was full of dusky shadows. There were three doors: one led to the dressing room, one to the corridor, and the third was locked on the outside. He knew that it opened upon a flight of narrow stairs that communicated with the library, having been built for the convenience of a studious Lennox long ago.

As he gazed about him, to his great amazement the door was seen to move. Slowly, noiselessly it opened, with no click of lock, no creak of hinge. Almost sure of seeing some ghostly visitant enter, he waited mute and motionless. A muffled hand and arm appeared and, stretching to their utmost, seemed to take something from the writing table that stood near this door. It was a human hand, and with a single leap Douglas was halfway across the room. But the door closed rapidly, and as he laid his hand upon it, the key turned in the lock. He demanded who was there, but not a sound replied; he shook the door, but the lock held fast; he examined the table, but nothing seemed gone, till, with an ominous thrill, he missed the iron ring. On reaching his chamber, he had taken it off, meaning to restore it to its place; had laid it down, to put Diana's rose in water; had forgotten it, and now it was gone!

Flinging on dressing gown and slippers, and taking a pistol from his traveling case, he left his room. The house was quiet as a tomb, the library empty, and no sign of intruders visible, till, coming to the door itself, he found that the rusty lock had been newly oiled, for the rusty key turned noiselessly, and the hinges worked smoothly, though the dust that lay thickly everywhere showed that this passage was still unused. Stepping into his room, Douglas gave a searching glance about him, and in an instant an expression of utter bewilderment fell upon his face, for there, on the exact spot which had been empty five minutes ago, there lay the iron ring!

≫ *Chapter IV* ≪

A SHRED OF LACE

LONG before any of the other guests were down, Diana stole into the garden on her way to the park. Hope shone in her eyes, smiles sat on her lips, and her heart sang for joy. She had long loved in secret; had believed and despaired alternately; and now her desire was about to be fulfilled, her happiness assured by a lover's voice. Hurrying through the wilderness of autumn flowers, she reached the shrubbery that divided park and garden. Pausing an instant to see if anyone awaited her beyond, she gave a great start, and looked as if she had encountered a ghost.

It was only Mrs. Vane; she often took early strolls in the park, followed by her man; Diana knew this, but had forgotten it in her new bliss. She was alone now, and as she seemed unconscious of her presence, Diana would have noiselessly withdrawn, if a glimpse of Mrs. Vane's face had not arrested and detained her. As if she had thrown herself down in a paroxysm of distress, sat Mrs. Vane, with both hands tightly clasped; her white lips were compressed, and in her eyes was a look of mingled pain, grief, and despair. The most careless observer would have detected the presence of some great anxiety or sorrow, and Diana, made generous by the assurance of her own happiness, for the first time felt a touch of pity for the woman of whom she had been both envious and jealous. Forgetting herself, she hastened forward, saying kindly, "Are you suffering, Mrs. Vane? What can I do for you?"

Mrs. Vane started as if she had been shot, sprang to her feet, and putting out her hands as if to keep the other off, cried, almost incoher-

ently, "Go back! Go back, and save yourself! For me you can do nothing
—it is too late!"

"Indeed, I hope not. Tell me your trouble, and let me help you
if I can," urged Diana, shocked yet not alarmed by the wildness of Mrs.
Vane's look and manner.

But she only clasped her hands before her face, saying despairingly,
"You can help both of us—but at what a price!"

"No price will be too costly, if I can honorably pay it. I have been
unjust, unkind; forgive it, and confide in me; for indeed, I pity you."

"Ah, if I dared!" sighed Mrs. Vane. "It seems impossible, and yet
I ought—for you, not I, will suffer most from my enforced silence."

She paused an instant, seemed to calm herself by strong effort, and,
fixing her mournful eyes upon Diana, she said, in a strangely solemn and
impressive manner, "Miss Stuart, if ever a woman needed help and pity,
it is I. You have misjudged, distrusted, and disliked me; I freely forgive
this, and long to save you, as I alone can do. But a sacred promise fetters
me—I dare not break it; yet if you will pledge your word to keep this
interview secret, I will venture to give you one hint, one warning, which
may save you from destroying your peace forever. Will you give me this
assurance?"

Diana shrank back, disturbed and dismayed by the appeal and the
requirement. Mrs. Vane saw her hesitation, and wrung her hands together in an agony of impotent regret.

"I knew it—I feared it. You will not trust me—you will not let me
ease my conscience by trying to save another woman from the fate that
darkens all my life. Go your way, then, and when the bitter hour comes,
remember that I tried to save you from it, and you would not hear me."

"Stay, Mrs. Vane! I do trust you—I will listen; and I give you my
word that I will conceal this interview. Speak quickly—I must go," cried
Diana, won to compliance even against her wishes.

"Stoop to me—not even the air must hear what I breathe. Ask Allan
Douglas the mystery of his life before you marry him, else you will rue
the hour that you became his wife."

"Allan Douglas! You know his name? You know the secret of his
past?" exclaimed Diana, lost in wonder.

"My husband knew him, and I— Hush! Someone is coming. Quick!
Escape into the park, or your face will betray you. I can command myself; I will meet and accost whoever comes."

Before the rapid whisper ended, Diana was gone, and when Douglas
came hastening to his tryst, he too found Mrs. Vane alone—and he too
paused a moment, surprised to see her there. But the picture he saw was

a very different one from that which arrested Diana. Great indeed must have been Mrs. Vane's command of countenance, for no trace of agitation was visible, and never had she looked more lovely than now, as she stood with a handful of flowers in the white skirt of her dress, her bright hair blowing in the wind, her soft eyes fixed on vacancy, while a tranquil smile proved that her thoughts were happy ones.

So young, so innocent, so blithe she looked that Douglas involuntarily thought, with a touch of self-reproach: "Pretty creature! What injustice my ungallant smile did her last night! I ask her pardon." Then aloud, as he approached, "Good morning, Mrs. Vane. I am off for an early stroll."

With the shy grace, the artless glance of a child, she looked up at him, offering a flower, and saying, as she smilingly moved on, "May it be a pleasant one."

It was not a pleasant one, however; and perhaps Mrs. Vane's wish had been sweetly ironical. Diana greeted her lover coldly, listened to his avowal with an air of proud reserve, that contrasted strangely with the involuntary betrayals of love and joy that escaped her. Entirely laying aside the chilly gravity, the lofty manner, which was habitual to him, Douglas proved that he could woo ardently, and forget the pride of the man in the passion of the lover. But when he sued for a verbal answer to his prayer, although he thought he read the assent in the crimson cheek half turned away, the downcast eyes, that would not meet his own, and the quick flutter of the heart that beat under his hand, he was thunderstruck at the change which passed over Diana. She suddenly grew colorless and calm as any statue, and freeing herself from his hold, fixed a searching look upon him, while she said slowly and distinctly, "When you have told me the mystery of your life, I will give my answer to your love—not before."

"The mystery of my life!" he echoed, falling back a step or two, with such violent discomposure in face and manner that Diana's heart sank within her, though she answered steadily:

"Yes; I must know it, before I link my fate with yours."

"Who told you that I had one?" he demanded.

"Lady Lennox. I had heard the rumor before, but never gave it thought till she confirmed it. Now I wait for your explanation."

"It is impossible to give it; but I swear to you, Diana, that I am innocent of any act that could dishonor my name, or mar your peace, if it were known. The secret is not mine to tell; I have promised to keep it, and I cannot forfeit my word, even for your sake. Be generous; do not let mere curiosity or pique destroy my hopes, and make you cruel when you should be kind."

So earnestly he spoke, so tenderly he pleaded, that Diana's purpose wavered, and would have failed her, had not the memory of Mrs. Vane's strange warning returned to her, bringing with it other memories of other mysterious looks, hints, and acts which had transpired since Douglas came. These recollections hardened her heart, confirmed her resolution, and gave her power to appear inexorable to the last.

"You mistake my motive, sir. Neither curiosity nor pique influenced me, but a just and natural desire to assure myself that in trusting my happiness to your keeping, I am not entailing regret upon myself, remorse upon you. I must know all your past, before I endanger my future; clear yourself from the suspicions which have long clung to you, and I am yours; remain silent, and we are nothing to each other from this day forth."

Her coldness chilled his passion, her distrust irritated his pride; all the old hauteur returned fourfold, his eye grew hard, his voice bitter, and his whole manner showed that his will was as inflexible as hers.

"Are you resolved on making this unjust, ungenerous test of my affection, Miss Stuart?"

"I am."

"You have no faith in my honor, then? No consideration for the hard strait in which my promise places me? No compassion for the loss I must sustain in losing the love, respect, and confidence of the woman dearest to me?"

"Assure me that you are worthy of love, respect, confidence, and I gladly accord them to you."

"I cannot, in the way you demand. Will nothing else satisfy you?"

"Nothing!"

"Then, in your words, we are nothing to one another from this day forth. Farewell, Diana!"

With an involuntary impulse, she put out her hand to detain him as he turned away. He took it, and bending, kissed it, with a lingering fondness that nearly conquered her. The act, the look that accompanied it, the tremor of the lips that performed it, touched the poor girl's heart, and words of free acceptance were rising to her lips, when, as he bent, a miniature, suspended by a chain of mingled hair and gold, swung forward from its hiding place in his breast, and though she saw no face, the haste with which he replaced it roused all her suspicions again, and redoubled all her doubts. Scorning herself for her momentary weakness, the gesture of recall was changed to one of dismissal, as she withdrew her hand, and turned from him, with a quiet "Farewell, then, forever!"

"One moment," he pleaded. "Do not let us destroy the peace of both our lives by an unhappy secret which in no way but this can do us harm. Bear with me for a few days, Diana; think over this interview, remember my great love for you, let your own generous nature appeal to your pride, and perhaps time may show you that it is possible to love, trust, and pardon me."

Glad of any delay which should spare her the pain of an immediate separation, she hesitated a moment, and then, with feigned reluctance, answered, "My visit was to have ended with the coming week; I will not shorten it, but give you till then to reconsider your decision, and by a full confession secure your happiness and my own."

Then they parted—not with the lingering adieus of happy lovers, but coldly, silently, like estranged friends—and each took a different way back, instead of walking blissfully together, as they had thought to do.

"Why so *triste*, Diana? One would think you had seen a ghost in the night, you look so pale and solemn. And, upon my word, Mr. Douglas looks as if he had seen one also," said Mrs. Berkeley, as they all gathered about the breakfast table two hours later.

"I did see one," answered Douglas, generously distracting general attention from Diana, who could ill sustain it.

"Last night?" exclaimed Mrs. Berkeley, full of interest at once.

"Yes, madam—at one o'clock last night."

"How charming! Tell us all about it; I dote upon ghosts, yet never saw one," said Mrs. Vane.

Douglas narrated his adventure. The elder ladies looked disturbed, Diana incredulous; and Mrs. Vane filled the room with her silvery laughter, as Harry protested that no ghost belonged to the house, and George explained the mystery as being the nightmare.

"I never have it; neither do I walk in my sleep, and seldom dream," replied Douglas. "I perfectly remember rising, partially dressing, and going down to the library, up the private stairs, and examining the door. This may be proved by the key, now changed to my side of the lock, and the train of wax which dropped from my candle as I hurried along."

"What woke you?" asked Mrs. Vane.

"I cannot tell; some slight sound, probably, although I do not remember hearing any, and fancy it was an instinctive sense of danger."

"That door could not have been opened without much noise, for the key was rusted in the lock. We tried to turn it the other day, and could not, so were forced to go round by the great gallery to reach that room."

Diana spoke, and for the first time since they parted in the park, Douglas looked at and addressed her.

"You have explored the private passage then, and tried the door? May I ask when?"

"Harry was showing us the house; anything mysterious pleased us, so we went up, tried the rusty key, and finding it immovable, we came down again."

"Of whom was the party composed?"

"My aunt, Mrs. Vane, and myself, accompanied by Harry."

"Then I must accuse Harry of the prank, for both key and lock have been newly oiled, and the door opens easily and noiselessly, as you may prove if you like. He must have had an accomplice among the housemaids, for it was a woman's hand that took the ring. She doubtless passed it to him, and while I was preparing to sally forth, both ran away —one to hide, the other to wait till I left my room, when he slipped in and restored the ring. Was that it, Hal?"

As Douglas spoke, all looked at Harry; but the boy shook his head, and triumphantly replied to his brother:

"George will tell you that your accusation is entirely unjust; and as he sat up till dawn, writing poetry, I could not have left him without his knowledge."

"True, Hal—you had nothing to do with it, I know. Did you distinctly see the hand that purloined your ring, Earl?" asked Lennox, anxious to divert attention from the revelation of his poetical amusements.

"No; the room was dusky, and the hand muffled in something dark. But it was no ghostly hand, for as it was hastily withdrawn when I sprang up, the wrapper slipped aside, and I saw white human flesh, and the outlines of a woman's arm."

"Was it a beautiful arm?" asked Lennox, with his eyes upon Mrs. Vane's, which lay like a piece of sculptured marble against the red velvet cushion of her chair.

"Very beautiful, I should say; for in that hasty glimpse it looked too fair to belong to any servant, and when I found this hanging to the lock, I felt assured that my spirit was a lady, for housemaids do not wear anything like this, I fancy," and Douglas produced a shred of black lace, evidently torn from some costly flounce or scarf.

The ladies put their heads together over the scrap, and all pronounced it quite impossible for any dressing maid to have come honestly by such expensive trimming as this must have been.

"It looks as if it had belonged to a deeply scalloped flounce," said Mrs. Vane. "Who of us wears such? Miss Stuart, you are in black; have I not seen you with a trimming like this?"

"You forget—I wear no trimming but crepe. This never was a part of a flounce. It is the corner of a shawl. You see how unequally rounded the two sides are; and no flounce was ever scalloped so deeply as this," returned Diana.

"How acute you are, Di! It is so, I really believe. See how exactly this bit compares with the corner of my breakfast shawl, made to imitate lace. Who wears a black lace shawl? Neither Di nor myself," said Mrs. Berkeley.

"Mrs. Vane often wears one."

Diana uttered the name with significance, and Douglas stirred a little, as if she put into words some vague idea of his own. Mrs. Vane shrugged her shoulders, sipped her coffee, and answered tranquilly, "So does Lady Lennox; but I will bear all the suspicions of phantom folly, and when I dress for dinner will put on every rag of lace I possess, so that you may compare this bit, and prove me guilty if it gives you pleasure. Though what object I could have in running about in the dark, oiling door locks, stealing rings, and frightening gentlemen is not as clear to me as it appears to be to you—probably because I am not as much interested in the sufferer."

Diana looked embarrassed, Lady Lennox grave, and, as if weary of the subject, Douglas thrust the shred of lace into his waistcoat pocket, and proposed a riding party. Miss Stuart preferred driving her aunt in the pony carriage, but Mrs. Vane accepted the invitation, and made George Lennox wretched by accepting the loan of one of Earl's horses in preference to his own, which she had ridden the day before. When she appeared, ready for the expedition, glances of admiration shone in the eyes of all the gentlemen, even the gloomy Douglas, as he watched her, wondering if the piquant figure before him could be the same that he had seen in the garden, looking like a lovely, dreaming child. Her black habit, with its velvet facings, set off her little lithe figure to a charm; her hair shone like imprisoned sunshine through the scarlet net that held it, and her face looked bewilderingly brilliant and arch in the shadow of a cavalier hat, with its graceful plume.

As Douglas bent to offer his hand in mounting her, she uttered an exclamation of pain, and caught at his arm to keep herself from falling. Involuntarily he sustained her, and for an instant she leaned upon him, with her face hidden in his breast, as if to conceal some convulsion of suffering.

"My dear Mrs. Vane, what is it? Let me take you in—shall I call for help?" began Douglas, much alarmed.

But she interrupted him and, looking up with a faint smile, answered quietly, as she attempted to stand alone, "It is nothing but the cramp in my foot. It will be over in a moment; Gabrielle fastened my boot too tightly—let me sit down, and I will loosen it."

"Allow me; lean on my shoulder; it's but a moment."

Down knelt Douglas; and, with one hand lightly touching his shoulder to steady herself, the other still closely folded, as if not yet out of pain, Mrs. Vane stood glancing from under her long lashes at Diana, who was waiting in the hall for her aunt, and observing the scene in the avenue with ill-concealed anxiety. The string was in a knot, and Douglas set about his little service very leisurely, for the foot and ankle before him were the most perfect he had ever seen. While so employed, Jitomar, Mrs. Vane's man, appeared, and, tossing him the gloves she had taken off, she signed to him to bid her maid bring her another pair, as some slight blemish in these had offended her fastidious taste. He comprehended with difficulty, it seemed, for words were useless to a deaf-mute, and the motions of his mistress's hands appeared at first without meaning to him. The idea came with a flash, and bowing, he bounded into the house, with his white robes streaming, and his scarlet slippers taking him along as if enchanted, while the grooms wondered, and Mrs. Vane laughed.

Jitomar hurried to his lady's room, delivered his message, and while Gabrielle went down with a fresh pair of gloves, he enacted a curious little scene in the deserted chamber. Carefully unfolding the discarded gloves, he took from the inside of one of them the shred of lace that Douglas had put into his waistcoat pocket at the breakfast table. He examined it with a peculiar smile; then going to a tiger-skin rug that lay beside the bed, he lifted it and produced a black lace shawl, which seemed to have been hastily hidden there. One corner was gone; but laying the torn bit in its place, it fitted exactly, and, as if satisfied, Jitomar refolded both, put them in his pocket, glided to his own room, prepared himself for going out, and, unobserved by anyone, took the next train to London. Mrs. Vane meanwhile had effaced the memory of her first failure by mounting her horse alone, with an elasticity and grace that filled her escort with astonishment and admiration. Laughing her enchanting laugh, she settled herself in the saddle, touched her hat to

Lady Lennox, and cantered away with Douglas, while Harry followed far behind, for George had suddenly remembered that an engagement would prevent his joining them, having no mind to see Mrs. Vane absorbed by another.

As they climbed a long hill, Mrs. Vane suddenly paused in her witty badinage, and after a thoughtful moment, and a backward glance at Harry, who followed apparently out of earshot, she said, earnestly yet timidly, "Mr. Douglas, I desire to ask a favor of you—not for myself, but for the sake of one who is dear to both of us."

"Mrs. Vane can ask no favor that I shall not be both proud and happy to grant for her own sake," returned Earl, eyeing her with much surprise.

"Well, then, I shall be most grateful if you will shun me for a few days; ignore my presence as far as possible, and so heal the breach which I fear I may unconsciously have caused between Miss Stuart and yourself."

"I assure you that you are mistaken regarding the cause of the slight coolness between us, and it is impossible to ignore the existence of Mrs. Vane, having once had the happiness of seeing her."

"Ah, you take refuge in evasion and compliments, as I feared you would; but it is my nature to be frank, and I shall compass my end by leaving you no subterfuge and no power to deny me. I met you both this morning, and read a happy secret in your faces; I hoped when next I saw you to find your mutual happiness secured. But no—I found you grave and cold; saw trouble in your eyes, jealousy and pain in Diana's. I have seen the latter sentiment in her eyes before, and could not but think that I was the unhappy cause of this estrangement. She is peculiar; she does not like me, will not let me love her, and wounds me in many ways. I easily forgive her, for she is not happy, and I long to help her, even against her will—therefore I speak to you."

"Again I assure you that you are wrong. Diana is jealous, but not of you alone, and she has placed me in a cruel strait. I, too, will be frank, and confess that she will not listen to me, unless I betray a secret that is not my own."

"You will not do this, having sworn to keep it?"

"Never! A Douglas cannot break his word."

"I comprehend now," said Mrs. Vane. "Diana wishes to test her power, and you rebel. It is not natural in both; yet I beseech you not to try her too much, because at a certain point she will become unmanageable. She comes of an unhappy race, and desperate things have been done in her family. Guard your secret, for honor demands it, but take my warning and shun me, that you may add nothing to the trouble she has brought upon herself."

"I have no wish to do so; but she also must beware of testing her power too severely, for I am neither a patient nor a humble man, and my will is inflexible when once I am resolved. She should see this, should trust me, and let us both be happy."

"Ah, if she truly loved, she would; for then one believes blindly, can think no ill, fear no wrong, desire no confidence that is not freely given. She does not know the bliss of loving with one's whole heart and soul, and asking no happier fate than to live for a man whose affection makes a heaven anywhere."

They had paused on the brow of the hill to wait for Harry, and as she spoke, Mrs. Vane's face kindled with a glow that made it doubly beautiful; for voice, eyes, lips, and gestures all betrayed how well *she* could love. Douglas regarded her with a curious consciousness of attraction and repulsion, feeling that had he met her before he saw and loved Diana, he never should have given his peace into the keeping of that exacting girl. An involuntary sigh escaped him; Mrs. Vane brightened instantly, saying:

"Nay, do not fall back into your gloomy mood again, or I shall think that I have increased, not lessened, your anxiety. I came to cheer you if I could, for though I have done with love myself, it gives me sincerest satisfaction to serve those who are just beginning to know its pleasant pain."

She was smiling as she spoke, but the lovely eyes lifted to her companion's face were full of tears. Remembering her loneliness, her loss, and with a grateful sense of all she desired to do for him, Douglas ungloved and offered her his hand, with an impulsive gesture, saying warmly, "You are very kind; I thank you, and feel already comforted by the thought that though I may have lost a lover, I have gained a friend."

Here Harry came up brimful of curiosity, for he had seen and heard more than they knew. After this they all rode on together, and when Douglas dismounted Mrs. Vane she whispered, "Remember, you are to shun me, no matter how pointedly. I shall forgive you, and she will be happier for our little ruse."

This speech, as well as the first uttered by Mrs. Vane when their serious conversation began, was overheard by Harry, and when Diana carelessly asked him if he had enjoyed his ride, he repeated the two remarks, hoping to gain some explanation of them before he told his brother, whose cause he heartily espoused. He knew nothing of Miss Stuart's love, and made her his confidante without a suspicion of the pang he was inflicting. She bade him forget what he had heard, but could not do so herself, and all that day those two sentences rang through her mind unceasingly.

Pausing that evening in the hall to examine one of the ancient portraits hanging there, Douglas heard a soft rustle, and turning, saw Mrs. Vane entering, as if from a moonlight stroll on the balcony. The night was cool, and over her head was drawn a corner of the black lace shawl that drooped from her shoulders. Her dress of violet silk was trimmed with a profusion of black lace, and wonderingly becoming to white skin and golden hair was the delicate tint and its rich decoration. Douglas went to her, saying, as he offered his hand, "You see how well I keep my word; now let me reward myself by taking you in. But, first, pray tell me if this is a picture of Sir Lionel."

He led her to the portrait that had excited his curiosity, and while she told him some little legend of it, he still lingered, held as much by the charm of the living voice as by the exploits of the dead knight. Standing thus, arm in arm, alone and engrossed in one another, neither, apparently, saw Diana pausing on the threshold of the library with an expression of deep displeasure in her face. Douglas did not see her; Mrs. Vane did, though not a sign betrayed it, except that in an instant her whole expression changed. As Douglas looked up at the picture, she looked up at him with love, grief, pain, and pity visibly contending in her beautiful face; then suddenly withdrawing her arm, she said, "I forgot, we are strangers now. Let me enter alone." And gliding from him with bent head, she passed into the drawing room.

Much amazed at her abrupt flight, Earl looked after her, saw Diana watching him, and inexpressibly annoyed by the contretemps, he started, colored, bowed coldly, and followed Mrs. Vane without a word. For a moment, Diana lingered with her head in her hands, thinking disconsolately: "What secret lies between them? She leaned and looked as if she had a right there. He is already more at ease with her than me, although they met but yesterday. Have they not met before? She asked some favor 'for the sake of one dear to both.' Who is it? He must shun her that someone may be happy, though deceived. Is that me? She knows his mystery, has a part in it, and I am to be kept blind. Wait a little! I too can plot, and watch, and wait. I can read faces, fathom actions, and play a part, though my heart breaks in doing it."

All that evening she watched them; saw that Douglas did not shun Mrs. Vane; also that he feigned unconsciousness of her own keen scrutiny, and seemed endeavoring to chase from her mind the memory of the morning's interview, or the evening's discovery. She saw Mrs.

Vane act surprise, pique, and displeasure at his seeming desertion, and console herself by making her peace with Lennox. To others, Diana appeared unusually animated and carefree, but never had an evening seemed so interminable, and never had she so gladly hailed the hour of separation.

She was standing by Lady Lennox when Mrs. Vane came up to say good night. Her ladyship did not like Diana, and did both love and pity the lonely little widow, who had endeared herself in so many ways. As she swept a curtsy, with the old-fashioned reverence that her hostess liked, Lady Lennox drew her nearer and kissed her with motherly affection, saying playfully as she did so, "No pranks tonight among the spirits, my dear, else these friends will think you and I are witches in good earnest."

"That reminds me, I have kept my promise, and Mr. Douglas can compare his telltale bit with my mother's, and, as you see, very precious in every respect."

Gravely exploring one pocket after another, Earl presently announced, with some chagrin, that the bit was lost, blown away while riding, probably. So nothing could be done, and Mrs. Vane was acquitted of lending her laces to the household ghost. Diana looked disappointed, and taking up a corner of the shawl, said, as she examined it narrowly, "As I remember the shred, it matched this pattern exactly. It is a peculiar one, and I observed it well. I wish the bit was not lost, for if people play such games with your clothes, they may take equal liberties with mine."

Seeing suspicion in her eyes, Mrs. Vane gathered the four corners of the shawl together, and with great care spread each over her violet skirt before Diana. Not a fracture appeared, and when she had done the same with every atom of trimming on her dress, she drew her slender figure up with an air of proud dignity, asking almost sternly, "Am I acquitted of this absurd charge, Miss Stuart?"

Entirely disconcerted by the quickness with which her distrust had been seen and exposed, Diana could only look guilty, apologize, and find herself convicted of an unjust suspicion. Mrs. Vane received her atonement graciously, and wrapping her shawl about her, went away to bed, with a mischievous smile shining in her eyes as she bowed to Douglas, whose glance followed her till the last glimpse of the violet dress disappeared.

❧ *Chapter V* ❧

TREASON

THE week passed gaily enough, externally, but to several of the party it was a very dreary and very memorable week. George Lennox basked in the light of Mrs. Vane's smiles, and his mother began to hope that Douglas would not take her at her word, but leave her son to woo and win the bonny widow, if he could. Earl watched and waited for Diana to relent, pleading with his eyes, though never a word of submission or appeal passed his lips. And poor Diana, hoping to conquer him, silenced the promptings of her reason, and stood firm, when a yielding look, a tender word, would have overcome his pride, and healed the breach. She suffered much, but told no one her pain till the last day came. Then, driven by the thought that a few hours would seal her fate, she resolved to appeal to Mrs. Vane. She knew the mystery; she professed to pity her. She was a woman, and to her this humiliation would not be so hard, this confession so impossible.

Diana haunted the hall and drawing rooms all that morning, hoping to find Mrs. Vane alone. At last, just before lunch, she caught her playing with Earl's spaniel, while she waited for Lennox to bring her hat from the garden seat where she had left it.

"Be so kind as to take a turn with me on the balcony, Mrs. Vane. I wish much to say a few words to you," began Diana, with varying color and anxious eyes, as she met her at the great hall door.

"With pleasure. Give me your arm, and let us have our little chat quite comfortably together. Can I do anything for you, my dear Miss Stuart? Pray speak freely, and, believe me, I desire to be your friend."

So kind, so cordial was the tone, the look, that poor Diana felt comforted at once; and bending her stately head to the bright one at her

side, she said, with a sad humility, which proved how entirely her love
had subdued her pride, "I hope so, Mrs. Vane, for I need a friend. You,
and you alone, can help me. I humble myself to you; I forget not my
own misgivings. I endeavor to see in you only a woman younger, yet
wiser than myself, who, knowing my sore necessity, will help me by
confessing the share she bears in the secret that is destroying my peace."

"I wish I could! I wish I dared! I have thought of it often; have
longed to do it at all costs; and then remembering my vow, I have held
my peace!"

"Assure me of one thing and I will submit. I will ask Allan to forgive me, and I will be happy in my ignorance, if I can. He told me that
this mystery would not stain his honor, or mar my peace if it were
known. Mrs. Vane, is this true?" asked Diana solemnly.

"No; a man's honor is not tarnished in his eyes by treachery to a
woman, and he believes that a woman's peace will not be marred by
the knowledge that in God's sight she is not his wife, although she may
be in the eyes of the world."

"Mrs. Vane, I conjure you to tell me what you mean! I have a right
to know; it is your duty to save me from sin and sorrow if you can, and
I will make any promise you exact to keep eternally secret whatever
you may tell me. If you fear Douglas, he shall never know that you have
broken your vow, whether I marry or discard him. Have pity upon me,
I implore you, for this day must make or mar my life!"

Few women could have withstood the desperate urgency of Diana's
prayer; Mrs. Vane did not. A moment she stood, growing paler as some
purpose took shape in her mind, then drew her companion onward,
saying hurriedly, as George Lennox appeared in the avenue, "Invite me
to drive out alone with you after lunch, and then you shall know all.
But, O Miss Stuart, remember that you bring the sorrow upon yourself
if you urge this disclosure. I cannot think it right to see you give yourself
to this man without a protest; but you may curse me for destroying your
faith in him, while powerless to kill your love. Go now, and if you retract your wish, be silent; I shall know."

They parted, and when Lennox came up, the balcony was deserted.

"My love, you get so pale and spiritless that I am quite reconciled
to our departure; for the air here does not suit you, and we must try the
seashore," said Mrs. Berkeley, as they rose from the table after lunch.

"I shall be myself again soon, Aunt. I need more exercise, and if
Mrs. Vane will allow me, I should enjoy a long drive with her this
afternoon," returned Diana, growing still paler as she spoke.

Mrs. Vane bowed her acceptance, and as she left the room a curious shiver seemed to shake her from head to foot as she pressed her hands together and hurried to her chamber.

The two ladies drove in silence, till Diana said abruptly, "I am ready, Mrs. Vane; tell me all, and spare nothing."

"Your solemn oath first, that living or dying, you will never reveal to any human soul what I shall tell you." And as she spoke, Mrs. Vane extended her hand.

Diana gave her own, and took the oath which the other well knew she would keep inviolate.

"I shall not torture you by suspense," Mrs. Vane began, "but show you at once why I would save you from a greater suffering than the loss of love. Miss Stuart, read that, and learn the mystery of your lover's life."

With a sudden gesture, she took from her bosom a worn paper, and unfolding it, held before the other's eyes the marriage record of Allan Douglas and Virginie Varens.

Not a word passed Diana's lips, but with the moan of a broken heart she covered up her face, and slowly, tremulously, the voice at her side went on, "You see here the date of that mysterious journey to Paris, from which he returned an altered man. There, too, is his private seal. That long lock of hair, that stained slipper, belonged to Virginie; and though he said he had never seen her, the lie cost him an effort, and well it might, for I sat there before him, and I am Virginie."

Diana's hands dropped from her pallid face, as she shrank away from her companion, yet gazed at her like one fascinated by an awful spell.

"Hear my story, and then judge between us," the voice continued, so melancholy, yet so sweet that tears came to the listener's eyes, as the sad story was unfolded. "I am of a noble family, but was left so poor, so friendless, that but for a generous boy I should have perished in the streets of Paris. He was a dancer, his poor earnings could not support us both. I discovered this, and in my innocence, thought no labor degrading that lessened my great debt to him. I, too, had become a dancer. I had youth, beauty, health, and a grateful heart to help me on. I made money. I had many lovers, but Victor kept me safe, for he, too, loved, but in secret, till he was sure I could give him love, not gratitude. Then Allan came, and I forgot the world about me; for I loved as only a girl of seventeen can love the first man who has touched her heart. He offered me his hand and honorable name, for I was as wellborn as himself, and even in my seeming degradation, he respected me. We were married, and for a year I was as happy as an angel. Then my boy was born, and for a time I lost my beauty. That cooled Allan's waning passion. Some fear of consequences, some later regret for his rash act, came over him, and made him very bitter to me when I most needed tenderness. He told me that our marriage had been without witnesses, that our faith was different, and that vows pronounced before a Catholic priest alone were not binding upon him. That he was weary of me, and having been recalled to Scotland, he desired to return as free as he went. If I would promise solemnly to conceal the truth, he would support the boy and me abroad, until I chose to marry; that I must destroy the record of the deed, and never claim him, or he would denounce me as an impostor, and take away the boy. Miss Stuart, I was very ignorant and young; my heart was broken, and I believed myself dying. For the child's sake, I promised all things, and he left me; but remorse haunted him, and his peace was poisoned from that hour."

"And you? You married Colonel Vane?" whispered Diana, holding her breath to listen.

"No, I have never married, for in my eyes that ceremony made me Allan's wife, and I shall be so till I die. When I was most forlorn, Colonel Vane found me. He was Allan's friend; he had seen me with him, and when we met again, he pitied me; and finding that I longed to hide myself from the world, he took me to India under an assumed name, as the widow of a friend. My boy went with me, and for a time I was as happy as a desolate creature could be. Colonel Vane desired to marry me; for, though I kept my promise, he suspected that I had been deceived and cruelly deserted, and longed to atone for his friend's perfidy by his own devotion. I would not marry him; but when he was dying, he begged me to take his name as a shield against a curious world, to take his fortune, and give my son the memory of a father when his own had cast him off. I did so; and no one knew me there except under my false name. It was believed that I had married him too soon after my husband's death to care to own it at once, and when I came to England, no one denied me the place I chose to fill."

"Oh, why did you come?" cried Diana, with a tearless sob.

"I came because I longed to know if Allan had forgotten me, if he had married, and left his poor boy fatherless. I saw him last winter, saw that you loved him, feared that he would love you, and when I learned that both were coming here, I resolved to follow. It was evident that Allan had not forgotten me, that he had suffered as well as I; and perhaps if he could bring himself to brave the pity, curiosity, and criticism of the world, he might yet atone for his deceit, and make me happy. We had met in London; he had told me to remember my vow; had confessed that he still loved me, but dared not displease his haughty family by owning me; had seen his boy, and reiterated his promise to provide for us as long as we were silent. I saw him no more till we met here, and this explains all that has seemed so strange to you. It was I who entered his room, but not to juggle with the ring. He invented that tale to account for the oiled lock, and whatever stir might have been overheard. I went to implore him to pause before he pledged himself to you. He would not yield, having gone too far to retract with honor, he said. Then I was in despair; for well I knew that if ever the knowledge of this passage in his life should come to you, you would feel as I feel, and regard that first marriage as sacred in God's eye, whatever the world might say. I gave him one more opportunity to spare you by the warning I whispered in the park. That has delayed the wrong, but you would have yielded had not other things roused suspicion of me. I had decided to say no more, but let you two tangle your fates as you would. Your appeal this morning conquered me, and I have broken every vow, dared every danger, to serve and save you. Have I done all this in vain?"

"No; let me think, let me understand—then I will act."

For many minutes they rolled on silently, two pale, stern-faced women, sitting side by side looking out before them, with fixed eyes that saw nothing but a hard task performed, a still harder one yet to be done. Diana spoke first, asking, "Do you intend to proclaim your wrong, and force your husband to do you justice?"

"No, I shall not ask that of him again, but I shall do my best to prevent any other woman from blindly sacrificing her happiness by marrying him, unconscious of my claim. For the boy's sake I have a right to do this."

"You have. I thank you for sparing me the affliction of discovering that man's perfidy too late. Where is your boy, Mrs. Douglas?"

Steadily she spoke; and when her lips pronounced the name she had hoped to make her own, a stern smile passed across her white face, and left a darker shadow behind. Mrs. Vane touched her lips with a warning gesture, saying pitifully, yet commandingly: "Never call me that until he gives me the right to bear it openly. You ask for my boy; will you come and see him? He is close by; I cannot be parted from him long, yet must conceal him, for the likeness to his father would betray him at once, if we were seen together."

Turning down a grassy lane, Mrs. Vane drove on till the way became too narrow for the carriage. Here they alighted, and climbing a wooded path, came to a lonely cottage in a dell.

"My faithful Jitomar found this safe nook for me, and brings me tidings of my darling every day," whispered Mrs. Vane, as she stole along the path that wound round the house.

Turning a sharp corner, a green, lawnlike bit of ground appeared. On a vine-covered seat sat an old French *bonne,* knitting as she nodded in the sun. But Diana saw nothing but a little figure tossing buttercups into the air, and catching them as they fell with peals of childish laughter. A three-year-old boy it was, with black curls blowing round a bold bright face, where a healthful color glowed through the dark skin, and brilliant eyes sparkled under a brow so like that other that she could not doubt that this was Allan's son. Just then the boy spied his mother, and with a cry of joy ran to her, to be gathered close, and covered with caresses.

There was no acting here, for genuine mother love transformed Mrs. Vane from her usual inexplicable self into a simple woman, whose heart was bound up in the little creature whom she loved with the passionate fondness of an otherwise cold and superficial nature.

Waving off the old *bonne* when she would have approached, Mrs. Vane turned to Diana, asking, "Are you satisfied?"

"Heaven help me, yes!"

"Is he not like his father? See, the very shape of his small hands, the same curve to his baby mouth. Stay, you shall hear him speak. Darling, who am I?"

"Mamma, my dear mamma," replied the little voice.

"And who is this?" asked Mrs. Vane, showing a miniature of Douglas.

"Oh, Papa! When will he come again?"

"God only knows, my poor baby. Now kiss Mamma, and go and make a pretty daisy chain against I come next time. See, love, here are bonbons and new toys; show them to Babette. Quick, let us slip away, Miss Stuart."

As the boy ran to his nurse the ladies vanished, and in silence regained the carriage. Only one question and answer passed between them, as they drove rapidly homeward.

"Diana, what will you do?"

"Go tomorrow, and in silence. It is all over between us, forever. Mrs. Vane, I envy you, I thank you, and I could almost *hate* you for the kind yet cruel deed you have done this day."

A gloomy darkness settled down on her altered face; despair sat in her eyes, and death itself could not have stricken hope, energy, and vitality out of it more utterly than the bitter truth which she had wrung from her companion.

George Lennox and Douglas were waiting at the door, and both ran down to help them alight. Diana dragged her veil over her face, while Mrs. Vane assumed an anxious, troubled air as the carriage stopped, and both gentlemen offered a hand to Miss Stuart. Putting Earl's aside with what seemed almost rude repugnance, she took George's arm, hurried up the steps, and as her foot touched the threshold of the door, she fell heavily forward in a swoon.

Douglas was springing toward her, when a strong grasp detained him, and Mrs. Vane whispered, as she clung to his arm tremblingly, "Do not touch her; she must not see you; it will kill her."

"Good heavens! What is the cause of this?" he asked, as Lennox carried Diana in, and help came flocking at his call.

"O Mr. Douglas, I have had an awful drive! She terrified me so by her wild conversation, her fierce threats of taking her own life, that I drove home in agony. You saw how she repulsed you, and rushed away to drop exhausted in the hall; imagine what it all means, and spare me the pain of telling you."

She spoke breathlessly, and glanced nervously about her, as if still in fear. Earl listened, half bewilderingly at first, then, as her meaning broke upon him, his dark cheek whitened, and he looked aghast.

"You do not mean that she is mad?" he whispered, recalling her fierce gesture, and the moody silence she had preserved for days.

"No, oh, no, I dare not say that *yet*; but I fear that her mind is unsettled by long brooding over one unhappy thought, and that the hereditary taint may be upon the point of showing itself. Poor girl!"

"Am I the cause of this outbreak? Is our disagreement the unhappy thought that has warped her reason? What shall I, what ought I to do?" Earl asked in great distress, as Diana's senseless body was carried up the stairs, and her aunt stood wringing her hands, while Lady Lennox dispatched a servant for medical help.

"Do nothing but avoid her, for she says your presence tortures her. She will go tomorrow. Let her leave quietly, and when absence has restored her, take any steps toward a reconciliation that you think best. Now I must go to her; do not repeat what I have said. It escaped me in my agitation, and may do her harm if she learns that her strange behavior is known."

Pressing his hand with a sympathizing glance, Mrs. Vane hurried in, and for an hour busied herself about Diana so skillfully that the physician sent all the rest away and gave directions to her alone. When recovered from her faint, Diana lay like one dead, refusing to speak or move, yet taking obediently whatever Mrs. Vane offered her, as if a mutual sorrow linked them together with a secret bond. At dusk she seemed to fall asleep, and leaving Gabrielle to watch beside her, Mrs. Vane went down to join the others at a quiet meal.

≈ *Chapter VI* ≈

A DARK DEATH

THE party separated early. Diana was still sleeping, and leaving her own maid to watch in the dressing room between their chambers, Mrs. Berkeley went to bed. As he passed them down the gallery to his apartment, Earl heard Mrs. Vane say to the maid, "If anything happens in the night, call me." The words made him anxious, and instead of going to bed, he sat up writing letters till very late. It was past midnight when the sound of a closing door broke the long silence that had filled the house. Stepping into the gallery, he listened. All was still, and nothing stirred but the heavy curtain before the long window at the end of the upper hall; this swayed to and fro in the strong current of air that swept in. Fearing that the draft might slam other doors and disturb Diana, he went to close it.

Pausing a moment to view the gloomy scene without, Douglas was startled by an arm flung violently about his neck, lips pressed passionately to his own, and a momentary glimpse of a woman's figure dimly defined on the dark curtain that floated backward from his hand. Silently and suddenly as it came, the phantom went, leaving Douglas so amazed that for an instant he could only stare dumbly before him, half breathless, and wholly bewildered by the ardor of that mysterious embrace. Then he sprang forward to discover who the woman was and whither she had gone. But, as if blown outward by some counterdraft, the heavy curtain wrapped him in its fold, and when he had freed himself, neither ghost nor woman was visible.

Earl was superstitious, and for a moment he fancied the spirit of Diana had appeared to him, foretelling her death. But a second thought assured him that it was a human creature, and no wraith, for the soft arms had no deathly chill in them, the lips were warm, living breath had passed across his face, and on his cheek he felt a tear that must have fallen from human eyes. The light had been too dim to reveal the partially shrouded countenance, or more than a tall and shadowy outline, but with a thrill of fear he thought, "It was Diana, and she is mad!"

Taking his candle, he hurried to the door of the dressing room, tapped softly, and when the sleepy maid appeared, inquired if Miss Stuart still slept.

"Yes, sir, like a child, it does one's heart good to see her."

"You are quite sure she is asleep?"

"Bless me, yes, sir, I've just looked at her, and she hasn't stirred since I looked an hour ago."

"Does she ever walk in her sleep, Mrs. Mason?"

"Dear, no, sir."

"I thought I saw her just now in the upper gallery. I went to shut the great window, lest the wind should disturb her, and someone very like her certainly stood for a moment at my side."

"Lord, sir! You make my blood run cold. It couldn't have been her, for she never left her bed, much less her room."

"Perhaps so; never mind; just look again, and tell me if you see her, then I shall be at ease."

Mrs. Mason knew that her young lady loved the gentleman before her, and never doubted that he loved her, and so considering his anxiety quite natural and proper, she nodded, crept away, and soon returned, saying, with a satisfied air, "She's all right, sir, sleeping beautifully. I didn't speak, for once when I looked at her, she said, quite fierce, 'Go away, and let me be until I call you.' So I've only peeped through the curtain since. I see her lying with her face to the wall, and the coverlet drawn comfortably round her."

"Thank God! She is safe. Excuse my disturbing you, Mrs. Mason, but I was very anxious. Be patient and faithful in your care of her; I shall remember it. Good night."

"Handsome creeter; how fond he is of her, and well he may be, for she dotes on him, and they'll make a splendid couple. Now I'll finish my nap, and then have a cup of tea."

With a knowing look and a chilly shiver, Mrs. Mason resettled herself in a luxurious chair, and was soon dozing.

Douglas meanwhile returned to his room, after a survey of the house, and went to bed, thinking with a smile and frown that if all spirits came in such an amicable fashion, the fate of a ghost seer was not a hard one.

In the dark hour just before the dawn, a long shrill cry rent the silence, and brought every sleeper under that roof out of his bed, trembling and with fright. The cry came from Diana's room, and in a moment the gallery, dressing room, and chamber were filled with pale faces and half-dressed figures, as ladies and gentlemen, men and maids came flocking in, asking breathlessly, "What is it? Oh, what is it?"

Mrs. Berkeley lay on the floor in strong hysterics, and Mrs. Mason, instead of attending to her, was beating her hands distractedly together, and running wildly about the room, as if searching for something she had lost. Diana's bed was empty, with the clothes flung one way and the pillows another, and every sign of strange disorder, but its occupant was nowhere to be seen.

"Where is she?" "What has happened?" "Why don't you speak?" cried the terrified beholders.

A sudden lull fell upon the excited group, as Mrs. Vane, white, resolute, and calm, made her way through the crowd, and laying her hand on Mrs. Mason's shoulder, commanded her to stand still and explain the mystery. The poor soul endeavored to obey, but burst into tears, and dropping on her knees, poured out her story in a passion of penitent despair.

"You left her sleeping, ma'am, and I sat as my lady bid me, going now and then to look at Miss. The last time I drew the curtain, she looked up and said, sharp and short, 'Let me be in peace, and don't disturb me till I call you.' After that, I just peeped through the crack, and she seemed quiet. You know I told you so, sir, when you came to ask, and oh, my goodness me, it wasn't her at all, sir, and she's gone! She's gone!"

"Hush! Stop sobbing, and tell me how you missed her. Gabrielle and Justine, attend to Mrs. Berkeley; Harry, go at once and search the house. Now, Mrs. Mason."

Mrs. Vane's clear, calm voice seemed to act like a spell on the agitation of all about her, and the maids obeyed; Harry, with the menservants, hurried away, and Mrs. Mason more coherently went on:

"Well, ma'am, when Mr. Douglas came to the door asking if Miss was here, thinking he saw her in the hall, I looked again, and thought she lay as I'd left her an hour before. But oh, ma'am, it wasn't her, it was the pillow that she'd fixed like herself, with the coverlet pulled round it, like she'd pulled it round her own head and shoulders when she spoke last. It looked all right, the night lamp being low, and me so sleepy, and I went back to my place, after setting Mr. Douglas's mind at rest. I fell asleep, and when I woke, I ran in here to make sure she was safe, for I'd had a horrid dream about seeing her laid out, dead and dripping, with weeds in her hair, and her poor feet all covered with red clay, as if she'd fallen into one of them pits over yonder. I ran in here, pulled up the curtain, and was just going to say, 'Thank the Lord,' when, as I stooped down to listen if she slept easy, I saw she wasn't there. The start took my wits away, and I don't know what I did, till my lady came running in, as I was tossing the pillows here and there to find her, and when I told what had happened, my lady gave one dreadful scream, and went off in a fit."

There was a dead silence for a moment, as Mrs. Mason relapsed into convulsive sobbing, and everyone looked into each other's frightened face. Douglas leaned on Lennox, as if all the strength had gone out of him, and George stood aghast. Mrs. Vane alone seemed self-possessed, though an awful anxiety blanched her face, and looked out at her haggard eyes.

"What did you see in the hall?" she asked of Douglas. Briefly he told the incident, and Lady Lennox clasped her hands in despair, exclaiming, "She has destroyed herself, and that was her farewell."

"Your ladyship is mistaken, I hope, for among the wild things she said this afternoon was a longing to go home at once, as every hour here was torture to her. She may have attempted this in her delirium. Look in her wardrobe, Mrs. Mason, and see what clothes are gone. That will help us in our search. Be calm, I beg of you, my lady; I am sure we shall find the poor girl soon."

"It's no use looking, ma'am; she's gone in the clothes she had on, for she wouldn't let me take 'em off her. It was a black silk with crepe trimmings, and her black mantle's gone, and the close crepe bonnet. Here's her gloves just where they dropped when we laid her down in her faint."

"Is her purse gone?" asked Mrs. Vane.

"It's always in her pocket, ma'am; when she drives out, she likes to toss a bit of money to the little lads that open gates, or hold the ponies while she gets flowers, and such like. She was so generous, so kind, poor dear!"

Here Harry came in, saying that no trace of the lost girl was visible in the house. But as he spoke, Jitomar's dark face and glittering eyes looked over his shoulder with an intelligent motion, which his mistress understood, and put into words.

"He says that one of the long windows in the little breakfast room is unfastened and ajar. Go, gentlemen, at once, and take him with you; he is as keen as a hound, and will do good service. It is just possible that she may have remembered the one o'clock mail train, and taken it. Inquire, and if you find any trace of her, let us know without delay."

In an instant they were gone, and the anxious watchers left behind traced their progress by the glimmer of the lantern, which Jitomar carried low, that he might follow the print her flying feet had left here and there in the damp earth.

A long hour passed, then Harry and the Indian returned, bringing the good news that a tall lady in black had been seen at the station alone, had not been recognized, being veiled, and had taken the mail train to London. Douglas and Lennox had at once ordered horses, and gone with all speed to catch an early train that left a neighboring town in an hour or two. They would trace and discover the lost girl, if she was in London.

"There can be no doubt that it was she, no lady would be traveling alone at such an hour, and the station people say that she seemed in great haste. Now let us compose ourselves, hope for the best, and comfort her poor aunt."

As Mrs. Vane spoke, Harry frankly looked his admiration of the cheerful, courageous little woman, and his mother took her arm, saying affectionately, "My dear, what should we do without you? For you have the nerves of a man, the quick wit of a woman, and presence of mind enough for us all."

The dreary day dawned, and slowly wore away. A dull rain fell, and a melancholy wind sighed among the yellowing leaves. All occupations flagged, all failed, except the one absorbing hope. The servants loitered, unreproved, and gossiped freely among themselves about the sad event. The ladies sat in Mrs. Berkeley's room, consoling her distress, while Harry haunted the station, waiting for an arrival or a telegram. At noon the letter came.

"The lady in black not Diana. On another scent now. If that fails, home at night."

No one knew how much they leaned upon this hope, until it failed and all was uncertainty again. Harry searched house, garden, park, and riverside, but found no trace of the lost girl beyond the point where her footprints ended on the hard gravel of the road. So the long afternoon wore on, and at dusk the gentlemen returned, haggard, wet, and weary, bringing no tidings of good cheer. The lady in black proved to be a handsome young governess, called suddenly to town by her father's dangerous illness. The second search was equally fruitless, and nowhere had Diana been seen.

Their despondent story was scarcely ended when the bell rang. Every servant in the house sprang to answer it, and every occupant of the drawing room listened breathlessly. A short parley followed the ring; then an astonished footman showed in a little farmer lad, with a bundle under his arm.

"He wants to see my lady, and would come in," said the man, lingering, as all eyes were fixed on the newcomer.

The boy looked important, excited, and frightened, but when Lady Lennox bade him to do his errand without fear, he spoke up briskly, though his voice shook a little, and he now and then gave a nervous clutch at the bundle under his arm.

"Please, my lady, Mother told me to come up as soon as ever I got home, so I ran off right away, knowing you'd be glad to hear something, even if it weren't good."

"Something about Miss Stuart, you mean?"

"Yes, my lady, I know where she is."

"Where? Speak quickly, you shall be paid for your tidings."

"In that pit, my lady," and the boy began to cry.

"No!"

Douglas spoke, and turned on the lad a face that stopped his crying, and sent the words to his lips faster than he could utter them, so full of mute entreaty was its glance of anguish.

"You see, sir, I was here this noon, and heard about it. Mrs. Mason's dream scared me, because my brother was drowned in the pit. I couldn't help thinking of it all the afternoon, and when work was done, I went home that way. The first thing I saw were tracks in the red clay, coming from the lodge way. The pit has overflowed and made a big pool, but just where it's deepest, the tracks stopped, and there I found these."

With a sudden gesture of the arm, he shook out the bundle; a torn mantle, heavily trimmed, and a crushed crepe bonnet dropped upon the floor. Lady Lennox sank back in her chair, and George covered up his face with a groan; but Earl stood motionless, and Mrs. Vane looked as if the sight of these relics had confirmed some wordless fear.

"Perhaps she is not there, however," she said below her breath. "She may have wandered on and lost herself. Oh, let us look!"

"She *is* there, ma'am, I see her sperrit," and the boy's eyes dilated as they glanced fearfully about him while he spoke. "I was awful scared when I see them things, but she was good to me, and I loved her, so I took 'em up and went on round the pool, meaning to strike off by the great ditch. Just as I got to the bit of brush that grows down by the old clay pits, something flew right up before me, something like a woman, all black but a white face and arms. It gave a strange screech, and seemed to go out of sight all in a minute, like as if it vanished in the pits. I know it warn't a real woman, it flew so, and looked so awful when it wailed, as Granny says the sperrits do."

The boy paused, till Douglas beckoned solemnly, and left the room with the one word "Come."

The brothers went, the lad followed, Mrs. Vane hid her face in Lady Lennox's lap, and neither stirred nor spoke for one long dreadful hour.

"They are coming," whispered Mrs. Vane, when at length her quick ear caught the sound of many approaching feet. Slowly, steadily they came on, across the lawn, up the steps through the hall; then there was a pause.

"Go and see if she is found, I cannot," implored Lady Lennox, spent and trembling with the long suspense.

There was no need to go, for as she spoke, the wail of women's voices filled the air, and Lennox stood in the doorway with a face that made all question needless.

He beckoned, and Mrs. Vane went to him as if her feet could hardly bear her, while her face might have been that of a dead woman, so white and stony had it grown. Drawing her outside, he said, "My mother must not see her yet. Mrs. Mason can do all that is necessary, if you will give her orders, and spare my mother the first sad duties. Douglas bade me come for you, for you are always ready."

"I will come; where is she?"

"In the library. Send the servants away, in pity to poor Earl. Harry can't bear it, and it kills me to see her look so."

"You found her there?"

"Yes, quite underneath the deepest water of the pool. That dream was surely sent by heaven. Are you faint? Can you bear it?"

"I can bear anything. Go on."

Poor Diana! There she lay, a piteous sight, with stained and dripping garments, slimy weeds entangled in her long hair, a look of mortal woe stamped on her dead face, for the blue lips were parted, as if by the passage of the last painful breath, and the glassy eyes seemed fixed imploringly upon some stern specter, darker and more dreadful even than the most desperate death she had sought and found.

A group of awestricken men and sobbing women stood about her. Harry leaned upon the high arm of the couch where they had laid her, with his head down upon his arm, struggling to control himself, for he had loved her with a boy's first love, and the horror of her end un-manned him. Douglas sat at the head of the couch, holding the dead hand, and looking at her with a white tearless anguish, which made his face old and haggard, as with the passage of long and heavy years.

With an air of quiet command, and eyes that never once fell on the dead girl, Mrs. Vane gave a few necessary orders, which cleared the room of all but the gentlemen and herself. Laying her hand softly on Earl's shoulder, she said, in a tone of tenderest compassion, "Come with me, and let my try to comfort you, while George and Harry take the poor girl to her room, that these sad tokens of her end may be removed, and she made beautiful for the eyes of those who loved her."

He heard, but did not answer in words, for waving off the brothers, Earl took his dead love in his arms, and carrying her to her own room, laid her down tenderly, kissed her pale forehead with one lingering kiss, and then without a word shut himself into his own apartment.

Mrs. Vane watched him go with a dark glance, followed him up-stairs, and when his door closed, muttered low to herself, "He loved her better than I knew, but she has made my task easier than I dared to hope it would be, and now I can soon teach him to forget."

A strange smile passed across her face as she spoke, and still, with-out a glance at the dead face, left the chamber for her own, whither Jitomar was soon summoned, and where he long remained.

❧ *Chapter VII* ❧

THE FOOTPRINT
BY THE POOL

T HREE sad and solemn days had passed, and now the house was still again. Mr. Berkeley had removed his wife, and the remains of his niece, and Lennox had gone with him. Mrs. Vane devoted herself to her hostess, who had been much affected by the shock, and to Harry, who was almost ill with the excitement and the sorrow. Douglas had hardly been seen except by his own servant, who reported that he was very quiet, but in a stern and bitter mood, which made solitude his best comforter. Only twice had he emerged during those troubled days. Once, when Mrs. Vane's sweet voice came up from below singing a sacred melody in the twilight, he came out and paced to and fro in the long gallery, with a softer expression than his face had worn since the night of Diana's passionate farewell. The second time was in answer to a tap at his door, on opening which he saw Jitomar, who with the graceful reverence of his race, bent on one knee, as with dark eyes full of sympathy, he delivered a lovely bouquet of the flowers Diana most loved, and oftenest wore. The first tears that had been seen there softened Earl's melancholy eyes, as he took the odorous gift, and with a grateful impulse stretched his hand to the giver. But Jitomar drew back with a gesture which signified that his mistress sent the offering, and glided away. Douglas went straight to the drawing room, found Mrs. Vane alone, and inexpressibly touched by her tender thought of him, he thanked her warmly, let her detain him for an hour with her soothing conversation, and left her, feeling that comfort was possible when such an angel administered it.

On the third day, impelled by an unconquerable wish to revisit the

lonely spot hereafter, and forever to be haunted by the memory of that
tragic death, he stole out, unperceived, and took his way to the pool. It
lay there dark and still under a gloomy sky, its banks trampled by many
hasty feet; and in one spot the red clay still bore the impress of the pale
shape drawn from the water on that memorable night. As he stood there,
he remembered the lad's story of the spirit which he believed he had
seen. With a dreary smile at the superstition of the boy, he followed his
tracks along the bank as they branched off toward the old pits, now
half-filled with water by recent rains. Pausing where the boy had passed
when the woman's figure sprang up before him with its old-witch cry,
Douglas looked keenly all about, wondering if it were possible for any
human being to vanish as the lad related. Several yards from the clump
of bushes and coarse grass at his feet lay the wide pit; between it and
the spot where he stood stretched a smooth bed of clay, unmarked by
the impress of any step, as he first thought. A second and more scrutinizing glance showed him the print of a human foot on the very edge of
the pit. Stepping lightly forward, he examined it. Not the boy's track,
for he had not passed the bushes, but turned and fled in terror, when
the phantom seemed to vanish. It was a child's footprint, apparently, or
that of a very small woman; probably the latter, for it was a slender,
shapely print, cut deep into the yielding clay, as if by the impetus of a
desperate spring. But whither had she sprung? Not across the pit, for
that was impossible to any but a very active man, or a professional gym-
nast of either sex. Douglas took the leap, and barely reached the other
side, though a tall agile man. Nor did he find any trace of the other
leaper, though the grass that grew to the very edge of that side might
have concealed a lighter, surer tread than his own.

With a thrill of suspicion and dread, he looked down into the turbid
water of the pit, asking himself if it were possible that two women had
found their death so near together on that night. The footprint was not
Diana's; hers was larger, and utterly unlike; whose was it, then? With a
sudden impulse he cut a long, forked pole, and searched the depths of
the pit. Nothing was found; again and again he plunged in the pole and
drew it carefully up, after sweeping the bottom in all directions. A dead
branch, a fallen rod, a heavy stone were all he found.

As he stood pondering over the mysterious mark, having recrossed
the pit, some sudden peculiarity in it seemed to give it a familiar aspect.
Kneeling down, he examined it minutely, and as he looked, an expression of perplexity came into his face, while he groped for some
recollection in the dimness of the past, the gloom of the present.

"Where have I seen a foot like this, so dainty, so slender, yet so strong, for the tread was firm here, the muscles wonderfully elastic to carry this unknown woman over that wide gap? Stay! It was not a foot, but a shoe that makes this mark so familiar. Who wears a shoe with a coquettish heel like this stamped here in the clay? A narrow sole, a fairy-like shape, a slight pressure downward at the top, as if the wearer walked well and lightly, yet danced better than she walked? Good heavens! Can it be? That word 'danced' makes it clear to me—but it is impossible—unless—can she have discovered me, followed me, wrought me fresh harm, and again escaped me? I will be satisfied at all hazards, and if I find her, Virginie shall meet a double vengeance for a double wrong."

Up he sprang, as these thoughts swept through his mind, and like someone bent on some all-absorbing purpose, he dashed homeward through bush and brake, park and garden, till, coming to the lawn, he restrained his impetuosity, but held on his way, turning neither to the right nor the left, till he stood in his own room. Without pausing for breath, he snatched the satin slipper from the case, put it in his breast, and hurried back to the pool. Making sure that no one followed him, he cautiously advanced, and bending, laid the slipper in the mold of that mysterious foot. It fitted exactly! Outline, length, width, even the downward pressure at the toe corresponded, and the sole difference was to the depth of heel, as if the walking boot or shoe had been thicker than the slipper.

Bent on assuring himself, Douglas pressed the slipper carefully into the smooth clay beside the other print, and every slight peculiarity was repeated with wonderful accuracy.

"I am satisfied," he muttered, adding, as he carefully effaced both the little tracks, "no one must follow this out but myself. I have sworn to find her and her accomplice, and henceforth it shall be my life business to keep my vow."

A few moments he stood buried in dark thoughts and memories, then putting up the slipper, he bent his steps toward the home of little Wat, the farmer's lad. He was watering horses at the spring, his mother said, and Douglas strolled that way, saying he desired to give the boy something for the intelligence he brought three days before. Wat lounged against the wall, while the tired horses slowly drank their fill, but when he saw the gentleman approaching, he looked troubled, for his young brain had been sadly perplexed by the late events.

"I want to ask you a few questions, Wat; answer me truly, and I will thank you in a way you will like better than words," began Douglas, as the boy pulled off his hat and stood staring.

"I'm ready; what will I say, sir?" he asked.

"Tell me just what sort of a thing or person the spirit looked like when you saw it by the pit."

"A woman, sir, all black but her face and arms."

"Did she resemble the person we were searching for?"

"No, sir; leastways, I never saw Miss looking so; of course she wouldn't when she was alive, you know."

"Did the spirit look like the lady afterward? When we found her, I mean?"

The boy pondered a minute, seemed perplexed, but answered slowly, as he grew a little pale, "No, sir, then she looked awful, but the spirit seemed scared like, and screamed as any woman would if frightened."

"And she vanished in the pit, you say?"

"She couldn't go nowhere else, sir, 'cause she didn't turn."

"Did you see her go down into the water, Wat?"

"No, sir, I only see her fly up out of the bushes, looking at me over her shoulder, and giving a great leap, as light and easy as if she hadn't no body. But it started me, so that I fell over backward, and when I got up, she was gone."

"I thought so. Now tell me, was the spirit large or small?"

"I didn't mind, but I guess it wasn't very big, or them few bushes wouldn't have hid it from me."

"Was its hair black or light?"

"Don't know, sir, a hood was all over its head, and I only see the face."

"Did you mind the eyes?"

"They looked big and dark, and scared me horridly."

"You said the face was handsome but white, I think?"

"I didn't say anything about handsome, sir; it was too dark to make out much, but it was white, and when she threw up her arms, they looked like snow. I never see any live lady with such white ones."

"You did not go down to the edge of the pit to leap after her, did you?"

"Lord, no, sir. I just scud the other way, and never looked back till I see the lodge."

"Is there any strange lady down at the inn, or staying anywhere in the village?"

"Not as I know, sir. I'm down there every day, and guess I'd hear of it if there was. Do you want to find anyone, sir?"

"No, I thought your spirit might have been some live woman, whom you frightened as much as she did you. Are you quite sure it was not?"

"I shouldn't be sure, if she hadn't flown away so strange, for no woman could go over the pit, and if she'd fell in, I'd have heard the splash."

"So you would. Well, let the spirit go, and keep away from the pit and the pool, lest you see it again. Here is a golden thank-you, my boy, so good-bye."

"Oh, sir, that's a deal too much! I'm heartily obliged. Be you going to leave these parts, please, sir?"

"Not yet; I've much to do before I go."

Satisfied with his inquiries, Douglas went on, and Wat, pulling on his torn hat as the gentleman disappeared, fell to examining the bit of gold that had been dropped into his brown palm.

"Do you want another, my lad?" said a soft voice behind him, and turning quickly, he saw a man leaning over the wall, just below the place where he had lounged a moment before.

The man was evidently a gypsy; long brown hair hung about a brown face with black eyes, a crafty mouth, and glittering teeth. His costume was picturesquely ragged and neglected, and in his hand he held a stout staff. Bending farther over, he eyed the boy with a nod, repeating his words in a smooth low tone, as he held up a second half-sovereign between his thumb and finger.

"Yes, I do," answered Wat sturdily, as he sent his horses trotting homeward with a chirrup and a cut of his long whip.

"Tell me what the gentleman said, and you shall have it," whispered the gypsy.

"You might have heard for yourself, if you'd been where you are a little sooner," returned Wat, edging toward the road—for there was something about the swarthy-faced fellow that he did not like, in spite of his golden offer.

"I was there," said the man with a laugh, "but you spoke so low I couldn't catch it all."

"What do you want to know for?" demanded Wat.

"Why, perhaps I know something about that spirit woman he seemed to be asking about, and if I do, he'd be glad to hear it, wouldn't he? Now I don't want to go and tell him myself, for fear of getting into trouble, but I might tell you, and you could do it. Only I must know what he said, first; perhaps he has found out for himself what I could tell him."

"What are you going to give me that for, then?" asked Wat, much reassured.

"Because you are a clever little chap, and were good to some of my people here once upon a time. I'm rich, though I don't look it, and I'd like to pay for the news you give me. Out with it, and then here's another yellow boy for you."

Wat was entirely conquered by the grateful allusion to a friendly act of his own on the previous day, and willingly related his conversation with Douglas, explaining as he went on. The gypsy questioned and cross-questioned, and finished the interview by saying, with a warning glance, "He's right; you'd better not tell anyone you saw the spirit—it's a bad sign, and if it's known, you'll find it hard to get on in the world. Now here's your money; catch it, and then I'll tell you my story."

The coin came ringing through the air, and fell into the road not far from Wat's feet. He ran to pick it up, and when he turned to thank the man, he was gone as silently and suddenly as he had come. The lad stared in amaze, listened, searched, but no gypsy was heard or seen, and poor bewildered Wat scampered home as fast as his legs could carry him, believing that he was bewitched.

That afternoon Douglas wrote a long letter, directed it to "M. Antoine Duprès, Rue Saint Honoré, Paris," and was about to seal it when a servant came to tell him that Mrs. Vane desired her adieus, as she was leaving for town by the next train. Anxious to atone for his seeming negligence, not having seen her that day, and therefore being in ignorance of her intended departure, he hastily dropped a splash of wax on his important letter, and leaving it upon his table hurried down to see her off. She was already in the hall, having bidden Lady Lennox farewell in her boudoir—for her ladyship was too poorly to come down. Harry was giving directions about the baggage, and Gabrielle chattering her adieus in the housekeeper's room.

"My dear Mrs. Vane, forgive my selfish sorrow; when you are settled in town let me come to thank you for the great kindness you have shown me through these dark days."

Douglas spoke warmly; he pressed the hand she gave him in both his own, and gratitude flushed his pale face with a glow that restored all its lost comeliness.

Mrs. Vane dropped her beautiful eyes, and answered, with a slight quiver of the lips that tried to smile, "I have suffered for you, if not with you, and I need no thanks for the sympathy that was involuntary. Here is my address; come to me when you will, and be assured that you will always find a welcome."

He led her to the carriage, assiduously arranging all things for her comfort, and when she waved a last adieu, he seized the little hand, regardless of Harry, who accompanied her, and kissed it warmly as he said, "I shall not forget, and shall see you soon."

The carriage rolled away, and Douglas watched it, saying to the groom, who was just turning stableward, "Does not Jitomar go with his mistress?"

"No, sir; he's to take some plants my lady gave Mrs. Vane, so he's to go in a later train—and good riddance to the sly devil, I say," added the man, under his breath, as he walked off.

Had he turned his head a moment afterward, he would have been amazed at the strange behavior of the gentleman he had left behind him. Happening to glance downward, Douglas gave a start, stooped suddenly, examining something on the ground, and as he rose, struck his hands together like one in great perplexity or exultation, while his face assumed a singular expression of mingled wonder, pain, and triumph. Well it might, for there, clearly defined in the moist earth, was an exact counterpart of the footprint by the pool.

❧ *Chapter VIII* ❧

ON THE TRAIL

THE packet from Havre was just in. It had been a stormy trip, and all the passengers hurried ashore, as if glad to touch English soil. Two gentlemen lingered a moment, before they separated to different quarters of the city. One was a stout, gray-haired Frenchman, perfectly dressed, blandly courteous, and vivaciously grateful, as he held the other's hand, and poured out a stream of compliments, invitations, and thanks. The younger man was evidently a Spaniard, slight, dark, and dignified, with melancholy eyes, a bronzed, bearded face, and a mien as cool and composed as if he had just emerged from some elegant retreat, instead of the cabin of an overcrowded packet, whence he had been tossing about all day.

"It is a thousand pities we do not go on together; but remember I am under many obligations to Señor Arguelles, and I implore that I may be allowed to return them during my stay. I believe you have my card; now *au revoir*, and my respectful compliments to Madame your friend."

"Adieu, Monsieur Dupont—we shall meet again."

The Frenchman waved his hand, the Spaniard raised his hat, and they separated.

Antoine Duprès, for it was he, drove at once to a certain hotel, asked for M. Douglas, sent up his name, and was at once heartily welcomed by his friend, with whom he sat in deep consultation till very late.

Arguelles was set down at the door of a lodging house in a quiet street, and admitting himself by means of a latchkey, he went noiselessly upstairs and looked about him. The scene was certainly a charming one, though somewhat peculiar. A bright fire filled the room with its ruddy light; several lamps added their milder shine; and the chamber was a flush of color, for carpet, chairs, and tables were strewn with brilliant costumes. Wreaths of artificial flowers strewed the floor; mock jewels glittered here and there; a lyre, a silver bow and arrow, a slender wand of many colors, a pair of ebony castanets; a gaily decorated tambourine lay on the couch; little hats, caps, bodices, jackets, skirts, boots, slippers, and clouds of rosy, blue, white, and green tulle were heaped, hung, and scattered everywhere. In the midst of this gay confusion stood a figure in perfect keeping with it. A slight blooming girl of eighteen she looked, evidently an actress—for though busily sorting the contents of two chests that stood before her, she was *en costume,* as if she had been reviewing her wardrobe, and had forgotten to take off the various parts of different suits which she had tried on. A jaunty hat of black velvet, turned up with a white plume, was stuck askew on her blond head; scarlet boots with brass heels adorned her feet; a short white satin skirt was oddly contrasted with a blue-and-silver hussar jacket; and a flame-colored silk domino completed her piquant array.

A smile of tenderest joy and admiration lighted up the man's dark features, as he leaned in, watching the pretty creature purse up her lips and bend her brows, in deep consideration, over a faded pink-and-black Spanish dress, just unfolded.

"Madame, it is I."

He closed the door behind him, as he spoke, and advanced with open arms.

The girl dropped the garment she held, turned sharply, and surveyed the newcomer with little surprise but much amazement, for suddenly clapping her hands, she broke into a peal of laughter, exclaiming, as she examined him, "My faith! You are superb. I admire you thus; the melancholy is becoming, the beard ravishing, and the *tout ensemble* beyond my hopes. I salute you, Señor Arguelles."

"Come, then, and embrace me. So long away, and no tenderer welcome than this, my heart?"

She shrugged her white shoulders, and submitted to be drawn close, kissed, and caressed with ardor, by her husband or lover, asking a multitude of questions the while, and smoothing the petals of a crumpled camellia, quite unmoved by the tender names showered upon her, the almost fierce affection that glowed in her companion's face, and lavished itself in demonstrations of delight at regaining her.

"But tell me, darling, why do I find you at such work? Is it wise or needful?"

"It is pleasant, and I please myself now. I have almost lived here since you have been gone. At my aunt's in the country, they say, at the other place. The rooms there were dull; no one came, and at last I ran away. Once here, the old mania returned; I was mad for the gay life I love, and while I waited, I played at carnival."

"Were you anxious for my return? Did you miss me, *carina?*"

"That I did, for I needed you, my Juan," she answered, with a laugh. "Do you know we must have money? I am deciding which of my properties I will sell, though it breaks my heart to part with them. Mother Ursule will dispose of them, and as I shall never want them again, they must go."

"Why will you never need them again? There may be no course but that in the end."

"My husband will never let me dance, except for my own pleasure," she answered, dropping a half-humble, half-mocking curtsy, and glancing at him with a searching look.

Juan eyed her gloomily, as she waltzed away clinking her brass heels together, and humming a gay measure in time to her graceful steps. He shook his head, threw himself wearily into a chair, and leaned his forehead upon his hand. The girl watched him over her shoulder, paused, shook off her jaunty hat, dropped the red domino, and stealing toward him, perched herself upon his knee, peering under his hand with a captivating air of penitence, as she laid her arm about his neck and whispered in his ear, "I meant you, *mon ami*, and I will keep my promise by-and-by when all is as we would have it. Believe me, and be gay again, because I do not love you when you are grim and grave, like an Englishman."

"Do you ever love me, my—"

She stopped his mouth with a kiss, and answered, as she smoothed the crisp black curls off his forehead, "You shall see how well I love you, by-and-by."

"Ah, it is always 'by-and-by,' never now. I have a feeling that I never shall possess you, even if my long service ends this year. You are so cold, so treacherous, I have no faith in you, though I adore you, and shall until I die."

"Have I ever broken the promise made so long ago?"

"You dare not; you know the penalty of treason is death."

"Death for you, not for me. I am wiser now; I do not fear you, but I need you, and at last I think—I love you."

As she added the last words, the black frown that had darkened the man's face lifted suddenly, and the expression of intense devotion returned to make it beautiful. He turned that other face upward, scanned it with those magnificent eyes of his, now soft and tender, and answered with a sigh, "It would be death to me to find that after all I have suffered, done, and desired for you, there was no reward but falsehood and base ingratitude. It must not be so; and in that thought I will find patience to work on for one whom I try to love for your sake."

A momentary expression of infinite love and longing touched the girl's face, and filled her eyes with tenderness. But it passed, and settling herself more comfortably, she asked, "How have you prospered since you wrote? Well, I know, else I should have read it at the first glance."

"Beyond my hopes. We crossed together; we are friends already, and shall meet as such. It was an inspiration of yours, and has worked like a charm. Monsieur from the country has not yet appeared, has he?"

"He called when I was out. I did not regret it, for I feel safer when you are by, and it is as well to whet his appetite by absence."

"How is this to end? As we last planned?"

"Yes; but not yet. We must be sure, and that we only can be through himself. Leave it to me. I know him well, and he is willing to be led, I fancy. Now I shall feed you, for it occurs to me that you are fasting. See, I am ready for you."

She left him and ran to and fro, preparing a dainty little supper, but on her lips still lay a smile of conscious power, and in the eyes that followed her still lurked a glance of disquiet and distrust.

Mrs. Vane was driving in the park—not in her own carriage, for she kept none—but having won the hearts of several amiable dowagers, their equipages were always at her command. In one of the most elegant of these she was reclining, apparently unconscious of the many glances of curiosity and admiration fixed upon the lovely face enshrined in the little black tulle bonnet, with its frill of transparent lace to heighten her blond beauty.

Two gentlemen were entering the great gate as she passed by for another turn; one of them pronounced her name, and sprang forward. She recognized the voice, ordered the carriage to stop, and when Douglas came up, held out her hand to him, with a smile of welcome. He touched it, expressed his pleasure of meeting her, and added, seeing her glance at his companion, "Permit me to present my friend, M. Dupont, just from Paris, and happy in so soon meeting a countrywoman."

Duprès executed a superb bow, and made his compliments in his mother tongue.

Mrs. Vane listened with an air of pretty perplexity, and answered, in English, while she gave him her most beaming look, "Monsieur must pardon me that I have forgotten my native language so sadly that I dare not venture to use it in his presence. My youth was spent in Spain, and since then England or India has been my home; but to this dear country I must cordially welcome any friend of M. Douglas."

As she turned to Earl, and listened to his tidings of Lady Lennox, Duprès fixed a searching glance upon her. His keen eyes ran over her from head to foot, and nothing seemed to escape his scrutiny. Her figure was concealed by a great mantle of black velvet; her hair waved plainly away under her bonnet; the heavy folds of her dress flowed over her feet; and her delicately gloved hands lay half buried in the deep lace of her handkerchief. She was very pale, her eyes were languid, her lips sad even in smiling, and her voice had lost its lightsome ring. She looked older, graver, more pensive and dignified than when Douglas last saw her.

"You have been ill, I fear?" he said, regarding her with visible solicitude, while his friend looked down, yet marked every word she uttered.

"Yes, quite ill; I have been through so much in the last month that I can hardly help betraying it in my countenance. A heavy cold, with fever, has kept me a prisoner till these few days past, when I have driven out, being still too feeble to walk."

Earl was about to express his sorrow when Duprès cried, "Behold! It is he—the friend who so assuaged the tortures of that tempestuous passage. Let me reward him by a word from M. Douglas, and a smile from Madame. Is it permitted?"

Scarcely waiting for an assent, the vivacious gentleman darted forward and arrested the progress of a gentleman who was bending at the moment to adjust his stirrup. A few hasty words and emphatic gestures prepared the stranger for the interview, and with the courtesy of a Spaniard, he dismounted and advanced bareheaded, to be presented to Madame. It was Arguelles; and even Douglas was struck with his peculiar beauty, and the native pride that was but half veiled by the Southern softness of his manners. He spoke English well, but when Mrs. Vane addressed him in Spanish, he answered with a flash of pleasure that proved how grateful to him was the sound of his own melodious tongue.

Too well-bred to continue the conversation in a language which excluded the others, Mrs. Vane soon broke up the party by inviting Douglas and his friend to call upon her that evening, adding, with a glance toward the Spaniard, "It will gratify me to extend the hospitalities of an English home to Señor Arguelles, if he is a stranger here, and to enjoy again the familiar sound of the language which is dearer to me than my own."

Three hats were lifted, and three grateful gentlemen expressed their thanks with smiles of satisfaction; then the carriage rolled on, the *señor* galloped off, looking very like some knightly figure from a romance, and Douglas turned to his companion with an eager "Tell me, is it she?"

"No; Virginie would be but one-and-twenty, and this woman must be thirty if she is a day, ungallant that I am to say so of the charming creature."

"You have not seen her to advantage, Antoine. Wait till you meet her again tonight in full toilet, and then pronounce. She has been ill; even I perceive the great change this short time has wrought, for we parted only ten days ago," said Douglas, disappointed, yet not convinced.

"It is well; we will go; I will study her, and if it be that lovely devil, we will cast her out, and so avenge the past."

At nine o'clock, a cab left Douglas at the door of a handsome house in a West End square. A servant in livery admitted him, and passing up one flight of stairs, richly carpeted, softly lighted, and decorated with flowers, he entered a wide doorway, hung with curtains of blue damask, and found himself in a charming room. Directly opposite hung a portrait of Colonel Vane, a handsome, soldierly man, with such a smile upon his painted lips that his friend involuntarily smiled in answer and advanced as if to greet him.

"Would that he were here to welcome you."

The voice was at his side, and there stood Mrs. Vane. But not the woman whom he met in Lady Lennox's drawing room; that was a young and blooming creature, festally arrayed—this a pale, sad-eyed widow, in her weeds. Never, surely, had weeds been more becoming, for the black dress, in spite of its nunlike simplicity, had an air of elegance that many a balldress lacks, and the widow's cap was a mere froth of tulle, encircling the fair face, and concealing all the hair but two plain bands upon the forehead. Not an ornament was visible but a tiny pearl brooch which Douglas himself had given his friend long ago, and a wedding ring upon the hand that once had worn the opal also. She, too, was looking upward toward the picture, and for an instant a curious pause fell between them.

The apartment was an entire contrast to the gay and brilliant drawing rooms he had been accustomed to see. Softly lighted by the pale flame of antique lamps, the eye was relieved from the glare of gas, while the graceful blending of blue and silver, in furniture, hangings, and decorations, pleased one as a change from the more garish colors so much in vogue. A few rare pictures leaned from the walls; several statues stood cool and still in remote recesses; from the curtained entrance of another door was blown the odorous breath of flowers; and the rustle of leaves, the drip of falling water, betrayed the existence of a conservatory close at hand.

"No wonder you were glad to leave the country, for a home like this," said Douglas, as she paused.

"Yes, it is pleasant to be here; but I should tell you that it is not my own. My kind friend Lady Leigh is in Rome for the winter, and knowing that I was a homeless little creature, she begged me to stay here, and keep both servants and house in order till she came again. I was very grateful, for I dread the loneliness of lodgings, and having arranged matters to suit my taste, I shall nestle here till spring tempts me to the hills again."

She spoke quite simply, and seemed as thankful for kindness as a solitary child. Despite his suspicions, and all the causes for distrust— nay, even hatred, if his belief was true—Douglas could not resist the wish that she might be proved innocent, and somewhere find the safe home her youth and beauty needed. So potent was the fascination of her presence that when with her his doubts seemed unfounded, and so great was the confusion into which his mind was thrown by these conflicting impressions that his native composure quite deserted him at times.

It did so then, for, leaning nearer, as they sat together on the couch, he asked almost abruptly, "Why do I find you so changed, in all respects, that I scarcely recognize my friend just now?"

"You mean this?" and she touched her dress. "As you have honored me with the name of friend, I will speak frankly, and explain my seeming caprice. At the desire of Lady Lennox, I laid aside my weeds, and found that I could be a gay young girl again. But with that discovery came another, which made me regret the change, and resolve to return to my sad garb."

"You mean that you found that the change made you too beautiful for George's peace? Poor lad—I knew his secret, and now I understand your sacrifice," Earl said, as she paused, too delicate to betray her young lover, who had asked and been denied.

She colored beautifully, and sat silent; but Douglas was possessed by an irresistible desire to probe her heart as deeply as he dared, and quite unconscious that interest lent his voice and manner an unusual warmth, he asked, thinking only of poor George, "Was it not possible to spare both yourself and him? You see I use a friend's privilege to the utmost."

She still looked down, and the color deepened visibly in her smooth cheek as she replied, "It was not possible, nor will it ever be, for him."

"You have not vowed yourself to an eternal widowhood, I trust?"

She looked up suddenly, as if to rebuke the persistent questioner, but something in his eager face changed her own expression of displeasure into one of half-concealed confusion.

"No, it is so sweet to be beloved that I have not the courage to relinquish the hope of retasting the happiness so quickly snatched from me before."

Douglas rose suddenly, and paced down the room, as if attracted by a balmy gust that just then came floating in. But in truth he fled from the siren by his side, for despite the bitter past, the late loss, the present distrust, something softer than pity, warmer than regard, seemed creeping into his heart, and the sight of the beautiful blushing face made his own cheek burn with a glow such as his love for Diana had never kindled. Indignant at his own weakness, he paused halfway down the long room, wheeled about, and came back, saying, with his accustomed tone of command disguised by a touch of pity, "Come and do the honors of your little paradise. I am restless tonight, and the splash of that fountain has a soothing sound that tempts me to draw nearer."

She went with him, and standing by the fountain's brim talked tranquilly of many things, till the sound of voices caused them to look toward the drawing room. Two gentlemen were evidently coming to join them, and Earl said with a smile, "You have not asked why I came alone; yet your invitation included Arguelles and Dupont."

Again the blush rose to her cheek, and she answered hastily, as she advanced to meet her guests, "I forgot them, now I must atone for my rudeness."

Down the green vista came the gentlemen—the stout Frenchman tripping on before, the dark Spaniard walking behind, with a dignity of bearing that made his companion's gait more ludicrous by comparison. Compliments were exchanged, and then, as the guests expressed a desire to linger in the charming spot, Mrs. Vane led them on, doing the honors with her accustomed grace.

Busied in translating the names of remarkable plants into Spanish for Arguelles, they were somewhat in advance of the other pair; and after a sharp glance or two at Douglas, Duprès paused behind a young orange tree, saying, in a low whisper, "You are going fast, Earl. Finish this business soon, or it will be too late for anything but flight."

"No fear; but what can *I* do? I protest I never was so bewildered in my life. Help me, for heaven's sake, and do it at once!" replied Douglas, with a troubled and excited air.

"Chut! You English have no idea of *finesse;* you bungle sadly. See, now, how smoothly I will discover all I wish to know." Then aloud, as he moved on, "I assure you, *mon ami,* it is an orange, not a lemon tree. Madame shall decide the point, and award me yonder fine flower if I am right."

"Monsieur is correct, and here is the prize."

As she spoke, Mrs. Vane lifted her hand to break the flower which grew just above her. As she stretched her arm upward, her sleeve slipped back, and on her white wrist shone the wide bracelet once attached to the opal ring. As if annoyed by its exposure, she shook down her sleeve with a quick gesture, and before either gentleman could assist her, she stepped on a low seat, gathered the azalea, and turned to descend. Her motion was sudden, the seat frail; it broke as she turned, and she would have fallen, had not Arguelles sprung forward and caught her hands. She recovered herself instantly, and apologizing for her awkwardness, presented the flower with a playful speech. To Earl's great surprise, Duprès received it without his usual flow of compliments, and bowing, silently settled it in his buttonhole, with such a curious expression that his friend fancied he had made some unexpected discovery. He had— but not what Douglas imagined, as he lifted his brows inquiringly when Mrs. Vane and her escort walked on.

"Hush!" breathed Duprès in answer. "Ask her where Jitomar is, in some careless way."

"Why?" asked Earl, recollecting the man for the first time.

But his question received no reply, and the entrance of a servant with refreshments offered the desired pretext for the inquiry.

"Where is your handsome Jitomar? His Oriental face and costume would give the finishing touch to this Eastern garden of palms and lotus flowers," said Douglas, as he offered his hostess a glass of wine, when they paused at a rustic table by the fountain.

"Poor Jitomar—I have lost him!" she replied.

"Dead?" exclaimed Earl.

"Oh, no; and I should have said happy Jitomar, for he is on his way home to his own palms and lotus flowers. He dreaded another winter here so much that when a good opportunity offered for his return, I let him go, and have missed him sadly ever since—for he was a faithful servant to me."

"Let us drink the health of the good and faithful servant, and wish him a prosperous voyage to the torrid land where he belongs," cried Duprès, as he touched his glass to that of Arguelles, who looked somewhat bewildered both by the odd name and the new ceremony.

By some mishap, as Duprès turned to replace his glass upon the table, it slipped from his hand and fell into the fountain, with a splash that caused a little wave to break over the basin's edge, and wet Mrs. Vane's foot with an unexpected bath.

"Great heavens—what carelessness! A thousand pardons! Madame, permit me to repair the damage, although it is too great an honor for me, *maladroit* that I am," exclaimed the Frenchman, with a gesture of despair.

Mrs. Vane shook her dress and assured him that no harm was done; but nothing could prevent the distressed gentleman from going down upon his knees, and with his perfumed handkerchief removing several drops of water from the foot of his hostess—during which process he discovered that, being still an invalid, she wore quilted black silk boots, with down about the tops; also that though her foot was a very pretty one, it was by no means as small as that of Virginie Varens.

When this small stir was over, Mrs. Vane led the way back to the saloon, and here Douglas was more than ever mystified by Duprès's behavior. Entirely ignoring Madame's presence, he devoted himself to Arguelles, besetting him with questions regarding Spain, his own family, pursuits, and tastes; on all of which points the Spaniard satisfied him, and accepted his various invitations for the coming days, looking much at their fair hostess the while, who was much engrossed with Douglas, and seemed quite content.

Arguelles was the first to leave, and his departure broke up the party. As Earl and Duprès drove off together, the former exclaimed, in a fever of curiosity, "Are you satisfied?"

"Entirely."

"She is not Virginie, then?"

"On the contrary, she *is* Virginie, I suspect."

"You suspect? I thought you were entirely satisfied."

"On another point, I am. She baffles me somewhat, I confess, with her woman's art in dress. But I shall discover her yet, if you let me conduct the affair in my own way. I adore mystery; to fathom a secret, trace a lie, discover a disguise, is my delight. I should make a superb detective. Apropos to that, promise me that you will not call in the help of your blundering constabulary, police, or whatever you name them, until I give the word. They will destroy the éclat of the *dénouement,* and annoy me by their stupidity."

"I leave all to you, and regret that the absence of this Jitomar should complicate the affair. What deviltry is he engaged in now, do you think? Not traveling to India, of course, though she told it very charmingly."

His companion whispered three words in his ear.

Earl fell back and stared at him, exclaiming presently, "It is impossible!"

"Nothing is impossible to me," returned the other, with an air of conviction. "That point is clear to my mind; one other remains, and being more difficult, I must consider it. But have no fear; this brain of mine is fertile in inventions, and by morning will have been inspired with a design which will enchant you by its daring, its acuteness, its romance."

≽ *Chapter IX* ≼

MIDNIGHT

FOR a week the three gentlemen haunted the house of the widow, and were much together elsewhere. Duprès was still enthusiastic in praise of his new-made friend, but Douglas was far less cordial, and merely courteous when they met. To outside observers this seemed but natural, for the world knew nothing of his relations to Diana, nor the sad secret that existed between himself and Mrs. Vane. And when it was apparent that the Spaniard was desperately in love with that lady, Douglas could not but look coldly upon him as a rival, for according to rumor the latter gentleman was also paying court to the bewitching widow. It was soon evident which was the favored lover, for despite the dark glances and jealous surveillance of Arguelles, Mrs. Vane betrayed, by unmistakable signs, that Douglas possessed a power over her which no other man had ever attained. It was impossible to conceal it, for when the great passion for the first time possessed her heart, all her art was powerless against this touch of nature, and no timid girl could have been more harassed by the alternations of hope and fear, and the effort to hide her passion.

Going to their usual rendezvous somewhat earlier than usual one evening, Duprès stopped a moment in an anteroom to exchange a word with Gabrielle, the coquettish maid, who was apt to be in the way when the Frenchman appeared. Douglas went on to the drawing room, expecting to find Mrs. Vane alone. The apartment was empty, but the murmur of voices was audible in the conservatory, and going to the curtained arch, he was about to lift the drapery that had fallen from its fastening, when through a little crevice in the middle he saw two figures that arrested him, and, in spite of certain honorable scruples, held him motionless where he stood.

Mrs. Vane and the Spaniard were beside the fountain; both looked excited. Arguelles talked vehemently; she listened with a hard, scornful expression, and made brief answers that seemed to chafe and goad him bitterly. Both spoke Spanish, and even if they had not, so low and rapid were their tones that nothing was audible but the varied murmur rising or falling as the voices alternated. From his gestures, the gentleman seemed by turns to reproach, entreat, command; the lady to recriminate, refuse, and defy. Once she evidently announced some determination that filled her companion with despair; then she laughed, and in a paroxysm of speechless wrath he broke from her, hurrying to the farthest limits of the room, as if unconscious whither he went, and marking with scattered leaves and flowers the passage of his reckless steps.

As he turned from her, Mrs. Vane dipped her hands in the basin and laid them on her forehead, as if to cool some fever of the brain, while such a weight of utter weariness came over her that in an instant ten years seemed to be added to her age. Her eyes roved restlessly to and fro, as if longing to discover some method of escape from the danger or the doubt that oppressed her.

A book from which Douglas had read to her lay on the rustic table at her side, and as her eye fell on it, all her face changed beautifully, hope, bloom, and youth returned, as she touched the volume with a lingering touch, and smiled a smile in which love and exultation blended. A rapid step announced the Spaniard's return; she caught her hand away, mused a moment, and when he came back to her, she spoke in a softer tone, while her eyes betrayed that now she pleaded for some boon, and did not plead in vain. Seizing both her hands in a grasp more firm than tender, Arguelles seemed to extort some promise from her with sternest aspect. She gave it reluctantly; he looked but half satisfied, even though she drew his tall head down and sealed her promise with a kiss; and when she bade him go, he left her with a gloomy air, and some dark purpose stamped upon his face.

So rapidly had this scene passed, so suddenly was it ended, that Douglas had barely time to draw a few paces back before the curtain was pushed aside and Arguelles stood in the arch. Unused to the dishonorable practices to which he had lent himself for the completion of a just work, Earl's face betrayed him.

The Spaniard saw that the late interview had not been without a witness, and forgetting that they had spoken in an unknown tongue, for a moment he looked perfectly livid with fear and fury. Some recollection suddenly seemed to reassure him, but the covert purpose just formed appeared to culminate in action, for, with ungovernable hatred flaming up in his eyes, he said, in a suppressed voice that scarcely parted his white lips, "Eavesdropper and spy! I spit upon you!" And advancing one step struck Douglas full in the face.

It had nearly been his last act, for, burning with scorn and detestation, Earl took him by the throat, and was about to execute swift retribution for both the old wrong and the new when Duprès came between them, whispering, as he wrenched Earl's arm away, "Hold! Remember where you are. Come away, señor, I am your friend in this affair. It shall be arranged. Douglas, remain here, I entreat you."

As he spoke, Duprès gave Earl a warning glance, and drew Arguelles swiftly from the house. Controlling a desperate desire to follow, Douglas remembered his promise to let his friend conduct the affair in his own way, and by a strong effort composed himself, though his cheek still tingled with the blow, and his blood burned within him. The whole encounter had passed noiselessly, and when after a brief pause Douglas entered the conservatory, Mrs. Vane still lingered by the fountain, unconscious of the scene which had just transpired. She turned to greet the newcomer with extended hand, and it was with difficulty that he restrained the rash impulse to strike it from him. The very effort to control this desire made the pressure of his own hand almost painful as he took that other, and the strong grasp sent a thrill of joy to Mrs. Vane's heart, as she smiled and glowed under his glance like a flower at the coming of the sun. The inward excitement, which it was impossible to wholly subdue, manifested itself in Earl's countenance and manner more plainly than he knew, and would have excited some of ill in his companion's mind had not love blinded her, and left none but prophecies of good. A little tremble of delight agitated her, and the eyes that once were so coldly bright and penetrating now were seldom lifted to the face that she had studied so carefully, not long ago. After the first greetings, she waited for him to speak, for words would not come at her will when with him; but he stood thoughtfully, dipping his hand into the fountain as she had done, and laying the wet palm against his cheek, lest its indignant color should betray the insult he had just received.

"Did you meet Señor Arguelles as you came in?" she asked presently, as the pause was unbroken.

"He passed me, and went out."

"You do not fancy him, I suspect."

"I confess it, Mrs. Vane."

"And why?"

"Need I tell *you?*"

The words escaped him involuntarily, and had she seen his face just then, her own would have blanched with fear. But she was looking down, and as he spoke the traitorous color rose to her forehead, though she ignored the betrayal by saying, with an accent of indifference, "He will not annoy you long. Tomorrow he fulfills some engagement with a friend in the country, and in the evening will take leave of me."

"He is about to return to Spain, then?"

"I believe so. I did not question him."

"You will not bid him adieu without regret?"

"With the greatest satisfaction, I assure you, for underneath that Spanish dignity of manner lurks fire, and I have no desire to be consumed." And the sigh of relief that accompanied her words was the most sincere expression of feeling that had escaped her for weeks.

Anxious to test his power to the utmost, Douglas pursued the subject, though it was evidently distasteful to her. Assuming an air of loverlike anxiety, he half timidly, half eagerly inquired, "Then when he comes again to say farewell, you will not consent to go with him to occupy the 'castle in Spain' which he has built up for himself during this short week?"

He thought to see some demonstration of pleasure at the jealous fear his words implied, but her color faded suddenly, and she shivered as if a chilly gust had blown over her, while she answered briefly, with a little gesture of the hand as she set the topic decidedly aside, "No, he will go alone."

There was a momentary pause, and in it something like pity knocked at the door of Earl's heart, for with all his faults he was a generous man, and as he saw this woman sitting there, so unconscious of impending danger, so changed and beautiful by one true sentiment, his purpose wavered, a warning word rose to his lips, and with an impetuous gesture he took her hand, and turned away with an abrupt "Pardon me— it is too soon—I will explain hereafter."

The entrance of a servant with coffee seemed to rouse him into sudden spirits and activity, for begging Mrs. Vane to sit and rest, he served her with assiduous care.

"Here is your own cup of violet and gold; you see I know your fancy even in trifles. Is it right? I took such pains to have it as you like it," he said, as he presented the cup with an air of tender solicitude.

"It does not matter, but one thing you have forgotten, I take no sugar," she answered, smiling as she tasted.

"I knew it, yet the line 'Sweets to the sweet' was running in my head, and so I unconsciously spoiled your draft. Let me retrieve the error?"

"By no means. I drink to you." And lifting the tiny cup to her lips, she emptied it with a look which proved that his words had already retrieved the error.

He received the cup with a peculiar smile, looked at his watch, and exclaimed, "It is late, and I should go, yet—"

"No, not yet; stay and finish the lines you began yesterday. I find less beauty in them when I read them to myself," she answered, detaining him.

Glad of an excuse to prolong his stay, Earl brought the book, and sitting near her, lent to the poem the sonorous music of his voice.

The last words came all too soon, and when Douglas rose, Mrs. Vane bade him good night with a dreamy softness in her eyes which caused a gleam of satisfaction to kindle in his own. As he passed through the anteroom, Gabrielle met him with a look of anxious though mute inquiry in her face. He answered it with a significant nod, a warning gesture, and she let him out, wearing an aspect of the deepest mystery.

Douglas hurried to his rooms, and there found Duprès with Major Mansfield, who had been put in possession of the secret, and the part he was expected to play in its unraveling.

"What in heaven's name did you mean by taking the wrong side of the quarrel, and forcing me to submit quietly to such an indignity?" demanded Earl, giving vent to the impatience which had only been curbed till now, that he might perform the portion of the plot allotted to him.

"Tell me first, have you succeeded?" said Duprès.

"I have."

"You are sure?"

"Beyond a doubt."

"It is well; I applaud your dexterity. Behold the major, he knows all, he is perfect in his role. Now hear yours. You will immediately write a challenge."

"It is impossible! Antoine, you are a daft to ask me to meet that man."

"Bah! I ask you to meet, but not to honor him by blowing his brains out. He is a dead shot, and thirsts for your blood, but look you, he will be disappointed. We might arrest him this instant, but he will confess nothing, and that clever creature will escape us. No, my little arrangement suits me better."

"Time flies, Duprès, and so perhaps may this crafty hind that you are about to snare," said the major, whose slow British wits were somewhat confused by the Frenchman's *finesse*.

"It is true; see then, my Earl. In order that our other little affair may come smoothly off without interference from our friend, I propose to return to the *señor*, whom I have lately left writing letters, and amuse myself by keeping him at home to receive your challenge, which the major will bring about twelve. Then we shall arrange the affair to take place at sunrise, in some secluded spot out of town. You will be back here by that time, you will agree to our plans, and present yourself at the appointed time, when the grand *dénouement* will take place with much éclat."

"Am I not to know more?" asked Douglas.

"It would be well to leave all to me, for you will act your part better if you do not know the exact program, because you do not perform so well with Monsieur as with Madame. But if you must know, the major will tell you, while you wait for Hyde and the hour. I have seen him, he has no scruples; I have ensured his safety, and he will not fail us. Now the charming *billet* to the *señor*, and I go to my post."

Douglas wrote the challenge; Duprès departed in buoyant spirits; and while Earl waited for the stranger, Hyde, the major enlightened him upon the grand finale.

The city clocks were striking twelve as two men, masked and cloaked, passed up the steps of Mrs. Vane's house and entered noiselessly. No light beamed in the hall, but scarcely had they closed the door behind them when a glimmer shone from above, and at the stairhead appeared a woman beckoning. Up they stole, as if shod with velvet, and the woman flitted like a shadow before them, till they reached a door to the second story. Opening this, she motioned them to enter, and as they passed in, she glided up another flight, as if to stand guard over her sleeping fellow servants.

One of the men was tall and evidently young, the other a bent and withered little man, whose hands trembled slightly as he adjusted his mask, and peered about him. It was a large still room, lighted by a night lamp, burning behind its shade, richly furnished, and decorated with warm hues, that produced the effect of mingled snow and fire. A luxurious nest it seemed, and a fit inmate of it looked the beautiful woman asleep in the shadow of the crimson-curtained bed. One white arm pillowed her head; from the little cap that should have confined it flowed a mass of golden hair over neck and shoulders; the long lashes lay dark against her cheek; the breath slept upon her lips; and perfect unconsciousness lent its reposeful charm to both face and figure.

Noiselessly advancing, the taller man looked and listened for a moment, as if to assure himself that this deep slumber was not feigned; then he beckoned the other to bring the lamp. It flickered as the old man took it up, but he trimmed the wick, removed the shade, and a clear light shone across the room. Joining his companion, he too looked at the sleeping beauty, shook his gray head, and seemed to deplore some fact that marred the pretty picture in his sight.

"Is there no danger of her waking, sir?" he whispered, as the light fell on her face.

"It is impossible for an hour yet. The bracelet is on that wrist; we must move her, or you cannot reach it," returned the other; and with a gentle touch drew the left arm from underneath her head.

She sighed in her sleep, knit her brows, as if a dream disturbed her, and turning on her pillow, all the bright hair fell about her face, but could not hide the glitter of the chain about her neck. Drawing it forth, the taller man started, uttered an exclamation, dragged from his own bosom a duplicate of the miniature hanging from that chain, and compared the two with trembling intentness. Very like they were, those two young faces, handsome, frank and full of boyish health, courage, and blithesomeness. One might have been taken a year after the other, for the brow was bolder, the mouth graver, the eye more steadfast, but the same charm of expression appeared in both, making the ivory oval more attractive even to a stranger's eye than the costly setting, or the initial letters *A. D.* done in pearls upon the back. A small silver key hung on the chain the woman wore, and as if glad to tear his thoughts from some bitter reminiscence, the man detached this key, and glanced about the room, as if to discover what lock it would be.

His action seemed to remind the other of his own task, for setting down the lamp on the little table where lay a prayer book, a bell, and a rosary, he produced a case of delicate instruments and a bunch of tiny keys, and bending over the bracelet, examined the golden padlock that fastened it. While he carefully tried key after key upon that miniature lock, the chief of this mysterious inspection went to and fro with the silver key, attempting larger locks. Nowhere did it fit, till in passing the toilet table his foot brushed its draperies aside, disclosing a quaint for-eign-looking casket of ebony and silver. Quick as thought it was drawn out and opened, for here the key did its work. In the upper tray lay the opal ring in its curiously thick setting, beside it a seal, rudely made from an impression in wax of his own iron ring, and a paper bearing its stamp. The marriage record was in hand, and he longed to keep or destroy it, but restrained the impulse; and lifting the tray, found below two or three relics of his friend Vane, and some childish toys, soiled and broken, but precious still.

"A child! Good God! What have I done?" he said to himself, as the lid fell from his hand.

"Hush, come and look, it is off," whispered the old man, and hastily restoring all things to their former order, the other relocked and replaced the casket, and obeyed the call.

For a moment a mysterious and striking picture might have been seen in that quiet room. Under the crimson canopy lay the fair figure of the sleeping woman, her face half hidden by the golden shadow of her hair, her white arm laid out on the warm-hued coverlet, and bending over it, the two masked men, one holding the lamp nearer, the other pointing to something just above the delicate wrist, now freed from the bracelet, which lay open beside it. Two distinctly traced letters were seen, *V. V.*, and underneath a tiny true-lover's knot, in the same dark lines.

The man who held the lamp examined the brand with minutest care, then making a gesture of satisfaction, he said, "It is enough, I am sure now. Put on the bracelet, and come away; there is nothing more to be done tonight."

The old man skillfully replaced the hand, while the other put back locket and key, placed the lamp where they found it; and with a last look at the sleeper, whose unconscious helplessness appealed to them for mercy, both stole away as noiselessly as they had come. The woman reappeared the instant they left the room, lighted them to the hall door, received some reward that glittered as it passed from hand to hand, and made all fast behind them, pausing a moment in a listening attitude, till the distant roll of a carriage assured her that the maskers were safely gone.

≫ *Chapter X* ≪

IN THE SNARE

T HE first rays of the sun fell on a group of five men, standing together on a waste bit of ground in the environs of London. Major Mansfield and Duprès were busily loading pistols, marking off the distance, and conferring together with a great display of interest. Douglas conversed tranquilly with the surgeon in attendance, a quiet, unassuming man, who stood with his hand in his pocket, as if ready to produce his case of instruments at a moment's notice. The Spaniard was alone, and a curious change seemed to have passed over him. The stately calmness of his demeanor was gone, and he paced to and fro with restless steps, like a panther in his cage. A look of almost savage hatred lowered on his swarthy face; desperation and despair alternately glowed and gloomed in his fierce eye; and the whole man wore a look of one who after long restraint yields himself utterly to the dominion of some passion, dauntless and indomitable as death.

Once he paused, drew from his pocket an ill-spelled, rudely written letter, which had been put into his hand by a countryman as he left his hotel, reread the few lines it contained, and thrust it back into his bosom, muttering, "All things favor me; this was the last tie that bound her; now we must stand or fall together."

"Señor, we are prepared," called Duprès, advancing, pistol in hand, to place his principal, adding, as Arguelles dropped hat and cloak, "our custom may be different from yours, but give heed, and at the word 'Three,' fire."

"I comprehend, monsieur," and a dark smile passed across the

Spaniard's face as he took his place and stretched his hand to receive the weapon.

But Duprès drew back a step—and with a sharp metallic click, around that extended wrist snapped a handcuff. A glance showed Arguelles that he was lost, for on his right stood the counterfeit surgeon, with the well-known badge now visible on his blue coat, behind him Major Mansfield, armed, before him Douglas, guarding the nearest outlet of escape, and on his left Duprès, radiant with satisfaction, exclaiming, as he bowed with grace, "A thousand pardons, Monsieur Victor Varens, but this little ruse was inevitable."

Quick as a flash that freed left hand snatched the pistol from Duprès, aimed it at Douglas, and it would have accomplished its work had not the Frenchman struck up the weapon. But the ball was sped, and as the pistol turned in his hand, the bullet lodged in Victor's breast, sparing him the fate he dreaded more than death. In an instant all trace of passion vanished, and with a melancholy dignity that nothing could destroy, he offered his hand to receive the fetter, saying calmly, while his lips whitened, and a red stain dyed the linen on his breast, "I am tired of my life; take it."

They laid him down, for as he spoke, consciousness ebbed away. A glance assured the major that the wound was mortal, and carefully conveying the senseless body to the nearest house, Douglas and the detective remained to tend and guard the prisoner, while the other gentlemen posted to town to bring a genuine surgeon and necessary help, hoping to keep life in the man till his confession had been made.

At nightfall, Mrs. Vane, or Virginie, as we may now call her, grew anxious for the return of Victor, who was to bring her tidings of the child, because she dared not visit him just now herself.

When dressed for the evening, she dismissed Gabrielle, opened the antique casket, and put on the opal ring, carefully attaching the little chain that fastened it securely to her bracelet, for the ring was too large for the delicate hand that wore it. Then with steady feet she went down to the drawing room to meet her lover and her victim.

But some reproachful memory seemed to start up and haunt the present with a vision of the past. She passed her hand across her eyes, as if she saw again the little room, where in the gray dawn she had left her husband lying dead, and she sank into a seat, groaning half aloud, "Oh, if I could forget!"

A bell rang from below, but she did not hear it; steps came through the drawing room, yet she did not heed them; and Douglas stood before her, but she did not see him till he spoke. So great was her surprise, that with all her power of dissimulation she would have found difficulty in concealing it, had not the pale gravity of the newcomer's face afforded a pretext for alarm.

"You startled me at first, and now you look as if you brought ill news," she said, with a vain effort to assume her usual gaiety.

"I do" was the brief reply.

"The señor? Is he with you? I am waiting for him."

"Wait no longer, he will never come."

"Where is he?"

"Quiet in his shroud."

He thought to see her shrink and pale before the blow, but she did neither; she grasped his arm, searched his face, and whispered, with a look of relief, not terror, in her own, "You have killed him?"

"No, his blood is not upon my head; he killed himself."

She covered up her face, and from behind her hands he heard her murmur, "Thank God, he did not come! I am spared that."

While he pondered over the words, vainly trying to comprehend them, she recovered herself, and turning to him said, quite steadily though very pale, "This is awfully sudden; tell me how it came to pass. I am not afraid to hear."

"I will tell you, for you have a right to know. Sit, Mrs. Vane; it is a long tale, and one that will try your courage to the utmost.

"Six years ago I went abroad to meet my cousin Allan," Douglas began, speaking slowly, almost sternly. "He was my senior by a year, but we so closely resembled each other that we were often taken for twin brothers. Alike in person, character, temper, and tastes, we were never so happy as when together, and we loved one another as tenderly as women love. For nearly a year we roamed east and west, then our holiday was over, for we had promised to return. One month more remained; I desired to revisit Switzerland, Allan to remain in Paris, so we parted for a time, each to our own pleasures, appointing to meet on a certain day at a certain place. I never saw him again, for when I reached the spot where he should have met me, I found only a letter, saying that he had been called from Paris suddenly, but that I should receive further intelligence before many days. I waited, but not long. Visiting the Morgue that very week, I found my poor Allan waiting for me there. His body had been taken from the river, and the deep wound in his breast showed that foul play was at the bottom of the mystery. Night and day I labored to clear up the mystery, but labored secretly, lest publicity should warn the culprits, or bring dishonor upon our name, for I soon found that Allan had led a wild life in my absence, and I

feared to make some worse discoveries than a young man's follies. I
did so; for it appeared that he had been captivated by a singularly beautiful girl, a *danseuse*, had privately married her, and both had disappeared with a young cousin of her own. Her apartments were searched,
but all her possessions had been removed, and nothing remained but a
plausible letter, which would have turned suspicion from the girl to
the cousin, had not the marriage been discovered, and in her room two
witnesses against them. The handle of a stiletto, half consumed in the
ashes, which fitted the broken blade entangled in the dead man's clothes,
and, hidden by the hangings of the bed, a woman's slipper, with a
bloodstain on the sole. Ah, you may well shudder, Mrs. Vane; it is an
awful tale."

"Horrible! Why tell it?" she asked, pressing her hand upon her
eyes, as if to shut out some image too terrible to look upon.

"Because it concerns our friend Arguelles, and explains his death,"
replied Earl, in the same slow stern voice. She did not look up, but he
saw that she listened breathlessly, and grew paler still behind her hand.

"Nothing more was discovered then. My cousin's body was sent
home, and none but our two families ever knew the truth. It was believed by the world that he died suddenly of an affection of the heart—
poor lad! it was the bitter truth—and whatever rumors were about
regarding his death, and the change it wrought in me, were speedily
silenced at the time, and have since died away. Over the dead body of
my dearest friend, I vowed a solemn vow to find his murderer and
avenge his death. I have done both."

"Where? How?"

Her hand dropped, and she looked at him with a face that was
positively awful in its unnatural calmness.

"Arguelles was Victor Varens. I suspected, watched, ensnared him,
and would have let the law avenge Allan's death, but the murderer
escaped by his own hand."

"Well for him it was so. May his sins be forgiven. Now let us go
elsewhere, and forget this dark story and its darker end."

She rose as she spoke, and a load seemed lifted off her heart; but
it fell again, as Douglas stretched his hand to detain her, saying, "Stay,
the end is not yet told. You forget the girl."

"She was innocent—why should she suffer?" returned the other,
still standing as if defying both fear and fate.

"She was *not* innocent—for she lured that generous boy to marry
her, because she coveted his rank and fortune, not his heart, and, when
he lay dead, left him to the mercies of wind and wave, while she fled

away to save herself. But that cruel cowardice availed her nothing, for though I have watched and waited long, at length I have found her, and at this moment her life lies in my hand—for you and Virginie are one!"

Like a hunted creature driven to bay, she turned on him with an air of desperate audacity, saying haughtily, "Prove it!"

"I will."

For a moment they looked at one another. In his face she saw pitiless resolve; in hers he read passionate defiance.

"Sit down, Virginie, and hear the story through. Escape is impossible—the house is guarded, Duprès waits in yonder room, and Victor can no longer help you with quick wit or daring hand. Submit quietly, and do not force me to forget that you are my cousin's—wife."

She obeyed him, and as the last words fell from his lips a new hope sprang up within her, the danger seemed less imminent, and she took heart again, remembering the child, who might yet plead for her, if her own eloquence should fail.

"You ask me to prove that fact, and evidently doubt my power to do it; but well as you have laid your plots, carefully as you have erased all traces of your former self, and skillfully as you have played your new part, the truth has come to light, and through many winding ways I have followed you, till my labors end here. When you fled from Paris, Victor, whose mother was a Spaniard, took you to Spain, and there, among his kindred, your boy was born."

"Do you know that, too?" she cried, lost in wonder at the quiet statement of what she believed to be known only to herself, her dead cousin, and those far-distant kindred who had succored her in her need.

"I know everything," Earl answered, with an expression that made her quail; then a daring spirit rose up in her, as she remembered more than one secret, which she now felt to be hers alone.

"Not everything, my cousin; you are keen and subtle, but I excel you, though you win this victory, it seems."

So cool, so calm she seemed, so beautifully audacious she looked, that Earl could only resent the bold speech with a glance, and proceed to prove the truth of his second assertion with the first.

"You suffered the sharpest poverty, but Victor respected your helplessness, forgave your treachery, supplied your wants as far as possible, and when all other means failed, left you there, while he went to earn bread for you and your boy. Virginie, I never can forgive him my cousin's death, but for his faithful, long-suffering devotion to you, I honor him, sinner though he was."

She shrugged her shoulders, with an air of indifference or displeasure, took off the widow's cap, no longer needed for a disguise, and letting loose the cloud of curls that seemed to cluster round her charming face, she lay back in her chair with all her former graceful ease, saying, as she fixed her lustrous eyes upon the man she meant to conquer yet, "I let him love me, and he was content. What more could I do, for I never loved *him?*"

"Better for him that you did not, and better for poor Allan that he never lived to know it was impossible for you to love."

Earl spoke bitterly, but Virginie bent her head till her face was hidden, as she murmured, "Ah, if it were impossible, this hour would be less terrible, the future far less dark."

He heard the soft lament, divined its meaning, but abruptly continued his story, as if he ignored the sorrowful fact which made her punishment heavier from his hand than from any other.

"While Victor was away, you wearied of waiting, you longed for the old life of gaiety and excitement, and, hoping to free yourself from him, you stole away, and for a year were lost to him. Your plan was to reach France, and under another name dance yourself into some other man's heart and home, making him your shield against all danger. You did reach France, but weary, ill, poor, and burdened with the child, you failed to find help, till some evil fortune threw Vane in your way. You had heard of him from Allan, knew his chivalrous nature, his passion for relieving pain or sorrow, at any cost to himself, and you appealed to him for charity. A piteous story of a cruel husband, desertion, suffering, and destitution you told him; he believed it, and being on the point of sailing for India, offered you the place of companion to a lady sailing with him. Your tale was plausible, your youth made it pathetic, your beauty lent it power, and the skill with which you played the part of a sad gentlewoman won all hearts, and served your end successfully. Vane loved you, wished to marry you, and would have done so had not death prevented. He died suddenly; you were with him, and though his last act was to make generous provision for you and the boy, some devil prompted you to proclaim yourself his wife, as soon as he was past denying it. His love for you was well-known among those with whom you lived, and your statement was believed."

"You are a magician," she said suddenly. "I have thought so before; now I am sure of it, for you must have transported yourself to India, to make these discoveries."

"No—India came to me in the person of a Hindoo, and from him I learned these facts," replied Douglas, slow to tell her of Victor's perfidy, lest he should put her on her guard, and perhaps lose some revelation which in her ignorance she might make. Fresh bewilderment seemed to fall upon her, and with intensest interest she listened, as that ruthless voice went on.

"Your plan was this: From Vane you had learned much of Allan's family, and the old desire to be 'my lady' returned more strongly than before. Once in England, you hoped to make your way as Colonel Vane's widow, and if no safe, sure opportunity appeared of claiming your boy's right, you resolved to gain your end by wooing and winning another Douglas. You were on the point of starting with poor Vane's fortune in your power (for he left no will, and you were prepared to produce forged papers, if your possession was questioned in England), when Victor found you. He had traced you with the instinct of a faithful dog, though his heart was nearly broken by your cruel desertion. You saw that he could not serve you; you appeased his anger and silenced his reproaches by renewed promises to be his when the boy was acknowledged, if he would aid you in that project. At the risk of his life, this devoted slave consented, and disguised as an Indian servant came with you to England. On the way, you met and won the good graces of the Countess Camareena; she introduced you to the London world, and you began your career as a lady under the best auspices. Money, beauty, art served you well, and as an unfortunate descendant of the noble house of Montmorenci, you were received by those who would have shrunk from you as you once did from the lock of hair of the plebeian French *danseuse,* found in Allan's bosom."

"I *am* noble," she cried, with an air that proved it, "for though my mother was a peasant, my father was a prince, and better blood than that of the Montmorencis flows in my veins."

He only answered with a slight bow, which might be intended as a mocking obeisance in honor of her questionable nobility, or a grave dismissal of the topic.

"From this point the tale is unavoidably egotistical," he said, "for through Lady Lennox you heard of me, learned that I was the next heir to the title, and began at once to weave the web in which I was to be caught. You easily understood what was the mystery of my life, as it was called among the gossips, and that knowledge was a weapon in your hands, which you did not fail to use. You saw that Diana loved me, soon learned my passion for her, and set yourself to separate us, without one thought of the anguish it would bring us, one fear of the consequences of such wrong to yourself. You bade her ask of me a confession that I could not make, having given my word to Allan's mother that her son's name should not be tarnished by the betrayal of the rash act that cost his life. That parted us; then you told her a tale of skillfully mingled truth and falsehood, showed her the marriage record on which a name and date appeared to convict me, took her to the boy whose likeness to his father, and therefore to myself, completed the cruel deception, and drove that high-hearted girl to madness and to death."

"I did not kill her! On my soul, I never meant it! I was terror-stricken when we missed her, and knew no peace or rest till she was found. Of that deed I am innocent—I swear it to you on my knees."

The haunting horror of that night seemed again to overwhelm her; she fell down upon her knees before him, enforcing her denial with clasped hands, imploring eyes, and trembling voice. But Douglas drew back with a gesture of repugnance that wounded her more deeply than his sharpest word, and from that moment all traces of compassion vanished from his countenance, which wore the relentless aspect of a judge who resolves within himself no longer to temper justice with mercy.

"Stand up," he said. "I will listen to no appeal, believe no oath, let no touch of pity soften my heart, for your treachery, your craft, your sin deserve nothing but the heavy retribution you have brought upon yourself. Diana's death lies at your door, as much as if you had stabbed her with the same dagger that took Allan's life. It may yet be proved that you beguiled her to that fatal pool, for you were seen there, going to remove all traces of her, perhaps. But in your hasty flight you left traces of yourself behind you, as you sprang away with an agility that first suggested to me the suspicion of Virginie's presence. I tried your slipper to the footprint, and it fitted too exactly to leave me in much doubt of the truth of my wild conjecture. I had never seen you. Antoine Duprès knew both Victor and yourself. I sent for him, but before the letter went, Jitomar, your spy, read the address, feared that some peril menaced you both, and took counsel with you how to delude the newcomer, if any secret purpose lurked behind our seeming friendliness. You devised a scheme that would have baffled us, had not accident betrayed Victor. In the guise of Arguelles he met Duprès in Paris, returned with him, and played his part so well that the Frenchman was entirely deceived, never dreaming of being sought by the very man who would most desire to shun him. You, too, disguised yourself, with an art that staggered my own senses, and perplexed Duprès, for our masculine eye could not fathom the artifices of costume, cosmetics, and consummate acting. We feared to alarm you by any open step, and resolved to oppose craft to craft, treachery to treachery. Duprès revels in such intricate affairs, and I yielded, against my will, till the charm of success drew me on with increasing eagerness and spirit. The day we first met here, in gathering a flower you would have fallen, had not the Spaniard sprung forward to save you; that involuntary act betrayed him, for the momentary attitude he assumed recalled to Duprès the memory of a certain pose which the dancer Victor often assumed. It was too peculiar to be accidental, too striking to be easily forgotten, and the entire unconsciousness of its actor was a proof that it was so familiar as to be quite natural. From that instant Duprès devoted himself to the Spaniard; this first genuine delusion put Victor off his guard with Antoine; and Antoine's feigned friendship was so adroitly assumed that no suspicion woke in Victor's mind till the moment when, instead of offering him a weapon with which to take my life, he took him prisoner."

"He is not dead, then? You lie to me; you drive me wild with your horrible recitals of the past, and force me to confess against my will. Who told you these things? The dead alone could tell you what passed between Diana and myself."

Still on the ground, as if forgetful of everything but the bewilderment of seeing plot after plot unfolded before her, she had looked up and listened with dilated eyes, lips apart, and both hands holding back the locks that could no longer hide her from his piercing glance. As she spoke, she paled and trembled with a sudden fear that clutched her heart, that Diana was not dead, for even now she clung to her love with a desperate hope that it might save her.

Calm and cold as a man of marble, Douglas looked down upon her, so beautiful in all her abasement, and answered steadily, "You forget Victor. To him all your acts, words, and many of your secret thoughts were told. Did you think his love would endure forever, his patience never tire, his outraged heart never rebel, his wild spirit never turn and rend you? All day I have sat beside him, listening to his painful confessions, painfully but truthfully made, and with his last breath he cursed you as the cause of a wasted life, and ignominious death. Virginie, this night your long punishment begins, and that curse is a part of it."

"Oh, no, no! You will have mercy, remembering how young, how friendless I am? For Allan's sake you will pity me; for his boy's sake you will save me; for your own sake you will hide me from the world's contempt?"

"What mercy did you show poor Diana? What love for Allan? What penitence for your child's sake? What pity for my grief? I tell you, if a word would save you, my lips should not utter it!"

He spoke passionately now, and passionately she replied, clinging to him, though he strove to tear his hands away.

"You have heard Victor's confession, now hear mine. I *have* longed to repent; I did hope to make my life better, for my baby's sake; and oh, I did pity you, till my cold heart softened and grew warm. I should have given up my purpose, repaid Victor's fidelity, and gone away to grow an honest, happy, humble woman, if I had not loved *you.* That made me blind, when I should have been more keen-sighted than ever; that kept me here to be deceived, betrayed, and that should save me now."

"It will not; and the knowledge that I detest and despise you is to add bitterness to your threefold punishment; the memory of Allan, Victor, and Diana is another part of it; and here is the heaviest blow which heaven inflicts as a retribution that will come home to you."

As he spoke, Douglas held to her a crumpled paper, stained with a red stain, and torn with the passage of a bullet that ended Victor's life. She knew the writing, sprang up to seize it, read the few lines, and when the paper fluttered to the ground, the white anguish of her face betrayed that the last blow *had* crushed her as no other could have done. She dropped into a seat, with the wail of tearless woe that breaks from a bereaved mother's heart as she looks on the dead face of the child who has been her idol, and finds no loving answer.

"My baby gone—and I not there to say good-bye! Oh, my darling, I could have borne anything but this!"

So utterly broken did she seem, so wild and woeful did she look, that Douglas had not the heart to add another pang to her sharp grief by any word of explanation or compassion. Silently he poured out a glass of wine and placed it nearer, then resumed his seat and waited till she spoke. Soon she lifted up her head, and showed him the swift and subtle blight that an hour had brought upon her. Life, light, and beauty seemed to have passed away, and a pale shadow of her former self alone remained. Some hope or some resolve had brought her an unnatural calmness, for her eyes were tearless, her face expressionless, her voice tranquil, as if she had done with life, and neither pain nor passion could afflict her now.

"What next?" she said, and laid her hand upon the glass, but did not lift it to her lips, as if the former were too tremulous, or the latter incapable of receiving the draft.

"Only this," he answered, with a touch of pity in his voice. "I will not have my name handed from mouth to mouth, in connection with an infamous history like this. For Allan's sake, and for Diana's, I shall

keep it secret, and take your punishment into my hands. Victor I leave
to a wiser judge than any human one; the innocent child is safe from
shame and sorrow; but you must atone for the past with the loss of
liberty and your whole future. It is a more merciful penalty than the law
would exact, were the truth known, for you are spared public contempt,
allowed time for repentance, and deprived of nothing but the liberty
which you have so cruelly abused."

"I thank you. Where is my prison to be?"

She took the glass into her hand, yet still held it suspended, as she
waited for his answer, with an aspect of stony immobility which troubled
him.

"Far away in Scotland I own a gray old tower, all that now remains
of an ancient stronghold. It is built on the barren rock, where it stands
like a solitary eagle's eyrie, with no life near it but the sound of the wind,
the scream of the gulls, the roll of the sea that foams about it. There
with my faithful old servants you shall live, cut off from all the world,
but not from God, and when death comes to you, may it find you ready
and glad to go, a humble penitent, more fit to meet your little child than
now."

A long slow tremor shook her from head to foot, as word by word
her merciful yet miserable doom was pronounced, leaving no hope, no
help but the submission and repentance which it was not in her nature
to give. For a moment she bowed her head, while her pale lips moved,
and her hands, folded above the glass, were seen to tremble as if some
fear mingled even in her prayers. Then she sat erect, and fixing on him
a glance in which love, despair, and defiance mingled, she said, with
all her former pride and spirit, as she slowly drank the wine, "Death
cannot come too soon; I go to meet it."

Her look, her tone, awed Douglas, and for a moment he regarded
her in silence, as she sat there, leaning her bright head against the dark
velvet of the cushioned chair. Her eyes were on him still brilliant and
brave, in spite of all that had just passed; a disdainful smile curved her
lips, and one fair arm lay half extended on the table, as it fell when
she put the glass away. On this arm the bracelet shone; he pointed to it,
saying, with a meaning glance, "I know that secret, as I know all the
rest."

"Not all; there is one more you have not discovered—yet."

She spoke very slowly, and her lips seemed to move reluctantly,
while a strange pallor fell on her face, and the fire began to die out of
her eyes, leaving them dim, but tender.

"You mean the mystery of the iron ring; but I learned that last night, when, with an expert companion, I entered your room, where you lay buried in the deep sleep produced by the drugged coffee which I gave you. I saw my portrait on your neck, as I wear Allan's, ever since we gave them to each other, long ago, and beside the miniature, the silver key that opened your quaint treasure casket. I found the wax impression of my signet, taken, doubtless, on the night when, as a ghost, you haunted my room; I found the marriage record, stamped with that counterfeit seal, to impose upon Diana; I found relics of Vane, and of your child; and when Hyde called me, I saw and examined the two letters on your arm, which he had uncovered by removing the bracelet from it."

He paused there, expecting some demonstration. None appeared; she leaned and listened, with the same utter stillness of face and figure, the same fixed look and deathly pallor. He thought her faint and spent with the excitement of the hour, and hastened to close the interview, which had been so full of contending emotions to them both.

"Go now, and rest," he said. "I shall make all necessary arrange ments here, all proper explanations to Lady Leigh. Gabrielle will prepare for your departure in the morning; but let me warn you not to attempt to bribe her, or to deceive me by any new ruse, for now escape is impossible."

"I have escaped!"

The words were scarcely audible, but a glance of exultation flashed from her eyes, then faded, and the white lids fell, as if sleep weighed them down. A slight motion of the nerveless hand that lay upon the table drew Earl's attention, and with a single look those last words were explained. The opal ring was turned inward on her finger, and some unsuspected spring had been touched when she laid her hands together; for now in the deep setting appeared a tiny cavity, which had evidently contained some deadly poison. The quick and painless death that was to have been Victor's had fallen to herself, and, unable to endure the fate prepared for her, she had escaped, when the net seemed most securely drawn about her. Horror-stricken, Douglas called for help; but all human aid was useless, and nothing of the fair, false Virginie remained but a beautiful, pale image of repose.

A Marble Woman

~ *or* ~

THE MYSTERIOUS MODEL

❧ *Chapter I* ❧

LITTLE CECIL

"WHAT do you mean by pulling the bell fit to bring the house down?" demanded gruff old Anthony, as he flung the door open and found himself confronted with a large trunk and a small girl holding a letter in her hand.

"It was the coachman, please, sir" was the composed answer.

"Well, what do you want, child?"

"I wish to come in. This is my luggage; I'll help you with it."

The small personage laid hold of one handle with such perfect good faith in her own strength that it produced a chuckle from the old servant as he drew the trunk in with one hand, the child with the other, and shut the door, saying more respectfully, "Now, ma'am, what next?"

Smoothing her disordered dress with dignity, the little girl replied, as if repeating a carefully learned lesson, "You are to give this letter to Mr. Bazil Yorke, and say Miss Stein has come. Then I am to wait till he tells me what to do."

"Are you Miss Stein?" asked Anthony, bewildered by the appearance of a child in that lonely house.

"Yes, sir; and I've come to live here if Mr. Yorke will keep me," said the little girl, glancing wistfully about her as if waiting for a welcome.

"Are you a relation of Master's?" questioned Anthony, still more mystified.

"No, sir. He knew my papa and mamma, but he never saw me. That's all I know about it."

The old man shook his head with an air of resignation as he mut-

tered to himself, "Some whim of Master's; it's just like him." Then
aloud, "I'll take up the letter, but you'd better play out here till you're
wanted; for when Master gets busy up aloft, it's no use trying to fetch
him down before the time."

Leading her through the hall, he opened a glass door and ushered
her into a city garden, where a few pale shrubs and vines rustled in the
wind. The child glanced listlessly about her as she walked, for nothing
was in bloom, and the place had a neglected air. Suddenly a splendid,
full-blown rose softly brushed her cheek and fell at her feet. With an
exclamation of pleasure she caught it up and looked skyward to see what
friendly fairy had divined her wish and granted it.

"Here I am," called a laughing voice, and turning about she saw
a boy leaning on the low wall that divided Mr. Yorke's garden from an
adjoining one. A rosy, bright-eyed boy about her own age he seemed,
full of the pleasant audacity which makes boyhood so charming, and
in a neighborly mood just then; for as she looked up wondering, he
nodded, smiled, and said merrily, "How are you? Do you like the rose?"

"Oh, yes! Did you mean it for me?"

"I thought you looked as if you needed one, so I tossed it over. It's
very dismal down there. Suppose you come up here, and then you can
see my garden while we talk a bit. Don't be afraid of me; just give me
your hand and there you are."

There was something so winning in voice, face, and gesture that
little Miss Stein could not resist the invitation. She gave her hand, and
soon sat on the wide coping of the wall, regarding her new friend with
a shy yet confiding look as he did the honors of the place with well-bred
eagerness. Neither asked the other's name, but making the rose their
master of ceremonies, introduced themselves through that pretty me-
dium, and soon forgot that they had been entire strangers five minutes
before.

"Do you like my garden?" asked the boy, as the girl smelled her
flower and smiled down upon the blooming plot below her.

"Very much; I wish Mr. Yorke would have one like it."

"He don't care for such things; he's odd and busy, and a genius,
you know."

"I hope that's nothing bad, because I'm going to live with him.
Tell me all about him, for I never saw him in my life."

"He's a sculptor and makes splendid statues up in that tower where
nothing but the sun and sparrows can see him. He never shows them,
and no one would ever see them if they didn't beg and tease and give
him no peace till they do."

"Is he kind and pleasant?" asked the girl.

"He looks precious grim with his long hair and beard, but he's got kind eyes, though his face is dark and strange."

"Has he got a wife and any little children?"

"Oh, dear, no! He lives here with old Tony and Mrs. Hester, the maid. I heard my mother tell a lady that Mr. Yorke had a love trouble and can't bear women, so none dare go near him. He's got a splendid great dog, but he's as fierce as a wolf to everyone but his master and Tony."

"I wish I hadn't come. I don't like odd people, and I'm afraid of dogs," sighed Miss Stein.

"Mr. Yorke will be kind to such a little thing as you, and make old Judas like you, I dare say. Perhaps you won't have to stay long if you don't like it. Is your home far away?"

"I've got no home now. Oh, Mamma! Mamma!" And covering her face with her little black frock, the child broke into such sudden, bitter sobs that the boy was stricken with remorse. Finding words vain, he sprang impetuously off the wall, and filling his hands with his choicest flowers, heaped them into the child's lap with such demonstrations of penitence and goodwill that she could not refuse to be comforted.

Just then Anthony called her, and with a hasty good-bye she turned to obey, but the boy detained her for a moment to say, "Don't forget to ask Mr. Yorke if you may play with me, because you'll be very dull all by yourself, and I should like you for my little sweetheart."

"Alfred! Alfred! It is rather too soon for that," called a smiling lady from a window of the adjoining house, whereat the boy sprang down, laughing at the unexpected publicity of his declaration, and Miss Stein walked away, looking much disturbed by Anthony's chuckles.

"The master will be down to his tea directly, so you can look out a winder and not meddle till he comes," said the old man as he left her.

The memory of the pretty lad warmed the child's heart and seemed to shed a ray of cheerfulness over the somber room. A table was spread with care, and beside one plate lay a book, as if "the master" was in the habit of enlivening his solitary meals with such society as the full shelves about afforded him. The furniture was ancient, the window hangings dark, the pictures weird or gloomy, and the deep silence that reigned through the house oppressed the lonely child. Approaching the table she ventured to examine the book. It proved intelligible and picturesque; so establishing herself in the armchair, she spread the volume before her, and soon became happily forgetful of orphanage and solitude.

So intent was she that a man came to the door unobserved, and pausing there, scrutinized her from head to foot. Had she looked up she would have seen a tall, athletic figure and a singularly attractive face, though it was neither beautiful nor gentle. The dark, neglected hair was streaked with gray at thirty; the forehead was marked with deep lines, and under the black brows were magnificent yet melancholy eyes, that just then looked as if some strong emotion had kindled an unwonted fire in their depths. The lower part of the face gave flat contradiction to the upper, for the nose was disdainful, the chin square and grim, the whole contour of the mouth relentless, in spite of the softening effect of a becoming beard. Dressed in velvet cap and paletot, and framed in the dark doorway, he looked like a striking picture of some austere scholar aged with care or study, not with years; yet searching closer, one would have seen traces of deep suffering, latent passion, and a strange wistfulness, as if lonely eyes were forever seeking something they had lost.

For many minutes Bazil Yorke watched the unconscious child, as if there was some strong attraction for him in the studious little figure poring over the book with serious eyes, one hand turning the pictured pages, the other pushing back the wavy hair from a blooming cheek and a forehead possessing delicate brows and the harmonious lines about the temples which artists so love. The man's eyes softened as he looked, for the child's patient trust made her friendlessness the more pathetic. He put out his hand as if to draw her to him, then checked the impulse, and the hard mouth grew grimmer as he swept off the cap, saying coldly, "Miss Stein, I am ready now."

His guest started, shut the book, slipped down, and went to meet her host, offering her hand as if anxious to atone for the offense of meddling.

Like one unused to such acts, Mr. Yorke took the small hand, gave it a scarcely perceptible pressure, and dropped it without a word. The action grieved the child, yet nothing betrayed the pang of disappointment it gave her except a slight tremor in the voice that timidly asked, "Did you get the letter, sir?"

"I did. Your mother wished me to keep you till you were eighteen, when you were to choose a guardian for yourself. Her family will not receive you, and your father's family is far away; but your mother and myself were old friends many years ago, and she hoped I would take you for a time."

"Will you, sir? I'll try not to be a trouble."

"No, I cannot. This is no place for a child; nor am I a fit guardian if it was. I will find some better home for you tomorrow. But as you will remain here tonight, you may take off your hat and cloak, or whatever it is."

Half pityingly, half impatiently he spoke, and eyed the child as if he longed to yet dared not keep her. The little hat was taken off, but the ribbons of the mantle were in a knot, and after pulling at it for a moment, she turned to her companion for help. As he stooped to give it with a curious reluctance in his manner, she scanned the face so near her own with innocent freedom, and presently murmured, as if to herself, "Yes, the boy was right; his eyes *are* kind."

With a wrench that tore the silk, and caused the child to start, Mr. Yorke broke the knot, and turning away, rang the bell with vehemence.

"What is your name?" he asked, carefully averting his eyes as the little girl sat down.

"Cecilia Bazil Stein."

"What an ominous conjunction!"

She did not understand the scornful exclamation and proceeded to explain.

"Mamma's name was Cecilia, yours is Bazil, and Papa's was Stein. You can call me Celia as Mamma did, if you please, sir."

"No, I shall call you Cecil. I dislike the other name."

Quick tears sprang to the child's eyes, but none fell, and lowering her voice she said, with trembling lips, "Mamma wished me to tell you that she sent her love, and the one precious thing she had as a keepsake, and hoped you'd take it in memory of the happy days when you and she were friends."

Mr. Yorke turned his back upon her for several minutes, then asked abruptly, "Where have you been this last year?"

"Here in America. We were in England before that, because Mamma did not like Germany since Papa died, and we were tired of going about."

"Your father died when you were a baby, I think. Have you been with your mother ever since?" asked Mr. Yorke with a half-smile, as the little creature spoke of these countries as composedly as if they were neighboring towns.

"Yes, I was always with her, and we were very happy staying in all sorts of new and pleasant places. But Mamma wished to save up some money for me, so we came here and lived very plainly in the country till she—"

The child stopped there, for her lips trembled and she did not wish to disgrace herself by crying twice in one hour. He saw that she controlled herself, and the little trait of character pleased him as did the pretty mixture of innocent frankness and good breeding betrayed by her manner and appearance.

"When did she leave you?" he ventured to ask, carefully avoiding the hard word "die."

"Three weeks ago."

"How old are you, Cecil?" he said presently, in order to change the current of her thoughts, although the question was an unnecessary one.

"Nearly twelve, sir."

"Twelve years, twelve long years since I saw her last, and then gave up the world."

He spoke low to himself, and his thoughts seemed to wander from the present to the past, as, bending his head upon his breast, he stood mute and motionless till Anthony announced, "Tea is ready, master."

Looking up with the melancholy shadow gloomier than ever in his eyes, Yorke led the child to the table, filled her cup, put everything within her reach, and opening a book, read more than he ate. Twilight was deepening in the room; the oppressive silence made the meal unsocial, and Cecil's heart was heavy, for she felt doubly forlorn, bereft of the protection she had hoped to find and the familiar name her mother's voice had endeared to her. She ate a few morsels, then leaned back in her chair, looking drearily about and wondering what would happen next. She did not wait long before a somewhat startling incident occurred.

As her eye roved to and fro it was arrested by the sudden appearance of a face at one of the windows. A strange, uncanny face, half concealed by a black beard that made the pallor of the upper part more striking. It was gone again instantly, but Cecil had only time to catch her breath and experience a thrill of alarm, when the long curtains that hung before the other half-open window stirred as if a hand grasped them, and through the narrow aperture between the folds the glitter of an eye was plainly visible. Fascinated by fear, the child sat motionless, longing to cry out, yet restrained by timidity and the hope that her companion would look up and see the intruder for himself.

He seemed absorbed in his book, and utterly unconscious of the hidden watcher, till an involuntary gesture caused another movement of the curtains, as if the hand loosened its grasp, for the eye vanished and Cecil covered her face with a long sigh of relief. Mr. Yorke glanced up, mistook the gesture for one of weariness, and evidently glad of an excuse to dispose of the child, he said abruptly, "You have come a long way today, and must be tired. Will you go to bed?"

"Oh, yes, I shall be glad to go," cried Cecil, eager to leave what to her was now a haunted room.

Taking a lamp, he led her along dimly lighted halls, up wide staircases, into a chamber that seemed immense to its small occupant, while the darkly curtained bed was so like a hearse she instantly decided that it would be impossible to sleep in it. Mr. Yorke glanced about as if desirous of making her comfortable, but quite ignorant how to set about it.

"The old woman who would have attended you is sick, but if you want anything, ring for Anthony. Good night."

Cecil was on the point of lifting her face for the good-night kiss she had been accustomed to receive from other lips, but remembering the careless pressure of his hand, the cold welcome he had given her, she restrained the impulse, and let him leave her with no answer but a quiet echo of his own "Good night."

The moment his steps died away, she opened the door again and watched the light mount higher and higher as he wound his way up a spiral flight of stairs that evidently led to the tower. Cecil longed to follow, for she was sleepless with the excitement of novelty and a lingering touch of fear (for the face still haunted her), and she now reproached herself for not having spoken to Mr. Yorke. She was about to make this an excuse for following him, when the sound of noises from above made her hesitate.

"I'll wait till he comes down, or till the person goes, for he ought to know about the man I saw, because it might be a thief," she thought.

After lingering on the threshold till she was tired, Cecil seated herself in an easy chair beside the door, and amused herself by examining the pictures on the wall. But she was more weary than she knew; the chair was luxuriously cushioned, the steady murmur of voices very soothing, and she soon lapsed away into a drowse.

The certainty that someone had touched her suddenly startled her wide awake. An instant's thought recalled her purpose, and fearing to be up too late, she ran into the upper hall, hoping to find Mr. Yorke descending. No one was in sight, however, yet so sure was she that a hand had touched her and a footstep sounded in the room that she looked over the balustrade, intending to call. Not a word left her lips, however, for neither Mr. Yorke nor Anthony appeared; but a man was going slowly down, wrapped in a cloak, with a shadowy hat drawn low over his brows. A slender hand shone white against the dark cloak, and as he reached the hall below he glanced over his shoulder, showing Cecil the same colorless face with its black beard and glittering eyes that had frightened her before, though he evidently did not see her now.

It alarmed her again, for it was a singularly sinister face in spite of its beauty. Never pausing to see what became of him, and conscious of nothing but an uncontrollable longing to be near Mr. Yorke, Cecil climbed the winding stairs without a pause till she reached an arched doorway, and seemed to see a gathering of ghosts beyond. The long, large room was filled with busts, statues, uncut blocks, tools, dust, and disorder, in the midst of which stood Mr. Yorke, dressed in a suit of gray linen, and intent on modeling something from a handful of clay. Many children would have been more alarmed at these inanimate figures than at the other, but Cecil found so much that was inviting, she forgot fear in delight, and boldly entered. A smiling woman seemed to beckon to her, a winged child to offer flowers, and all about the room pale gods and goddesses looked down upon her from their pedestals with what to her beauty-loving eye seemed varying expressions of welcome. Judas, the great dog, lay like a black statue on a tawny tiger skin, and the strong glow from a chandelier shone on his master as he worked with a swift dexterity that charmed Cecil.

Eager to ask questions, she began her explanations with a sudden "Bazil, I came up to—"

But got no further, for with a start that sent the model crumbling to the floor, he turned upon her almost angrily, demanding, "Who calls me by that name?"

"It's me; Mamma always said Bazil, and so I got used to it. What can I call you, sir?"

"Simply *Yorke*, as others do. I forbid that hateful name. Why are you here?"

"Indeed, I could not help it. I was so lonely and so frightened down there. I saw a face at the window, and wanted to tell you, but heard someone talking up here and I waited. But when I waked I saw the same face going down the stairs, and so I ran to you."

Yorke listened with curious intentness to her story, asked a question or two, mused a moment, then said, pointing to a half-finished athlete, "The man is my model for that. He is a strange person, and does odd things, but you need not fear him."

A quick-witted woman would have seen at a glance that dust lay thick on the clay figure, and have known that the slender hand grasping the cloak could never have belonged to the arm that served as a model for the brawny athlete. But Cecil's childish eyes saw no discrepancy between the two, and she believed the explanation at once. With a sigh

of mingled satisfaction and relief, she looked about her, and said beseechingly, "Please let me stop and see your work. I like it so much, so very
much!"

"What do you know about it, child?" Yorke answered, wondering
at her interest and sudden animation.

"Why, I used to do it; Mamma taught me as you taught her, with
wax first, then pretty brown clay like this; and I was very happy doing it,
because I liked it best of all my plays."

"Your mother taught you! Why, Cecil?" And Yorke's grave face
kindled with an expression that won the child to franker speech at once.

"She liked it as well as I, and always called me little Bazil when
I made pretty things. She was fond of it because she used to be very
happy doing it a long time ago. She often told me about you when you
lived in her father's house; how you hated lessons, and loved to make
splendid things in wax and wood and clay; how you didn't care to eat
or sleep when you were busy, and how you made an image of her, but
broke it when she was unkind to you. She didn't tell me what she did,
but I wish you would, so that I may be careful not to do it while I'm
here."

He laughed such a bitter laugh, it both touched and troubled her,
as he answered harshly, "No fear of that; I never can be hurt again as
she hurt me thirteen years ago." Then with a sudden change in countenance and manner, he sat down on a block of marble with a half-finished
angel's head looking out of it, drew Cecil toward him, and looked at her
with hungry eyes as he said eagerly, "Tell me more. Did she talk of me?
Did she teach you to care for me? Child, speak fast—I vowed I would
ask no questions, but I must!"

His voice rose, his glance searched her face, his stern mouth grew
tremulous, and the whole man seemed to wake and glow with an unconquerable desire. Reassured by this sudden thaw in the frosty aspect
of her guardian, Cecil leaned confidingly against his knee and softly
answered, with her hand upon his shoulder, "Yes, Mamma often spoke
of you; she wished me to love you dearly—and the last thing she said was
that about the keepsake. I think she will be sorry if you send me away,
because she thought you'd care for me as you once did for her."

Some strange emotion rushed warm and tender over Bazil Yorke,
and as if the words, the gentle touch, had broken down some barrier
set up by pride or will, he took the child into his arms with an impetuous
gesture, saying brokenly, "She remembered me—and she sent me her all.
Surely I may keep the gift and put one drop of sweetness into this bitter
life of mine."

Bewildered, yet glad, Cecil clung to him, drawn by an attraction that she could not understand. For a moment Yorke hid his face in her long hair, then put her away as abruptly as he had embraced her, and returned to his work as if unused to such betrayals of feeling and ashamed of them. He merely said, as he took up his tools, "Amuse yourself as you please; I must work."

Quite contented, Cecil roved about the room till curiosity was satisfied; made timid advances toward the great dog, which were graciously received; and at length gathering up the crumbled clay that fell from Yorke's hand, she sat down beside Judas and began to mold as busily as the master.

Presently a little voice broke the silence, humming a song that Yorke remembered well. Softly as it was sung, Judas pricked up his ears, his master paused in his work, and leaning with folded arms, listened till the long hush recalled the singer from her happy reverie. She stopped instantly, but seeing no displeasure in the altered face above her, she held out her work, asking shyly, "Is it very bad, sir?"

It was a bunch of grapes deftly fashioned by small fingers that needed no other tool than their own skill, and though swiftly done, it was as graceful as if the gray cluster had just been broken from a vine. Yorke examined it critically, lifted the child's face and studied it intently for a moment, kissed it gravely on the forehead so like his own, and said, with an air of decision, "It is well done; I shall keep both it and you. Will you stay and work with me, Cecil, and be content with no friend but myself, no playmate but old Judas?"

Cecil read the yearning of the man's heart in his eyes with the quick instinct of a child, and answered it by exclaiming heartily, "Yes, I will; and be very happy here, for I like this place, I like Judas, and I love you already, because you make these lovely things, and are so kind to me now."

"Are you a discreet girl, Cecil? Can you see and hear things, and yet not ask questions or tell tales?" asked Yorke, somewhat anxiously.

"I think I am."

"So do I. Now I have a mind to keep you, for you are one of my sort; but I wish you to understand that nothing which goes on in my house is to be talked about outside of it. I let the world alone, and desire the world to do the same by me; so remember if you forget your promise, you march at once."

"I always keep my promises. But may I ask two questions now before I promise? Then I'll never do it anymore."

"Well, my inquisitive little person, what is it?"

"I want to know if I can sometimes see the pleasant boy who gave me this rose."

"And kissed you on the wall," added Yorke, with such a satirical look that Cecil colored high and involuntarily exclaimed, "Did you see us? I thought you couldn't from this high place."

"I see everything that happens on my premises. If you do not gossip you may see the boy occasionally. What is the other question?"

"Will that disagreeable man come here often—the model, I mean? He frightens me, and I don't want to see him unless you wish me to."

"You will not see him anymore. I shall not work at this figure for the present, so there will be no need of him. Make yourself easy; I shall never wish you to see or speak to him."

"You are very kind. I'll try to please you and not peep or ask questions. Can I wash my hands and look at this pretty book? I'll go quietly away to bed when I get sleepy."

With very much the air of a man who had undertaken the care of a butterfly, Yorke established her with the coveted portfolio on her lap, and soon entirely forgot her.

Accustomed to the deep reveries of a solitary life, hour after hour passed unheeded, and the city clocks tolled their warnings to deaf ears. After glancing once at the little chair and finding the child gone, he thought no more of her, till rising to rest his cramped limbs he saw her lying fast asleep on the tiger skin. One arm embraced the dog's shaggy neck, her long hair swept the dusty floor, and the rosy warmth of slumber made the childish face blooming and beautiful.

"Truly I am a fit guardian for a little creature like this," Yorke muttered, as he watched her a moment; then he covered her with a cloak and began to pace the room, busied with some absorbing thought. Once he paused and looked at the sleeper with an expression of grim determination, saying to himself as he eyed the group, "If I had power to kill the savage beast, skill to subdue the fierce dog, surely I can mold the child as I will, and make the daughter pay the mother's debt."

His face darkened as he spoke, the ruthless look deepened, and the sudden clenching of the hand boded ill for the young life he had taken into his keeping.

All night the child lay dreaming of her mother, all night the man sat pondering over an early wrong that had embittered a once noble nature, and dawn found them unchanged, except that Cecil had ceased to smile in her sleep, and Bazil Yorke had shaped a fugitive emotion into a relentless purpose.

≽ *Chapter II* ≼

THE BROKEN
CUPID

FIVE years later, a new statue stood in the studio; we might have said two new statues, though one was a living creature. The marble figure was a lovely, Psyche-bending form, and with her graceful hand above her eyes, as if she watched her sleeping lover. Of all Bazil Yorke's works this was the best, and he knew it, for, surrounded by new influences, he had wrought at it with much of his youthful ardor—had found much of the old happiness while so busied, and was so proud of his success that no offer could tempt him to part with it—no certainty of fame persuade him to exhibit it, except to a chosen few.

The human figure was Cecil, changed from a rosy child into a slender, deep-eyed girl. Colorless, like a plant deprived of sunshine, strangely unyouthful in the quiet grace of her motions, the sweet seriousness of her expression, but as beautiful as the Psyche and almost as cold. Her dress heightened the resemblance, for the white folds draped her from neck to ankle; not an ornament marred its severe simplicity, and the wavy masses of her dark hair were gathered up with a fillet, giving her the head of a young Hebe. It was a fancy of Yorke's, and as few eyes but his beheld her, she dressed for him alone, unconscious that she served as a model for his fairest work. Standing in the one ray of sunshine that shot athwart the subdued light of the studio, she seemed intent upon a little Cupid exquisitely carved in the purest marble. She was not working now, for the design was finished, but seemed to be regarding it with mingled satisfaction and regret—satisfaction that it was done so well, regret that it was done so soon. The little god was just drawing an arrow from his quiver with an arch smile, and the girl watched him with one almost as gay. A rare sight upon her lips, but some happy fancy seemed to bring it, and more than once she gave the graceful figure a caressing touch, as if she had learned to love it.

"Don't fire again, little Cupid, I surrender," suddenly exclaimed a blithe voice behind her, and, turning, Cecil saw her friend and neighbor, Alfred, now a tall young man, though much of the boyish frankness and impetuosity still remained.

"Do you like it, Alf?" she asked, with a quiet smile of welcome, and a repose of manner contrasting strongly with the eagerness of the newcomer's.

"You know I do, Cecil, for it has been my delight ever since you began it. The little god is perfect, and I must have him at any cost. Name your price, and let it be a high one."

"Yorke would not like that, neither should I. You have more than paid for it by friendly acts and words through these five years, so let me give it to you with all my heart."

She spoke tranquilly, and offered her hand as if transferring to him the lovely figure it had wrought. He took the white hand in both his own, and with a sudden glow on his cheek, a sudden ardor in his eye, said, in an impulsive voice, "With all your heart, Cecil? Let me take you at your word, let me claim, not only the image of love, but the reality, and keep this hand as mine."

A soft tinge of color touched the girl's cheek as she drew her hand away, but the quiet smile remained unchanged, and she still looked up at him with eyes as innocent and frank as any child's.

"I did not mean that, Alf; we are too young for such things yet, and I know nothing of love except in marble."

"Let me teach you then; we never are too young to learn that lesson," he urged eagerly. "I meant to wait another year before I spoke, for then I shall be my own master, and have a home to give you. But you grow so lovely and so dear, I must speak out and know my fate. Dear Cecil, what is it to be?"

"I cannot tell; this is so new and strange to me, I have no answer ready."

She looked troubled now, but more by his earnestness than by any maidenly doubts or fears of her own, and leaning her head upon her hand seemed to search for an answer, and search in vain. Alfred watched her a moment, then broke out indignantly, "No wonder it seems new and strange, for you have led a nun's life all these years, and know nothing of the world outside these walls. Yorke lets you read neither romance nor poetry, gives you no companions but marble men and women, no change but a twilight walk each day, or a new design to work out in this gloomy place. You never have been told you have a heart and a right to love like other women. Let me help you to know it, and find an answer for myself."

"Am I so different from other girls? Is my life strange and solitary? I've sometimes thought so, but I never felt quite sure. What *is* love, Alfred?"

"This!" And opening his arms her young lover would have answered her wistful question eloquently, but Cecil shrank a little, and put up her hand to check his impulse.

"Not so, tell me in words, Alf, how one feels when one truly loves."

"I only know how *I* feel, Cecil. I long for you day and night; think of you wherever I am; see no one half so beautiful, half so good as you; care for nothing but being here, and have no wish to live unless you will make life happy for me."

"And that is love?" She spoke low, to herself, for as he answered her face had slowly been averted, a soft trouble had dawned in her eyes, and a deeper color risen to her cheek, as if the quiet heart was waking suddenly.

"Yes; and you do love me, Cecil? Now I know it—now you will not deny it."

She looked up, pale but steady, for the child's expression was quite gone, and in her countenance was all a woman's pain and pity, as she said decidedly, "No, Alf, I do not love you. I know myself now, and feel that it is impossible."

But Alfred would not accept the hard word "impossible," and pleaded passionately, in spite of the quiet determination to end the matter, which made Cecil listen almost as coldly as if she did not hear. Anger succeeded surprise and hope, as the young man bitterly exclaimed, "You might make it possible, but you will not try!"

"No, I will not, and it is unkind of you to urge me. Let me be in peace—I'm happy with my work, and my nun's life was pleasant till you came to trouble it with foolish things."

She spoke impatiently, and the first glimpse of passion ever seen upon her face now disturbed its quietude, yet made it lovelier than ever.

"Well said, Cecil; my pupil does honor to her master."

Both started as the deep voice sounded behind them, and both turned to see Bazil Yorke leaning in the doorway with a satirical smile on his lips. Cecil made an involuntary motion to go to him, but checked herself as Alfred said hotly, "It is not well said! And but for the artful training you have given her, she would be glad to change this unnatural life, though she dare not say so, for you are a tyrant, in spite of your seeming kindness!"

"Do you fear me too much to tell the truth, Cecil?" asked Yorke, quite unmoved.

"No, master."

"Then decide between us two, now and forever, because I will not have your life or mine disturbed by such scenes as this. If you love Alfred, say so freely, and when my guardianship ends I will give you to his. If you prefer to stop with me, happy in the work you are wonderfully fitted to perform, content with the quiet life I deem best for you, and willing to be the friend and fellow laborer of the old master, then come to him and let us hear no more of lovers or of tyrants."

As he spoke Cecil had listened breathlessly, and when he paused, she went to him with such a glad and grateful face, such instant and entire willingness, that it touched him deeply, though he showed no sign of it except to draw her nearer, with a caressing gesture which he had not used since she ceased to be a child.

The words, the act, wounded the young lover to the heart, and he broke out, in a voice trembling with anger, sorrow, and reproach, "I might have known how it would be; I should have known if my own love had not blinded me. You have taught her something beside your art —have made too sure of her to fear any rival, and when the time comes you will change the guardian to a husband, and become her master in earnest."

"Not I! My day for such folly is long since past. Cecil will never be anything to me but my ward and pupil, unless some more successful lover than yourself should take her from me."

Yorke laughed scornfully at the young man's accusation, but looked down at the girl with an involuntary pressure of the arm that held her, for despite his careless manner, she was dearer to him than he knew.

"I will never leave you for any other—never, my dear master."

Alfred heard her soft whisper, saw her cling to Yorke, knew that there was no hope for him, and with a broken "Good-bye, Cecil, I shall not trouble you again," he was gone.

"Poor lad, he takes it hardly, but he'll soon forget. I should have warned him, had I not been sure it would have hastened what I desired to prevent. It is over at last, thank heaven, so look up, foolish child; there are no lovers here to frighten you now."

But Cecil did not look up, she hid her face and wept quietly, for Alfred had been her only young friend since the day he gave the rose and made the new home pleasant by his welcome.

Yorke let her tears flow unreproved for a few moments, then his patience seemed exhausted, and placing her in a seat, he turned away to examine the Cupid which Alfred had not accepted. As he looked at it he smiled, then frowned, as if some unwelcome fancy had been conjured up by it, and asked abruptly, "What suggested the idea of this, Cecil?"

"You did!" was the half-audible answer.

"I did? Never to my knowledge."

"Your making Psyche suggested Cupid, for though you did not tell me the pretty fable, Alf did, and told me how my image should be made. I could not do a large one, so I pleased myself with trying a little winged child with the bandage and the bow."

"Why would you not let me see it till it was done?"

"At first because I hoped to make it good enough to give you, then I thought it too full of faults to offer, so I gave it to Alf; but he would not have it without me, and now I don't care for it anymore."

Yorke smiled, as if well pleased at this proof of her indifference to the youth, then with a keen glance at the drooping face before him, he asked, "Are you quite sure that you do not care for Alfred?"

"Very sure, master."

"Then what has changed you so within a week or two? You sang yesterday like an uncaged bird, a thing you seldom do. You smile to yourself as you work, and when I wished to use your face as a model not an hour ago, you could not fix your eyes on me as I bade you, and cried when I chid you. What is it, Cecil? If you have anything upon your mind, tell me, and let nothing disturb us again if possible."

If the girl had been trained to repress all natural emotions and preserve an unvarying calmness of face, voice, and manner, she had also been taught to tell the truth, promptly and fearlessly. Now it was evident that she longed to escape the keen eye and searching questions of her master, as she loved to call him, but she dared not hesitate, and answered slowly, "I should have told you something before, only I did not like to, and I thought perhaps you knew it."

"Well, well, stop blushing and speak out; I know nothing but this boy's love and the change in you." Yorke spoke impatiently, and wore an anxious look, as if he dreaded more tender confessions, for Cecil never lifted her eyes as she rapidly went on:

"A week ago, as we came in from our evening walk, you stopped at the corner to call Judas, and I went on to open the door for you. Just as I put the key into the latch, a hand took mine, as if to slip something into it, but I was so startled I let the paper drop, and should have called to you if someone had not wrapped me in a cloak so closely that I could not speak, though I was kissed more than once and called 'my darling' in a very tender voice. It all happened in a minute, and before I knew what to do, the man was gone, and I ran in, too frightened to wait for you."

As she paused, Cecil looked up, and was amazed to see no wonder on Yorke's face, but an expression of pain and indignation that she could not understand. "Back again and I not know it," he muttered to himself, then aloud, almost sternly, "why did you not tell me this before?"

"You were busy that night, and when I'd thought of it a little I did not like to speak of it, because I remembered that you called me silly when I told you that people made me uncomfortable by looking at me as I walked in the day. I thought I'd wait, but it troubled me and made me seem unlike myself, I suppose."

"Are you sure it was not Alfred, playing some foolish prank in the twilight?" asked Yorke.

"I know it was not Alf; he wears no beard, and is not tall like this strange man."

"It could not have been Anthony?"

"Oh, no, that is impossible. Old Tony's hands are rough; these were soft though very strong, and the voice was too low and kind for his."

"Have you no suspicion who it might have been?" asked Yorke, searching her thoughtful face intently.

She blushed deeper than before, but answered steadily, "I did think of you, master, for you are tall and strong, you wear a beard and cloak, and your hand is soft. But your voice never is like that voice, and you never say 'my darling' in that tender way."

Yorke knit his brows, saying, a little bitterly, "You seem to have forgiven this insolent stranger already because of that, and to reproach me that I never use such sentimental phrases, or embrace my ward upon my doorstep. Shall I tell you who this interesting phantom probably was? The model, whom you disliked so much that I dismissed him when you came."

Cecil turned pale, for her childish terror had remained as fresh in her memory as the events that wakened it; and though she had merely caught glimpses of the man as he occasionally glided into Yorke's private room during the past five years, she still felt a curious mixture of interest and fear, and often longed to break her promise and ask questions concerning him and his peculiar ways.

"Why do you let him come?" she said, forgetting everything but surprise, as Yorke spoke as he had never done before.

"I wish I could prevent it!" he answered, eyeing her half sadly, half jealously. "I've bidden him to go, but he *will* come back to harass me. Now I'll end it at any cost."

"But why does he care for me?" asked Cecil, finding that her first question had received an answer.

"Because you are beautiful and—" There Yorké caught back the coming words, and after a pause said coldly, "Remember your promise— no more of this."

For several minutes he went to and fro, busied with anxious thoughts, while Cecil mused over the mystery, and grieved for Alfred's disappointment. Suddenly Yorke paused before her.

"Do you understand to what you pledge yourself when you say you will never leave me, Cecil?"

"I think I do" was the ready answer.

"Nothing is to be changed, you know."

"I hope not."

"No romances—no poetry to be allowed."

"I do not want them."

"No frivolities and follies like other women."

"I can be happy without."

"No more Cupids of any sort."

"Shall I break this one?"

"No, leave it as a warning, or send it to poor Alf."

"What else, master?" she asked wistfully.

"Only this: Can you be content year after year with study, solitude, steady progress, and in time fame for yourself, but never any knowledge of love as Alfred paints it?"

"*Never*, Yorke?"

"*Never*, Cecil!"

She shivered, as if the words fell cold upon her heart, all the glad light and color faded from her face, and she looked about her with longing eyes, as if the sunshine had gone out of her life forever. Yorke saw the change, and a momentary expression of pity softened the stern determination of his face.

"This never would have happened but for that romantic boy," he thought. "There shall be no more of it, and a little pain now shall spare us all misunderstanding hereafter."

"Cecil," he said aloud, "love makes half the misery of the world; it has been the bane of my life—it has made me what I am, a man without ambition, hope, or happiness—and out of my own bitter experience I warn you to beware of it. You know nothing of it yet, and if you are to stay with me you never will, unless this boy's folly has done more harm than I suspect. Carving Cupid has filled your head with fancies that will do you no good; banish them and be what I would have you."

"A marble woman like your Psyche, with no heart to love you, only grace and beauty to please your eye and bring you honor; is that what you would have me?"

He started, as if she had put some hidden purpose into words; his eye went from the gleaming statue to the pale girl, and saw that he had worked out his design in stone, but not yet in that finer material given him to mold well or ill. He did not see the pain and passion throbbing in her heart; he only saw her steady eyes; he only heard her low spoken question, and answered it, believing that he served her better than she knew.

"Yes, I would have you beautiful and passionless as Psyche, a creature to admire with no fear of disturbing its quiet heart, no fear of endangering one's own. I am kinder than I seem in saying this, for I desire to save you from the pain I have known. Stay with me always, if you can, but remember, Cecil, I am done with love."

"I shall remember, sir."

Yorke left her, glad to have the task over, for it had not been as easy as he fancied. Cecil listened and answered with her usual submission, stood motionless till the sound of a closing door assured her that he was gone, then a look of sharp anguish banished the composure of her face, and a woman's passionate pride trembled in her voice as she echoed his last words.

"I am done with love!" And lifting the little Cupid let it drop broken at her feet.

❧ *Chapter III* ❧

GERMAIN

FOR a week Cecil saw little of Yorke, as, contrary to his custom, he was out a greater part of each day, and when at home was so taciturn and absorbed that he was scarcely more than a shadow in the house. She asked no questions, appeared unconscious of any change, and worked busily upon a new design, thinking bitter thoughts the while. Alfred never came, and Cecil missed him; but Yorke was well satisfied, for the purpose formed so long ago had never changed; and though the young man's love endangered its fulfillment, that cloud had passed by, leaving the girl all his own again. She too seemed to cherish some purpose, that soon showed its influence over her; for her face daily grew more cold and colorless, her manner quieter, her smiles fewer, her words briefer, her life more nunlike than ever, till unexpected events changed the current of her thoughts, and gave her new mysteries to brood over.

One evening, as Cecil sat drawing, while Yorke paced restlessly up and down, he said suddenly, after watching her for several minutes, "Cecil, will you do me a great favor?"

"With pleasure, if I can and ought," she answered, without pausing in her work.

"I am sure you can, I think you ought, yet I cannot explain why I ask it, although it will annoy and perplex you. Will you have faith in me, and believe that what I do is done for the best?"

"I trust you, sir; you have taught me to bear in silence many things that perplex and annoy me, so I think I can promise to bear one more."

Something in her meek answer seemed to touch him like a reproach, for his voice softened, as he said regretfully, "I know I am not all I might be to you, but the day may come when you will see that I have spared you greater troubles, and made my dull home a safer shelter than it seems."

He took a turn or two, then stopped again, asking abruptly, "A gentleman is to dine with me tomorrow; will you do the honors of the house?"

It was impossible to conceal the surprise which this unusual request produced, for during all the years they had been together, few strangers had been admitted, and Cecil, being shy, had gladly absented herself on these rare occasions. Now she laid down her pencil and looked up at him, with mingled reluctance and astonishment in her face.

"How can I, when I know nothing of such things? Hester has always suited you till now."

"I have neglected many womanly accomplishments which you should have acquired, this among them; now you shall learn to be the little mistress of the house, and leave Hester in her proper place. Will you oblige me, Cecil?"

Yorke spoke as if discharging a painful duty which had been imposed upon him; Cecil was quick to see this, and any pleasure she might have felt in the proposal was destroyed by his uneasy manner.

"As you please, sir" was all her answer.

"Thank you; now one thing more. Haven't you a plain gray gown?"

"Yes."

"Be kind enough to wear it tomorrow, instead of that white one, which is more becoming, but too peculiar to appear in before strangers. This, also, I want altered; let me show you how."

He untied the band that held her hair, and as it fell upon her shoulders, he gathered the dark locks plainly back into a knot behind, smoothing away the ripples on her forehead, and the curls that kept breaking from his hold.

"Wear it so tomorrow. Look in the glass, and see how I mean," he said, as he surveyed the change he had effected.

She looked, and smiled involuntarily, though a vainer girl would have frowned, for the alteration added years to her age, apparently; destroyed the beautiful outline of her face, and robbed her head of its most graceful ornament.

"You wish me to look old and plain, I see. If you like it, I am satisfied."

He looked annoyed at her quickness in divining his purpose, and shook out the curls again, as he said hastily, "I do wish it, for my guest worships beauty, and I have no desire for more love passages at present."

"No fear of that till poor Alf's forgotten."

She spoke proudly, and took up her pencil as if weary of the subject. Yorke stood for a moment, wondering if she found it hard to forget "poor Alf," but he said no more, and sat down as if a load were off his mind. Opening a book, he seemed to read, but Cecil heard no leaves turned, and a covert glance showed him regarding the page with absent eyes and a melancholy expression that troubled her. There had been a time when she would have gone to him with affectionate solicitude, but not now; and though her heart was full of sympathy, she dared not show it, so sat silent till the clock struck ten, then with a quiet "Good night" she was gone.

"We shall dine at six; I'll ring for you when Germain comes," said Yorke, as they came in from their walk the following day.

"I shall be ready, sir."

Cecil watched and waited for the stranger's arrival, in a flutter of expectation, which proved that in spite of Yorke's severe training, feminine curiosity was not yet dead. She heard Anthony admit the guest, heard Yorke receive him, and heard the old woman who came to help Hester on such occasions ejaculate from behind a door, "Bless me, what a handsome man!" But minute after minute passed, and no bell rang, no summons came for her. The clock was on the stroke of six, and she was thinking, sorrowfully, that he had forgotten her, when Yorke's voice was heard at the door, saying with unusual gentleness, "Come, Cecil; it is time."

"I thought you were to ring for me," she said, as they went down together.

"And I thought it more respectful to come and wait upon the little mistress, than to call her like a servant. How your heart beats! You need fear nothing. I shall be near you, child."

He took her by the hand with a protecting gesture that surprised her, but a moment later she understood both speech and action. A gentleman was standing at the far end of the room, and as they noiselessly approached, Cecil had time to mark the grace and strength of his tall figure, the ease of his attitude, the beauty of the hands loosely locked together behind him, before Yorke spoke.

"Germain, my ward, Miss Stein."

He turned quickly, and the eyes that Cecil was shyly averting, dilated with undisguised astonishment, for a single glance assured her that Germain was the mysterious model. Her hand closed over Yorke's, trembling visibly, as the stranger, in a singularly musical voice and with an unmistakably highbred air, paid his compliments to Miss Stein.

"Control yourself, and bear with this man for my sake, Cecil," whispered Yorke, as he led her to a seat, and placed himself so as to screen her for a moment.

She did control herself, for that had been her earliest lesson, and she had learned it well. She did bear with this man, for whom she felt such an aversion, and when he offered his arm to lead her in to dinner, she took it, though her eyes never met his, and she spoke not a word. It was long before she ventured to steal a look at him, and when she did so, it was long before she looked away again. The old woman was right, he *was* a handsome man; younger apparently than his host, and dressed with an elegance that Yorke had never attempted. Black hair and beard, carefully arranged, brilliant dark eyes, fine features, and that persuasive voice, all helped to make a most attractive person, for now the sinister expression was replaced by one of the serenest suavity, the stealthy gait and gestures exchanged for a graceful carriage, and some agreeable change seemed to have befallen both the man and his fortunes, as there was no longer any appearance of mystery or poverty about him. Cecil observed these things with a woman's quickness, and smiled to think she had ever feared the gay and gallant gentleman. Then she turned to examine Yorke, and saw that the accustomed gravity of his face was often disturbed by varying emotions; for sometimes it was sad, then stern, then tender, and more than once his eye met hers with a grateful look, as if he thanked her for granting him a greater favor than she knew.

Cecil performed her duties gracefully and well, but said little, and listened attentively to the conversation, which never strayed from general subjects. Though interested, she was not sorry when Yorke gave her the signal to withdraw, and went away into the drawing room. Here, leaning in an easy chair before the fire, she hoped to enjoy a quiet half hour at least, but was disappointed. Happening to lift her eyes to the mirror over the low chimneypiece, to study the effect of the plain bands of hair, she saw another face beside her own, and became aware that Mr. Germain was intently watching her in the glass, as he leaned upon the high back of her chair. Meeting her eyes, he came and stood upon the rug, which Judas yielded to him with a surly growl. Cecil arrested the dog, feeling a sense of security while he was by, for the childish dread was not yet quite gone, and despite his promise, Yorke did not appear. Germain seemed to understand the meaning of her hasty glance about the room, and answered it.

"Your guardian will follow presently, and sent me on to chat with you, meantime. Permit me."

As he spoke, Anthony entered, bringing coffee, but Germain brought Cecil's cup himself, and served her with an air of devotion that both confused and pleased her by its novelty. Drawing a chair to the other side of the tiny table between them, he sat down, and before she knew it, Cecil found herself talking to this dreaded person, shyly at first, then frankly and with pleasure.

"How was the great Rachel last night, Miss Stein?"

"I did not see her, sir."

"Ah, you prefer the opera, as I do, perhaps?"

"I never went."

"Then Yorke should take you, if you love music."

"I do next to my art, but I seldom hear any."

"Your art—then you are to be a sculptor?"

"I hope to be in time, but I have much to learn."

"You will go to Italy before long, I fancy? That's part of every artist's education."

"No, sir, I shall not go. Yorke has been, and can teach me all I need."

"You have no desire for it, then? Or do you wait till some younger guardian appears, who has not seen Italy, and can show it to you as it should be shown?"

"I shall never have any guardian but Yorke, we have already settled that—"

Here Cecil paused, for Germain looked at her keenly, smiled, and said significantly, "Pardon me, I had not learned that he intended to end his romance in the good old fashion, by making his fair ward his wife. I am an early friend, and have a right to take an interest in his future, so I offer my best wishes."

"You mistake me, sir; I should not have said that. Yorke is my guardian, nothing more, nor will he ever be. I have no father, and he tries to be one to me."

Cecil spoke with a bashful eagerness, burning cheeks, and downcast eyes, unconscious of the look of relief that passed over her companion's face as she explained.

"A thousand pardons; my mistake was natural, and may prove a prophecy. Now let me atone for it by asking how the Psyche prospers. Is it worthy of its maker and its model?"

"It is done, and very beautiful; everyone who sees it thinks it worthy of its maker, except me. I know he will do nobler things than that. He had no model but his own design; you have seen that, perhaps?"

"I see it now," he answered, bowing.

"Indeed, I am not; he never makes a model of me now, except for a moment. He has had none since you left."

A curious expression swept over Germain's face, and he exclaimed, with ill-disguised satisfaction, "You recognize me then? I was not sure that you had ever seen me, though I used to haunt the house like a restless spirit, as I am."

"Yes, I knew you at once, because I never could forget the fright you gave me years ago, peeping in, the night I came. Since then I've seen you several times, but never heard your name until yesterday."

"That is like Yorke. He hides his good deeds, and when I was most unfortunate, he befriended me, and more than once has kept me from what fate seems bent on making me, a solitary vagabond. The world goes better with me now, and one day I hope to take my proper place again; till then, I must wait to pay the debt I owe him."

This impulsive speech went straight to Cecil's heart, and banished the last trace of distrust. In the little pause that followed, she found time to wonder why Yorke did not come, and thinking of him, she asked if he would approve all she had been saying. A moment's recollection showed her that she had unconsciously given her companion many hints of the purpose, pursuits, and prospects of her life, during that seemingly careless conversation. She felt uncomfortable, and hoping Yorke had not heard her, sat silent until Germain spoke again.

"I see an instrument yonder. Let me lead you to it, for having owned that you love music, you cannot deny me the pleasure of listening to it."

Fearing to commit herself again, if she continued to talk, Cecil complied, but as they crossed the room together, she saw Yorke standing in the shadow of a curtained window. He made a warning sign, that caused her to hesitate an instant, trying to understand it; Germain's quick eye followed hers like a flash, and kindled with sudden fire; but before either could speak, Yorke advanced, saying gravely, "Will you venture, Cecil? Germain is a connoisseur in music."

"Then I dare not try; please let me refuse," she answered, drawing back, for now she comprehended that she was not to sing.

But Germain led her on, saying, with his most persuasive air, "You will not refuse me presently, when I have given you courage by doing my part first."

He sat down as he spoke, and began to sing; Cecil was stealing back to her seat, but paused in the act to listen; for a moment stood undecided, then turned, and slowly, step by step, drew nearer, like a fascinated bird, till she was again beside him, forgetful now of everything but the wonderful voice that filled the room with its mellow music. As it ceased, she gave a long sigh of pleasure, and exclaimed like a delighted child, "Oh! Sing again; it is so beautiful!"

Germain flashed a meaning glance over his shoulder at Yorke, who stood apart, gloomily watching them.

"Sit then, and let me do my best to earn a song from you." And placing a chair for her, he gave her music such as she had never dreamed of, as song after song poured from his lips, stirring her with varying emotions, as the airs were plaintive, passionate, or gay.

"Now may I claim my reward?" he said at length, and Cecil, without a thought of Yorke, gladly obeyed him.

Why she chose a little song her mother used to sing she could not tell; it came to her, and she sang it with all her heart, giving the tender words with unwonted spirit and sweetness. Sitting in his seat, Germain leaned his arm upon the instrument and watched her with absorbing interest. Unconsciously, she had pushed away the heavy bands that annoyed her, and now showed again the fair forehead with the delicate brow; her cheeks were rosy with excitement, her eyes shone, her lips smiled as she sang, and in spite of the gray gown with no ornament but a little knot of pansies, Cecil had never looked more beautiful than now. When she ended, she was surprised to see that this strange man's eyes were full of tears, and instead of compliments, he only pressed her hand, saying with lowered voice, "I cannot thank you as I would for this."

Yorke called the girl to him, and Germain slowly followed. At dinner he had led the conversation, now he left it to his host, saying little, but sitting with his eyes on Cecil, who, to her own surprise and Yorke's visible disquiet, did not feel abashed or offended by the pertinacious gaze. He lingered long, and went with evident reluctance, bidding Cecil good night in a tone so like the mysterious "my darling" that she retreated hastily, convinced that it must have been uttered by himself alone.

"How do you like this gentleman?" asked Yorke, returning from a somewhat protracted farewell in the hall.

"Very much. But why didn't you tell me who I was to see?"

"I had a fancy to test your powers of self-control, and I was satisfied."

"I will take care that you shall be, sir," she answered, with set lips and a flash of the eye.

"You seem to have quite outlived your old dislike, and quite forgotten his last offense," continued Yorke, as if ill pleased.

"I am no longer a silly child, and I have not forgotten his offense; but as you overlooked the insult, I could not refuse to meet your guest when you bade me to bear with him for your sake."

There was an air of dignity about her, and a touch of sarcasm in her tone, that was both new and becoming, yet it ruffled Yorke, though he disdained to show it.

"Of one thing I am satisfied. Seclude a woman as you may; when an opportunity comes, she will find her tongue. I did not know my silent girl tonight."

"You heard me, then? I am sorry, but I did not know what I was doing till it was done. You gave me a part to play, and I am no actress, as you see. Is the masquerade over now?"

"Yes, and it has not proved as successful as I hoped, yet I am glad it was no worse."

"So am I," and Cecil shook down her hair with an aspect of relief.

"Where are your pansies?" Yorke asked suddenly.

"They fell out as I was singing, they must have dropped just here," and she looked all about, but no pansies were visible.

"I thought so," muttered Yorke. "I shall repent this night's experiment, I fear, but God knows I did it for the best."

Cecil stood, thoughtfully coiling a dark lock around her finger for a moment, then she asked wistfully, "Will Mr. Germain come again? He said he hoped to do so, when he went."

"He will not, rest assured of that," answered Yorke grimly, adding, as if against his will, "he is a treacherous and dangerous man, in spite of his handsome face and charming manners. Beware of him, child, and shun him, if you would preserve your peace; mine is already lost."

"Then why do you—" There she checked herself, remembering that she was not to ask questions.

"Why do I bring him here? you would ask. That I shall never tell you, and it will never happen again, for the old spell is as strong as ever, I find."

He spoke bitterly, because in the girl's face he saw the first sign of distrust, and it wounded him deeply. It had been a hard evening for him, and he had hoped for a different result, but his failure was made manifest, as Cecil bowed her mute good-night, and went away more perplexed than ever.

≫ *Chapter IV* ≪

IN THE DARK

DAYS passed and Germain did not reappear, though Cecil strongly suspected that he had endeavored to do so more than once; for now the door was always locked. Anthony often mounted guard in the hall; Yorke seldom went out, and when they walked together chose a new route each day, while his face wore a vigilant expression as if he were perpetually on the watch. These changes kept the subject continually before the girl's mind, though not a word was spoken. More than once she caught glimpses of a familiar figure haunting the street, more than once she heard the mellow voice singing underneath her window, and more than once she longed to see this strange Germain again.

Standing at the window one somber afternoon, she thought of these things as she watched her guardian giving orders to Anthony, who was working in the garden. As Yorke turned to enter the house, she remembered that the studio was not lighted as he liked to find it, and hurried away to have it ready for his coming. Halfway up the first flight she stopped a moment, for a gust of fresh air blew up from below as if from some newly opened door or window. The hall was dusky with early twilight, and looking downward she saw nothing.

"Is that you, Yorke?" she asked, but no one answered, and she went on her way. At the top of the second flight she paused again, fancying that she heard steps behind her. The sound ceased as she stopped, and thinking to herself, "It's Judas," she ran up the spiral stairs leading to the tower. These were uncarpeted, and in a moment the sound of steps was distinctly audible behind her; neither the slow tread of Yorke, nor the quick patter of the dog, but soft and stealthy footfalls as of someone anxious to follow unsuspected. She paused, and the steps paused also; she went on and the quick sound began again; she peered downward through the gloom, but the stairs wound abruptly round and round, and nothing could be seen. She called to Yorke and the dog again, but there was no reply except the rustle of garments brushing against the wall, and the rapid breathing of a human creature. A nervous thrill passed over her; the thought of Germain flashed into her mind, and the early terror woke again, for time and place suggested the forbidding figure she had seen lurking there so long ago. Fearing to descend and meet him, she sprang on, hoping to reach the studio in time to call Yorke from the window and lock the door. As she darted upward, the quick tread of a man's foot was plainly heard, and when she flung the door behind her, a strong hand prevented it from closing, a tall figure entered, the key was turned, and Germain's well-remembered voice exclaimed:

"Do not cry out. I have risked my life by entering at a window, for I must speak to you, and Yorke guards you like a dragon."

"Why do you come if he forbids it, following and frightening me in the dark?" cried Cecil, grasping vainly for a lamp as Germain placed himself between her and the window.

"Because he keeps you from me, and he has no right to do it. I love you as he never can, yet though I plead day and night, and promise anything, he will not let me see you, even for an hour. Do not fear or shun me, but come to me, little Cecil, come to me, and let me feel that you are mine."

With voice and gesture of intensest love and longing, he advanced as if to claim her, but Cecil, terrified by this impetuous wooing, fled before him to an inner room, bolted the door, and rang the bell until it broke. Vainly Germain shook the door and implored her to hear him; she neither answered nor listened, but called for help till the room rang again.

Soon, very soon, Yorke's familiar step came leaping up the stairs, and his voice demanded, in tones of wonder and alarm, "Cecil, where are you? Speak to me, and open instantly."

"I cannot come—it is Germain—"

More she could not say, for with the arrival of help her strength deserted her, and she dropped down upon the floor, faint but not unconscious. Lying thus, she heard the outer door give way, heard a wrathful exclamation from Yorke, an exultant laugh from Germain, then hurried conversation too low for her to catch a word, till suddenly both voices rose, one defiant, the other determined.

"I tell you, Bazil, I *will* see her!"

"Not if I can prevent it."

"Then I swear I will use force!"

"I swear you shall not!"

A quick movement followed, and the terrified listener heard unmistakable sounds of a fierce but brief struggle in the darkened room, the stamp of feet, the hard breathing of men wrestling near at hand, the crash of a falling statue and a human body, a low groan, then sudden silence. In that silence Cecil lost her consciousness, for her quiet life had ill prepared her for such scenes. Only for a moment, however; the sound of retreating footsteps recalled her, and trying to control the frightened flutter of her heart, she listened breathlessly. What had happened? Where was Yorke? These questions roused her, and the longing to answer them gave her courage to venture from her refuge.

Softly drawing the bolt, she looked out. Nothing could be seen but the pale glimmer of stars through the western window; all near at hand was hidden by the deep shadow of a tall screen that divided the studio. A moment she stood trembling with apprehension lest Germain had not gone, then stole a few steps forward, whispering, "Yorke, are you here?"

There was no answer, but as the words left her lips she stumbled over something at her feet, something that stirred and faintly sighed. Losing fear in an all-absorbing anxiety, Cecil sprang boldly forward, groped for a match, lighted the lamp with trembling hands, and looked about her. The beautiful Psyche lay headless on the ground, but the girl scarcely saw it, for half underneath it lay Yorke, pale and senseless. How she dragged him out she never knew; superhuman strength seemed given her, and self-possession to think and do her best for him. Throwing up the window, she called to Anthony still busy in the garden, then bathed the white face, fanned the breathless lips, chafed the cold hands, and soon had the joy of seeing Yorke's eyes open with a conscious look.

"It is I. Where are you hurt? What shall I do for you, dear master?"

"Tell them the Psyche fell, nothing more," he answered, painfully, but with a clear mind and a commanding glance.

She understood and obeyed him when the old man arrived. With many exclamations of concern and much wonderment as to how the accident could have occurred, Anthony laid his master on the couch, gave him such restoratives as were at hand, and then went to fetch a surgeon and find Hester, who was gossiping in a neighbor's kitchen, according to her wont.

"Tell me what happened, my poor child," whispered Yorke when they were alone, and Cecil sat beside him with a face almost as pallid as his own.

"Not now, you are not fit. Wait awhile," she began.

But he interrupted her, saying with a look she dared not disobey, "No, tell me now—I must know it!"

She told him, but he seemed too weak for indignation, and looked up at her with a faint glimmer of his old sarcastic smile.

"Another lover, Cecil, and a strange one; but you need not fear him, for though as rash and headstrong as a boy, he will not harm you." Then Yorke's face changed and darkened as he said, earnestly, "Promise me that you will never listen to him, never meet him, or countenance his mad pursuit of you. No good can come of it to you, and only the bitterest disappointment to me. Promise me this, I implore you, Cecil."

She hesitated, but his face grew haggard with suspense, and something in her own heart pleaded for him more persuasively than his anxious eyes or urgent words.

"I promise this. Now rest and let me fan you, for your lips are white with pain."

He did not speak again till steps and voices were heard approaching; then he drew her down to him, whispering, "Not a word of Germain to anyone; keep near me till I am up again, then I will take measures to prevent the recurrence of a scene like this."

For several days Yorke saw no one but the doctor and his servants, for the fall and the heavy weight upon his chest had seriously injured him. He rebelled against the order to be still, finding a single week's confinement very irksome with no society but Hester, no occupation but a book or his own thoughts. Cecil did not come to nurse him as she used to do when slighter indispositions kept him in his rooms. She sent no little gifts to tempt his appetite or enliven his solitude; she made daily inquiries for his health, but nothing more. He missed his familiar spirit and her gentle ministrations, but would not send for her, thinking, with a mixture of satisfaction and regret, "She takes me at my word, and perhaps it's better so, for absence will soon cure any girlish pique my frankness may have caused her."

But though he would not call her, he left his room sooner than was wise, and went to find her in the studio. Everything was in its accustomed order, Cecil at her place, and his first exclamation one of pleasant surprise.

"Why, here's my Psyche mended and mounted again! Many thanks, my little girl."

She went to take the hand he offered, saying very quietly, "I am glad to see you, master, and to find you like what I have done."

"I never thought my Psyche would cause me so much suffering, but I forgive her for her beauty's sake," answered Yorke, laughing, for an unusual cheerfulness possessed him, and it was pleasant to be back in his old haunt again. "Well, what do you see in it?" he asked, observing that the girl stood with her eyes fixed on the statue.

"I see my model."

He remembered his own words, and was glad to change the conversation by a question or two.

"How have you got on through these days that have been so wearisome to me? Have you missed the old master?"

"I have been busily at work, and I have missed you, for I often want help, and Tony cannot always walk with me."

Yorke felt slightly disappointed both at the answer and her welcome, but showed no sign of it as he said, "Nothing has been seen of Germain since his last freak, I fancy?"

"He has been here."

"The deuce he has!" ejaculated Yorke, looking amazed. "Did you see him, Cecil?"

"Yes; I could not help it. I was watching for the doctor one day, and hearing a ring, I opened the door, for Tony and Hester were with you. Germain stepped quickly in and asked, 'Is Yorke alive?' I said yes. 'I thank God for that!' he cried. 'Tell him to get well in peace; I'll not disturb him if I can keep away—' Then Anthony appeared and he was gone as quickly as he came."

"That was like him, reckless and generous, fierce and gentle by turns. Pity that so fine a nature should be so early wrecked."

Yorke mused a moment, and Cecil, as if anxiety or pity made her forget her promise, asked suddenly, "Shall you let him go unmolested after such an outrage as this?"

"Yes, even if he had half murdered me or maimed me for life, I would not lift a finger against him. God knows I have my faults, and plenty of them, but I can forgive blows like his easier than some that gentler hands have dealt me."

Cecil made no answer, but seemed lost in wonderment, till Yorke, observing how pale and heavy-eyed she looked, said kindly, "Have you, too, been ill? I asked for you every day, and Hester always gave a good report. Is anything amiss? Tell me, child."

"I am not ill, and nothing is amiss except that I do not sleep, owing to want of exercise, perhaps."

"This must be mended; I'll give you sleep tonight, and tomorrow we will have a long drive together."

Going to an ancient cabinet, he took from it a quaint flask, poured a few drops of some dark liquid into a tiny glass, and mingling it with water, brought it to her.

"It is bitter, but it will bring you deep and dreamless sleep. Drink, little wakeful spirit, drink and rest."

Without offering to take the glass, she bent and drank, not the first bitter draft his hand had given her.

"I think you would drink hemlock without a question if I gave it to you," he said, smiling at her mute obedience.

"I think I should. But I asked no questions now because I knew that this was laudanum. Mamma used it when in pain, and I have often tasted it, playing that I made it sweet for her."

Yorke turned hastily away as if to replace the flask and cup, and when he spoke again he was his gravest self. "Go now, and sleep, Cecil. Tomorrow the old quiet life shall begin again."

It did begin again, and week after week, month after month passed in the same monotonous seclusion. They went nowhere, saw scarcely anyone; Yorke's genius was almost unknown, Cecil's beauty blooming unseen; and so the year rolled slowly by.

❧ *Chapter V* ❧

GOSSIP

P
UTTING his head into the studio where Cecil was at work as usual, and Yorke lounged on the sofa in a most unwonted fit of indolence, "Mrs. Norton's compliments, and can she see the master for a few minutes?" said Anthony.

"Alfred's mother! What next? I'll come, Tony," answered the master, turning to observe the effect of this announcement upon the girl.

But she scarcely seemed to have heard the question or answer, and went on smoothing the rounded limbs of a slender Faun, with an aspect of entire absorption.

"What an artist I have made of her, if a lump of clay is more interesting than the news of her first lover," thought her guardian, as he left the room with a satisfied smile.

Since Alfred's disappointment, there had been a breach between the neighbors, and his mother discontinued the friendly calls she had been wont to make since Cecil came. She was a gray-haired, gracious lady, with much of her son's frankness and warmth of manner. After a few moments spent in general inquiries, she said, with some embarrassment but with her usual directness, "Mr. Yorke, I have felt it my duty to come and tell you certain things, of which I think you should be informed without delay. You lead such a secluded life that you are not likely to hear any of the injurious rumors that are rife concerning Cecil and yourself. They are but natural, for any appearance of mystery or peculiarity always excites curiosity and gossip, and as a woman and a neighbor, I venture to warn you of them, because I take a deep interest in the girl, both for her own sake and my son's."

"I thank you, Mrs. Norton, and I beg you will speak freely. I am entirely ignorant of these rumors, though I know that tattling tongues find food for scandal in the simplest affairs."

The guest saw that the subject was distasteful to her host, but steadily continued, "While she was a child, the relationship of guardian and ward was all sufficient; but now that she is a woman, and so beautiful a woman, it strikes outside observers that you are too young a man to be her sole companion. It is known that you live here together with no society, few friends, and those chiefly gentlemen; that you have neither governess nor housekeeper, only an old female servant. Cecil goes nowhere, and never walks without yourself or Anthony; while her beauty attracts so much attention that interest and curiosity are unavoidably aroused and increased by the peculiarity of her life. It would be a trying task to repeat the reports and remarks that have come to me; you can imagine them, and feel how much pain they cause me, although I know them to be utterly groundless and unjust."

Intense annoyance was visible in Yorke's face, as he listened and answered haughtily, "Those who know me will need no denial of these absurd rumors. I care nothing for the idle gossip of strangers, nor does Cecil, being too innocent to dream that such things exist."

"But you know it, sir, and you know that a man may defy public opinion, and pass scatheless, a woman must submit and walk warily, if she would keep her name unsullied by the breath of slander. A time may come when she will learn this, and reproach you with unfaithfulness to your charge, if you neglect to surround her with the safeguards which she is, as yet, too innocent to know that she needs."

Mrs. Norton spoke earnestly, and her maternal solicitude for the motherless girl touched Yorke's heart, for he *had* one, though he had done his best to starve and freeze it. His manner softened, his eye grew anxious, and he asked, with the air of one convinced in spite of himself, "What would you have me do? I sincerely desire to be faithful to my duty, but I begin to fear that I have undertaken more than I can perform."

"May I suggest that the presence of a respectable gentlewoman in your house would most effectually silence busy tongues, and might be a great advantage to Miss Stein, who must suffer for the want of female society?"

"I have tried that plan and it failed too entirely to make me willing to repeat the experiment."

A slight flush on Yorke's dark cheek and a disdainful curl of the lips told the keen-eyed lady as plainly as words that the cause of the dismissal of a former governess had been too much devotion to the guardian, too little to the ward. Mrs. Norton was silent a moment, and then said, with some hesitation, "May I ask you a very frank question, Mr. Yorke?"

"Your interest in Cecil gives you a right to ask anything, madam," he replied, bowing with the grace of manner which he could assume at will.

"Then let me inquire if you intend to make this girl your wife, at some future time?"

"Nothing can be further from my intentions" was the brief but decided reply.

"Pardon me; Alfred received an impression that you were educating her for that purpose, and I hoped it might be so. I can suggest nothing else, unless some other gentleman is permitted to give the protection of his name and home. My poor boy still loves her, in spite of absence, time, and efforts to forget; he is still eager to win her, and I would gladly be a mother to the sweet girl. Is there no hope for him?"

"None, I assure you. She loves nothing but her art, as I just had an excellent proof; for when you were announced, and your son's name mentioned, she seemed to hear nothing, remember nothing, but worked on, undisturbed."

Mrs. Norton rose, disappointed and disheartened by the failure of her mission.

"I have ventured too far, perhaps, but it seemed a duty, and I have performed it as best I could. I shall not intrude again, but I earnestly entreat you to think of this, for the girl's sake, and take immediate steps to contradict these injurious rumors. Call upon me freely, if I can aid you in any way, and assure Cecil that I am still her friend, although I may have seemed estranged since Alfred's rejection."

Yorke thanked her warmly, promised to give the matter his serious consideration, and bade her adieu, with a grateful respect that won her heart, in spite of sundry prejudices against him.

As the door closed behind her, he struck his hands impatiently together, saying to himself, "I might have known it would be so! Why did I keep the child until I cannot do without her, forgetting that she would become a woman, and bring trouble as inevitably as before? I'll not have another companion to beset me with the romantic folly I've forsworn; neither will I marry Cecil to silence these malicious gossips; I'll take her away from here, and in some quiet place we will find the old peace, if possible."

In pursuance of this purpose, he announced that he was going away upon business that might detain him several days, and after many directions, warnings, and misgivings, he went. He was gone a week, for the quiet place was not easily found, and while he looked, he saw and heard enough to convince him that Mrs. Norton was right. He took pains to gather, from various sources, the reports to which she had alluded, and was soon in a fever of indignation and disgust. Her words haunted him; he soon saw clearly the wrong he had been doing Cecil, felt that his present plan would but increase it, and was assured that one of two things must be done without delay, either provide her with a chaperon or marry her himself, for he rebelled against the idea of giving her to any other. The chaperon was the wisest but most disagreeable expedient, for well he knew that a third person, however discreet and excellent, would destroy the seclusion and freedom which he loved so well, and had enjoyed so long. It was in every respect repugnant to him, and he believed it would be to Cecil also. The other plan to his own surprise did not seem so impossible or distasteful, and the more he thought of it, the more attractive it became. Nothing need be changed except her name, slander would be silenced, and her society secured to him for life. But would she consent to such a marriage? He recalled with pleasure the expression of her face when she went to him, saying, "I will never leave you, my dear master, never"; and half regretted that he had checked the growth of the softer sentiment, which seemed about to take the place of her childish affection. He did not love her as a husband should, but he felt how sweet it was to be beloved, knew that she was happy with him, and longed to keep his little ward, at any cost, to himself.

Still undecided, but full of new and not unpleasurable fancies, he hurried home, feeling a strong curiosity to know how Cecil would regard this proposition should he make it. No one ran to meet him, as he entered, no one called out a glad welcome, and the young face that used to brighten when he came was nowhere visible.

"Where is Miss Cecil?" he asked of Hester.

"In the garden, master," she answered, with a significant nod, that sent him to the nearest window that opened on the garden.

Cecil was walking here with Alfred, and Yorke's face darkened ominously, as a jealous fear assailed him that she was about to solve the question for herself. He eyed her keenly, but her face was half averted, and he could see that she listened intently to her companion, who talked rapidly, and with an expression that made his handsome face more eloquent than his ardent voice.

"Cecil!" called Yorke sharply, unwilling to prolong a scene that angered him, more than he would confess even to himself.

Alfred looked up, bowed with a haughty, half-defiant air, said a few words to Cecil, and leaped the wall again. But she, after one glance upward, went in so slowly that her guardian chafed at the delay, and when at length she came to him with a cold handclasp, and a tranquil "Home so soon?" he answered, almost harshly, "Too soon, perhaps. Why do I find that boy here? I thought he was away again."

"He is going soon, and came because he could not keep away, he said. Poor Alf, I wish he did not care for me so much."

While she was speaking, Yorke examined her with a troubled look, for that brief absence made him quick to see the changes a year had wrought, unobserved till now. Something was gone that once made her beauty a delight to heart as well as eye; some nameless but potent charm that gave warmth, grace, and tenderness to her dawning womanhood. He felt it, and for the first time found a flaw in what he had thought faultless until now. There was no time to analyze the feeling, for drawing away the hand he had detained, she brought him from her desk three letters, directed to herself, in a man's bold writing.

"Germain!" exclaimed Yorke, as his eye fell on them. "Has he dared to write, when he swore he would not? Have you read them?"

She turned them in his hand, and showed the seals unbroken. A flash of pleasure banished the disquiet from his face, and there was no harshness in his voice as he asked, "How did they come? I forbade Tony to receive any communication he might venture to make."

"Tony knows nothing of them. One came in a bouquet, which was tossed over the wall the very day you went; one was brought by a carrier dove soon afterward; the bird came pecking at my window, and thinking it was hurt, I took it in; the third was thrust into my hand by someone whom I did not see, as I was walking with Hester yesterday. I suspected who they were from, and did not open them, because I promised not to listen to this man."

"Rare obedience in a woman! Have you no wish to see them? Will you give me leave to look at them before I burn them?"

"Do what you like, I care nothing for them now."

She spoke so confidingly, and smiled so contentedly, as she stood folding up his gloves, that Yorke felt his purpose strengthening every instant. The letters confirmed it, for as he flung the last into the fire, he said to himself, "There is no way but this; there will be peace for neither of us while Alfred and Germain have hopes of her. Once mine, and I shall have a legal right to defy and banish both."

Turning with decision, he drew her down to a seat beside him, saying, in a tone he had not used since the Cupid was broken, "Sit here and listen, for I've many things to tell you, my little girl. You are eighteen tomorrow, and according to your mother's desire may choose what guardian you will. I leave you free, having no right to influence you, but while I have a home it always will be yours, if you are happy here."

She turned her face away, and for an instant some inward agitation marred its habitual repose, but she answered steadily, though there was an undertone of pain in her voice, "I know it, Yorke, and you are very kind. I am happy here, but I cannot stay, because hard things are said of us, things that wrong you and wound me, more than tongue can tell."

"Who told you this?" he demanded, angrily.

"Alfred; he said I ought to know it, and if you would not follow his mother's advice, I should choose another guardian."

"And will you, Cecil?"

"Yes, for your sake as well as my own."

The tone of resolution made her soft voice jar upon his ear, and convinced him that she would keep her word.

"Whom will you choose?" he gravely asked.

"It is hard to tell; I have made no friends in all these years, and now I have nowhere to go, unless I turn to Mrs. Norton. She will be a mother to me, Alfred a very gentle guardian, and in time I may learn to love him."

Yorke felt both reproached and satisfied; reproached, because it was his fault that the girl had made no friends, and satisfied because there was as much regret as resolution in her voice, and his task grew easier as he thought of Alfred, whom she should never learn to love.

"But you promised to stay with me, and I want you, Cecil."

"I did promise, but then I knew nothing of all this. I want to stay, but now I cannot, unless you do something to make it safe and best."

"Something shall be done. Will you have another governess or an elderly companion?" he asked, wishing to assure himself of her real feeling before he spoke more plainly.

She sighed, and looked all the repugnance that she felt, but answered sorrowfully, "I dread it more than you do, but there is no other way."

"One other way. Shall I name it?"

"Oh, yes, anything is better than another Miss Ulster."

"If my ward becomes my wife, gossip will be silenced, and we may still keep together all our lives."

He spoke very quietly, lest he should startle her, but his voice was eager, and his glance wistful in spite of himself. The eager eyes that had been lifted to his own fell slowly, a faint color came up to her cheek, and she answered with a slight shake of the head, as if more perplexed than startled, "How can I, when we don't care for one another?"

"But we do care for one another. I love you as if you were a child of my own, and I think if nothing had disturbed us that you would have chosen me to be your guardian for another year, at least, would you not?"

"Yes, you are my one friend, and this is home."

"Then stay, Cecil, and keep both. Nothing need be changed between us; to the world we can be husband and wife, here guardian and ward, as we have been for six pleasant years. No one can reproach or misjudge us then; I shall have the right to protect my little pupil, she to cling to her teacher and her friend. We are both solitary in the world. Why can we not go on together in the old way, with the work we love and live for?"

"It sounds very pleasant, but I am so ignorant I cannot tell if it is best. Perhaps you will regret it if I stay, perhaps I shall become a burden when it is too late to put me away, and you may tire of the old life, with no one but a girl to share it with you."

Her face was downcast, and he did not see her eyes fill, her lips tremble, or the folded hands, pressed tight together, as she listened to the proposition which gave her a husband's name, but not a husband's heart. He saw that she thought only of him, forgetful of herself—knew that he offered very little in exchange for the liberty of this young life, and began to think that he had been mistaken in supposing that she loved him, because she showed so little emotion now; but in spite of all this, the purpose formed so long ago was still indomitable, and though forced by circumstances to modify it, he would not relinquish his design. The relentless look replaced all others, as he rose to leave her, though he said, "Do not answer yet, think well of this, be assured that I desire it, shall be happy in it, and see no other course open, unless you choose to leave me. Decide for yourself, my child, and when we meet tomorrow morning, tell me which guardian you have chosen."

"I will."

Cecil was usually earliest down, but when the morrow came, Yorke waited for her with an impatience that he could not control, and when she entered, he went to meet her, with an inquiring eye, an extended hand. She put her own into it without a word, and he grasped the little hand with a thrill of joy that surprised him as much as did the sudden impulse which caused him to stoop and kiss the beautiful, uplifted face that made the sunshine of his life.

Ashamed of this betrayal of his satisfaction, he controlled himself, and said, with as much of his usual composure as he could assume, "Thank you, Cecil; now all is decided, and you never shall regret this step, if I can help it. We will be married privately, and at once, then let the gossips tattle as they please."

"Are you quite satisfied with me for choosing as I have done?" she asked, as he led her to her place.

"Quite satisfied, quite proud and happy that my ward is to be mine forever. Is she content?"

"Yes, I chose what was pleasantest, and will do my best to be all you would have me, to thank you for giving me so much."

No more was said, and very soon all trace of any unusual emotion had vanished from Cecil's face; not so with Yorke. A secret unrest possessed him, and did not pass away. He thought it was doubt, anxiety, remorse, perhaps, for what he was about to do, but try as he would, the inward excitement kept him from his usual pursuits, and made him long to have all over without delay. Feeling that he owed Mrs. Norton some explanation of his seeming caprice, he went to her, frankly stated his reasons for the change, and took counsel with her upon many matters. With the readiness of a generous nature, she put aside her own disappointment, and freely did her best for her peculiar neighbor, glad that she had served the girl so well.

She soon convinced him that it would be better not to have a private wedding, but openly to marry and give the young wife a gay welcome home, that nothing mysterious or hasty should give fresh food for remark. He yielded, for Cecil's sake, and the good lady, with a true woman's love of such affairs, soon had everything her own way, much to Yorke's annoyance, and Cecil's bewilderment. Alfred was gone, and his mother wisely left him in ignorance of the approaching marriage, and stifled many a sigh, as she gave her orders and prepared the little bride.

Great was the stir and intense the surprise among the sculptor's few friends when it was known what was afloat, and Yorke was driven half wild with questions, congratulations, and praises of his betrothed. So much interest and goodwill pleased even while it fretted him; and bent on righting both himself and Cecil, in a manner that should preclude all further misconception, he asked friends and neighbors from far and near to his wedding, thinking, with a half-sad, half-scornful smile, "Let them come, they will see that she is lovely, will think that I am happy, and never guess what a mockery it is to me."

They did come, did think the bride beautiful, the bridegroom happy; and would have had no suspicion of the mockery, but for one little incident that had undue effect upon the eager-eyed observers. Among the guests was one whom none of the others knew; a singularly handsome man, who glided in unannounced, just before the ceremony, and placed himself in the shadow of the draperies that hung before a deep window in the drawing room. Two or three of the neighbors whispered together, and nodded their heads significantly, as if they had suspicions; but the entrance of the bridal pair hushed the whispers, and suspended the nods for a time at least. As they took their places, Cecil was seen to start and change color when her eye fell on the stranger, leaning in the purple gloom of the recess; Yorke did the same, then he frowned; she drew her veil about her, and stern bridegroom and pale bride appeared to compose themselves for the task before them.

The instant the ceremony was over, one gossip whispered to another, "I told you so, it is the same person who used to sing under her window, and watch the house for hours. A lover, without doubt, and why she preferred this gloomy Mr. Yorke to that devoted creature passes my comprehension."

"It's my opinion that she didn't prefer him, but was persuaded into it. He's far too old and grave for such a young thing, and I suspect she agrees with me. Did you see her turn as pale as her dress when she saw that fine-looking man in the recess? Poor thing, it's plain to see that she is marrying from gratitude, or fear, or something of that sort."

This romantic fancy soon took wing, and flew from ear to ear, although the stranger vanished as suddenly as he came. Yorke caught a hint of it, but only smiled disdainfully, and watched Cecil with a keen sense of satisfaction, in the knowledge that she was all his own. Not only was his eye gratified by her beauty that day, but his pride also, for the admiration she excited would have satisfied the most enamored bridegroom. She seemed to have grown a woman suddenly, for gentle dignity replaced her former shyness, and she bore herself like a queen; pale as the flowers in her bosom, calm as the marble Psyche that adorned an alcove, and so like it that more than one enthusiastic gentleman begged Yorke to part with the statue, now that he possessed the beautiful model. All this flattered his pride as man and artist, enhanced his pleasure in the events of the day, roused his ambition that had slept so long, and banished his last doubt regarding the step he had so hastily taken.

When all was over, and the house quiet again, he roamed through the empty rooms, still odorous and bright with bridal decorations, looking for his wife, and smiling, as he spoke the word low to himself, for the pleasant excitement of the day was not yet gone. But nowhere did he see the slender white figure in the misty veil; her little glove lay where she dropped it when the ring was put on, her bouquet of roses and orange flowers was fading in the seat she left, and an array of glittering gifts still stood unexamined by their new mistress. Thinking she was worn out and had gone to rest, he went slowly toward the studio, wondering if he should not feel more like his old self in that familiar place. Passing Cecil's room, he saw that the door was open, and no one within but the newly hired maid, who was busy folding up the silvery gown.

"Where is Miss Cecil?" he asked.

"Mrs. Yorke is in the tower, sir," answered the woman, with a simper at his mistake.

He bit his lip, and went on; but as he climbed the winding stairs, he passed his hand across his eyes, remembering a happy time, nineteen years ago, when that name had almost been another and a dearer woman's. Dressed in the plain gray gown, and with no change about her but the ring on the hand that caressed the dog's shaggy head, Cecil sat reading as if nothing had disturbed the usual quiet routine of her day. If she had looked up with a word of welcome or a smile of pleasure, it would have pleased him well, for his heart was very tender just then, and she was very like her mother. But she seemed unconscious of his presence till he stood before her, regarding her with the expression that was so attractive and so rare.

"Are you worn out with the bustle of the day, and so come here to rest and find yourself, as I do?" he asked, stroking the soft waves of her hair.

"Yes, I am tired, but I was never more myself than I have been today," she answered, turning a leaf, as if waiting to read on.

"What did it all seem like, Cecil?"

"A pretty play, but I was glad to have it over."

"It was a pretty play, though Germain might have spoiled it if I had not warned him away. But it is not quite over, as I was reminded on my way up. We must remember that before others I am your husband, and you my little wife, else I shall call you 'Miss Cecil' again, and you say 'master,' as you did half an hour ago."

"What would you have me do? I know I shall forget, for there is nothing to remind me but this," and she turned the ring to and fro upon her finger, adding, as he thought, regretfully, "It begins to make a difference already, and you said nothing would be changed."

"Nothing shall be changed, except that," he answered, chilled by her coldness, and turning sharply round, he seized chisel and mallet, and fell to work, regardless of bridal broadcloth and fine linen.

≫ *Chapter VI* ≪

CECIL'S SECRET

IT was easy to say that nothing should be changed, but they soon found it very hard to prevent decided alterations in the lives of both. Yorke's friends, rejoicing in the new tie that seemed about to give him back to the world he had shunned so long, did everything in their power to help on the restoration by all manner of festivities after the wedding. Having yielded once or twice by Mrs. Norton's advice, Yorke found it both difficult and irksome to seclude himself again, for it seemed as if a taste of the social pleasures neglected for so many years had effectually roused him from his gloom and given him back his youth again. But the chief cause of the change was Cecil. Wherever she went she won such admiration that his pride was fostered by the praise it fed on, and regarding her as his best work, he could not deny himself the satisfaction of beholding the homage paid his beautiful young wife. She submitted with her usual docility, yet expressed so little interest in anything but her art that he soon grew jealous of it, and often urged her to go pleasuring lest she should grow old and gray before her time, as he had done.

"Look your loveliest tonight, Cecil, for there will be many strangers at Coventry's, and I have promised him that my handsome wife would come," he said, as he came into the drawing room one tempestuous afternoon and found her looking out into the deserted street where the rain fell in torrents and the wind blew gustily.

"It is so stormy, need we go?"

"We must. The wind will fall at dark, and one does not mind rain in a closed carriage. You wonder at me, I dare say, and so do I at myself;

but I think I'm waking up and growing young again. Now I shall be old Yorke and read studiously for an hour."

He laughed as he spoke and laid himself on the couch, book in hand. But he read little, for Cecil's unusual restlessness distracted his attention, and he had fallen into a way of observing her lately while she worked or studied and he sat idle. She too opened a book, but soon put it down; she made a sketch, but seemed ill pleased with it, and threw it in the fire; she worked half a flower at her embroidery frame, turned over two or three portfolios with a listless air, then began to wander up and down the room so noiselessly that it would not have disturbed him had he been as absorbed as he seemed. Watching her covertly, he saw her steps grow rapid, her eyes wistful, her whole face and figure betray impatience and an intense desire for something beyond her reach. Several times she seemed about to follow an almost uncontrollable impulse, but checked herself on the way to the door and resumed her restless march, pausing with each turn to look out into the storm.

"What is it, Cecil? You want something. Can I get it for you?" he said at last, unable to restrain the question.

"I do want something, but you cannot get it for me," she answered, pausing with an expression of mingled doubt and desire infinitely more becoming than her usual immobility.

"Come here and tell me what it is; you so seldom ask anything of me I am curious to know what this may be."

Drawing her down upon the couch where he still lay, he waited for her request with an amused smile, expecting some girlish demand. But she delayed so long that he turned her face to his, saying, as he studied its new aspect, "Is it to stay at home tonight, little girl?"

"No, it is to go out now, and alone."

"Alone, and in this raging storm? You are crazy, child."

"I like the storm; I'm tired of the house. Please let me go for just half an hour."

"Why do you wish to be alone, and where are you so eager to go?"

"I cannot tell you. Be kind and don't ask me, Yorke."

"A secret from me! That's something new. When shall I know it?"

"Never, if I can help it."

He lay looking at her with a curious feeling of wonder and admiration, for this sudden earnestness made her very charming, and he found it extremely pleasant to while away an idle hour discovering the cause of this new waywardness in Cecil.

"I think you will tell me like an obedient little wife, and ask me prettily to go with or for you."

"I cannot tell you, and you must not come with me. Dear Yorke, let me go, please let me go!"

She folded her hands, dropped on her knees before him, and pleaded so earnestly with voice, and eyes, and outstretched hands, that he sat up amazed.

"What does it mean, Cecil? You have no right to keep a secret from me, and I cannot let you go out in such a storm on such a mysterious errand as this. A month ago you promised to obey me. Will you rebel so soon, and risk your health if nothing else by this strange freak?"

There was a sudden kindling of the eye as she rose and turned away with a resolute, white face, saying, in a tone that startled him, "I have the same right to my secret as you have to yours, and I shall keep it as carefully. A month ago I did promise to love, honor, and obey; but the promises meant nothing, and your will is not my law, because though my husband before the world, you are only my guardian here. I harm no one but myself in doing this, and I *must* go."

"Will you go if I forbid it?" he asked, rising in real perplexity and astonishment.

"Yes," she answered, steadily.

"How if I follow you?"

"I shall do something desperate, I'm afraid."

She looked as if she might, and he dared not insist. Entreaties and commands had failed; perhaps submission might succeed, and he tried it.

"Go, then; I shall not follow. I trust you in this, as you have trusted me more than once, and hope you will be as worthy of confidence as I try to be."

He thought he had conquered, for as he spoke, gravely yet kindly, she covered up her face as if subdued, and expecting a few tears, an explanation, and penitence, he stood waiting and recalling scenes of childish waywardness which had always ended so. No, not so; for to his unspeakable surprise Cecil left the room without a word. Five minutes later the hall door closed, and he saw her fighting her way against wind and rain with the same intense longing, the same fixed resolution in her face.

For an hour he watched and waited, racking his brain to discover some clue to this mysterious outbreak. Several trifling events now returned to his memory and deepened his perplexity. Just before they were married he brought her home a pretty bonbonnière to hold the comfits for which she still had a childish fancy. Having filled it for her, he was about to drop it into one of the ornamented pockets of the little apron she wore, but as he touched it a paper rustled, and as if the sound recalled some forgotten secret, she had clutched the pocket in a sudden panic and begged him to stop. He had accused her of having love letters from Alfred hidden there, and she had indignantly denied it, but hurried away as if to put her secret under lock and key. Later she had ventured out alone once or twice, always asking pardon when reproved for these short flights, but repeating them till strictly forbidden. Since then she had grown more taciturn than ever, and often went away to her own room to read or rest, she said. How she did spend the long hours passed there, Yorke was too proud to ask either mistress or maid, though he had felt much curiosity to know. The present mystery recalled these lesser ones, but gave no help in explaining anything, and he could only roam about the room and watch the storm more restlessly than Cecil.

Another hour passed and he began to feel anxious, for twilight gathered fast and still she did not come. A third hour rolled slowly by; the streetlamps glimmered through the mist, but among the passing figures no familiar one appeared, and he was fast reaching that state of excitement which makes passive waiting impossible when, as he stood peering out into the wild, wet night, a slight rustle was heard behind him, and a soft voice broke the long silence.

"I am ready, Yorke."

Turning with a start, he saw that all his fears had been in vain, for no storm-beaten figure stood before him, but Cecil shining in festival array.

"Thank heaven you are safe! I've been watching for you, but I did not see you come," he said, eyeing her with renewed wonder.

"No, I took care that you should not, and have been busy for an hour making myself pretty, as you bade me. Are you satisfied?"

He would have been hard to please if he was not satisfied with the fair apparition standing in the light of the newly kindled chandelier. A rosy cloud seemed to envelop her, bridal pearls gathered up the dark hair, shone on graceful neck and arms, and glimmered here and there among the soft-hued drapery. A plumy fan stirred in her hand, and a white down-trimmed cloak half covered shoulders almost as fair, for Yorke adorned his living statue with a prodigal hand. He could not but smile delightedly and forgive her, though she asked no pardon, for he was too glad to have her back to think of questions or reproaches.

"I am more than satisfied. Now come and let me play hostess among the teapots, for you are too splendid for anything but to be looked at, and you must need refreshment after your wild walk."

"No, I want nothing; let Hester fill my place. I'll wait for you here, and enjoy the pleasant fire you have made for me."

She knelt down before it, and he went slowly away, looking backward at the pretty picture the firelight showed him. When he rejoined her after tea and toilet, she was lying in a deep chair looking straight before her with a singular expression, dreamy, yet intense, blissfully calm, yet full of a mysterious brightness that made her face strangely beautiful. He examined her keenly, but she did not see him, he spoke, but she did not hear him, and not until he touched her did she seem conscious of his presence. Then the rapt look passed away, and she roused herself with an effort.

But Yorke could not forget it, and later in the evening when Coventry's rooms were full of friends and strangers, he stepped aside into a corner to observe Cecil from a distance and receive the compliments that now were so welcome to him. Two gentlemen paused nearby and, unconscious who was overhearing them, spoke freely of his ward.

"Where is Yorke's statue as they call her? A dozen people are waiting for my opinion, and I must not disappoint them," said the elder of the two, with the air of an experienced connoisseur.

"She is sitting yonder. Do you see her, Dent? The dark-haired angel with the splendid eyes," returned the younger, speaking with artistic enthusiasm.

Dent took a survey, and Yorke waited for his opinion, feeling sure that it would be one of entire and flattering approval.

"As a work of art she is exquisite, but as a woman she is a dead failure. Why in heaven's name didn't Yorke marry one of his marble goddesses and done with it?"

"They say he has," laughed Ascot, as Dent put down his glass with a shake of the head. "He fell in love with her beauty, and is as proud of it as if he had carved the fine curves of her figure and cut the clear outline of her face. If it were not for color and costume, she might be mounted on a pedestal as a mate for that serenely classical Pallas just behind her."

"Now to my eye," said Dent, "that rosy, sweet-faced little woman sitting near her is far lovelier than this expressionless, heartless-looking beauty. See how young Mrs. Vivian kindles and glows with every passing emotion; look at her smile, hear her laugh, see her meet her husband's eye with a world of love in her own, and then contrast her with your statuesque Mrs. Yorke."

"Every man to his taste. I admire the sculptor's, but I don't envy him his handsome wife unless he possesses the art of warming and waking his Galatea. I doubt it, however, for he hasn't the look of a Pygmalion, though a very personable man. Come and introduce me to charming Mrs. Vivian; I've looked at the snow image till I'm positively chilled."

They passed on, and Yorke sent a glance after them that might have hastened their going had they met it. He had heard nothing but praise before, and this was quite a revelation to him. He was hurt and angry, yet ashamed of being so, and drawing back into his corner, began to contrast Cecil with her neighbor. The gentlemen were right; that indefinable something which she had once possessed was gone now, and her beauty had lost its magic. The woman near her was all they had said, young, blooming, blithe, and tender, with her new happiness shining in her face, and making her far more winsome than her fairer neighbor. He watched her look up at her husband with her heart in her eyes, and felt a sense of wrong because he had never met a glance like that in the dark eyes he knew so well. He saw the young pair dance together, and as they floated by, forgetful of everything but one another, he sighed involuntarily, remembering that he had done with love. He looked long at Cecil, and began to wonder if he did possess the power to animate his statue. For the first time he forgot his purpose, and yielding to the impulse of the moment, crossed the room, bent over her, and asked, "Cecil, can you waltz?"

"Yes; poor Alf taught me."

The tone in which the name was uttered roused the old jealous feeling, for she never spoke *his* name in that softened voice.

"Come, then, and waltz with me," he said, with a masterful air as novel as the request.

"With you? I thought you never danced."

"I will show you that I do. Lean on my arm, and let me see if I can bring some color into those white cheeks of yours."

She glanced up at him with a curious smile, for he looked both melancholy and excited; the next minute she forgot his face to wonder at his skill, for with a strong arm and steady foot he bore her round and round with a delightsome sense of ease and motion as the music rose and fell and their flying feet kept time. Yorke often looked down to mark the effect of this on Cecil, and was satisfied, for soon she glowed with the soft excitement of exercise and pleasure; the mysterious brightness returned to her eyes again and shone upon her face. Once he paused purposely before Dent and Ascot, and as he waited as if to catch the time, he heard the young man whisper, "Look at her now and own that she is beautiful."

"That she is, for this is nature and not art. The man *can* animate his statue and I envy him," returned the other, drawing nearer to watch the brilliant creature swaying on her husband's arm as Yorke swept her away, wearing an expression that caused more than one friend to smile and rejoice.

"Rest a little, then we will dance again," he said, when he seated her, and leaning on her chair began to ply the fan, still bent on trying his power, for the test interested him.

"Do you see Mrs. Vivian yonder, Cecil? Tell me what you think of her."

"I think she is very pretty, and that her husband loves her very much."

"Don't you envy her?"

"No."

"Now that you have seen something of the world, and tasted many of its pleasures, do you never regret that you tied yourself to me so young, never reproach me for asking you to do it?" He leaned nearer as he spoke and looked deep into her eyes; they looked back at him as if they read his heart, and something in their lustrous depths stirred him strangely; but he saw no love there, and she answered in that undemonstrative voice of hers, "I am contented, Yorke."

"Call me Bazil; I am tired of the other, and it is too ugly for your lips."

She smiled to herself, remembering a time when Bazil was forbidden, and asked a question in her turn.

"Who are the gentlemen just passing?"

"Dent and Ascot, artists, I believe. Why do you ask?"

"I thought they were friends of yours, they seem to take so much interest in us."

"They are no friends of mine. Shall I tell you what they say of us?"

"Yes, Bazil, if you like."

He did not answer for a moment, because the long unused name came very sweetly from her lips, and he paused to enjoy it. Then he told her; but she only smoothed the ruffled plumage of the fan he had been using, and looked about her undisturbed.

"Mrs. Vivian tries to please her husband by being fond and gay; I try to please mine by being calm and cool. If both are satisfied, why care for what people say?"

"But I do care, and it displeases me to have you criticized in that way. Be what you like at home, but in public try to look as if you cared for me a little, because I will not have it said that I married you for your beauty alone."

"Shall I imitate Mrs. Vivian? You are hard to please, but I can try."

He laughed a sudden and irrepressible laugh, partly at her suggestion, partly at his own request, and she smiled for sympathy, so blithe and pleasant was the sound.

"What a capricious fool I am becoming," he said. "I no longer know myself, and shall begin to think my gray hairs have come too soon if this goes on. *Am* I very old and grave, Cecil?"

"Eight-and-thirty is not old, Bazil, and if you always dressed as carefully as tonight, and looked as happy, no one would call you my old husband, as a lady did just now."

Yorke glanced at a mirror opposite and fancied she was right; then his face clouded over, and he shook his head as if reproaching himself for a young man's folly. But the reflection he saw was that of a stately-looking man, with fine eyes and a thoughtful countenance which just then wore a smile that made it singularly attractive. Here their host was seen approaching with the strangers, and Yorke whispered suddenly, "Imitate Mrs. Vivian if you can; I want to try the effect upon these gentlemen."

She bowed and held the fan above her eyes a moment, as if to screen them from the light. When it dropped, as the newcomers were presented, they saw a blooming, blushing face, with smiles on the lips, light in the eyes, and happiness in every tone of the youthful voice. Amazed at the rapidity of the change, yet touched by her obedience and charmed with her address, her husband could only look and listen for the first few minutes, wondering what spirit possessed the girl. So well did she act her part that he soon entered heartily into his own, and taking young Vivian for his model, played the devoted husband so successfully that Dent and Ascot lingered long, and went away at last to report that Mrs. Yorke was the most charming woman in the room, and the sculptor the happiest man.

"Was my imitation a good one? Is that what you wish me to be in public?" asked Cecil, dropping back into her accustomed manner the instant they were alone, though her face still wore its newly acquired charm.

"It was done to the life, and you quite took my breath away with your 'loves' and 'dears,' and all manner of small fascinations. Where did you learn them? What possesses you tonight, Cecil?"

"An evil spirit. I have called it up, and now I cannot lay it."

She laid her hands against her cheeks, where a color like the deep heart of a rose burned steadily, while her eyes glittered and the flowers on her bosom trembled with the rapid beating of her heart, and some inward excitement seemed to kindle her into a life and loveliness that startled Yorke and half frightened herself. She saw that her words bewildered him still more than her actions, and, as if anxious to make him forget both, she rose, saying with an imperious little gesture, "We have sat apart in this nook too long; it is ill-bred. Come and dance with me."

He obeyed as if they had changed places, and for an hour Cecil danced like a devotee, delighting and surprising those about by the gaiety and grace with which she bore her part in the brilliant scene. When not with her, Yorke lingered nearby, longing to take her home, for her spirits seemed unnatural to him, and a half-painful, half-pleasurable sentiment of tender anxiety replaced his former pride in her. She had blossomed so suddenly he scarcely knew his quiet pupil, and while her secret perplexed him, this new change both charmed and troubled him, and kept him hovering about her till she came to him flushed and breathless, saying in the same excited manner as before, "Take me home, Bazil, or I shall dance myself to death. I want to be quiet now, for my head aches and burns, and I'm so tired I shall fall asleep before I know it."

Making their adieus, he took her to a quiet anteroom and left her to rest while he went to find his carriage. He was absent many minutes, being detained by the way, and when he returned it was to find Cecil fast asleep. Her fan and gloves had fallen from her hands, and she lay with her disordered hair scattered on the pillow, her white arms folded under her head, looking as if an unconquerable drowsiness had overpowered her. Wrapping her in her cloak Yorke took her away half awake, let her sleep undisturbed on his shoulder during the drive, and reluctantly gave her into the hands of her maid when they reached home.

Very little sleep did he get that night, for Cecil's figure was continually dancing before his eyes, sometimes as he first saw it that evening in the firelight, then as it looked when she played Mrs. Vivian with such spirit, or when she answered with that strange expression, "An evil spirit. I have called it up, and now I cannot lay it." But oftenest as he watched it by the light of the streetlamps, with a soft cheek against his own, and recollections of that other Cecil curiously blended with thoughts of the one sleeping on his shoulder. Calling himself a fool, with various adjectives attached, and resolutely fixing his mind on other things, having failed to bring repose, he lighted both lamp and meerschaum and read till dawn.

His first question when he met Victorine in the morning was "How is Mrs. Yorke?"

"Still asleep, sir, and I haven't called her, for the only thing she said last night was to bid me let her rest all day unless she woke."

"Very well, let her be quiet, and tell me when she rises."

He went to his studio, but could settle to nothing, and found the day wearisomely long, for Cecil did not rise. He asked for her at dinner, but she was still asleep, and hoping for a long evening with her, he resigned himself to a solitary afternoon. The clock was on the stroke of six when Victorine came in, looking frightened.

"I think Mrs. Yorke is ill, sir."

"Is she awake?" he asked, starting up.

"I've tried to wake her, but I can't. Perhaps you could, sir, for something must be amiss—she looks so strangely and hasn't stirred since morning."

Before the last sentence was out of her mouth Yorke was halfway upstairs, and in another minute at Cecil's bedside. A great change had come over her since he saw her last, a change that alarmed him terribly. The restless sleep had deepened into a deathlike immobility; the feverish flush was gone, and violet shadows gave her closed eyes a sunken look; through her pale lips slow breaths came and went; and when he felt her pulse her hand dropped heavily as he relinquished it. Stooping, he whispered gently yet urgently, "Cecil, wake up, it is time."

But there was no sign of waking, and nothing stirred but the faint flutter of her breath. He raised her, brushed the damp hair from her forehead, and cried in a voice tremulous with fear, "My darling, speak to me!"

But she lay mute and motionless. With a desperate sort of energy he flung up the window, rolled the bed where a fresh wind blew in, laid her high on the pillows, bathed her head and face, held pungent salts to her nostrils, and chafed her hands. Still all in vain; not a sound or motion answered him, and all his appeals, now tender, now commanding, could not break the trance that held her. Desisting suddenly from his fruitless efforts, he sent Victorine for a physician, and till he came suffered the most terrible suspense. Before Dr. Home could open his lips Yorke explained hurriedly, and bade him do something for heaven's sake.

The old gentleman took a long survey, touched pulse and temples, listened to her breathing, and then asked, though his own medicine case was in his hand, "Do you keep laudanum in the house?"

"I have some that I've had a long time. I'll get it for you." And Yorke was gone in spite of Victorine's offer of assistance. But he returned with a fresh anxiety, for the little flask was empty.

"It was half full two days ago; no one goes to that cabinet but myself. I don't understand it," he began.

"I do."

And there was something in the doctor's tone that caused the bottle to drop from Yorke's hand as he whispered, with a look of incredulity and dismay, "Do you think she has taken it?"

"I have no doubt of it."

Yorke seized the old man's arm with a painful grip, asking in a terror-stricken tone, "Do you mean she tried to destroy herself?"

"Nothing of the sort; she has only taken an overdose and must sleep it off."

"Doctor, you deceive me! I know enough of this perilous stuff to know that the bottle under my feet contained enough to kill a man."

"Perhaps so, but not your wife; and the fact that she is still alive proves that I am right."

Terror changed to intense relief as Yorke asked with an appeasing gesture, "Can you do nothing for her? Will she not sleep herself to death?"

"I assure you there is no danger; she will wake in a few hours, weak and languid, but all the better for the lesson she has unintentionally given herself. It's a dangerous habit, and I advise you to put a stop to it."

"To what? I don't understand you, sir."

The doctor looked up from the powder he was preparing, saw Yorke's perplexity, and answered with a significant nod, "I see you don't, but you shall, for she is too young for such things yet. Your wife eats opium, I suspect."

For a moment Yorke stared at him blankly, then said impetuously, "I'll not believe it!"

"Ask the maid," returned the doctor, but Victorine spoke for herself.

"Upon my word, sir, I know nothing of it. Mrs. Yorke sleeps a deal some days and is very quiet, but I never saw her take anything but the little comfits."

"Hum! She is more careful than I suspected. I'm sure of it, however, and perhaps you can satisfy yourself if you choose to look."

The doctor cast a suggestive glance about the room. Yorke understood it, and taking Cecil's keys began his search, saying sternly, "I have a right to satisfy myself and save her from further danger if it is so."

He did not look long, for in a corner of the drawer where certain treasures were kept he found a paper which had evidently been a wrapper for something that left a faintly acrid odor behind. A few grayish crumbs were shaken from the folds, and Dr. Home tasted them with a satisfied "I thought so."

Yorke crushed the paper in his hand, asking in a tone of mingled pain and perplexity, "Why should she do it?"

"A whim, perhaps, ennui, wakefulness; a woman's reasons for such freaks are many. You must ask her and put a stop to it, though I think this may break up the habit."

"What led you to suspect her of it?" asked Yorke, trying to find his way out of the mystery.

"I detected laudanum in her breath; that explained the unnatural sleep. The fact that it had not already killed her assured me that she was used to it, for, as you said, a dose like that would kill a man, but not a woman who had been taking opium for months. I can do nothing now; keep the room cool, let her wake naturally, then give her this, and if she is not comfortable tomorrow, let me know."

With that the doctor left him, Victorine began her watch beside the pale sleeper, and Yorke went away to wander through the silent house haunted by thoughts that would not let him rest.

❧ *Chapter VII* ❦

HEART FOR HEART

D R. Home was right; Cecil's heavy sleep gradually passed into a natural one, and in the morning she woke, wan and nerveless, but entirely ignorant that she had lost a day. A misty recollection of some past excitement remained, but brought no explanation of her present lassitude, except a suspicion that she had taken more opium than was prudent. Finding herself alone when she woke, she did not ring for Victorine, but made her toilet hastily, rubbed a transient color into her pale cheeks, drew her hair low on her temples to conceal her heavy eyes, and went down fearing that it was very late.

Yorke sat in his place with a newspaper in his hand, but he was not reading, and there was something in his face that made Cecil pause involuntarily to examine it. It seemed as if years had been added to his age since she saw him last; his mouth was grave, his eye sad; a weary yet resolute expression was visible, but also the traces of some past suffering that touched the girl and caused her to lay her hand upon his shoulder, saying in her gentlest tone, "Good morning, Bazil; forgive me for being so wilful yesterday. I am punished for my fault by finding you so grave and tired now."

"I am only tired of waiting for my breakfast" was all the answer she got, but she felt him start and saw the paper rustle in his hand as she spoke, though whether surprise or displeasure caused these demonstrations she could not tell, and fancying him in one of his moody fits, took her place in silence. His coffee stood untouched till it was cold before he looked up and said, with a keen glance which made her eyes falter and fall, "Are you quite rested, Cecil?"

"Not quite; I danced too much last night."

"The night before last, you mean."

"We were at Coventry's last evening, Bazil."

"No, on Monday evening."

"Yes, and today is Tuesday."

He turned the paper toward her and Wednesday stared her full in the face. She looked incredulous, then bewildered, and putting her hand to her forehead seemed trying to recollect, while a foreboding fear came over her.

"Then what became of yesterday? I remember nothing of it," she asked with a troubled look.

"You slept it away."

"What! All day?"

"For six-and-thirty hours, without a word, almost without a motion."

His eye was still upon her, his voice was ominously quiet, and as he spoke her wandering glance fell on an open book that lay beside him. She read its title—*Confessions of an Opium-Eater*—and overcome by a painful blending of shame and fear, she covered up her face without a word.

"Is it true, Cecil?"

"Yes, Bazil."

"How long has it been?"

"A year."

"What tempted you to try such a dangerous cure, or pleasure?"

"Yourself."

"I! How? When?"

"You gave me laudanum when I could not sleep. I liked its influence, and after that I tried it whenever I was sad or tired."

"Was this the secret I nearly discovered once, the cause of your solitary walks, the evil spirit that possessed you at Coventry's?"

"Yes; I had opium in my pocket that day, and was so frightened when I thought you would discover it, because I knew you would be angry. I went out those times to get it, for I dared not trust anyone. Last night, no, Monday night, I had none, and I longed for it so intensely I could not wait. I disobeyed you, but the storm was too much for me, and I was just turning back in despair, when I remembered the little flask. You seldom go to the cabinet, never use the laudanum, and I thought I could replace it by-and-by."

"But, child, had you no fear of consequences when playing such perilous pranks with yourself? You might have killed yourself, as you came near doing just now."

"I was used to it because Mamma often had it, and at first I was very careful; but the habit grew upon me unconsciously, and became so fascinating I could not resist it. In my hurry I took too much, and was frightened afterward, for everything seemed strange. I don't know what I did, but nothing seemed impossible to me, and it was a splendid hour; I wish it had been my last."

Tears fell between her fingers, and for a moment she was shaken by some uncontrollable emotion. Yorke half rose as if to go to her, but checked the impulse and sat down again with the air of a man bent on subduing himself at any cost. Cecil was herself again almost immediately, and wiping away her tears, seemed to await his reproof with her accustomed meekness.

But none came, for very gently he said, "Was this kind to yourself or me?"

"No; forgive me, Bazil. I will amend my fault."

"And promise never to repeat it?"

"I promise, but you cannot know how hard a thing it is to give up when I need it so much."

"Why, Cecil?"

"Because—" she stopped an instant, as if to restrain some impetuous word, and added, in an altered tone, "because I find it hard to tame myself to the quiet, lonely life you wish me to lead. I am so young, so full of foolish hopes and fancies, that it will take time to change me entirely, and what I have seen of the world lately makes it still more difficult. Have patience with me, and I shall be wiser and more contented soon."

He had left the table as if to throw up a window, and lingered for a moment to enjoy the balmy air, perhaps to conceal or conquer some pang of self-reproach, some late regret for what he had done. When he returned, it was to say, with an undertone of satisfaction in his grave voice, "Yes, it is too soon to ask so much of you, and if you give up this dangerous comforter, surely I can give up a little of the seclusion that I love. It is hard to break off such a habit. I will help you, and for a time we will forget these troubles in new scenes and employments. Will you go to the seashore for a month, Cecil, and so make home pleasanter by absence?"

"Oh, so gladly! I love the sea, and it will do me good. You are very kind to think of it, and I thank you so much, Bazil!"

She did thank him, with eyes as well as lips, for her face brightened like a prisoner's when the key turns in the lock and sunshine streams into his cell. Yorke saw the joy, heard the tone of gratitude, and stifled a sigh, for they showed him what a captive he had made of her, and betrayed how much she had suffered silently.

"Shall I go with you?" he asked, in a curiously unauthoritative tone, but with a longing look that might have changed her reply had she seen it.

"If you care to, I shall feel safer; but do not unless it is pleasant to you."

"It *is* pleasant. We will go tomorrow," he said decidedly. "Rest and prepare today; take Victorine with you, and leave your troubles all behind, and in a month we will come back our happy selves again."

"I hope so" was all her answer, and the change was settled without more words.

"The charm does not work," sighed Yorke within himself, as he looked down at Cecil leaning on his arm while they went pacing along the smooth beach seven days later, with the great waves rolling up before them, a fresh wind blowing inward from the sea, and summer sunshine brooding over the green islands of the bay. The week had brought no change to Cecil; air and bathing, exercise and change of scene, thoughtful care and daily devotion on her husband's part, all seemed to have failed, and she walked beside him with the old quietude and coldness intensified instead of lightened.

"What shall I do with you, Cecil? You don't get strong and rosy as I hoped you would, and you often have a longing look as if you wanted your opium again; but you know I dare not give it to you."

"I shall learn to do without it in time, or find something else to take its place. Hark!"

As the words left her lips, her hand arrested him, her eyes kindled, a smile broke over her face, and her whole figure seemed to start into life. He stood still wondering, but instantly he learned what magic had wrought the spell, for on the wings of the wind came the fitful music of a song from a solitary boatman whose skiff lay rocking far out in the bay. Both recognized the voice, both watched the white sail gliding nearer, and both faces altered rapidly; Cecil's warmed and brightened as she listened with head erect and detaining hand, but Yorke's darkened with the blackest frown it had ever worn as he drew her away with an impatient gesture and peremptory "Come in; it is too warm to linger here for a fisherman's song!"

The smile broke into a laugh as she said, following with evident reluctance, "Do fishermen sing Italian and go fishing in costumes like that?"

"Your ears and eyes must be keener than mine if you can discover what I neither hear nor see," he answered almost petulantly. But still smiling, she looked backward as she began to sing like a soft echo of the stranger's voice, and let him lead her where he would. Till sunset he kept her in their rooms, busy with pencil, book, or needle, blind to the wistful glances she often sent seaward, and deaf to hints that they were losing the hours best suited for sketching. Victorine came in at last, bringing Cecil's hat and mantle, and, as if the nod she gave him was a preconcerted signal, Yorke rose at once, saying promptly, "Yes, now we can go, without fear of sun or—"

"Fishermen," added Cecil, with a slightly scornful smile.

"Exactly." And Yorke put on her mantle without a sign of displeasure at her interruption. She seemed upon the point of refusing the stroll that now had no charm for her, but yielded, and they went out together, leaving Victorine to lift her hands and wonder afresh at the strange behavior of her master and mistress.

"I have a fancy to walk upon the rocks; can I, Bazil?" were the first words Cecil uttered, as they came into the splendor of the evening hour that bathed sea and sky within its ruddy glow.

A single sail was skimming down the bay, and not a figure sat or stood among the rocks. Yorke saw this, and answered with a gracious smile, "Walk where you will; I leave the path to you."

She climbed the cliffs and stood watching the lonely boat until it vanished round the rocky point where the lighthouse tower showed its newly kindled spark. Then she turned and said wearily, "Let us go home. I find it chilly here."

He led her down another path than that by which they came, but stopped suddenly, and she felt his hand tighten its hold as he exclaimed, "Go back; it is not safe. Go, I beg of you!"

It was too late, for she had seen a figure lying on a smooth ledge of the cliff, had recognized it, and glided on with a willful look, a smile of satisfaction. He set his teeth and sprang after her, but neither spoke, for Germain lay asleep, and the entire repose of his fine face not only restrained their tongues, but riveted their beauty-loving eyes. Cecil was touched to see how changed he was; for all the red glow shining over him, his face was very pale; the wind blew back the hair from his temples, showing how hollow they had grown; and stooping to brush an insect from his forehead, she saw many gray hairs among the dark locks scattered on the stone. His mouth was half hidden by the black beard, but the lips smiled as if some happy dream haunted his sleep, and in the hands folded on his broad chest, she saw a little knot of ribbon that had dropped from her dress that morning as she listened to his song.

Yorke saw it, also, and made an involuntary gesture to pluck it from the sleeper's hold, but Cecil caught his arm, whispering sharply, "Let him keep it! You care nothing for it, and he needs something to comfort him, if I read his face aright."

Yorke stood motionless an instant, then seemed to take some sudden resolution, for drawing her gently aside, he said with a mildness that was as new as winning, "You are right; he does need comfort, and he shall have it. Go on alone, Cecil; I will follow soon."

She obeyed him, but glancing backward as she went, she saw him turn his face to the cliff behind him, and lay his head down on his arm in an attitude of deep dejection or of doubt. He stood so till the last sound of her light step died away, then he stopped and touched the sleeper, with a low-spoken "August, it is I."

Germain leaped to his feet as if the slight touch had been a blow, the quiet call a pistol shot, and his hand went to his breast with an instinctive motion that half revealed a hidden weapon. A single glance seemed to reassure him, for though his heart beat audibly, and his very lips were white, he laughed and offered the hand that had just been ready to deal death to some imaginary captor. Yorke did not take it, and, as if the discourtesy reminded him of something, Germain drew back, bowed with the grace that was habitual to him, and said coolly, "Pardon me; your sudden waking makes me forgetful. I was dreaming of you, and in the dream we were friends as of old."

"Never again, August; it is impossible. But I will do my best for you now, as before, if I may trust you."

"Have I not kept my word this time? Have I not left you in peace for nearly a year? Did I not obey you today when you bade me shun you, though the merest accident betrayed your presence to me?"

"You have done well for one so tempted and so impetuous; but you forget the letters written to Cecil in my absence, and lying down to sleep in our very path is not putting the bay between us as I bade you."

"Forgive the letters; they did no harm, for she never read them, I suspect. Ah, you smile! Then I am right. As for finding me here, it was no plot of mine. I thought you always walked on the beach, so I crept up to catch one glimpse of her unseen, before I went away for another year, perhaps. Be generous, Bazil. You have made her all your own; do not deny me this poor boon."

"I will not. Promise me to keep our secret sacredly, and you shall see her when you will. But you must control yourself, eye, tongue, voice, and manner, else I must banish you again. Remember your life is in my hands, and I will give you up rather than let harm come to her."

"I swear it, Bazil. You may safely indulge me now, for I shall not haunt you long; my wanderings are almost over, and you may hear Death knocking at my heart."

Real solicitude appeared in Yorke's face as the other spoke with a melancholy smile, and obeying a kindly impulse, he laid his hand on Germain's shoulder.

"I hope not, for it is a very tender heart, in spite of all its wayward-ness and past offenses. But if it be so, you shall not be denied the one happiness that I can give you. Come home with me, and for an hour sun yourself in Cecil's presence. I do not fear you in this mood, and there is no danger of disturbing her; I wish there was!"

"God bless you, Bazil! Trust me freely. The wild devil is cast out, and all I ask is a quiet time in which to repent before I die. Take me to her; I will not mar her peace or yours. May I keep this? It is my only relic."

He showed the ribbon with a beseeching look, and remembering Cecil's words, Yorke bowed a mute assent as he led the way down the rude path and along the beach where slender footprints were still visible in the damp sand.

She was waiting in the softly lighted room, with no sign of impa-tience as she sat singing at the instrument. It was the air Germain had sung, and pausing behind her, he blended the music of his voice with hers in the last strains of the song. She turned then, and put out her hand, but caught it back and glanced at Yorke, for the recollection of the struggle in the dark returned to check the impulse that prompted her to welcome this man whom she could not dislike, in spite of mystery, violence, and unmistakable traces of a turbulent life. Yorke saw her doubt and answered it instantly.

"Give him your hand, Cecil, and forgive the past; there is no ill will between us now, and he will not forget himself again."

Germain bowed low over the little hand, saying in the tone that always won its way, "Rest assured of that, Mrs. Yorke, and permit me to offer my best wishes, now that my prophecy has been fulfilled."

In half an hour Yorke saw the desired change, for Germain worked the miracle, and Cecil began to look as she had done a year ago. Sitting a little apart, he watched them intently, as if longing to learn the secret, for he had failed to animate his statue since the night when for a time he believed he had some power over her, but soon learned that it was to opium, not to love, that he owed his brief success. Cecil paid no heed to him, but seemed forgetful of his presence, as Germain entertained her with an animation that increased the fascination of his manner. An irresistible mingling of interest, curiosity, and compassion attracted her to him. Yorke's assurance, as well as his own altered demeanor, soon removed all misgivings from her mind, and the indescribable charm of his presence made the interview delightful, for he was both gay and gentle, devoted and respectful. The moment the hour struck, he rose and went, with a grateful glance at Yorke, a regretful one at Cecil. She did not ask now as before, "Will he come again?" but her eyes looked the question.

"Yes, he will come tomorrow, if you like. He is ill and lonely, and not long for this world; so do your best for him while you may."

"I will, with all my heart, for indeed I pity him. It is very generous of you to forget his wrongdoing, and give me this pleasure."

"Then come and thank me for it a la Mrs. Vivian."

He spoke impulsively and held his hands to her, but she drew back, swept him a stately little curtsy, and answered with her coolest air, "We are not in public now, so, thank you, guardian, and good night."

She smiled as she spoke, but he turned as if he had been struck, and springing out of the low window, paced the sands until the young moon set.

They had come to the seaside before the season had begun, but now the great hotel was filling fast, and solitude was at an end. Cecil regretted this, and so did Yorke, for the admiration which she always excited no longer pleased but pained him, because pride had changed to a jealous longing to keep her to himself. In public she was the brilliant, winning wife, in private, the cold, quiet ward, and nothing but Germain's presence had power to warm her then. He came daily, seeming to grow calmer and better in the friendly atmosphere about him. Cecil enjoyed his society with unabated pleasure, and Yorke left them free after being absent for hours and apparently intent upon some purpose of his own. Of course, there were many eyes to watch, many tongues to comment upon the actions of the peculiar sculptor and his lovely wife. Germain was known to be a friend; it was evident that he was an invalid, and no longer young; but flirting young ladies and gossiping old ones would make romances, while the idle gentlemen listened and looked on. Cecil soon felt that something was amiss, for though her secluded life had made her singularly childlike in some things, she was fast learning to know herself, and understand her relations to the world. She wondered if Yorke heard what was said, and hoped he would speak if anything displeased him; but till he did, she went on her way as if untroubled, walking, sailing, singing, and driving with Germain, who never forgot his promise, and who daily won from her fresh confidence and regard. So the days passed till the month was gone, and with a heavy heart Cecil heard her husband give orders to prepare for home.

"Are you ready?" he asked, coming in as she stood recalling the pleasant hours spent with Germain, and wondering if he would come to say farewell.

"Yes, Bazil, I am ready."

"But not glad to go?"

"No, for I have been very happy here."

"And home is not made pleasanter by absence?"

"I shall try to think it is pleasanter."

"And I shall try to make it so. Here is the carriage. Shall we go?"

As they rolled away, Cecil looked back, half suspecting to see some signal of adieu from window, cliff, or shore, but there was none, and Yorke said, interpreting the look aright, "It is in vain to look for him; he has already gone."

"It is much better so. I am glad of it," she said decidedly, as she drew down her veil, and leaning back, seemed to decline all further conversation. Her companion consoled himself with Judas, but something evidently filled him with a pleasant excitement, for often he smiled unconsciously, and several times sang softly to himself, as if well pleased at some fancy of his own. Cecil thought her disappointment amused him, and much offended, sat with her eyes closed behind her veil, careless of all about her, till the sudden stopping of the carriage roused her, and looking up, she saw Yorke waiting to hand her out.

"Why stop here? This is not home," she said, looking at the lovely scene about with wondering eyes.

"Yes, this is home," he answered, as leading her between blooming parterres and up the wide steps, he brought her into a place so beautiful that she stood like one bewildered. A long, lofty hall, softly lighted by the sunshine that crept in through screens of flowers and vines. A carpet, green and thick as forest moss, lay underfoot; warm-hued pictures leaned from the walls, and all about in graceful alcoves stood Yorke's fairest statues, like fit inhabitants of this artist's home. Before three wide windows airy draperies swayed in the wind, showing glimpses of a balcony that overhung the sea, whose ever-varying loveliness was a perpetual joy, and on this balcony a man sat, singing.

"Does it please you, Cecil? I have done my best to make home more attractive by bringing to it all that you most love."

Yorke spoke with repressed eagerness, for his heart was full, and try as he might, he could not quite conceal it. Cecil saw this, and a little tremor of delight went through her; but she only took his hand in both her own, exclaiming gratefully, "It is too beautiful for me! How shall I thank you? This is the work you have been doing secretly, and this is why you sent Germain before us to give me a sweet welcome. How thoughtful, and how beautiful it was of you."

He looked pleased but not satisfied, and led her up and down, showing all the wonders of the little summer palace by the sea. Everywhere she found her tastes remembered, her comfort consulted, her least whim gratified, and sometimes felt as if she had four 1 something dearer than all these. Still no words passed her lips warmer than gratitude, and when they returned to the hall of statues, she only pressed the generous hand that gave so much, and said again, "It is too beautiful for me. How can I thank you for such kindness to your little ward?"

"Say wife, Cecil, and I am satisfied."

"Pardon me, I forgot that, and like the other best because it is truer. Now let me go and thank Germain."

She went on before him, and coming out into the wide balcony, saw nothing for a moment but the scene before her. Below, the waves broke musically on the shore, the green islands slept in the sunshine, the bay was white with sails, the city spires glittered in the distance, and beyond, the blue sea rolled to meet the far horizon.

"Has he not done well? Is it not a charming home to live and die in?" said Germain, as she turned to greet him, with both hands extended, and something more than gratitude in her face. That look, so confiding and affectionate, was too much for Germain; he took the hands and bent to give her a tenderer greeting, remembering his promise just in time, and with a half-audible apology, hurried away, as if fearing to trust himself.

Cecil looked after him sorrowfully, but when Yorke approached, asking in some surprise, "Where is Germain?" she answered reproachfully, "He is gone, and he must not come again."

"Why not?"

"Because he cannot forget, and others see it as well as I. You might have spared him this, and for my sake have remembered that it is not always wise to be kind."

"Ah, they gossip again, do they? Let them; I've done one rash and foolish thing to appease Mrs. Grundy, and now I shall trouble myself no further about her or her tongue."

Leaning on the balustrade, he did not look at her, though he held his breath to catch her reply, but seemed intent on watching leaf after leaf float downward to the sea. His careless tone, his negligent attitude wounded Cecil as deeply as his words; her eyes kindled, and real resentment trembled in her voice.

"Who should care, if not you? Do you know what is said of us?"

"Only what is said of every pretty woman at a watering place." And he leaned over to watch the last leaf fall.

"You do not care, then? It gives you no pain to have it said that I am happier with Germain than with you?"

He clenched the hand she could not see, but shrugged his shoulders and looked far off at sea, as if watching a distant sail.

"For once, rumor tells the truth, and why should I deny it? My pride may be a little hurt, but I'm not jealous of poor Germain."

If he had seen her hold her lips together with almost as grim a look as his own often wore, and heard her say within herself, "I will prove that," he would have carried his experiment no further. But he never turned his head, and Cecil asked, with a touch of contempt in her voice that made him wince, "Do you wish this mysterious friend of yours to go and come as freely as he has done of late?"

"Why not, if he is happy? He has not long to enjoy either life or love."

"And I am to receive him as before, am I?"

"As you please. If his society is agreeable to you, I have no desire to deprive you of it, since mine is burdensome and Alfred away."

Something in the emphasis unconsciously put upon the last name caused a smile to flit over Cecil's face, but it was gone instantly, and her voice was cold as ice.

"Thank you; and you have no fear of the consequences of this unparalleled generosity of yours?"

"None for myself or my snow image. Has she for herself?"

"I fear nothing for myself; I have no heart, you know."

She laughed a sudden laugh that made him start, and as she vanished behind the floating curtains, he struck his hand on the iron bar before him with a force that brought blood, saying, in an accent of despair, "And she will never know that I have one, till she has broken it!"

❧ *Chapter VIII* ❧

MASKS

"CECIL, the world begins to wonder why Mrs. Yorke does not admit it to a glimpse of her new home."

"Mrs. Yorke is supremely indifferent to the world's wonder or its wishes."

She certainly looked so, as she sat in the couch corner singing to herself, and playing with a useless fan—for the room was breezy with sea airs, though an August sun blazed without. Yorke was strolling from alcove to alcove, as if studying the effects among his statues, and Germain lounged on the wide step of the balcony window, with a guitar across his knee, for he still came daily, as neither master nor mistress had forbidden him.

"I think I have proved my indifference, but people annoy me with questions, and I suspect we shall have no peace till we give some sort of an entertainment, and purchase freedom hereafter by the sacrifice of one evening now."

"You are right, Yorke; I, too, have been beset by curious inquirers, and I suggest that you end their suspense at once. Why not have a masquerade? These rooms are admirably fitted for it, there has been none this season, and the moon is at the full next week. What does 'my lady' say?"

Germain spoke in his persuasive voice, and Cecil looked interested now.

"If we must have anything let it be that. I like such things, and it is pleasant to forget oneself sometimes. Does the fancy suit you, Bazil?"

"Anything you please, or nothing at all. I only spoke of it, thinking you might find some pleasure in pleasing others," he returned, still busy with the piping Faun that had a place among the finer works of his own hands.

"I used to do so, and tried very hard to please, but no good came of it, so now I enjoy myself, and leave others to do likewise. What characters shall we assume, Germain?"

As she asked the question, her voice changed as abruptly as her manner, and languid indifference was replaced by lively interest.

"I shall assume none, I have not spirits enough for it, but in a domino can glide about and collect compliments for you. Your husband must take the brilliant part, as a host should."

"He had better personate Othello; the costume would be becoming, and the character an easy one for him to play, he is such a jealous soul."

She spoke ironically, and he answered in the same tone.

"No, thank you, I prefer Hamlet, but you would succeed well as the princess in the fairy tale, who turned to stone whenever her husband approached her, though a very charming woman to all others. Perhaps, however, you would prefer to personate some goddess; I can recommend Diana, as a cool character for a sultry summer evening."

"I hate goddesses, having lived with them all my life. Everyone will expect me to be some classical creature or other, so I shall disappoint them, and enjoy myself like a mortal woman. I'll imitate the French marquise whom we saw last winter at the theater; she was very charming, and the dress is easily prepared, if one has jewels enough."

Germain laughed involuntarily at the idea of Cecil in such a character, and she laughed also, a lighthearted laugh, pleasant to hear.

"You think I cannot do it? Wait and see. I am a better actress than you think; I've had daily practice since I was married, and Bazil will testify that I do my part well."

"So well that sometimes it is impossible not to mistake art for nature. When shall this fete take place, Madame la Marquise?"

"Next week; four days are enough for preparation, and if we wait longer, I shall get tired of the fancy, and give it up."

"Next week it shall be then."

Yorke stood looking down the long room at the pretty tableau at the end, for Germain was leaning on the back of the couch now, dropping odorous English violets into the white hands lifted to catch them, and Cecil looked as if she was already enjoying herself as a mortal woman. Standing apart among the statues, he wondered if she remembered the time when his will was law, and it was herself who obeyed with a weakness he had not yet learned. Now this was changed, and he called himself a fool for losing his old power, yet gaining no new hold upon her. She ruled him, but seemed not to know it, and keeping her smiles for others, showed her darkest side to him, being as lovely and as thorny as any brier rose. Presently she sprang up, saying with unusual animation, "I will go and consult with Victorine, and then we will drive to town and give our orders. You must come with me, Germain. I want your taste in my selection; Bazil has none, except in stones."

"One cannot doubt that, with such proofs all about one," answered Germain, as he followed her toward the door. "When shall we have another statue, Yorke? You have been idle of late."

"Never busier in my life; I have a new design in my mind, but it takes time to work it out. Wait a few weeks longer, and I will show you something that shall surpass all these."

"Unless you have lost your skill."

Yorke's face had kindled as he spoke, but it fell again when Cecil whispered these words in passing, with a glance that seemed to prophesy a failure for the new design, whatever it might be. A flush of passionate pain passed across his face, and he lifted his arms as if to hurl poor Psyche down again, but the sight of the bruised hand seemed to recall some purpose, and calm him by its spell.

For four days there was much driving to and fro between the city and the beach; the great hotel was all astir, and the villas along the shore were full of busy tongues and needles, for summer is the time for pleasure, and the Yorkes' masquerade was the event of the season. On the appointed evening all things were propitious, the night was balmy, the sky cloudless, the moon lent her enchantment to the scene, and the lonely home beside the sea wore its most inviting aspect, for the hall of statues was brilliant with lights, blooming with flowers, and haunted by the fitful music of a band concealed among the shrubbery without. Yorke, looking stately and somber as the melancholy Dane, and Germain in a plain black silk domino, stood waiting for Cecil, mask in hand. Presently she came rustling down, in a costume both becoming and piquant, for the powdered hair made her fair skin dazzling, and the sweeping brocades of violet and silver set off her slender figure. She wore no ornaments, but a profusion of rich lace upon the dress, white plumes in her hair, and a cluster of roses on her bosom. With the costume she seemed to have assumed the coquetry of the French marquise, and greeted her companions in broken English, spoken with a charming accent and sprightly grace that caused Germain to compliment her on her skill, and Yorke to survey her with undisguised pride, as he said, with a significant smile, "Let me put the last touch to this ravishing toilet of yours, and prove that you were right in saying I had some taste in stones."

Cecil bent her beautiful neck to let him clasp a diamond necklace about it, and held out a pair of lovely arms to receive their glittering fetters, with a little cry of pleasure, and a characteristic *"Merci, monsieur!* You are too gallant in so revenging yourself upon me for my idle words. These are superb, I kiss your munificent hands," and as he essayed to fasten in the brooch, she touched his hand with her lips. The pin dropped, Germain took it up, and turning to him, she said, in her own voice, "Put it in my hair just here, there is no room for it below; diamonds are best on the head, and roses on the heart."

As he deftly fastened it above her white forehead, she drew out a flower broken by Yorke's unskillful hand, and tying it to the ribbon of Germain's domino, she said, "Wear this, else among so many black dominoes I shall not know my friend, and make my confidences to wrong ears."

"Now I am prouder of my rose than you of your jewels, madame, and thank you for it heartily," he replied, surveying it with delight.

"Shall I wear not your favor, also?" asked Yorke, with extended hand.

"Oh, yes, but not that one, because it does not suit you. There's rue for you; and here's some for me, but we may wear our rue with a difference."

As she quoted poor Ophelia's words, from a vase nearby she gathered a flowerless sprig, and gave it to him with a glance that cut him to the heart. He took it silently, and instantly resuming her gay manner, she exclaimed, as the roll of a carriage was heard, "It is the Coventrys, they come early, because I asked them to play the host and hostess for an hour to increase the bewilderment of our guests, and give us greater freedom. She is to be Juno, and while she is masked, no one will suspect that it is not I. Come, Germain, let us slip away, and return later."

The rooms filled rapidly, and the mock host and hostess did the honors so well that the guests had no doubt of their identity, while the real master of the house moved among them unsuspected, watching impatiently for the arrival of the marquise and her friend. He waited long, but at last the white plumes were seen approaching, and many eyes followed the brilliant figure that entered, not on the arm of a black domino, but a young courtier in the picturesque costume of Elizabeth's time. Yorke saw at a glance that this was not Germain; who was it then? Alfred flashed into his mind, but he was across the water, and not expected to return for months. No new-made acquaintance of Cecil's carried himself with such a gay and gallant air; for the disguise seemed to sit easily upon him, and he wore doublet and hose, velvet cloak and lovelocks, ruff and sword with none of the awkwardness that most men exhibit when in costume. Nor was this all he saw to disturb him; the charming marquise leaned upon the arm of this debonair Sir Walter Raleigh, talking with an animation that attracted attention, while the devotion of her escort, and the grace of both, roused much curiosity concerning this striking young couple. Hamlet followed them like a shadow, but their conversation was in whispers, and they went their way as if unconscious of anything but themselves. Yorke soon met the black domino with the white rose dangling on his breast, and drew him apart to ask eagerly, "Who is that with Cecil?"

"I have no idea."

"Where did she meet him?"

"I cannot tell you."

"But you went away together, and were to return together. When and how did you part?"

"We went to the music room to wait a little, but soon she sent me for her fan, which had been forgotten. I was gone some time, for the maid was busy with the ladies; when I returned Madame had disappeared, and I saw no more of her till she came in with Sir Walter."

"Rude to you, that is not like her!"

"I was to blame, if anyone; she grew tired of waiting, doubtless, and finding some friend, left me to follow her. I am glad she did, for he is a fitter escort for youth and beauty than I. They look like a prince and princess out of a fairy tale, and it does one's heart good to watch them."

Yorke made no reply, but stood motionless beside Germain, looking where *he* looked, for the dancing had begun, and the young pair were slowly circling round the room to the sound of music, inspiring enough to stir the coldest blood. Twice the marquise floated by, with a glance over her shoulder as she passed; but the third time she looked in vain, for the two dark figures were gone, and a splendid Cleopatra held her court in the deserted recess.

"I am out of breath; let us stroll about and hear people's comments on me and mine; that will be amusing," she said, pausing, and her escort obeyed.

It was amusing, and something more, for as they passed through the glittering throng, or mingled with the groups gathered about each statue-haunted alcove, Cecil saw and heard the wonder, admiration, and reverence her husband's genius inspired. This was the first time his works had been exhibited, and there was something so romantic in the fact that these fine statues had stood unknown, unseen, till they were brought to decorate his wife's home, as if love alone could make him care for fame, that their beauty seemed increased fourfold in the spectators' eyes; and so warm were the commendations bestowed upon the marbles, so varied and beautiful the tributes paid the man, that Cecil glowed behind the mask, and was glad of that screen to hide her smiles and tears. From many lips she heard the same story, sorrow, love, and fame, with endless embellishments, but always the same contrast between romance and reality for her. If he loved her, why so careless about Germain? What was the mystery that bound the two so closely together, with such a strange mingling of dislike and gratitude, forbearance and submission? Had she not a right to solve the secret if she could, now that her happiness depended on it? These thoughts saddened and silenced her so visibly that her companion soon perceived it.

"Where are all your spirits gone? Have I really offended you by coming? Or do these chattering people weary you? Tell me, Cecil, and let me do my best to make you gay again," he whispered, bending till his curling locks touched her shoulder.

"Neither, Sir Walter; the heat oppresses me, so take me out into the garden, and leave me to rest, while you play the cavalier to some other lady, lest your devotion to one should give offense."

"If I submit now, I may join you when I've done penance in a single dance, may I not? Remember how short my time is, and how much I have to say."

"You may come if you will forget the past, and think only of the future."

"I can safely promise that, for it is now the desire of my heart," and with a curious blending of joy and regret in his voice, Sir Walter left the marquise on the broad steps that led down into the garden. Moonlight flooded the terrace, grove, and flowery paths where changing figures wandered to and fro, or sat in the green nooks, each group making a graceful picture in that magic light. Here a troubadour sang to his guitar, as knights and ladies listened to his lay; there glided a monk or nun, somber and silent, as if blind and deaf to the gaiety about them; elves glittered in the grove; Mephistopheles followed a blond Margaret; Louis Fourteenth and Marie Stuart promenaded with stately pace along the terrace; and Rebecca the Jewess was flirting violently with Cardinal Wolsey on the steps. Enjoying the mirth and mystery with a divided mind, Cecil wandered on, declining all courteous offers of companionship from fellow wanderers, and came at last to a retired nook, where a rustic seat stood under a leafy arch before the little fountain that sparkled in the moonlight. Scarcely was she seated, however, before a long shadow fell across the path, and turning, she saw a black domino behind her.

"Does Madame recognize me?"

The voice was feigned, nothing but the outline of the figure was visible, and no badge distinguished this domino from a dozen others, but after a moment's pause and a brief scrutiny, Cecil seemed satisfied, and removing her mask, exclaimed with an air of perfect confidence, "It is Germain; you cannot hide yourself from me."

"Is Madame sure?"

"Yes, I know you by the rapid beating of your heart. You forget that, *mon ami*."

"Does no other heart beat fast when it approaches you, lovely marquise?"

"None but yours, I fancy. You have been dancing, and I bade you not, it is dangerous. Come now, and rest with me; the music is delicious from this distance, and the night too beautiful to waste in crowded rooms."

With an inviting gesture she swept her silken train aside, that he might share the little seat, and as he took it, put up her hand to remove his mask, with the smile still shining on her face, the friendly tone still softening her voice.

"Take off that ugly thing, it impedes your breathing, and is bad for you."

But he caught the hand, and imprisoned it in both his own, while the heartbeats grew more audible, and some inward agitation evidently made it difficult to speak quietly.

"No, permit me to keep it on; I cannot show as calm a face as you tonight, so let me hide it."

Something in the touch and tone caused Cecil to look closer at the mask, which showed nothing but glittering eyes and glimpses of a black beard.

"Where is the sign that will assure me you are Germain?" she demanded.

"Here," and turning to a fold of the black domino she saw the rose still hanging as she had tied it.

"No wonder you did not care to show your badge, it is so faded. Break a fresh one from the trellis yonder, and I will place it better for you."

"Give me one from your bouquet, that is fresher and sweeter to me than any other in the garden or the world."

"Moonlight and masquerading make you romantic; I feel so too, and will make a little bargain with you, since you prize my rose so highly. You shall take your choice of these I wear, if you will answer a few questions."

"Ask anything—" he began eagerly, but caught back the words, adding, "put your questions, and if I can answer them without forfeiting my word, I will, truly and gladly."

"Ah, I thought that would follow. If I forfeit my word in asking, surely you may do the same in answering. I promised Bazil to control my curiosity; I have kept my promise till he broke his, now I am free to satisfy myself."

"What promise has he broken?"

"I will answer that when you have earned the rose. Come, grant my wish, and then you may question in return."

"Speak, I will do my best."

"Tell me then what tie binds you to Yorke?"

"The closest, yet most inexplicable."

"You are his brother?"

"No."

"He cannot be your father, that is impossible?"

"Decidedly, as there are but a few years difference between our ages."

She heard a short laugh as this answer came, and smiled at her own foolish question.

"Then you must be akin to me, and so bound to him in some way. Is that it?"

"I am not akin to you, yet I am bound to you both, and thank God for it."

"What is the mystery? Why do you haunt me? Why does Yorke let you come? And why do I trust you in spite of everything?"

"The only key I can give you to all this is the one word, love."

She drew back, as he bent to whisper it, and put up her hand as if to forbid the continuance of the subject, but Germain said warmly, "It is because I love you that I haunt you. Yorke permits it, because he cannot prevent it, and you trust me, because your heart is empty and you long to fill it. Is not this true? I have answered your questions, now answer mine, I beg of you."

"No, it is not true."

"Then you do love?"

"Yes."

"Whom, Cecil, whom?"

"Not you, Germain, believe that, and ask no more."

"Is it a younger, comelier man than I?"

"Yes."

"And you have loved him long?"

"For years."

"He is here tonight?"

"He is. Now let us go in, I am tired of this."

"Not yet, stay and answer me once more. You shall not go till I am satisfied. Tell me, have you no love for Yorke?"

His sudden violence terrified her, for, as she endeavored to rise, he held her firmly, speaking vehemently, and waiting her reply, with eyes that flashed behind the mask. Remembering his wild nature, and fearing some harm to Bazil, she dared not answer truly, and hoping to soothe him, she laid her hand upon his arm, saying, with well-feigned coldness, "How can I love him, when I have been taught for years only to respect and obey him? He has been a stern master, and I never can forget my lesson. Now release me, Germain, and never let this happen again. It was my fault, so I forgive you, but there must be no more of it."

There was no need to bid him release her, for as the words left her lips, like one in a paroxysm of speechless repentance, grief, or tenderness, he covered her hands with passionate tears and kisses, and was gone as suddenly as he had come. Cecil lingered a moment to recover herself and readjust her mask, and hardly had she done so when down the path came Hamlet, as if in search of her. The difference between the two had never been more strongly marked than now, for Germain had been in his most impetuous mood, and Yorke seemed unusually mild and calm, as Cecil hurried toward him, with a pleasant sense of safety as she took his arm, and listened to his quiet question.

"What has frightened you, my child?"

"Germain, he is so violent, so strange, that I can neither control nor understand him, and he must be banished, though it is hard to do it."

"Poor Germain, he suffers for the sins of others as well as for his own. But if he makes you unhappy, he shall go, and go at once. Why did you not tell me so before?"

"I did, but you said, let him stay. Have you forgotten that so soon?" Yorke laughed low to himself.

"It seems that I have forgotten. It was kind of me, however, to let him stay where he was the happiest; did you not think so, Cecil?"

"No, I thought it very unwise. I was hurt at your indifference, and tried to show you your mistake; but I have done harm to Germain, and he must go, although in him I lose my dearest friend, my pleasantest companion. I am very proud, but I humble myself to ask this favor of you, Bazil."

"Gentle heart, how can he ever thank you for your compassion and affection? Be easy, he shall go; but as a last boon, give him one more happy day, and I will make sure that he shall not offend again, as he seems to have done tonight. I, too, am proud, but I humble myself, Cecil, to ask this favor of you."

So gently he spoke, so entirely changed he seemed, that Cecil's eyes filled, for her heart felt very tender, and before she could restrain it, an impulsive exclamation escaped her.

"Ah, Bazil, if you were always as kind as now, how different my life would be."

"So would mine, if I dared be kind." The answer was impulsive as the exclamation, and he made a gesture as if to take her to himself; but something restrained him, and with a heavy sigh he walked in silence.

"Dared to be kind?" she echoed, in a grieved and wondering tone. "Are you afraid to show that you care for me a little?"

"Mortally afraid, because I cannot tell you all. But, thank heaven, there will come a time when I may speak, and for that hour I long, though it will be my last."

"O Bazil, what do you mean by such strange words?"

"I mean that when I lie dying, I can tell my miserable mystery, and you will pity and pardon me at last."

"But you once said you would never tell me."

"Did I? Well, then Germain shall tell you when he dies. You'll not have long to wait."

Cecil shivered at the ominous words, and started with a faint cry, for they seemed confirmed, as her eye fell on a dark figure lying with hidden face among the grass, not far from the solitary path they had unconsciously chosen. There was something so pathetic about the prostrate figure, flung down as if in the abandonment of despair, that Cecil was on the point of going to offer comfort, when her companion detained her, whispering earnestly, "Leave him to me, and go on alone. It is time for the unmasking, and we shall be missed. I'll follow soon, and bring him with me."

She obeyed, and went on, more heavyhearted than when she came. Within, the gaiety was at its height, and as she entered, Sir Walter was instantly at her side, leading her away for the last dance before the masks were removed. Presently silence fell upon the motley throng, and all stood ready to reveal themselves, when a signal came. A single horn sounded a mellow blast, and in a moment the room brightened with smiling faces, as the black masks fell, while a general peal of laughter filled the air. Cecil glanced about her for her husband and Germain. They were standing together near the door, both unmasked now, and both more mysterious to her than ever. Neither looked as she expected to see them; Yorke was grim and pale, with smileless lips and gloomy eyes; Germain leaned near him, smiling his enchanting smile, and wearing the indescribable air of romance which always attached to him, and even now, rendered him a more striking figure than many of the gayer ones about him.

"Shall I ever understand them?" she sighed to herself, as her eyes turned from them to Sir Walter, standing beside her, one hand on his sword hilt, the other still holding the half-mask before his face, as if anxious to preserve his incognito as long as possible. Yorke's eye was upon him, also, as he waited with intense impatience to see his suspicion confirmed; but in the confusion of the moment, he lost sight of the marquise and her attendant before this desire was gratified. Making his way through the crowd as fast as frequent salutations, compliments, and jests permitted, he came at last to the balcony. A single glance assured him that his search was ended, and stepping into the deep shadow of the projecting wall, he eyed the group before him with an eye that boded ill to the unconscious pair.

Cecil's face was toward him, and it wore a look of happiness that had long been a stranger to it, as she spoke earnestly but in so low a tone that not a word was audible. Her companion listened intently, and made brief replies; he was unmasked now, but the long plume of his hat drooping between his face and the observer still prolonged his suspense. Only a few moments did they stand so, for, as if bidding him adieu, Cecil waved her hand to him, and reentered the hall through the nearest window. Sir Walter seated himself on the wide railing of the balcony, flung his hat at his feet, and turned his face full to the light, as if enjoying the coolness of the sea breeze. One instant he sat humming a blithe cavalier song to himself, the next, a strong hand clutched and swung him over the low balustrade, as a face pale with passion came between him and the moon, and Yorke's voice demanded fiercely, "What brings you here? Answer me truly, or I will let go my hold, and nothing but my hand keeps you from instant death."

It was true, for though Alfred's feet still clung to the bars, his only support was the arm, inflexible as iron, that held him over the rocky precipice, below which rolled the sea. But he was brave, and though his face whitened, his eye was steady, his voice firm, as he replied unhesitatingly, "I came to see Cecil."

"I thought so! Are you satisfied?"

"Fully satisfied."

"That she loves you as you would have her love?"

"Yes, as I would have her love."

"You dare say this to me!" and Yorke's grip tightened, as a savage light shot into his black eyes, and his voice shook with fury.

"I dare anything. If you doubt it, try me."

Alfred's blood was up now, and he forgot himself in the satisfaction it gave him to inflict a pang of jealousy as sharp as his own had been.

"What was she saying to you as she left?" demanded Yorke, under his breath.

"I shall answer no questions, and destroy no confidences" was the brief reply.

"Then I swear I will let go my hold!"

"Do it, and tell Cecil I was true to the end."

With a defiant smile, Alfred took his hands from the other's arm, and hung there only by that desperate clutch. The smile, the words, drove Yorke beyond himself; a mad devil seemed to possess him, and in the drawing of a breath, the young man would have been dashed upon the jagged cliffs below, had not Germain saved them both. Where he came from, neither saw, nor what he did, for with inconceivable rapidity Yorke was flung back, Alfred drawn over the balustrade, and planted firmly on his feet again. Then the three looked at one another: Yorke was speechless with the mingled rage, shame, and grief warring within him; Alfred still smiling disdainfully; Germain pale and panting with the shock of surprise at such a sight, and the sudden exertion which had spared the gay evening a tragic close. He spoke first, and as one having authority, drawing the young man with him, as he slowly retreated toward the steep steps that wound from the balcony to the cliff that partially supported it.

"Go, Bazil, and keep this from Cecil; I have a right to ask it, for half the debt to you is canceled by saving you from this act, that would have made your life as sad a failure as my own. I shall return tomorrow for the last time; till then I shall guard this boy, for you are beside yourself."

With that they left him, and he let them go without a word, feeling that indeed he was beside himself. How long he stood there, he did not know; a stir within recalled him to the necessity of assuming composure, and fighting down the agitation that must be controlled, he went in to play the courteous host at his own table, and answer to the toasts drunk to the health and happiness of himself and his fair wife. He went through with his duties with a desperate sort of gaiety that deceived careless observers, but not Cecil. She too was feverishly restless for Alfred did not appear, and Germain was gone also; but she hid her disquiet better than Yorke, and the effort made her so brilliantly beautiful and blithe that the old fancy of "Yorke's statue" was forgotten, and "Yorke's wife" became "the star of the goodly companie."

The evening came to an end at last, and Yorke's long torment was over. Early birds were beginning to twitter, and the short summer night was nearly past, as the latest guest departed, leaving the weary host and hostess alone. Cecil's first act was to unclasp the diamonds, and offer to restore them to the giver, saying gratefully, yet with gravity, "I thank you for your generous thought of me, and have tried to do honor to your gift, but please take them back now, they are too costly ornaments for me."

"Too heavy chains, you mean," and with a sudden gesture, he sent the glittering handful to the ground, adding, in a tone that made her start, "Did you bring that boy here?"

"Do you mean the gallant Sir Walter?"

"I mean Alfred Norton."

"No, I did not ask him."

"You knew he was coming?"

"I only hoped so."

The dark veins rose on Yorke's forehead, he locked his hands tightly together behind him, and fixed on her a look that she never could forget, as he said slowly, as if every word was wrung from him, "You must see him no more. I warn you, harm will come of it if you persist."

A smile broke over her face, and with a shrug of her white shoulders, and an accent of merry malice that almost drove him frantic, she answered nonchalantly, "Why mind him more than poor Germain? If he comes, I cannot shun him, unless my lord and master has turned jealous, and forbids it; does he?"

"Yes."

Yorke left the room, as he uttered the one word that was both an answer and a confession; had he looked backward, he would have seen Cecil down upon her knees gathering up the scattered diamonds, with that inexplicable smile quenched in tears, and on her face that tender expression he so longed to see.

♣ *Chapter IX* ♣

ON THE RACK

THE house was not astir till very late next day, for master and mistress breakfasted in their own rooms at noon, and seemed in no haste to meet. A more miserable man than Yorke the sun did not shine on. Oppressed with remorse for last night's violence, shame at last night's betrayal of jealousy, and bitter sorrow for last night's defeat, he longed yet dreaded to see Cecil, feeling that all hope of winning her heart was lost, and nothing but the resignation of despair remained for him.

Fearing that Alfred might venture back, he haunted house and garden like a restless ghost, despising himself the while, yet utterly unable to resist the power that controlled him. No one came, however; not even Germain, and the afternoon was half over before Cecil appeared. He knew the instant she left her room, for not a sound escaped him; he saw her come down into her boudoir looking so fresh and fair he found it hard to feign unconsciousness of her presence, till he was composed enough to meet her as he would. The windows of her room opened on the shady terrace where he had been walking for an hour. After passing and repassing several times, in hopes that she would speak to him, he pulled his hat low over his brows, and looking in, bade her "Good morning." She answered with unusual animation, but her eye did not meet his, and she bent assiduously over her work as if to hide her varying color. Yorke was quick to see these signs of disquiet, but the thought of Alfred made him interpret them in his own way, and find fresh cause of suffering in them.

Both seemed glad to ignore last night, for neither spoke of it, though conversation flagged, and long pauses were frequent, till Yorke, in sheer desperation, took up a book, offering to read aloud to her. She thanked him, and leaning on the window ledge he opened at random and began to read. Of late, poems and romances had found their way into the house, apparently introduced by Germain, and to her surprise Yorke allowed Cecil to read them, which she did with diligence, but no visible effect as yet. In five minutes Yorke wished she had refused his offer, for the lines he had unwittingly chosen were of the tenderest sort, and he found it very hard to read the tuneful raptures of a happy lover, when his own heart was heaviest. He hurried through it as best he could, and not till the closing line was safely delivered did he venture to look at Cecil. For the first time she seemed affected by the magic of poetry; her hands lay idle, her head was averted, and her quickened breath stirred the long curls that half hid her face.

"She thinks of Alfred," groaned Yorke, within himself, and throwing down the book, he abruptly left her for another aimless saunter through the garden and the grove. He did not trust himself near her again, but lying in the grass where he could see her window, he watched her unobserved. Still seated at her embroidery frame, she worked at intervals, but often dropped her needle to look out as if longing for someone who did not come. "She waits for Alfred," sighed Yorke, and laying his head down on his arm, he fell to imagining how different all might have been had he not marred his own happiness by blindly trying to atone for one wrong with another. The air was sultry, the soft chirp of insects very soothing; the weariness of a wakeful night weighed down his eyelids, and before he was aware of its approach, a deep sleep fell upon him, bringing happier dreams to comfort him than any his waking thoughts could fashion.

A peal of thunder startled him wide awake, and glancing at his watch, he found he had lost an hour. Springing up, he went to look for Cecil, as he no longer saw her at her window. But nowhere did he find her, and after a vain search he returned to the boudoir, thinking some clue to her whereabouts might be discovered there. He did discover a clue, but one that drove him half mad with suspense and fear. Turning over the papers on her writing table, hoping to find some little message such as she often left for him, he came upon a card bearing Alfred's name, and below it a single line in French.

"At five, on the beach. Do not fail."

Yorke's face was terrible as he read the words that to his eyes seemed a sentence of lifelong desolation, for, glancing despairingly about the room, he saw that Cecil's hat was gone, and understood her absence now. A moment he stood staring at the line like one suddenly gone blind; then all the pain and passion passed into an unnatural calmness as he thrust the card into his pocket and rang like a man who has work to do that will not brook delay.

"Where is Mrs. Yorke?" was the brief question that greeted Anthony when he appeared.

"Gone to the beach, I think, sir."

"How long ago?"

"Nearly an hour, I should say. It was half past four when I came home; she was here then, for I gave her the note; but she went out soon after, and now it's half past five."

"What note was that?"

"An answer to one I carried to the hotel, sir."

"To Mr. Alfred, was it not?"

"Yes, sir."

"Did you see him, Anthony?"

"Gave it into his own hand, sir, as Mistress bade me, for it was important, she said."

"Very important! He answered it, you say?"

"Yes, sir. I met him on the lawn, and when he'd read the note, he just wrote something outlandish on his card and told me to hurry back. Is anything wrong, master?"

"Mrs. Yorke has gone boating with him, I believe, and I am anxious about her, for a storm is blowing up and Mr. Alfred is no sailor. Are you sure she went that way?"

"Very sure, sir; she had her boat cloak with her, and went down the beach path. I thought she spoke to you lying under the pine, but I suppose you were asleep, so she didn't wake you."

"She stopped, did she?"

"Yes, sir, several minutes, and stooped down as if speaking to you."

"You were watching her, it seems. Why was that?"

"Beg pardon, sir, but I couldn't help it; she looked so gay and pretty it did my old eyes good to look at her."

"You may go."

The instant he was alone, Yorke caught up a delicate lace handkerchief that lay on a chair, and calling Judas, showed it to him with a commanding "Find her." The dog eyed his master intelligently, smelled the bit of cambric, and with nose to the ground, dashed out of the house, while Yorke followed, wearing the vigilant, restless look of an Indian on the war trail. Under the pine Judas paused, snuffed here and there, hurried down the path, and set off across the beach, till coming to a little cove, he seemed at fault, ran to and fro a minute, then turned his face seaward and gave a long howl as if disappointed that he could not follow his mistress by water as by land. Yorke came up breathless, looked keenly all about him, and discovered several proofs of the dog's sagacity. Cecil's veil lay on a rocky seat, large and small footprints were visible in the damp sand, and a boat had been lately drawn up in the cove, for the receding tide had not washed the mark of the keel away.

"She could not be so treacherous—she has gone with Germain—I will not doubt her yet." But as the just and generous emotion rose, his eye fell on an object which plainly proved that Alfred *had* been there. A gold sleeve button lay shining at his feet; he seized it, saw the initials *A. N.* upon it, and doubted no longer, as the hand that held it closed with a gesture full of ominous significance, and turning sharply, he went back more rapidly than he came. Straight home he hurried, and calling Anthony, alarmed the old man as much by his appearance as by the singular orders he gave.

"If Germain comes, tell him to wait here for me; if young Norton comes, do not admit him; if Mrs. Yorke comes, put a light in the little turret window. I am going to look for her, and shall not return till I find her, unless the light recalls me."

"Lord bless us, sir! If you're scared about Mistress, let someone go with you. I'll be ready in a jiffy."

"No; I shall go alone. Get me the key of the boathouse, and do as I tell you."

"But, master, they'll put in somewhere when they see the squall coming on. Better send down to the hotel, or ride round to the Point. It's going to be a wild night, and you don't look fit to face it."

But Yorke was deaf to warnings or suggestions, and hastily preparing himself for the expedition, he repeated his orders, and left Anthony shaking his head over "Master's recklessness."

As he unmoored the boat, Judas leaped in, and standing in the bow, looked into the dim distance with an alert, intent expression, as if he shared the excitement of his companion. Up went the sail, and away flew the *Sea Gull,* leaving a track of foam behind, and carrying with it a heart more unquiet than stormy sea or sky. Across the bay skimmed the boat, and landing on the now deserted beach, Yorke went up to the hotel, so calm externally that few would have suspected the fire that raged within.

"Is young Norton here?" he asked of a clerk lounging in the office.

"Left this afternoon, sir."

"Rather sudden, wasn't it? Are you sure he's gone?"

"Don't know about the suddenness, Mr. Yorke, but I do know that he paid his bill, sent his baggage by the four-thirty train, and said he should follow in the next."

"Did he say anything about coming over to the Cliffs? I expected him today."

"I heard nothing of it, and the last I saw of him he was going toward the beach to bid the ladies good-bye, I supposed."

"Thank you, Gay. I had a message for him, but I can send it by mail." And Yorke sauntered away as if his disappointment was a very trifing one. But the instant he was out of sight his pace quickened to a stride, and he made straight for the depot, cursing his ill-timed sleep as he went. Another official was soon found and questioned, but no young gentleman answering to Alfred's description had purchased a ticket; of this the man was quite sure, as very few persons had left by either of the last trains.

"Well planned for so young a head, but Judas and his master will outwit him yet," muttered Yorke between his teeth, concentrating all his wrath on Alfred, for he dared not think of Cecil.

Stopping at Germain's lodging, he was told that his friend had gone to town at noon, and had not yet returned. This intelligence settled one point in his mind and confirmed his worst fear. Regardless of the gathering storm, he put off again, shaping his course for the city, led by a conviction that the lovers would endeavor to conceal themselves there for a time at least. A strange pair of voyagers went scudding down the harbor that afternoon: the great black hound, erect and motionless at the bow, though the spray dashed over him, and the boat dipped and bounded as it drove before the wind; the man erect and motionless at the helm, one hand on the rudder and one on the sail, his mouth grimly set, and his fiery eye fixed on the desired haven with an expression which proved that an indomitable will defied both danger and defeat. Craft of all sorts were hurrying into port, and more than one belated pleasure boat crossed Yorke's track. The occupants of each were scanned with a scrutinizing glance, and once or twice he shouted an inquiry as they passed. But in none appeared the faces he sought, no answer brought either contradiction or confirmation of his fear, and no backward look showed him the welcome light burning in the little turret window. Coming at last to the wharf where they always landed, he questioned the waterman to whose care he gave his boat.

"Aye, aye, sir; this squall line sent more than one philandering young couple home in a hurry. The last came in twenty minutes ago, just in time to save the crew from more water than they bargained for."

"Did you observe them? Was the lady beautiful? The gentleman young? Did you catch the name of either? Where—"

"Drop anchor there, sir, till I overhaul the first cargo of questions," broke in the man, for Yorke was hurrying one inquiry upon the heels of another without waiting for an answer to any. "Did I observe 'em? No, I didn't, particularly. Was the lady pretty? Don't know; she was wrapped up and scared. Was the gentleman young? Not more than three-and-twenty, I should say. Did I catch their names? Not a name, being busy with the boats."

"Did they seem fond of one another? Were they in a hurry? Which way did they go?"

"Uncommon fond, and in a devil of a hurry. Which way they went I can't tell; it was no business of mine, so I didn't look. Anything more, sir?" said the man good-humoredly.

"Yes; take this for your trouble, and show me the boat they came in."

"Thanky, sir; that's it over yonder. The lad must have been half-seas over with love or liquor, to bring his sweetheart all the way from the Point in a cockleshell like that."

"From the Point? It is a hotel boat, then?"

"Aye, sir; I know 'em all, and the *Water Witch* is the worst of the lot, but her smart rigging gives her a rakish look to them that don't know a mud scow from a wherry."

"Did the young man give you any orders about the boat?"

"Only to keep her till she was called for."

"And you have no idea which way they went?"

"No, sir; they steered straight ahead as far as the corners, but what course they took then I can't say."

Yorke was gone before the man had finished his sentence, and with Judas at his heels, turned toward his old home, feeling little doubt but he should find the fugitives at Mrs. Norton's close by; for though she was absent for the summer, her house was accessible to her son. Admitting himself without noise, he searched his own premises, and from the garden reconnoitered the adjoining ones. Every window was closely shuttered; no light anywhere appeared, and the house was evidently unoccupied. Hester, when called, had heard and seen nothing of Mr. Alfred for months, and was much surprised at her master's sudden appearance, though he fabricated a plausible excuse for it. Out he went again into the storm that now raged furiously, and for several hours searched every place where there was the least possibility of finding those he sought. He looked also for Germain, hoping he might lend some help; but he was in none of his usual haunts, and no clue to the lost wife was found.

Drenched, despairing, and exhausted with his fruitless quest, he stepped into a lighted doorway for shelter, while he took a moment's thought what course to pursue next. As he stood there, Ascot, the young artist, came from the billiard room within; he had been Yorke's guest the night before, and recognizing his host in the haggard, weatherbeaten man standing in the light, he greeted him gaily.

"Good evening, ancient mariner; you look as if your last voyage had not been a prosperous one. I can sympathize with you, for thanks to that confounded *Water Witch,* we nearly went to the bottom in the squall this afternoon."

"The *Water Witch?*" cried Yorke, checking himself in the act of abruptly quitting Ascot, whose gaiety was unbearable just then.

"Yes, I warn you against her. We came over from the Point in her, and had a narrow escape of being made 'demd, damp, moist, unpleasant bodies,' as Manteline says."

"This afternoon, Ascot? At what time?"

"Between five and six."

"Did you leave the boat at the lower wharf where we usually land?"

"Yes; and there she may stay till doomsday, though we ought to be grateful to her, after all."

"We? Then you were not alone?"

"No, my Grace was with me—" There Ascot stopped, looking half embarrassed, half relieved, but added, with a frank laugh, "I never could keep a secret, and as I have betrayed myself, I may as well confess that I took advantage of the storm and danger to make myself a very happy man. Give me joy, Yorke; Grace Coventry is mine."

"Joy! Your torment has but just begun," with which gloomy answer Yorke left the astonished young gentleman to console himself with love dreams and a cigar.

"Have I lost my senses as well as my heart, that I go chasing shadows, and deluding myself with jealous fears and fancies, when perhaps there is no mystery or wrong but what I conjure up?" mused Yorke, as he crossed the deserted park, intent upon a new and hopeful thought. Having made one mistake, he began to believe that he had made another, and wasted time and strength in looking for what never had been lost. Weariness calmed him now, the rain beating on his uncovered head cooled the fever of his blood, and the new hope seemed to brighten as he cherished it.

"I'll go back and wait; perhaps she has already come, or tidings of her. Anything is better than this terrible suspense," he said, and set about executing his design in spite of all obstacles.

It was nearly midnight now, too dark and wild to attempt returning by water, and the last train had left; but only a few miles lay between him and home, and neither weariness nor tempest could deter him. Soon mounted on a powerful horse, he was riding swiftly through the night, recalling legends of the Wild Huntsman to the few belated travelers who saw the dark horseman dash by them, with the dark hound following noiselessly behind. The storm was in accordance with his mood, and he liked it better than a summer night, though the gusts buffeted him and the rain poured down with unabated violence. At the first point where the Cliffs were visible, he reined up and strained his eyes to catch a glimpse of the light that should assure him of Cecil's safety. But a thick mist obscured land and sea, and no cheering ray could pierce the darkness. A mile nearer his eye was gladdened by the sight of a pale gleam high above the lower lights that glimmered along the shore. Brighter and brighter it grew as he approached, and soon, with a thrill of joy that made his heart leap, he saw that it shone clear and strong from the little turret window. An irrepressible shout broke from his lips as he galloped up the steep road, leaped the gate, and burst into the hall before man or maid could open for him.

"Where is she?" he cried, in a voice that would have assured the wanderer of a tender welcome had she been there to hear and answer it.

Anthony started from a restless doze in his chair, and shook his gray head as he eyed his master pitifully.

"She ain't here, sir, but we've had news of her; so I lit the lamp to bring you home."

Yorke dropped into a seat as if he had been shot, for with the loss of his one hope, all strength seemed to desert him, and he could only look at Anthony with such imploring yet despairing eyes that the old man's hard face began to work as he said below his breath, "After you'd gone, sir, I went down to the Point and stayed round there till dark. Just as I was coming away, old Joe came in bringing a sail he'd picked up halfway down the harbor. There were several of us standing about the pier, and naturally we asked questions. Then it come out from one and another that the sail belonged to the boat Mr. Alfred took this afternoon. He left there alone, but one of the men saw him with a lady afterward, and by his description I knew it was Mistress."

Yorke covered up his face as if he knew what was coming and had not courage to meet it; but soon he said, brokenly, "Go on," and Anthony obeyed.

"The man wasn't quite sure about Mr. Alfred, as he don't know him, and didn't mind him much; but he was sure of Mistress, and could swear to the boat and sail, for he helped rig it, and his sweetheart made the streamer. I'd like to think he was wrong, but as Mr. Alfred hired the boat, and the dear lady was seen in it, I'm awfully afraid they were wrecked in the squall."

How still the house seemed as the words dropped slowly from Anthony's lips. Nothing stirred but poor Judas panting on his mat, and nothing broke the silence but the soft tick of a clock and the sobbing of the wind without. Yorke had laid down his head as if he never cared to lift it up again, and sat motionless in an attitude of utter despair, while the old servant stood respectfully silent, with tears rolling down his withered cheeks, for his gentle mistress had won his heart, and he mourned for her as for a child of his own.

Suddenly Yorke looked up and spoke.

"Have you sent anyone to look for them?"

"Yes, master, long ago, and—"

"What is it? You keep something back. Out with it, man; I can bear anything but suspense."

"They found the boat, and it was empty, master."

"Where was it? Tell me all, Anthony."

"Just outside the little bay, where the gale would blow hardest and the tide run strongest. The mast was broken short off, the boat half full of water, and one broken oar still hung in the rowlock, but there was no signs of anyone except this."

Turning his face away, Anthony offered a little silken scarf, wet, torn, and stained, but too familiar to be mistaken. Yorke took it, looked at it with eyes out of which light and life seemed to have died, then put it in his breast, and turning to the faithful hound, said in a tone the more pathetic for its calmness: "Come, Judas; we went together to look for her alive, now let us go together and look for her dead."

Before Anthony could detain him he had flung himself into the saddle and was gone. All that night he haunted the shores, looking long after others had relinquished the vain search, and morning found him back in the city, inquiring along the wharves for tidings of the lost.

Taking his own boat, he turned homeward at last, feeling that he could do no more, for the reaction had begun, and he was utterly spent. The storm had passed, and dawn was breaking beautifully in the east; the sea was calm, the sky cloudless; the wind blew balmily, and the sea gull floated along a path of gold as the sun sent its first shaft of light over the blue waste. A strange sense of peace came to the lonely man after that wild night of tempest and despair. The thought of Cecil quiet underneath the sea was more bearable than the thought of Cecil happy with another, for in spite of repentance and remorse, he could not accept his punishment from Alfred's hand, and clung to the belief that she was dead, trying to find some poor consolation for his loss in the thought that life was made desolate by death, not by treachery. So sailing slowly through the rosy splendor of a summer dawn, he came among the cluster of small islands that lay midway between the city and the little bay. Some were green and fair, some were piles of barren rocks; none were inhabited, but on one still stood a rude hut, used as a temporary shelter for pleasure parties or such fishermen as frequented the neighborhood. Yorke saw nothing of the beauty all about him; his eyes were fixed upon the white villa that once was home; his mind was busy with memories of the past, and he was conscious of nothing but the love that had gone down into that shining sea. Judas was more alert, for, though sitting with his head on his master's knee, as if trying to comfort him by demonstrations of mute affection, he caught sight of a little white flag fluttering from the low roof of the hut, and leaped up with a bound that nearly took him overboard. The motion roused Yorke, and following the direction of the dog's keen eye, he saw the signal—saw, also, a woman wrapped in a dark cloak sitting in the doorway, with her head upon her knees, as if asleep.

In an instant both dog and man were trembling with excitement, for there was something strangely familiar about the cloak, the bent head with its falling hair, the slender hands folded one upon another. Like one inspired with sudden life, Yorke plied his oars with such energy that a few vigorous strokes sent the boat high upon the pebbly shore, and leaping up the bank, while Judas followed baying with delight, he saw the figure start to its feet, and found himself face to face with Cecil.

≥ *Chapter X* ≤

AT LAST

WHILE Yorke slept, on the previous afternoon, Cecil met Alfred on the beach, talked with him for half an hour, and when he left her, hastily, she stood waving her hand till he was out of sight; then she looked about her, as if in search of someone, and her face brightened as she saw Germain approaching.

"I am glad you are come," she said, "for I was just trying to find a man to take this boat home, and here I find a gentleman. Alfred came in it, but delayed so long that he had only time to run across the cliffs and catch the train. Will you ferry me over to the Point, and add another favor to the many I already owe you?"

"Nothing would please me better, but instead of landing so soon, let me take you down below the lighthouse, as I promised you I would. This will be my only opportunity, for I go away tomorrow, and you know you said I should have one more happy day."

"Did Bazil tell you that?" asked Cecil, looking disturbed, as his words recalled last night's adventure.

"No, but I am well aware that I trouble you—that you wish me gone, and I shall obey; but give me this last pleasure, for I may never come again."

The smile he gave her was both melancholy and submissive; she longed to bid him stay but dared not, yet remembering Bazil's wish that she should bear with him a little longer, she was glad to grant it, for she felt her power over this man, and feared nothing for herself. A moment's hesitation, then she went toward the boat, saying, in her friendliest tone, "I trust you, and you shall have your pleasure; but, believe me, if I wish you gone it is for your own sake, not mine."

"I know it—I am grateful for your pity, and I will not disturb your confidence by any violence. Indeed, I think I'm done with my old self, and grow quieter as the end approaches."

Cecil doubted that, as she remembered the scene before the fountain, but Germain was certainly his gentlest self now, and as they sailed across the bay before the freshening wind she found the hour full of real rest and enjoyment despite her care. Absorbed in animated conversation, and unconscious of the lapse of time, they glided past the Point, the pleasant islands, the city with its cloud of smoke, the lighthouse on its lonely rock, and were floating far down the harbor, when the growling of distant thunder recalled them from the delights of a musical discussion to the dangers of an impending storm. A bank of black clouds was piled up in the west, the wind came in strong gusts, the waves rolled in long swells, and sea and sky portended a summer squall.

"How careless I have been," exclaimed Germain, looking anxiously about him. "But I fancy we need fear nothing except a drenching, for it will take some time to return in the teeth of this gale. Wrap your cloak about you, and enjoy the fine sight, while I do my best to atone for my forgetfulness."

Cecil had no fear, for Germain was a skillful boatman, and she loved to watch the grand effects of light and shade as the thunderous clouds swept across the sky, blotting out the blue and making the water somber with their shadows. An occasional flash seemed to rend the dark wall, but no rain fell, and by frequent tacking Germain was rapidly decreasing the distance between them and home. Safely past the city they went, for Cecil would not land there lest Yorke should be alarmed at her long absence, and as the storm still delayed, she hoped to reach shelter before it broke.

"Once past the islands and we are quite safe, for the little bay is quiet, and we can land at any point if the rain begins. A few minutes more of this rough work, and we can laugh at the gale. Bend your head, please, I must tack again else—"

The rest of the sentence was lost in a crash of thunder like the report of cannon, as a fierce gust swept down upon them, snapping the slender mast like a bulrush, and carrying Germain overboard wrapped in the falling sail. With a cry of horror Cecil sprang up, eager yet impotent to save either herself or him; but in a moment he appeared, swimming strongly, cleared away the wreck of the sail, righted the boat, and climbed in, dripping but unhurt.

"Only another of my narrow escapes. I'm surely born to die quietly in my bed, for nothing kills me," he said coolly, as he brushed the wet hair from his eyes and took breath.

"Thank heaven! You are safe. Land anywhere, for now the sail is gone we must not think of reaching home," cried Cecil, looking about her for the nearest shore.

"We will make for the lower island; the storm will not last long, and we can find shelter there. Unfortunate that I am, to make my last day one of danger and discomfort for you."

"I like it, and shall enjoy relating my adventures when we are at home. Let me row, it is too violent exercise for you," she said, as he drew out the oars and took off his coat.

"It will not hurt me—or if it does what matter? I would gladly give my life to see you safe."

"No, no, you must not do it. Let the boat drift, or give me an oar; I am strong; I fear nothing; let me help you, Germain."

"Take the rudder then and steer for the island; that will help me, and the sight of you will give me strength for a short tussle with the elements."

Cecil changed her seat, and with her hand upon the helm, her steady eyes upon the green spot before them, sat smiling at the storm, so fair and fearless that the sight would have put power into any arm, courage into any heart. For a time it seemed to inspire Germain, and he pulled stoutly against wind and tide; but soon, to his dismay, he felt his strength deserting him, each stroke cost a greater effort, each heartbeat was a pang of pain. Cecil watched the drops gather on his forehead, heard his labored breathing, and saw him loosen the ribbon at his throat, and more than once dash water over his face, alternately deeply flushed and deadly pale. Again and again she implored him to desist, to let her take his place, or trust to chance for help, rather than harm himself by such dangerous exertion. But to all entreaties, suggestions, and commands, he answered with a gentle but inflexible denial, an utter disregard of self, and looks of silent love that Cecil never could forget.

The rain fell now in torrents, the gale steadily increased, and the waves were white with foam as they dashed high against the rocky shore of the island which the little boat was struggling to reach. Nearer and nearer it crept, as Germain urged it on with the strength of desperation, till, taking advantage of a coming billow, they were carried up and left upon the sand, with a violence that nearly threw them on their faces. Cecil sprang out at once; Germain leaned over the broken oars panting heavily, as if conscious of nothing but the suffering that racked him.

Her voice roused him, but only to fresh exertion, for seizing her hand he staggered up the bank, flung open the door of the hut, and dropped down at her feet as if in truth he had given his life to save her. For a moment she was in despair; she ran out into the storm, called, waved her handkerchief, and looked far and near, hoping some passing boat might bring help. But nothing human was in sight; the nearest point of land was inaccessible, for an ebbing wave had washed the boat away, and she was utterly alone with the unconscious man upon the barren island. She had a brave spirit, a quick wit, and these were her supporters now, as, forgetting her own fears, she devoted herself to her suffering comrade. Fortunately, her vinaigrette was in her pocket, and water plentiful; using these simple remedies with skill, the deathlike swoon yielded at last, and Germain revived.

With the return of consciousness he seemed to remember her situation before his own, and exert himself to lighten its discomforts by feeble efforts to resume his place as protector. As soon as he had breath enough to speak, he whispered, with a reassuring glance, "Do not be afraid, I will take care of you. The pain has gone for this time, and I shall be better soon."

"Think of yourself, not me. If I only had a fire to dry and warm you I should be quite happy and content," answered Cecil, looking round the gloomy place that darkened momentarily.

With the courtesy as native to him as his impetuosity, Germain tried to rise as he took out a little case and pointed toward a corner of the hut.

"You need fire more than I; here are matches, there is wood; help me a little and you shall be 'quite happy and content.'"

But as he spoke the case dropped from his hand, and he fell back with a sharp pang that warned him to submit.

"Lie still and let me care for you; I like to do it, and the exercise will keep me warm. Here is wood enough to last all night, and with light and heat we shall be very comfortable till morning and help comes."

With the heartiness of a true woman when compassion stirs her, Cecil fell to work, and soon the dark hut glowed with a cheery blaze, the wooden shutter was closed, excluding wind and rain, the straw scattered here and there was gathered into a bed for Germain, and with her cloak over him, he lay regarding her with an expression that both touched and troubled her, so humble, grateful, and tender was it. When all was done, she stepped to the door, thinking she heard the sound of passing oars; nothing appeared, however, but as she listened on the threshold Germain's voice called her with an accent of the intensest longing.

"Do not leave me! Come back to me, my darling, and let nothing part us anymore."

She thought he was wandering, and gave no answer but a soothing "Hush, rest now, poor Germain."

"Never that again; call me Father, and let me die happy in my daughter's arms."

"Father?" echoed Cecil, as a thrill of wonder, joy, and blind belief shook her from head to foot.

"Yes, I may claim you at last, for I am dying. Let our heart speak; come to me, my little Cecil, for as God lives I am your father."

He struggled up, spread wide his arms, and called her in a tone of tenderness that would have carried conviction to the most careless listener. Cecil's heart did speak; instinct was quicker than memory or reason. In an instant she understood the attraction that led her to him, owned the tender tie that bound them, and was gathered to her father's bosom, untroubled by a doubt or fear. For a time there were only broken exclamations, happy tears, and demonstrations of delight, as father and daughter forgot everything but the reunion that gave them back to one another. Soon Cecil calmed herself for his sake, made him lie down again, and while she dried his hair and warmed his cold hands in her own, she began to question eagerly.

"Why was I never told of this before?" she sorrowfully said, regretting the long years of ignorance that had deferred the happiness which made that hour so bright, in spite of darkness and danger.

"My life depended upon secrecy, and this knowledge would have been no joy, but a shame and sorrow to you, my poor child."

"Mamma always told me that you died when I was a baby; did she believe it?"

"No, she knew I was alive, but in one sense I did die to her, and all the world, for a convict has no country, home, or friends."

"A convict!" And Cecil shrank involuntarily.

He saw it, but clung to her, saying imploringly, "Hear me before you cast me off. Try to pity and forgive me, for with all his sins your father loves you better than his life."

"I do not cast you off—I will love, pity, and forgive; believe this, and trust your daughter, now that she is yours again."

Cecil spoke tenderly, and tried to reassure him with every affectionate demonstration she could devise, for the one word "father" had unlocked her heart, and all its pent-up passion flowed freely now that a natural vent was found. Lying with her hand in his, August Stein told the story of the past, and Cecil learned the secret of her father's and her husband's life.

"Dear, nineteen years ago Bazil and your mother were betrothed. The gifted young man was a fit mate for the beautiful girl, and but for me they might have been a happy pair this day. In an evil hour I saw her, loved her, and resolved to win her in spite of every obstacle, for my passions ruled me, and opposition only made me the more resolute and reckless. I used every art to dazzle, captivate, and win her, even against her will, and I succeeded; but the brief infatuation was not love, and though she fled with me, she soon discovered that her heart still clung to Bazil. Well it might, for though we had wronged him deeply he took no revenge, and would have helped us in our sorest strait. We were not happy, for I led a wild life, and your mother longed for home. Her father disowned her, when our secret marriage was discovered, her friends deserted her, and for a year we wandered from place to place, growing poorer and more wretched as hope after hope failed. I had squandered my own fortune, and had no means of earning a livelihood except my voice. That had won me my wife, and I tried to sing my way to competence for her sake. To do this, I was obliged to leave her; I always did so reluctantly, for the birth of my little daughter made the mother dearer than before. Cecil, always remember that I loved you both with all the fervor of an undisciplined nature, and let that fact lighten your condemnation of what follows."

"I shall remember, Father."

"Coming home unexpectedly one day, I found Bazil there. He had discovered us and, seeing our poverty, generously offered help. I should have thanked and honored him for that, but knowing that he did it for Cecilia's sake I hated and distrusted him, refused his kindness, and forbade him the house. He bore with me, promised your mother that he would befriend her, and went away, hoping I would relent when I was calmer. His nobleness made my own conduct seem more base; the knowledge that my wife reproached me for destroying her happiness wounded me deeply; and the thought that Bazil saw my failure and pitied me rankled in my heart and made me miserable. I had been brooding darkly over these things as I returned from my distasteful work a night or two later, and was in a desperate mood. As I entered quietly, I saw a man bending over the cradle where my baby lay; I thought it was Bazil, my wrath rose hot against him, some devil goaded me to it, and I felled him with a single blow. But when the light shone on his dead face I saw that it was not Bazil but the young surgeon who had saved both wife and child for me."

There was a long pause, broken only by Stein's fluttering breath and Cecil's whisper.

"Do not go on; be quiet and forget."

"I cannot forget or be quiet till I tell you everything. I was tried, sentenced to imprisonment for life, and for ten years was as dead to the world as if I had lain in my grave. I raged and pined like a savage creature in my prison, made many desperate attempts to escape, and at last succeeded. I left Australia, and after wandering east and west, a homeless vagabond for two weary years, I ventured back to England, hoping to learn something of my wife, as no tidings of her had reached me all those years. I could not find her, and dared not openly inquire; Yorke tells me she concealed herself from everyone, accepted nothing even from him, but devoted herself to you, and waited patiently till it pleased heaven to release her."

"Poor Mamma! Now I know how heavy her burden must have been, and why she longed to lay it down."

"Child, she did not find it half so heavy as I found mine, nor long to lay it down as bitterly as I have longed for eighteen years. If she had loved me it would have saved us both, for affection can win and hold me as nothing else has power to do. It has done much for me already, because, since I knew you, my darling, I have learned to repent and, for your sake, to atone, as far as may be, for my wasted life."

"It is very sweet to hear you say that, Father, and to feel that I have helped you, even unconsciously. Now leave the sorrowful past, and tell me how you found Bazil and myself."

"Growing bold, after two years of safety, I ventured to inquire for Yorke, thinking that he could tell me something of your mother. He had left Germany, where we first met, and had gone home to America. I followed, and found him leading the solitary life you know so well. He was so changed I hardly recognized him; I was still more altered, and trusting to the disguise which had baffled keener eyes than his, I offered myself as a model, feeling curiously drawn to him as the one link between Cecilia and myself. He accepted my services, and paid me well, for I was very poor; he pitied me, knowing only that I was a lonely creature like himself, and so generously befriended me that I could not harden my heart against him; but overpowered by remorse and gratitude I betrayed myself, and put my life into his hands, only asking to see or hear of my wife. He knew nothing of her then, but with a magnanimity that bound me to him forever, he kept my secret, and endeavored to forgive the wrong which he never could entirely forget."

"O Bazil, so generous, so gentle, why did I not know this sooner, and thank you as I ought?"

The tender words were drowned in sudden tears, as Cecil hid her face, weeping with mingled self-reproach and joy over each revelation that showed her something more to love and honor in her husband. But she soon dried her tears to listen, for her father hurried on as if anxious to be done.

"I saw you, my child, the night you came, and was sure you were mine, you were so like your mother. I implored Bazil to let me have you, when I knew that she was gone, but he would not, having promised to guard you from me, and never let your life be saddened by the knowledge of your convict father. He has kept that promise sacredly, and bound me to an equal silence, under penalty of betrayal if I break it, except as I do now, when I have nothing more to fear. He let me see you secretly, when you slept, or walked, or were busy at your work, for he had not the heart to deny me that. Ah, Cecil, you never knew how near I often was to you—never guessed what right I had to love you, or how much I longed to tell you who I was. More than once I forgot myself, and would have broken my word at any cost, but something always checked me in time, and Bazil's patience was long-suffering. The night he let me see and sing to you did me more good than years of prison life, for you unconsciously touched all that was best in me, and by the innocent affection that you could not control made that hour more beautiful and precious than I can tell you. Since then, whether near or absent, gloomy or gay, I have regarded you as my saving angel, and tried in my poor way to be more worthy of you, and earn a place in your memory when I am gone."

Such love and gratitude shone in his altered face that Cecil could only lay her head upon his shoulder, praying that he might be spared for a longer, better life, and a calmer death at last. Soon her father spoke again, smiling the old sweet smile, as he caressed the beautiful head that leaned against him as if its place were there.

"Did my little girl think me a desperate lover, with my strange devices to attract and win her? Bazil told me that I frightened you, and I tried to control myself; but it was so hard to stand aside and see my own child pass me like a stranger, that I continually forgot your ignorance and betrayed how dear you were to me. What did you think of that mysterious Germain?"

"What could I think but that he loved me? How could I dream that you were my father when all my life I had believed you dead? Even now I almost doubt it, you are so young, so charming and lighthearted when you please."

"I am past forty, Cecil, and what I am is only the shadow of what I was, a man endowed with many good gifts; but all have been wasted or misused, owing to a neglected education, a wayward will, an impetuous nature, and a sanguine spirit, which has outlived disgrace and desolation, suffering and time."

"And this is the mystery that has perplexed me for so long. I think you might have told me as well as Bazil, and let me do my part to make you happy, Father."

"I longed to do so, and assured him that we might trust you; but he would not break his promise to your mother. It was wise, though very hard to bear. I was not a fit guardian for a beautiful young girl like mine, and I knew it, yet I wanted you, and made his life a burden to him by my importunity. Love him, Cecil, love him faithfully, for he has spared you much sorrow, and through you has saved your father."

She did not answer, but looking into her face, he was satisfied. Thus opening their hearts to one another, the night wore on, yet neither found it long, and when at last Stein slept, exhausted, Cecil sat beside him, thinking happy thoughts, while the wind raved without, the rain beat on the low roof, the sea thundered round the island, and Yorke went searching for her far and wide.

Morning dawned at last, and as her father still slept, she opened the little window, that the balmy air might refresh him, put up her signal of distress, and sat down to watch and wait. The sound of hurrying feet roused her from her reverie, and looking up, she saw her husband coming toward her, so changed and haggard that her joy turned to fear. Dreading to excite her father, she instantly glanced over her shoulder, and barred the entrance with her extended arm. Her gesture, her expression, instantly arrested Yorke, and while Judas fawned delightedly about her feet, he stood apart, with the sad certainty that she was not alone, to mar his joy at finding her.

"Is he there?" was his first question, sternly put.

"Yes; he is ill and sleeping; you must not disturb him. Blame me if you will, but he shall be left in peace."

She spoke resolutely, and closed the door between them and the sleeper, keeping her place upon the threshold, as if ready to defend him, for Yorke's manner alarmed her even more than his wild appearance. The action seemed to affect him like an insult; he seized her arm, and holding it in a painful grasp, eyed her almost fiercely, as he said, with a glance that made her tremble, "Then you did leave me sleeping, and go away with this man, to be wrecked here, and so be discovered?"

"Yes; why should I deny it?"

"And you love him, Cecil?"

"With all my heart and soul, and you can never part us anymore."

As she answered, with a brave, bright smile, and a glad voice, she felt Yorke quiver as if he had received a blow, saw his face whiten, and heard an accent of despair in his voice, when he said slowly, "You will leave him, if I command it?"

"No—he has borne enough. I can make him happy, and I shall cling to him through everything, for you have no right to take me from him."

"No right?" ejaculated Yorke, loosening his hold, with a bewildered look.

"None that I will submit to, if it parts us. You let me know him, let me learn to love him, and now, when he needs me most, you would take me from him. Bazil, you have been very generous, very kind to both of us, and I am truly grateful, but while he lives, I must stay with him, because I have promised."

He looked at her with a strange expression, at first as if he felt his senses going, then he seemed to find a clue to her persistency. A bitter laugh escaped him, but his voice betrayed wounded pride and poignant sorrow.

"I understand now; you intend to hold me to my bond, and see in me nothing but your guardian. You are as ignorant as headstrong, if you think this possible. I gave up that foolish delusion long ago, and tried to show you a truer, happier tie. But you were blind and would not see, deaf and would not hear, hardhearted and would not relent."

"You bade me be a marble woman, with no heart to love you, only grace and beauty, to please your eye and do you honor. Have I not obeyed you to the letter?"

Coldly and quietly she spoke, yet kept her eyes on the ground, her hand on her breast, as if to hold some rebellious emotion in check. As the soft voice reechoed the words spoken long ago, all that scene came back to Yorke, and made the present moment doubly hard to bear.

"You have, you have! God forgive me for the wrong I did you. I tried to atone for it, but I have failed, and this is my punishment."

He spoke humbly, despairingly, and his proud eyes filled as he turned his face to hide the grief he was ashamed to show. Cecil stood with bent head, and face half hidden by her falling hair, but though she trembled, she compelled voice and features to obey her with the ease which long practice had made second nature.

"If you had cared to teach me a gentler lesson, I would have gladly learned it; but you did not, and having done your best to kill love in my heart, you should not reproach me if you are disappointed now, or wonder that I turn to others for the affection without which none of us can live."

"I will not reproach; I do not wonder, but I cannot give you up. Cecil, there is still time to relent, and to return; let me tell you how hard I have tried to make you love me, in spite of my own decree, and perhaps my patience, my penitence, may touch your heart. I will not urge my right as husband, but plead as lover. Will you listen?"

"Yes."

Cecil stole a glance at him as she spoke, and a curious smile touched her lips, though she listened with beating heart to words poured out with the rapidity of strong emotion.

"When you came to me, I kept you because you were like your mother, whom I loved, and who deserted me. That loss embittered my whole nature, and I resolved to make your life as loveless as my own. It seemed a small atonement for a great wrong, and believing that it was just to visit the sins of the parents upon the children, I carried out my purpose with a blind persistency that looks like madness to me now. But the sentiment I had forsworn revenged itself upon me, and while trying to cheat you of love, it crept into my own heart, and ruled me like a tyrant. Unconsciously, I loved you long before I knew it; that was why I disliked Alfred, why I was so willing to marry you, and why I was so disappointed when others found in you the same want that I felt yet would not own. The night I watched beside you, fearing you would never wake, I found the key to my own actions, saw my delusion, and resolved to conquer it."

He paused for breath, but Cecil did not speak, though the hidden face brightened, and the heart fluttered like a caged bird.

"I could not conquer it, for it was my master. You can never know how hard I tried, how rebellious my pride was, or how firm my purpose, but all failed, and I was forced to own that my happiness, my peace, depended upon you. Then I determined to undo my six years' work, to teach you how to love, and make my wife mine in heart as in name. I gave myself wholly to the task of winning you; I studied your tastes, gratified your whims, and tried every art that can attract a woman. You were tired of the old home, and I gave you a new one; you enjoyed Germain's society, and I let him come, in defiance of my better judgment; you had some pride in my talent, for your sake I displayed it; you loved pleasure, and I labored to supply it freely; I even tried to lure you with splendor and bribe you with diamonds. But I had lost my skill, and all my efforts were in vain, for no veritable marble woman could have received my gifts more coldly, or ignored my unspoken love more utterly than you. One smile like those you daily gave Germain would have repaid me, but you never shed it over me; one frank word or affectionate look would have brought me to your feet; but all the compassion, confidence, and tenderness were given to others—for me you had only indifference, gratitude, and respect. Cecil, I have suffered one long torment since I married you, longing for my true place, yet not daring to claim it, lest I should rouse aversion and not love."

Still with her head bent, her face hidden, and her hand upon her heart, she stood, and Yorke went on, more passionately than before.

"I know that I have forfeited my right to expect affection or demand obedience, but I implore you to forget this infatuation, and retrieve this rash step. You do not know what you are doing, for this will mar your whole life, and make mine worthless. Cecil, come back to me, and let me try again to win you! I will work and wait for years, will be your servant, not your master, will bear and suffer anything if I may hope to touch your heart at last. Is this impossible? Do you love Alfred more than reputation, home, or husband?"

"I never have loved Alfred."

"Then who, in God's name, is this man to whom you will cling through everything?"

"My father."

She looked up now, and turned on him a face so full of hope and joy, that he stood dumb with astonishment as she drew nearer and nearer, with outstretched hands, beaming eyes, and tender voice.

"O Bazil! I know all; the past is forgiven, your long labor and atonement are over, and there is no need for you to work or wait, because my heart always has been yours."

If the dead Cecilia had come to him in the youthful guise she used to wear, it would not have more amazed and startled him than did these words from his wife's lips, and not till he felt her clinging to him so trustfully, so tenderly, did he fully realize his happiness.

"What does it mean? Why keep this from me so long? Did you not see I loved you, Cecil?"

"It means that I, too, tried to conquer myself, and failed. Till very lately, I was not sure you loved me, and I could not bear to be repulsed again."

"Ah, there is the thorn that has vexed you! You are a true woman, in spite of all my training, and you could not forget that hour, so I had to suffer till you were appeased. Is it possible that my innocent, artless girl could lay such plots, and wear a mask so long, that she might subdue her guardian's proud heart?"

"Everything is possible to a woman when she loves, and you were only conquered with your own weapons, Bazil. Let me make my confession now, and you shall see that you have not suffered, worked, and waited all alone. When you bade me renounce love, I found it very hard to kill the affection that had grown warmer than you chose to have it. But I did my best to seem what you desired me to be, and your lessons of self-control stood me in good stead. I chilled and hardened myself rigorously; I forced myself to be meek, cold, and undemonstrative to you, whatever I might be to others; I took opium, that I might forget my pain, and feign the quietude I could not feel, and I succeeded beyond my hopes. When you asked me to marry you, I was half prepared for it, because Alfred insisted that you loved me. I wished to believe it; I wanted to stay, and would have frankly owned how dear you were to me, if you had not insisted upon offering me protection, but no love. That night I resolved to show you your mistake, to prove to you that you had a heart, and teach you a better lesson than any you had taught your pupil."

"You have done so, little dearest, and I am your scholar henceforth. Teach me gently, and I will study all my days. What more, Cecil?"

"I found it very hard to resist when you grew so kind, and should have been sure you loved me, but for Germain. Why you let him come, and showed no displeasure at my delight in his society, was so inexplicable to me that I would not yield till I was satisfied. Last night my father told me all, and if anything could make you dearer, it would be the knowledge of the great debt we owe you. My generous, patient husband, how can I thank you as I ought?"

He showed her how, and for several minutes they stood in the sunshine, very silent, very happy, while the waves broke softly on the shore, as if all storms had passed away forever. Yorke spoke first.

"One thing more, Cecil, lest I forget it, for this sudden happiness has turned my brain, I think, and nothing is clear to me but that you are mine. What does this mean?" And drawing out the card, he held it before her eyes, with some anxiety dimming the brightness of his own.

She took it, tore it up, and as the white shreds went flying away on the wind, she said smiling, "Let all your jealous fears go with them, never to come back again. What a miserable night you must have had, if you believed that I had left you for Alf."

"An awful night, Cecil," and he told her all the wanderings and his fears.

"I will not say that you deserved it for harboring such a thought, because you have suffered enough, and it is so much sweeter to forgive than to reproach. But you must promise never to be jealous anymore, not even of 'poor Alf.'"

The happy-hearted laugh he had so longed to hear gladdened his ear, as she looked up at him with the arch expression that made her charming.

"I'll try," he answered meekly, "but keep him away till I am very sure you love me, else I shall surely fling him into the sea, as I nearly did the night Sir Walter and the marquise tormented me. Why did he come? And why did you meet him yesterday?"

"He came to tell me that he had replaced my image with a more gracious one, for when he heard that I was married, he cast me off, and found consolation in his pretty cousin's smiles. His was a boyish love, ardent but short-lived, and he is happy now, with one who loves him as I never could have loved. Hearing of our masque, he planned to come in disguise, and tell his story as a stranger, that he might the better watch its effect on me. But I knew him instantly, and we enjoyed mystifying those about us, till I forgot him in my own mystification. You did not wish him to come again, so I wrote to him, saying good-bye, and begging him to go at once. The disobedient boy had more to tell me, and sent word he should be on the beach at five. I knew he would come to the house unless I met him, and fearing a scene—for you have grown very tragic, dear—I went. He delayed so long that he had only time to hurry across to the lower depot for the last train, leaving his boat to Father and myself."

"What misery the knowledge of this would have spared me! Why did you not tell me, when we were together yesterday, that Alfred had forgotten you?"

"I meant to do so, but you gave me no opportunity, for you were so restless and strange I was half afraid of you. Besides, since you had confessed jealousy, I hoped you would confess love also, and I waited, thinking it would come."

"How could I own it, when *you* had confessed you loved a younger man than I, and my eyes were blinded by Alfred's silence and your own?"

"I did not tell you that it was my father. Did he betray me?"

She looked perplexed, and Yorke half ashamed, as he confessed another proof of his affection.

"It was I, Cecil, who came to you in the garden, who questioned you, and was stabbed to the heart by your answers. Good heavens, how blind I've been!"

"Never reproach me with treachery, after that. Why did you change dresses? To try me?"

"Yes; and as you sat there so near me, so gentle, frank, and beautiful, I found it almost impossible to sustain my character; but I knew if I revealed myself, you would freeze again, and all the charm be gone. Heaven knows I was a miserable man that night, for you disappointed me, and Alfred drove me half mad; but your father saw my folly, and saved me from myself. God bless him for that!"

"Yes, God bless him for that, and for saving me to be your happy wife. Come now and wake him; he has been very ill, and needs care."

They went, and kneeling by him, Cecil called him gently, but he did not answer; and taking her into his arms, her husband whispered tenderly, "Dear, he will never wake again."

Never again in this world, for the restless heart was still at last, and the sunshine fell upon a face of such reposeful beauty that it was evident the long sleep had painlessly deepened into death.

The Skeleton in the Closet

"LOUIS, to whom does that château belong?" I asked, as we checked our horses under the antique gateway, and my eye, following the sweep of the lawn, caught a glimpse of the mansion embosomed in a blooming paradise of flowers and grand old trees.

"To Mme. Arnheim, the loveliest widow in all France," Louis answered, with a sigh.

"And the cruelest, I fancy, or you would have been master here," I replied, interpreting the sigh aright, for my friend was a frequent captive to the gentle sex.

"Never its master, Gustave—I should always have remained a slave while Mathilde was there," he answered, with a moody glance through the iron gates that seemed to bar him from the heaven of his desire.

"Nay, Louis, come down from the clouds and tell me something of the Circe whose spells have ensnared you; come hither and sit on this little knoll where we have a better view of the château, and while our horses rest, you shall tell the story of your love, as the romances have it." And dismounting as I spoke, I threw myself upon the green sward opposite the flowery lawn that sloped up to the terraces whereon the château stood.

Louis flung himself beside me, saying abruptly, "There is no tale to tell, Gustave. I met Mathilde at the general's a year ago—loved her, of course, and of course without success. I say of course, for I am not the only one that has laid siege to her cold heart, and got frostbitten in the attempt. She is a marble image, beautiful and cold, though there are rare flashes of warmth that win, a softness that enchants, which make her doubly dangerous. She lives yonder with her old duenna, Mlle. D'Aubigny, caring little for the world, and seldom blessing it with her presence. She has made an Eden, but desires no Adam, and is content to dwell year after year solitary in her flowery nook like the English poet's Lady of Shalott."

"And trust me, like that mysterious lady, she, too, will one day see—

> *"A bow-shot from her bower-eaves,*
> *Riding 'mong the barley-sheaves,*
> *The sunlight dazzling thro' the leaves,*
> *And flashing on his greaves*
> *A bold Sir Lancelot.*
> *She'll leave her web, and leave her loom,*
> *She'll make three paces thro' the room,*
> *She'll see the water-lilies bloom,*
> *She'll see the helmet and the plume,*
> *And follow down to Camelot,"*

chanted I, making a free translation of the lines to suit my jest.

"There she is! Look, Gustave, look!" cried Louis, springing to his feet, with an eager gesture toward the lawn.

I looked, almost expecting to behold the shadowy lady of the poet's song, so fully had the beauty of the spot enchanted me. A female figure was passing slowly down the broad steps that led from terrace to terrace into the shaded avenue. Silently I drew Louis into the deep shadow of the gateway, where we could look unperceived.

The slender, white-robed figure came slowly on, pausing now and then to gather a flower, or caress the Italian greyhound tripping daintily beside her. My interest was excited by my friend's words, and I looked eagerly for the beauty he extolled. She *was* beautiful—and when she paused in the shadow of a drooping acacia, and stood looking thoughtfully toward the blue lake shining in the distance, I longed to be an artist, that I might catch and keep the picture.

The sunshine fell upon her through the leaves, turning her hair to gold, touching the soft bloom of her cheek, and rendering more fair the graceful arms half bared by the fresh wind tossing the acacia boughs. A black lace scarf was thrown about her, one end drawn over her blond hair, as the Spanish women wear their veils; a few brilliant flowers filled her hands, and gave coloring to her unornamented dress. But the chief charm of her delicate face was the eyes, so lustrous and dark, so filled with the soft gloom of a patient grief that they touched and won my heart by their mute loveliness.

We stood gazing eagerly, forgetting in our admiration the discourtesy of the act, till a shrill neigh from my horse startled us, and woke Mme. Arnheim from her reverie. She cast a quick glance down the avenue, and turning, was soon lost to us in the shelter of a winding path.

"Come, Louis, come away before we are discovered; it was a rude act, and I am ashamed of it," I cried, drawing him away, though my eye still watched the lover, hoping for another glance.

Louis lingered, saying bitterly, "Gustave, I envy that dog the touch of her hand, the music of her voice, and proud as I am, would follow her like a hound, even though she chid me like one, for I love her as I never loved before, and I have no hope."

Wondering no longer at the passion of my friend, I made no reply to his gloomy words, but turning away, we mounted, and with a lingering look behind, departed silently. Louis returned to Paris; I to my friend General Moreau, at whose hospitable home I was visiting to recruit my health, shattered by long illness.

The general's kind lady, even amid her cares as hostess to a mansion full of friends, found time to seek amusement for her feeble guest, and when I had exhausted her husband's stock of literature, as if prompted by some good angel she proposed a visit to Mme. Arnheim to bespeak for me admission to her well-stored library.

Concealing my delight, I cheerfully accompanied Mme. Moreau, asking sundry questions as we drove along, concerning the fair recluse. There was a slight reserve in Madame's manner as she answered me.

"Mathilde has known much sorrow in her short life, *mon ami*, and seeks to forget the past in the calmness of the present. She seldom visits us except we are alone—then she comes often, for the general regards her with a fatherly affection; and in her society I feel no want of other friends."

"Has she been long a widow?" I asked, impelled by a most unmasculine curiosity to learn yet more.

"Seven years," replied Madame. "Her husband was a German—but I know little of her past life, for she seldom speaks of it, and I have only gathered from the few allusions she has made to it, that she married very young, and knew but little happiness as a wife."

I longed to ask yet more, and though courtesy restrained my tongue, my eyes betrayed me; Mme. Moreau, who had taken the invalid to her motherly heart, could not resist that mute appeal, for, as she drew up the window to shield me from the freshening breeze, she said smilingly:

"Ah, my child, I may repent this visit if I lead you into temptation, for boy as you seem to me, there is a man's heart in this slight frame of yours and a love of beauty shining in these hollow eyes. I cannot satisfy you, Gustave—she came hither but two years ago, and has lived secluded from the world, regardless of many solicitations to quit her solitude and widowhood. Your friend Louis was one of her most earnest suitors, but, like the rest, only procured his own banishment, for Mathilde only desires friends and not lovers. Therefore, let me warn you, if you desire the friendship of this charming woman, beware of love. But see, we have arrived, so bid adieu to ennui for a while at least."

Up the wide steps and over the green terraces we passed into a room whose chief charm was its simplicity; no costly furniture encumbered it, no tasteless decorations marred it; a few rare pictures enriched its walls, and a few graceful statues looked out from flowery nooks. Light draperies swayed to and fro before the open casements, giving brief glimpses of bloom and verdure just without. Leafy shadows flickered on the marble floor, and the blithe notes of birds were the only sounds that broke the sunny silence brooding over the whole scene.

Well as I fancied I remembered Mme. Arnheim, I was struck anew with the serene beauty of her face as she greeted us with cordial courtesy.

A rapt pity seemed to fill the pensive eyes as Madame spoke of my long illness, and her whole manner was full of interest, and a friendly wish to serve that captivated me and made me bless the pallid face that wore so sweet a pity for me.

We visited the library, a fascinating place to me, full of rare old books, and the soft gloom of shade and silence so dear to a student's heart. A few graceful words made me welcome here, and I promised myself many blissful hours in a spot so suited to my taste and fancy.

"Come now to the chapel, where M. Novaire will find another friend whose sweet discourse may have power to beguile some hours of their slow flight," said Mme. Arnheim, as she led the way into a little chapel rich in Gothic arches and stained windows, full of saintly legends that recalled the past.

"Ah, yes, here is indeed a treasure for you, Gustave—I had forgotten this," said Mme. Moreau, as our hostess led me to a fine organ, and with a smile invited me to touch its tempting keys.

With a desire to excel never experienced before, I obeyed, and filled the air with surges of sweet sound that came and went like billows breaking melodiously on the strand. Mme. Arnheim listened with drooping eyes and folded hands; and as I watched her standing in the gloom with one mellow ray of sunlight falling on her golden hair, she seemed to my excited fancy a white-robed spirit with the light of heaven shining on its gentle head.

The beautiful eyes were full of tender dew as they met mine in thanking me, and a certain deference seemed to mark her manner, as if the music I had power to create were a part of myself, and still lingered about me when the organ keys were mute.

Returning toward the château, we found a dainty little feast spread on a rustic table in the shadow of a group of foreign trees. No servants appeared, but Mme. Arnheim served us herself with a cordial ease that rendered doubly sweet the light wines she poured for us, and the nectarines she gathered from the sunny wall.

It was a new and wonderfully winning thing to me to see a creature beautiful and gifted—so free from affectation, so unconscious of self, so childlike, yet so full of all the nameless charms of gracious womanhood. To an imaginative temperament like mine it was doubly dangerous, and I dreaded to depart.

I sat apparently listening to the low dash of the fountain, but eye, ear, and mind were all intent on her; watching the pliant grace of her slender form, listening to the silvery music of her voice, and musing on the changeful beauty of her countenance. As I thus regarded her, my eye was caught by the sole ornament she wore, an ornament so peculiar and so ill-suited to its gentle wearer that my attention was arrested by it.

As she refilled my glass, a bracelet slipped from her arm to her wrist, and in that brief moment I had examined it attentively. It was of steel, delicately wrought, clasped by a golden lock, the tiny key of which hung by a golden chain. A strange expression stirred the sweet composure of her face as she saw the direction of my glance, and with a sudden gesture she thrust the trinket out of sight.

But as her hands moved daintily among the fruit in serving us, the bracelet often fell with a soft clash about her slender wrist, and each time she thrust it back, till her white arm was reddened with the marks of its slight links.

It seemed a most unfitting ornament, and as I watched her closely, I fancied some sad memory was connected with it, for the sight of it seemed painful, and all notice irksome to her. Ah, I little knew to what a fate it fettered her!

As we stood upon the terrace, awaiting the carriage, I turned from the château with its airy balconies without, and its inviting apartments within, to the blooming scene before me, exclaiming with enthusiasm, "This is the loveliest spot in France! A perfect picture of a peaceful, happy home. Ah, madame, many must envy you this tranquil retreat from the cares and sorrows of the world."

Mme. Arnheim's dark eyes wandered over the fair home I admired, and again I saw that strange expression flit across her face, but now more vividly than before. Pain, abhorrence, and despair seemed to sit for an instant on those lovely features; a swift paroxysm of mute anguish seemed to thrill through her whole figure; and I saw the half-hidden hands clenched as if controlling some wild impulse with an iron will. Like a flash it came and went, and with a long, deep sigh she answered slowly, "Do not envy me, for you have all the world before, free to choose a home where fancy leads. This is my world, and is often wearisome for all its loveliness."

There was a mournful cadence in her voice that saddened me, and a black shadow seemed to fall across the sunny landscape as I listened. The carriage came, and when she turned to say adieu, no trace of gloom marred the sweet serenity of her pale countenance.

"Come often and come freely, Monsieur Novaire," she said, adding, with a smile that would have won from me any boon I had the power to bestow, "My books, my organ, and my gardens are most sincerely at your service, and I only claim the right to listen when you fill my little chapel with the melody I love so well."

I could only thank her in words that sounded very poor and cold, remembering the sweetness of her own, and we drove away, leaving her in the shadow of the hall, still smiling her adieu.

Frankly as the favor had been granted, I accepted it, and went often to the château which soon became a "Castle Dangerous," and its fair mistress the one beloved object in the world to me. Day after day I went to muse in the quiet library, or to soothe my restless spirit with the music of the chapel organ. Mme. Arnheim I but seldom saw until I learned the spell which had power to lure her to my longing eyes. At the château she was the stately hostess, always courteous and calm, but when I sat alone in the chapel, filling the air with the plaintive or triumphal melody, I never failed to see a shadow gliding past the open door, or hear the light fall of a step along the echoing aisles, and with an altered mien she came to listen as I spoke to her in the tenderest strains heart could devise or hand execute.

This filled me with a sense of power I exulted in, for, remembering Mme. Moreau's warning words, "If you desire Mathilde's friendship, beware of love," I concealed my growing passion, and only gave it vent in the music that lured her to my side, and spoke to her in accents that never could offend. Slowly the coldness of her manner vanished, and though still chary of her presence, she came at last to treat me as a friend. At rare intervals some sudden interest in the book I read, some softened mood produced by the song I sang, the strain I played, gave me glimpses of a nature so frank and innocent, and a heart so deep and tender, that the hope of winning it seemed vain, and I reproached myself with treachery in accepting thus the hospitalities of her home and the blessing of her friendship, while so strong a love burned like a hidden fire in my breast.

Calmly the days flowed by, and nothing marred my peace till a slight incident filled me with restless doubts and fears. Wandering one day among the gardens, led by the desire of meeting Mathilde, I struck into an unfrequented path which wound homeward round a wing of the château which I had never visited and which I had believed unused. Pausing on the hillside to examine it, my eye fell on an open window opposite the spot where I was standing, and just within it I beheld Mathilde sitting with bent head and averted face. Eager to catch a glimpse of that beloved countenance, I stood motionless, screened by a drooping tree. As I peered further into the shaded room a jealous pang shot through me and my heart stood still, for in the high carved chair beside Mathilde I saw the arm and shoulder of a man. With straining eyes I watched it, and set my teeth fiercely when I saw the arm encircle her graceful neck, while the hand played idly with a tress of sunny hair I would have given worlds to touch. The arm was clothed in the sleeve of a damask robe de chambre, somber yet rich, and the hand seemed delicate and white; its motions were languid and I heard the murmur of a low voice often broken by faint laughter.

I could not move, but stood rooted to the spot till Mathilde dropped the curtain, and a moment after her voice rose soft and sweet, singing to that unknown guest, then I turned and dashed into the wood like one possessed.

From that day my peace was gone, for though Mathilde was unchanged, between us there always seemed to rise the specter of that hidden friend or lover, and I could not banish the jealous fears that tortured me. I knew from Mme. Moreau that Mathilde had no relatives in France, and few friends beside the general and his wife. The unknown was no cousin, no brother then, and I brooded over the mystery in vain. A careless inquiry of a servant if there were any guests at the château received a negative reply, given with respectful brevity and a quick, scrutinizing glance—while, as he spoke, down through hall and corridor floated the sound of Mathilde's voice singing in that far-off room.

Once more, and only once, I watched that window, waiting long in vain, but the curtain was thrown back at length, and then I saw

Mathilde pacing to and fro with clasped hands and streaming eyes, as if full of some passionate despair; while the low laughter, I remember well, seemed mocking her great sorrow.

She came to the casement and flung it wide, leaning far out, as if to seek consolation in the caressing breath of the balmy air and the soft sighing of the pines. As she stood thus, I saw her strike her fettered arm a cruel blow upon the strong stone balcony enclosing the window—a blow which left it bruised; though she never heeded it, but turned again into the room, as if in answer to some quick command.

I never looked again—for whatever secret sin or sorrow was there concealed, I had no right to know it, for by no look or word did Mathilde ever seek my sympathy or aid; but with a growing paleness on her cheek, a deepening sadness in her eye, she met me with unaltered kindness, and listened when I played as if she found her only solace there.

So the summer passed, and silently the hidden passion that possessed me did its work, till the wan shadow that once mocked me from my mirror was changed into the likeness of an ardent, healthful man, clear of eye, strong of arm, and light of foot. They said it was the fresh air of the hills; I knew it was the healing power of a beloved presence and the magic of an earnest love.

One soft September day, I had wandered with Mathilde into the deep ravine that cleft a green hill not far from the château. We had sat listening to the music of the waterfall as it mingled pleasantly with our conversation, till a sudden peal of thunder warned us home. Shut in by the steep cliffs, the gathering clouds had been unobserved until the tempest was close at hand. We hastily wound our way up from below, and paused a moment to look out upon the wildly beautiful scene.

Standing thus, there came a sudden glare before my eyes, followed by a deafening crash that brought me faint and dizzy to the ground. A flood of rain revived me, and on recovering I was conscious that Mathilde's arms encircled me, and my head was pillowed on her bosom; I felt the rapid beating of her heart, and heard the prayers she was murmuring as she held me thus. Her mantle was thrown about me, as if to shield me from the storm, and shrouded in its silken folds I lay as if in a dream, with no fear of thunderbolt or lightning flash—conscious only of the soft arms enfolding me, the faint perfume of her falling hair, and the face so near my own that every whispered word fell clearly on my ear.

How long I should have remained thus I cannot tell, for warmer drops than rain fell on my cheek and recalled me to myself. Putting aside the frail screen she had placed between me and the sudden danger, I staggered to my feet, unmindful of my dizzy brain and still half-blinded eyes.

"Not dead! Not dead! Thank God for that" was the glad cry that broke from Mathilde's lips, as I stood wild-eyed and pale before her. "O Gustave, are you unscathed by that awful bolt which I thought had murdered you before me?"

I reassured her, and felt that it was now my turn to shelter and protect, for she clung to me trembling and tearful, so changed that the calm, cold Mme. Arnheim of the fair château and the brave, tenderhearted creature on the cliff seemed two different women, but both lovely and beloved.

Swiftly and silently we hurried home, and when I would have quitted her she detained me with gentle force, saying, "You must remain my guest tonight, I cannot suffer you to leave my roof in such a storm as this."

Old Mlle. D'Aubigny bustled to and fro, and after refreshment and repose left us together by the cheerful firelight on the library hearth.

Mathilde sat silent, as if wrapped in thought, her head bent on her hand. I sat and looked at her till I forgot all but my love, and casting prudence to the winds, spoke out fervently and fast.

"Mathilde," I said, "deal frankly with me, and tell me was it *fear* or *love* that stirred this quiet heart of yours, and spoke in words of prayerful tenderness when you believed me dead? Forgive me if I pain you, but remembering that moment of unlooked-for bliss, I can no longer keep the stern silence I have imposed upon myself so long. I have loved you very truly all these months of seeming coldness, have haunted this house not in search of selfish ease, but to be near you, to breathe the air you breathed, to tread the ground you trod, and to sun myself in the light of your beloved presence. I should have been silent still, knowing my unworthiness, but as I lay pillowed on your bosom, through the tumult of the storm, a low voice from your heart seemed to speak to mine, saying 'I love you.' Tell me, dearest Mathilde, did I hear aright?"

An unwonted color dawned upon her cheek, a world of love and longing shone upon me in her glance, while a change as beautiful as it was brief passed over her, leaving in the stately woman's place a tender girl, whose heart looked from her eyes, and made her broken words more full of music than the sweetest song.

"Gustave, you heard aright; it was not fear that spoke." She stretched her hand to me, and clasping it in both my own I bent to kiss it with a lover's ardor—when between my eager lips and that fair hand dropped the *steel bracelet* with a sharp metallic sound.

With a bitter cry, Mathilde tore herself from my hold, and covering up her face shrank away, as if between us there had risen up a barrier visible to her alone.

"Mathilde, what is it? What power has this bauble, to work such a change as this? See! It is off and gone forever; for this hand is mine now, and shall wear no fetter but the golden one I give it," I cried, as kneeling on the cushion at her feet I repossessed myself of her passive hand, and unlocking the hateful bracelet, flung it far away across the room.

Apparently unconscious of my presence, Mathilde sat with such mute anguish and despair in every line of her drooping figure that a keen sense of coming evil held me silent at her feet, waiting some look or word from her.

A sharp struggle must have passed within her, for when she lifted up her face, all light and color had died out, and the whole countenance was full of some stern resolve, that seemed to have chilled its beauty into stone. Silently she motioned me to rise, and with a statelier mien than I had ever seen her wear, she passed down the long room to where the ominous steel bracelet glittered in the light. Silently she raised it, reclasped it on her arm, then with rapid motion rent away the tiny key and flung it into the red embers glowing on the hearth.

A long, shuddering sigh heaved her bosom as it vanished, a sound more eloquent of patient despair than the bitterest tears that ever fell. Coming to my side, she looked into my eyes with such love and pity shining through the pale determination of her face that I would have folded her to my breast, but with a swift gesture of that fettered arm she restrained me, saying slowly as if each word wrung her heart:

"God forgive me that I could forget the solemn duty this frail chain binds me to. Gustave, I never meant to wrong you thus, and will atone for it by giving you the confidence never bestowed on any human being. Come and see the secret anguish of my life, the haunting specter of my home, the stern fate which makes all love a bitter mockery, and leaves me desolate."

Like a shadow she flitted from me, beckoning me to follow. The storm still raged without, but all was bright and still within as we passed through gallery and hall into that distant wing of the château. The radiance of shaded lamps fell on the marble floors—graceful statues gleamed among the flowers, and the air was full of perfume, but I saw no beauty anywhere, for between me and the woman whom I loved an unknown phantom seemed to stand, and its black shadow darkened all the world to me.

Mathilde paused in a silent corridor at length, and looking back at me, whispered imploringly, "Gustave, do not judge me till I have told you all." Then before I could reply, she passed before me into a dimly lighted room, still beckoning me to follow.

Bernhardt, an old servant whom I had seldom seen, rose as she entered, and at a motion from Mathilde bade me be seated. Mechanically I obeyed, for all strength seemed to desert me as I looked upon the scene before me.

On the floor, clothed in the dress I well remembered, sat a man playing with the childish toys that lay around him. The face would have been a young and comely one, were it not for the awful blight which had fallen on it; the vacant gaze of his hollow eyes, the aimless movements of his feeble hands, and the unmeaning words he muttered to himself, all told the fearful loss of that divine gift—reason.

Mathilde pointed to the mournful wreck, saying, with a look of desolation which few human faces wear, "Gustave, am I not a widow?"

Then I knew that I saw the husband of my Mathilde—and he an idiot!

A brief sensation of mingled disgust, despair, and rage possessed me, for I knew how powerless I was to free the heart I coveted from this long slavery; one thought of Mathilde recalled me, one glance into those eyes so full of pain and passion banished every feeling but a tender pity for her cruel lot, and a redoubled love and admiration for the patient strength which had borne this heavy weight of care all those years. I could not speak, I only took that fettered hand and kissed it reverently.

The imbecile (I cannot say husband) rose, when he saw Mathilde, and creeping to her side filled her hands with toys, still smiling that vacant smile, so pitiful to see in eyes that have shone unclouded upon such a wife, still muttering those senseless words so dreadful to hear, from lips that should have spoken with a man's wisdom and a husband's tenderness to her.

My heart ached, as I saw that young, fair woman sit near that wreck of manhood, soothing his restless spirit with the music of her voice, while his wandering hands played with the one ornament she wore, that bracelet whose slight links were so strong a chain to bind her to a bitter duty, so sorrowful a badge of slavery to a proud soul like hers.

Sleep fell suddenly on that poor, wandering mind, and with a few words to old Bernhardt, Mathilde led me back into the quiet room we left.

I sank into a chair, and dropping my head upon my folded arms, sat silent, knowing now what lay before us.

The storm rolled and crashed above our heads, but in the silence of the room, the voice I loved so well spoke softly at my side, as Mathilde told the story of her life.

"Gustave, I was an orphan, and my stern guardian found his ward an irksome charge. He looked about him for some means of relief, and but two appeared, marriage or a convent. I was but sixteen then, blithe of heart, and full of happy dreams; the convent seemed a tomb to me, and any fate a blessed one that saved me from it. I had a friend—heaven forgive her the wrong she did me!—and this friend influenced my guardian's choice, and won for me the husband you have seen. She knew the fearful malady that cursed him even then, but bade him conceal it from my guardian and me. He loved me, and obeyed her, and thus she led me into that dark web of woe where I have struggled all these years.

"I had innocently won a heart that she coveted, and though I did not listen to that lover's suit, he was lost to her, and for that she hated me. I knew nothing of her passion then, and trusted her implicitly. We were in Germany, and I, a stranger in a strange land, followed where she pointed, and so walked smilingly to my doom. Reinhold Arnheim was a gentle but weakhearted man, guided by his cousin Gertrude, my false friend. He loved me with all the ardor of his feeble nature, and I, seeing a free future before me, thought I gave him my heart, when it was but a girlish affection for the man who saved me from the fate I dreaded.

"My guardian's last illness coming suddenly upon him, he desired to see me safe in a husband's home, before he left me forever. I was married, and he died, believing me a happy wife—I, a child, betrothed one little month.

"Nine years ago, that marriage mockery took place, but to me it seems a lifetime full of pain. Ah! I should have been a happier woman in a nun's narrow cell than a wife worse than widowed, with a secret grief like this!" Mathilde paused, and for a moment nothing broke the silence but the wind, as it swept moaning away across the lake.

"Let me pass lightly over the two years that followed that unhappy bridal," she continued hurriedly. "I was frantic with indignation and dismay when I learned the secret Gertrude's wickedness and Reinhold's weakness had withheld from me. I had no friends to flee to, no home but my husband's, and too proud to proclaim the wrongs for which I knew no redress, I struggled to conceal my anguish, and accept my fate.

"My husband pleaded with me to spare him, the victim of a hereditary curse. I knew he loved me, and pity for his misfortune kept me silent. For years, no one knew the secret of his malady but Gertrude, his physician, Bernhardt, and myself.

"We seemed a happy pair, for Reinhold was truly kind, and I played my part well, proud to show my false friend that her cruel blow had failed to crush me.

"Gustave, tongue can never tell how I suffered—how I prayed for strength and patience; love would have made it easier to bear, but when those years of trial made a woman of the careless girl, and looking into my heart for some affection to sustain me, I found only pity and aversion, then I saw the error I had committed in my ignorance—I never loved him, and this long suffering has been my punishment for that great sin. Heaven grant it may atone!

"Gustave, I tried to be a patient wife—I tried to be a cheerful companion to poor Reinhold in his daily life, a brave comforter in those paroxysms of sharp agony which tortured him in secret—but all in vain. I could not love him, and I came at length to see my future as it stretched before me black and barren.

"Tied for life, to a man whose feeble mind left no hope of comforting companionship in our long pilgrimage, and with whom duty, unsweetened by affection, grew to a loathsome slavery—what wonder that I longed to break away and flee from my prison by the only outlet left to my despair?

"I wavered long, but resolved at length to end the life now grown too burdensome to bear. I wrote a letter to my husband, asking forgiveness for the grief I caused him, and freely pardoning the great wrong he had done me. No reproaches embittered my last words, but tenderly and truthfully I showed him all my heart, and said farewell forever.

"But before I could consummate my sinful purpose, I was seized with what I fondly hoped would prove a mortal illness, and while lying unconscious of all grief and care, Reinhold found and read that letter. He never told me the discovery he had made, but hid the wound and loved me still—never kinder than when he watched beside me with a woman's patient tenderness, as I slowly and reluctantly came back to life and health again.

"Then when he deemed me strong enough to bear the shock, he kissed me fondly one sad day, and going out with dogs and gun, as if to his favorite sport, at nightfall was brought home a ghastly spectacle.

"To all but his old servant it seemed a most unhappy accident, but in the silence of the night, as we watched beside what we believed to be his dying bed, old Bernhardt told me, that from broken words and preparations made in secret, he felt sure his master had gone out that day intending never to return alive—choosing to conceal his real design under the appearance of a sad mischance, that no remorse might poison my returning peace.

"With tears the old man told his fears, and when I learned that Reinhold had read that fatal letter, I could no longer doubt. It was a sad and solemn sight to me—for sitting in the shadow of death, I looked back upon my life, and seeing clearly where I had failed in wifely duty and in Christian patience, I prayerfully devoted my whole future to the atonement of the wrong I had committed against God, my husband, and myself.

"Reinhold lived, but never knew me again, never heard my entreaties for pardon, or my tender assurances of pity and affection—all I could truly offer even then. The grief my desperate resolve had caused him and the shock of that rash act were too much for his weak body and weak brain, and he rose up from that bed of suffering the mournful wreck you see him now.

"Gustave, I have kept my vow, and for seven long years have watched and guarded him most faithfully. I could not bear the pity of those German friends, and after wandering far and wide in search of health for my unhappy husband, I came hither unknown and friendless, bringing my poor husband to a quiet home, where no rude sound could disturb, no strange face make afraid. I was a widow in the saddest sense of that sad word, and as such I resolved henceforward to be known.

"The few who knew of the existence of the shadow you have seen believe him to be my brother, and I have held my peace, making a secret sorrow of my past, rather than confess the weakness and wickedness of those most near to me; I may have erred in this, but wronging no one, I hoped to win a little brightness to my life, to find a brief oblivion of my grief.

"I fled from the world; seeking to satisfy the hunger of my heart with friendship, and believing myself strong to resist temptation, I welcomed you and tasted happiness again, unconscious of love's subtle power, till it was too late to recall the heart you made your own. Gustave, I shunned you, I seemed cold and calm, when longing to reply to the unspoken passion shining in your glance; I felt my unseen fetters growing too heavy to be borne, and my life of seeming peace a mockery whose gloom appalled and tortured me.

"Heaven knows I struggled to be firm, and but for that unguarded moment of today, when death seemed to have bereft me of the one joy I possessed, I should still have the power to see you go unsaddened by a hopeless love, unburdened by a tale of grief like this. O my friend, forgive and pity me! Help me to bear my burden as I should, and patiently accept the fate heaven sends."

We had sat motionless, looking into each other's eyes as the last words fell from Mathilde's lips; but as she ceased and bent her head as if in meek submission, my heart overflowed. I threw myself before her, and striving to express the sympathy that mingled with my love, could only lay my throbbing forehead on her knee, and weep as I had not wept for years.

I felt her light touch on my head, and seemed to gather calmness from its soothing pressure.

"Do not banish me, Mathilde," I said, "let me still be near you with a glance of tenderness, a word of comfort for your cheer. There is a heavy shadow on your home. Let me stay and lighten it with the love that shall be warm and silent as the summer sunshine on your flowers."

But to my prayer there came a resolute reply, though the face that looked into my own was eloquent with love and grief.

"Gustave, we must part at once, for while my husband lives I shall guard his honorable name from the lightest breath. You were my friend, and I welcomed you—you are my lover, and henceforth are banished. Pardon me, and let us part unpledged by any vow. You are free to love whenever you shall weary of the passion that now rules your heart. I am bound by a tie which death alone can sever; till then I wear this fetter, placed here by a husband's hand nine years ago; it is a symbol of my life, a mute monitor of duty, strong and bright as the hope and patience which now come to strengthen me. I have thrown away the key, and its place is here till this arm lies powerless, or is stretched free and fetterless to clasp and hold you mine forever!"

"Give me some charm, some talisman, to keep my spirit brave and cheerful through the separation now before us, and then I will go," I cried, as the chapel clock tolled one, and the last glimmer died upon the hearth.

Mathilde brushed the hair back from my eager face, and gazed long and earnestly into my eyes, then bent and left a kiss upon my forehead, saying, as she rose, "It is a frank, true countenance, Gustave, and I trust the silent pledge it gives me. God keep you, dearest friend, and grant us a little happiness together in the years to come!"

I held her close for one moment, and with a fervent blessing turned to go, but pausing on the threshold, I looked back. The storm had died, and through the black clouds broke the moon with sudden radiance. A silvery beam lit that beloved face, and seemed to lure me back. I started to return, but Mathilde's clear voice cried farewell; and on the arm that waved a last adieu, the steel bracelet glittered like a warning light. Seeing that, I knew there was no return. I went out into the night a better and a happier man for having known the blessedness and pain of love.

Three years went by, but my hidden passion never wavered, never died—and although I wandered far and wide over the earth, I found no spot so beautiful to me as the sunny château in its paradise of flowers, and no joy so deep as the memory of Mathilde.

I never heard from her, for, though I wrote as one friend to another, no reply was returned. I lamented this, but could not doubt the wisdom of her silence, and waited patiently for my recall.

A letter came at length, not to welcome, but to banish me forever. Mathilde had been a widow, and was a wife again. Kindly she told me this, speaking of my love as a boyish passion, of her own as a brief delusion—asking pardon for the pain she feared to give, and wishing for me a happiness like that she had now won.

It almost murdered me, for this hope was my life. Alone in the Far East, I suffered, fought, and conquered, coming out from that sharp conflict with no faith, no hope, no joy, nothing but a secret love and sorrow locked up in my wounded heart to haunt me like a sad ghost, till some spell to banish it was found.

Aimlessly, I journeyed to and fro, till led by the longing to again see familiar faces, I returned to Paris and sought out my old friend Moreau. He had not left the city for his summer home, and desiring to give him a glad surprise, I sprang up the stairs unannounced and entered his saloon.

A lady stood alone in the deep window, gazing thoughtfully upon the busy scene below. I knew the slender figure draped in white, the golden hair, the soft dark eyes, and with a sharp pang at my heart, I recognized Mathilde—more lovely and serene than ever.

She turned, but in the bronzed and bearded man did not recognize the youth she parted from, and with a glance of quiet wonder waited for me to speak. I could not, and in a moment it was needless, for eye spoke to eye, heart yearned to heart, and she remembered. A sudden color flushed her cheek as she leaned toward me with dilated eyes; the knot of Parmese violets upon her bosom rose and fell with her quickened breath, and her whole frame thrilled with eagerness as she cried joyfully, "Gustave! Come back to meet me at last!"

I stirred to meet her, but on the arms outstretched to greet me no steel bracelet glittered, and recollecting all my loss I clasped my hands before my face, crying mournfully, "O Mathilde, how can you welcome me, when such a gulf has parted us forever? How smile upon the friend whose love you have so wronged, whose life you have made so desolate?"

A short silence ensued, and then Mathilde's low voice replied, still tenderly, but full of pain, "Gustave, there is some mystery in this; deal frankly with me, and explain how I have wronged, how made you desolate?"

"Are you not married, and am I not bereft of the one dear gift I coveted? Did not your own hand part us and give the wound that still bleeds in my faithful heart, Mathilde?" I asked, with a glance of keen inquiry.

"Gustave, I never doubted your truth, though years passed, and I received no answer to the words of cheer I sent to comfort your long exile—then why doubt mine? Some idle rumor has deceived you, for I am now free—free to bestow the gift you covet, free to reward your patient love, if it still glows as warmly as mine."

Doubt, fear, and sorrow fled at once; I cared for nothing, remembered nothing, desired nothing, for Mathilde was free to love me still. That was rapture enough for me, and I drank freely of the cup of joy offered, heedless of unanswered doubts, unraveled mysteries and fears.

A single hour lifted me from gloom and desolation to blessedness again, and in the light of that returning confidence and peace all that seemed dark grew clear before our eyes. Mathilde had written often, but not one word from her had reached me, and not one line of mine had gladdened her. The letter telling of her marriage she had never penned, but knew now to whom she owed the wrong; and pale with womanly indignation told me that the enemy who had schemed to rob us of our happiness was Louis my friend.

He had met her again in Paris, and the passion, smothered for a long time, blazed up afresh. He never spoke of it in words lest he should again be banished, but seemed content to be her friend, though it was evident he hoped to win a warmer return in time.

Poor Reinhold died the year we parted, and was laid to rest in the quiet chapel where sunlight and silence brooded over his last sleep. Mathilde had written often to recall me, but when no reply to those fond missives came, she ceased, and waited hopefully for my return. Louis knew of my friendship with Mathilde, and must have guessed our love, for by some secret means he had thus intercepted letters, which would have shortened my long exile, and spared us both much misery and doubt.

More fully to estrange us he had artfully conveyed through other lips the tidings of my falsehood to Mathilde, hoping to destroy her faith in me and in her sorrow play the comforter and win her to himself. But she would not listen to the rumors of my marriage, would not doubt my truth, or accept the friendship of a man who could traduce a friend.

But for that well-counterfeited letter I too had never doubted, never suffered, and my ireful contempt rose fiercely as I listened to these proofs of Louis's treachery and fraud.

He was absent on some sudden journey, and ere he could return I won Mathilde to give me the dear right to make her joys and griefs my own. One soft, spring morning we went quietly away into a neighboring church, and returned one in heart and name forever.

No one but our old friends the general and his wife knew the happy truth, for Mathilde dreaded the gossip of the world, and besought me not to proclaim my happiness till we were safe in our quiet home, and I obeyed, content to know her mine.

The crimson light of evening bathed the tranquil face beside me as we sat together a week after our marriage, full of that content which comes to loving mortals in those midsummer days of life—when suddenly a voice we both remembered roused us from our happy reverie. Mathilde's eye lit, her slender figure rose erect, and as I started with a wrathful exclamation on my lips, she held me fast, saying, in the tones that never failed to sway me to her will, "Let me deal with him, for he is not worthy of your sword, Gustave; let me avenge the wrong he did us, for a woman's pity will wound deeper than your keenest thrust; promise me, dearest Gustave, that you will control yourself for love of me, remembering all the misery you might bring down upon us both!"

She clung to me with such fond entreaty that I promised, and standing at her side endeavored to be calm, though burning with an indignation nothing but the clasp of that soft hand had power to restrain.

Singing a blithe song Louis entered, but with arrested step and half-uttered greeting paused upon the threshold, eyeing us with a glance of fire, and struggling to conceal the swift dismay that drove the color from his cheek, the power from his limbs.

Mathilde did not speak, and with an effort painful to behold, Louis regained composure; for some sudden purpose seemed to give him courage and sent a glance of triumph to his eye, as with a mocking smile he bowed to the stately woman at my side, saying with malicious emphasis, "I come to present my compliments to Mme. Arnheim on my return from Germany, from Frankfort, her old home—and I bear to her the tenderest greetings from our fair friend Mme. Gertrude Steinburg. Will Madame accept as gladly as I offer them?"

"A fit messenger from such a friend?" icily replied Mathilde.

With a quick perception of her meaning, and a warning pressure of my clenched hand, Louis threw himself into a seat, and with an assumption of friendly ease, belied by the pallor of his countenance and the fierce glitter of the eye, continued with feigned sympathy—determined to leave no bitter word unsaid:

"She is a charming woman, and confided much to me that filled me with surprise and grief. What desolation will be carried to the hearts of Madame's many lovers when they learn that she is no lovely widow, but a miserable wife bound to an idiotic husband—how eagerly will they shun the fair château where Madame guards the secret shame and sorrow of her life, and how enviable must be the feelings of my friend when he discovers the deception practiced upon him and the utter hopelessness of his grand passion."

His keen eye was upon me as he spoke, and seeing the conflict which raged within me, mistook it for dismay and fear. A sardonic laugh broke from his lips, and before Mathilde could reply, he said, "I little thought, when listening to the cheerful story Mme. Steinburg told with such grace, how speedy and agreeable a use I should have power to make of it. Believe me, madame, I sympathize with your misfortunes, and admire the art which renders you all ice to one lover, and all fire to another."

Mathilde dropped my hand, and stood with folded arms, lofty pride in her mien, calm pity in her eye, and cool contempt upon her lips, as she replied in clear, cold tones:

"I am not what you think me, sir, and your generous sympathy comes too late. I was a widow; for the husband whose misfortune should have made his name sacred even to you died three years ago—I am a wife, happy in the love doubt could not estrange or time destroy. Your dark designs have failed, and for every year of needless separation we forgive you, since it renders our affection doubly strong, our union doubly blessed. Your absence at Mme. Steinburg's side removed the only barrier that could have kept us still asunder. Let me thank both of those false friends for the one kind deed that crowned our happiness. Gustave has left your punishment to me. See! It is this."

With a gesture of impassioned grace she threw herself upon my breast, and looking out from that fond shelter with a countenance all radiant with love, and pride, and joy, she cried, "Go! We pity you, and from the fullness of our bliss we pardon all."

She had avenged us well, for in the glance my proud eyes met, I read passion, humiliation, and despair, as Louis gazed upon us for a moment, and then vanished, the last cloud that dimmed our sky.

Paris lay behind us, and we stood on the green terrace looking over the fair domain now so full of peace and promise to our eyes.

Remembering the look of hopeless anguish that had stirred the face I loved in that same spot so long ago, I looked down to read its lineaments afresh.

It was there, close beside me, bright with happiness, and beautiful with the returning bloom that banished its former pensive charm. Trust spoke in the clinging touch upon my arm, joy beamed in the blithe smile of her lips, and love sat like a glory in her tender eyes.

She met my glance, and with a sudden impulse folded her hands, saying softly, "The shadow has departed, Gustave, never to return, and I am free at last. May I be truly grateful for my happy lot."

"No, dearest Mathilde, you are a captive still, not to duty, but to love, whose thralldom shall be to you as light as the fetter I now bind you with." And as I spoke I clasped a slender chain of gold upon the fair arm where for nine bitter years lay the weight of that steel bracelet.

A Whisper
in the Dark

AS we rolled along, I scanned my companion covertly, and saw much to interest a girl of seventeen. My uncle was a handsome man, with all the polish of foreign life fresh upon him; yet it was neither comeliness nor graceful ease which most attracted me; for even my inexperienced eye caught glimpses of something stern and somber below these external charms, and my long scrutiny showed me the keenest eye, the hardest mouth, the subtlest smile I ever saw—a face which in repose wore the look that comes to those who have led lives of pleasure and learned their emptiness. He seemed intent on some thought that absorbed him, and for a time rendered him forgetful of my presence, as he sat with folded arms, fixed eyes, and restless lips. While I looked, my own mind was full of deeper thought than it had ever been before; for I was recalling, word for word, a paragraph in that half-read letter:

> At eighteen Sybil is to marry her cousin, the compact having been made between my brother and myself in their childhood. My son is with me now, and I wish them to be together during the next few months, therefore my niece must leave you sooner than I at first intended. Oblige me by preparing her for an immediate and final separation, but leave all disclosures to me, as I prefer the girl to remain ignorant of the matter for the present.

That displeased me. Why was I to remain ignorant of so important an affair? Then I smiled to myself, remembering that I did know, thanks to the willful curiosity that prompted me to steal a peep into the letter that Mme. Bernard had pored over with such an anxious face. I saw only a single paragraph, for my own name arrested my eye; and, though wild to read all, I had scarcely time to whisk the paper back into the reticule the forgetful old soul had left hanging on the arm of her chair. It was enough, however, to set my girlish brain in a ferment, and keep me gazing wistfully at my uncle, conscious that my future now lay in his hands; for I was an orphan and he my guardian, though I had seen him but seldom since I was confided to Madame a six years' child.

Presently my uncle became cognizant of my steady stare, and returned it with one as steady for a moment, then said, in a low, smooth tone, that ill accorded with the satirical smile that touched his lips, "I am a dull companion for my little niece. How shall I provide her with pleasanter amusement than counting my wrinkles or guessing my thoughts?"

I was a frank, fearless creature, quick to feel, speak, and act, so I answered readily, "Tell me about my cousin Guy. Is he as handsome, brave, and clever as Madame says his father was when a boy?"

My uncle laughed a short laugh, touched with scorn, whether for Madame, himself, or me I could not tell, for his countenance was hard to read.

"A girl's question and artfully put; nevertheless I shall not answer it, but let you judge for yourself."

"But, sir, it will amuse me and beguile the way. I feel a little strange and forlorn at leaving Madame, and talking of my new home and friends will help me to know and love them sooner. Please tell me, for I've had my own way all my life, and can't bear to be crossed."

My petulance seemed to amuse him, and I became aware that he was observing me with a scrutiny as keen as my own had been; but I smilingly sustained it, for my vanity was pleased by the approbation his eye betrayed. The evident interest he now took in all I said and did was sufficient flattery for a young thing, who felt her charms and longed to try their power.

"I, too, have had my own way all my life; and as the life is double the length, the will is double the strength of yours, and again I say no. What next, mademoiselle?"

He was blander than ever as he spoke, but I was piqued, and resolved to try coaxing, eager to gain my point, lest a too early submission now should mar my freedom in the future.

"But that is ungallant, Uncle, and I still have hopes of a kinder answer, both because you are too generous to refuse so small a favor to your 'little niece,' and because she can be charmingly wheedlesome when she likes. Won't you say yes now, Uncle?" And pleased with the daring of the thing, I put my arm about his neck, kissed him daintily, and perched myself upon his knee with most audacious ease.

He regarded me mutely for an instant, then, holding me fast, deliberately returned my salute on lips, cheeks, and forehead, with such warmth that I turned scarlet and struggled to free myself, while he laughed that mirthless laugh of his till my shame turned to anger, and I imperiously commanded him to let me go.

"Not yet, young lady. You came here for your own pleasure, but shall stay for mine, till I tame you as I see you must be tamed. It is a short process with me, and I possess experience in the work; for Guy, though by nature as wild as a hawk, has learned to come at my call as meekly as a dove. Chut! What a little fury it is!"

I was just then; for exasperated at his coolness, and quite beside myself, I had suddenly stooped and bitten the shapely white hand that held both my own. I had better have submitted; for slight as the foolish action was, it had an influence on my afterlife as many another such has had. My uncle stopped laughing, his hand tightened its grasp, for a moment his cold eye glittered and a grim look settled round the mouth, giving to his whole face a ruthless expression that entirely altered it. I felt perfectly powerless. All my little arts had failed, and for the first time I was mastered. Yet only physically; my spirit was rebellious still. He saw it in the glance that met his own, as I sat erect and pale, with something more than childish anger. I think it pleased him, for swiftly as it had come the dark look passed, and quietly, as if we were the best of friends, he began to relate certain exciting adventures he had known abroad, lending to the picturesque narration the charm of that peculiarly melodious voice, which soothed and won me in spite of myself, holding me intent till I forgot the past; and when he paused I found that I was leaning confidentially on his shoulder, asking for more, yet conscious of an instinctive distrust of this man whom I had so soon learned to fear yet fancy.

As I was recalled to myself, I endeavored to leave him; but he still detained me, and, with a curious expression, produced a case so quaintly fashioned that I cried out in admiration, while he selected two cigarettes, mildly aromatic with the herbs they were composed of, lit them, offered me one, dropped the window, and leaning back surveyed me with an air of extreme enjoyment, as I sat meekly puffing and wondering what prank I should play a part in next. Slowly the narcotic influence of the herbs diffused itself like a pleasant haze over all my senses; sleep, the most grateful, fell upon my eyelids, and the last thing I remember was my uncle's face dreamily regarding me through a cloud of fragrant smoke. Twilight wrapped us in its shadows when I woke, with the night wind blowing on my forehead, the muffled roll of wheels sounding in my ear, and my cheek pillowed upon my uncle's arm. He was humming a French *chanson* about "love and wine, and the Seine tomorrow!" I listened till I caught the air, and presently joined him, mingling my girlish treble with his flutelike tenor. He stopped at once and, in the coolly courteous tone I had always heard in our few interviews, asked if I was ready for lights and home.

"Are we there?" I cried; and looking out saw that we were ascending an avenue which swept up to a pile of buildings that rose tall and dark against the sky, with here and there a gleam along its gray front.

"Home at last, thank heaven!" And springing out with the agility of a young man, my uncle led me over a terrace into a long hall, light and warm, and odorous with the breath of flowers blossoming here and there in graceful groups. A civil, middle-aged maid received and took me to my room, a bijou of a place, which increased my wonder when told that my uncle had chosen all its decorations and superintended their arrangement. "He understands women," I thought, handling the toilet ornaments, trying luxurious chair and lounge, and ending by slipping my feet into the scarlet-and-white Turkish slippers, coquettishly turning up their toes before the fire. A few moments I gave to examination, and, having expressed my satisfaction, was asked by my maid if I would be pleased to dress, as "the master" never allowed dinner to wait for anyone. This recalled to me the fact that I was doubtless to meet my future husband at that meal, and in a moment every faculty was intent upon achieving a grand toilette for this first interview. The maid possessed skill and taste, and I a wardrobe lately embellished with Parisian gifts from my uncle which I was eager to display in his honor.

When ready, I surveyed myself in the long mirror as I had never done before, and saw there a little figure, slender, yet stately, in a dress of foreign fashion, ornamented with lace and carnation ribbons which enhanced the fairness of neck and arms, while blond hair, wavy and golden, was gathered into an antique knot of curls behind, with a carnation fillet, and below a blooming dark-eyed face, just then radiant with girlish vanity and eagerness and hope.

"I'm glad I'm pretty!"

"So am I, Sybil."

I had unconsciously spoken aloud, and the echo came from the doorway where stood my uncle, carefully dressed, looking comelier and cooler than ever. The disagreeable smile flitted over his lips as he spoke, and I started, then stood abashed, till beckoning, he added in his most courtly manner, "You were so absorbed in the contemplation of your charming self that Janet answered my tap and took herself away unheard. You are mistress of my table now. It waits; will you come down?"

With a last touch to that unruly hair of mine, a last, comprehensive glance and shake, I took the offered arm and rustled down the wide staircase, feeling that the romance of my life was about to begin. Three covers were laid, three chairs set, but only two were occupied, for no Guy appeared. I asked no questions, showed no surprise, but tried to devour my chagrin with my dinner, and exerted myself to charm my uncle into the belief that I had forgotten my cousin. It was a failure, however, for that empty seat had an irresistible fascination for me, and more than once, as my eye returned from its furtive scrutiny of napkin, plate, and trio of colored glasses, it met my uncle's and fell before his penetrative glance. When I gladly rose to leave him to his wine—for he did not ask me to remain—he also rose, and, as he held the door for me, he said, "You asked me to describe your cousin. You have seen one trait of his character tonight; does it please you?"

I knew he was as much vexed as I at Guy's absence, so quoting his own words, I answered saucily, "Yes, for I'd rather see the hawk free than coming tamely at your call, Uncle."

He frowned slightly, as if unused to such liberty of speech, yet bowed when I swept him a stately little curtsy and sailed away to the drawing room, wondering if my uncle was as angry with me as I was with my cousin. In solitary grandeur I amused myself by strolling through the suite of handsome rooms henceforth to be my realm, looked at myself in the long mirrors, as every woman is apt to do when alone and in costume, danced over the mossy carpets, touched the grand piano, smelled the flowers, fingered the ornaments on étagère and table, and was just giving my handkerchief a second drench of some refreshing perfume from a filigree flask that had captivated me when the hall door was flung wide, a quick step went running upstairs, boots tramped overhead, drawers seemed hastily opened and shut, and a bold, blithe voice broke out into a hunting song in a tone so like my uncle's that I involuntarily flew to the door, crying, "Guy is come!"

Fortunately for my dignity, no one heard me, and hurrying back I stood ready to skim into a chair and assume propriety at a minute's notice, conscious, meanwhile, of the new influence which seemed suddenly to gift the silent house with vitality, and add the one charm it needed—that of cheerful companionship. "How will he meet me? And how shall I meet him?" I thought, looking up at the bright-faced boy, whose portrait looked back at me with a mirthful light in the painted eyes and a trace of his father's disdainful smile in the curves of the firm-set lips. Presently the quick steps came flying down again, past the door, straight to the dining room opposite, and, as I stood listening with a strange flutter at my heart, I heard an imperious young voice say rapidly, "Beg pardon, sir, unavoidably detained. Has she come? Is she bearable?"

"I find her so. Dinner is over, and I can offer you nothing but a glass of wine."

My uncle's voice was frostily polite, making a curious contrast to the other, so impetuous and frank, as if used to command or win all but one.

"Never mind the dinner! I'm glad to be rid of it; so I'll drink your health, Father, and then inspect our new ornament."

"Impertinent boy!" I muttered, yet at the same moment resolved to deserve his appellation, and immediately grouped myself as effectively as possible, laughing at my folly as I did so. I possessed a pretty foot, therefore one little slipper appeared quite naturally below the last flounce of my dress; a bracelet glittered on my arm as it emerged from among the lace and carnation knots; that arm supported my head. My profile was well cut, my eyelashes long, therefore I read with face half averted from the door. The light showered down, turning my hair to gold; so I smoothed my curls, retied my snood, and, after a satisfied survey, composed myself with an absorbed aspect and a quickened pulse to await the arrival of the gentlemen.

Soon they came. I knew they paused on the threshold, but never stirred till an irrepressible "You are right, sir!" escaped the younger.

Then I rose prepared to give him the coldest greeting, yet I did not. I had almost expected to meet the boyish face and figure of the picture; I saw instead a man comely and tall. A dark moustache half hid the proud mouth; the vivacious eyes were far kinder, though quite as keen as his father's; and the freshness of unspoiled youth lent a charm which the older man had lost forever. Guy's glance of pleased surprise was flatteringly frank, his smile so cordial, his "Welcome, cousin!" such a hearty sound that my coldness melted in a breath, my dignity was all forgotten, and before I could restrain myself I had offered both hands with the impulsive exclamation "Cousin Guy, I know I shall be very happy here! Are you glad I have come?"

"Glad as I am to see the sun after a November fog."

And bending his tall head, he kissed my hand in the graceful foreign fashion he had learned abroad. It pleased me mightily, for it was both affectionate and respectful. Involuntarily I contrasted it with my uncle's manner, and flashed a significant glance at him as I did so. He understood it, but only nodded with the satirical look I hated, shook out his paper, and began to read. I sat down again, careless of myself now; and Guy stood on the rug, surveying me with an expression of surprise that rather nettled my pride.

"He is only a boy, after all; so I need not be daunted by his inches or his airs. I wonder if he knows I am to be his wife, and likes it."

The thought sent the color to my forehead, my eyes fell, and despite my valiant resolution I sat like any bashful child before my handsome cousin. Guy laughed a boyish laugh as he sat down on his father's footstool, saying, while he warmed his slender brown hands, "I beg your pardon, Sybil. (We won't be formal, will we?) But I haven't seen a lady for a month, so I stare like a boor at sight of a silk gown and highbred face. Are those people coming, sir?"

"If Sybil likes, ask her."

"Shall we have a flock of people here to make it gay for you, Cousin, or do you prefer our quiet style better; just riding, driving, lounging, and enjoying life, each in his own way? Henceforth it is to be as you command in such matters."

"Let things go on as they have done then. I don't care for society, and strangers wouldn't make it gay to me, for I like freedom; so do you, I think."

"Ah, don't I!"

A cloud flitted over his smiling face, and he punched the fire, as if some vent were necessary for the sudden gust of petulance that knit his black brows into a frown, and caused his father to tap him on the shoulder with the bland request, as he rose to leave the room, "Bring the portfolios and entertain your cousin; I have letters to write, and Sybil is too tired to care for music tonight."

Guy obeyed with a shrug of the shoulder his father touched, but lingered in the recess till my uncle, having made his apologies to me, had left the room; then my cousin rejoined me, wearing the same cordial aspect I first beheld. Some restraint was evidently removed, and his natural self appeared. A very winsome self it was, courteous, gay, and frank, with an undertone of deeper feeling than I thought to find. I watched him covertly, and soon owned to myself that he was all I most admired in the ideal hero every girl creates in her romantic fancy; for I no longer looked upon this young man as my cousin, but my lover, and through all our future intercourse this thought was always uppermost, full of a charm that never lost its power.

Before the evening ended Guy was kneeling on the rug beside me, our two heads close together, while he turned the contents of the great portfolio spread before us, looking each other freely in the face, as I listened and he described, both breaking into frequent peals of laughter at some odd adventure or comical mishap in his own travels, suggested by the pictured scenes before us. Guy was very charming, I my blithest, sweetest self, and when we parted late, my cousin watched me up the stairs with still another "Good night, Sybil," as if both sight and sound were pleasant to him.

"Is that your horse Sultan?" I called from my window next morning, as I looked down upon my cousin, who was coming up the drive from an early gallop on the moors.

"Yes, bonny Sybil; come and admire him," he called back, hat in hand, and a quick smile rippling over his face.

I went, and standing on the terrace, caressed the handsome creature, while Guy said, glancing up at his father's undrawn curtains, "If your saddle had come, we would take a turn before 'my lord' is ready for breakfast. This autumn air is the wine you women need."

I yearned to go, and when I willed the way soon appeared; so careless of bonnetless head and cambric gown, I stretched my hands to him, saying boldly, "Play young Lochinvar, Guy; I am little and light; take me up before you and show me the sea."

He liked the daring feat, held out his hand, I stepped on his boot toe, sprang up, and away we went over the wide moor, where the sun shone in a cloudless heaven, the lark soared singing from the green grass at our feet, and the September wind blew freshly from the sea. As we paused on the upland slope, that gave us a free view of the country for miles, Guy dismounted, and standing with his arm about the saddle to steady me in my precarious seat, began to talk.

"Do you like your new home, Cousin?"

"More than I can tell you!"

"And my father, Sybil?"

"Both yes and no to that question, Guy; I hardly know him yet."

"True, but you must not expect to find him as indulgent and fond as many guardians would be to such as you. It's not his nature. Yet you can win his heart by obedience, and soon grow quite at ease with him."

"Bless you! I'm that already, for I fear no one. Why, I sat on his knee yesterday and smoked a cigarette of his own offering, though Madame would have fainted if she had seen me; then I slept on his arm an hour, and he was fatherly kind, though I teased him like a gnat."

"The deuce he was!"

The morning ride on the moors

With which energetic expression Guy frowned at the landscape and harshly checked Sultan's attempt to browse, while I wondered what was amiss between father and son, and resolved to discover; but finding the conversation at an end, started it afresh by asking, "Is any of my property in this part of the country, Guy? Do you know I am as ignorant as a baby about my own affairs; for, as long as every whim was gratified and my purse full, I left the rest to Madame and Uncle, though the first hadn't a bit of judgment, and the last I scarcely knew. I never cared to ask questions before, but now I am intensely curious to know how matters stand."

"All you see is yours, Sybil" was the brief answer.

"What, that great house, the lovely gardens, these moors, and the forest stretching to the sea? I'm glad! I'm glad! But where, then, is your home, Guy?"

"Nowhere."

At this I looked so amazed that his gloom vanished in a laugh, as he explained, but briefly, as if this subject were no pleasanter than the first, "By your father's will you were desired to take possession of the old place at eighteen. You will be that soon; therefore, as your guardian, my father has prepared things for you, and is to share your home until you marry."

"When will that be, I wonder?" And I stole a glance from under my lashes, wild to discover if Guy knew of the compact and was a willing party to it.

His face was half averted, but over his dark cheek I saw a deep flush rise, as he answered, stooping to pull a bit of heather, "Soon, I hope, or the gentleman sleeping there below will be tempted to remain a fixture with you on his knee as 'Madame my wife.' He is not your own uncle, you know."

I smiled at the idea, but Guy did not see it; and seized with a whim to try my skill with the hawk that seemed inclined to peck at its master, I said demurely, "Well, why not? I might be very happy if I learned to love him, as I should, if he were always in that kindest mood of his. Would you like me for a little mamma, Guy?"

"No!" short and sharp as a pistol shot.

"Then you must marry and have a home of your own, my son."

"Don't, Sybil! I'd rather you didn't see me in a rage, for I'm not a pleasant sight, I assure you; and I'm afraid I shall be in one if you go on. I early lost my mother, but I love her tenderly, because my father is not much to me, and I know if she had lived I should not be what I am."

Bitter was his voice, moody his mien, and all the sunshine gone at once. I looked down and touched his black hair with a shy caress, feeling both penitent and pitiful.

"Dear Guy, forgive me if I pained you. I'm a thoughtless creature, but I'm not malicious, and a word will restrain me if kindly spoken. My home is always yours, and when my fortune is mine you shall never want, if you are not too proud to accept help from your own kin. You are a little proud, aren't you?"

"As Lucifer, to most people. I think I should not be to you, for you understand me, Sybil, and with you I hope to grow a better man."

He turned then, and through the lineaments his father had bequeathed him I saw a look that must have been his mother's, for it was womanly, sweet, and soft, and lent new beauty to the dark eyes, always kind, and just then very tender. He had checked his words suddenly, like one who has gone too far, and with that hasty look into my face had bent his own upon the ground, as if to hide the unwonted feeling that had mastered him. It lasted but a moment, then his old manner returned, as he said gaily, "There drops your slipper. I've been wondering what kept it on. Pretty thing! They say it is a foot like this that oftenest tramples on men's hearts. Are you cruel to your lovers, Sybil?"

"I never had one, for Madame guarded me like a dragon, and I led the life of a nun; but when I do find one I shall try his mettle well before I give up my liberty."

"Poets say it is sweet to give up liberty for love, and they ought to know," answered Guy, with a sidelong glance.

I liked that little speech, and recollecting the wistful look he had given me, the significant words that had escaped him, and the variations of tone and manner constantly succeeding one another, I felt assured that my cousin was cognizant of the family league, and accepted it, yet with the shyness of a young lover, knew not how to woo. This pleased me, and quite satisfied with my morning's work, I mentally resolved to charm my cousin slowly, and enjoy the romance of a genuine wooing, without which no woman's life seems complete—in her own eyes at least. He had gathered me a knot of purple heather, and as he gave it I smiled my sweetest on him, saying, "I commission you to supply me with nosegays, for you have taste, and I love wild flowers. I shall wear this at dinner in honor of its giver. Now take me home; for my moors, though beautiful, are chilly, and I have no wrapper but this microscopic handkerchief."

Off went his riding jacket, and I was half smothered in it. The hat followed next, and as he sprang up behind I took the reins, and felt a thrill of delight in sweeping down the slope with that mettlesome creature tugging at the bit, that strong arm around me, and the happy hope that the heart I leaned on might yet learn to love me.

The day so began passed pleasantly, spent in roving over house and grounds with my cousin, setting my possessions in order, and writing to dear old Madame. Twilight found me in my bravest attire, with Guy's heather in my hair, listening for his step, and longing to run and meet him when he came. Punctual to the instant he appeared, and this dinner was a far different one from that of yesterday, for both father and son seemed in their gayest and most gallant mood, and I enjoyed the hour heartily. The world seemed all in tune now, and when I went to the drawing room I was moved to play my most stirring marches, sing my blithest songs, hoping to bring one at least of the gentlemen to join me. It brought both, and my first glance showed me a curious change in each. My uncle looked harassed and yet amused; Guy looked sullen and eyed his father with covert glances.

The morning's chat flashed into my mind, and I asked myself, "Is Guy jealous so soon?" It looked a little like it, for he threw himself upon a couch and lay there silent and morose; while my uncle paced to and fro, thinking deeply, while apparently listening to the song he bade me finish. I did so, then followed the whim that now possessed me, for I wanted to try my power over them both, to see if I could restore that gentler mood of my uncle's, and assure myself that Guy cared whether I was friendliest with him or not.

"Uncle, come and sing with me; I like that voice of yours."

"Tut, I am too old for that; take this indolent lad instead. His voice is fresh and young, and will chord well with yours."

"Do you know that pretty *chanson* about 'love and wine, and the Seine tomorrow,' cousin Guy?" I asked, stealing a sly glance at my uncle.

"Who taught you that?" And Guy eyed me over the top of the couch with an astonished expression which greatly amused me.

"No one; Uncle sang a bit of it in the carriage yesterday. I like the air, so come and teach me the rest."

"It is no song for you, Sybil. You choose strange entertainment for a lady, sir."

A look of unmistakable contempt was in the son's eye, of momentary annoyance in the father's, yet his voice betrayed none as he answered, still pacing placidly along the room, "I thought she was asleep, and unconsciously began it to beguile a silent drive. Sing on, Sybil; that Bacchanalian snatch will do you no harm."

But I was tired of music now they had come, so I went to him, and passing my arm through his, walked beside him, saying with my most persuasive aspect, "Tell me about Paris, Uncle; I intend to go there as soon as I'm of age, if you will let me. Does your guardianship extend beyond that time?"

"Only till you marry."

"I shall be in no haste, then, for I begin to feel quite homelike and happy here with you, and shall be content without other society; only you'll soon tire of me, and leave me to some dismal governess, while you and Guy go pleasuring."

"No fear of that, Sybil; I shall hold you fast till some younger guardian comes to rob me of my merry ward."

As he spoke, he took the hand that lay upon his arm into a grasp so firm, and turned on me a look so keen, that I involuntarily dropped my eyes lest he should read my secret there. Eager to turn the conversation, I asked, pointing to a little miniature hanging underneath the portrait of his son, before which he had paused, "Was that Guy's mother, sir?"

"No, your own."

I looked again, and saw a face delicate yet spirited, with dark eyes, a passionate mouth, and a head crowned with hair as plenteous and golden as my own; but the whole seemed dimmed by age, the ivory was stained, the glass cracked, and a faded ribbon fastened it. My eyes filled as I looked, and a strong desire seized me to know what had defaced this little picture of the mother whom I never knew.

"Tell me about her, Uncle; I know so little, and often long for her so much. Am I like her, sir?"

Why did my uncle avert his eyes as he answered, "You are a youthful image of her, Sybil"?

"Go on, please, tell me more; tell me why this is so stained and worn; you know all, and surely I am old enough now to hear any history of pain and loss."

Something caused my uncle to knit his brows, but his bland voice never varied a tone as he placed the picture in my hand and gave me this brief explanation:

"Just before your birth your father was obliged to cross the Channel, to receive the last wishes of a dying friend. There was an accident; the vessel foundered, and many lives were lost. He escaped, but by some mistake his name appeared in the list of missing passengers; your mother saw it, the shock destroyed her, and when your father returned he found only a motherless little daughter to welcome him. This miniature, which he always carried with him, was saved with his papers at the last moment; but though the seawater ruined it he would never have it copied or retouched, and gave it to me when he died in memory of the woman I had loved for his sake. It is yours now, my child; keep it, and never feel that you are fatherless or motherless while I remain."

Kind as was both act and speech, neither touched me, for something seemed wanting. I felt yet could not define it, for then I believed in the sincerity of all I met.

"Where was she buried, Uncle? It may be foolish, but I should like to see my mother's grave."

"You shall someday, Sybil," and a curious change came over my uncle's face as he averted it.

"I have made him melancholy, talking of Guy's mother and my own; now I'll make him gay again if possible, and pique that negligent boy," I thought, and drew my uncle to a lounging chair, established myself on the arm thereof, and kept him laughing with my merriest gossip, both of us apparently unconscious of the long dark figure stretched just opposite, feigning sleep, but watching us through half-closed lids, and never stirring except to bow silently to my careless "Good night."

As I reached the stairhead, I remembered that my letter to Madame, full of the frankest criticisms upon people and things, was lying unsealed on the table in the little room my uncle had set apart for my boudoir; fearing servants' eyes and tongues, I slipped down again to get it. The room adjoined the parlors, and just then was lit only by a ray from the hall lamp.

I had secured the letter, and was turning to retreat, when I heard Guy say petulantly, as if thwarted yet submissive, "I *am* civil when you leave me alone; I *do* agree to marry her, but I won't be hurried or go a-wooing except in my own way. You know I never liked the bargain, for it's nothing else; yet I can reconcile myself to being sold, if it relieves you and gives us both a home. But, Father, mind this, if you tie me to that girl's sash too tightly I shall break away entirely, and then where are we?"

"I should be in prison and you a houseless vagabond. Trust me, my boy, and take the good fortune which I secured for you in your cradle. Look in pretty Sybil's face, and resignation will grow easy; but remember time presses, that this is our forlorn hope, and for God's sake be cautious, for she is a headstrong creature, and may refuse to fulfill her part if she learns that the contract is not binding against her will."

"I think she'll not refuse, sir; she likes me already. I see it in her eyes; she has never had a lover, she says, and according to your account

The compact overheard

a girl's first sweetheart is apt to fare the best. Besides, she likes the place, for I told her it was hers, as you bade me, and she said she could be very happy here, if my father was always kind."

"She said that, did she? Little hypocrite! For your father, read yourself, and tell me what else she babbled about in that early *tête-à-tête* of yours."

"You are as curious as a woman, sir, and always make me tell you all I do and say, yet never tell me anything in return, except this business, which I hate, because my liberty is the price, and my poor little cousin is kept in the dark. I'll tell her all, before I marry her, Father."

"As you please, hothead. I am waiting for an account of the first love passage, so leave blushing to Sybil and begin."

I knew what was coming and stayed no longer, but caught one glimpse of the pair. Guy in his favorite place, erect upon the rug, half laughing, half frowning as he delayed to speak, my uncle serenely smoking on the couch; then I sped away to my own room, thinking, as I sat down in a towering passion, "So he does know of the baby betrothal and hates it, yet submits to please his father, who covets my fortune—mercenary creatures! I can annul the contract, can I? I'm glad to know that, for it makes me mistress of them both. I like you already, do I, and you see it in my eyes? Coxcomb! I'll be the thornier for that. Yet I do like him; I do wish he cared for me, I'm so lonely in the world, and he can be so kind."

So I cried a little, brushed my hair a good deal, and went to bed, resolving to learn all I could when, where, and how I pleased, to render myself as charming and valuable as possible, to make Guy love me in spite of himself, and then say yes or no, as my heart prompted me.

That day was a sample of those that followed, for my cousin was by turns attracted or repelled by the capricious moods that ruled me. Though conscious of a secret distrust of my uncle, I could not resist the fascination of his manner when he chose to exert its influence over me; this made my little plot easier of execution, for jealousy seemed the most effectual means to bring my wayward cousin to subjection. Full of this fancy, I seemed to tire of his society, grew thorny as a brier rose to him, affectionate as a daughter to my uncle, who surveyed us both with that inscrutable glance of his, and slowly yielded to my dominion as if he had divined my purpose and desired to aid it. Guy turned cold and gloomy, yet still lingered near me as if ready for a relenting look or word. I liked that, and took a wanton pleasure in prolonging the humiliation of the warm heart I had learned to love, yet not to value as I ought, until it was too late.

One dull November evening as I went wandering up and down the hall, pretending to enjoy the flowers, yet in reality waiting for Guy, who had left me alone all day, my uncle came from his room, where he had sat for many hours with the harassed and anxious look he always wore when certain foreign letters came.

"Sybil, I have something to show and tell you," he said, as I garnished his buttonhole with a spray of heliotrope, meant for the laggard, who would understand its significance, I hoped. Leading me to the drawing room, my uncle put a paper into my hands, with the request "This is a copy of your father's will; oblige me by reading it."

He stood watching my face as I read, no doubt wondering at my composure while I waded through the dry details of the will, curbing my impatience to reach the one important passage. There it was, but no word concerning my power to dissolve the engagement if I pleased; and, as I realized the fact, a sudden bewilderment and sense of helplessness came over me, for the strange law terms seemed to make inexorable the paternal decree which I had not seen before. I forgot my studied calmness, and asked several questions eagerly.

"Uncle, did my father really command that I should marry Guy, whether we loved each other or not?"

"You see what he there set down as his desire; and I have taken measures that you *should* love one another, knowing that few cousins, young, comely, and congenial, could live three months together without finding themselves ready to mate for their own sakes, if not for the sake of the dead and living fathers to whom they owe obedience."

"You said I need not, if I didn't choose; why is it not here?"

"I said that? Never, Sybil!" and I met a look of such entire surprise and incredulity it staggered my belief in my own senses, yet also roused my spirit, and, careless of consequences, I spoke out at once.

"I heard you say it myself the night after I came, when you told Guy to be cautious, because I could refuse to fulfill the engagement, if I knew that it was not binding against my will."

This discovery evidently destroyed some plan, and for a moment threw him off his guard; for, crumpling the paper in his hand, he sternly demanded, "You turned eavesdropper early; how often since?"

"Never, Uncle; I did not mean it then, but going for a letter in the dark, I heard your voices, and listened for an instant. It was dishonorable, but irresistible; and if you force Guy's confidence, why should not I steal yours? All is fair in war, sir, and I forgive as I hope to be forgiven."

"You have a quick wit and a reticence I did not expect to find under that frank manner. So you have known your future destiny all these months then, and have a purpose in your treatment of your cousin and myself?"

"Yes, Uncle."

"May I ask what?"

I was ashamed to tell; and in the little pause before my answer came, my pique at Guy's desertion was augmented by anger at my uncle's denial of his own words the ungenerous hopes he cherished, and a strong desire to perplex and thwart him took possession of me, for I saw his anxiety concerning the success of this interview, though he endeavored to repress and conceal it. Assuming my coldest mien, I said, "No, sir, I think not; only I can assure you that my little plot has succeeded better than your own."

"But you intend to obey your father's wish, I hope, and fulfill your part of the compact, Sybil?"

"Why should I? It is not binding, you know, and I'm too young to lose my liberty just yet; besides, such compacts are unjust, unwise. What right had my father to mate me in my cradle? How did he know what I should become, or Guy? How could he tell that I should not love someone else better? No! I'll not be bargained away like a piece of merchandise, but love and marry when I please!"

At this declaration of independence my uncle's face darkened ominously, some new suspicion lurked in his eye, some new anxiety beset him; but his manner was calm, his voice blander than ever as he asked, "Is there then someone whom you love? Confide in me, my girl."

"And if there were, what then?"

"All would be changed at once, Sybil. But who is it? Some young lover left behind at Madame's?"

"No, sir."

"Who, then? You have led a recluse life here. Guy has no friends who visit him, and mine are all old, yet you say you love."

"With all my heart, Uncle."

"Is this affection returned, Sybil?"

"I think so."

"And it is not Guy?"

I was wicked enough to enjoy the bitter disappointment he could not conceal at my decided words, for I thought he deserved that momentary pang; but I could not as decidedly answer that last question, for I would not lie, neither would I confess just yet; so, with a little gesture of impatience, I silently turned away, lest he should see the telltale color in my cheeks. My uncle stood an instant in deep thought, a slow smile crept to his lips, content returned to his mien, and something like a flash of triumph glittered for a moment in his eye, then vanished, leaving his countenance earnestly expectant. Much as this change surprised me, his words did more, for, taking both my hands in his, he gravely said, "Do you know that I am your uncle by adoption and not blood, Sybil?"

"Yes, sir; I heard so, but forgot about it," and I looked up at him, my anger quite lost in astonishment.

"Let me tell you then. Your grandfather was childless for many years, my mother was an early friend, and when her death left me an orphan, he took me for his son and heir. But two years from that time your father was born. I was too young to realize the entire change this might make in my life. The old man was too just and generous to let me feel it, and the two lads grew up together like brothers. Both married young, and when you were born a few years later than my son, your father said to me, 'Your boy shall have my girl, and the fortune I have innocently robbed you of shall make us happy in our children.' Then the family league was made, renewed at his death, and now destroyed by his daughter, unless—Sybil, I am forty-five, you not eighteen, yet you once said you could be very happy with me, if I were always kind to you. I can promise that I will be, for I love you. My darling, you reject the son, will you accept the father?"

If he had struck me, it would scarcely have dismayed me more. I started up, and snatching away my hands, hid my face in them, for after the first tingle of surprise an almost irresistible desire to laugh came over me, but I dared not, and gravely, gently he went on.

"I am a bold man to say this, yet I mean it most sincerely. I never meant to betray the affection I believed you never could return, and would only laugh at as a weakness; but your past acts, your present words, give me courage to confess that I desire to keep my ward mine forever. Shall it be so?"

He evidently mistook my surprise for maidenly emotion, and the suddenness of this unforeseen catastrophe seemed to deprive me of words. All thought of merriment or ridicule was forgotten in a sense of guilt, for if he feigned the love he offered it was well done, and I believed it then. I saw at once the natural impression conveyed by my conduct; my half confession and the folly of it all oppressed me with a regret and shame I could not master. My mind was in dire confusion, yet a decided "No" was rapidly emerging from the chaos, but was not uttered; for just at this crisis, as I stood with my uncle's arm about me, my hand again in his, and his head bent down to catch my answer, Guy swung himself gaily into the room.

A glance seemed to explain all, and in an instant his face assumed that expression of pale wrath so much more terrible to witness than the fiercest outbreak; his eye grew fiery, his voice bitterly sarcastic, as he said, "Ah, I see; the play goes on, but the actors change parts. I congratulate you, sir, on your success, and Sybil on her choice. Henceforth I am *de trop*, but before I go allow me to offer my wedding gift. You have taken the bride, let me supply the ring."

He threw a jewel box upon the table, adding, in that unnaturally calm tone that made my heart stand still:

"A little candor would have spared me much pain, Sybil; yet I hope you will enjoy your bonds as heartily as I shall my escape from them. A little confidence would have made me your ally, not your rival, Father. I have not your address; therefore I lose, you win. Let it be so. I had rather be the vagabond this makes me than sell myself, that you may gamble away that girl's fortune as you have your own and mine. You need not ask me to the wedding, I will not come. Oh, Sybil, I so loved, so trusted you!"

And with that broken exclamation he was gone.

The stormy scene had passed so rapidly, been so strange and sudden, Guy's anger so scornful and abrupt, I could not understand it, and felt like a puppet in the grasp of some power I could not resist; but as my lover left the room I broke out of the bewilderment that held me, imploring him to stay and hear me.

It was too late, he was gone, and Sultan's tramp was already tearing down the avenue. I listened till the sound died, then my hot temper rose past control, and womanlike asserted itself in vehement and voluble speech. I was angry with my uncle, my cousin, and myself, and for several minutes poured forth a torrent of explanations, reproaches, and regrets, such as only a passionate girl could utter.

My uncle stood where I had left him when I flew tc the door with my vain cry; he now looked baffled, yet sternly resolved, and as I paused for breath his only answer was "Sybil, you ask me to bring back that headstrong boy; I cannot; he will never come. This marriage was distasteful to him, yet he submitted for my sake, because I have been unfortunate, and we are poor. Let him go, forget the past, and be to me what I desire, for I loved your father and will be a faithful guardian to his daughter all my life. Child, it must be—come, I implore, I command you."

He beckoned imperiously as if to awe me, and held up the glittering betrothal ring as if to tempt me. The tone, the act, the look put me quite beside myself. I did go to him, did take the ring, but said as resolutely as himself, "Guy rejects me, and I have done with love. Uncle, you would have deceived me, used me as a means to your own selfish ends. I will accept neither yourself nor your gifts, for now I despise both you and your commands." And as the most energetic emphasis I could give to my defiance, I flung the ring, case and all, across the room; it struck the great mirror, shivered it just in the middle, and sent several loosened fragments crashing to the floor.

"Great heavens! Is the young lady mad?" exclaimed a voice behind us. Both turned and saw Dr. Karnac, a stealthy, sallow-faced Spaniard, for whom I had an invincible aversion. He was my uncle's physician, had been visiting a sick servant in the upper regions, and my adverse fate sent him to the door just at that moment with that unfortunate exclamation on his lips.

"What do you say?"

My uncle wheeled about and eyed the newcomer intently as he repeated his words. I have no doubt I looked like one demented, for I was desperately angry, pale and trembling with excitement, and as they fronted me with a curious expression of alarm on their faces, a sudden sense of the absurdity of the spectacle came over me; I laughed hysterically a moment, then broke into a passion of regretful tears, remembering that Guy was gone. As I sobbed behind my hands, I knew the gentlemen were whispering together and of me, but I never heeded them, for as I wept myself calmer a comforting thought occurred to me. Guy could not have gone far, for Sultan had been out all day, and though reckless of himself he was not of his horse, which he loved like a human being; therefore he was doubtless at the house of a humble friend nearby. If I could slip away unseen, I might undo my miserable work, or at least see him again before he went away into the world, perhaps never to return. This hope gave me courage for anything, and dashing away my tears, I took a covert survey. Dr. Karnac and my uncle still stood before the fire, deep in their low-toned conversation; their backs were toward me; and hushing the rustle of my dress, I stole away with noiseless steps into the hall, seized Guy's plaid, and, opening the great door unseen, darted down the avenue.

Not far, however; the wind buffeted me to and fro, the rain blinded me, the mud clogged my feet and soon robbed me of a slipper; groping for it in despair, I saw a light flash into the outer darkness; heard voices calling, and soon the swift tramp of steps behind me. Feeling like a hunted doe, I ran on, but before I had gained a dozen yards my shoeless foot struck a sharp stone, and I fell half stunned upon the wet grass of the wayside bank. Dr. Karnac reached me first, took me up as if I were a naughty child, and carried me back through a group of staring servants to the drawing room, my uncle following with breathless entreaties that I would be calm, and a most uncharacteristic display of bustle.

I was horribly ashamed; my head ached with the shock of the fall, my foot bled, my heart fluttered, and when the doctor put me down the crisis came, for as my uncle bent over me with the strange question "My poor girl, do you know me?" an irresistible impulse impelled me to push him from me, crying passionately, "Yes, I know and hate you; let me go! Let me go, or it will be too late!" Then, quite spent with the varying emotions of the last hour, for the first time in my life I swooned away.

Coming to myself, I found I was in my own room, with my uncle, the doctor, Janet, and Mrs. Best, the housekeeper, gathered about me, the latter saying, as she bathed my temples, "She's a sad sight, poor thing, so young, so bonny, and so unfortunate. Did you ever see her so before, Janet?"

"Bless you, no, ma'am; there was no signs of such a tantrum when I dressed her for dinner."

"What do they mean? Did they never see anyone angry before?" I dimly wondered, and presently, through the fast disappearing stupor that had held me, Dr. Karnac's deep voice came distinctly, saying, "If it continues, you are perfectly justified in doing so."

"Doing what?" I demanded sharply, for the sound both roused and irritated me, I disliked the man so intensely.

"Nothing, my dear, nothing," purred Mrs. Best, supporting me as I sat up, feeling weak and dazed, yet resolved to know what was going on. I was "a sad sight" indeed: my drenched hair hung about my shoulders, my dress was streaked with mud, one shoeless foot was red with blood, the other splashed and stained, and a white, wild-eyed face completed the ruinous image the opposite mirror showed me. Everything looked blurred and strange, and a feverish unrest possessed me, for I was not one to subside easily after such a mental storm. Leaning on my arm, I scanned the room and its occupants with all the composure I could collect. The two women eyed me curiously yet pitifully; Dr. Karnac stood glancing at me furtively as he listened to my uncle, who spoke rapidly in Spanish as he showed the little scar upon his hand.

That sight did more to restore me than the cordial just administered, and I rose erect, saying abruptly, "Please, everybody, go away; my head aches, and I want to be alone."

"Let Janet stay and help you, dear; you are not fit," began Mrs. Best; but I peremptorily stopped her.

"No, go yourself, and take her with you; I'm tired of so much stir about such foolish things as a broken glass and a girl in a pet."

"You will be good enough to take this quieting draft before I go, Miss Sybil."

"I shall do nothing of the sort, for I need only solitude and sleep to be perfectly well," and I emptied the glass the doctor offered into the fire.

He shrugged his shoulders with a disagreeable smile, and quietly began to prepare another draft, saying, "You are mistaken, my dear young lady; you need much care, and should obey, that your uncle may be spared further apprehension and anxiety."

My patience gave out at this assumption of authority; and I determined to carry matters with a high hand, for they all stood watching me in a way which seemed the height of impertinent curiosity.

"He is not my uncle! Never has been, and deserves neither respect nor obedience from me! I am the best judge of my own health, and you are not bettering it by contradiction and unnecessary fuss. This is my house, and you will oblige me by leaving it, Dr. Karnac; this is my room, and I insist on being left in peace immediately."

I pointed to the door as I spoke; the women hurried out with scared faces; the doctor bowed and followed, but paused on the threshold, while my uncle approached me, asking in a tone inaudible to those still hovering round the door, "Do you still persist in your refusal, Sybil?"

"How dare you ask me that again? I tell you I had rather die than marry you!"

"The Lord be merciful to us! Just hear how she's going on now about marrying Master. Ain't it awful, Jane?" ejaculated Mrs. Best, bobbing her head in for a last look.

"Hold your tongue, you impertinent creature!" I called out; and the fat old soul bundled away in such comical haste I laughed, in spite of languor and vexation.

My uncle left me, and I heard him say as he passed the doctor, "You see how it is."

"Nothing uncommon; but that virulence is a bad symptom," answered the Spaniard, and closing the door locked it, having dexterously removed the key from within.

I had never been subjected to restraint of any kind; it made me reckless at once, for this last indignity was not to be endured.

"Open this instantly!" I commanded, shaking the door. No one answered, and after a few ineffectual attempts to break the lock I left it, threw up the window and looked out; the ground was too far off for a leap, but the trellis where summer vines had clung was strong and high, a step would place me on it, a moment's agility bring me to the terrace below. I was now in just the state to attempt any rash exploit, for the cordial had both strengthened and excited me; my foot was bandaged, my clothes still wet; I could suffer no new damage, and have my own way at small cost. Out I crept, climbed safely down, and made my way to the lodge as I had at first intended. But Guy was not there; and returning, I boldly went in at the great door, straight to the room where my uncle and the doctor were still talking.

"I wish the key of my room" was my brief command.

Both started as if I had been a ghost, and my uncle exclaimed, "You here! How in heaven's name came you out?"

"By the window. I am no child to be confined for a fit of anger. I will not submit to it; tomorrow I shall go to Madame; till then I will be mistress in my own house. Give me the key, sir."

"Shall I?" asked the doctor of my uncle, who nodded with a whispered "Yes, yes; don't excite her again."

It was restored, and without another word I went loftily up to my room, locked myself in, and spent a restless, miserable night. When morning came, I breakfasted abovestairs, and then busied myself packing trunks, burning papers, and collecting every trifle Guy had ever given me. No one annoyed me, and I saw only Janet, who had evidently received some order that kept her silent and respectful, though her face still betrayed the same curiosity and pitiful interest as the night before. Lunch was brought up, but I could not eat, and began to feel that the exposure, the fall, and excitement of the evening had left me weak and nervous, so I gave up the idea of going to Madame till the morrow; and as the afternoon waned, tried to sleep, yet could not, for I had sent a note to several of Guy's haunts, imploring him to see me; but my messenger brought word that he was not to be found, and my heart was too heavy to rest.

When summoned to dinner, I still refused to go down; for I heard Dr. Karnac's voice, and would not meet him, so I sent word that I wished the carriage early the following morning, and to be left alone till then. In a few minutes, back came Janet, with a glass of wine set forth on a silver salver, and a card with these words: "Forgive, forget, for your father's sake, and drink with me, 'Oblivion to the past.'"

It touched and softened me. I knew my uncle's pride, and saw in this an entire relinquishment of the hopes I had so thoughtlessly fostered in his mind. I was passionate, but not vindictive. He had been kind, I very willful. His mistake was natural, my resentment ungenerous. Though my resolution to go remained unchanged, I was sorry for my part in the affair; and remembering that through me his son was lost to him, I accepted his apology, drank his toast, and sent him back a dutiful "Good night."

I was unused to wine. The draft I had taken was powerful with age, and, though warm and racy to the palate, proved too potent for me. Still sitting before my fire, I slowly fell into a restless drowse, haunted by a dim dream that I was seeking Guy in a ship, whose motion gradually lulled me into perfect unconsciousness.

Waking at length, I was surprised to find myself in bed, with a shimmer of daylight peeping through the curtains. Recollecting that I was to leave early, I sprang up, took one step, and remained transfixed with dismay, for the room was not my own! Utterly unfamiliar was every object on which my eyes fell. The place was small, plainly furnished, and close, as if long unused. My trunks stood against the wall, my clothes lay on a chair, and on the bed I had left trailed a fur-lined cloak I had often seen on my uncle's shoulders. A moment I stared about me bewildered, then hurried to the window. It was grated!

A lawn, sere and sodden, lay without, and a line of somber firs hid the landscape beyond the high wall which encompassed the dreary plot. More and more alarmed, I flew to the door and found it locked. No bell was visible, no sound audible, no human presence near me, and an ominous foreboding thrilled cold through nerves and blood, as, for the first time, I felt the paralyzing touch of fear. Not long, however. My native courage soon returned, indignation took the place of terror, and excitement gave me strength. My temples throbbed with a dull pain, my eyes were heavy, my limbs weighed down by an unwonted lassitude, and my memory seemed strangely confused; but one thing was clear to me: I must see somebody, ask questions, demand explanations, and get away to Madame without delay.

With trembling hands I dressed, stopping suddenly with a cry; for lifting my hands to my head, I discovered that my hair, my beautiful, abundant hair, was gone! There was no mirror in the room, but I could feel that it had been shorn away close about face and neck. This outrage was more than I could bear, and the first tears I shed fell for my lost charm. It was weak, perhaps, but I felt better for it, clearer in mind and readier to confront whatever lay before me. I knocked and called. Then, losing patience, shook and screamed; but no one came or answered me; and wearied out at last, I sat down and cried again in impotent despair.

An hour passed, then a step approached, the key turned, and a hard-faced woman entered with a tray in her hand. I had resolved to be patient, if possible, and controlled myself to ask quietly, though my eyes kindled, and my voice trembled with resentment, "Where am I, and why am I here against my will?"

"This is your breakfast, miss; you must be sadly hungry" was the only reply I got.

"I will never eat till you tell me what I ask."

"Will you be quiet, and mind me if I do, miss?"

"You have no right to exact obedience from me, but I'll try."

"That's right. Now all I know is that you are twenty miles from the Moors, and came because you are ill. Do you like sugar in your coffee?"

"When did I come? I don't remember it."

"Early this morning; you don't remember because you were put to sleep before being fetched, to save trouble."

"Ah, that wine! Who brought me here?"

"Dr. Karnac, miss."

"Alone?"

"Yes, miss; you were easier to manage asleep than awake, he said."

I shook with anger, yet still restrained myself, hoping to fathom the mystery of this nocturnal journey.

"What is your name, please?" I meekly asked.

"You can call me Hannah."

"Well, Hannah, there is a strange mistake somewhere. I am not ill—you see I am not—and I wish to go away at once to the friend I was to meet today. Get me a carriage and have my baggage taken out."

"It can't be done, miss. We are a mile from town, and have no carriages here; besides, you couldn't go if I had a dozen. I have my orders, and shall obey 'em."

"But Dr. Karnac has no right to bring or keep me here."

"Your uncle sent you. The doctor has the care of you, and that is all I know about it. Now I have kept my promise, do you keep yours, miss, and eat your breakfast, else I can't trust you again."

"But what is the matter with me? How can I be ill and not know or feel it?" I demanded, more and more bewildered.

"You look it, and that's enough for them as is wise in such matters. You'd have had a fever, if it hadn't been seen to in time."

Sybil imprisoned in the madhouse

"Who cut my hair off?"

"I did; the doctor ordered it."

"How dared he? I hate that man, and never will obey him."

"Hush, miss, don't clench your hands and look in that way, for I shall have to report everything you say and do to him, and it won't be pleasant to tell that sort of thing."

The woman was civil, but grim and cool. Her eye was unsympathetic, her manner businesslike, her tone such as one uses to a refractory child, half soothing, half commanding. I conceived a dislike to her at once, and resolved to escape at all hazards, for my uncle's inexplicable movements filled me with alarm. Hannah had left my door open, a quick glance showed me another door also ajar at the end of a wide hall, a glimpse of green, and a gate. My plan was desperately simple, and I executed it without delay. Affecting to eat, I presently asked the woman for my handkerchief from the bed. She crossed the room to get it. I darted out, down the passage, along the walk, and tugged vigorously at the great bolt of the gate, but it was also locked. In despair I flew into the garden, but a high wall enclosed it on every side; and as I ran round and round, vainly looking for some outlet, I saw Hannah, accompanied by a man as gray and grim as herself, coming leisurely toward me, with no appearance of excitement or displeasure. Back I would not go; and inspired with a sudden hope, swung myself into one of the firs that grew close against the wall. The branches snapped under me, the slender tree swayed perilously, but up I struggled, till the wide coping of the wall was gained. There I paused and looked back. The woman was hurrying through the gate to intercept my descent on the other side, and close behind me the man, sternly calling me to stop. I looked down; a stony ditch was below, but I would rather risk my life than tamely lose my liberty, and with a flying leap tried to reach the bank; failed, fell heavily among the stones, felt an awful crash, and then came an utter blank.

For many weeks I lay burning in a fever, fitfully conscious of Dr. Karnac and the woman's presence; once I fancied I saw my uncle, but was never sure, and rose at last a shadow of my former self, feeling pitifully broken, both mentally and physically. I was in a better room now, wintry winds howled without, but a generous fire glowed behind the high closed fender, and books lay on my table.

I saw no one but Hannah, yet could wring no intelligence from her beyond what she had already told, and no sign of interest reached me from the outer world. I seemed utterly deserted and forlorn, my spirit was crushed, my strength gone, my freedom lost, and for a time I succumbed to despair, letting one day follow another without energy or hope. It is hard to live with no object to give zest to life, especially for those still blessed with youth, and even in my prison house I soon found one quite in keeping with the mystery that surrounded me.

As I sat reading by day or lay awake at night, I became aware that the room above my own was occupied by some inmate whom I never saw. A peculiar person it seemed to be; for I heard steps going to and fro, hour after hour, in a tireless march that wore upon my nerves, as many a harsher sound would not have done. I could neither tease nor surprise Hannah into any explanation of the thing, and day after day I listened to it, till I longed to cover up my ears and implore the unknown walker to stop, for heaven's sake. Other sounds I heard and fretted over: a low monotonous murmur, as of someone singing a lullaby; a fitful tapping, like a cradle rocked on a carpetless floor; and at rare intervals cries of suffering, sharp but brief, as if forcibly suppressed. These sounds, combined with the solitude, the confinement, and the books I read, a collection of ghostly tales and weird fancies, soon wrought my nerves to a state of terrible irritability, and wore upon my health so visibly that I was allowed at last to leave my room.

The house was so well guarded that I soon relinquished all hope of escape, and listlessly amused myself by roaming through the unfurnished rooms and echoing halls, seldom venturing into Hannah's domain; for there her husband sat, surrounded by chemical apparatus, poring over crucibles and retorts. He never spoke to me, and I dreaded the glance of his cold eye, for it looked unsoftened by a ray of pity at the little figure that sometimes paused a moment on his threshold, wan and wasted as the ghost of departed hope.

The chief interest of these dreary walks centered in the door of the room above my own, for a great hound lay before it, eyeing me savagely as he rejected all advances, and uttering his deep bay if I approached too near. To me this room possessed an irresistible fascination. I could not keep away from it by day, I dreamed of it by night, it haunted me continually, and soon became a sort of monomania, which I condemned, yet could not control, till at length I found myself pacing to and fro as those invisible feet paced overhead. Hannah came and stopped me, and a few hours later Dr. Karnac appeared. I was so changed that I feared him with a deadly fear. He seemed to enjoy it; for in the pride of youth and beauty I had shown him contempt and defiance at my uncle's, and he took an ungenerous satisfaction in annoying me by a display of power. He never answered my questions or entreaties, regarded me as being without sense or will, insisted on my trying various mixtures and experiments in diet, gave me strange books to read, and weekly received Hannah's report of all that passed. That day he came, looked at me, said, "Let her walk," and went away, smiling that hateful smile of his.

Soon after this I took to walking in my sleep, and more than once woke to find myself roving lampless through that haunted house in the dead of night. I concealed these unconscious wanderings for a time, but an ominous event broke them up at last and betrayed them to Hannah.

I had followed the steps one day for several hours, walking below as they walked above; had peopled that mysterious room with every mournful shape my disordered fancy could conjure up; had woven tragical romances about it, and brooded over the one subject of interest my unnatural life possessed with the intensity of a mind upon which its uncanny influence was telling with perilous rapidity. At midnight I woke to find myself standing in a streak of moonlight, opposite the door whose threshold I had never crossed. The April night was warm, a single pane of glass high up in that closed door was drawn aside, as if for air; and as I stood dreamily collecting my sleep-drunken senses, I saw a ghostly hand emerge and beckon, as if to me. It startled me broad awake, with a faint exclamation and a shudder from head to foot. A cloud swept over the moon, and when it passed the hand was gone, but shrill through the keyhole came a whisper that chilled me to the marrow of my bones, so terribly distinct and imploring was it.

"Find it! For God's sake find it before it is too late!"

The hound sprang up with an angry growl; I heard Hannah leave her bed nearby; and with an inspiration strange as the moment, I paced slowly on with open eyes and lips apart, as I had seen *Amina* in the happy days when kind old Madame took me to the theater, whose mimic horrors I had never thought to equal with such veritable ones. Hannah appeared at her door with a light, but on I went in a trance of fear; for I was only kept from dropping in a swoon by the blind longing to fly from that spectral voice and hand. Past Hannah I went, she following; and as I slowly laid myself in bed, I heard her say to her husband, who just then came up, "Sleepwalking, John; it's getting worse and worse, as the doctor foretold; she'll settle down like the other presently, but she must be locked up at night, else the dog will do her a mischief."

The man yawned and grumbled; then they went, leaving me to spend hours of unspeakable suffering, which aged me more than years. What was I to find? Where was I to look? And when would it be too late? These questions tormented me; for I could find no answers to them, divine no meaning, see no course to pursue. Why was I here? What motive induced my uncle to commit such an act? And when should I be liberated? were equally unanswerable, equally tormenting, and they haunted me like ghosts. I had no power to exorcise or forget. After that I walked no more, because I slept no more; sleep seemed scared away, and waking dreams harassed me with their terrors. Night after night I paced my room in utter darkness—for I was allowed no lamp—night after night I wept bitter tears wrung from me by anguish, for which I had no name; and night after night the steps kept time to mine, and the faint lullaby came down to me as if to soothe and comfort my distress. I felt that my health was going, my mind growing confused and weak; my thoughts wandered vaguely, memory began to fail, and idiocy or madness seemed my inevitable fate; but through it all my heart clung to Guy, yearning for him with a hunger that would not be appeased.

At rare intervals I was allowed to walk in the neglected garden, where no flowers bloomed, no birds sang, no companion came to me but surly John, who followed with his book or pipe, stopping when I stopped, walking when I walked, keeping a vigilant eye upon me, yet seldom speaking except to decline answering my questions. These walks did me no good, for the air was damp and heavy with vapors from the marsh; for the house stood near a half-dried lake, and hills shut it in on every side. No fresh winds from upland moor or distant ocean ever blew across the narrow valley; no human creature visited the place, and nothing but a vague hope that my birthday might bring some change, some help, sustained me. It did bring help, but of such an unexpected sort that its effects remained through all my afterlife. My birthday came, and with it my uncle. I was in my room, walking restlessly—for the habit was a confirmed one now—when the door opened, and Hannah, Dr. Karnac, my uncle, and a gentleman whom I knew to be his lawyer entered, and surveyed me as if I were a spectacle. I saw my uncle start and turn pale; I had never seen myself since I came, but if I had not suspected that I was a melancholy wreck of my former self, I should have known it then, such sudden pain and pity softened his ruthless countenance for a single instant. Dr. Karnac's eye had a magnetic power over me; I had always felt it, but in my present feeble state I dreaded, yet submitted to it with a helpless fear that should have touched his heart—it was on me then, I could not resist it, and paused fixed and fascinated by that repellent yet potent glance.

Hannah pointed to the carpet worn to shreds by my weary march, to the walls which I had covered with weird, grotesque, or tragic figures to while away the heavy hours, lastly to myself, mute, motionless, and scared, saying, as if in confirmation of some previous assertion, "You see, gentlemen, she is, as I said, quiet, but quite hopeless."

I thought she was interceding for me; and breaking from the bewilderment and fear that held me, I stretched my hands to them, crying with an imploring cry, "Yes, I *am* quiet! I *am* hopeless! Oh, have pity on me before this dreadful life kills me or drives me mad!"

Dr. Karnac came to me at once with a black frown, which I alone could see; I evaded him, and clung to Hannah, still crying frantically—for this seemed my last hope—"Uncle, let me go! I will give you all I have, will never ask for Guy, will be obedient and meek if I may only go to Madame and never hear the feet again, or see the sights that terrify me in this dreadful room. Take me out! For God's sake take me out!"

My uncle did not answer me, but covered up his face with a despairing gesture, and hurried from the room; the lawyer followed, muttering pitifully, "Poor thing! Poor thing!" and Dr. Karnac laughed the first laugh I had ever heard him utter as he wrenched Hannah from my grasp and locked me in alone. My one hope died then, and I resolved to kill myself rather than endure this life another month; for now it grew clear to me that they believed me mad, and death of the body was far more preferable than that of the mind. I think I *was* a little mad just then, but remember well the sense of peace that came to me as I tore strips from my clothing, braided them into a cord, hid it beneath my mattress, and serenely waited for the night. Sitting in the last twilight I thought to see in this unhappy world, I recollected that I had not heard the feet all day, and fell to pondering over the unusual omission. But if the steps had been silent in that room, voices had not, for I heard a continuous murmur at one time: the tones of one voice were abrupt and broken, the other low, yet resonant, and that, I felt assured, belonged to my uncle. Who was he speaking to? What were they saying? Should I ever know? And even then, with death before me, the intense desire to possess the secret filled me with its old unrest.

Night came at last; I heard the clock strike one, and listening to discover if John still lingered up, I heard through the deep hush a soft grating in the room above, a stealthy sound that would have escaped ears less preternaturally alert than mine. Like a flash came the thought, "Someone is filing bars or picking locks: will the unknown remember me and let me share her flight?" The fatal noose hung ready, but I no longer cared to use it, for hope had come to nerve me with the strength and courage I had lost. Breathlessly I listened; the sound went on, stopped; a dead silence reigned; then something brushed against my door, and with a suddenness that made me tingle from head to foot like an electric shock, through the keyhole came again that whisper, urgent, imploring, and mysterious, "Find it! For God's sake find it before it is too late!" Then fainter, as if breath failed, came the broken words, "The dog—a lock of hair—there is yet time."

Eagerness rendered me forgetful of the secrecy I should preserve, and I cried aloud, "What shall I find? Where shall I look?" My voice, sharpened by fear, rang shrilly through the house; Hannah's quick tread rushed down the hall; something fell; then loud and long rose a cry that made my heart stand still, so helpless, so hopeless was its wild lament. I had betrayed and I could not save or comfort the kind soul who had lost liberty through me. I was frantic to get out, and beat upon my door in a paroxysm of impatience, but no one came; and all night long those awful cries went on above, cries of mortal anguish, as if soul and body were being torn asunder. Till dawn I listened, pent in that room which now possessed an added terror; till dawn I called, wept, and prayed, with mingled pity, fear, and penitence; and till dawn the agony of that unknown sufferer continued unabated. I heard John hurry to and fro, heard Hannah issue orders with an accent of human sympathy in her hard voice; heard Dr. Karnac pass and repass my door; and all the sounds of confusion and alarm in that once quiet house. With daylight all was still, a stillness more terrible than the stir; for it fell so suddenly, remained so utterly unbroken, that there seemed no explanation of it but the dread word death.

At noon Hannah, a shade paler but grim as ever, brought me some food, saying she forgot my breakfast, and when I refused to eat, yet asked no questions, she bade me go into the garden and not fret myself over last night's flurry. I went, and passing down the corridor, glanced furtively at the door I never saw without a thrill; but I experienced a new sensation then, for the hound was gone, the door was open, and with an impulse past control, I crept in and looked about me. It was a room like mine, the carpet worn like mine, the windows barred like mine; there the resemblance ended, for an empty cradle stood beside the bed, and on that bed, below a sweeping cover, stark and still a lifeless body lay. I was inured to fear now, and an unwholesome craving for new terrors seemed to have grown by what it fed on: an irresistible desire led me close, nerved me to lift the cover and look below—a single glance—then with a cry as panic-stricken as that which rent the silence of the night, I fled away, for the face I saw was a pale image of my own. Sharpened by suffering, pallid with death, the features were familiar as those I used to see; the hair, beautiful and blond as mine had been, streamed long over the pulseless breast, and on the hand, still clenched in that last struggle, shone the likeness of a ring I wore, a ring bequeathed me by my father. An awesome fancy that it was myself assailed me; I had plotted death, and with the waywardness of a shattered mind, I recalled legends of spirits returning to behold the bodies they had left.

Glad now to seek the garden, I hurried down, but on the threshold of the great hall door was arrested by the sharp crack of a pistol; and as a little cloud of smoke dispersed, I saw John drop the weapon and approach the hound, who lay writhing on the bloody grass. Moved by compassion for the faithful brute whose long vigilance was so cruelly repaid, I went to him, and kneeling there, caressed the great head that never yielded to my touch before. John assumed his watch at once, and leaning against a tree, cleaned the pistol, content that I should amuse myself with the dying creature, who looked into my face with eyes of almost human pathos and reproach. The brass collar seemed to choke him as he gasped for breath, and leaning nearer to undo it, I saw, half hidden in his own black hair, a golden lock wound tightly round the collar, and so near its color as to be unobservable, except upon a close inspection. No accident could have placed it there; no head but mine in that house wore hair of that sunny hue—yes, one other, and my heart gave a sudden leap as I remembered the shining locks just seen on that still bosom.

"Find it—the dog—the lock of hair," rang in my ears, and swift as light came the conviction that the unknown help was found at last. The little band was woven close. I had no knife, delay was fatal. I bent my head as if lamenting over the poor beast and bit the knot apart, drew out a folded paper, hid it in my hand, and rising, strolled leisurely back to my own room, saying I did not care to walk till it was warmer. With eager eyes I examined my strange treasure trove. It consisted of two strips of thinnest paper, without address or signature, one almost illegible, worn at the edges and stained with the green rust of the collar; the other fresher, yet more feebly written, both abrupt and disjointed, but terribly significant to me. This was the first:

I have never seen you, never heard your name, yet I know that you are young, that you are suffering, and I try to help you in my poor way. I think you are not crazed yet, as I often am; for your voice is sane, your plaintive singing not like mine, your walking only caught from me, I hope. I sing to lull the baby whom I never saw; I walk to lessen the long journey that will bring me to the husband I have lost—stop! I must not think of those things or I shall forget. If you are not already mad, you will be; I suspect you were sent here to be made so; for the air is poison, the solitude is fatal, and Karnac remorseless in his mania for prying into the mysteries of human minds. What devil sent you I may never know, but I long to warn you. I can devise no way but this; the dog comes into my room sometimes, you sometimes pause at my door and talk to him; you may find the paper I shall hide about his collar. Read, destroy, but obey it. I implore you to leave this house before it is too late.

The other paper was as follows:

I have watched you, tried to tell you where to look, for you have not found my warning yet, though I often tie it there and hope. You fear the dog, perhaps, and my plot fails; yet I know by your altered step and voice that you are fast reaching my unhappy state; for I am fitfully mad, and shall be till I die. Today I have seen a familiar face; it seems to have calmed and strengthened me, and though he would not help you, I shall make one desperate attempt. I may not find you, so leave my warning to the hound, yet hope to breathe a word into your sleepless ear that shall send you back into the world the happy thing you should be. Child! Woman! Whatever you are, leave this accursed house while you have power to do it.

That was all. I did not destroy the papers, but I obeyed them, and for a week watched and waited till the propitious instant came. I saw my uncle, the doctor, and two others follow the poor body to its grave beside the lake, saw all depart but Dr. Karnac, and felt redoubled hatred and contempt for the men who could repay my girlish slights with such a horrible revenge. On the seventh day, as I went down for my daily walk, I saw John and Dr. Karnac so deep in some uncanny experiment that I passed out unguarded. Hoping to profit by this unexpected chance, I sprang down the steps, but the next moment dropped half stunned upon the grass; for behind me rose a crash, a shriek, a sudden blaze that flashed up and spread, sending a noisome vapor rolling out with clouds of smoke and flame.

Aghast, I was just gathering myself up when Hannah fled out of the house, dragging her husband senseless and bleeding, while her own face was ashy with affright. She dropped her burden beside me, saying, with white lips and a vain look for help where help was not, "Something they were at has burst, killed the doctor, and fired the house! Watch John till I get help, and leave him at your peril." Then flinging open the gate she sped away.

"Now is my time," I thought, and only waiting till she vanished, I boldly followed her example, running rapidly along the road in an opposite direction, careless of bonnetless head and trembling limbs, intent only upon leaving that prison house far behind me. For several hours,

I hurried along that solitary road; the spring sun shone, birds sang in the blooming hedges, green nooks invited me to pause and rest; but I heeded none of them, steadily continuing my flight, till spent and footsore I was forced to stop a moment by a wayside spring. As I stooped to drink, I saw my face for the first time in many months, and started to see how like that dead one it had grown, in all but the eternal peace which made that beautiful in spite of suffering and age. Standing thus and wondering if Guy would know me, should we ever meet, the sound of wheels disturbed me. Believing them to be coming from the place I had left, I ran desperately down the hill, turned a sharp corner, and before I could check myself passed a carriage slowly ascending. A face sprang to the window, a voice cried "Stop!" but on I flew, hoping the traveler would let me go unpursued. Not so, however; soon I heard fleet steps following, gaining rapidly, then a hand seized me, a voice rang in my ears, and with a vain struggle I lay panting in my captor's hold, fearing to look up and meet a brutal glance. But the hand that had seized me tenderly drew me close, the voice that had alarmed cried joyfully, "Sybil, it is Guy: Lie still, poor child, you are safe at last."

Then I knew that my surest refuge was gained, and too weak for words, clung to him in an agony of happiness, which brought to his kind eyes the tears I could not shed.

The carriage returned; Guy took me in, and for a time cared only to soothe and sustain my worn soul and body with the cordial of his presence, as we rolled homeward through a blooming world, whose beauty I had never truly felt before. When the first tumult of emotion had subsided, I told the story of my captivity and my escape, ending with a passionate entreaty not to be returned to my uncle's keeping, for henceforth there could be neither affection nor respect between us.

"Fear nothing, Sybil; Madame is waiting for you at the Moors, and my father's unfaithful guardianship has ended with his life."

Then with averted face and broken voice Guy went on to tell his father's purposes, and what had caused this unexpected meeting. The facts were briefly these: The knowledge that my father had come between him and a princely fortune had always rankled in my uncle's heart, chilling the ambitious hopes he cherished even in his boyhood, and making life an eager search for pleasure in which to drown his vain regrets. This secret was suspected by my father, and the household league was formed as some atonement for the innocent offense. It seemed to soothe my uncle's resentful nature, and as years went on he lived freely, assured that ample means would be his through his son. Luxurious, self-indulgent, fond of all excitements, and reckless in their pursuit, he took

At the spring

no thought for the morrow till a few months before his return. A gay
winter in Paris reduced him to those straits of which women know so
little; creditors were oppressive, summer friends failed him, gambling
debts harassed him, his son reproached him, and but one resource remained—Guy's speedy marriage with the half-forgotten heiress. The boy
had been educated to regard this fate as a fixed fact, and submitted, believing the time to be far distant; but the sudden summons came, and
he rebelled against it, preferring liberty to love. My uncle pacified the
claimants by promises to be fulfilled at my expense, and hurried home
to press on the marriage, which now seemed imperative. I was taken to
my future home, approved by my uncle, beloved by my cousin, and, but
for my own folly, might have been a happy wife on that May morning
when I listened to the unveiling of the past. My mother had been melancholy mad since that unhappy rumor of my father's death; this affliction had been well concealed from me, lest the knowledge should prey
upon my excitable nature and perhaps induce a like misfortune. I believed her dead, yet I had seen her, knew where her solitary grave was
made, and still carried in my bosom the warning she had sent me,
prompted by the unerring instinct of a mother's heart. In my father's will
a clause was added just below the one confirming my betrothal, a clause
decreeing that, if it should appear that I inherited my mother's malady,
the fortune should revert to my cousin, with myself a mournful legacy,
to be cherished by him whether his wife or not. This passage, and that
relating to my freedom of choice, had been omitted in the copy shown
me on the night when my seeming refusal of Guy had induced his father
to believe that I loved him, to make a last attempt to keep the prize by
offering himself, and, when that failed, to harbor a design that changed
my little comedy into the tragical experience I have told.

Dr. Karnac's exclamation had caused the recollection of that clause
respecting my insanity to flash into my uncle's mind—a mind as quick to
conceive as fearless to execute. I unconsciously abetted the stratagem,
and Dr. Karnac was an unscrupulous ally, for love of gain was as strong
as love of science; both were amply gratified, and I, poor victim, was
given up to be experimented upon, till by subtle means I was driven
to the insanity which would give my uncle full control of my fortune
and my fate. How the black plot prospered has been told; but retribution
speedily overtook them both, for Dr. Karnac paid his penalty by the sudden death that left his ashes among the blackened ruins of that house
of horrors, and my uncle had preceded him. For before the change of
heirs could be effected my mother died, and the hours spent in that
unhealthful spot insinuated the subtle poison of the marsh into his blood;

years of pleasure left little vigor to withstand the fever, and a week of suffering ended a life of generous impulses perverted, fine endowments wasted, and opportunities forever lost. When death drew near, he sent for Guy (who, through the hard discipline of poverty and honest labor, was becoming a manlier man), confessed all, and implored him to save me before it was too late. He did, and when all was told, when each saw the other by the light of this strange and sad experience—Guy poor again, I free, the old bond still existing, the barrier of misunderstanding gone— it was easy to see our way, easy to submit, to forgive, forget, and begin anew the life these clouds had darkened for a time.

Home received me, kind Madame welcomed me, Guy married me, and I was happy; but over all these years, serenely prosperous, still hangs for me the shadow of the past, still rises that dead image of my mother, still echoes that spectral whisper in the dark.

Perilous Play

"IF someone does not propose a new and interesting amusement, I shall die of ennui!" said pretty Belle Daventry, in a tone of despair. "I have read all my books, used up all my Berlin wools, and it's too warm to go to town for more. No one can go sailing yet, as the tide is out; we are all nearly tired to death of cards, croquet, and gossip, so what shall we do to while away this endless afternoon? Dr. Meredith, I command you to invent and propose a new game in five minutes."

"To hear is to obey," replied the young man, who lay in the grass at her feet, as he submissively slapped his forehead, and fell a-thinking with all his might.

Holding up her finger to preserve silence, Belle pulled out her watch and waited with an expectant smile. The rest of the young party, who were indolently scattered about under the elms, drew nearer, and brightened visibly, for Dr. Meredith's inventive powers were well-known, and something refreshingly novel might be expected from him. One gentleman did not stir, but then he lay within earshot, and merely turned his fine eyes from the sea to the group before him. His glance rested a moment on Belle's piquant figure, for she looked very pretty with her bright hair blowing in the wind, one plump white arm extended to keep order, and one little foot, in a distracting slipper, just visible below the voluminous folds of her dress. Then the glance passed to another figure, sitting somewhat apart in a cloud of white muslin, for an airy burnoose floated from head and shoulders, showing only a singularly charming face. Pale and yet brilliant, for the Southern eyes were magnificent, the

(579)

clear olive cheeks contrasted well with darkest hair; lips like a pomegranate flower, and delicate, straight brows, as mobile as the lips. A cluster of crimson flowers, half falling from the loose black braids, and a golden bracelet of Arabian coins on the slender wrist were the only ornaments she wore, and became her better than the fashionable frippery of her companions. A book lay on her lap, but her eyes, full of a passionate melancholy, were fixed on the sea, which glittered round an island green and flowery as a summer paradise. Rose St. Just was as beautiful as her Spanish mother, but had inherited the pride and reserve of her English father; and this pride was the thorn which repelled lovers from the human flower. Mark Done sighed as he looked, and as if the sigh, low as it was, roused her from her reverie, Rose flashed a quick glance at him, took up her book, and went on reading the legend of "The Lotus Eaters."

"Time is up now, Doctor," cried Belle, pocketing her watch with a flourish.

"Ready to report," answered Meredith, sitting up and producing a little box of tortoiseshell and gold.

"How mysterious! What is it? Let me see, first!" And Belle removed the cover, looking like an inquisitive child. "Only bonbons; how stupid! That won't do, sir. We don't want to be fed with sugarplums. We demand to be amused."

"Eat six of these despised bonbons, and you *will* be amused in a new, delicious, and wonderful manner," said the young doctor, laying half a dozen on a green leaf and offering them to her.

"Why, what are they?" she asked, looking at him askance.

"Hashish; did you never hear of it?"

"Oh, yes; it's that Indian stuff which brings one fantastic visions, isn't it? I've always wanted to see and taste it, and now I will," cried Belle, nibbling at one of the bean-shaped comfits with its green heart.

"I advise you not to try it. People do all sorts of queer things when they take it. I wouldn't for the world," said a prudent young lady warningly, as all examined the box and its contents.

"Six can do no harm, I give you my word. I take twenty before I can enjoy myself, and some people even more. I've tried many experiments, both on the sick and the well, and nothing ever happened amiss, though the demonstrations were immensely interesting," said Meredith, eating his sugarplums with a tranquil air, which was very convincing to others.

"How shall I feel?" asked Belle, beginning on her second comfit.

"A heavenly dreaminess comes over one, in which they move as if on air. Everything is calm and lovely to them: no pain, no care, no fear of anything, and while it lasts one feels like an angel half asleep."

"But if one takes too much, how then?" said a deep voice behind the doctor.

"Hum! Well, that's not so pleasant, unless one likes phantoms, frenzies, and a touch of nightmare, which seems to last a thousand years. Ever try it, Done?" replied Meredith, turning toward the speaker, who was now leaning on his arm and looking interested.

"Never. I'm not a good subject for experiments. Too nervous a temperament to play pranks with."

"I should say ten would be about your number. Less than that seldom affects men. Ladies go off sooner, and don't need so many. Miss St. Just, may I offer you a taste of Elysium? I owe my success to you," said the doctor, approaching her deferentially.

"To me! And how?" she asked, lifting her large eyes with a slight smile.

"I was in the depths of despair when my eye caught the title of your book, and I was saved. For I remembered that I had hashish in my pocket."

"Are you a lotus-eater?" she said, permitting him to lay the six charmed bonbons on the page.

"My faith, no! I use it for my patients. It is very efficacious in nervous disorders, and is getting to be quite a pet remedy with us."

"I do not want to forget the past, but to read the future. Will hashish help me to do that?" asked Rose with an eager look, which made the young man flush, wondering if he bore any part in her hopes of that veiled future.

"Alas, no. I wish it could, for I, too, long to know my fate," he answered, very low, as he looked into the lovely face before him.

The soft glance changed to one of cool indifference and Rose gently brushed the hashish off her book, saying, with a little gesture of dismissal, "Then I have no desire to taste Elysium."

The white morsels dropped into the grass at her feet; but Dr. Meredith let them lie, and turning sharply, went back to sun himself in Belle's smiles.

"I've eaten all mine, and so has Evelyn. Mr. Norton will see goblins, I know, for he has taken quantities. I'm glad of it, for he don't believe in it, and I want to have him convinced by making a spectacle of himself for our amusement," said Belle, in great spirits at the new plan.

"When does the trance come on?" asked Evelyn, a shy girl, already rather alarmed at what she had done.

"About three hours after you take your dose, though the time varies with different people. Your pulse will rise, heart beat quickly, eyes darken and dilate, and an uplifted sensation will pervade you generally. Then these symptoms change, and the bliss begins. I've seen people sit or lie in one position for hours, rapt in a delicious dream, and wake from it as tranquil as if they had not a nerve in their bodies."

"How charming! I'll take some every time I'm worried. Let me see. It's now four, so our trances will come about seven, and we will devote the evening to manifestations," said Belle.

"Come, Done, try it. We are all going in for the fun. Here's your dose," and Meredith tossed him a dozen bonbons, twisted up in a bit of paper.

"No, thank you; I know myself too well to risk it. If you are all going to turn hashish-eaters, you'll need someone to take care of you, so I'll keep sober," tossing the little parcel back.

It fell short, and the doctor, too lazy to pick it up, let it lie, merely saying, with a laugh, "Well, I advise any bashful man to take hashish when he wants to offer his heart to any fair lady, for it will give him the courage of a hero, the eloquence of a poet, and the ardor of an Italian. Remember that, gentlemen, and come to me when the crisis approaches."

"Does it conquer the pride, rouse the pity, and soften the hard hearts of the fair sex?" asked Done.

"I dare say now is your time to settle the fact, for here are two ladies who have imbibed, and in three hours will be in such a seraphic state of mind that 'No' will be an impossibility to them."

"Oh, mercy on us; what *have* we done? If that's the case, I shall shut myself up till my foolish fit is over. Rose, you haven't taken any; I beg you to mount guard over me, and see that I don't disgrace myself by any nonsense. Promise me you will," cried Belle, in half-real, half-feigned alarm at the consequences of her prank.

"I promise," said Rose, and floated down the green path as noiselessly as a white cloud, with a curious smile on her lips.

"Don't tell any of the rest what we have done, but after tea let us go into the grove and compare notes," said Norton, as Done strolled away to the beach, and the voices of approaching friends broke the summer quiet.

At tea, the initiated glanced covertly at one another, and saw, or fancied they saw, the effects of the hashish, in a certain suppressed excitement of manner, and unusually brilliant eyes. Belle laughed often, a silvery ringing laugh, pleasant to hear; but when complimented on her good spirits, she looked distressed, and said she could not help her merriment; Meredith was quite calm, but rather dreamy; Evelyn was pale, and her next neighbor heard her heart beat; Norton talked incessantly, but as he talked uncommonly well, no one suspected anything. Done and Miss St. Just watched the others with interest, and were very quiet, especially Rose, who scarcely spoke, but smiled her sweetest, and looked very lovely.

The moon rose early, and the experimenters slipped away to the grove, leaving the outsiders on the lawn as usual. Some bold spirit asked Rose to sing, and she at once complied, pouring out Spanish airs in a voice that melted the hearts of her audience, so full of fiery sweetness or tragic pathos was it. Done seemed quite carried away, and lay with his face in the grass, to hide the tears that would come; till, afraid of openly disgracing himself, he started up and hurried down to the little wharf, where he sat alone, listening to the music with a countenance which plainly revealed to the stars the passion which possessed him. The sound of loud laughter from the grove, followed by entire silence, caused him to wonder what demonstrations were taking place, and half resolve to go and see. But that enchanting voice held him captive, even when a boat put off mysteriously from a point nearby, and sailed away like a phantom through the twilight.

Half an hour afterward, a white figure came down the path, and Rose's voice broke in on his midsummer night's dream. The moon shone clearly now, and showed him the anxiety in her face as she said hurriedly, "Where is Belle?"

"Gone sailing, I believe."

"How could you let her go? She was not fit to take care of herself!"

"I forgot that."

"So did I, but I promised to watch over her, and I must. Which way did they go?" demanded Rose, wrapping the white mantle about her, and running her eye over the little boats moored below.

"You will follow her?"

"Yes."

"I'll be your guide then. They went toward the lighthouse; it is too far to row; I am at your service. Oh, say yes," cried Done, leaping into his own skiff and offering his hand persuasively.

She hesitated an instant and looked at him. He was always pale, and the moonlight seemed to increase this pallor, but his hat brim hid his eyes, and his voice was very quiet. A loud peal of laughter floated over the water, and as if the sound decided her, she gave him her hand and entered the boat. Done smiled triumphantly as he shook out the sail, which caught the freshening wind, and sent the boat dancing along a path of light.

How lovely it was! All the indescribable allurements of a perfect summer night surrounded them: balmy airs, enchanting moonlight, distant music, and, close at hand, the delicious atmosphere of love, which made itself felt in the eloquent silences that fell between them. Rose seemed to yield to the subtle charm, and leaned back on the cushioned seat with her beautiful head uncovered, her face full of dreamy softness, and her hands lying loosely clasped before her. She seldom spoke, showed no further anxiety for Belle, and soon seemed to forget the object of her search, so absorbed was she in some delicious thought which wrapped her in its peace.

Done sat opposite, flushed now, restless, and excited, for his eyes glittered; the hand on the rudder shook, and his voice sounded intense and passionate, even in the utterance of the simplest words. He talked continually and with unusual brilliancy, for, though a man of many accomplishments, he was too indolent or too fastidious to exert himself, except among his peers. Rose seemed to look without seeing, to listen without hearing, and though she smiled blissfully, the smiles were evidently not for him.

On they sailed, scarcely heeding the bank of black cloud piled up in the horizon, the rising wind, or the silence which proved their solitude. Rose moved once or twice, and lifted her hand as if to speak, but sank back mutely, and the hand fell again as if it had not energy enough to enforce her wish. A cloud sweeping over the moon, a distant growl of thunder, and the slight gust that struck the sail seemed to rouse her. Done was singing now like one inspired, his hat at his feet, hair in disorder, and a strangely rapturous expression in his eyes, which were fixed on her. She started, shivered, and seemed to recover herself with an effort.

"Where are they?" she asked, looking vainly for the island heights and the other boat.

"They have gone to the beach, I fancy, but we will follow." As Done leaned forward to speak, she saw his face and shrank back with a sudden flush, for in it she read clearly what she had felt, yet doubted until now. He saw the telltale blush and gesture, and said impetuously, "You know it now; you cannot deceive me longer, or daunt me with your pride! Rose, I love you, and dare tell you so tonight!"

"Not now—not here—I will not listen. Turn back, and be silent, I entreat you, Mr. Done," she said hurriedly.

He laughed a defiant laugh and took her hand in his, which was burning and throbbing with the rapid heat of his pulse.

"No, I *will* have my answer here, and now, and never turn back till you give it; you have been a thorny Rose, and given me many wounds.

I'll be paid for my heartache with sweet words, tender looks, and frank confessions of love, for proud as you are, you do love me, and dare not deny it."

Something in his tone terrified her; she snatched her hand away and drew beyond his reach, trying to speak calmly, and to meet coldly the ardent glances of the eyes which were strangely darkened and dilated with uncontrollable emotion.

"You forget yourself. I shall give no answer to an avowal made in such terms. Take me home instantly," she said in a tone of command.

"Confess you love me, Rose."

"Never!"

"Ah! I'll have a kinder answer, or—" Done half rose and put out his hand to grasp and draw her to him, but the cry she uttered seemed to arrest him with a sort of shock. He dropped into his seat, passed his hand over his eyes, and shivered nervously as he muttered in an altered tone, "I meant nothing; it's the moonlight; sit down, I'll control myself— upon my soul I will!"

"If you do not, I shall go overboard. Are you mad, sir?" cried Rose, trembling with indignation.

"Then I shall follow you, for I *am* mad, Rose, with love—hashish!"

His voice sank to a whisper, but the last word thrilled along her nerves, as no sound of fear had ever done before. An instant she regarded him with a look which took in every sign of unnatural excitement, then she clasped her hands with an imploring gesture, saying, in a tone of despair, "Why did I come! How will it end? Oh, Mark, take me home before it is too late!"

"Hush! Be calm; don't thwart me, or I may get wild again. My thoughts are not clear, but I understand you. There, take my knife, and if I forget myself, kill me. Don't go overboard; you are too beautiful to die, my Rose!"

He threw her the slender hunting knife he wore, looked at her a moment with a far-off look, and trimmed the sail like one moving in a dream. Rose took the weapon, wrapped her cloak closely about her, and crouching as far away as possible, kept her eye on him, with a face in which watchful terror contended with some secret trouble and bewilderment more powerful than her fear.

The boat moved round and began to beat up against wind and tide; spray flew from her bow; the sail bent and strained in the gusts that struck it with perilous fitfulness. The moon was nearly hidden by scudding clouds, and one-half the sky was black with the gathering storm. Rose looked from threatening heavens to treacherous sea, and tried to be ready for any danger, but her calm had been sadly broken, and she could not recover it. Done sat motionless, uttering no word of encouragement, though the frequent flaws almost tore the rope from his hand, and the water often dashed over him.

"Are we in any danger?" asked Rose at last, unable to bear the silence, for he looked like a ghostly helmsman seen by the fitful light, pale now, wild-eyed, and speechless.

"Yes, great danger."

"I thought you were a skillful boatman."

"I am when I am myself; now I am rapidly losing the control of my will, and the strange quiet is coming over me. If I had been alone I should have given up sooner, but for your sake I've kept on."

"Can't you work the boat?" asked Rose, terror-struck by the changed tone of his voice, the slow, uncertain movements of his hands.

"No. I see everything through a thick cloud; your voice sounds far away, and my one desire is to lay my head down and sleep."

"Let me steer—I can, I must!" she cried, springing toward him and laying her hand on the rudder.

He smiled and kissed the little hand, saying dreamily, "You could not hold it a minute; sit by me, love; let us turn the boat again, and drift away together—anywhere, anywhere out of the world."

"Oh, heaven, what will become of us!" and Rose wrung her hands in real despair. "Mr. Done—Mark—dear Mark, rouse yourself and listen to me. Turn, as you say, for it is certain death to go on so. Turn, and let us drift down to the lighthouse; they will hear and help us. Quick, take down the sail, get out the oars, and let us try to reach there before the storm breaks."

As Rose spoke, he obeyed her like a dumb animal; love for her was stronger even than the instinct of self-preservation, and for her sake he fought against the treacherous lethargy which was swiftly overpowering him. The sail was lowered, the boat brought round, and with little help from the ill-pulled oars it drifted rapidly out to sea with the ebbing tide.

As she caught her breath after this dangerous maneuver was accomplished, Rose asked, in a quiet tone she vainly tried to render natural, "How much hashish did you take?"

"All that Meredith threw me. Too much; but I was possessed to do it, so I hid the roll and tried it," he answered, peering at her with a weird laugh.

"Let us talk; our safety lies in keeping awake, and I dare not let you sleep," continued Rose, dashing water on her own hot forehead with a sort of desperation.

"Say you love me; that would wake me from my lost sleep, I think.

I have hoped and feared, waited and suffered so long. Be pitiful, and answer, Rose."

"I do; but I should not own it now."

So low was the soft reply he scarcely heard it, but he felt it and made a strong effort to break from the hateful spell that bound him. Leaning forward, he tried to read her face in a ray of moonlight breaking through the clouds; he saw a new and tender warmth in it, for all the pride was gone, and no fear marred the eloquence of those soft, Southern eyes.

"Kiss me, Rose, then I shall believe it. I feel lost in a dream, and you, so changed, so kind, may be only a fair phantom. Kiss me, love, and make it real."

As if swayed by a power more potent than her will, Rose bent to meet his lips. But the ardent pressure seemed to startle her from a momentary oblivion of everything but love. She covered up her face and sank down, as if overwhelmed with shame, sobbing through passionate tears, "Oh, what am I doing? I am mad, for I, too, have taken hashish."

What he answered she never heard, for a rattling peal of thunder drowned his voice, and then the storm broke loose. Rain fell in torrents, the wind blew fiercely, sky and sea were black as ink, and the boat tossed from wave to wave almost at their mercy. Giving herself up for lost, Rose crept to her lover's side and clung there, conscious only that they would bide together through the perils their own folly brought them. Done's excitement was quite gone now; he sat like a statue, shielding the frail creature whom he loved with a smile on his face, which looked awfully emotionless when the lightning gave her glimpses of its white immobility. Drenched, exhausted, and half senseless with danger, fear, and exposure, Rose saw at last a welcome glimmer through the gloom, and roused herself to cry for help.

"Mark, wake and help me! Shout, for God's sake—shout and call them, for we are lost if we drift by!" she cried, lifting his head from his breast, and forcing him to see the brilliant beacons streaming far across the troubled water.

He understood her, and springing up, uttered shout after shout like one demented. Fortunately, the storm had lulled a little; the lighthouse keeper heard and answered. Rose seized the helm, Done the oars, and with one frantic effort guided the boat into quieter waters, where it was met by the keeper, who towed it to the rocky nook which served as harbor.

The moment a strong, steady face met her eyes, and a gruff, cheery voice hailed her, Rose gave way, and was carried up to the house, looking more like a beautiful drowned Ophelia than a living woman.

"Here, Sally, see to the poor thing; she's had a rough time on't. I'll take care of her sweetheart—and a nice job I'll have, I reckon, for if he ain't mad or drunk, he's had a stroke of lightnin', and looks as if he wouldn't get his hearin' in a hurry," said the old man as he housed his unexpected guests and stood staring at Done, who looked about him like one dazed. "You jest turn in yonder and sleep it off, mate. We'll see to the lady, and right up your boat in the morning," the old man added.

"Be kind to Rose. I frightened her. I'll not forget you. Yes, let me sleep and get over this cursed folly as soon as possible," muttered this strange visitor.

Done threw himself down on the rough couch and tried to sleep, but every nerve was overstrained, every pulse beating like a trip-hammer, and everything about him was intensified and exaggerated with awful power. The thundershower seemed a wild hurricane, the quaint room a wilderness peopled with tormenting phantoms, and all the events of his life passed before him in an endless procession, which nearly maddened him. The old man looked weird and gigantic, his own voice sounded shrill and discordant, and the ceaseless murmur of Rose's incoherent wanderings haunted him like parts of a grotesque but dreadful dream.

All night he lay motionless, with staring eyes, feverish lips, and a mind on the rack, for the delicate machinery which had been tampered with revenged the wrong by torturing the foolish experimenter. All night Rose wept and sang, talked and cried for help in a piteous state of nervous excitement, for with her the trance came first, and the after-agitation was increased by the events of the evening. She slept at last, lulled by the old woman's motherly care, and Done was spared one tormenting fear, for he dreaded the consequences of this folly on her, more than upon himself.

As day dawned he rose, haggard and faint, and staggered out. At the door he met the keeper, who stopped him to report that the boat was in order, and a fair day coming. Seeing doubt and perplexity in the old man's eye, Done told him the truth, and added that he was going to the beach for a plunge, hoping by that simple tonic to restore his unstrung nerves.

He came back feeling like himself again, except for a dull headache, and a heavy sense of remorse weighing on his spirits, for he distinctly recollected all the events of the night. The old woman made him eat and drink, and in an hour he felt ready for the homeward trip.

Rose slept late, and when she woke soon recovered herself, for her dose had been a small one. When she had breakfasted and made a hasty toilet, she professed herself anxious to return at once. She dreaded yet longed to see Done, and when the time came armed herself with pride, feeling all a woman's shame at what had passed, and resolving to feign forgetfulness of the incidents of the previous night. Pale and cold as a statue she met him, but the moment he began to say humbly, "Forgive me, Rose," she silenced him with an imperious gesture and the command "Don't speak of it; I only remember that it was very horrible, and wish to forget it all as soon as possible."

"All, Rose?" he asked, significantly.

"Yes, *all*. No one would care to recall the follies of a hashish dream," she answered, turning hastily to hide the scarlet flush that would rise, and the eyes that would fall before his own.

"*I* never can forget, but I will be silent if you bid me."

"I do. Let us go. What will they think at the island? Mr. Done, give me your promise to tell no one, now or ever, that I tried that dangerous experiment. I will guard your secret also." She spoke eagerly and looked up imploringly.

"I promise," and he gave her his hand, holding her own with a wistful glance, till she drew it away and begged him to take her home.

Leaving hearty thanks and a generous token of their gratitude, they sailed away with a fair wind, finding in the freshness of the morning a speedy cure for tired bodies and excited minds. They said little, but it was impossible for Rose to preserve her coldness. The memory of the past night broke down her pride, and Done's tender glances touched her heart. She half hid her face behind her hand, and tried to compose herself for the scene to come, for as she approached the island, she saw Belle and her party waiting for them on the shore.

"Oh, Mr. Done, screen me from their eyes and questions as much as you can! I'm so worn out and nervous, I shall betray myself. You will help me?" And she turned to him with a confiding look, strangely at variance with her usual calm self-possession.

"I'll shield you with my life, if you will tell me why you took the hashish," he said, bent on knowing his fate.

"I hoped it would make me soft and lovable, like other women. I'm tired of being a lonely statue," she faltered, as if the truth was wrung from her by a power stronger than her will.

"And I took it to gain courage to tell my love. Rose, we have been near death together; let us share life together, and neither of us be any more lonely or afraid?"

He stretched his hand to her with his heart in his face, and she gave him hers with a look of tender submission, as he said ardently, "Heaven bless hashish, if its dreams end like this!"

The Unknown Thrillers of Louisa May Alcott

TITLE	CENTRAL THEME(S)
"Pauline's Passion and Punishment" Anonymous	Manipulating Heroine
"A Whisper in the Dark" Anonymous	Mind Control
"V. V.: or, Plots and Counterplots" By A Well Known Author	Manipulating Heroine
"A Marble Woman: or, The Mysterious Model" By A. M. Barnard	Manipulating Hero Opium Addiction
"Behind a Mask: or, A Woman's Power" By A. M. Barnard	Manipulating Heroine

FIRST PUBLICATION	REPRINT HISTORY
Frank Leslie's Illustrated Newspaper, Vol. XV, Nos. 379 & 380 (January 3 & 10, 1863). Stern 27 *	*Behind a Mask* (From file of *Leslie's* at New York Public Library and New York Historical Society)
Frank Leslie's Illustrated Newspaper, Vol. XVI, Nos. 401 & 402 (June 6 & 13, 1863). Stern 30	*A Modern Mephistopheles and A Whisper in the Dark* (Boston: Roberts Brothers, 1889). BAL 219 †
	Plots and Counterplots (From Stern copy of *A Modern Mephistopheles and A Whisper in the Dark*)
The Flag of Our Union, Vol. XX, Nos. 5, 6, 7, 8 (February 4, 11, 18, 25, 1865). Stern 47	*Ten Cent Novelette*, No. 80, By A. M. Barnard (Boston: Thomes & Talbot, *ca.* 1870). BAL 165
	Plots and Counterplots (From copy of *Ten Cent Novelette* at New York Public Library, Rare Book Division)
The Flag of Our Union, Vol. XX, Nos. 20, 21, 22, 23 (May 20, 27, June 3, 10, 1865). Stern 51	*Plots and Counterplots* (From issues of *The Flag of Our Union* at Houghton Library, Harvard University)
The Flag of Our Union, Vol. XXI, Nos. 41, 42, 43, 44 (October 13, 20, 27, November 3, 1866). Stern 53	*Behind a Mask* (From issues of *The Flag of Our Union* at American Antiquarian Society)

TITLE	CENTRAL THEME(S)
"The Abbot's Ghost: or, Maurice Treherne's Temptation" By A. M. Barnard	Gothic Romance
"The Skeleton in the Closet" By L. M. Alcott	Madness
"The Mysterious Key, and What It Opened" By L. M. Alcott	Italianate Englishman Gothic Devices
"Perilous Play" By L. M. A.	Hashish Experimentation

FIRST PUBLICATION	REPRINT HISTORY
The Flag of Our Union, Vol. XXII, Nos. 1, 2, 3, 4 (January 5, 12, 19, 26, 1867). Stern 55	*Behind a Mask* (From issues of *The Flag of Our Union* in Rare Book Division, Library of Congress)
Ten Cent Novelette, No. 49 (Boston: Elliott, Thomes & Talbot [1867]). Trailer to *The Foundling* by Perley Parker. Stern 60; BAL 151	*Plots and Counterplots* (From copy in Alderman Library, University of Virginia)
Ten Cent Novelette, No. 50 (Boston: Elliott, Thomes & Talbot [1867]. Stern 64; BAL 152	*The Leisure Hour Library,* No. 382 (New York: F. M. Lupton, *ca.* 1900). *Behind a Mask* (From copy of *Ten Cent Novelette* in Alderman Library, University of Virginia, previously owned by Carroll A. Wilson)
Frank Leslie's Chimney Corner, Vol. VIII, No. 194 (February 13, 1869). Stern 94	*Frank Leslie's Popular Monthly,* Vol. II, No. 5 (November, 1876). *Plots and Counterplots* (From issue of *Frank Leslie's Chimney Corner* in New York Public Library)

---

* Stern numbers refer to numbered items in the Alcott Bibliography appended to Madeleine B. Stern, ed., *Louisa's Wonder Book: A Newly Discovered Alcott Juvenile* (Mount Pleasant, Michigan: Clarke Historical Library, Central Michigan University, 1975).

† BAL numbers refer to *Bibliography of American Literature,* compiled by Jacob Blanck (New Haven: Yale University Press, 1955) Vol. I.

ABOUT THE AUTHOR

LOUISA MAY ALCOTT was born in Germantown, Pennsylvania, in 1832, the daughter of Amos Bronson Alcott, the philosopher, innovative educator, and a contemporary of Emerson and Thoreau; and of Abby May Alcott, known in her day as a radical thinker and early feminist.

Determined to become a writer, Alcott published her first book, *Flower Fables*, at the age of sixteen. Eight years later she garnered some success with *Hospital Sketches*, which described her experiences as a Civil War nurse. Her first novel, *Moods*, appeared in 1865, but true—and lasting—fame arrived with the publication of *Little Women*, a novel based on many real-life incidents concerning Alcott herself, her sisters, and her parents.

Although she wrote a total of 291 novels, serials, short stories, poems, and articles, it is for *Little Women* that Louisa May Alcott is really remembered. The book was an immediate success and, since its publication, has been translated into more than twenty languages—a sure sign of its universal appeal; *Little Women* is still one of the most popular and widely read books ever written for girls. Alcott continued to write after the great success of *Little Women*, publishing her last novel, *A Garland for Girls*, in 1888. She died later that same year, on March 6th, at the age of fifty-six.